TELEVENGE

a novel

PAMELA KING CABLE

SATYA HOUSE PUBLICATIONS

Hardwick, Massachusetts

SATYA HOUSE PUBLICATIONS
Post Office Box 122
Hardwick, Massachusetts 01037
www.satyahouse.com

10 9 8 7 6 5 4 3 2 1
FIRST EDITION

ISBN 978-1-935874-16-4
ISBN 978-1-935874-13-3 (ebook)

Cover image © Philcold | Dreamstime.com
Author photo © Michael Cable
Printed in the United States of America

PUBLISHER'S CATALOGING-IN-PUBLICATION DATA
(*Prepared by The Donohue Group, Inc.*)

Cable, Pamela King.
    Televenge : a novel / Pamela King Cable. — 1st ed.

    p. ; cm.

    Issued also as an ebook.
    ISBN: 978-1-935874-16-4(pbk.)

    1. Christian women—Southern States—Fiction. 2. Television in religion—
Fiction. 3. Evangelists—Fiction. 4. Southern States—Fiction. 5. Mystery fiction.
8. Religious fiction. I. Title.

PS3603.A34 T45 2012
813.6

TELEVENGE

Also by Pamela King Cable
Southern Fried Women

For Aaron and Jillian
and
For Lily

In Memory of Jaclyn Michelle Cable
1978 - 1997

ACKNOWLEDGEMENTS

Televenge would not have been written without the following individuals who believed in this story from the beginning and worked so hard to see it in print, I wish to relay a heartfelt thank you . . .

To Julie Murkette, Publisher at Satya House, who spent several days in 2008 immersed within the pages of *Televenge* and immediately began a quest of her own: to publish this book. I want to thank Julie and Joe Murkette who never gave up. I want to thank them for their pursuit, their diligence, and for recognizing and understanding the incredible amount of blood, sweat, and tears that went into this story. Thank you for putting up with my obsessive nature and for embracing my dream. For laying it all on the line and going the extra mile. I'm grateful beyond measure for your undying passion and all your hard work. There's none like you. None.

To Satya House Publications. I'm so blessed to have you on my side. Thank you to the entire team who commented, copyedited, proofread, designed, promoted, and spent untold hours on every detail.

To Cristy Bertini for her meticulous copyediting. I'm indebted to Desiree Harrington and Laine Cunningham, freelance editors, for taking on the monumental task of earlier drafts.

To Claudine Wolk whose kindness and understanding, not to mention patience, helped me through Social Media 101, and for an incredible social media campaign.

To the early team of readers who cheered me on, supported my efforts, and sometimes kicked my butt as I wrote this story: Jackie Stanley, Dena Harris, Tina Rich, Elaine Ober, Gail Gurley, Bobbie Rossi, Bette Lou Nicholson, Lorin Oberweger, Beth Hanggeli, Debra Doda, and Kathy Mendenhall.

To Diana Gabaldon, for encouraging me to not be so concerned about book length, but to write the story of my heart as it should be written.

To Literary Agent Katharine Sands, for letting me drive her around Winston-Salem, Greensboro, and Raleigh many years ago from one writing conference to the next, listening to my "perfect pitch", and coming up with the title.

To Literary Agent Donald Maass who many years ago posed just the right questions that sent the story off into its own direction—raising it to a new level, and to Literary Agent Rita Rosenkranz for her friendship and encouragement early on and for proving to me that some agents really do care.

To Aaron, Annie, and Lily Ober, Jillian Ober, and to Christopher, Nicole, Andrew, and Lauren Cable, children and grandchildren I cherish to the depths of me. Thank you for your love and support. You are the heart of this book. Aaron and Jillian, I hope someday when you are old and I am long gone, you will read this book and remember what is true and what is not, and that despite it all your mother loved you beyond words.

To Tina Rich. What can I say? From the time we sat together in the church nursery with our babies on our laps and then walked out of that place forever, you've been more than my best friend. I cannot imagine my life without you. For crying with me and believing in me early on when nobody else did. For reading every draft and keeping my dream alive, you are my treasure.

To Elaine Ober, for being such a champion of this story, for laboring through every line and word over and over again, and for your consistent love and enthusiasm over the years, I'm forever grateful.

To Darrel and Joyce King, my father and mother, for their goodness, their courage to leave a megachurch many years ago, and for their unwavering faith in the face of adversity. And for giving me my voice.

A special thank you to the many who broke from legalistic and manipulative churches and cults and shared with me your struggle for freedom. Your heartbreaking oral accounts contributed and helped to shape this book. You shall forever remain anonymous.

And last, but never least, I want to thank Michael Cable. If it had not been for your unfailing love and unswerving patience there would be no *Televenge*. None of this could have been possible had you not picked me out of the miry clay many years ago and given me this whole new wonderful life. Your constant devotion made it possible for me to be a writer. Not once in over ten years did you complain of my endless hours of writing. Your uncompromising belief in me is mind-boggling, and your sacrifice epitomizes what it means to love me as Christ loves the church. Thank you for never allowing me to give up. With you, I found unconditional love and the true meaning of the word, *husband*. I'm grateful to be made from your rib, a man of extraordinary integrity, insight, and strength, the vessel through whom God has chosen to love me in ways I never thought possible. There are no words.

Names for God
used in TELEVENGE

Adonai-Jehovah: The Lord Our Sovereign

El-Elyon: The Lord Most High

El-Olam: The Everlasting God

El-Shaddai: The God Who is Sufficient for the Needs of His People

Jehovah-Elohim: The Eternal Creator

Jehovah-Jireh: The Lord Our Provider

Jehovah-Nissi: The Lord Our Banner

Jehovah-Ropheka: The Lord Our Healer

Jehovah-Shalom: The Lord Our Peace

Jehovah-Tsidkenu: The Lord Our Righteousness

Jehovah-Mekaddishkem: The Lord Our Sanctifier

Jehovah-Sabaoth: The Lord of Hosts

Jehovah-Shammah: The Lord is Present

Jehovah-Rohi: The Lord Our Shepherd

Jehovah-Hoseenu: The Lord Our Maker

Jehovah-Eloheenu: The Lord Our God

Beware of false prophets, which come to you in sheep's clothing, but inwardly they are ravening wolves. Ye shall know them by their fruits. . . . Not every one that saith unto me Lord, Lord, shall enter into the kingdom of heaven; but he that doeth the will of my Father which is in heaven. Many will say to me in that day, Lord, Lord, have we not prophesied in thy name? And in thy name have cast out devils? And in thy name done many wonderful works? And then will I profess unto them, I never knew you. Depart from me, ye that work iniquity.

— Matthew 7:15-23 KJV

CONTENTS

Dearly beloved, avenge not yourselves, but rather give place unto wrath:
for it is written, Vengeance is mine; I will repay, saith the Lord.
— Romans 12:19 KJV

PART ONE
In The Beginning

1972
DAYDREAM BELIEVER

Andie Parks Oliver

Never had there been a time when I was riper for love than the summer of my fourteenth birthday. I drew boys like beetles to magnolias. Nature, lust, puppy love . . . folks always had a name for this phenomenon. But for a young girl from Winston-Salem, North Carolina, it was the moment my hormones wept at the altar of my womanhood. I shouted and my eyes sparkled with the covenant of God embedding itself into the deepest regions of my heart. The gangly girl dissolved, leaving only a sanctified goddess, and in that instant—I met Joe.

I attended church at the House of Praise on the outskirts of the city with my younger sister, Caroline, and occasionally with my father. But my mother, who I called Dixie because that's what she wanted us to call her, never missed a service. From a tender age, I had scanned the pews for a husband. Church boys were more handsome, and most descended from upstanding Southern families, which in my estimation, made good husbands, fathers, and providers.

I approached a row of sophomore boys slouched like lanky pups on the back pew in the sanctuary.

"You're sitting on my Bible."

"Sorry . . . I don't see your name on it."

I snatched my white leather King James from the pick of the litter. "It's Andie Parks."

"It's nice to meet ya, Andie."

"Likewise."

"Ain't ya gonna ask my name?"

"I already know your name, Joe Oliver."

"Then I'm glad I sat on your Holy Bible."

"I'm glad I put it there for you to sit on, silly."

So, on my sixteenth birthday when Joe placed a silver promise ring with its diamond chip on my left hand, my future was set in that tiny stone. Dixie then permitted me to spend certain weekends in Salisbury—a town full of Southerners with lineages back to Stonewall Jackson and beyond.

Maudy and Al Oliver welcomed me into their home. They had prayed long and hard for God to show favor to their three evangelical sons. As a result of their fervent prayers, they believed Jehovah-Jireh provided their eldest son with a gift of music, their middle son with a gift of intellect, and their youngest son with a church girl, saved and filled with the Holy Ghost.

Maudy had made me a bed on the couch, and that's where she expected to find me in the morning. "Sleep well?" She towered over me with wire-brush curlers wrapped tight to her head.

"Fine, thanks." I hadn't slept at all.

Joe discovered an old mattress in the attic. In luminous moonlight streaming through open windows and reflecting off yellowed, peeling wallpaper, he promised before God to love me forever. He was unshakable about his promises and I believed him. I'd been brought up to trust in spiritual things so I returned his promises—that no matter our future, I'd love him until the end of my days and beyond. I rolled to my back and pulled Joe onto my naked breasts. I knew someday we'd recall that moment; our moment of commitment, of purest love, when we reached for the hem of God, knowing we would marry and be one flesh forever. I closed my eyes and promised Joe openly and God silently, that I'd never love another.

The sizzle and smell of sausage frying jolted my senses and I rolled off the couch with a nubby blanket wrapped around my shoulders. *I love you, Andie Rose.* I scampered to the bathroom with Joe's voice penetrating my thoughts. Splashing cool water on my face, I wiped away streaked mascara with a towel as my promise ring flickered in the mirror and in my eyes.

"Breakfast, Andie!" Maudy's voice rang from the kitchen.

I shivered.

He had held me until morning's first light, chancing discovery, not wanting to let go. He told me I was smart and pretty and sweet. He loved me. I knew it. Slipping out of his arms, I whispered against his cheek, "What will your mama say if she finds us making love up here?" Naked except for a pair of wispy blue panties, I stood in the steeply pitched attic and pulled on Joe's sweatshirt, and then crept down the narrow staircase, careful not to make too much noise. The old house creaked as if threatening to expose my escapade. An hour had passed when I heard Joe leave for work at the Esso station, and before I had a chance to respond to his kiss on my forehead.

Maudy knocked on the bathroom door. "Breakfast, darlin'. Come get it while it's hot."

Startled, I shook myself. "I'll be right out." I smelled him, the remnants of Joe lodged in every part of me.

§

I washed down my first bite of Maudy's biscuits and gravy with coffee and a replay of the previous night's church service. Calvin Artury's sermon to the youth expounded on the sin of premarital sex. The Friday marathon service had bothered some—I'd overheard the gossip after the altar call. It seemed our pastor enjoyed preaching about sex; proclaiming Christians had the best sex lives. But I concurred with Calvin—it was "better to marry than burn," and if there was one thing I knew for sure, it was that Joe and I were burning.

I also agreed with Calvin's views on the unnecessary pursuit of a higher education. Every Bible-Belt evangelical worth their salt held fast to the blessed hope that Jesus was coming back and right soon. As a result, Joe and I had been invited to more than a dozen teenage weddings—a common occurrence at the House of Praise. Progressing from high school to homemaker fit into my plans, too. More than anything, I wanted a wedding. A beautiful home. A good husband. Well-raised children. Everything my mother had.

Maudy fidgeted with the kitchen radio. I sat at the table, recalling the day I grew deeper in love with the Oliver family. The day Maudy enlightened me as to the family's commitment to Christ. Riveted, I felt my heart would burst at the seam watching my future mother-in-law's tears drip like a leaky spigot. "The Lord healed me from the cancer in '66 when Reverend Artury first came to town and touched me during a service in the tabernacle. I'll praise God's name forever," she cried. "We Olivers don't need what the world offers. We search for a deeper walk with the Almighty. It's no secret our neighbors think we're crazy because we speak in unknown tongues and drive an hour to church when we could've joined the First Baptist Church in Salisbury. It's the price we've chosen to pay for saving the lost at any cost. We've dedicated our lives to furthering the ministry of Reverend Artury."

Daddy and I never called him Reverend Artury. Daddy said it was just too uppity for any man to call himself *Reverend*. And until the moment Maudy explained her devotion to the House of Praise and its *Reverend*, I had also viewed the Olivers' allegiance as a deformity. Like they had three eyeballs, and everyone stared at them because of it. Suddenly it all made sense and I wanted to be one of them—a proud and dedicated member of the church. A believer. An Oliver.

Still, I'd heard the talk in the ladies' restroom, the lobby, and the parking lot. Rumors that Calvin possessed all nine gifts of the Holy Spirit. I reasoned preachers got the gifts like most folks were blessed with a talent. But it was the gift of discernment that troubled me most. The possibility of Calvin peering inside my soul—knowing my motives, Christian and otherwise—if it was true, I didn't want him within twenty feet. I figured I had fulfilled Maudy and Al's unspoken requirements as a marriage candidate for their son, accepting Jesus Christ as my Savior and missing only an occasional church service. That was all Calvin needed to know about me.

I snapped out of my stupor when Maudy turned up the static on the AM radio station.

"Wide is the road to Hell! But narrow is the gate to Glory! Dedicate your lives to God, consecrate your minds to Him, or face an eternity where the worm never dies!" Calvin's pre-recorded sermon pierced the air as Maudy sliced more biscuits. Her eyes watched me until I gave her the look. That look all good Pentecostals have down pat when they feel the Spirit move. Shoulders raised, a slight shake of the head, and the anointed smile that purses our lips.

I was baffled. After enduring three endless church services every week, why did we need to listen to him on Saturday morning radio? Calvin's evangelizing voice droned on. I swallowed the bite of biscuit in my mouth and put the rest down on my plate. Daddy's blasphemous words vibrated inside my head. *Hell, the Olivers would spit on the sidewalk if Calvin told 'em to do it.* Not a devoted churchgoer, Bud Parks refused to tolerate the House of Praise at times and opted for church attendance on his own terms, even at the risk of losing his soul. I admired Daddy's honesty, yet prayed for his redemption. I wanted to be a good Christian, but my hands trembled carrying breakfast dishes to the sink.

§

In the spring of my senior year, Joe and I set a wedding date: July 1, 1972, one month after my high school graduation and one month before my eighteenth birthday. As the day approached, not a soul questioned how we'd survive. Our sole possession, Joe's God-awful green 1970 AMC Javelin, had lost its hubcaps to some Rowan County ditch months before. With no savings and no real employment, we decided to live on love, because, after all, we believed in Bible prosperity, mustard-seed faith, and miracles. Calvin had promised—as long as Jesus Christ and the House of Praise remained the bedrock of our life, Jehovah-Jireh would meet our every need.

§

Days before the wedding, I retreated to my favorite spot—the Oliver porch swing. Basking in the glow of dusk, I heard the crunch of footsteps on the gravel behind me. It was Joe, with his hair combed back and wet from his after-work shower. He collapsed into the swing, exhausted, slipped his arm around me and rested his head on my shoulder. Soft rain fell from the few purple clouds dotting the sunlit evening, and I sat still and quiet, hoping our future held endless moments like that one wrapped in each other's arms.

The landscape faded further into nightfall when I saw the house lights come on. "I'd better help your mama with supper," I said.

"Don't go. Not yet." Joe simply strengthened his grasp and watched the evening shadows thicken, without saying another word. As if trapping the moment deep in his memory.

I started to wiggle out of his embrace, but Joe slid his arm under my legs and held me on his lap. Clutched against him, I felt the warmth of his shower on his skin and smelled the gasoline and oil set into the cracks of his hands. Soothed by his relaxed mood, my head against his chest, I drifted easily into my favorite pastime—daydreaming. The old swing rocked back and forth, the rust-covered chains screeching out familiar tunes while soundless rain dripped from clematis wound around splintered porch posts. Cradled in my fiancé's arms, I shut out the world and fantasized.

In sweetheart fashion, we remained entwined for what seemed like forever until a few insatiable daydreams popped out of my mouth like bubble gum. "I know you want me to work, but when the babies come—" I paused and smiled, lifting my face to his. "We *are* building a house, right? We talked about it. Remember?"

"What will we build it with, Andie, honey, our fat bank account? I know you got big dreams, but can we talk about houses and kids later? At least until I find a better-paying job. You ain't trailer trash, I know that, but it don't mean you can't live in one for a while. Besides two can live as cheap as one, if we don't eat much."

I didn't push. *Ladies must sometimes go through the back door to a man's heart.* I'd learned that from Dixie. *Joe loves me.* I believed the rest would come in time.

Quiet again, I smiled at the dozen rocking chairs that greeted guests like a flock of ducks floating on a wooden pond. Strewn the length of the Olivers' deep wrap-around porch, the chairs had comforted me as I spent endless evenings there, dreaming about making babies with Joe, spending holidays with the Olivers, and about the sisters-in-law I was sure to have—envious girls my own age who would fuss over my beautiful child as Joe rocked it to sleep on that same porch. I thanked God I'd soon be a part of the old house and the Oliver family. I kept my goals simple and uncomplicated, and preferred my life to remain that way.

§

President of Future Homemakers of America, I also led my own special club—one of nine girls in the Class of '72 planning a wedding. Marriage was every young girl's destiny and I pitied college-bound girls with no boyfriends. Between homework assignments, I clipped pictures of gowns and flower arrangements from *Bride* magazine. Pouring through Dixie's *House Beautiful* magazines, I organized and decorated rooms for my dream house, and every night I tied up the phone with my best friend in the whole wide world.

"Mavis! Just because you're black doesn't mean you can't be my Maid of Honor!"

"Mavis! Maudy said to invite the whole congregation. What do you think?"

"Mavis! Of course, Joe agreed with me. Two boys, two girls and a big house!"

Her less-than-enthusiastic responses annoyed me, but all was forgotten as I became increasingly absorbed in wedding plans. *Mrs. Joe Oliver* had been scribbled over the phone book, my notebooks, and my tennis shoes. Nothing could keep me from it. My intentions were as clean and clear as Dixie's living room picture window. I followed a neat and tidy little path with no divergence. Nobody had to tell me to pick up my clothes or finish my homework. I had brushed my hair 100 strokes every night from the time I was old enough to wash it by myself. Making my bed seemed as natural as scrubbing my face, and I wore my choice of marriage over college like a badge of honor. Studying and straight A's came as easy as breathing. Still, there were no plans to further my education. Daddy and Dixie had discussed my potential, but Lord knows, they never breathed a word of it to me. A wedding was far cheaper than potential.

It didn't matter anyway. At seventeen, my love for Joe filled my head and my heart, leaving room for little else. I had no desire to squeeze into Patty Lou's Volkswagen after graduation and head to Myrtle Beach; there'd be no beach-blanket stories to tell, no up-all-night frolics to remember with friends. No secrets to keep. No bridges to burn. I wanted none of that wild and crazy stuff. It hindered my plans to marry Joe, bear his children, and build a new home with a picket fence, a fancy front door, cathedral ceilings, a stone fireplace, a frost-free freezer, and a color TV and princess phone in every room.

July 1972
A Bargain Wedding

Andie

My wedding cost one thousand dollars, almost to the penny. The way Dixie carried on about it, it was as if she had given me the entire tobacco crop profit from Forsyth County. Dixie and Daddy were middle-class folk who had pulled themselves out of poverty. They'd shopped for a bargain wedding—an unfortunate by-product of their frugal present due to their meager past.

Mavis refused to attend the ceremony. "Colored people at your wedding will jus' make the white folks nervous." I knew it was an excuse. For reasons unknown, she didn't like Joe. After some begging, I convinced her to take pictures at the reception. Mavis had two obsessions: singing and photography. She'd won a ribbon at the 1970 State Fair in Raleigh for a black and white photograph of her parents working in their tobacco field. After that, Mavis's camera became an extension of her arm.

The summer of 1972 broke records in heat and humidity. My fourteen-year-old sister and sole bridesmaid suffered in the high temperatures. Lanky and lean, Caroline looked nothing like me. Her amber eyes matched her thick coppery ringlets that stuck to her face and neck like hot tar on a shoe, while sweat poured down her neck in tiny streams. Dixie had picked out a dress for flat-chested Caroline, and then proceeded to stuff my sister's bra with Kleenex. Long sleeves and a high neck only added to Caroline's misery. The green gingham dress looked like a picnic tablecloth, and the magnolia blossoms she carried wilted right along with her attitude.

It was a short, simple wedding. Ted, Joe's oldest brother and the House of Praise pianist until he'd left for the Marine Corps, had secured a three-day pass to play *We Have This Moment* on the organ. A song made popular by evangelists, Richard and Patti Roberts. I wanted to walk down the aisle to a recording of Karen Carpenter singing *Close to You*, or at least *Here Comes the Bride*, but Maudy axed them both. Worldly music was not allowed in our church, she'd said. And she was furious with Ray, the middle Oliver son, who was always late and bolted in at the last minute to stand as Joe's best man. But when my princess-white dress floated through the double doors at the back of the church, I heard Maudy's gasp over that of the guests.

Holding tight to Daddy's arm and a bouquet of pink roses, I walked step-pause-step-pause toward the altar in the midst of a fairy tale daydream while my girlish grin beamed through the blusher covering my face. Daddy, regal in a black tuxedo, escorted his seventeen-year-old daughter down the 100-foot aisle without a smile. Passing my hand to Joe, Daddy turned and quietly retreated up the aisle and out the back door. Later he said he was sick and needed air. I figured he needed a cigarette. My mother smiled as if her husband's flight out of the church was a rehearsed part of the ceremony.

Calm and composed, next to a yellow pew bow designating her assigned seat, Dixie sat poised like the belle she was, coiffed and proper in pink chiffon, her wedding up-do curled, shellacked, and tucked under a wide-brimmed hat.

After traditional nuptials, Calvin, without warning, shed unexpected tears during his final prayer and blessing. His emotion touched and surprised us all. But when he called for wedding guests to receive Jesus and join the church, my cheeks flushed hot. Embarrassed at my pastor's boldness, I quickly reasoned we owed that much of our ceremony to the Lord. I knew somehow I'd have to acquire the Olivers' thick skin and unswerving allegiance to the House of Praise. Until then, I would drink in the glory of the day. The day of my dreams.

§

In ninety-degree heat, the rented fellowship hall at the edge of town provided giant oscillating fans to blow perspiration off the faces of our sweltering guests. Joe had stripped off his crushed-velvet jacket and tie, but I was destined to suffer in my long-sleeved, tight-bodiced, hoop-skirted wedding dress. I tried to recall what possessed me to buy it, other than Dixie saying it was on sale. The spiral curls cascading to the middle of my back had turned spaghetti-like in the heat. I needed air. Shoving the heavy wooden doors wide, I stepped outside the reception hall and cooled off while sultry breezes blew my bleached-blonde hair away from my tan face. I had prided myself as a Julie Barnes (from *The Mod Squad*) look-alike. Except I never liked the freckles scattered across my nose—faint little dots like the final touches on a watercolor painting. At five-foot-three, I was no long-legged ballerina.

Standing with my arms held out from my sides, I blew sweaty bangs off my forehead. Perspiration dripped from under my veil, slid to my neck, and down the curve of my back. Fanning myself with a wedding program, I leaned against the warm brick building, gazing at the rising moon. It glowed a soft see-through white, like a baby's bitty toenail.

"Hey, wife, I've been looking all over for you."

"I was hot."

"Hot for me?" Joe wrapped his arms around my waist, kissed me deeply, and smothered his face on my neck, slick with sweat.

I gently pushed him away. "Stop. We should get back inside. There's guests to greet and we need to eat."

He pulled me back and smiled, holding my hips tight against his own and murmuring into my hair. "I only want to eat you. We're legal now, you know. We can do it anytime we want."

I giggled and squirmed. "By the way, what did Calvin talk to you about before the ceremony?"

Joe's smile evaporated quick as a flash, and I immediately regretted the question. He lifted his head and stared past me, out into the parking lot. "How'd you know that?"

"Your mama told me. What'd he have to say that was so all-fired important?"

He gave me a sigh of impatience. "Men talk. Forget it."

"No, really, what'd he say? Why didn't he talk to both of us?"

"He was just doing his job; he talked about being a good husband and—forget it, okay?"

Wrapping my arms around his neck, I breathed in the clinging scent of Hai Karate on his sweat-soaked shirt. Forcing his head to bend to my upturned face, I saw that his countenance was as smooth and blank as a wall. My new husband's mind was elsewhere. "I've not had a moment alone with you since we said 'I do.' I'm Mrs. Joe Oliver. Imagine that." I pulled up his left hand from around my waist, scrubbed free of grease and gasoline, and kissed his shiny new wedding ring. "I want you to remember this promise."

He smiled, finally. "I've a feeling you won't let me forget it. Kiss me, I'm starved for you, not barbecue."

I kissed him, then laid my head on his chest, feeling his warmth again and the strength of his arms. We stood locked together for a moment, swaying in the hot breeze. "Oh Joe, I'm going to make you the perfect wife. Our home will be more beautiful than anything you can imagine; full of love just like Calvin said it would be, because we're special. Special to God. You'll be so proud of me. I love you, Joe. I love you to the moon."

"I want to give you the moon, Andie Rose." The tenderness in his voice was overwhelming.

"You already have."

§

Guests lined up at the buffet table and dined on local barbecue and potato salad. They drank alcohol-free punch and fellowshipped, casting occasional glances at Joe and me. Other than some distant cousins of Daddy's, Dixie's friends, and a few girls from school, I hardly knew any of our guests—church and townsfolk Maudy made me invite.

I made a beeline for Mavis and insisted we fix plates for her parents. Their shyness almost kept them from attending, so it was no surprise when they didn't get in line for supper. Rupert and Loretta were not readily accepted outside their own church and family circle. Of course, it had a lot to do with the fact that Rupert was white and Loretta was a very dark black woman.

Mavis balanced their plates in her hands, and I couldn't help but notice how she had inherited her mother's flawless complexion and raw exquisiteness. Her eyes sprang to mine, wide and attempting to cover her many insecurities. "Where's the Reverend?" No matter how hard I tried to make Mavis believe she was truly talented and gorgeous, I knew she continued to fight the feeling that deep down, she was just a nobody.

I nodded politely to guests and led Mavis back to her table. "Calvin doesn't go to wedding receptions."

"That against your religion? Say it in the Bible somewhere?"

"You know it doesn't. I think it's to make him seem more mysterious," I said.

"Personally, I'm glad the blonde bombshell ain't here."

"Quit calling him that; it's disrespectful. Somebody might hear you." I found Mavis's parents perched at a table like two parrots with nobody to talk to except Daddy. It wasn't a surprise Daddy had chosen to sit with the Dumass family since he and Rupert had been best friends since childhood.

"Where's the band?" Mavis asked.

Daddy grinned. "House of Praise folk don't believe in dancing or drinking. Or smoking." He lit his unfiltered Camel and blew a straight line of smoke into the hot air above his head. "Ain't that right, Rosebud?"

I smiled at Daddy, despite his shrewd comment. He'd called me Rosebud since I was a baby, a combination of both of our names.

Mavis laughed out loud. "You can't be serious." Loretta shot her a look. "Sorry, Mama," she said. "Andie, you want me to sing? How about a little *Proud Mary*?" Mavis clicked her fingers and boogied in her seat to the music in her head.

I stood to leave, kissing my friend on her forehead. "Ike and Tina would be honored, but I doubt my guests would appreciate your joke."

"Who's joking?" She grabbed her camera and snapped my picture.

I turned my attention to Joe, mingling with guests. The uncomfortable look on his face was my cue. "My husband needs me." I giggled at the sound of my words. "Rupert and Loretta, enjoy your supper. Daddy, behave yourself and smoke outside, okay?" I managed a tremulous smile. "Mavis, be happy for me!"

She shook her head. "Go on. Go to Church Boy before he struts over here. I'm not up to congratulating him for taking you to Salisbury."

"It's only an hour down the road. Besides, you're the one heading for New York!" I said as I walked away.

Mavis yelled something that left me, as well as a few nearby guests in shock. "You can annul this stupid thing tomorrow and go with me!"

I pretended not to hear because otherwise, I would've walked back and slapped her. I stayed away from Mavis the rest of the night, and never called to say goodbye the next morning before she left for New York City. Something for which I will never forgive myself.

August 1972
REALITY GRABS HOLD

Andie

    Shady Acres was shady, but not with trees. Several low-income families had parked their homes in the rusted tin-can village on the north side of Salisbury. Children played in the street while women hung clothes from lines strung between their trailers, gossiped, and drank beer on concrete-slab patios. I smiled at the neighbors and vowed to act lady-like, a little sour with the knowledge they were all staring at me as I followed behind Joe and the realtor. After peering down at the lone flowerbed of weeds and late-summer tomatoes next to the porch, I sighed. The bleak reality of my new living conditions hit me hard. I broke my vow after stepping inside and covering my nose with my hand. "It stinks in here."

    "It's got a gas stove." The realtor fumbled with the knobs.

    "It smells like eggs," I said.

    "I'll have it checked."

    The realtor's lop-sided apology went unacknowledged. The kitchen reeked, no argument please. Following Joe into the living room, I watched him nod and smile. Tears puddled in my eyes. "Orange carpet and drapes? Royal blue couch? I think I'll choose what's behind door number three!" The rental agent excused himself and slipped out to the porch for a smoke.

    "Very funny," Joe said.

    Observing our possible new love nest with a critical eye, I couldn't help it. I cringed at the thought of even sitting on the furniture. Turning sharp on my heel, I walked back through the trailer and smirked. "A bedroom *and* a bathroom. Ain't we lucky?"

    "Not bad for a trailer though." Joe followed me with his hands in his back pockets.

    Purple shag rugs and a matching fuzzy toilet cover did not distract from the lime green circles on the bathroom wallpaper. "I can't live in a crayon box, Joe. Dixie will just die if she sees this. It's awful. You can't expect me to live here, honey . . . please?"

    "Yes, I do. Can we stop the sarcasm?"

    "No!" I walked into the bedroom and pointed to the picture over the bed. "Velvet Elvis has to go." I didn't mean to spout off, but my words just burst out like a vengeful sneeze.

    Joe rubbed his head. "I need aspirin. Listen to me, Andie. We can't live like your folks. We ain't got that kind of money. They were poor when they started out, remember? Took a few years until your daddy made good. It'll be the same with us. This place is a hundred dollars a month. We can't afford more. Look at this way . . . it's the best trailer in the lot."

    I crossed my arms in front of my chest like a stop sign and hung my head. I couldn't speak. Joe pulled me into his arms and kissed my cheek. His sweetness along with his endearing words moved me into submission. "We got to make do . . . at least for a while," he said. "We'll both be at work all the time anyhow. Shoot, Mama expects us over for supper most nights. She knows we ain't got a pot to piss in. Live within your means until God provides the increase. Reverend Artury preached about it, remember? We got to pay our dues like everybody else, Andie. You can do this for me, right?"

I nodded and followed him back to the living room, watched him flop into a chair and cross his feet on the plastic coffee table. Much to my surprise, I smiled at him.

"C'mon, now," he said. "It's not so bad. It's a dadgum twelve by sixty foot trailer. We got more room in here than most of the apartments we looked at."

I finally got it. Joe had a keen eye for tacky. He never understood décor or quality, and he loved cheap. He reeked of it as much as the kitchen did of rotten eggs.

"I know this ain't what you're used to, but you'll fix it up," he said. "Shoot, someday when we're living high on the hog, we'll look back and laugh about this place."

It didn't make me feel better. The single-wide—no matter what I thought of it—sat within walking distance to Joe's work. My fantasy house faded into the sunset of my best daydream. I had no idea what made me expect better on what we earned.

Joe backed the Javelin out of the gravel driveway. I rested my head in the crook of my arm and leaned out the open window. We'd have to buckle down; never miss church. Maybe God would see our dedication. Give us a break. I recalled Calvin's recent sermon. He'd said to give out of our need, look for a blessing, and we'd surely be blessed. A little act of trust. *Give, and it shall be given unto you; good measure, pressed down, shaken together, and running over, shall men give into your bosom. For with the same measure that you give it shall be measured to you again. Somewhere in Luke's gospel, I think.* Prideful, I gave up my life as Bud Parks' daughter and settled for less as Joe's wife. Driving out of Shady Acres that day, I stared at the one-size-fits-all trailer in the rear-view mirror. I figured I'd swallow Calvin's definition of faith and see what comes out the other end.

§

We moved into the trailer park a week later. Two days before my eighteenth birthday. The pig-naked truth of our pitiful finances fell hard on me, yet I agreed with Joe. We had to tithe. Together we resolved to give ten percent of our gross earnings to God, or rather the House of Praise, hoping God would honor our newfound faith, help us pay our bills, and put some beans and cornbread in our bellies.

November 1972
JOE

Andie

He wasn't the average Joe. Smaller than his brothers, what he lacked in size he made up in beauty—sharp and serrated, like the gleaming edge of his bowie knife. A brilliant smile of perfect teeth, Joe's chiseled cheeks reflected light and shimmered with health when clean-shaven. Hair the color of Carolina sand, his striking cat-green eyes were as big and round as my aqua blues. I saw an infinite capacity for kindness in Joe's eyes. At 5 feet 11 inches, he weighed 170 pounds, most of it carried in his chest and shoulders from working on tobacco farms in his youth. He had a permanent suntan and lived in Levi's, white T-shirts, and a ball cap and boots, even in the summer. Barely twenty-one, he turned heads everywhere he went.

Joe dedicated himself to the task at hand. A natural handyman, he became hell-bent on finding a good-paying job to reclassify himself as a successful man in the eyes of his family and the members of his church. My young husband's desperate job search—one that didn't need a college degree—prompted bouts of depression and abrupt changes in his personality. His brothers' achievements only served to emphasize Joe's lack of any. His boss, Coot, began buying him a few beers after work—*an employee benefit*, he'd said. Joe said it also eased the pressure to be perfect. I liked it that Joe wasn't perfect. My daddy kept Pabst Blue Ribbon in his refrigerator and I never saw the sin in it. But Joe kept a written record of his sins and of every dime he spent in his pocket ledger and demanded I do the same. He told me he wanted us to have more out of life than what he had to offer. So, on nights at home in his underwear on the couch, he drank a beer, asked God to forgive him for it, and then worked on his lists. To-do lists, to-buy lists, to-find lists. Still, his aspirations for a better life left no extra money for me.

I remained quiet about our living conditions, and resigned myself to the sacrifice of my husband's dreams for a new and improved lifestyle. Momentary poverty did not stop me from enjoying my new marital status until the first evening Joe arrived home, drunk and burbling like a baby. Soon, Saturday nights became a ritual. Supper with Maudy and Al concluded with Joe promising to return home early. By three in the morning, I was holding my husband's head over the toilet while he begged my forgiveness, swore he loved me, and apologized for his behavior. By dawn I would have him in shape for Sunday services. The cycle continued every week. I chose to deal with Joe's depression alone, hiding it from our families.

But after a particularly long Friday night service, the drive home gave me the captive audience I needed. The November air had turned as crisp and chilly as Joe's mood. "I don't understand," I said. "You were raised in this church, yet it's like you wear a mask. What's wrong with being yourself?"

"Are you calling me a hypocrite?"

"No. You're a good ol' boy beneath a Godly exterior you created and can't possibly live up to. It's making you crazy."

"But I got to quit sinning," Joe said. "Who I am is not good enough. When the rapture comes, I want to be ready. *Be ye therefore perfect, even as your Father, which is in Heaven, is perfect.* The gospel of Matthew is plain. It takes living a perfect life to get into Glory. The Bible says *sin will not enter in.* At some point, God's gonna quit forgiving me for backsliding every week."

"That's ridiculous. We all make mistakes. I believe the true meaning of perfect is *to be looked upon as good.* Not sinless. Nobody's sinless. What about God's grace? Doesn't the Bible say His mercies are renewed every morning? You've got to quit beating yourself up."

"You think you're so damn smart. Your daddy teach you that? I keep forgetting you weren't born into this ministry like I was. There's no excuse for sin; Reverend Artury said so."

"Crap, Joe, we're not trying to get into a country club. God doesn't just love Calvin."

Joe slammed on the brakes at a red light. "Would you please quit calling him by his first name! Show some respect, how 'bout it?"

"Okay, sorry, but you're putting too much pressure on yourself. If this is about money, I'll find a job, soon. Maybe we should move to Raleigh. Make a fresh start. Work harder."

"We're not moving anywhere. And I'm already working as hard as I can. Six days a week for minimum wage." He looked away and stared at the road. His next words burst off his tongue like spit. "I should've stayed at home a while, not married, gone to school."

My eyes filled with hot tears. "You regret marrying me? Is that what you're saying?"

Joe's hands choked the wheel. "Trying to get to Heaven and providing for you at the same time ain't easy. I wish we would've waited, that's all I'm saying."

"Supporting a wife and children makes it worse for *you*, that's what you mean."

"Shi—shoot-fire! Why are you always putting words in my mouth? A wife's all I can handle right now. Don't you dare get pregnant. Don't you dare. You take those pills. You hear?"

"Uh-huh." I'd yearned for a baby from the time I stopped playing with dolls. Grim, silent tears crusted on my cheeks by the time we arrived home.

§

As time passed, Joe's admiration for Calvin increased to believing the House of Praise was his only means to peace of mind, and yet his fight to live free from sin grew harder every week. The more he tried, the more depressed he became and the more demands our pastor made from his pulpit to live holy. One Sunday morning, Calvin prophesied the miracle hand of Jehovah-Rohi was on the youth at the House of Praise; that God had great plans in store for us. That's when Joe stopped talking about wanting more out of life, and a yearning to break free from Calvin's powerful grasp invaded my daily thoughts. But after a quiet supper one evening, the yearning turned into a chill that rippled from my head to my feet.

Joe scraped food off his plate into the garbage pail. "God wants my total attention," he said. "Reverend Artury has asked me to work in audio control, recording the services on tape. So I said I'd do it. He's sending me to a community college to take classes. I feel like God has answered my prayers. I'll still work for Coot, but I'll also learn a new trade."

I gave him the best smile I could muster. "Are you getting paid to record the services?"

"Didn't you hear me? I said I'm still working for Coot. Can you quit thinking about getting rich for a second? I'm taking classes in sound engineering all paid for by the House of Praise. I like the idea. Our tithing is paying off. Things'll get better, Andie. You'll see. I feel God's call. He's leading me into a new profession. I'm not leading Him for a change."

Two nights later, he lay on the bathroom floor, drunk, while I sank to the fuzzy rug beside him. "What's going on?" I asked. "Why are you doing this? Please, Joe. I need help understanding—"

"You need help?" His forehead was dotted with beer sweat. Eyes swollen and red, Joe glared at me. "Why do *you* need help? I love you, Andie, damn it. But it's me who needs help. Me! What's wrong with me? Don't you dare call Mama. I never want my family to know. Promise me."

I ran my hands through my uneven bangs. "I promise."

§

Maudy sensed our rocky relationship and assured me all marriages started out that way. I viewed my rocks as boulders. The road ahead appeared dark and impassable on nights my husband suffered through his black moods. Then, without warning, the clouds gave way to sunny dispositions. I learned how to live with him, and said little when the depression held him captive. Maudy encouraged me to make sure Joe stayed in church. That was the easy part.

To Joe, church was a drug. He got high talking about God. His buzz lasted long into the night telling me how fortunate we were to be members of Calvin Artury's ministry. I only listened and blinked, my head heavy on my pillow. He believed like the rest of the congregation—that we were better than everybody else. "We'll arrive in Heaven long before the Baptists, Presbyterians, Methodists, and certainly the Catholics, if those idolaters get in at all."

I swallowed a yawn. "What about the rest of the world's religions?" I found Joe's beliefs confusing. I'd heard Calvin allude to the congregation's superiority, but as the daughter of Bud Parks I refused to believe in elitism, especially where Jesus was concerned.

"The Jehovah's Witnesses and Mormons are racing each other to Hell, as far as I can see," he said. "I've heard if you even look at a Buddhist or a Hare Krishna you can become demon possessed, needing salvation all over again.

I know men in the church who wouldn't hesitate to shoot an Atheist if they knew what one looked like."

I snickered. "Who?"

"Well, me and a few others."

"You wouldn't shoot anybody. I know you better than that, Joe Oliver."

"Don't be so sure. I'd do anything for the cause of Christ," he said. "I've dedicated myself to God's will. I'm a disciple. *And it shall come to pass in the last days, saith God, I will pour out my Spirit upon all flesh* . . . I don't want to be a lukewarm Christian, Andie. I want His smile on my life. A life without a spot or wrinkle."

"This conversation is too heavy for me. I'm sleepy." I waited for him to put his arm around my waist, hoping to add more than two days a week to our lovemaking, but my see-through nighty wasn't working.

"I feel like reading my Bible awhile. You sleep," he said.

The sudden light from the living room cast strange shadows in the bedroom's darkness. My hope for a better tomorrow waned and my heart cried to bury every uncertainty in his arms. Wishing Joe would change his mind and lay down the second chapter of Acts to lay with me, I felt my eyes grow heavy. Church turned him on far more than I did and we'd not even seen our first anniversary. *How can I possibly be so jealous of God and still call myself a Christian?*

May 1973
A Nonexistent Indiscretion

Andie

Joe proclaimed he finally beat the blues and his need for alcohol; that he had become the man God wanted him to be. But I grew despondent watching him add a new sin to his list—gawking at girls in the car's rear-view mirror. Attracted to Barbie dolls everywhere he went, Joe flirted with the young women at church and pushed the limits of his marital boundaries. He was drawn to pretty females, like I was to donuts and Oreos.

And then there was Candace Cooper, a beautician at the local beauty shop who lived across the road. Joe dashed out the door like a dog after a bitch in heat every time Candace and her skinny legs, tight pants, teased hair, and double-D cups arrived home with a load of groceries. Of course, women who live in trailer parks can't keep a secret to save their lives. With all the open windows during the warm months, stories floated out of Shady Acres, around town, and eventually to Maudy that Candace was a bona fide hussy. "She's twice divorced," Maudy said, "and her fourteen-year-old daughter smokes pot. They're trailer trash. The absolute worst."

I mentioned my annoyance about Candace to Joe, but he blew it off. "Stop bringing this up," he said, giving me one of his goofy grins. "Mama would disown me if I ever cheated on you." I smiled a bland, half-smile, satisfied until the afternoon I discovered naked girls under our bed. In magazines. At first, it surprised me. I understood how it could be a turn-on, especially to a man. Except smut had moved into our trailer like a drunken uncle with more than a few winks and wet kisses on his mind. Three or four nights a week, Joe opened his *Hustler* to a big-busted woman spread across two glossy pages and made love to her while I watched from my side of the bed like a submissive puppy and said nothing.

I questioned whether something lacking in me caused Joe to need the kind of stimulation he found in those smutty pictures. Wasn't I pretty enough or sexy enough? I'd gained a little weight, but I didn't think anybody noticed. One morning I stuffed a note into his lunch bucket. *Would you like to counsel with Calvin about your magazine problem?*

The next morning he left a note of his own: *FYI, I've already talked to Reverend Artury. He referred me to Hebrews 13:4. Marriage is honorable in all, and the bed undefiled. Nothing we do as a married couple is a sin. Nothing. I know we can't afford them. So I'll stop.*

I balled up the note and pitched it into the trash, my cheeks fiery. "It's not the money, Joe. Damn it! It's how it makes me feel!" Later I discovered most of the magazines under the bed were gone—along with a large storage box I had used to move my cookbooks into the trailer after the wedding.

June 1973
ANNOUNCEMENT

Andie

Blonde-headed and covered with strawberry freckles from head to foot, my mother-in-law smelled like soap and sunshine. Maudy's unruly hair had thinned by her forty-ninth birthday and her scalp burnt every summer. The most interesting part about her was that she believed, wholeheartedly, in divine healing. She believed a prayed-over bad back could be made whole overnight and a bad attitude could be cast out with a Bible verse. She also believed walking barefoot cured warts, drinking rainwater repaired split ends, and good bowel movements prevented migraines. Her strong, homespun beliefs had endured economic hardship. At least, that's what I'd been told. Maudy flaunted herself as queen mother of three handsome, sandy-haired sons and demanded their attention come Hell or high water. Her passionate interests—once missionary work and saving the souls of heathens and starving children—were suddenly her boys.

Maudy's rubber-soled slippers slid and squeaked like basketball shoes on a gymnasium floor as she dashed around the kitchen preparing supper. We'd spent the afternoon scrubbing and waxing her worn linoleum and then snapping beans. Taking an occasional sip from her coffee cup, she updated me on the weekly news from town and church, while I sat on one of her six mismatched chairs at the chrome-legged table near the open window and watched Joe work on our car. In the center of the oilcloth-covered table sat a sugar bowl, a plastic tub of margarine, a bottle of Red Hot, and a ceramic daisy napkin holder that I filled while Maudy talked.

Next thing I knew, Ray drove into the yard like a man on a mission. He parked his yellow '69 Camaro beside a giant oak, stepped out and stood in a 'James Dean lean' against the tree, his shirt collar upright, arms crossed, and a lit cigarette between his fingers. Shaking his head, he tossed his cigarette into the driveway and extinguished it with the toe of his shoe. I was only too happy Maudy didn't see him do it. Walking toward his daddy's backyard body shop, he rubbed the back of his neck like he was edgy about something and hollered, "Hey, Daddy!" Southern to the root of his soul and proud of it, Ray loved Tar Heel basketball, deer season, and was pre-law. But he was neither bullheaded nor aggressive. Always clean-shaven, he possessed impeccable manners, and never forgot to praise his mama's good cooking. And like Ted, he played flawless piano. I knew Joe was jealous of his brothers, but we never talked about it.

Al hugged both of his sons into a football huddle before sitting on a pile of scrap metal to shoot the breeze with Ray. My father-in-law stood a head and a half taller than his wife. He was an eroded, old version of Joe with sagging earlobes and the same crew cut he wore when he stormed the beach at Normandy. Fifty years of tears and smiles had engraved deep wrinkles into Al's rugged face. Kindhearted, poetic and philosophical, he had worked most of his adult life in his shop, repairing cars and welding farm machinery for Rowan County farmers until his clothes and skin smelled of smoke and metal. He was a gentle giant and I loved him.

Moments later, Ray meandered through the back door. "What's for supper? Hey, Andie."

I glanced up from my coffee to catch my brother-in-law grabbing the spoon out of Maudy's hush puppy batter.

"Hold off, suppah's almost ready," Maudy said.

Blushing, Ray kissed his mother's cheek and handed her the spoon before beginning his well-rehearsed speech. "Mama, guess what?"

"Don't make me guess, Raymond. You know I don't like guessing games."

"Seems Reverend Artury's secretary has been trying to get in touch with me all week. I called Fannie back after class today. They want me to play piano for the choir. You know they've been needing somebody since Ted went to Nam."

When Maudy and Al's oldest son left home to join the Marines, the church went through several piano players hoping for his quick return. Ted astonished everybody and reenlisted as his tour of duty in Vietnam ended. Stationed at Camp Lejeune, Ted rarely phoned home and his letters were few and far between.

"Why that's plumb wonderful." Tossing her dish towel on the table, Maudy cackled like a hen in a feed mill. A sizeable woman, she put a serious strain on her housedress seams, laughing and carrying on about Ray's news. "My, my—Ray Oliver, the new House of Praise pianist," she chortled. "When do you start?"

"Hold on, Mama. I'm not sure I want to."

"And why not?" Her smile quickly receded into the folds of her mouth. A choir member herself, Maudy no doubt had a heavy hand in getting Ray on the church platform. I was sure of it.

"Now don't get upset. My school schedule's tight. I can't make all those services, and you know how they are about missing church. Besides, I just met a girl. *The* girl."

Maudy's elation converted to one of faked pleasure. "Oh? My, Ray—"

Al bolted in from the back porch with Joe behind him. My father-in-law shot me a wink and a grin before scrubbing his hands in the kitchen sink. "I'm starved. Let's eat."

"Put a sock in it, Al. Now Ray, as for attending church, I'm sure you can arrange your schedule to put God first." Maudy turned to her husband. "Our son has something to tell us."

"Make it snappy; I'm famished." Another broad smile lit Al's ruddy face.

Maudy untied her apron and eased herself down on a chair, her eyes fixed on Ray. Al sat by me and drummed his fingers on the oilcloth, his eyes alight with enthusiasm, which told me he already knew what Ray was about to say.

Joe leaned against the refrigerator with his hands in his pockets. "Good God, Ray. You finally find a girl to put up with your bull crap?"

Ray tilted his head toward his brother with a look of warning. Raking his fingers through his hair, he cleared his throat. "Well. Where do I start? Her name. Her name is Libby. Elizabeth Stewart from Chapel Hill." He said it like he was singing it. "She's studying to be a veterinarian. We met on campus. I—I'm sure I'm in love with her."

The quiet room gave me goose bumps, so I spoke up. "Well? What's she like?"

Ray looked at me and smiled. "She's intelligent with a wonderful sense of humor and from a big family in Virginia. The Stewarts own two horse farms up there and one here in North Carolina, near Burlington. I knew the minute I met her we were more than friends. I want y'all to meet her. Did I say she's smart? She made the Dean's List. And she's as pretty as you, Andie."

I blushed.

Maudy held her jaw rigid. "Does she go to church? Is she a Christian?"

"Yes, Mama, she's a good Christian. She goes to church."

"Where?" Her eyes bore into Ray's.

He hesitated, and then let it all out in one long breath. "She attends the Church of the Immaculate Heart of Mary in Chapel Hill. She's Catholic, Mama."

Silence prevailed, except for the hush puppies popping in the fryer.

Al jumped to his feet. "Anyone ready to eat? Smells good, Maudy. You make enough?"

Ray's face went white as rice. He turned to Joe. "That's it? No comments?"

Joe shrugged. "I guess any girl you pick, you ol' dog, will have to get by Mama."

At that, Maudy's blank expression changed to a feeble smile. "I'm sure she's a lovely girl. Bring her by the house as soon as you can. Will she at least attend church with you?"

Ray hesitated. "Sure, Mama. Especially when she finds out I'm the new pianist."

Maudy reached across the table and patted her son's hand. She didn't ask if Libby was saved and filled with the baptism in the Holy Ghost. I was sure she already knew the answer to that question because as far we could tell, Catholics didn't raise their arms when they prayed or preach a salvation message or speak in tongues. That inquisition would wait for another day.

A Conditional Marriage

Andie

In 1973, a pretty face was as good as a résumé. Eleven months into marriage, I landed my first real job. The manager at the First National Bank of Salisbury took a shine to my *delightful personality*, despite my obvious inexperience. He stared at my chest, handed me a new employee packet, and I became an official bank teller thrilled to take home my first paycheck of one hundred seven dollars after taxes. My optimism soared.

"It's a start, Joe. Maybe I can take some night classes, visit Dixie next week; buy some new shoes—" I stopped as Joe's expression went sour.

"What the devil are you talking about?" He dropped his supper plate into the sink. "You're bringing home barely enough money to pay the bills I can't cover and buy a few extra cans of beans. Ain't no money for shoes. Get your head outta your ass and stop buying donuts. We don't need that shit. Especially you. I've been meaning to talk to you. How much you weigh now? You eat as much as me, for Christ's sake."

My mouth flew open.

"I don't want a fat wife. Stop stuffing your face so damn much and we'll save a few dollars. As far as night classes go, who's paying for those? And we sure as hell don't have extra money for you to drive to Dixie's or buy shoes. You got enough gas to get to work and that's it! Quit your damn crying!" His boot met the refrigerator with a swift kick. Then he shoved me hard enough that I stumbled and fell, ramming my leg into an open kitchen drawer.

The shock of the shove paralyzed me, but only for a moment. I shot to my feet and grabbed my jacket. "You bastard!" Swallowing a list of dirty names I wanted to heave at him, I fled the trailer and traipsed a mile to the gas station at the end of the street, hoping he'd run after me. To apologize. But he didn't. *Damn him! What'd I do to make him so angry?* I directed my fury first at myself, then at Joe. And at God. And of course, at Calvin. *The tithe comes out first, the rest waits.* Calvin Artury got my shoe money.

Taking a quarter from my jacket pocket, I bought a Snickers from the vending machine. Sulking like a little kid on the slow walk home, I recalled a tender time of promises and vows, "… *no matter our future, Joe, I'll love you until the end of my days and beyond.*" For all my youth, my determination to make my marriage work was an innate obsession. Though anger pulsed in my veins, love reigned supreme. Joe had also made a promise. *He promised to love me forever.* A promise that could not be squandered away, even over a shove.

When I returned home, the car was gone. Standing in the doorway, I resolved, once again, to make the best of my situation—be brave, lose weight, and work harder. Exercise caution. Be all Joe wanted me to be. He didn't want a fat wife. *Am I fat?* I stared into the bathroom mirror, and then stepped on the scale. One hundred thirty-five pounds. I'd gained fifteen pounds since graduation. Sliding down the wall to the fuzzy purple rug, I pulled my knees to my chest. *So this is marriage. Don't I have a say?* It wasn't the partnership I envisioned.

I needed to talk to someone. Calling Dixie was not possible under the circumstances. I needed a friend, someone other than Maudy who, of course, was biased toward her son. I needed Mavis who had left me for New York City. I wrote her a letter every week, but Mavis, not being much of a writer, seldom replied. *God, I miss you, Mavis.* I needed to believe the success of my marriage was not conditional on how much I weighed or if I missed church. I needed to cry. So I did. For a long, long time.

§

Joe came tripping in the door at midnight, smelling like cigarettes and beer, sinking into the couch and kicking off his mud-caked boots. I stared at the clumps of dirt I'd have to vacuum before work in the morning. Keeping a tidy house was an inherited curse.

"I'm an asshole," he said, slurring his words.

I curled up in the recliner, tucked my feet under, and pulled my nightgown over the fresh bruise on my leg. A lock of hair fell to my cheek and I pushed it behind my ear.

Joe cocked his head and frowned. "Say something."

"What do you want me to say?"

He lit a cigarette. "I saw Coot. Told him about our fight. He said I'm an asshole. I guess I am. We got to watch our money. That's all I'm saying. That, and—sorry."

Albeit a lame apology, it moved me. "Okay. I'm sorry, too. Sorry for complaining about money. And, well—I'll start a diet. Let's not argue anymore, at least not tonight. I have to go to work in the morning."

Joe stood, pulled me into the bedroom and pressed firmly into me. With my back against the paneled wall, I shoved thoughts of sin and religion out of my head. Romantic lovemaking, like we did in his mama's attic before we were married, was all but forgotten. The smell of beer on his breath I usually despised, excited me. I was ready for him. Passion spread through me like grease on a hot skillet as I pulled his shirt loose from beneath his belt and ran my hands over his chest. His nipples grew hard in a second. He unbuttoned my nightgown letting it fall to the floor, pulled my bra straps off my shoulders, and in one quick movement unhooked the back. My swelling breasts offered a definite invitation. While he cupped and rubbed them, I fumbled with his belt, then his pants, yanking him naked. He lifted my one 135-pound body in his arms, and then laid me on the bed. I wrapped my fingers around his neck and pulled him down on top of me. "You take your pill?" he asked in a rush of breath.

"Yes," I said, and guided him in.

Joe pushed into me hard and swift. With his second thrust, all thought vanished as my body took him in, wrapping around him like a velvet blanket. My senses exploded as the smell of Joe was absorbed into my skin, the feel of him, and the soft sound of his breathing, the taste of his body as I opened my mouth against his face and throat.

"Oh, Andie Rose," he said, squeaking like he'd just inhaled a lungful of helium.

I drew myself closer to him. That time, at least, he'd left his *Hustler* under the bed.

§

The air grew heavy with sleep. Joe leaned over to kiss me. "I do love you. You got a pretty face, prettier than any girl I've ever seen. But you're getting a bit chubby in the ass. Please lose weight," he said. "Guys make fun of other guys with fat wives."

I yawned and plumped my pillow. "Okay."

Switching off the light, he turned to me once more. "By the way, Mama called. She wants us over for supper Saturday night. She's making peach ice cream for Daddy's birthday. It's his favorite."

I sighed. *Mine too. Damn.*

June 1974
SUCCESSFUL EVANGELISM

Andie

Calvin P. Artury was no ordinary man of God. Nobody knew what the *P* stood for, but he was educated and well-traveled, drove a new Cadillac every year, and as far as everyone knew he owned one home. A modest brick two-story in the suburbs.

To preach, he wore an immaculate three-piece suit, black with a white shirt, a red tie, a blood red boutonniere, and polished leather boots. With broad shoulders and a thick neck, he looked shorter than he really was. He advanced straight at his congregation, his head forward with a considerable stoop and a cast-iron glare like a dueling western legend. Once, to Joe's chagrin, I called him Cowboy Calvin. The six-foot Reverend had big, brilliant blue eyes and bushy blonde hair slicked back into waves behind childlike ears. Handsome to a degree, his curls fell down around his shirt collar, and he spoke with a Southern accent not unlike my own.

He first wheeled and dealed his way into radio. Admired and respected by his audience, Calvin was our first link to Heaven, our own religious psychic. No one dared to cross him; many believed he alone had the ear of God. I don't remember where I first heard that Calvin was the son and grandson of bootleggers. Everyone knew his virtuous and churchgoing mama spoiled him rotten because he'd said as much. A perfect mama's boy, he accompanied her to church every week, yet he seldom mentioned his parents or his past. He did, however, admit to an indulgence in alcohol and dancing before he got saved and before God healed him from some unknown disease that supposedly left him at death's door. He said that's when Jesus appeared to him in a vision, commanding him to save as many souls for the kingdom as there were grains of sand on the shore. He said he had lots of visions after that.

Calvin's attractive wife, Vivian Artury, called Vivi by those who knew her, was a gifted pianist. She directed the choir in beautifully embroidered robes of the finest silks and imported materials from Europe and Asia. Her daddy, a judge and campaign organizer for President Eisenhower, adored his only child, giving her the best of life. Maudy said a rumor traveled the church circuit that Vivi's daddy believed Calvin was the next Billy Graham. But Calvin was beholden to no denomination, obtaining his divinity degree on his own and proclaiming his nondenominational status after their marriage. Strident fundamentalism brought him to power.

At every public appearance, Calvin's trophy wife hung on his arm. If the rumor mill of the Triad was to be believed, an unhappy Vivi threw herself into gospel music and other religious diversions. No two stories alike, the churchwomen believed she wanted a child and Calvin was opposed to it. The Arturys' cleaning lady told Dixie the Reverend and his wife slept in separate beds, which for some reason made my mother laugh when she heard it. I liked Vivi. Mostly because she made a beeline for me whenever I stepped into the sanctuary. I was just a bitty girl, but I remember her hugging me into her hip and saying to anyone within earshot, "Look at this pretty little thing, doesn't she have the most lovely blue eyes you ever did see?"

Calvin became a widower early in his career when Vivi died from cancer. No one knew what kind of cancer, just that it had killed her. When Vivi first became ill, Calvin proclaimed God would heal her. When God didn't, he told the congregation it was God's will and we all accepted it; then he buried her with more pomp and circumstance than royalty. White-gloved volunteers stood guard over her pink and silver-plated casket for five days prior to a four-hour funeral and burial on the church grounds under an imported twenty-foot high marble statue of Jesus commissioned by Calvin and carved in Greece.

About that time, Dixie let her loose lips fly. "He has the nerve to talk about the statues in the Catholic Church. Nice to know our tithe went to buy a big statue instead of putting food in a poor child's belly. I kept my mouth shut when they redecorated the church with velvet draperies and pew cushions and gold-plated the pulpit and the piano, but Vivi's funeral was a disgrace!"

Daddy summed it up nicely. "Seems Calvin's gone a little crazy in the head. That man just ain't wrapped right." The sad thing was, Calvin grieved for his wife, dedicating a year's worth of sermons to her memory. It got old. Vivi's death evolved into an unusual marketing strategy to increase church membership and gain sympathetic momentum. I would've rather had my head sewn to the carpet before sitting through another tear-jerking, three hours of poor-me-I-lost-my-wife-but-God-will-raise-up-this-ministry-because-of-her-death sermon. Except I listened anyway, like the rest of the members who sat in his pews.

In time, Calvin became an Elvis-type preacher. He shook, rattled, and rolled down every aisle, yanking people out of their seats and casting out evil spirits for everything from cancer, to a plain case of earwax build-up. Forceful in his approach, he'd motion for the sick person to raise their arms, then he'd shriek, "Thou foul spirits, COME OUT!" and smack their forehead with the palm of his hand. The healing process usually ended with the person falling backward, while ushers caught the prayed-over believer and lowered them to the new purple carpet. Sometimes, the floors were laid out head-to-toe with people having been slain in the Spirit. It always looked like one big miracle massacre to me.

But here's the kicker: I saw that God honored faith wherever He found it, because people did appear to get healed of all types of sickness and disease in Calvin's endless services. It was his major drawing card, attracting folks like flies to cake crumbs. Most came and never left. Because of the miracles, they believed whatever Calvin told them. That he lived perfect before God; that he was the chosen vessel through which Jehovah's divine gift of healing flowed. Simply put, people either believed or they didn't. Anyone who didn't was ridiculed for giving in to "lies of Satan." It was creepy. Calvin's voice, powerful and haunting, also declared himself anointed of God. I wasn't sure if he was anointed, but I'd seen him scare the shit out of folks and dangle them over Hell on numerous occasions. His prophetic messages predicted gloom and doom causing even the most righteous churchgoers to doubt their salvation, answer his altar calls, and cry out for forgiveness of unknown sins.

He preached about an irate, flood-heaving, fire-breathing God who insisted on getting ten percent of everything we made. A God who used unspeakable plagues, a den of lions and a fiery furnace to test the faith and conviction of His people. To me, the Old Testament God who only spoke to prophets, destroyed an army with the jawbone of an ass and whole cities with the breath of His nostrils, seemed so ruthless and just plain underhanded. A God who called for blood sacrifices didn't sound like a God I wanted to pray to, let alone worship. Daddy said House of Praise people tended to forget the dispensation of grace we lived in, that they loved their brimstone, and that Calvin wanted his flock believing they were a sin or two away from burning in Hell like a pig on a spit. It was funny and oh, so true. Calvin was a devout advocate of *scare 'em to death* religion. Even the church walls pulsated with fear and trembling. Yet, despite his cunning and talented use of fear, the congregation esteemed him. With immense affection, everyone called him *Reverend*. Everyone except me.

His church overflowed with believable testimonies, but Calvin was his own best publicist, exuding unbridled hope and ceaseless energy. When he mixed his North Carolina heritage and shining eyes with his down-home preaching style and proclaimed faith, it transformed multitudes of Americans from visitors into full-fledged House of Praise members. Rich and poor, young and old, red and yellow, black and white—it seemed he had the whole wide world in his hands. And yet, like Calvin, the House of Praise was anything but ordinary.

Unlike primitive tent revivals and clapboard steepled structures, the glitz and glamour of Calvin's church attracted folks of every class. Enormous crowds, rivaling those of big names in evangelism like Oral Roberts and Billy Graham, arrived in buses, car caravans, or by any means possible. Multitudes packed the pews like spectators at the Super Bowl. Blazing lights in the mammoth ceiling lit the sanctuary with brilliant illumination. An army of uniformed ushers, male and female, busied themselves with pre-service tasks: seating visitors, distributing tithe envelopes, and keeping a watchful eye on possible troublemakers. Polished, vacuumed, and adorned with large vases of fresh flowers, the House of Praise was a showcase fit for the wealthy. As much as Calvin embraced society's elite, he also opened his arms to the poor and the destitute, feeding them with hopes of a bountiful life and an eternity with Jesus. A constant flow of new folk joined the church until the parking lot, like Hell, had to be enlarged several times. By 1973, it was standing room only in the overflowing sanctuary.

Some believed Calvin was a type of Old Testament prophet or a modern-day apostle. When he strut into the sanctuary like a celebrity, people shot to their feet. A standing ovation began every service, as well as a heaping portion of piano and organ music. It rang out as he pranced roundabout his gold-plated pulpit, flinging his arms and singing old-timey gospel songs in his strange tenor voice. Often he broke into tongues and interpretation, foregoing any previously planned sermon. He frequently spoke of God using one of His Hebrew names, El-Shaddai, Jehovah-Rohi and others. The congregation learned to use them. It made us feel superior to the Baptists down the street who only knew God as—God. I believe Calvin did this to flaunt his relationship with the Almighty. It was like calling Vice President Ford, Jerry, or President Nixon, Dick.

The House of Praise Reverend commanded respect and attention, and declared he saw angels and demons entering or exiting the sanctuary. He claimed to hear the audible voice of God and preached Bible fasting with vim and vigor. "The scripture says, *this kind goeth not out but by prayer and fasting!*" I didn't think for a minute Calvin skipped any meals; at least I never saw him lose any weight to speak of. It was just another rule for being a good Christian, and as time wore on, those rules became harder to follow.

I soon sensed a change in his ambitions. He birthed a new urgency, a call to evangelism, spending as much as an hour or more collecting 'love offerings' separate from the tithe—thousands of dollars pledged for his projects: buildings, missions, and the ramp-up for television. For many, pledges were paid before the rent or mortgage. Unpaid pledges, according to Calvin, resulted in withheld blessings. Like a Veg-O-Matic salesman, he marketed Christianity like canned soup. Folks ate it up. He picked the pockets of the poor and the elderly, drained the middle-class of their savings, and preached the seed-sowing prosperity message to the masses. Every week he scooped up buckets full of tax-free money. People rose out of their pews with their fingers clutched around hard-earned cash, and while the music played on, they marched toward Calvin and tossed their love offerings into one of a dozen buckets lined up on the carpeted altar. A mass of believers giving with the hopes that it'd be enough for a better job, a newer car, or a bigger house. Though for some, with the miracle of sight, sound, or a sick child hanging in the balance, no amount was too great to give.

But what set Calvin apart from the rest of the religious world was the rapture. It was his favorite scare tactic to prevent folks from slacking off in their church attendance. We were told the chance for those who were left behind to make Heaven was slim to none. He said salvation was not enough. You had to speak in tongues, a heavenly language, to be caught up with Jesus in the clouds. No other church taught this. As a result, frightened multitudes jammed the aisles and the altar at the end of every service. With eyes shut tight, raised arms, stammering lips, tear-drenched faces, and sweaty bodies, folks tarried for hours, begging God for the gift of tongues with one or more Holy Ghost coaches shouting into their ears, "Praise you, Jesus. Praise you, Jesus. Praise you, Jesus. That's it! That's it! That's the Holy Ghost talking!"

One way or another, his growing congregation worried themselves into a tizzy about making Heaven, finding it difficult at times to live in the real world. With no board of elders, no deacons, and no governing body for him to answer to, Calvin pastored as he pleased. Members sometimes waited weeks for counseling, because according to Calvin—nobody else was spiritually qualified to counsel the sin-sick soul. Nobody except him.

But it was the children who suffered the most. A crying baby in the sanctuary was forbidden. Noise of any kind, unless Spirit-led, was not tolerated. Children under age twelve were sent to windowless Sunday school rooms in the church basement. Large male ushers yanked disrespectful teens out of their seats and planted them firmly in a front pew and no one said boo about it. The organized church, in my mind, had become a religious dictatorship.

In time, the hellfire and damnation beaded up and rolled off my back like spilled milk on a fresh-waxed floor. I grew bored and restless and escaped by way of secular paperbacks, believing every rip in my heart could be sewed up with a romance novel. Smuggling them inside my Bible cover, I figured reading a good Harlequin during church was no worse than the folks who managed to sneak out for a cigarette. While the congregation fled to the altar for their weekly weeping, wailing and gnashing of teeth, I refused to play Calvin's games. Although some held tight to the belief that God gave him power to read our minds, I wasn't so sure.

The one thing that worried me the most, however, was Calvin's affection for Joe. It held my young husband spellbound. He had known the Oliver boys from their early childhood, with Joe at his disposal to run church errands, mow the church lawn, or drive a church bus. No doubt it made Joe feel more special than his brothers, and since he was the only Oliver son with no career direction, I felt sure Calvin had used it to his advantage. He also wanted me immersed in his brewing religious efforts, his plan that included television, asking Joe if I had any special talents and keeping tabs on my whereabouts by way of Maudy. It galled me. Calvin had sucked us in and swooped us up in his three-ring circus and I soon wanted nothing to do with any of it. Every week I hid my growing unbelief and kept my mouth shut for the sake of the Oliver family.

Going through the motions, the boil festered. I tried to believe Joe would seek a better job with real career prospects, but I suspected he knew about certain plans the pious Reverend had for him. Other young couples in Salisbury had built new homes, bought new cars, and started their families. I still wore my clothes from high school, lived in a tenement on wheels, and drove a car with more Bondo than paint. We bowed to Calvin's wishes and followed his rules, never daring to ask why, and that didn't seem to bother Joe one bit.

Then, after years of complaining, Daddy decided he wasn't giving up his Camels for any preacher who wailed against the evil of cigarettes, especially in tobacco country. It didn't take much to convince Dixie to quit the church. She'd stomped on her soapbox, shooting off her mouth until I couldn't keep her backslidden condition out of the gossip circuit any longer. Joe said, "Give 'em a good lettin' alone." So I cut back on visits, but shunning my parents wasn't something I did easily. As an Oliver, I was tied to Calvin's ministry, and up until then I had only dreaded church. Suddenly, I hated it. It scared me that I hated it.

Still, Calvin's grip on Joe grew stronger. Trapped in a religious well of discontent, I splashed a smile on my face every Friday and Sunday. I had settled for so little, feeling stripped of character while the dreams of my adolescence vanished, and I quickly came to understand the meaning of long-suffering. As the months passed, Joe's depression loomed as thick as storm clouds and split us in two. It confused and exhausted me. But damn it, I loved him. No matter what I felt about Calvin and his House of Praise, I was comforted feeling Joe next to me on that church pew. As much as I faked my religious experience, my love for Joe refused to die. Nothing was more important than that. Not even my own happiness. I'd made my choice. I just had to find a way to live with it. Maybe some thought I was weak, and undeserving of sympathy. And maybe I was. But the day I met Joe, the spark of God's optimism embedded itself in my heart and refused to go out. Unconditional love vibrated through every nerve in my young body; it was the lifeblood of all that mattered.

LONG DISTANCE CALL

Andie

My knuckles cracked lifting the pressure cooker to the stove. A mess of green beans, ham and tiny red potatoes took little effort to prepare, except I wished I had another onion—and more bacon grease. Every Saturday, I contributed something for supper at Maudy's. After turning the flame down on the stove, I pulled off my sweaty T-shirt, unsnapped my bra, yanked my hair out of its ponytail, and headed for a badly needed shower. Wrapped in a towel, I stepped on the scale. I thought it was broken or that my eyes had gone bad. One hundred fifty pounds. I stood in the cool shower, and cried.

I had become one of the women in my neighborhood. Scrambling to find something to wear, I avoided the mirror. With no money to visit a salon, I cut my own hair. Lipstick scraped out of the bottom of the tube doubled as blusher. My mascara, like my patience, was all but used up. For the first time, I regretted marrying at seventeen.

Lying on the bed was like trying to rest in a steam bath. I carried a glass of sweet tea, more ice than tea, outside to wait for Joe and to catch an evening breeze. The sun was a big neon peach, its rays heating the scattering of mobile homes like ovens. I remember asking Coot who came up with the name Shady Acres. He'd said a former owner had planned on planting more trees, but ran out of money. When the phone rang, I bolted back inside.

"Andie Rose? It's your old pal . . . Motown Mama."

I hesitated, "Who?"

"Has it been that long, girl? It's me, Mavis."

"Mavis!" Mavis Grace Dumass—my confidante since birth. A total opposite in every way. Destined to protect me from the first day of second grade. The day she beat the snot out of a boy for calling me a nigger-lover. Mavis was a spitfire. Her face fixed in a constipated grin, my best friend had made a fist and dared anyone to call her Mavis Dumb Ass. As she grew older, her Diahann Carroll-beauty and Gladys Knight-talent became known in churches all over the Triad. I knew her gift of song would send her to places I would never go. "Lord, Mavis, you come home?"

Her laugh sounded tired and strained. "Nah, still singing in a dive bar with a band. Place sucks a big weenie, but it pays my rent. You know . . . paying my dues. I'm taking pictures with a local photographer on the side, though. Making extra between gigs. Thanks for your letters. I called Dixie. She gave me your number, and here I am! Can we talk? You busy?"

"You know me. Busier than a cat covering crap on linoleum," I said.

Mavis's laugh was comforting nonetheless.

"I've missed you, Mavis. I'm glad you got my letters."

"Look forward to them every week. Hey, you knocked up yet? Church Boy still whistling *Dixie* and flying his Confederate flag? Dang redneck. Why didn't he get drafted?"

I seldom mentioned Joe in letters to Mavis. She had voiced her opinion months before the wedding, declaring I was marrying beneath me for the man on top of me. Writing to Mavis about Joe would've been a waste of good paper. Ignoring her spiteful and crude comments, I shot back with my best Carolina drawl. "No babies yet, sugah. Cain't afford 'em. For your information, the draft ended a while ago. Thank you, precious, for inquiring 'bout my husband. *Joe's* fine. We're fine. I'm . . . fine. Mavis, you still smoke?"

Silence.

I stretched out on the couch and listened to my friend exhale cigarette smoke at the other end of the phone line, a sound like wind blowing through pine trees.

Mavis mocked my twang. "Have to support the family business somehow. Forget that, I had a feelin' you weren't . . . *fine.*"

"What makes you think that?"

"You silly goose, I can read you like we used to read those trashy *True Story* magazines you stole from Dixie. Anyway, thought I'd call and tell you to leave that bastard and get your butt to New York. Stay with me. You got to do your own thing before you're too old to do it. Lots of jobs in this city. Hey, you still working at the bank? There's a place here called Wall Street. Banks and shit like that. Men in suits. Cute, smart ones. Good God, Andie. You're not white trash. Aren't you sick of the South?" Mavis had barely taken a breath.

I disregarded her white trash comment, because it struck me that even though I'd not been raised that way, it was certainly what I'd become. I wasn't admitting anything to Mavis. "I've never been anywhere else. My family lives here. Why should I leave?"

"'Cause you're not happy." A bona fide hard-ass, Mavis knew me better than anyone.

I changed the subject. "It's hot as the hinges on Hell's back door. We were supposed to be at Maudy's for supper an hour ago and Joe isn't home from work yet."

"When's the last time you ate in a nice restaurant?" she asked. "You bought any new clothes since you married that bum?"

My mother had told Mavis more than my phone number. The interrogation gave me pause. I wasn't sure it was right to take out my anger on Mavis who only spoke the truth. Preoccupied with unreadable thoughts, Joe and his moods fluctuated cold and hot and I'd lain awake too many nights wondering why. I gritted my teeth and tried again to lighten the dialogue.

"Come on, that's enough," I sighed. "He's been as good as they get down here, I guess. I try not to complain. I'm paying my dues here too, you know. I'm glad you called. Will you be visiting your folks anytime soon?"

Mavis's tone changed. "I take it you haven't heard."

"Heard what?"

"Mama died a week ago. The cancer got her. Daddy had her cremated. No service; no money for one, I 'spect. I wanted to call, in case Dixie forgot to tell you, as usual."

I felt sick. "Oh my God, Mavis, I'm so sorry. It seems I've been out of touch with the whole world. I didn't know or I'd have gone to see your daddy. Are you coming home?" I made a mental note to call my mother and ask her why she hadn't phoned me about Loretta's death, and did she send a casserole or a pie to the family? Did anybody go to the funeral? My heart hurt for Rupert, and I listened for some hint of sorrow in Mavis's voice.

"Nah, Daddy's busy farming his tobacco. The tough old buzzard needed a son. Never got one. I can't come home. I can't get stuck in Hicktown again. I'd as soon live in Hell with my back broke than live in the South. Besides, I can't see Daddy needy. He'll be okay. Aunt Lula's at the farm with him. You 'member Mama's sister, Lula? She'll cook and clean for him."

Joe exploded through the front door. A hot gasoline-smelling breeze blew in with him. "You ready to go? I'll hop in the shower. Why you got them pants on, woman? It's 100 degrees outside. Who's on the phone?"

"Mavis. She's calling from New York City."

"Tell that darlin' piece of brown sugah hey from Joe." He stripped naked, leaving a trail of greasy clothes and dirty boots, then slammed the bathroom door behind him.

"Sorry. It's Joe; he just got home. He says hey, though."

"I heard him. Still one charming son of a bitch."

"He can be. He really can be."

"It's *fine*, Andie. I got to go anyway. Just wanted to check on you, and make sure you heard about Mama. Tell Church Boy to take better care of you, or I'll make an exception and come to Hicktown to punch in his pretty face. And he knows goddamn well I can do it."

More silence. I wished Mavis wasn't jealous of Joe. I wished she knew him better, knew the good part of him I was hanging on to.

"When you wallow with pigs, expect to get dirty," she said. Mavis's statement encased the nutmeg flavor of her mama's wit we both knew so well.

"Loretta teach you that?"

"Yeah." She paused. Then she just spit it out. "He treats you like a two-year-old with no sense. I hate him."

"But you don't know him. He's my life," I said, because it was 1974 and he was still my husband and we lived in the Bible Belt and I had always submitted to him, as God said to do.

"Shuh. Dawg life better, if you axe me."

"I ain't asking. I'm real sorry about your mama, though."

"Thanks." Mavis hesitated like she wanted to tell me something. "Take care, Andie."

I felt the sting of God's spark and took a deep breath. "I will. You do the same."

July 1974
LIBBY

Andie

The air felt parched from a cloudless sky and relentless sun. It painted the Piedmont in shades of brown as the season wore on with no rain. In the heat of the day, fat June bugs flew blind into the trailers at Shady Acres, sounding like someone throwing stones at the siding. Maudy gave me a flat of petunias, but I couldn't remember to water them and Joe had refused. Their spindly necks withered in the heat. Weeds grew in the driveway and patio cracks like litter, and a neighbor's sprinkler dribbled water over a patch of grass that looked as hard and buzzed as Al's crew cut. The air-conditioned First National Bank provided heat relief at work, but I drooped like my unwatered petunias walking to the car at five o'clock. Sliding behind the wheel, I burnt my legs on the vinyl upholstery and my blouse stuck to my back like a thick coat of Turtle wax. God, it was hot. I glanced in the rear-view mirror and wiped sweat off my face with my hand, anxious to get to Maudy's cooler house and her backyard full of shade trees.

The evening slugged by, just as vicious and sticky. I carried glasses of iced coffee to the front porch for Ray and Joe, and then sprawled out the length of the swing and stretched like a cat. My magazine in my lap, I imagined Joe talking about me the way Ray chattered on about Libby. He cherished her. I heard it in his voice. I had admired Libby's independence and drive as a woman and wanted to say so the next chance I got, but Joe got his digs in first.

"I think she's uppity. You need to put a harness on her head and a bit in her mouth. Rein her in from time to time."

Ray stood abruptly. "Don't you think it's about time you shut the hell up and grew the hell up?"

I raised my head from my *Good Housekeeping* in time to see Joe flip his brother the finger.

Ray snapped his head toward me. "I swear, Andie, how do you put up with him?" The screen door's spring screamed obscenities as he nearly yanked it from its hinges, stormed back inside and allowed it to smack the door jam behind him.

"I think I pissed him off." Joe's green eyes looked my way for sympathy.

I squeaked my tongue against my teeth and grinned at his sheepish expression. "Uh-huh."

§

On Fridays, the girls at the bank took turns bragging about their plans for the weekend. They appeared surreal as magazine models in the break room, wearing bright smiles and the latest fashions. Their weekends consisted of parties, movies, and nice restaurants. Picnicking in the mountains or shopping at the beach. My plans were always the same: church on Friday night, supper with the Olivers on Saturday, back to church on Sunday. I had lived in North Carolina all my life and had never seen its beaches. I hated weekends.

But I did look forward to sharing my back pew with Libby whenever she showed up at the House of Praise. Resembling a rare flower that busts up through hard-packed Carolina clay, Libby spread fields of wild fragrance and color without knowing it. I loved her belly laugh. It rolled out of her small frame to bathe those nearest her in absolute joy. Like warm rain dripping from the fingers of God on unworthy faces. Along with her deep-purplish eyes, her hair was the color of coal, and her gold watch, simple gold earrings, and alligator loafers meant she had the upper-class look squared away. Libby was one of the few females who dared to wear pants to church. Pressed slacks, a crisp sleeveless blouse, and a sweater tied at her shoulders, she possessed a liberated attitude that put most people off. Her intelligence and quiet elegance intimidated even me. She was only a year or two older, but we had traveled different paths. Her dream for a college degree came before her desire for marriage, children, anything. I found her way of thinking unusual, but I envied her ability and determination to make unpopular choices. Libby was a mystery, a fascinating young woman living in a world of opportunity that I, on occasion, saw in a movie or read about in a paperback.

She attended only two church services a month with Ray: far less than Maudy had hoped for. I was not surprised when Calvin requested Ray remain seated on the platform near the gold-plated piano, explaining he never knew when the mood for a song would strike him. I suspected it had everything to do with Libby, and that we'd see snowballs in Hell before we'd see Ray sitting next to an unsaved, liberated woman in the House of Praise. Calvin wouldn't allow it. He liked Ray's Ryan O'Neal looks and demeanor, and meant to keep him as altar decoration. It bowled me over that my brother-in-law put up with it. I knew Ray's devotion to his mother was what kept him at the House of Praise and its so-called anointed piano. But when his love for Libby surpassed it all, he'd leave. I knew that, too.

Libby neither commented on the services, nor participated. Calvin couldn't cast out her Catholicism, no matter how hard he preached at her. Hands folded in her lap, she smiled only when Ray looked her way. I was dying to know what she thought. Of Calvin. Of all of it. One Friday night as the herd of praise and worshippers headed to the altar, I reached for Libby's hand and whispered, "Be honest, what do you think of our pastor?"

She squeezed my fingers and said, "The best sermons are lived, not preached. You're brave to sit under this agony. Hold on as long as you can. Maybe you'll win your tug of war."

CONCESSION

Andie

One cool summer evening, I observed my mother-in-law's pained face deep in thought. Up to my elbows in dish suds, I broke the silence between us. "What's wrong, Maudy?"

"I was thinking Ray will probably leave the House of Praise and go with Libby. I don't like it none. What can I do? He always did what Al and I told him not to."

"He's a good man," I said. "It's plain to see Ray and Libby love each other."

"I know, I know. Really, I hope they move to Chapel Hill. Better yet, Virginia, near her folks. Best everybody think Ray left the church because of a new job rather than believe he backslid because of a Catholic woman. At least you and Joe will stay at the House of Praise, like me and Al, right?"

My heart sank and my eyes filled with tears as Maudy trumpeted her vision of our future. I couldn't speak. I took a short breath and looked my mother-in-law in the eye, attempting to smile, when all I wanted was for a little of Ray to rub off on Joe.

Maudy wiped my tears away with a dish towel. "Thank you, sugah. I knew you would. Once you've been healed by the touch of the Master's hand, you never forget where your loyalty lies. For me, that's with the man of God, Reverend Artury. I praise God's holy name every day knowing you and Joe will raise your babies in the fear and admonition of the Lord, as we did. I've prayed so hard for my Joe to become the missionary I wanted to be." Maudy gave my arm a gentle squeeze. Her eyes brimmed with tears. Then she grinned, nodded a little with her chin, and lowered her voice as if she were about to reveal a secret. "I've spoken to Reverend about Joe. He agrees the call of God is on his life. I'm proud of the way you two are standing for Jesus. Hold on to the horns of the altar, my sweet daughter. Your day will come."

My day? What had come was pure frustration, manifesting itself in weight gain and plenty of sleepless nights. I'd worn myself to a stump, begging Joe to tell me what plagued him, but he wouldn't open his heart. Not even a little. We fought like pit bulls. Frustrated as he was tormented, I couldn't patch up our marriage, so I scrubbed and scoured every room in our trailer like a woman gone mad, then sat with the lights off, quiet and alone, and cried until dawn.

Maudy didn't see the side of Joe I saw. His dark side. His staying-out-until-two-in-the-morning side. His nasty temper side. Joe had forbidden me to tell her any of it. All Maudy saw was *Holy Joe*, prostrate on the altar every Sunday, pouring out his heart to Jesus. I hated to spoil her vision of her perfect son, but she'd probably not see any grandbabies from us. Calvin's strange and powerful influence was real and Maudy had no idea the damage she'd done by pushing her precious Reverend down all of our throats. I suspected Joe didn't want kids. I wasn't sure, but the thought of bringing up the subject of children again frightened me.

§

Miraculously, two weeks passed with no black moods, no alter ego, and no drinking binges for Joe. We'd even had supper in town two Saturdays in a row. I'd lost five pounds and suddenly, when Joe spoke, he looked at my face instead of staring right through me at everything more interesting. Church life had improved for him, too. Not only was he awarded the privilege of recording the services, but he had also been asked to tape the choir on Tuesday nights during their practice. Even Coot had given him a small pay raise. When Joe was happy, I was happy.

But a roadblock loomed in the distance on Joe's street of contentment. His long string of good days ended the moment I jokingly mentioned I'd forgotten to take my birth control pill. The battle commenced while supper dishes crusted in the sink of my otherwise tidy kitchen.

"Kids mean even less money, and an even fatter wife!"

"But I didn't do it on purpose!"

"You can't be this careless since . . . well . . . since I've decided we're not having kids."

"*You've* decided? How can you make this decision without me?" My voice cracked. "What about how I feel? You're never home, Joe. I'm sick of being alone. You knew I wanted children. You *knew* it!"

My husband was suddenly an unmasked stranger. His eyes turned murky and expressionless, but his coldness had become all too familiar. "I knew nothing! We were young and stupid. We still are, don't you see? We can't bring kids into this world because *you're* lonely. Reverend Artury—"

"For God's sake! Leave him out of our lives for a change!"

"You really don't get it, do you? He's our Shepherd. He is the voice of God in my life, and he should be in yours, too. If Reverend says this world is not a place to bring children into, then I believe him. I trust him. He's known me all my life."

"Well, hot damn for you! He sure hasn't known me or he'd know I want children!"

"Stop it, Andie. Look around! The world's a mess. You really want to bring up children in this sick world? There's so much to be done before Christ returns. How many times will you ignore the fact Jesus is coming back soon? Having kids will get in the way of our efforts."

"Whose way? Yours? Certainly not mine! This is not okay with me, Joe. I've always wanted children and you knew it!"

"I also know we can change our minds. I've changed mine. If you want to stay married to me, there'll be no kids. And don't you dare recruit my mama to convince me otherwise. Keep our parents out of our personal life. You've got to get right with God, Andie. Seek His face. I know you struggle. You've seen *me* struggle. I want to draw closer to the Lord. If you love me, you'll do this for me." Joe pulled his Bible off the coffee table. "Amos chapter three, verse three; '*Can two walk together, except they be agreed?*' This subject is not open for discussion. No children, not now, not ever. Don't forget to take your pill again, you hear?"

Stiff-shouldered, I sat motionless on the couch. Joe's low and disturbing tone hid the anguish in his words, the pain in his voice I was not privy to—it all frightened me.

He got down on his knees, swallowed hard and folded his fingers over mine. "Please, Jesus. Let my sweet Andie Rose see. Help her to be a Proverbs thirty-one woman for me. Open her eyes and show her Your will for our lives. I don't want to walk this road without her." He looked up at me and smiled. I returned his smile with little compassion as my vision blurred with unshed tears, watching my white picket fence disappear before my eyes. I'd never heard him pray out loud. When he laid his head on my lap, my hands, soft and weak, stroked his hair, but a response evaded me. My tongue pressed hard against my closed lips. After two years of marriage, I barely knew him.

Joe pulled himself up and sat at my feet. "I had a long talk with Reverend Artury I've been meaning to tell you about." He looked into my eyes and smiled again, like a child. But his face had become mature and more handsome even in the fault-finding light of the trailer. I had always adored his smile. I adored every bit of him. My resistance softened.

"Reverend has plans for me, for us. We're heading fast toward television. I may be asked to work on his full-time staff, televising miracle services to the world. Can you imagine when people tune in and see the deaf hear and the lame walk? In their living rooms? It'll turn the world upside down. The ministry will explode overnight, proving there is a God, and that He works through our pastor! Our pastor, Andie." His hands clutched his hair. "Think about it."

I raised my brow, but said nothing. The back of my throat grew dry, and I swallowed several times. It didn't help.

"Reverend's going to travel the globe. I'm going with him. It's a high honor and God will reward your sacrifice, as well."

With that revelation, my stomach soured at the idea of Joe traveling away from home, away from me for days at a time. But it all made sense. Calvin sending Joe to school. Molding him for the television ministry. I'd noticed Joe had worked hard at losing his strong Southern accent. He'd feathered back his hair and traded in his T-shirts, Levi's and boots for button-downs, khakis and loafers. There was no escaping our destiny. The path became plain.

"Reverend said religious TV broadcasting is the future. I'll have a real career, better than if I'd spent years in college. After all the stupid, meaningless, low-class jobs I've had, this is a new beginning. For both of us. It's big money."

Shedding a steady stream of new tears, I shuddered. "Yeah? What's it pay?"

He handed me a Kleenex. "Does it matter? I didn't ask him. It has to be a might better than what Coot pays me. I'll be working for the Lord. I've got to put God first, above everything and everybody."

Even me. I closed my eyes, pulled in a deep breath. Maybe it was wrong to refuse my husband this chance for a career in full-time ministry. Who was I to limit God and put Him in a box? Despite how I felt about Calvin, maybe a prestigious job working for a well-known preacher would help Joe feel better about himself and about us. Once again, I'd find a way to fit in and be happy. Life wouldn't be what I'd hoped for, but I'd adjust. Maybe Joe did indeed possess the missionary heart his mama had prayed for, and like it or not, I'd got part of what I wanted at least—a marriage, albeit a weak one. Maybe we'd find a new place to live. With a white picket fence at least. Half a daydream-come-true was better than nothing.

Telegram

Andie

"It's blowing up a big one." Al tossed the newspaper onto the floor and got up from his recliner to close the living room windows.

The screen door moaned and snapped back as I stepped out to the porch. A sensation of sorrow and heaviness surrounded me. "Look at the sky. That's the darkest horizon I've ever seen." I shivered and looked at Maudy whose expression told me she sensed it, too.

"Weatherman on the radio said we're in for severe weather this evening. It's like the four horsemen of the Apocalypse could ride out of those storm clouds. Best be ready, Jesus is coming soon to rapture His saints," Maudy reminded us. "You know what Reverend says; if you're left behind, you'll either give your head to make Heaven, or take the mark of the beast and doom your soul to the Lake of Fire." The woman loved biblical prophecy and the book of Revelation. She perched on the edge of her pew, entranced, whenever Calvin preached about the rapture.

The first streaks of lightning crossed the sky and I counted to ten before hearing thunder.

"Suppah's ready. Let's go in before this hits," Maudy said, standing and removing her apron. As she opened the screen door, a car entered the driveway. "You expecting comp'ny, Al?" Al and Maudy descended the porch steps to greet our visitors while the rest of us stood in unison and ceased our chatter. The license plate indicated they were government officials. My heart rose to my throat. Ray put his arm around Libby, and I headed for Joe. He grabbed my hand, and we raced behind his parents to the car.

The driver remained seated while the other man opened the passenger door. A military man, he put on his hat as he exited the dull-green vehicle. He had a chest full of medals and was missing his left arm from the elbow down. He didn't smile. Just a head nod, first to Al, then Maudy. "Mr. and Mrs. Oliver?" Maudy's face had turned the color of ice.

"Yes, we're the Olivers." Al's voice quivered. "And you are?"

"Major Tim Holderman, War Department. I've news for you, sir, ma'am." Shaking Al's hand, he nodded again to Maudy. "Would you like to go inside? Looks like we're about to get hit with this storm."

Maudy couldn't speak, so Al said, "Just tell us what you came to say, Major."

The Major had a folder under the stump of his left arm. He reached inside and pulled out a smaller envelope. "It is not a pleasant task delivering this telegram to you, Mr. and Mrs. Oliver. One I have had to carry out all too often these past twelve years in service to our country. I regret to inform you, your son, Sergeant Theodore Oliver, has been killed in a helicopter training accident."

My hand flew to my mouth. Maudy's knees buckled, and she fell to the gravel. A gasp tore from Al's throat.

"Please accept our country's condolences, and know the Red Cross will return his body to you for burial as quickly as can be arranged. I have a letter for you from General Anthony Zinni. If you need assistance, or have questions regarding your son's death, please feel free to call the number on the letter. I am very sorry for your loss."

Tears streamed the length of Al's rugged cheeks. He shook Major Holderman's hand once more, then looked at his family and said, "The Lord gives, and the Lord takes away. Blessed be the name of the Lord." Ray and Libby knelt and wrapped their arms around Maudy. For one awful moment, I froze on the verge of hysteria. Joe knelt by Ray. Al dropped to his wife with me at his side, sobbing into his shoulder. In one huddled heap of sorrow, our grief was like the storm rolling over our heads. Powerful, dark, and intense. With one year remaining in his reenlistment, Ted had remained at Camp Lejeune to train young Marines. Instead of dying in the rice paddies of Vietnam, he died in a farmer's peach orchard, somewhere in South Carolina.

I didn't notice the Major's car backing out of the driveway or the amount of time that passed. Clustered near Maudy, we pulled at her to get her to stand or at least move off the gravel where she fell. She wouldn't budge. She had curled up in a ball, rocked back and forth, her hands clasped together over the back of her head as lightning flashed and rain fell like judgment.

Exasperated, I reached for Maudy's head and took it in my hands. "Look at me, Maudy, look at me!" She opened her swollen eyes; the rain had soaked our bodies. Everyone watched as I screamed, "Hold on to *me*, Maudy, hold on to *me*, take my strength. Ted wants you to stand!"

She grabbed my arms and like a newborn colt, wobbled to her feet, drenched and trembling. She spoke. "I will not curse God and die. We will stand together as a family and know that Ted is in a better place. We will find strength in the Lord, and in Reverend Artury's counsel." Maudy looked at me with lifeless eyes, glazed over from the rain and her tears. "Let's get out of the storm."

§

I had never known such sorrow. My sleep was filled with ghastly dreams of the crash while the horror of it was magnified by my insistent imagination. My heart heavy, I watched time pass. Within the week, the Red Cross delivered Ted's body to a funeral home in Salisbury, and the Oliver family laid him to rest in a Baptist cemetery a mile from their home. The 100 acres surrounding the House of Praise did not include a cemetery. The sole grave on the property belonged to Vivian Artury. The church didn't have a fellowship hall either, because Calvin didn't believe in serving food on church grounds.

Of course, Calvin officiated at Ted's funeral, finding it necessary to use eulogy time to save souls from the fire of Hell. I imagined myself leaping to my feet and screaming—stop! The family needs to feel loved, not cursed! We need a message of healing, not another sermon of doom! But instead, I shrank into the background and said nothing.

It also bothered me that within the House of Praise there were no funeral committees to assist families in their hour of need. Calvin's congregation seldom fellowshipped with one another, let alone the rest of the world. Only Maudy's twin brother from Atlanta and the few people in Salisbury who knew Ted brought food to the Oliver home. I approached Maudy about it. "Your neighbor, Leola, told me the ladies at the Baptist church make sure their grieving families are taken care of. She said the church family should be an extension of your own." Maudy politely ignored me, kissed me swiftly on the forehead, and strode off to make coffee.

Dixie arrived with a peach cobbler and intentions of helping me organize food. I also knew my mother wanted the gory details of Ted's death. Sitting at the picnic table alone when I arrived with coffee for her, she smiled an unreliable smile. "You a size fourteen now? Isn't it time to buy some clothes that fit?"

I reached for a piece of cobbler. "You want to donate to the 'Andie Oliver Clothing Fund?'"

Clearly agitated, my mother clicked her tongue and said, "Always the smart-ass."

Hurt welled up in my throat. "Dixie, you got a beetle up your butt or what?"

"Should I send your sister down here for a week or two? Remind you of your own family?"

"There's no room for Caroline at my place and you know it. I should come to see you more often, I know. Except Joe only gives me a little money every week for gas and groceries."

Dixie reached for her purse under the Olivers' picnic table. "Here, take this twenty. Buy some gas and get a new pair of shoes at the Kmart or something. You look like the dickens. You been sick?"

I kissed her cheek, picked up my plate, and then stormed into the house. Maudy and Al were torn to pieces over the loss of their son, and all my mother could talk about was how shitty I looked.

September 1974
CONFESSIONS

Andie

Early September had been gray and drizzly, matching my mood. On the morning the skies cleared, Ray called and asked me to meet him for coffee. It didn't take him long to ask all the right questions. "You still hoping to move out of that trailer park? You and Joe thinking about having kids?"

I shook my head. "No kids. Joe's determined to work for Calvin—I mean, Reverend Artury. Full-time. Our crazy preacher hates kids. Kids mean less time and money you can give to the church. He wants no distractions: an army of young childless couples devoted without question." Ray raised his eyebrows. I had said too much. "I'm sorry. I didn't mean crazy. I—"

"Forget it, I agree with you," he said.

I sat back in my chair and blinked, my mouth open.

Ray stirred cream into his coffee. His green eyes, the same color and shape as Joe's, flashed and held their gaze on me. "Don't look so surprised. I detest him for taking Daddy's hard-earned money. *You* don't have any money. So what do you think the Reverend wants *you* to give?" His stare pierced right through me. "Joe. He wants you to give Joe. Which it seems to me, you already have. Now what, Andie? My brother spends every waking moment with that nut case. Why don't you get busy working on something worth giving *your* time to. Look, I was born an Oliver; I love God as much as the rest. I've cleared the cobwebs out of my head. Libby's helped me see my path a little plainer."

I looked hard at Ray, my eyes asking. Ray didn't need to hear my question to answer it.

"No, I'm not turning Catholic, and Libby's not taking up holy rolling anytime soon. But, I think it's what happened to Ted. His head cleared out. It's why he reenlisted. When you can step back, get away from it . . ." Ray's expression grew solemn. He teared up. It was clear he missed his brother. "Ted didn't want to get stuck in that mess again. It's a cult. I wish Mama saw it for what it is."

The word hit me full force. Ray had the balls to say out loud what few thought and even fewer dared to utter.

Cult.

The word rang in my head and wedged in my throat. "You really feel that way?"

"You bet I do. That's why I'm getting out."

"You're leaving? For real?"

"I can't take it anymore. Libby hates it. Be careful, though. The House of Praise is a subtle cult. Artury's slick, *and* he's a genius. He's much more dangerous than the Hare Krishnas he wails on about. His objective is control and manipulation. Money is a by-product. Don't be swayed by his religious exterior, no matter how many souls he saves or sick folk he heals." Ray bit into his jelly donut and wiped his mouth with his napkin. "Watch your back, Andie. I plan to talk to Mama and Daddy about it once they've grieved a little more over Ted. I can't make them do what they don't want to do. But if I can get them to leave, maybe Joe will, too."

"Oh, Ray." I took a deep breath. "That'd be an answer to my prayers. I can never call it a *cult* around Joe, though." I gave my brother-in-law an embittered nod. My eyes glistened with tears as I whispered my next words. "He might hit me." I looked away from him, and then down at my coffee.

Ray reached over the table and gently lifted my chin, forcing me to look into his eyes. "Joe's not like me. He's different. If he ever hits you, sweetie, you knock him into next week." He stared at me for several odd seconds. "Brother or no brother, you never let a man lay a hand on you other than for love, you understand me?"

"Sure."

"You have to do something with your life, little sister. Go back to school. Someday you may not have a choice but to be the breadwinner. Take the reins from Joe. Start thinking about your future. Force the issue with him, otherwise you'll be working for minimum wage and living at Shady Acres ten years from now."

I was touched, yet stung, by Ray's concern. Fear of my future struck me silent. When I was little I'd been told all women had crosses to bear. Crosses secretly strapped to their backs by men so they could swoop in, save the day, make themselves look like heroes. I never dreamed I'd have to save myself.

"Libby and I, well, we care about you. I don't want to see you hurt, by my brother or anybody. Only you can decide what you really want out of life."

The coffee shop window reflected a flush in my cheeks. My face burned with the truth. I caved. Leaning forward, I spoke in a voice barely above a whisper, but with the power of a scream. "I want a baby." I sat back and sipped at my coffee, watching a smile grow across Ray's face. "I stopped taking the pill. I've not told a soul. I figure it's time to lay my burdens at Jesus's feet. Let God decide, not Calvin or anybody else, whether we have kids. Or not."

Ray threw his head back and laughed out loud. He reached across the table and squeezed my arm. "Well, it'll serve that bugger brother of mine right. I don't see him making anyone happy but himself. I can't believe I'm talking that way about my own kin, but it don't take much to see what's going on."

My eyes narrowed and I wondered what Ray *wasn't* saying. "What do you mean?"

"Never mind. Get yourself a baby if you want one."

§

Unlike the cool wave of Labor Day, September's end ushered in more dog days of summer, escalating the petulance in both man and beast. Insects hummed a monotonous chirr, a round-robin of song in the heat of the day. Clear blue skies, scorching sun, and not a gust of wind, the South came to yet another standstill. Insufferable waves of heat floated above the blacktop parking lots and roads. Even Al took a break from the shop for a week. The high temperatures were too much under his welding helmet.

After nearly two months of mourning, Maudy had become a weeping wreck. Her pain was unbearable for all of us. I stopped after work one muggy evening to remind my mother-in-law she still had two sons who were alive, loved her, and couldn't stand to see her so distraught. When I walked inside, she stood by the window air conditioner in her sun-bleached housedress that had seen better days, arms folded, and peering out across the highway. Oblivious to my presence, she slipped her arms into the sleeves of her powder-blue sweater and pulled it close. Her hair shot in every direction. She didn't speak until I touched her shoulder, startling her.

"Maudy? Is the heat getting to you?"

With one hand she tucked a flyaway curl into the loose knot at the nape of her neck. An immediate rush of tears welled in her eyes. She spun around and darted out the front door to the porch, collapsing into a rocking chair. Rubbing her temples with the tips of her fingers, Maudy didn't want Al to overhear our conversation, so I closed the door tight behind me.

"It's not the heat. It's Ted. I keep reliving our last conversation. He said he hated Reverend Artury. He said when his tour of duty was up he wasn't coming home. I told him—I told him his daddy and I would disown him." Her confession sounded like a foreign language.

I shook my head. "What?"

"Last time he was home on leave, for your wedding, he dropped that bomb on us; said he was never going back to church. I went plumb crazy on him. It's my fault. My fault he's dead."

I stood motionless as Maudy wept into her hands. I had no idea what to say next, except the obvious. "Why? Why'd you say that to him?"

Maudy lifted her head and reached for a tissue in her apron pocket. A vein pulsed in her forehead. She wasn't pretty anymore. Her tormented face had aged over the past weeks. Agony had set her lips into scant straight lines, pencil-thin and bloodless under lipstick the color of raw hamburger, and her eyes were still lifeless. "Because I raised my sons to work for the Lord! You know that. I want to see my sons in Heaven because God knows the rest of my alcoholic family won't be there!"

"You've not disowned Ray," I said. "And you *know* he's leaving the church."

"That's right. Because of Ted, I swore I'd never again shun my sons for any reason. Ted was furious. I'll never forget the look on his face. He called us liars. Frauds. Hypocrites. Vietnam had hardened him, made him angry. I wish to God I handled it better than I did. But you know Al," she snickered. "Always been such a positive thinker. He thought Ted would come to his senses and we'd discuss it again when he came home. We never got the chance. We never got the chance." Maudy sobbed and when I handed her another tissue, I felt her tremor.

"Please talk to somebody about this. It's killing you."

"Al refuses to discuss it. I've tried to get an appointment with Reverend. It's impossible. This is my fault entirely. Now Ted is gone forever and I'll never be able to tell him how sorry I am. My God, Andie. What have I done?" Maudy bent her face to her knees and wailed.

I rushed for my broken-hearted mother-in-law whose back curled like a cashew. "I'll tell you what you did. You loved him with a true mother's love. When Teddy was a baby you held his hand, wiped his bottom, and handed him the world. You stood beside Al, raised your boys and never complained a day in your life. You made the best decisions you could make. Ted knows you're sorry. I know he loved you. I know he still does. And if he were here, he'd tell you himself. You have to forgive yourself, and Al has to do the same. It's time you practice what you preach. Time to hold on to the horns of the altar and get some strength from the God you serve."

Maudy lifted her head and looked at me with red eyes and tear-stained cheeks. "You *are* precious to me, daughter. I know Joe hasn't been what you'd hoped for." She blew her nose. "But someday he'll get it through his thick Oliver skull how blessed he is to have you. He'll come around. Thank you, sugah. I'll be okay. I have to be."

I wrapped my arms around her shoulders and breathed in her spicy scent of cloves and cinnamon. "Yes, yes you do," I winked. "Because you're about to be a grandma."

She squealed like a kindergartner. "Oh, Andie, bless you! Does Joe know?"

"No, and don't tell him. I have to find a way to break it gently."

"Joe will make a *good* daddy, you'll see. Can we tell Al? Oh, we must. It'll take his mind off Ted. Now we've something to look forward to; a new life in the Oliver family. A life."

Next to Mavis, I loved my mother-in-law more than any woman I knew. We were close. We were friends. We were Ruth and Naomi ... *thy people shall be my people, and thy God, my God*. On her wide front porch in the quiet dusk, Maudy and I watched the sun hover behind high thin clouds offering a spectacular sunset, and then sink into the sweltering Carolina landscape. From the corner of my eye, I saw her lift her face to the Heavens and sigh. "You must've conceived about the time Ted died. God knew. He knew." She turned and reached for my hand. "Now listen, God knows I'm no prophet, but I believe, Andie; I believe this child you're carrying will change the course of your life."

I sensed the warm unction of her statement. "I suppose you're right," I said. But leaning back against my chair, I knew I was not to have a beautiful experience carrying a child, and I felt something else—a cold, dark winter.

October 1974
A HEARTBEAT AWAY

Andie

The Piedmont basked in an autumn sun, showing off the reds and golds of its counties. The sky over North Carolina, blue enough to drown in, pitched and rolled as far as the eye could see. The air grew warm and sugared as the new season floated down from the mountains. Town windows displayed cutouts of jack-o'-lanterns and ghosts. A grinning cardboard skeleton with accordion-pleated legs swung from the entrance of Dr. Otis Eshelman's office in Lexington.

I took a day off work and drove to my doctor appointment. A family practitioner, Dr. Eshelman wasn't expensive and he was country at heart. I buttoned my shirt after the exam while he stood nearby with my chart.

"Have you told your husband?"

I wouldn't meet his eyes as I hopped down from the exam table.

"You're almost twelve weeks, and you're showing now, missy. Doesn't he notice when he sees you without your clothes on?"

"Don't matter. Joe just thinks I'm getting fatter. We only have sex when he's desperate. The lights are out." I spoke before I had a chance to think about what I was saying. There was no one else to talk to. Mavis, Libby, and Ray were all long-distance calls. So were my parents. Maudy would never understand. I carried my fear alone. Dr. Eshelman didn't flinch. I figured he'd heard worse.

"If you two need counseling, I can recommend somebody."

Avoiding my doctor's eyes again, I said, "I'm okay. It's Joe who's got problems. Somebody needs to help me tell him he's going to be a daddy. I can't find that somebody." I fled the exam room before Dr. Eshelman could respond.

§

The old car's squeaks and the rattles on the ride home kept me company and hid the quiet. The radio hadn't worked in months. Joe had attempted to fix it by beating the dashboard. The gaping hole from his fist exemplified his worsening temper. I missed the radio and the Joe I used to know.

There was only one beat that mattered to me anyway. A beat that stopped time. A beat to keep time to the tune of love songs and lullabies sung by mothers to their infants all over the world. It had rhythm and I could dance to it. A simple beat passed down for thousands of generations. A beat that belonged to me. I could listen to the echo of it forever. A heartbeat, the most angelic sound I'd ever heard.

My fingers moved over my stomach as I drove. Come springtime my baby would lie in my arms. My dream of motherhood hovered only months away. It was time to share the news with Joe, the other half of the heartbeat.

SOMETHING TO TELL YOU

Andie

"If you want to hide during service, you should stay home."

"Love to," I mumbled. I sensed Joe's annoyance as he hurried to the parking lot, not even so much as opening the car door for me.

The long service ended at eleven. I had spent the last two hours throwing up in the restroom, but not before I confided in a friendly usherette that my pregnancy would require frequent trips to the toilet. She promised to keep my secret, but I caught whiffs of her perfume around every corner.

Joe never allowed me to miss a service. Staying home was out of the question. The Olivers had to remain without spot or wrinkle after the way Ray had embarrassed the family and left the church for a Catholic girl.

Joe drove home with one hand on the wheel and the other holding up his head, his elbow cocked on the door. He needed sleep, but I sensed he had other plans, roaming off to only God knew where. His eyes glazed and cold, he never held my hand anymore when he drove. At midnight, he pulled into the driveway and stopped. "I'm going 'round the corner to fill up the gas tank, then talk to Coot about work tomorrow."

"Coot's at the shop at this hour? You know that for sure, do ya?" Down to my bones, I knew he was lying.

"Go to bed. Or go slurp up a couple bowls of ice cream and slap a few more pounds on your thighs. I'll be back in an hour or so."

Fed up with his extra-curricular activities, I was too tired to care where Joe insisted he had to go at that late hour. With a distended belly and bursting waistband, I ignored his cruel comment.

He gave me a quick peck on the cheek. "I'm sorry. I didn't mean it. But I can't get you to lose weight. Mama says I need to be patient, but you're trying my patience. Go to bed. I'll be back in a while."

His patience? I shot him a pissed-off look he didn't see. He stared straight ahead, waiting for me to get out of the car. Without saying another word I opened the door, stepped out and watched him drive off, the car's tail lights flickering as red as any devil's eyes. Trudging up the porch steps in the moonlight, I fumbled inside my purse for the trailer key. "He doesn't even have the decency to keep the headlights on until I get inside. Damn him." Finding my way to the couch, I collapsed. *It's coming unglued.* A film grew across my eyes—the beginning of tears. I sank deeper into the worn cushions, realizing my continuous quest to fix my marriage was not only foolish, but I'd made everything worse. And to top it off, I had no idea how to break it to him that, like it or not, he was about to have a baby.

§

Two nights later, I pulled the plug on Joe's world. "Where're you going?"

"I told Coot I'd meet him at the garage to work on an Impala that just came in." Clean-shaven, polished boots, the same pressed shirt he wore the last time we ate out—immediately I erected a wall of suspicion and covered it with pictures of cheap, slinky women. *Adultery is a sin, he won't risk it; I know he won't.*

"You smell awfully nice to go work in a grease pit."

"We're also meeting a new Nascar client tonight. Coot wanted me to look decent."

"Oh." I followed him from room to room in my house shoes and pink terrycloth robe. He nearly tripped over me as he whirled around to check his hair in the mirror.

"What now, Andie?" A sharp edge had crept into his voice.

"You work all day, and now you're working nights, too. I need to talk to you. It's important. Can you be a little late?"

"How long's this going to take?" Joe leaned against the door with his hand on the knob.

"I . . . can you at least sit for a second?"

He threw his car keys on the kitchen table and parked himself on our tattered couch.

"Do you love me, Joe?"

"Jesus, Andie, what kind of a question is that?"

"Just answer it. Do you love me?"

"Of course I do. Now what's so important that it can't wait 'til later?"

"When is later with you? I never see you other than an occasional supper at your folks. And this can't wait any longer. You need to know." I bit at my bottom lip and twisted the tissue in my hand, unable to bear it any longer. A sharp twinge of dread burned in my stomach. My eyes heavy with tears and a defeated countenance revealed my secret within seconds.

Joe's face turned as pale as school paste. He stared at me across a sudden ringing silence. "Are you—are you pregnant?"

I nodded, wiped tears from my eyes, and gave him a pathetic whimper. "Yes."

Watching Joe's reaction to my pitiful *yes* was like watching werewolf movies as a child. I'd cover my eyes when Lon Chaney's body contorted into deformities of fangs, claws, and wild eyes. Joe's body twitched and shook. His face flushed; he shot me a vicious glare. I couldn't move. Fear and sweat trickled down my spine.

"You did this to me on purpose, didn't you? You think now we'll move away—be one big happy family. That I'm going to turn into somebody like your daddy. Now I know why you're as big as a goddamn cow. I thought it was all the ice cream. You fucking liar. You promised me. You agreed with me. No kids! How could you do this to me? You know how important my future is with Reverend Artury. He specifically told me to never get you pregnant. I should leave your sorry ass!" Joe stood, his eyes flashing fire and daggers aimed at my heart. He moved toward me and stopped inches from my face. "You promised me! You said you'd never forget your pill again!" That's when he grabbed my throat with both hands.

My eyes wide, I fought to loosen Joe's fingers from around my neck, my body flailing beneath his powerful grip. I tried to speak, but I sounded as though I was screaming from the bottom of a lake. I was no match for his strength. I had expected him to yell or kick the refrigerator again, but I never expected him to choke his pregnant wife. Managing to turn my body, I looked into his eyes and mouthed the words, *please, Joe . . . stop.*

He let go and backed against the wall. My hand at my throat, I watched him grab his keys off the table. Spitting bullets into my eyes and hair he screamed, "If I stay here, I'll kill you!"

Afraid to move, I stood in my robe still clutching my throat. He stormed out, slamming the front door so hard our wedding picture jumped off its nail and shattered on the floor. Staggering to the kitchen table, I pulled out a chair to sit, but my legs wouldn't work. The room swirled. Sweat poured down my face in fast streams and I slid to the floor. Reaching over my head, I grabbed the phone off the counter. Barely able to see the numbers, I dialed Maudy. No answer. Then I called my parents, only telling them I was pregnant, Joe was angry, and I was sick. Could they come? An hour later they stood at my front door, ready to lynch Joe.

"Why didn't you tell us sooner?" Daddy asked, helping me to the couch. Dixie swept up the glass, and then gave the trailer a quick look-see before examining me.

"I had to tell Joe first." I neglected to mention Maudy and Al had known for weeks.

"Bud, let's pack her stuff and take her home. The child is a mess. Look at this place. Godamighty, Andie, how do you stand it? I knew your trailer was a dump, but I'd thought you'd have fixed it up by now. You haven't bought a thing since I was here last, when was that?" Accustomed to perfectly matched rooms of furniture and accessories, Dixie went from room to room with her hands on her hips, shaking her head.

"It's clean. I keep it clean. It's just—well—not very pretty, I guess."

"That's for *damn* sure. Where do you plan on putting a baby in here? What does he do with your money? Does he save any of it?" Questions I was sure she'd been dying to ask.

"I don't see what happens to it. I give him my paycheck, and he gives me an allowance. I don't know what to say to you, Dixie." I cried like a child with a bad stomach ache and sobbed into my daddy's chest while he rubbed my back.

My mother gathered my things. "Write Joe a note and tell him you'll be in Winston with us for a few days. If he cares. Where's your suitcase?"

"Grocery sacks in the corner by the fridge. Use those."

Dixie was about to make another remark when Daddy held up his hand and said, "Stop."

My mother stomped off to root through my closet.
I searched for a pen to write Joe a note.

§

Daddy said little during the ride to Winston-Salem. I watched him from the back seat, grinding his teeth while he chain-smoked. He pinched every cigarette between his lips, the smoke making him squint as he assessed my situation. I knew he'd find a time to approach Joe about his pending date with fatherhood. Fortunately for Joe, there were no bruises on my body Daddy could see. Dixie, on the other hand, kept nothing inside. Disregarding my emotional state, she babbled on and on about nursery themes, layettes, breast or bottle, cloth or disposables, girls' names, boys' names, a baby shower, on and on. It didn't stop.

I couldn't think. Joe had ripped out my heart and shoved it down my aching throat, rendering me speechless, and my mother wouldn't shut up. Not until I tuned her out with imaginary duct tape slapped over her mouth. I wanted to yell, I wanted to sleep for a week, and I wanted to remember what it felt like to be happy.

When she ran out of baby things to talk about, Dixie felt the need to fill me in on Caroline's high school activities, her handsome new boyfriend, and her perfect report cards. She let me know I'd thrown myself into a world of Olivers and forgot about my sister. She was right.

Just add it to the list, Dixie.

That night I broke down in my old bed, missing the man I married. Where did he go? What happened to him? I had loved Joe, it seemed, all my young life. At that moment, I despised him. Maybe as much as Mavis did. *Oh God— Mavis. She'll have a field day with this.*

Where is he? Why does Coot give him so much overtime? How come I don't see any overtime pay? What does he really do until two in the morning? For the first time, I wanted a straightforward explanation. I wanted honest answers. I wanted the truth.

Lying awake and feeling like a speck of nothing, I realized I hadn't bought a pair of shoes or a new dress in nearly two years. I'd been sewing simple outfits for work with Maudy's old sewing machine and thrift shop remnants. Threadbare described my marriage and my underwear. Drowsy, I floated between thought and sleep, my mind drifting back and forth in time. *I made a promise. To love him—'til the end of my days.* Feeling his hands around my throat, I wasn't sure I could keep that promise any longer. *Where is Your love, God? Where is Your faithfulness?* No answer. Just a hollow feeling in the silence of a room that smelled like my childhood and made me wish I could go back. Even back to my mother's womb. And start over.

Deal With It

Andie

Friday came too soon. My head ached from little sleep. My eyes swollen and cried out, I spent the morning throwing up, and then I called my boss at the bank. I needed a sick day. From work and from church. Although missing a Friday night church service was an unwritten sin, it was also the bright spot in the gloom of my current situation. Sitting at the breakfast bar, I bit into a piece of dry toast and jumped when the wall phone rang beside my head.

Dixie wiped my crumbs off the counter. "You want me to answer it? You know it's him."

"No, I might as well get this over with." I picked up the receiver. "Joe?"

"Andie, it's me, Coot." *Coot. Of all people to call.* "What the hell happened last night? Joe's drunker than I've ever seen him. He's been a-layin' on the garage floor since early this morning. I tried calling yer trailer, then I called Maudy. She's on her way to git him. She's worried sick and said fer me to call."

I licked away the tears that slid to my lips. "Is he okay, other than drunk?"

"Lord, yes. He'll be a-sleepin' this one off all day. Unless his mama gits a hold of him."

I looked over my shoulder to see if Dixie was listening, but thankfully she'd left the kitchen to wake Caroline for school. "Coot, Joe and I are having a baby and he's not happy about it. That's what this is about. Make sure Maudy takes him home. I'll try to come to Salisbury today to talk to him. Otherwise, I'll be staying with my parents until Monday."

"I'm jus' glad yer okay. Joe needs his ass kicked a couple times. He'll git over it."

"Not this time," I said. I heard the traffic on Innes Street through the phone. "I need to know something, Coot. Has Joe been working nights for you?"

He hesitated. "I guess it's 'bout time to give him his first kick. No, I ain't got that much work fer him. Jus' enough to keep us both busy during the day and that's 'bout it. Best be asking him yer own self where he goes at night. I got a customer. I need to git."

"But, I—"

"I'm sorry, Andie. I really got a customer."

"Okay, thanks."

Coot might have kicked Joe's ass, but he had kicked mine as well. It was as much my fault as it was Joe's. I'd let him get away with it, turning a deaf ear and ignoring the warnings for the past two years. There was no denying the truth any longer. Whether we stayed together or not, Joe's unfaithfulness outweighed my getting pregnant without his permission. If I couldn't get him to leave the church I'd at least get him to own up to his responsibilities as a father. His parents would take my side; make him straighten up. Maudy would do that. I was sure of it.

§

I found my mother in the laundry room, pressing Daddy's shirts and singing one of her favorite hymns. Her voice was the thing I loved about her the most. "*I'll fly away . . .*" She stopped when she saw me.

"Mind if I borrow your car, go to the library and check out a book on babies?" I lied.

"Drop your sister off at school on the way. She's about to wear me to a frazzle. I want you to get to know her a little. Caroline wants to be like you. Maybe you can talk her out of it."

In a split second I'd gone from wanting to hug her to wishing I could swing my fist at her. It made no sense. Dixie had taught Caroline and me our purpose in life meant marriage and babies. *Now she's ashamed of me?* "Sure, Dixie, I'll tell her to be like you."

My mother sprinkled the next shirt with water and frowned. "I just meant she needs to marry someone with a little more money than Joe Oliver."

"Fine. I'll tell my sister to marry for money. That'll make her happy."

Dixie's steam iron hissed like a snake. "Well it didn't hurt me none, now did it?"

My voice hardened. "Daddy didn't have money when you married him."

"But I had no doubt he would. He was one semester shy of a degree with job offers." Hanging Daddy's blue pinstripe on a hanger, she sighed and said, "Last shirt!"

I wanted to spit. Instead, I tossed an overlooked button-down onto her ironing board. "You missed one."

Pivoting on my heel, I left the room, my footsteps echoing on Dixie's beautiful hardwood floors. I had better things to do than fight with my mother. I had to make a phone call before taking Caroline to school and driving to Salisbury. A call to circle my wagons, head Joe off at the pass, and shoot first.

§

I arrived in Salisbury at eleven. Turning onto Innes Street, McGraw's Garage sat next to the only vacant lot. Coot's hand-painted sign peeled like his shop's brown garage doors, already hoisted and exposing the cave-like inside that smelled of exhaust fumes and gasoline. My palms sweating, I watched him walk toward my car, motioning for me to roll the window down.

Coot was somewhere in his forties and barrel-chested, his hair mid-way along its route from coal-dust black to old-man gray. He lifted his Confederate flag ball cap to drag his bare arm across his sweaty brow. A ring of dirt had sunk into the pores of his bright white forehead. His murky brown eyes behind coke-bottle lenses looked like tadpoles swimming in a water jar.

Peering down at his watch, Coot replaced his ball cap and said, "Maudy done took him home, 'bout two hours ago. She said to hightail it up to the house and talk this out." Not even noon, and his Grateful Dead T-shirt already showed half-moon bands of sweat under the armpits. A chaw between his gum and bottom lip, he spit a bullet of chew into an empty RC Cola bottle and grinned. "She weren't too happy with him."

I nodded. "Thanks for your help."

Coot scratched his day-old chin stubble with a dirty fingernail. "I hope everything turns out. Tell that goober to be at work Monday. No excuses or I'll be obliged to whip his ass my own self."

In spite of his redneck ways, I loved Coot. The greasy old goat had more common sense than all the slick-haired politicians in Raleigh. There wasn't an ounce of pretense in his whole nasty-smelling body.

§

Speeding into the Olivers' driveway, I spied Maudy rushing down the front porch steps with a glass of what looked like iced tea. She dumped it into her petunia bed and raced toward me like a hunter after a moving target. Before I could even put the car in park, Maudy reached inside my open window, took hold of my head, and planted a wet kiss on my cheek. "I'm sorry for all this, sugah. We gave him a good talking to. That boy's in a foul mood like I never seen. Al tried to pray with him, and he just up and left the room. He's got himself a super hangover, but it serves that sinner right. He's got a whole lot of forgiveness to be asking for."

I stepped out of the car, wiping the tattoo of her lips off my face. "I didn't come to fight with Joe; we just need to talk." I heard the back door slam. It was Joe, hoofing it straight toward me. He stared into my eyes as if wanting to strangle me again. I stared back, not knowing what to say and glad I wasn't alone with him.

"Mama, go on inside. I need to talk to Andie."

"Be kind to her, Joe. She's your wife and you're having a baby whether you like it or not. I won't see her mistreated. I mean it."

"We're just going to talk."

"You best not lose your temper, young man. Your daddy's watching you like a hawk."

"I ain't a kid, Mama. Now go on—please."

I stood frozen by the side of Dixie's car and cried as Maudy walked away.

"Stop crying." At his cold drill sergeant command, I gulped and hiccupped every tear back into my head. Joe placed his foot on the car's bumper and his hand on the hood. He leaned in to speak, private-like, pinning me against the car with his words. "I'm calling Reverend Artury on the phone after I sober up a little. I want him to talk to you. You've no idea the pain you're putting me through." He pressed the heel of his other hand into his forehead. "Fuck! My head is killing me." Staring a hole through me with his bloodshot eyes, he said, "I need a few days away from you. I'm hoping Reverend can help me, 'cause I'm having a real hard time accepting what you've done to me."

The only words that blared into my ears were *I, me, my,* and *I'm*. It was all about Joe. My feelings didn't matter a hoot. Darkness clouded the edges of my vision. Quickly, I pulled myself together remembering what Coot had said. And then I lit into him.

"What *I've* done? You lousy two-timing bastard. You want sympathy? You'll find it in the dictionary—between shit and syphilis!"

Joe stepped toward me ready to go for my throat again, but I backed up. I wasn't about to let him respond.

"Coot told me there's never been any overtime. What are you doing at night, Joe? Where are you really going? You think I'm stupid? Let's bring Maudy and Al out here. Let's see if I can get the truth out of you in front of them. I'm having a baby, *our* baby, and I'm not ashamed of it. I did nothing wrong by wanting to have a child. What happened to your promises, your vows; you remember any of them? What happened to you? Now who's a liar, huh?"

"I grew up! I'm making decisions—"

"Yeah, well, you've got a few more decisions to make, big boy. Your folks won't turn on their grandchild, and they'll hold you responsible for what happens to us, so deal with it!"

Joe clenched and unclenched his fists. Thank God his daddy stood at the shop door watching us. Otherwise, I would've had my first black eye right about then.

Looking back, I should've hightailed it to our trailer, packed everything I owned into Dixie's car and left him. But I didn't. Maybe it was the ignorance of my youth, something in my gene pool that created a stubbornness far worse than Joe's. I don't know. What I also didn't know, was my patience and the very core of my beliefs had yet to be tried by fire.

"Fine." His voice cracked, raising it a few octaves until he cleared his throat. "I'll tell you where I've been. Here, there—everywhere. Shooting pool at the bowling alley. Driving 'round, hanging out with a few friends, including a female friend of mine. She's only a friend. Nothing happened. Not that I wasn't tempted. I just couldn't stand the thought of going home to you. You nag and you look like shit. What happened to *you*?"

"Takes money to get my hair done and buy decent clothes and shoes."

"You manage to find money for ice cream. You want more money? Get a better job. I'm working for Coot until Reverend hires me full-time."

"So, it's my fault? You've lied to me for months about overtime when you've been with another woman, and it's *my* fault?"

Joe's expression grew hard and resentful. "Look, we're getting nowhere, and I'm not dealing with anything right now. I'm sure Reverend Artury will want to see you—"

"Oh, you can bet he does!"

"What—what do you mean?"

"I *know* how to use a phone. I called his secretary after breakfast. I've got an appointment Sunday morning before church. I'm telling him the truth."

Joe's eyes sparked with fury. "You think you can use Reverend against me?"

"Against you? Is that all you can think about—you? I'm going to see him, but not for you. I'm going for this baby and for me. But mark my words, Joe Oliver, Calvin better be willing to help us put our marriage back together, or at least turn you into a father, or I *will* spill my guts that you've been cheating on me. I doubt he'll hire an adulterer."

"I never said I cheated on you, and you don't have proof." Joe grabbed my arm. I jerked it away as Al stepped out of his shop.

"You okay, Andie?" Al's concern grew louder. "Andie?"

I nodded. "Fine, Al." Joe's daddy paused, and then ducked back into his shop.

"Look at me, Joe. I've been faithful to you. You know it, and so does everybody else, and now *we* are pregnant. Other than some good ol' boys, and some old gal you're doing *nothing* with, your family and church will be on my side on this one. You know that, too. And I'm sure I can get proof if I dig hard enough."

Joe rubbed his palms on his Levi's then pushed his hair off his forehead with such force, I knew it had to hurt. "I'm done talking for one day. I'll see you Monday at home," he said.

"Fine." I wavered, uncertain for a moment, but something in me had changed. I had to say it. The steadiness in my voice surprised me. "Oh, Joe, one last thing." I pulled my shirt away from my bruised neck. "You ever touch me again like that, I'll get Daddy's gun. You've seen me shoot. You know I don't miss."

I turned away, and that was it. I had won the first battle in my tug of war. Except I didn't feel victorious. Pondering a life for my unborn child and myself that didn't include Joe felt strange. I drove back to Winston-Salem, praying. *Oh God, please don't let this happen.* I knew he could change. If he wanted. If he could see his mistakes. If he could see what he was about to lose. Unfortunately, I needed Calvin's help with that. If Joe listened to anyone, it was his Reverend. And I would forgive him for touching another woman, if he promised before God never to do it again. But pulling into my parents' driveway and wiping at a different set of tears, I knew the direction of our lives was anybody's guess.

GIVE IT BACK

Andie

The one earthly thing Calvin loved was glamour. His fashion conscious House of Praise had no intentions of following the Pentecostal dress code. Though he wanted the ladies to dress respectably, no woman was forced to wear long hair and ugly shirtwaist dresses. Dixie had been in a rare mood that weekend and bought me five new outfits, underwear, and a suitcase at half-price from JCPenny. I was thrilled. And thankful. My belly had grown fast, and I no longer needed to hide it. But when Caroline saw the heels of my shoe worn down to the plastic, she offered me a pair of her own, as well as tubes of lipstick and mascara. "Keep them," she said. I was at the mercy of my teenage sister's handouts. Patting my belly, she sniffed back tears. "I hope it's a boy and looks like Daddy."

Slim-waisted and girlish, Dixie led me to the door and started fussing with my hair. "Just give me a pretty grandbaby, darlin'. One good thing about the Oliver men, they are definitely pretty." I accepted her odd comment as an *I love you*, and kept thanking her and thanking her for my new clothes until I heard Daddy start the car. Finally. Waving from the passenger seat, I was on my way to the House of Praise and my inescapable meeting with the right-hand man of God.

§

Daddy dropped me off at the side door of the church. My hands dripped with sweat. I felt a sudden wave of nausea as I pulled my suitcase out of the back seat. "Thanks, Daddy. I'll call you later."

He reached across the upholstery and grabbed my arm. "Listen Rosebud, I want you to know no matter what Dixie says, I'm still the king of my castle and you can always come home. I don't want you to live the way you're living. I want you happy. Here's a little money." Daddy slipped two twenty-dollar bills into my palm. "Don't take any crap off Calvin. He's just a man—human like the rest of us—no matter what anybody thinks. Want me to sit out here and wait?"

"No need," I said. "Maudy and Al will be here soon. I'm grateful for all you've done this weekend and I appreciate the money. I've got to try to make it work with Joe. Try as hard as I can. Who knows? I may need a room at Bud and Dixie's Motel after all." I stepped out of the car and blew him a kiss. His rust-colored eyes glistened with tears as he caught my kiss with his hand and then drove away.

§

I wondered if waiting outside President Ford's office felt any different than standing on the deep, plush carpet in the church office. Colorful foil wallpaper, three-dimensional in texture, glimmered in the dim light like a low-burning fire. The professionally decorated lobby, like Calvin, was a bit gaudy. The shoe fit. To my right, a maze of hallways meandered off to parts unknown. On the expanse of the longest wall in front of me, an exquisite painting entitled *The Apostle Paul* captured my attention.

Calvin had requested I arrive early. Fannie, the church secretary, wasn't there yet. Too early for members to arrive, I set my suitcase on the carpet and sat on a red velvet settee, staring at the Apostle Paul in the painting. His face harsh and twisted, his right hand stretched to the sky, his left pointing to a crowd of Roman soldiers; it was like looking into a madman's soul. I shuddered. The eerie sensation, as if being accused along with the Romans, unnerved me.

Feeling the way I did about Calvin, I had always avoided the church offices. I knew some people waited weeks to get an appointment and I questioned why it was so easy for me? I felt like Dorothy waiting to see the Wizard. My queasy stomach rumbled and I broke out in a sweat. Hearing voices from somewhere, I smoothed my hair behind my ears and pulled my new dress down around my knees, aware of a tiny run in my pantyhose. I crossed my legs, hoping no one noticed. The office door opened.

"Andie?"

Evan Preston, the Church Administrator, stood in the doorway. *Executioner*, I'd heard him called. Somewhere in his thirties, he wore a crisp, well-cut suit. His hair, styled and heavily sprayed, glowed the color of red wine. He had a soldier's body and the fine chiseled features of a politician or a movie star. Someone used to giving orders and living in the spotlight. Evan, like his boss, had incredible people skills and a chess-like outlook on evangelism. Or so I'd been told. Joe once said Evan knew where the well-known evangelists used to be in the ratings, where they were now, and where they were headed. Billy Graham, Pat Robertson, Kathryn Kuhlman, Oral Roberts, Rex Humbard—he knew them all. Calvin, I was sure, would have nothing less than a beautiful, articulate, and intelligent man like Evan for his second-in-command.

Should I stand and salute him or something? Instead, I answered softly, "Yes?"

"Reverend Artury will be here in a moment. Would you like to sit in Fannie's office?"

"No. No thanks. I'll wait out here."

"Fine. I'll let you know when he's in." I nodded and Evan disappeared down the hall.

I wasn't about to give Calvin a standing ovation when I saw him. The thought of it made me giggle, which made me feel better. After a twenty-minute wait though, my bladder was about to burst from the extra coffee I drank at breakfast. I fidgeted in my seat, watching Evan perform his own imitation of an Artury strut. He walked the halls and snapped demands at arriving staff, choir members, and ushers. *Who does this guy think he is?* I sighed. *Joe's boss someday, that's who he is.* My skin crawled.

With a whoosh, the office door opened again and there he stood. Calvin. Grinning at me as if I were his long-lost baby sister come to visit. His enticing smile encouraged mine in return and I stood on wobbly legs. He wore his wedding ring, but not his black suit. The gray pinstripe looked strange on him. He held out his hand to greet me and I shook it. His grip was strong and solid, but I felt no electricity, no power to slay me to the carpet. "Andie, so nice to see you this magnificent morning in the house of God. Won't you come in?" Calvin withdrew his warm hand, leaving mine feeling cool and empty. "Let's chat a while before service starts, shall we?" The sound of his deep voice jolted me and stoked my fear and dread of him. It filled the space around him with such rehearsed fervor and feeling that it seemed better suited for the Broadway stage than to preach God's word. I'd heard him bellow on behind his pulpit most of my life, but sitting on a back pew in his vast auditorium did not prepare me for hearing him up close and personal. I ambled forward. His blue eyes were almost turquoise, as well as sharp and assessing, and he stared at my stomach before ushering me into the *holy of holies*.

Calvin's office was a perfect box. Smaller than I had pictured, it contained an enormous mahogany desk engulfing the space around it. Strange enough, there was only one small window, but plenty of track lighting, and the far wall was covered in mirrored tiles. Silk flower arrangements and a framed picture of his wife sat on his desk. The room smelled like a familiar men's cologne and was uncomfortably warm. Black and white photos of Vivi in glamorous mink stoles and evening gowns, along with places they'd traveled to around the world, filled the wall behind him. A large oil painting of Jesus and the Samaritan woman at the well hung on the wall behind me, next to a larger portrait of Calvin. It gave me the creeps. His desk appeared clean and organized, and his Bible lay open on top of it. No other books could be seen.

"Have a seat." He pointed to an odd-looking gold leather chair across from his desk. I hovered on the edge of the chair's slick cushion as if sitting on a fence and watched him glide around his desk to relax in his own ridiculous mixture of desk chair and throne. I chuckled, imagining myself as Dorothy, shaking before Oz. He raised his eyebrows. "Is something funny?"

I jerked my eyes away. "No, I'm sorry. I never in my wildest dreams anticipated seeing the inside of this office." My smile faded. If Calvin could read my mind, it was time to find out. I sure didn't want him to know he made me feel like a rabbit squaring off against a copperhead.

He got quiet—eerily quiet—moving his head like he was listening to someone whisper into his ear. He stared at me a long time before he finally said, "Andie, let's talk openly. I'm glad you called. I want my young couples to reach out to me when they're in distress. I've gone before the Lord, sought His counsel for your situation. You know my feelings for Joe and his family and that includes you, of course. The Olivers have been a cornerstone of this ministry. They have all contributed at one time or another. Maudy worked toe-to-toe with the men in this church, laying the foundation and even nailing on the roof. I am grateful for all they've done."

"They've been wonderful to me, too."

He sighed, then continued. "I want Joe involved in the television ministry. El-Shaddai will bless you for sacrificing your husband to His work. Joe has a servant's heart and is consistently willing to do whatever is asked of him at any given moment."

"Yes, I know."

"Is Joe the head of your home?"

"Yes, I believe he is."

"I'm sure you're aware Joe called me. I hope you can understand why I was surprised to find you had gone behind your husband's back and allowed yourself to conceive. But I already knew about your pregnancy. My ushers tell me everything; you need to remember that."

"Thank you, I will. I don't know what Joe told you, but I'm sure his story is not exactly how this happened. Yes, I stopped taking the pill, but I never agreed with him *not* to have a child. He may have heard it that way, but I never agreed to it. I've always wanted children. He knew that."

"Nevertheless, you allowed conception without discussing it with him, did you not?"

"Yes, I suppose I did." I felt like I was being cross-examined and found guilty at the same time. My nerves clawed at my stomach.

"I also know that Joe is very distressed at the moment and I need his mind clear. He'll continue to train in audio and recording; be instrumental in the set-up and organization of our sound studios and production company as we begin the television ministry. He *must* continue to pray, fast, live in the Word and allow God to anoint him for the job ahead."

I had no doubt Joe could do anything he put his mind to. No doubt he dreamed of getting out of Coot's grease pit someday and believed the church was his golden opportunity. But I'd only heard my husband pray one measly prayer since I'd known him. He'd never fasted a meal or read more than a few chapters from the Bible to make a point with me or to please his mama.

"Eventually, I'll be in a position to hire him, but only if I know he is not distracted at home. This is a testing time for him."

I was ready to show him the bruises on my neck. "I'm a bit testy myself. Joe has said and done some awful things, I'd like to tell you—"

"Don't, Andie; don't dishonor your husband." Calvin held up both hands. "Whatever he has done, I'm sure he'll ask God and you to forgive him. It will pass. Joe needs your forgiveness and support right now."

"What about my support? Isn't he supposed to love me as Christ loved the church?"

"Yes, but you were to submit to his authority. God appointed him as head of your home, and you said that indeed, he is."

My legs trembled. "I called hoping you could help me. Help me and Joe, our marriage, I mean. The fact is, we're pregnant. I need Joe to be a loving husband, father, and—"

"God wants to heal your marriage." His smile made me quiver. "But you must bow to His will." He stopped a moment, as if to allow his words to penetrate my thick head. "What I'm about to say will take a strong woman to hear. You need to understand Jesus is building an army at the House of Praise to save the world before He comes back. We need to lead many souls into the safety of the ark before God sends the judgment rain. Do you know what I am saying to you?" He didn't wait for an answer. "We've got to put on the whole armor of God to fight the battles of the mind, Andie. To become sanctified soldiers in Christ. Though your husband struggles with many temptations at the moment, I know his heart. He wants the oil in his lamp, the seal of God. He wants to be a part of this mission. This is a divine mission I'm on and I'm taking those with me who want to work for God, will put God first in their life and deny every temptation of the flesh. Marriage is one thing, but children can be a vast distraction to those in the midst of ministry."

"How?"

"I'm not getting into that with you this morning. There isn't time. I will give this to you straight. You need to consider giving your baby back to God."

I sank in my chair while my stomach churned, preparing to retch. If I didn't get some air soon, I'd have to puke on his pretty desk. "What are you saying to me?"

He twisted a small gold ring around his swollen pinky finger next to his wedding ring. "There is a clinic in Raleigh, very discreet. The whole procedure takes only a matter of minutes. It's legal now. The doctor who runs the clinic is a friend of mine. I will pay the bill and you and Joe can go back to rebuilding your marriage."

"You're—you're asking me to have an abortion? Kill my baby? I know you don't want us to have children, but—don't you preach against abortion? How is this the will of God?" My mind flipped through the sermons I could remember. He'd spoken very little about abortion other than mentioning God preferred couples remain childless rather than to abort their children. Something about a woman's only choice is to honor God's plan for her life. Obviously, Calvin knew what that plan was. But his stand on abortion had never been clear. Come to think of it, he'd been vague on many issues I'd heard that other preachers wailed on about.

"What I preach is for the masses as a whole. God's ways are not our ways, His thoughts—not our thoughts. We cannot question His divine plan; we can only follow. And it's really not a baby. It's a fetus. It doesn't have a soul until it takes its first breath. There is no sin in taking an unwanted growth off your body. This is the same thing."

I stood. "My baby is not unwanted."

"Joe doesn't want it. He's angry and disappointed his wife did this to him. Genesis the third chapter, verse sixteen tells us, *Unto the woman God said: I will greatly multiply thy sorrow and thy conception; in sorrow thou shalt bring forth children; and thy desire shall be to thy husband, and he shall rule over thee.*"

I'd had all I could take. There was no question that I was having a baby in the midst of sorrow, and nobody was taking it or ruling over me. Not anymore. "You said I should give my baby back to God, then you called it a fetus. Which is it?"

"I'm not playing word games with you. It's a fetus until it's born. My first comment was a figure of speech." He raised his eyebrows for emphasis. "Do you want me to pray with you?"

"No, I'm a little sick. I need to use the restroom."

"Alright then. I'll talk to Joe and tell him to lighten up on you. Let me know what you decide. You'll need to do this soon. I'll be praying you make the right decision."

§

I moved as fast as my short, pudgy legs could carry me. In a frantic search for the nearest ladies' room, I turned the corner and ran smack into Evan Preston, knocking him back on his heels. He grabbed my arms as if to discipline a child. "Whoa, where're you running to, gal? You could hurt a person." I tried to pull free. "Don't you be running in these halls, now," he smirked, like I was some fifth-grader. I wasn't amused and he knew it, but he wouldn't let go. Until I threw up all over his nice Sunday suit. His eyes sparked with disdain and he growled like a dog, stepped back, and watched it drip from his silk tie to his snakeskin boots. Clutching my arm, he yanked open the ladies' room door behind him and shoved me hard enough that I fell to my knees. I stood slowly and staggered to the sink.

Fannie opened the ladies' room door and slipped my suitcase inside. "In case you need to clean yourself up," she said, offering no assistance and shaking her head as if it were my fault.

The hot-pink wallpapered ladies' room smelled like rotten oranges and my nausea intensified. After splashing cold water on my puffy face, I reached for a paper towel from the dispenser and knocked over a metal waste can. It struck the tiled floor with a crash loud enough to wake the dead, spilling trash over the floor. Dropping to my knees again, I scooped up the mess and uprighted the can. Then I dashed to the nearest toilet, vomiting the rest of my breakfast. Resting on the cool tile, I felt my nausea subsiding.

Thankful for my suitcase, I dug through it for a toothbrush, then stripped off my dress and proceeded to wash it out in the sink. Teetering on one foot, I peeled off my pantyhose and stuffed the entire mess inside the suitcase as best I could. Whispering a prayer nobody enter and see me standing in nothing but my bra and panties, I dressed quickly, slid my swollen feet into my shoes and ran a brush through my hair. By the time I trudged into the sanctuary the choir was into their third and final song. I squeezed into a pew with two dowdy women and an old man and his wife. The battle to keep my baby snug inside my womb had begun. I was at war.

I don't know if I walked the aisle that morning due to reckless faith or divine stupidity, but I felt a strange need to pray on the gold-velvet kneepad that followed the long curve of the altar. A place I was familiar with. An altar I had prayed at with Joe many times.

With my eyes closed, I heard Calvin shout and sing in his typical end-of-service-wild-man rant. I knew the process well. He walked back and forth laying hands on the people he could reach, the sick and sinners needing salvation, while choir members sang praise and worship choruses at the microphone in the choir loft. The sound of it was as recognizable as a Shake-n-Bake commercial, and I figured I just blended into the crowd. But when I felt someone standing in front of me, I looked up and gasped. It was Calvin, glaring down at me. He raised his hand to stop the music and singing. "People, let's pray for our little sister, Andie Oliver, this morning. She's needing the Lord like never before." So quick it scared me, he slapped my forehead with his palm and screamed, "LOOSE HER, SATAN!" My head snapped back, and like a crazy woman I yanked out of the ushers' hold and shot to my feet before Calvin had a chance to say another word or touch me again. He stared at me as if to ridicule, but I stared back just as hard.

Desperate and defiant, I wanted a sign from God. The real God, if there was one. I remained standing at that familiar altar, but far enough back in the crowd where Calvin couldn't reach me. I convinced myself there had to be a kinder God somewhere, a God who existed in the hearts of honest men and women even if they found themselves in a den of lions. When I shut my eyes, my morning sickness vanished. I felt as if I were floating in the midst of a dream. Although the multitude around me cried out, suddenly all sound stopped. A cool breeze blew and I was at peace. In my mind's eye a baby appeared. I saw its beating heart and the buds of its hands and feet. As instantly as it appeared, it disappeared and the sanctuary grew noisy again, like someone had switched on a radio.

I'd never had a vision before and still wasn't sure anybody really did. It didn't matter. It was my sign, my gift from God. In spite of Calvin and his barbaric urging, I was going to keep my baby. Wild horses from Hell couldn't drag me to Raleigh to *give it back to God*.

January 1975
Resentment

Andie

I listened to Maudy talk as though she and Calvin were the best of friends. "Reverend doesn't want the congregation to assume the baby isn't Joe's. He told Joe to be sweet to you. And of course he doesn't want a Spirit-filled man like Joe to ignore his responsibilities. You know how Reverend is about gossip of any kind, especially concerning his staff. He said scandal will destroy a ministry in no time flat."

Not knowing how to fight them and win, I remained quiet. In a few days, Joe returned home. He wasn't accepting the role of doting husband and expectant father, but I knew if he left me it would kill any chance of him working for Calvin. Joe knew it, too. Still, he refused to play house and offered no excuses as to where he went every night. So I withdrew from making any decisions about my marriage and concentrated, instead, on my pregnancy.

§

Christmas 1974 was not a happy holiday. Relieved to see 1975 arrive, I hoped for a better year. Libby pointed out that every new year brings new problems to solve. I wanted problems no more serious than diaper rash and teething. The baby kicked a lot. I mentioned it to Joe, but he ignored the bulge under my shirt. With the onset of fatherhood, his life took a turn for the worse. I battled just to get him to answer simple questions like do you want a turkey or ham sandwich in your lunch? Or, do you need clean socks?

Winter in North Carolina always came late and left early. During its short stay, it packed a punch I had not anticipated. In late January, an ice storm hit, the likes of which the state had not seen since Strom Thurmond was a boy. Duke Power worked twenty-four-hour shifts because the storm shut down power from the Outer Banks to the Blue Ridge. Tree limbs, electric and telephone lines snapped like peanut brittle. I stayed with Dixie the week the trailer froze over—a nice respite from living with Joe.

At the end of my seventh month, my boss called me into his office to say my pregnancy was too obvious to continue working at the bank. That since my job was in the public eye, they preferred the eyes of the public not see me get much bigger. As if bank customers would have to explain to their children how I got that way. Of course, they'd be happy to hold my position open for six weeks after the baby's birth. It was the excuse I needed to quit. At 175 pounds with swollen feet and the need to pee every hour, my pregnancy was far from glowing. Joe's reaction to my unemployment was to hold tight to his paycheck, giving me less money than ever before.

Al and Maudy slipped me extra cash every week, hoping to ease the pain of their son's hatefulness, while Dixie planned a February baby shower to be held in her home. But the best news of all was the wedding of Ray and Libby, scheduled for March.

Television evangelism infiltrated every avenue of our lives and was suddenly big business. But Calvin couldn't broadcast nationally until he was known nationally. In the spring of the new year, he took his faith-healing services on the road and headed to Georgia for his first miracle crusade. Like General Sherman, Calvin Artury invaded Atlanta and burned it to the ground with the hellfire of the Word of God.

PART TWO
God Created

February 1975
TRAVELING MAGIC PUPPET SHOW

Reverend Calvin Artury

"Oh Lamb of God, give me souls lest I die!"

Not all evangelists sound like hillbillies, the kind Northerners hear and think of ignorant rednecks. We don't all play with snakes, drink poison, or preach in old-fashioned circus tents with sawdust on the floor. Not all evangelists wear suits from Sears and shout Bible verses on street corners like homeless vagabonds. I'm not that kind of evangelist.

I handpicked my team for the Calvin Artury Miracle Crusades. An elite group of thirty male volunteers to travel with me on a mission to save the world for Jesus. Professionally-trained singers, musicians, TV cameramen, bus drivers, and stage crew. The newspapers called us the Great Artury and his Traveling Magic Puppet Show. But who's on the Lord's side? I am! And thank God for it. Those negative reviews only endeared me to the Christian world, drawing the masses like Jews to the Promised Land. My ministry team left Winston-Salem on custom-made buses every Friday after church, and arrived home early Monday morning in time for the men to report to their regular jobs, usually worn out and worthless. But they had pledged their souls to the cause of Christ and my miracle crusades and I loved each and every one of them.

The crusades were a wondrous production. Gardens of potted ferns, stage sets with miles of drapery, giant chandeliers, and a massive pulpit were hauled in one truck while another was packed with state-of-the-art video and audio equipment, as well as a grand Steinway piano, a Hammond organ, two sets of drums, horns, guitars and a massive amount of paraphernalia.

In a city hit with a publicity blitz about our upcoming crusade, TV cameras panned the garish magnificence of some recycled cinema, coliseum, or Masonic Temple. Audiences were filled to capacity with women donned in furs, pearls, overlarge hats, or simple housedresses. Men and boys in rumpled suits, designer fashions, or dirty blue jeans; all manner of couture entered the great arenas, primed for my entrance. A humble minister sent to preach a faith-healing and salvation message along with the imminent end-time apocalypse.

I spent an hour in prayer and two hours in makeup prior to every service. To keep my hair in place, my stylist slicked it back tight. It often appeared glued to my skull, and it hung in gelled curls to my shoulders. But no amount of makeup hid my ghostly appearance. My pale face had grown puffy from lack of sleep, especially in the soft patches under my eyes. Someone had to bear the burden of Jehovah's ministry and He had chosen me. As a result, a fretwork of wrinkles lined my forehead and my chin sagged. The stress of the ministry was beginning to show. Thankfully, every service was like a shot of adrenaline.

I could be as tired and worn out as Elmer Gantry's Bible, but as the shouts and praises from my massive audience resounded throughout the building, the Spirit of God fell on me like a great and mighty wind. While the Men of Praise quartet crooned their over-rehearsed gospel numbers throughout the opening hour, I pranced and paraded through my audience, pressed the flesh and acknowledged the revering words from my faithful. I was the main attraction. The star of the show. The jewel in the crown of Christ that folks came to see. Nobody else.

I had given up my black suit for a resplendent new look in the crusades: blue or white Italian three-piece suits, tailored and sleek. Yet, my attire was meek compared to my message and the zeal and sincerity with which I delivered it. Repeated every week and seldom unvaried in content, my sermons were just a precursor for the offerings that often lasted over an hour.

"Who will give one hundred dollars tonight? Who are my partners in this miracle ministry? Don't be held accountable on Judgment Day. This is not the time to fail. Not now, dear people. Give God your tithe and your offerings, for His promises are Yes and Amen!" Hallelujahs echoed off ornate ceilings as I chanted over and over, "Hold your money high! Show God your faith! Be my partner and help me reach the world with God's power and anointing to save the lost at any cost! Oh, people! There are millions of souls at stake!"

It was impossible, however, for the thundering crowds, which numbered in the thousands, to walk to my portable altar. An army of volunteer ushers, local churchmen and deacons dressed in dark slacks, stark-white shirts and fat ties, hustled up and down the aisles, gathering the loaves and the fishes from the multitude who believed into my white plastic buckets.

And so it came to pass, week after golden week, until *The Calvin Artury Hour of Power* was broadcast to a much larger congregation by way of radio and local television with prophetic preaching and music galore. Every message wrapped itself around giving to God and getting a miracle, losing nothing over the airwaves. Integrated both racially and economically, the audiences at home took it to heart. It pleased me greatly.

A phone number blinked at the bottom of the TV screen for prayer requests from those not fortunate enough to attend the crusades. The TV audience could pray with a trained counselor and then enroll in the Blessed Cloth Plan, according to the book of *Acts, chapter nineteen and verse twelve.* For one hundred dollars, they were eligible to receive a blessed cloth and join my book club. If they didn't have the money, it was payable in monthly or bi-weekly installments, and renewable every year. Faithful viewers ran to their phones to become part of the prayer loop. It was a sweet deal.

Back in Winston-Salem, my staff mailed the new members one of my books and a Blessed Cloth: a little swatch of white fabric cut with pinking sheers by volunteers and prayed over by me. Pinned to the cloth were my instructions on how to lay it on their body for a miracle.

My ministry's explosive growth, both in people and dollars, was enough to bring a chill of fear or envy to the soul of my most seasoned competitors.

Plans to invade every major metropolitan area in the United States and other countries with my ministry team went into effect. The Calvin Artury Miracle Crusades soon became The Calvin Artury Worldwide Miracle Ministry. It was nothing less than a miracle of *recreation*. In the beginning, God *recreated* me into an international superstar using one simple tool. Television.

§

Inevitably, I was forced to hire an assistant for Sunday services back home. When I first saw Pastor Tony DeSanto, he surprised me. Definitely not a Southerner, Tony grew up in New Jersey, was a former gang member, and ended up in a seminary after his conversion to Christ. I discovered he was divorced, childless, and had pastored a small nondenominational church in Miami for about six months. I insisted my congregation accept him with the same love and adoration they gave to me.

Of course, Tony's sermons were like decaf in comparison to the espresso tirades of my own. Beyond all that, he wasn't hard to look at. Tony's movie-star smile won the women over at the moment of introduction. My new Assistant Pastor's duties also included weddings and funerals, leaving me to concentrate on the crusades, the television ministry, and building an empire. But I assured my hometown flock, Friday nights belonged to me. Before my team and I departed to the next crusade destination, I would preach the Friday evening service to my faithful Winston-Salem congregation, the people who held my heart.

It was then that I promoted Evan Preston from Church Administrator to Chief Operations Officer, giving him full authority over my church staff and the all-volunteer ministry team. He ruled with an iron fist, making sure the men never pocketed a dime of the offerings they sat around and counted during the crusades. They cowered around Evan who had partnered with me to become the voice of God—no questions asked.

Yet, it was an exciting time for the bubbas who hailed from the rural parts of North Carolina. I offered them first-class tickets to Heaven in exchange for helping me achieve the largest following in the world. Each team member eventually lost interest in all things at home. They existed solely for the next crusade and I elevated them in status within the church. Especially Joe Oliver. He and the rest of my ministry team stayed in above-average hotels, ate in nicer restaurants and wore tailor-made suits at every crusade, all expenses paid by me. I maintained that God wanted his children to have the best, and for Joe—a poor boy from Salisbury, North Carolina—he'd hit pay dirt. And he knew it.

Homecoming

Andie

My daddy grew up in the high country of North Carolina, in Boone. I wanted a husband like Bud Parks and had often thought if President Ford was even mildly like Daddy, then the country was in good hands. A brilliant man, Daddy studied hard and valued his education. Laboring in middle management for the R. J. Reynolds Tobacco Company, he worked six days a week. Undeniably dark and handsome, Daddy stood an inch, or maybe more, under six feet and played the banjo like nobody's business. He'd nicknamed his seventeen-inch biceps his *guns*, and some said he could take down a man twice his size. He had smoked from the time he was ten and could grab hold of his lighter, fire it up, and drag hard, all within a split second. Or two. Cigarettes were as much a part of him as the dark hair on his head and upper lip. Tobacco and cotton still controlled the South, and he was at the constant beck and call of his Camels.

Daddy adored Dixie. I contended it was one of the mysteries of life. My mother was an orphan and a high school dropout who met Daddy in his senior year at Appalachian State. She swore girls all over campus took to their beds the day she married him. Blessed with a Grace Kelly face and Scarlett O'Hara charm, Dixie possessed the right amount of stubbornness to get what she wanted. Devoted to a comfortable lifestyle and one-upmanship, she kept her teased, blonde pageboy—and her house—perfect. Petite, she neither gained more than five pounds after a pregnancy, nor did she step one foot outside her house unless she applied lipstick to wide lips that made you want to keep on staring at them. Her deep-set, gray eyes had backed me against the wall on more than one occasion, and when she was tired, one of them wandered outward a little. Thirty-five and holding, my mother worked hard at her *Jackie O* image. Presentation was everything.

Dixie never discussed her life prior to her marriage, and Caroline and I learned to never ask. There were no pictures of her from her youth, other than the few Daddy kept in his wallet. My mother's past was the one hot button we never pushed. Dixie's explosions could keep you up all night like a bad case of food poisoning and we avoided them at all cost.

§

It was no surprise when Dixie used my baby shower as a chance to take guests on a guided tour of her home before ushering them to the sizeable sunroom overlooking her lush winter garden. Tables of bite-sized sandwiches, canapés, and ginger ale punch had been set up beneath the room's slow-turning ceiling fans that stirred the evening air. Scented candles flickered on aged oak tables next to white wicker furniture, and large hanging baskets of wandering Jew and asparagus ferns exuded Dixie's comfortable style.

Daddy had purchased the house for a steal. The Foursquare monstrosity boasted high ceilings, spacious rooms, crown moldings, built-in cabinets, and

Craftsman-style woodwork. A sweeping staircase and its gleaming walnut banisters curved gently to the upper story and its four bedrooms. Scattered throw rugs muffled squeaky heart pine floors, and antique curio cabinets in the living room displayed Dixie's Hummel figurine collection. Years of cigarette smoke had soaked into the walls of Daddy's study so Dixie kept the door closed to prevent the smell from reeking throughout the house. My emotional attachment to my parents' home, as well as its glossy-magazine-like contents, not only contributed to my storybook childhood, but also to my ideas of what women needed to build a proper nest.

The end of February had gone balmy and out of season, unlike its beginning. Dixie cracked open a few windows to keep the house cool. Before the shower, Caroline twisted pink and blue crêpe paper together and hung it from the banisters. Ribbon streamers hung from the light fixtures and baby booties decorated the *Welcome Baby Oliver* cake. Most guests were unaware of my tattered marriage, and I insisted Dixie keep her comments focused on the baby since her opinion of Joe was that he had the emotional equivalent of a door knob, possessed no paternal instinct, and lacked less chance than a kerosene cat in Hell to acquire it.

God, I missed Mavis. She was a good buffer between Dixie and me and could make me laugh like nobody else. It'd been over two years since I'd seen her, and I needed her more than ever. I would've given back all of my gifts just to have Mavis come home.

As the festivities ended, Maudy helped Dixie gather my gifts and display them properly in the living room. Like I was brought up to do, I thanked my guests profusely with sweet smiles and hugs while the women patted my belly and said their good-byes. My mother stood on the front porch, waving and giggling like a schoolgirl, her other hand caressing the etched glass window in the open front door. My sister and I knew the only thing Dixie loved more than her house was showing it off. For that reason alone, the baby shower was a success.

§

Late the next afternoon, I hunted empty corners and drawer space to store my baby gifts when the phone rang.

"Andie Rose, it's Mavis." She sounded out of breath.

"*Good Golly, Miss Molly.* Is everything okay?"

"Peachy; just in a hurry. Can you pick me up at the Winston bus station tomorrow morning at nine?"

"Can I? Of course I can! Oh, Mavis, you're coming home. I've missed you."

"Missed you more. Can't wait to see you."

"Dixie gave me a baby shower last night. Poop, I wish you could've come a day earlier." My hands started to shake and I nearly dropped the phone. "Gosh, it's been a long time."

"Too long. Haven't been home since your wedding. Not even when Mama passed. Remember, tomorrow morning at nine. You'll have to miss Sunday service. Is that a problem?"

"No problemo. I'll be there. Joe's on the road."

"I know."

"I guess I wrote to you about him; traveling with Calvin. Anyway, our assistant pastor doesn't pound on the pulpit as much. I miss church every chance I get these days."

"That's my girl. Glad to hear it. Well, then, I'll see you in the morning."

I giggled. "You sho' nuff will."

It was good to hear Mavis laugh as I hung up the phone.

§

I opened my eyes on Sunday morning with Mavis's voice in my head. It sounded strange. Urgent-like. As I drove north on Route 52 with heavy traffic, it started to downpour. Vehicles pulled off the road and parked beneath bridges and underpasses. I lowered my speed to keep my bald tires from hydroplaning and crept along below the speed limit. When I reached the city limits, the rain stopped and my belly turned rock hard as a Braxton Hicks contraction bore down. I relaxed my breathing and kept going.

Pulling into the loading zone at the bus station, I saw Mavis waiting on the sidewalk. Tall and stunning, she possessed the body of a dancer and the elegant grace of a gazelle. Her orange paisley bell-bottoms rode low on her hips and her see-through gauze top clung tight around her ample chest of caramel-colored flesh. She was a real jar of honey. Mavis made no effort to hide her bra. But she looked different, more sophisticated than when I saw her last. Her hair, no longer a relaxed flip, had been styled into a neat, short fro. Gold hoops hung low from her ears. She looked taller than I remembered until I caught a glimpse of her platform shoes peeking out from under her pant legs.

Mavis adjusted her shoulder bag, moving the strap from the left shoulder to the right. At the sight of my car, she brought her large pink-tinted sunglasses down low on her nose and smiled so big and wide all I could see were her Pepsodent teeth and two dimples, as if angelic fingers had squeezed her cheeks good and hard. Stopping short of plowing into the taxi in front of me, I burst out of my car squealing like a pig in a poke and ran to grab Mavis by the neck. A head taller than me, she bent and kissed my baby-filled belly. "Girl, you's big as a watermelon. You sho' they ain't two babies in dat belly?"

I giggled. "Just one. Look at you, though! Like a model, so worldly and citified."

Mavis smiled and patted her hair. "Like my do? Cost me a hundred bucks."

"That's my rent payment! Hey, feel like an early lunch? How about Kopper Kettle Diner?"

"Fine wid me." Turning off her Gullah, she shook her head at the old Javelin. "Well, well, Church boy still making you drive this piece of shit car."

"Godamighty, Mavis. You're not home ten minutes and you're wailing on Joe."

"Not like he don't deserve it. I guess I'm cranky. I don't think I've eaten much since I left the South. Yankee women don't eat like us Southerners. They throw up at least five times a day."

"What? Why?"

"To keep weight off. Fat's a big damn deal in New York. If you're young, you better not be fat. It's worse than being a colored woman in the South. Can't get a decent paying job, a man, or a good seat on the bus."

"Does it work?" I asked.

"I've lost twenty pounds since high school. Keep it off, too. Every time I feel myself getting a little pudgy, I puke. Works every time."

"That's awful. Don't puke around me. I can't stand the smell."

Mavis's laugh came from deep in her throat, a slightly hoarse laugh, a laugh I loved. She squirmed in her seat. "Soon as we eat, get me to Daddy's. I need a shower. Got me the worse case of swamp-ass from sitting on that bus all night."

"Did you call Rupert and tell him you were coming?"

"Yeah, you'd think Gerald and Betty Ford was coming to see him. Had Aunt Lula cleaning and cooking all day. I gone have me a fat ass fuh sho' 'fore I get back."

Mavis, who had always tried to be more white than black, had finally embraced her African-American roots. But the part of her white daddy she could not hide was her eyes. As bright and green as new tobacco leaves. Dewy with promise, her eyes smiled even before she did. "You best downshift this bucket of rust, or we's gone stall on dis here hill."

I giggled and downshifted. Mavis seemed a little uneasy, but I attributed it to her all-night bus ride and her swampy ass.

§

Ken Kopper limped over to greet us. The victim of a car accident, Ken dragged his leg behind him, and for as long as I could remember, he lit up whenever he saw Mavis. He'd always been sweet on her. Leading us to a familiar booth in the back, Ken and his toothy grin coaxed a smile from our faces. "Glad to see you both. Been a while—hey, Mavis?"

"Sure has. Good to see you too, Ken," Mavis answered.

We slid across orange-plastic benches opposite each other, a seat we wore as if it were a pair of old blue jeans, tattered and comfortable. Brushing off a scattering of imaginary crumbs from the wooden table, I reminded Mavis of how we'd studied together there, knew the menu like we knew every song The Supremes ever recorded, and drank fifty-cent cups of coffee when it was all the money we had. For a moment, our lives melded again. Bouts of laughter catapulted us into our past, reminiscing happier times. Mavis had me riveted to my seat with stories about living and working in Manhattan and I filled her in on Joe and the Olivers, keeping some of it to myself. Since she already despised Joe for reasons I couldn't explain, I felt no need to add fuel to her fire.

§

At noon, I drove Mavis home.

"I lost my job, Andie."

"What?"

"I say I lost my job." She shrugged and sighed. "Singing gig is over. Place shut down. Bars come and go in New York. And the photographer I work part-time for, Harry, he won't need me 'til late spring. I'm renting out my apartment for a couple months, so I won't have that expense while I'm here with Daddy. But my agent may call me any day and then I'm back to the city, and probably singing in another dive bar."

"So, is that why you came home?"

Mavis didn't answer. She stared out the window, her eyebrows forming a V as I pulled into the Dumass farm's red dirt driveway. I guessed that she missed her mama. From a distance, I saw Rupert and Aunt Lula come at a fast trot down the porch steps.

"Tell you what," Mavis said. "Pick me up tomorrow morning. We'll go see Dixie, have one of her killer breakfasts and talk some more. Then we'll head on down to your place, see all those baby gifts." She sighed a deep, almost sorrowful sigh. "You're such a natural mama."

I stopped the car. "We'll see how natural I am in about a month. You'll be a great mama someday, too, Mavis."

"Someday," she said. Her eyes filled with tears before she bent and kissed my belly again. "Poor thing, he can't help it his daddy's a prick. You know what? It took me two years of living in the meanest city in the world to realize how truly special you are."

I smiled thinking about it. "I'm not special, Mavis. I'm just a country girl. You're right about one thing, though—Joe's been a prick lately." I shrugged. "There's always hope."

"And you've always been so full of it."

I laughed. "Full of what? Shit?"

Mavis winked. "No, you silly goose. Hope," she said, stepping out of the car.

I waved to Rupert and Aunt Lula as they threw their arms around Mavis. I missed her already and I hadn't even backed out of the driveway. But at the Salisbury exit, I pulled over and lost my lunch on the side of the road. My thoughts had turned to Joe.

§

With Mavis home, I felt stronger and flat out refused to allow Joe to dictate every minute of my day. The job of paying the bills had become mine when he started traveling with the ministry team. Feeling the freedom to make decisions regarding our finances, I spoke up that Monday morning. "I'm going to be with Mavis today. I need the car."

"Too bad. I'm leaving Coot's early to go to the church this afternoon," Joe said.

"I'll take you and pick you up. I'm going to be with Mavis."

"How long is she staying? You can't be driving to Winston every day."

"Mavis will be here until her agent calls her back to New York City. I don't know how long that will be. And as long as the bills are paid and you've got a bologna sandwich to eat, I'm going to see Mavis when I want."

Joe had made a habit of slamming doors. That day's slam was no surprise.

§

I arrived back at the Dumass farm early as expected. Mavis glanced out the kitchen window and within seconds she came running to my car with her backpack slung over her shoulder.

Breakfast at Dixie's consisted of cat-head biscuits and sawmill gravy, sausage, grits, scrambled eggs, and fresh fruit. Mavis filled her plate and went back for seconds. "Them biscuits are truly as big as a cat's head, Miz Dixie. I gone be as big as this here house 'fore I get my fat ass back to New York."

"Your hiney is not fat, Mavis. Look at Andie's."

"Stop it, Dixie." I blasted her with my best look of exasperation.

My mother winked at Mavis. "I know she's missed you something awful. More than she misses any of us, that's for sure. Just eat and enjoy your time at home."

I poured more coffee, ignoring Dixie and watching Mavis smile while she sucked on a slice of cantaloupe. Her smile was her best feature; I'd forgotten how much I missed her face. Mavis had spent many hours as part of our family, and we talked the morning away reliving some of our treasured moments around the breakfast table. Though she seemed glad to be back, I sensed a change in her. Her restlessness to return to New York was hard to hide. We had grown up together, but Mavis was always bound for the bright lights of a Northern city to find her fortune while I would forever remain a small-town girl in the South.

Glamorous and talented, Mavis lived in two worlds, but was accepted by neither. Her never-ending struggle to fit in didn't end when she moved to New York City. Before auditions Mavis spent time in front of the mirror, deciding if she were white or black. She changed her hair, her dress, and her accent like she changed her underwear. Her adversity was not that Negro blood ran through her veins, but the way people used her skin color to limit her chances. Despite how I felt about my own life, I encouraged her to take those chances and chase her dreams. However, I knew deep down, the people Mavis cherished most were not in the big city she loved, but in the small North Carolina towns she loathed.

After the breakfast dishes were washed, dried, and put away, I waddled to the sunroom. Mavis followed with her coffee mug in hand, and we sunk into Dixie's wicker sofa. The baby kicked when she put both hands on my belly. "Now there's three of us," she said, leaving Joe out. "I've got something for you." She reached into her backpack.

The beautiful hoops in her ears and the rings on her pinkies and thumbs had siphoned the Carolina girl right out of her. She had made a little money in New York and it showed. Around both wrists several silver and gold bangle bracelets clinked together. The sound caught me off guard. As if she had the power to foresee her own future. She pulled out a box wrapped in blue tissue paper with a baby-blue bow tied neatly around the corners. Her dimples smiled. "For you mostly, but that little boy will enjoy it in a few years. Did I tell you I think it's a boy? Maybe someday they'll be able to tell us before it's born."

"I don't want to know. I like surprises," I said. Finding no card attached, I tore off the wrapping and lifted the lid. I didn't have to open the cover; I knew what it was. Mavis's gift to me was her love bound in a photo album. I pulled it out of the box and laid it on my lap, running my hands up and down the cover. She had cut out a pink rose from a magazine and decoupaged it to the front. Inscribed under the rose in her best handwriting it read, *To Andie Rose With Love*, barely legible.

"I've been saving photos of you and me for years," she said. "I figured the time had come to put them in an album."

Teary-eyed, Mavis snuggled up close and turned the pages for me. When the phone rang I pointed to it. "I'm afraid you need to get it. I'm too big to move."

Mavis answered it and I saw her eyes brighten from across the room. I hoped it wasn't her agent calling her back to New York and I gave her my best pout.

She knew what I was thinking and smiled. "It's Daddy."

Returning to the sofa, Mavis lowered her head and I waited. A feeling of angst spread through my chest and I blurt out a laugh that sounded more like a grunt. "What? I'm not turning another page in this album until you tell me what Rupert said."

"Holy moly!" Mavis gulped. "Seems I'm not just a lounge-singer after all. Mount Zion Baptist Church heard I'm in town. They want me to sing this Sunday with the choir. I'm sure Aunt Lula had a say in that. I told Daddy I'd do it. Better find my old Andraé Crouch tapes and clear out my lungs."

"See there, Mavis, you've come home a star. I'm going, too. It's not every day I get to hear my best friend sing." It was then I turned to a photograph that explained the basis for our abiding love. Why for as long as we lived, nothing would keep us apart or change the direction of our friendship. "Why the hell did you put this picture in here?" I growled. "I can still smell the metal trays and milk cartons."

"Story needs telling," Mavis said. "Your child should know how special you are."

"You would've done the same for me." It was a picture of me at sixteen wearing a thick, black hair net on my blonde head, serving large spoonfuls of macaroni and cheese to a lunch line of high school students.

Mavis pulled up my chin and looked deep into my eyes. She beamed a great smile. Her gentle fingers pushed away several strands of hair from my face. "It's not because you pulled me through school after I flunked the second grade, or because I spent more time at your house than I did my own. And it's not because you were my only friend. It's because you gave up your goodness for me, Miz Andie Rose. I took your hairnet picture so I would never forget what you did for me.

BLOOD PACT

Mavis Dumass

Andie's mind doesn't work like mine. We're as different as green beans and apple butter. That's what makes me love her. I'd hate her if she were like me. In some ways, she's as weak as a bug-bit kitten. But when it comes to me, she's Queen Esther, Joan of Arc, and Eleanor Roosevelt all rolled into one.

In exchange for free lunches my junior year, I worked two periods a day taking lunch money from students. Miss Alberta, the cafeteria monitor, balanced the metal lockbox full of cash before giving it to me to carry to the office where I stowed it safely in the file cabinet behind the school secretary's desk. One fine spring day, I walked out with the box under my arm, and telephoned the school to say I'd gone home sick. Then I took out the money, put a big rock in the box, and sunk it in the pond on our farm. The next day, when the principal discovered the lockbox was missing, he called in his number one suspect: me.

What the school officials didn't know was that I had already spent the money on a new 35-millimeter camera, and registration and entry fees for the photography competition at the North Carolina State Fair. I'd also called Andie and told her my daddy had bought me a new camera for my birthday. I'm sure she wondered how Rupert could come up with that kind of money all of a sudden since he was as poor as a church mouse with no church.

When Andie arrived at school the next day and heard I'd been accused of stealing the money, she knew I lied to her to protect her. She also knew I was about to lose more than my new camera.

I once traded a quick feel under my shirt to a boy for his Kodak Instamatic, and discovered my love of photography. With that cheap camera the desires of my heart became apparent. Whispering my plans to Andie during our sleepovers, I was going to move to New York City and work as a photographer, support myself through years of auditions and singing in nightclubs. I was the next Diana Ross. The world just didn't know it yet. Those dreams lingered on my lips until they consumed me. I was determined to find a way out of the South and truly believed stealing that lunch money was my only chance. Except I was looking at possible jail time or reform school and severely damaging my relationship with my folks. They had no resources to fight the charges or pay back the money.

Fitting into an all-white school had been difficult for me, and my window of opportunity to make something of my life was about to shut. My dreams were in the toilet, but Andie could not bear to see them flushed. She was quite aware her daddy had the money to keep her safe. Her biggest problem was Dixie. The decision for Andie became an easy one.

When she walked into the school office, I made the mistake of meeting her eyes. The visible panic on Andie's face about tore me up. Wanting to dispel her fear, I blinked and gave her a shrug, as if all of the hoopla around my thievery meant nothing. But that didn't stop her. She marched right up to me sitting behind the counter waiting for the sky to fall on my head. "Don't confess to anything," she whispered. Standing at the principal's office door, Andie took a deep breath and walked in without knocking. I watched with my mouth open in disbelief until the door closed with an audible *click* behind her. When she came out, her red and swollen eyes told me all I needed to know. She had confessed to the crime, declaring I had nothing to do with it, and that she knew I put the money in a file cabinet the secretary never remembered to lock. In martyred silence, Andie only shook her head when asked if she'd like to change her story.

Bud and Dixie were called in. That's when Andie confessed to giving all the money to a homeless family, hoping it would ease her punishment. It didn't.

Andie got a three-day suspension and mandatory school service the rest of the year. Working the lunch line all four periods was a small price to pay in her opinion. She was also required to stay an hour after school every day to make up her work for classes missed by slinging hash in the cafeteria. Bud paid the school the one hundred seventy-nine dollars I stole, and no charges were filed since Andie, up until that moment, had been an exemplary student.

It was Dixie who took a belt to her near-grown daughter, swinging in all directions, oblivious to where it landed. But Bud didn't believe Andie's story and confronted her with the truth. She made him promise to keep her secret. True, he wished she wouldn't have done it, but understood her risking her reputation out of loyalty to me, and he told Dixie to never hit her again. I was glad because that beating nearly had me undone. Then Bud told my parents he'd bought me the camera for my birthday. The incident was over. For me. But not for Andie.

Girls who had been jealous of her painted a scarlet letter T on her locker, branding Andie a thief for the rest of her time in high school. She dropped out of several clubs and was kicked off the school newspaper staff, and that's when she started spending all her spare time out of town—with Joe. My demons nearly got the best of me. Staring at the camera with its complex dials, levers and numbers etched around the rings, I came close to throwing it in the pond to sink next to the metal lockbox. I almost didn't follow through on the contest at the state fair, waiting until the last minute to submit my photograph. But Andie told me she wasn't slinging hash for nothing. So I won a blue ribbon in Raleigh that year, and realized her reasons for doing what she did were honest and pure. I also knew someday, sooner or later, I would repay her love.

§

"Remember our blood pact?"

"Still got the scar." Andie opened her right hand. A small scar ran across her palm, almost invisible to the eye. Nobody would notice it unless they were told what it was. I had rubbed at my own scar through the years, almost caressing it at times. It remained a constant reminder of our loyalty.

We clasped our hands together. "Sisters, forever," I said.

"Forever," Andie repeated.

The words impaled my heart before they ever made it out of my mouth. "I'd die for you."

Andie laughed. "Oh, please, let's hope you never have to."

Yet, I meant it. I had expected Joe at some point to love her and be good to her. But he was nothing short of a walking penis. I was finally going to tell Andie everything I knew about him. Absolutely everything. Of all the stunningly beautiful men and women I had met and worked with in New York, it was a pregnant little white woman living in North Carolina I treasured more than anyone in the world. Arriving home the winter of 1975, I realized when I was with Andie—I knew who I was. She had always loved me unconditionally and in return, I would save her from living with a man who did not love her.

CAUGHT

Mavis

We laughed like two pig-tailed girls skipping down Memory Lane that morning. Growing up, I had wanted Andie's soft corn-silk hair, blue eyes, and cotton-white skin. I tried to dress and look like her every day. What a sight we were back then. We howled at the pictures I had glued into the album. It wasn't until Joe called and demanded she pick him up at his parents' house that our grand day ended. Driving to Salisbury, Andie grew quiet. I sensed her broken spirit as I jabbered on about everything and nothing. When we reached the outskirts, I inquired about the Olivers, trying to get a clearer picture of things. "Haven't seen Mrs. Oliver since your wedding. How's she been since Ted died?"

"Some better. She spends most of her time making sure I stay in church."

I grunted. "Huh. Lot of good that's done."

"True," Andie said. "The only Oliver with a productive life and positive cash flow is Ray and God knows he'll never step foot in that place again. I wish I could leave like Ray did. I'm no masochist. But if there's the slightest chance for this baby to have some kind of a daddy, then I can't leave. Not right now."

"Mmm-mmm, what a pickle you're in. How does he do it?"

"How does who do what?"

"How does Calvin manipulate men to put the church before their own wives?"

"Good question," Andie said. "Maybe you should ask the Reverend yourself."

My mama's Gullah kicked in. "No suh, not me. He done gib me da heebie-jeebies when I sees him on da TV."

"You're so lucky, Mavis. Your time is your own. Your Sundays are free."

I lifted my brow before waving my hands at her words. "Don't I know it."

When we pulled into the Olivers' gravel drive I saw Joe in the welding shop with his daddy, hoisting the back end of a John Deere. Joe ambled toward the car as Andie parked where the driveway ended at a flowerbed surrounded by old railroad ties. Bending forward, he stuck his head in my open window. "Well, if it ain't Andie and her colored girlfriend. Hey, Mavis, how the hell are ya? I hear you're in town for a while." He opened the car door for me, leaving Andie to open her own. It pissed me off.

I didn't bother to smile. "I'm home for a bunch of reasons."

"Sorry to hear about your mama. How's your daddy?"

"Daddy's fine." It occurred to me that Joe and I had never had a conversation before. I glanced at Andie standing in the warm February sun, pressing her hands into her back. The weight of the baby clearly stressed her, not to mention her feet appeared swollen twice their normal size. But Joe couldn't peel his eyes off me to even acknowledge her.

Andie stood facing Joe in the middle of the driveway. "I know we're a little early. Would you two mind if I went inside and laid on the couch a while before we head back to Winston?" She was trying to tread carefully.

"Go ahead," Joe said. "You just missed Mama. She hung out the wash, then walked up to Leola's for her daily dose of gossip. Mavis and I can just sit out here in the yard and talk."

I suspected it was the longest string of words he'd spoken to his wife since she'd told him about her pregnancy.

Andie looked at me. "You okay with that?" Dark circles under her once bright eyes were a clear indication she needed rest and lots of it.

"Fine, sweetie. You go in and put your feet up."

She gave me a look of concern, but I promptly dispelled her fear. "Go on. Me and Joe, jus' gone chitchat. Right, Joe?"

Joe had already walked to a redwood chair under the coolness of a large oak.

"Okay, but play nice. Give me a half-hour, and then we'll head back." Andie gave me another look over her shoulder before she opened the back door to Maudy's house. I smiled and pooh-poohed her on inside with a wave of my hand.

Joe motioned for me to have a seat in a matching chair across from him. "You warm enough?" he asked.

I took the seat, but ignored him, and listened to Maudy's sheets snap on the clothesline instead. Moments later I placed my hands on my knees and stared into his eyes. "Look, I want to talk to you, Church Boy, but not about the weather."

"Okay," he said. "I'm all ears."

"You know I never liked you. What I really don't like is the way you treat Andie."

Joe made a fist with his hand. "I don't give a shit if you don't like me, and how I treat my wife is none of your damn business."

He chewed the inside of his cheek and I continued my head-on attack. "Oh, that's where you're wrong. I have something here in my backpack I think you might like to see." I pulled out my camera to get to an envelope on the bottom. I opened it, held up a five by seven-inch color photograph, and shot Joe my biggest smile.

He glared at it a few seconds, then looked behind him. I assumed to make sure his daddy hadn't stepped out of the shop. "Where the hell did you get that?"

I cocked my head. "I took the picture, Church Boy. Saw the entire performance. It is you in the picture, isn't it? I mean—it sure looks like you."

"You took it?"

"You deaf? Yes, I took it." Watching him lick at a line of sweat on his upper lip, I snickered. "That photo opportunity is nothing I'm proud of. I mean, it's not even my best work. But right now, my dearest friend in the wide world, who, by the way, I've known a lot longer than you have, is drowning in sorrow because she thinks her redneck husband doesn't love her. That little pregnant lady in there *is* my business, Church Boy."

I sat back in my chair, relaxed and confident in myself and my mission. I returned the photo and camera to my backpack then crossed my legs as I lit a cigarette, knowing he wanted one, but wouldn't dare smoke in front of his parents. "Religion is the dirtiest game in town, isn't it, Church Boy? I heard Calvin's crusade was coming to Philadelphia. Thought I'd take a trip over, see what you were up to. I watched you, you two-timing moron. Saw the whole thing. I came back to tell Andie all about you. I took the picture to pass on to your offspring. Let the child know what kind of a daddy he's really got."

White as the sheets behind him, Joe choked on his words. "So what's next?"

"Don't know. That depends on you. You need to start showing her a little love and kindness. She's about to drop your kid into this world, and you've done nothing but make her life a living Hell. Time you took a good look at what you are and decide if you want to ruin the life of someone you don't deserve. Personally, I'd just as soon shoot you as look at you, but my sweet Andie Rose has loved you a long time. God only knows why." I lifted my cigarette into the side of my mouth and took a long drag. I could see by the look on his face, I'd made my point.

I stood and took two hip-swinging steps toward him, leaned over so he could see my deep cleavage, and blew smoke in his face. "You make it right with her, Church Boy, or I will put this picture and story in the newspapers. I swear I will." I grinned. "I can see the headlines. Calvin Artury Ministry Team Member, Caught in the Act of Adultery. And during a miracle crusade!"

I turned around as Maudy stormed from the side of the house. By the look on her face, she'd heard more than she should have. I squatted and put out my cigarette in the driveway, then stood and pocketed the butt. Pensively, I glided up to her. "Hey there, Mrs. Oliver, nice to see you again." I held out my hand. But Maudy just stood there. She didn't say a word. "Well, I'll go in and get Andie off the couch; we should get Joe to Winston." I jogged to the back porch and up the steps. Once inside, I stood by the open kitchen window before waking Andie.

I watched Maudy stumble into the chair I had just occupied. Shaking her head at her son, she held up her finger. Her voice thundered across the yard. "Don't say a word. I heard it all. You hit that altar on Sunday, get on your knees, and confess this sin to God and NOBODY else! Don't you *ever* do this again. You get yourself squared away with your wife. You do it before Mavis does any more damage. Your daddy and I have worked too hard to be disgraced by both sons. What Ray did was bad enough; I never in my life thought you'd do worse." She stood and walked toward her worthless son, towering over him. "Mavis is right about one thing though; you start treating your wife with respect. Find some love for her and make it work, or I promise you, you will never work full-time for Reverend Artury!"

Joe shot up and fled to his car, revving the engine and honking the horn. I found Andie and nudged her awake then dashed out and jumped in the back seat behind Joe. Andie duck-walked down the porch steps, half-asleep, her ponytail swinging behind her. Falling into the passenger side, she barely got the door closed before Joe slammed the car into reverse and sped out the drive. He didn't speak, he just spun more rubber off his already bald tires.

§

None of us spoke the entire trip to Winston-Salem. The tension, thick as cow manure, made Andie squirm. She looked over at Joe and blinked, "What time do you want me to pick you up?"

"I'm working late. Coot's coming to get me at midnight after he hits a few bars. Take Mavis home, then go home yourself."

Andie peeked over her shoulder at me as Joe pulled into the parking lot at the House of Praise. I snickered. "Place still looks the same."

Joe glared at me in the rear-view mirror. "How the hell would you know?"

Almost immediately, I saw Calvin Artury standing by his Cadillac talking with two other men. Joe parked his rusted bomb two spots away from a shiny El Dorado in the space marked *Reserved for Reverend Artury.* I sank in my seat and slipped on my sunglasses and ball cap.

"Don't wait up," Joe snapped.

"Do I ever?" Andie snapped back. I was so proud of her. I'd never heard her do that. She stepped out and waddled around the front of the car to the driver's side.

I had one last chance. I whispered to the back of Joe's head. "Do yourself a favor. Get out of this Mickey Mouse church and make a life for your wife and child or I'll do it for you."

He whipped around and looked me straight in the face. "Go fuck yourself," he said. "I ain't afraid of niggras like you."

I shot back with a threatening smile. "Consider yourself warned, Church Boy." Inching out with my back to the Reverend, I slid around the rear of the car and dove into the front passenger seat.

Andie started the car. "Why is Calvin looking at you?"

"Who knows?" I said. "Let's go. This place gives me the creeps." I hunkered low in the seat as she drove out of the church lot.

Pastor, We Have A Problem

Reverend Calvin Artury

Silas Turlo, an accountant, landed a position on my staff as Chief Financial Officer. A fifty-year-old ex-Marine with "Semper Fi" tattooed across his left bicep, silver Brylcreemed hair and dark gray eyes to match, the man was a five-ten tank. Married thirty-some years to Sylvia, his wife had also finagled her way into my inner circle as my Head Usher. Silas smelled like cheap aftershave. Old Spice, I think. He wore a *Jesus is mine* tie-bar and was forever rolling a toothpick in his mouth. Every year he bought my old Cadillac. I met him when he used to raise hunting dogs and race stock cars on the weekends. That was right before God delivered him into my hands. Silas's tacky exterior had nothing to do with his brains. He was brilliant with numbers.

Late one afternoon I pulled into the church lot and found Evan and Silas in head-to-head confrontation. "I'd like to hire your son, Silas, but does Percy have any marketable skills?"

"He deserves a spot on the ministry team!" Silas's high-pitched voice always unnerved me.

I held up my hand to halt their conversation feeling a strange current surge through my body, as if my spirit was suddenly at war. Thunder rumbled in the distance when a car rolled into the lot. I watched Joe Oliver step out. His beautiful wife and a strangely familiar black woman was with him. They sped away as I motioned to Joe. Meeting him halfway down the sidewalk, my mind flipped to the Old Testament Book of First Samuel, chapter seventeen. The story of David and the giant. "You know that black girl?"

Joe shoved his hand through his hair. "Yes, sir. Unfortunately. Her name is Mavis Dumass. She and Andie have been friends for years."

"Just how good of friends are they?"

"Best friends. Reverend, can I talk to you about something?"

"Sure, son. Allow me to finish my meeting with Evan. We'll talk in my office."

§

Evan and Silas followed me inside, closing my office door behind them and leaving Joe at my secretary's desk. Joe would have to wait his turn. Editing videotapes of my new TV show, *The Calvin Artury Hour of Power*, suddenly took second place to an urgency building inside me.

"We may have a problem," I said. "Mavis is back in town. Joe said she's been Andie's friend for years."

Evan leaned against the edge of my desk. "How much do you think Andie knows? You want me to have her and Mavis followed?"

"No. No need to panic yet. Silas, get me the general ledgers from the past three crusades."

"Sure, but I think we need to bring DeSanto into this." Silas tugged at his shirt collar.

"Pastor DeSanto doesn't need to be called unless I deem it necessary; *if* I deem it necessary, then I'll call him."

I watched them leave my office. Evan looked first at Joe and then back at me. "Reverend, call me if you need to have a meeting tomorrow."

I nodded.

Gathering my thoughts, I poked my head around the corner. "Joe, I need to make a few phone calls. Can we talk after you're done editing?"

"Yes, sir."

"Come back at eleven o'clock tonight. I know that's late, but I have some things I need to take care of."

After retreating to the darkness of my office, I called Tony and told my Assistant Pastor to meet me in my office first thing in the morning. While I waited for Silas to bring me the ledgers, I opened my desk drawer and reached for an ivory-handled knife, a gift from my late wife on our last trip to Africa. The handle felt cool to the touch, and comforting to my soul.

ABSOLUTE PROOF

Andie

Something was wrong. "Was that an attempt to be invisible back there?"

Mavis shrugged. "I hate that guy. I mean I hate what he's done to you and Joe."

"Speaking of Joe, what happened at the house? Come on, tell me; you two threw silent daggers at each other all the way to the church."

"Let's just shop and have some fun. We'll talk later. I promise to tell you everything. Feel like a pair of new shoes?"

"Flip-flops maybe. It's all I can fit my feet into these days."

§

The mall announced its fifteen-minute-to-close jingle. I carried a bag of shiny-black flip-flops Mavis had charged on her BankAmericard for me. "You're going to need clothes after you have this baby," she said.

"I know. I've learned if we are to have anything in this life, it'll be me who gets it. Ray told me once I'd have to take the reins. He was right. In addition to working full-time, I've got to go back to school after this baby is born. Find a career. Something better than counting other people's money."

"How will you manage that? You got a baby sitter lined up?"

"Maudy volunteered for two days a week. I hear there's a daycare at the Baptist church. They only charge for diapers and lunches if you're poor. I'm sure we qualify. Should I take you home now?"

"No. Let's go to your place. I want to see those baby gifts."

"It's getting late, Mavis."

"It's okay. I'll call Aunt Lula. She bought a new Chevy Nova; she's dying to drive it. She'll pick me up before Joe gets home, I promise."

The temperature had dropped to winter again. Plumb tuckered out, I just wanted to crawl into bed. The baby had kicked the past hour and my back hurt. But I sensed Mavis had something on her mind. Obviously, it couldn't wait.

§

My shower gifts were stashed in closets and drawers, but I hauled each one out and cradled it like an infant.

"If you don't mind me asking, where's this baby going to sleep?" Mavis always had a way of asking questions I didn't have an answer for. "And how do you plan on washing diapers in here? I'm sure Joe won't give you money for Pampers."

I kicked off my shoes and crumpled on the old blue couch like a crushed paper cup. "I don't have it all figured out, but at least I'm organized."

"True enough. There's not an empty corner or crevice in this whole over-stuffed trailer." Mavis opened cold sodas for both of us, and then sat in the recliner across from me. She knew the answer to her next question, but asked it anyway. "How are you and Joe doing, really?"

"It's a strain. I'm sure you see it. We're not a normal couple. I think he intentionally lost his wedding band months ago—"

"Don't say another word." Mavis sighed. "There's something I have to tell you."

"This is the real reason you came home, isn't it?"

"Andie, you and Daddy are my life, and Aunt Lula, of course. I . . . I know things about Joe I can't keep from you any longer." Mavis rolled her Coke bottle between her palms. "You've never been to one of Calvin's crusades, right?"

"Never wanted to go." I squirmed and shut my eyes. I felt the least Mavis could do was see that I was exhausted and uninterested in her overblown imagination at the moment.

But she continued. "I went to the Philadelphia crusade last month. I had to see it for myself. Oh, Calvin's really something. I would guess there's a new crop of women every weekend at his faith-healing rallies. Or maybe they follow the buses across the country like those Mick Jagger and Jim Morrison groupies. Diesel sniffers I've heard them called, looking to get laid or find a husband; only these women are respectfully dressed, of course. A smorgasbord of good Christian women of every denomination under the sun. I saw how they marched down front to the altar. Uh-huh, all of 'em rejoicing and bringing in the sheaves." Sarcastic, Mavis hissed through her teeth. "Hundreds of pretty women served up like cherry pie. What straight man in his right mind wouldn't be tempted? He doesn't love you, Andie. He can't. No man can truly love his wife when he's screwing another woman."

I opened my eyes. I hadn't told Mavis about Joe cheating on me. I hadn't told anyone. Hoping it was behind me, I didn't even want to think about it anymore. Acting as though it was the first time I heard about his unfaithfulness, I shot her a surprised look. "What? What are you saying?"

"Just listen to me. I found a seat in the back of the auditorium and wore a big hat and sunglasses. No one recognized me; I looked like a reporter. I zeroed in on Joe, busy doing whatever it is he does. I kept him in sight. You know I never trusted him. Then I saw her. A redhead. Red like I'd never set eyes on before." Mavis set her Coke on the coffee table. "Gorgeous, sorry to say. Joe kept strolling over to where she sat, talking and laughing with her. Later, Calvin laid hands on her for a bad back. Can you imagine?" Mavis snickered. "Believe me, the broad didn't have a bad back. After the service I watched Joe put his hand on her shoulder and whisper into her ear. I had a hunch and followed her to the parking lot. A half-hour later, Joe comes whistling out the stage door, smiling like he's going on a turkey shoot. I hung behind and followed them in a taxi. First they stopped at McDonald's. Your husband, he's a real classy guy—knows how to show a girl a good time. Then he took her to a hotel in Philly called The Chesapeake. It's a dump. Lots of prostitutes use it."

Tears gathered on my eyelids like rain on lily pads. I wasn't shocked by Mavis's words.

"Do you want me to go on?" Mavis asked, watching my every movement.

"Yes."

"I'm sorry to have to tell you this. But you need to know."

I nodded and reached for a tissue.

"While they necked in the car after Church Boy ate his Happy Meal, I skedaddled into the hotel. I was in luck; I knew the night auditor. It was a guy I'd met at a bar in New York. In fact, he had wanted to date me once. But I guessed correctly. Joe was stupid enough to book a room in his own name. Of course Benny, my new friend, wasn't about to help me further until I promised him a blowjob. So I promised him. What? Don't look at me that way. I wanted to give you absolute proof. Benny not only provided me with their room number, he gave me access before they checked in. Seems the Chesapeake is famous for its rooms used by a sleazy X-rated film crew that got busted some months back. Room 220 is a creaky-floored hole in the wall. It had a . . . well . . . a hole in the wall. A one-way mirror, the kind the cops use, where I could sit and take pictures from the adjoining room. So I situated myself behind the wall while Benny delayed Joe and his redheaded hooker."

"I have pictures of the whole thing. You've got to get rid of him, Andie. You've got to get him out of your life. How could he do this to you? That's why I came home, to give you these." Mavis lifted her backpack to her lap and pulled out an envelope. "This shit ain't pretty, I know, but these photographs just might save you from a lifetime of heartache. I confronted Joe today. Needless to say, he was pissed! Andie, there's more I need to tell you, I . . ."

I didn't want to hear anymore. I couldn't. I jumped to my feet and dashed to the bathroom, holding my hand over my mouth.

Mavis ran after me. She pounded on the bathroom door while I vomited into the toilet. "Andie, let me in. Come on, I love you, girl. I just wanted to help you!" She pleaded. "Please Andie, I never meant to hurt you like this."

I finally opened the door, stooped over and drained of every drop of energy. I was sure Mavis could see I was sick. "You don't understand, do you?" I said. "I love him. I'll be damned if I know why, but I do. I have to go to bed now. Please, I can't take this. I have to go to bed. I don't want to end up in the hospital before I'm supposed to. I love you too, Mavis, but your timing really sucks. I have to . . . just . . . please . . . let me go to bed."

"Shuh, I'm gone shut up and put chu in da bed. No more talk 'bout dis tonight." She knew her mama's Gullah accent soothed me in the past. Mavis's eyes widened in alarm. Helping me into a fresh nightgown, she stared at my huge belly horizontally lined with deep purple stretch marks. She had not seen my naked body since high school. My belly button had disappeared— flattened was more like it. My breasts were twice their normal size, my swollen legs and feet looked like balloons ready to pop, and my fingers resembled fat link sausages.

"You poor little thing." Mavis pulled the bed covers down and helped me crawl in, then slipped out to make a quick call, I assumed to her Aunt Lula. I heard her tiptoe back through the trailer. She crawled on top of the bed with me, then wiped my brow with a cool wet cloth. Softly, she sang an old Negro spiritual her mother taught her as a little girl while they bent their backs together in dusty tobacco fields. A waterfall of tears streamed down my face onto the pillow and dropped to the sheet below. Mavis knew I was not well enough to hear the rest of whatever she came home to say. It would have to wait. Maybe until after the baby was born, and then again, maybe not even then. I knew what Joe was; she didn't need to tell me another thing. I heard Lula's car in the drive.

"I gots to go, Andie Rose. You gone be okay now. You sleep. Mavis gone take care of all dis nonsense. I sorry I hurt you, baby." She kissed my cheek.

I reached for her hand. "*You* didn't hurt me. You told me the truth. This was as hard for you to say, as much as it was for me to hear. I need rest, and I need to think." I yawned.

"Okay. I'll call you in a day or so. Before I sing at church on Sunday."

"Sure, that's fine. And Mavis?"

"Yes?"

"I don't want to see those pictures. I believe you without having to look at them."

"I know," she whispered.

"Thanks. Turn out the light in the living room and lock the door on your way out."

"Okay. Night, Andie."

"G'night."

Breathing took effort. I tried to quiet my mind, but it was as if suddenly the hand of God had curled into a fist. What had I done to deserve this? My brain filled with images of Joe and a redheaded woman, and I wondered how many women he'd really been with. I could scarcely feel the dozens of tears that rolled off my face. So much commotion rumbled inside my head, and yet I yearned for sleep to fill it like warm rising dough.

REVELATIONS

Reverend Calvin Artury

I shoved the beautifully carved handle of the knife back into my desk drawer. At eleven on the dot, I opened my office door. "Joe, come in. Have a seat."

"Thanks, Reverend. I really needed to talk to you tonight."

"Let's keep this short, shall we? It's late and I have an early morning appointment." I sank into my chair. "What's on your mind?"

Joe sat slowly and rubbed the back of his neck, confessing his affair; that Mavis Dumass had blackmailed him; that she'd followed him from the Philadelphia crusade to a hotel, took pictures, and threatened to put them in the newspaper. I practically bit my tongue in half as he apologized for his reckless actions. He wanted out of his marriage and lied through his teeth, accusing Andie of refusing him sex since her pregnancy. After he had puked it up, we sat in deafening silence.

Joe and a few other young men in my flock held a special piece of my heart. I had pushed him into marrying Andie, but I had not anticipated he would want to bolt so quickly. Of all the women in my church, I wanted Andie safe within its walls. She had always reminded me of my mother. She had the same soft round exterior, was quiet and headstrong, yet never a problem. Until now. I needed the mind of God on the mess Joe had dropped into my lap.

And just that quickly, I had it.

Sex was the Achilles heel of my ministry team. The leverage I needed to control them. I had to put a spark back in his marriage, keep them together at least temporarily while I put out a few smoldering fires.

"You and the rest of the team were warned, if you were caught with your pants down you would pay the price."

"I—I'm sorry, Reverend. I've asked God to forgive me."

"I can't condone your actions, son, any more than God can, but I can't afford to lose you either. Your work is critical to the ministry and I recognize your talent. It would take me months to replace you, and I don't have that luxury while I'm in the process of buying a television station. So this is what I propose. It's not time to end your marriage. I will let you know when that time is. Obviously, I was not able to enforce the abortion with Andie. I don't like it, but you've got a child on the way. It would be scandalous for you to leave your wife at this time. I told you a couple months ago to ease up on her, but it appears you have not. You can't expect to win her to the cause of Christ if she suspects you don't want to be married to her."

"But the fact is, I *don't* want to be married to her after what she did to me."

"You want my blessing for a divorce?"

"Yes, more than anything. I don't want to be married at all."

I strained to hide my irritation. I didn't like surprises from my ministry team. "Let's get one thing understood. If you want to work for me, you'll be a married man. I need a team of young married people. It looks good to the masses. You, Joe, will not create a scandal that will, and I repeat—that *will* bring ravenous reporters to our doors. You're on the verge of creating a nasty one for me to clean up. And if I have to clean up after you, you'll never work here. You got that?"

Joe had suddenly gone mute.

"Have you ever acted, Joe? Ever been in a school play, or taken any drama classes?"

A nervous chuckle escaped his lips. "No, can't say that I have."

"That's too bad, because you've got to become an Academy Award winner overnight. Think of it as part of your job. It'll help you get through it. I'll direct, you act." I stood and leaned forward, placing my hands square in the middle of my desk. "I want you to throw yourself at her swollen feet tomorrow morning, swallow your pride, and beg Andie to forgive you. Tomorrow morning without fail! Get back in her good graces to circumvent anymore gossip than we may already have. If we don't end up with too much of a mess, I will still consider you for full-time hire."

"How long—"

"The Jews wandered in the wilderness forty years because of their disobedience!"

Joe gave me a resigned shrug. "I hope it's not that long."

"You'll stay with Andie as long as Jehovah-Jireh wants. Or you can disobey the voice of God, and face an eternity in Hell. Your choice." I sat and leaned back in my chair to survey him coolly and loosen my tie. "Like I said, someday I'll allow you to leave her, but not now. Now is not the time."

"What about Mavis?"

"Leave Mavis Dumass to me. You say she's been friends with Andie a long time?"

"Since they were kids."

"Andie ever talk much about Mavis to you? Tell you anything about her, what she did, her hobbies, anything like that?"

"If she did, I never paid attention. I never liked her. And she certainly hates me."

"How long's she been in town?"

"Couple days. Andie says she won't be heading back to New York 'til her agent calls."

I made a few notes then focused my attention on the young man who from the time he was fifteen had followed me like a disciple into the River Jordan. "Go home, Joe. Get on your knees and *act* like you love your wife. We'll talk more as time goes on. You're important to me. I'll not allow you suffer too much. Besides, I know your parents want you to succeed where your brother has failed." I stood a final time to signal the meeting was over. Joe took a chance and met me halfway around my desk. I found myself embracing him, not wanting to let go, and speaking directly into his ear. "Keep it in your pants, Joe. Otherwise, I'll tell Evan to cut it off."

He stepped back and chuckled, as if I had told a joke. "Thanks, Reverend. I promise not to let you down." Leaving my office, Joe looked back.

I wasn't smiling.

§

The next morning I relaxed in the soft glow of my office at home and rested my head on the back of my leather chair. Mavis Dumass was a ticking time bomb—explosive—and Joe's behavior could light the fuse. I hoped I'd got my point across to Joe. I needed to take care of Mavis years ago, instead of believing she would return to New York and never be heard from again. She was never to come back. That was the deal.

I swiveled my chair around and faced the window. I had refused to allow my housekeeper to take down the lace panels. A long time ago I had shared the study with my wife, Vivi. Her tiny desk remained in the room, just as she had left it. Her sweater still hung on the back of the chair eerily filling the shoulders.

A fierce and powerful sun broke through the clouds. Its rays slanted low through the windows, bringing a tear of sad joy to my eyes. "I hope you can see me, Mama. I hope you're proud of your son. I miss you." I let out a deep and congested sigh. "Unlike you, I shall escape death. When He raptures me, I know you'll be there, waiting."

Switching on my desk lamp, I opened the Bible on my desk. *Time Magazine* was barking at my door for an interview. *The New York Times* said I was the 'one to watch' to take over as the country's leading evangelist. I already controlled the South and its mass of fundamentalist conservatives. I wanted the world, and no little black jezebel was going to ruin it for me. As He would have me do, I aspired to deity. To be viewed as the Pope, Abraham, Joseph Smith, Muhammad, Moses, John the Divine. I wanted my people to see that God's end-time calendar revolved around my ministry. The occasion was drawing near when my congregation and the world would realize it. I more than wanted the power and admiration Jesus had; I deserved it. It's what I lived for.

I would discuss Mavis with Pastor DeSanto. We had to resolve that problem, and then the Andie Oliver problem. One was becoming as bad as the other.

A Broken Dam

Andie

I woke early Tuesday morning with Joe asleep beside me. *Why isn't he at work?* Stumbling to the bathroom, I sat on the toilet until my legs went numb. Leaning against the sink, I splashed water on my bulging red eyes and heard him walk into the kitchen. In the next second, the electric can opener whirred and popped. *What's he doing?*

I waddled toward the noise. "Why are you home?"

"Oh, hey. I thought I'd make coffee. I told Coot I needed the day off."

I shook my head, thinking possibly I had water in my ears and hadn't heard him right. "What?"

"We need to talk. I took the day off."

"I'm not talking until I've had a shower and coffee."

Joe opened the refrigerator and peered in. "You get in the shower, I'll make breakfast."

"You'll what?"

He shut the refrigerator door with his elbow; his hands were full. "Make breakfast. I'm not totally helpless in a kitchen." He half-grinned and set the eggs and bread on the counter.

I made it to the bathroom without fainting. *This is the Twilight Zone.* He'd not said a kind word to me in months, at least not when we were alone. In front of someone, he could be cordial, but alone he'd been hell to live with. I'd broken lots of eggshells and felt like I'd just been flung from a nightmare because of him. Questions rolled through my head like words on a teleprompter. *Why is he so amiable all of a sudden?* Even before I stepped into the shower I heard him banging pans and rummaging through the refrigerator again.

Standing in the cool water, I nearly jumped out of my skin when Joe poked his head behind the shower curtain. "I can't find any of Mama's jam in the fridge." When I didn't respond he didn't bark at me for an answer. Instead, he made a funny noise with his throat. "Eggs, toast, and coffee are ready when you are," he said.

I sat in my bathrobe at the kitchen table wishing I had remembered to slip on my house shoes. My feet were cold and my hair was damp. My head felt fuzzy. I had to pee again. It was impossible to think about communicating with him; my brain had come to an emotional dead-end overnight.

Joe grabbed the percolator, placed his finger on the glass knob on top, and then tipped it sideways to fill my coffee cup. "Do you put anything in your coffee?"

We'd been married two and a half years, and he had no idea how I liked my coffee. "Black will be fine, thanks."

"Andie Rose . . . I . . . "

Suddenly my heart bulldozed through the dead-end. He hadn't called me Andie Rose in so long, I'd forgotten the sound of it. Tears formed in the corners of my eyes.

"Eat up. We'll talk after I take my turn in the shower."

I managed to swallow a few bites, then scrape the rest into the trash. Listening to him whistle in the shower, I put dishes in the sink then sprayed them with hot water and a green line of Palmolive. Running cold fingers through my tangled hair, I walked out to the front porch. I'd been standing a while in the warm morning sun, feeling numb, when a sudden bout of hopefulness intensified within me, then evaporated just as quickly. His good mood insulted me. The baby kicked. "Good morning, little one," I said, hand to my belly. "We've got some decisions to make, you and I. How much longer will we live with your daddy? Where do we go from here, huh? Why do you suppose he's so nice today?"

"Because I hope you'll forgive me," said Joe. I flipped around. He stood at the screen door. "Come in, Andie; let's talk." He held the door wide open as I stepped back inside. "More coffee?"

"I have to pee first."

Sitting at the kitchen table again, I watched sunlight stream through the windows, showcasing the dust balls on the floor I had neglected the past week. I wasn't about to forgive him. My emotions were like the dust balls: disgusting dried-up pieces of nothing.

"I know Mavis told you about Philadelphia. I know you think I've been cheating on you with lots of women."

"It doesn't matter if it were a hundred women or just one, Joe. I can't. I won't. I won't live like this. Why would you ask me to forgive you now? Why now? Because you've been caught? Again? Because Calvin is afraid of what people might say?"

Joe's eyes filled with worry. "I had a long talk with . . . a nice guy at church. I've got issues with marriage, Andie. I don't want to be married. But I am. And, well, after the shit hit the fan with Mavis yesterday, I realized she was right. I don't want to lose you, and I don't blame you if you hate me." His hand reached across the table, but there was nothing for him to hold. I didn't reach back. "Forgive me, Andie. Please. I'll change, please believe me. I'm not sure I can be with you for the baby's birth, but I'll be a better husband. And I'll really try . . . try to be a father."

I'd not heard words like those come out of his mouth for a long time. If he was lying, he was doing a damn good job. They were the exact words I'd wanted to hear since I told him about the baby months before. I sat up a little straighter and pushed my coffee away from me. I wasn't jumping into his arms unless I could see my reflection in his heart. In the past few months, I'd grown up and acquired a thicker skin. I'd learned some things about myself. Though I wanted to believe him, I would not. Not yet. Time would tell a true story. In the meantime, I would enjoy his peace treaty, and get through giving birth without having to walk on eggshells.

He slid off his chair onto his knees, landed in front of me, and for the first time in almost nine months he placed his hands on the huge mountain of baby that was my belly. The baby kicked and he smiled. "I'm sorry, to the both of you."

The dam broke and I pulled his hands off me, holding them, and taking them up to wipe my tears. I wanted him to feel my sorrow. "I'm not sure what's worse. The betrayal or the lies. Sorry won't do it for me, Joe. A five-minute apology will not heal the wounds you've created. I hope you're not lying. Time will tell. Unfortunately for you, I can't think of anything right now but this baby. You'll have to take a *back* seat. We'll try to get along, and then . . . we'll see. Who was the man you spoke to?"

"Some old guy at church; no ministry team member, if that's what you're thinking." Joe crawled back onto his chair. His eyes darted around the room like the shadows of a bird.

"Oh." I hesitated. "Do I know him?"

He swallowed. "No." He wouldn't look at me. "I don't remember his name even. I think he's a doctor."

Liar. He talked to Calvin, but won't admit it. Calvin didn't allow anybody within his congregation to counsel the members of his church. Especially his ministry team. It didn't matter at that moment; I'd leave things be until after the baby came and my strength returned. My impetuous nature would have to learn even more patience and see where this new turn of events with Joe was leading.

Starved for affection, I let the words slip out. "Do you love me, Joe?"

He got down on his knees again and leaned in close, his breath warm on my face. Staring into my eyes, he cupped my chin softly with his hands. "Yes," he said, and kissed me.

Sorry We're Open

Mavis

I called Andie on Tuesday evening and heard Joe asking her who was on the phone. We couldn't talk. So I told her to meet me for lunch the next day at the Sorry We're Open Diner in Welcome.

§

A long, skinny eatery with no booths, Sorry We're Open looked the same as the last time I ate there. Along the front by the windows, a row of twenty tables for four had been squished together on a black-and-white checkerboard floor. Red vinyl stools, some with duct-tape patches, sat on chrome pedestals beneath a long counter. Standing in line waiting to be seated, Andie closed her eyes as if to catch a quick nap. Her massive belly bumped against my hip. I sensed the baby was ready to pop out any day. "You seen your doctor lately?"

"I missed a couple appointments. Just don't have the money."

"Andie Rose, you make payments. Go see your doctor."

Her smile did not indicate compliance.

"Go see your doctor!"

"Okay, geez, I'll call him when I get home. I've been feeling kind of funny lately anyway."

"Funny, how?"

"I don't know. I never had a baby before. It doesn't kick much. No wiggle room, I suppose." She lowered her voice. "I feel kind of swollen *down there*, I guess."

"You guess? You *guess* your crotch feels kind of funny?"

"Shhh! God, Mavis. Does everyone in New York City say crotch that easy? I'll see the doctor as soon as I can. Happy?"

"Excuse me, but last time I checked the calendar it was 1975 not 1955!"

"Not down here. Not in the South. We roll about ten years behind the rest of the country."

"Dat's true, Miss Scarlett. Us dahkies in da South don't know nuttin' 'bout birthin' babies, ceptin' if you puts a knife under da bed, it cuts da pain in two." I loved making Andie laugh. "You gotta be tough to have a baby," I said.

She looked at me and cocked her head. "How would you know?"

"True; how the hell would I know?"

We were still laughing when we squeezed through the crowded diner behind a hostess to a table at the end of the lunch counter. Faded color photos of yellow scrambled eggs and beige link sausages lined the wall. Andie maneuvered into her chair like a bus backing into a parking spot. I handed the menus back to the waitress and told her to bring a pot of coffee, two bowls of bean soup, and a plate of cornbread and apple butter. Even though bean soup gave Andie gas, I figured Joe deserved a couple good stink bombs under his sheets.

"Thanks," said Andie. "I didn't want to decide on anything today. Not even food."

"I figured that. He fed you a line of crap, didn't he?"

"Maybe, but it sounded good."

I sighed. "Andie, look at me. He's a snake. He can't flush his meanness down the toilet and come out smelling like checkout-counter cologne. You really love him? After all I told you he done?" I peered at Andie over my coffee cup while I waited for an answer.

She shifted in her seat, palming her belly. "I don't know. I'm sorry; I just don't know. I'm not sure I can turn love off overnight, no matter what." Andie rested her elbows on the table and cupped her hands around teary eyes, shielding her embarrassment from nearby patrons. Her voice quivered. "I'll reserve making any decisions until after the baby comes. I'll never trust him again, that's for sure. This marriage may be over, but like I told Joe, time will tell me the truth. Maybe I *am* a fool, and a stupid one at that." She turned her head and stared out the window. A toddler in pink OshKosh overalls held tight to her mama's finger as she walked her into the restaurant. A young couple scurried to their car, the father's dark hair curled down his neck while his baby's button face beamed on his shoulder. "He told me he loved me," she said.

"Yeah, he loves ya, about as much as I love hoeing a row of tobacka, and that ain't much." I sulked in my seat believing Andie was indeed the stupidest fool I'd ever known. But that moment vanished quickly. I finally realized she loved Joe as she loved everyone in her life—unconditionally. There was no greater love than that. Andie possessed some kind of supernatural strength. A force I'd seen manifested from the time we were little. I admired her endurance, determination, and courage to stay in a God-forsaken marriage, no matter the steep price she had to pay for it. But I refused to believe Joe's confession of love. I'd talk to Church Boy again. Tell him to at least keep on faking it so Andie could be happy.

Then it occurred to me—maybe, if Church Boy were out of Calvin's reach, he might remember why he married her to begin with. I needed to go to the root of the problem. The man who controlled him. Namely, Calvin. I knew I'd have no difficulty getting bumped to the front of the line. Yes, Lord. It was time to get in the Reverend's face.

Andie stuffed a cracker in her mouth and smiled. "Look, it's Joe and Coot. I forgot they come here for lunch sometimes."

I turned to watch the hostess seat them at the other end of the diner.

"I'd rather not let them know we're here," she said. Not even Andie's casual shrug could hide the pain filling her watery blue eyes.

Edging out a half-smile and a sharp sigh, I used my thumb to wipe a crumb off Andie's cheek. "I have to use the restroom." Then I handed her the dessert menu. "Here. See what you want for your sugar rush today. I'll be right back." I walked, instead, to Joe's table.

"Excuse me, Joe?"

"Well, hey, Mavis. Andie with you?"

"Yeah, she's sitting over there."

"Coot, this is Andie's friend, Mavis. Mavis, this is my boss, Coot McGraw."

"Nice to meet cha, ma'am."

"Same here. Um, Joe, can I speak to you a second? Outside."

"Sure. Coot, order me a grilled cheese with tomato and a Coke. Tell her to put some home fries on the side."

"Got it." Coot returned to his menu.

"After you," Joe said to me, pointing to the door.

I led him to the parking lot where Andie couldn't see us. "Listen Joe, I know Andie's sticking with you 'til the bitter end. I won't upset her again."

He paled slightly and his mouth twitched, from either amusement or aggravation. "Glad to hear it. But I'd certainly love to give you a fist sandwich at least once before I die."

"Well, Church Boy, I might jus' give you that chance someday. Andie done told me about your lil' performance Tuesday morning. Mmm–mmm, you sho' is quite the actor. Know this, Church Boy. I know you lie. I ain't afraid of Calvin Artury and I plan to talk to him soon about all this. Ain't afraid to do right by Andie—ain't afraid of nothing. So you tell him that. In the meantime, you keep our girl happy, and I'll hold tight to the pretty pictures of your Philadelphia fling. 'Cause if you break her heart again, I'll publish those pictures, just before I slit your throat all the way down to your little white pecker. You 'member that, Church Boy."

Joe's anger exploded as he leaped forward to grab me by the arm, but I backed up quickly and he stumbled, making himself look silly. Two truckers in dirty jeans and ball caps, walking into the diner, stepped between us.

"You alright, ma'am? You need help?"

"No, thank you, gentlemen. I'm fine."

Escorting me into the restaurant, the two men gave Joe the evil eye, but I looked back and smiled my prettiest smile.

§

Joe charmed his way, casual-like, to our table.

"Hey, Andie. Seen you two sitting here. I'm buying you and Mavis lunch today." He lay ten dollars on the table, then stared down at me. I could feel him wanting to yank me off the chair and pummel me with his fist.

"Thank you," Andie said, distracting him.

I rolled my eyes. "Well, Mister Big Spender, if you're buying, then we're ordering pie and ice cream. Might want to add a few more dollars to that ten. And thanks. You're a peach."

Joe shot me a wry smile, then winked at Andie. "See you at home tonight."

Andie's eyes followed him.

"More coffee?" The waitress poured and chatted with Andie, but I glanced down the line of tables. Coot held his chili and slaw-dog with one hand and wiped sauce off his already spotted T-shirt with the other. Church Boy only drank his Coke, less than interested in his meal and his grease-monkey boss.

He would no doubt relay my message to Calvin. I drew in a breath, reluctant to listen to anything except what my gut was telling me. He would cut me down if he could. In the deepest part of me I felt shipwrecked. My insides rolled like seaweed tossing in stomach acid. I'd put up a good act. Not just afraid, but borderline terrified, I understood the man I was dealing with better than anyone. There was no turning back. I'd get what I came back to Winston-Salem for. Peace for Andie.

March 1975
A Song Of Faith

Andie

I rolled out of bed the first Sunday in March to another sun-drenched day pouring through the windows, yet biting as winter begged to hang around a few more weeks. I had promised to meet Mavis on the steps of Mount Zion Baptist Church at nine o'clock. St. Christopher's Catholic Church was located across the street, which was convenient because I had invited Libby and Ray to stop in after Mass to hear Mavis sing. She was going to sing my favorite church song. One that nobody at the House of Praise seemed to know. It'd been years since I'd heard Mavis sing with a backup choir, and I shivered with anticipation. I couldn't get dressed fast enough. Friends and family I loved under one roof, and in a fresh new church no less.

Joe had kissed me before leaving Friday night for a crusade. I felt nothing but wet lips. My wall had been built brick by brick, insult by insult: a fortress. It'd take more than a few quick kisses to tear it down. Broken and pieced back together, I'd leave the House of Praise, but not until I fought my best fight to take him with me. Even if we didn't end up together, I still wanted my baby's father freed from religious bondage. But I didn't want to think about Joe. I felt good and my spirits were up. I'd found a burst of energy waiting for my little one to make its arrival, and I started to sing—and not church songs. A little Lynyrd Skynyrd. A bit of Ronstadt. Some Janis Joplin mixed in with Aretha. Shoot, Dixie wasn't the only one in the family who could sing. Every song exploded from some unearthed happiness inside me. I almost skipped to the car.

Like a never-ending row of crucifixes, telephone poles lined the township road that took me to Route 52 and to Winston-Salem. Suddenly it was spring, with colors stretching toward the sky. Sun-kissed crocuses and daffodils poked through the ground and waved in the wind. Grateful for the cool breezes, if only for the next few weeks, I drove with my window down, dodging new potholes and inhaling deep breaths of freshly plowed Rowan County dirt. Though the air felt as crisp as a sheet on a winter clothesline, I knew summer's heat was not far away.

Following the highway signs, I found Mount Zion Baptist Church sitting in the middle of its own town square. The dandelion-dotted lawns were rich with the first new blades of spring grass. Ribbons of purple and yellow pansies cabled the walkways, twisting between blooming Bradford pear trees. Mavis waited for me on the church steps, beaming in her borrowed choir robe. My pride couldn't be contained in my head or my heart, watching her walk toward the choir loft, talking and laughing with folks she knew. It was a blessed day.

Rupert sat on a back pew, and I slid in next to him. At least Ray and Libby could easily see me when they entered the sanctuary later. I felt different, sitting in that church. I felt something I'd never felt before. I felt God dwelling there. And it was overflowing with tar-pit dark skin.

"Maybe Jesus is a black man," I said to Rupert.

Mavis's daddy gave me a slow, knowing smile. "Hmmm, now that's a thought. It'd be a big disappointment to the White South, wouldn't it?"

"You're telling me. It'd stink like a fart in church to some good ol' boys I know."

Rupert smiled wider that time. "Serve 'em right. Suit me just fine," he said.

Sitting there, I thought about the rural counties and small towns in the Carolinas where folks still flew Confederate flags on the steps of their courthouses and in their front yards. Single-storied houses and trailers spewed throughout the countryside—in need of paint or rusted-out, on blocks, with fans wedged into windows and not a soul in sight. I'd seen their dirt yards, their porches stocked with dented refrigerators and old couches. Tin roofs, tobacco barns, and cinder block buildings with neon Budweiser signs in the window; general stores that sold bait and tackle and chicken wings at the same counter. Places I'd been with Daddy when he'd pull up in his pickup, tag his deer, and fill his tank with unleaded. Collarless dogs had chased my car down many of those red dirt roads. Mavis had refused to drive through those areas, especially at night. She'd found it safer in New York, having moved above the Mason Dixon line.

My eyes adjusted to the light in the room. A gaggle of colorful hats nodded to one another like sunflowers with heavy heads, as if partaking in a religious ceremony all their own. In a sea of bright smiles filling the sanctuary, each woman over the age of thirty wore earrings to match their outfits, smudges of red rouge on their toffee cheeks, and dazzling shades of lipstick. Suddenly, I felt underdressed.

Mavis's Aunt Lula spotted me and dashed over. Her large-brimmed purple hat with a matching plume sat like a boat on her head and rocked back and forth as she pounded up the aisle. When she fell into the seat next to me, the pew creaked and vibrated. "Andie, chile', you gives ol' Aunt Lula a big hug."

"Aunt Lula, it's so good to see you. I can't wait to hear Mavis sing."

"Shuh, chile', me too. Been a long time. I'm fixing to cry mah eyes out. You bring a hankie?"

"Yes, ma'am. Two."

She patted my hand. "Well, you enjoy the service and ah be seeing you later." Touching Rupert's shoulder in hello, she stood, then wobbled back to her pew.

Seated next to Rupert, watching his face beam as Mavis chatted with the rest of the choir, I felt privileged to know such a man. A man who had been ostracized from a white world because he'd fallen in love with a black woman some twenty-five years before. They were tight communities of family, that church. I'd heard Rupert say as far as he was concerned, his world was in the black community. They accepted him, loved him, and would bury him next to the woman he had loved and called his wife.

I turned my gape to the interior of the church. Old and somewhat in need of repair, there were no elegant velvet draperies on the windows or soft cushions on the pews. The walls were cracked and peeling. Dog-eared songbooks and fans advertising a local funeral home rested in worn trays on the backs of pews that had held the members since before the turn of the century. Mount Zion Baptist Church had no carpet on the floor to absorb the sound of shoes or noise in general. The congregation greeted each other in the name of the Lord, laughed, and from my viewpoint, enjoyed their morning. Even their children sat in the sanctuary, giggling and visiting with other families. Dr. Goodwin, the pastor, already in his simple pine pulpit, arrived with no fanfare. He'd simply shown up, ready to start his service.

My whole body smiled as he tapped his microphone and said, "Welcome, brothers and sisters, into the House of the Lawd this fine morn. *For this is the day the Lawd has made, we shall be glad and reeejoice in it!*" The organist played perfectly harmonized chords. No planned music, just flats and sharps with voices all their own, blending together, making a melody in the heart of the man sitting at the organ. People clapped and lifted their hands for the joy of it. Moving and waving in perfect rhythm, they felt their music and their God. Goose bumps marched along my arms and I closed my eyes and felt it, too. All the way to my feet. My baby leaped in my belly and when I opened my eyes, my gaze fell on Mavis in the choir loft, shouting like she'd seen a glimpse of Jehovah Himself.

The festivities were far different than I was used to. The people appeared as though they wanted to be there, not because they were guilted into it. Dr. Goodwin, a pleasant enough man, was tall and wore thick black-rimmed glasses. He talked so loud he didn't need his microphone, crying out, "Chil'ren of Gawd, cast your burdens on Him, and He shall sustain thee." I loved the way he seemed to sing his sermon. The members rocked back and forth, or fanned themselves in their seats. Not one soul could sit still, and I too swayed in the sea of worshipers.

Dr. Goodwin threw his head back, Martin Luther King style. He raised his hands to the ceiling and from my pew at the back of the church, I could see his palms were pink as roses. His pastor voice pulsated, filling the sanctuary with electricity. "*They that wait upon the Lawd, shall renew their strength, they shall mount up with wings as the eagle. Yes Lawd, they shall run and not be weary, they shall walk and not faint, teach me Lawd . . . to wait upon Thee!*" The congregation repeated him; blessings and *amens* abounded in every pew, even among the littlest children. The power of their pastor's words captured their hearts. I nearly laughed out loud. And I did laugh when Dr. Goodwin, in good humor, apologized for forgetting to take up the offering. Fifteen minutes later, the plates were passed, the prayer said, and the service continued. I looked at Mavis, who looked back at me and broke into a wide, open grin. Even her dimples smiled.

Libby and Ray walked in the back just as the choir stood to sing. I motioned to them and they scooted into the pew as Mavis stepped to the microphone.

"This song is dedicated to my best friend who is here with me today, and to my daddy in memory of my mama." Mavis nodded to the pianist and began to sing.

"Great is Thy faithfulness . . ."

It was a song I recalled from my early childhood, a song my grandma Parks had sung to me long before my little feet ever touched House of Praise property. It had depth and meaning. Its beauty transcended time. Libby's hand patted my knee. Ray wiped his eyes. There was no angel in Heaven that morning that didn't stop and listen to Mavis praise her God and sing as though her life depended on it. She sang the song to me. It was love to her; it was life to her.

The congregation's shouts quieted when Mavis stepped up to the microphone again. Without warning or introduction she belted out the first words of Mahalia Jackson's signature song, *Move On Up A Little Higher.* People jumped to their feet, stomping, clapping, rocking, rolling, and waving their hankies. Anyone peeking in the windows would've thought the Mount Zion Baptist congregation of jubilation had gone a bit crazy in the head. I looked at Mavis, her hands raised to Heaven, tears streaming, chin quivering, and I knew. At that moment I knew Mavis had truly found the God she had sung about all her life. A sight I would treasure the rest of my days.

§

I didn't want pictures taken of my pregnant self, but we gathered outside after the service for Libby to snap photos of Mavis and me, standing in front of the church with our arms around each other. She took several pictures and then said to Mavis, "You were brilliant. The most beautiful voice I've ever heard." Smiling at Ray, Libby said, "Go ahead. Ask her. She can always say no."

Mavis grinned. "Ask me what?"

"I'm sure Andie told you, Libby and I are getting married next week in the Catholic church across the street, over there, by those tall pines," Ray pointed. "Our soloist had emergency surgery yesterday. She won't be well by next Saturday. So, would you . . . well, would you consider being our soloist? I'd be willing to pay for your services. And, of course, we insist you be our honored guest at the wedding."

I was about to bust, raising my eyebrows at Mavis.

Mavis laughed out loud and stuffed my head in the crook of her arm to give me a noogie. "Just look at Andie Rose, look at that face, how can I say no to that?"

AVE MARIA

Andie

For one full day, flat on my back, I braved sporadic pains that finally subsided by Friday morning. Mavis called early to check on me. "You sure you're not in labor?"

"God, Mavis, yes, I'm sure. I'm not due until April. For your information, I called my doctor and he asked if I still have my plug. I don't even know what a plug is. I'm actually feeling better than ever."

"Okay, fine. But call me if your water breaks, hear? I'll get you to the hospital lickety split. Just remember, first babies have a tendency to take forever to pop out. Or so I'm told."

"Thanks, but I think this is a false alarm. Lord, don't call Dixie. It's all I can do to keep her from moving in with me."

"Your mama's pushy, but she means well."

I heard the front door open. "I'll see you at the wedding tomorrow. Joe's home." I kissed Mavis goodbye through the phone and hung up as he walked into the bedroom.

"You need anything? Mama's expecting me for supper before I head to the church. Bus is leaving early tonight, but want me to bring you back a plate?"

"No, thanks," I said, pushing my wedding rings around a groove in my swollen finger.

Joe side-stepped to the edge of the bed. I hid my hands under the blanket. "I'm trying, Andie," he said before bending over and kissing me on the forehead.

I nodded.

While he showered and shaved, I stayed in bed smelling a healthy dose of cologne floating through the trailer—a gift of Calvin's favorite fragrance, Drakkar, given to his closest staff members. Joe walked back in, buck-naked, except for a few beads of water on his broad, muscular chest the color of cured tobacco leaves. He stepped into his boxers, pressed jeans, and then walked unzipped to the closet. He had spit-shined his leather boots, and blew off a bit of dust before he pulled them on. As he buttoned his clean shirt and packed for the next crusade, I pleaded with him one last time. "Please, Joe. Go with me to Ray and Libby's wedding. For me if not for Ray."

"Let's not argue about this again. You're supposed to support me in my work for the Lord, not Ray marrying a Catholic. Don't get me wrong; it's not Libby. I like her just fine; it's the Catholic part I hate. And her folks are highfalutin.'"

I handed him a stack of clean T-shirts. "I don't think Jesus hates Catholics, even highfalutin' ones."

"It's not the people; it's their ways. The way they practice their religion, worship Mary, read their prayers, all that fancy talk nobody knows what they're saying, kissing that Pope's ring and thinking he's God Almighty."

I couldn't help but think Calvin's church was pretty much the same way. I laid Joe's shaving kit next to his suitcase and watched him empty his sock drawer into his duffle bag. He always packed as if he were never coming home. I wasn't surprised by Calvin's unjust punishment of Ray, refusing to allow Joe to attend his brother's wedding. I was just filled with my usual disgust that the self-righteous Reverend had a say in our lives even in matters as private as a wedding. "It's a shame. Your only brother is to be married tomorrow and you won't be there."

"I choose to put God first."

"No you don't; you put Calvin first." I could feel his anger well up and get hot. I'd felt it too many times. That time was different, though. That time he didn't explode. He grit his teeth and forced a long breath through his nose like an agitated bull.

"You bet I do. He's the only man who ever helped me get anywhere in my lousy life. And if that means loyalty over my family, so what? Proverbs thirty-one, Andie. *The heart of her husband doth safely trust in her, so that he shall have no need of spoil.* I'll see you Monday," he said as he zipped his duffle bag. Seconds later he grabbed his jacket and keys and was gone.

No kiss goodbye. Not even a swear word. But I didn't cry. I was numb. All of Joe's kisses and words of love since the morning of his dramatic apology felt phony anyway. He still hadn't talked about the baby. He'd been quiet as usual, and somewhat nicer, but always with that obligatory kiss. No passion, just a kiss. Like a kiss from my daddy. And what was it about that Proverbs thirty-one woman that felt so unattainable for me? Made me feel so subservient.

Once again I had no desire to know where Calvin and his mighty men of valor were heading off to; it hurt less if I didn't know. I looked at my watch and laid my *Good Housekeeping* on the table by the bed. The pains had started again.

§

When the phone rang later that evening I figured it had to be Maudy. It was.

"Are you going to the rehearsal suppah tonight, sugah?"

I drew a deep breath before answering her. "No. I'm resting for the wedding tomorrow. I hear they're having surf 'n turf. Aren't you going?"

"No. Al and I figured we best go to our own Friday night service. For Joe's sake."

I bit my tongue. "Then I guess I'll see you at St. Christopher's tomorrow at three?"

"Oh, that sounds awful, doesn't it? St. Christopher's! I just can't get over it."

"Get over it, Maudy. Your son is marrying a wonderful woman. Be happy for him. You're aware they're having a dance band and champagne?"

"I know, don't remind me. You want to ride up with us tomorrow?"

"No, I'm driving myself. I'm staying with my folks tomorrow night after the wedding."

"Did Joe put them new tires on your car?"

I got up and peeked through the window. "Nope. Four new tires are still sitting on my porch."

Maudy growled with compassion. "Want me to send Al over?"

"No, I'll call Coot in the morning. He'll do it, or at least put them in the trunk and Daddy will put them on the car this weekend."

"Okay, sugah. I'll see you tomorrow then. Lord, help me."

"Bye, Maudy." I shook my head. It didn't matter that Libby was beautiful, intelligent, smart, and rich. It didn't even matter that Ray loved her. Maudy would never get over it, as hard as she tried. Her son was getting married in a Catholic church. *Ray might as well be a Buddhist.*

§

A soft kick woke me on Saturday morning. Opening a hand on my stomach, I caressed the absurdly large mound, but the baby had fallen asleep. Or so it seemed. Heavy with child, I hauled myself out of my warm bed and dressed the best I could for Ray and Libby's wedding. Pulling up my hair, I curled the back and allowed it to fall in ringlets down my neck. Dixie's gold earrings sat on my dresser. I slipped the tiny hoops into my ear lobes before pressing my best church dress. Made of a soft knit I'd sewed myself, the lapis blue dress offset my eyes and, thankfully, dusted the floor because my flip-flops were the only shoes that fit. Rooting through Joe's underwear drawer, I found two cotton hankies for the crying jags I felt sure to have during the ceremony. I crammed them into my patent-leather purse along with a couple dollars for gas and then called Coot.

When I opened my front door, Coot's '72 Barracuda peeled around the corner and screeched to a stop in my driveway. He lurched from the car, left the door ajar, and stomped up my porch steps to grab two tires. Business had picked up. All he had time to do was lug them to my car and throw them into the trunk. Hustling back for the last two tires, Coot spit a stream of tobacco juice into the yard. "Tars don't belong on a goddamn porch! Andie, I swear, that goober husband of yers shoulda put these on weeks ago. I need him to work fer *me* on Saturdays instead of that TV preacher. When I done *got* overtime fer him, he ain't around. I guess working on Harleys and welding stock car frames ain't where his dadgum head's at anymore. Damn it, Joe, you lil' bastard."

I knew Coot felt sorry for me.

"Make sure Bud puts these tars on 'fore you head back down here. Them old tars you got on that piece of shit car are 'bout as thin as baloney."

"I know. Thanks for buying them for us. I'll try and pay you back a little at a time."

"Don't you never mind. I bought 'em fer you, not Joe. He's been a-pissin' me off lately. Got himself a baby coming and his wife is a driving 'round on baloney tars."

"Well, how about I bring you some wedding cake then?"

"No, thanks, but kiss the bride fer me. Tell Ray I said congratulations."

"I will. Thanks again. I love ya, big guy."

Coot turned around with tears in his eyes. He kissed my cheek and said, "Nobody's told me that since my mama passed."

"Well then, you're overdue," I said.

"Guess so." Embarrassed and anxious to get back to work, Coot sprinted to his car. "You be careful," he yelled back at me. "Supposed to rain today. Shame too, on Ray's weddin' day."

§

The wedding of Ray and Libby began on an exquisite note. A trumpet, a violin, a piano, and an organ serenaded seven bridesmaids to *Canon in D* as they strolled down an aisle covered in rose petals. They wore ivory satin sheaths and carried daylilies on long stems tied with ribbon that coiled to the floor. Libby's sleeveless satin gown with mother-of-pearl trim and white lace gloves to match, conveyed elegance. Her short veil of tulle, fastened to tons of dark curls, framed her face. The dramatic contrast of Libby's hair with her dove-white skin reminded me of a bride doll I had once. So fragile and expensive, Dixie never allowed me to play with it. It stayed in a box in the closet. On occasion I'd sneak the doll out of the box, finger its shiny black ringlets, painted-on ruby lips and soft skin. Libby was my bride doll come to life.

Al and Maudy sat alone on the front pew, marked with a white satin pew bow and sprigs of baby's breath. I sat behind them, two rows back. Libby walked down the long aisle with her hand resting in the loving crook of her father's arm. Ray, in tux and tails, waited for his bride at the altar and cried. I'd never seen Joe cry. Ray's roommate from college filled in as his best man. It should've been Joe.

Candles and daylilies with white roses adorned the altar, in corners, and down the aisle. When Mavis stood to sing, I noticed she had pinned up her hair and was wearing her mama's pearl earrings. Her rented dress, baby-blue chiffon and strapless with sequins on the bodice, sparkled in the candlelight. Her long blue gloves only accentuated her slender arms. Red carpet movie stars in Hollywood paled in comparison to Mavis. As she sang *Ave Maria*—more of a religious experience than I *ever* had in church—it shot chills through the sanctuary. Her voice echoed over the altar and into the vestibule. The candles burned brighter and the air held the emotions of her audience, releasing them as tears on each face. Not a dry eye could be seen.

I smiled at Maudy, bristling in her pew when the priest dropped wafers on the tongues of guests who lined up with their hands folded in prayer. The ritual reminded me of a bird feeding its young, and I wondered why my dogmatic in-laws put up such fuss when people didn't worship the way they did. What was the difference, as long as they worshipped? I didn't understand much of what the priest said, but I couldn't take my eyes off of that communion. I watched as though I were the sole witness to some divine creation.

It was then Ray walked to the piano and sat. As a surprise to his bride and guests he began to play and sing. *"The first time ever I saw your face . . ."* By the time Ray finished singing the Roberta Flack song, guests were weeping again in their pews. Even Mavis sat dabbing at her eyes with a tissue. I wasn't sobbing like the rest. Dry-eyed, I sat in shock. Libby had what I so desperately wanted. I realized I had about as much chance as a firefly in a freezer to see any of Ray rub off on Joe. It finally sunk into my thick head; they were nothing alike and never would be. Joe had lusted after me; maybe even loved me a little in the beginning, at least enough to marry me. But only God knew if there was anything left of our marriage worth saving. I sighed, wiped the look of despair off my face, and smiled my best smile as Mr. and Mrs. Ray Oliver walked arm-in-arm up the aisle.

Ushered out of the sanctuary one pew at a time, guests stood in the reception line while I looped my arm through Mavis's and walked to the fellowship hall behind the church. "You were wonderful. I'm so proud of you, I can't tell you how much."

Mavis smiled through her tears. "I looked out over that sea of white faces and got so nervous I practically peed my pants, 'til I saw you. I knew I might be the only black woman in the whole place, but I was loved by somebody."

"Yes, you are." I bent my head toward Mavis's shoulder. "You truly are."

Mavis and I sat at a round table with four other guests we didn't know. She excused herself to go to the ladies room, and I watched as one guest after another stopped to compliment her performance.

"Someday she'll be a star," said a woman sitting next to me.

"She already is, to me," I said.

§

Holding up my water glass to the first of many champagne toasts, I heard thunder and turned to see the first drops of rain hit the reception hall windows. The band played soft music as black tie waiters served a salad of fresh greens, and a main course of lamb with mint or grilled lemon chicken and tiny broiled potatoes. A cheese, olive, and pickle tray sat on every table. Servers brought coffee, tea, and fresh drinks from the bar, and a seven-tiered wedding cake towered beside a fountain of rum punch.

Guests drank and danced throughout the evening. I sat comfortably at the table and recalled the story of Jesus turning water into wine, his first recorded miracle, at a wedding no less. I had to believe he danced and drank His wine and laughed with guests. It annoyed me that Christians had turned Jesus into a somber, priest-like eunuch, never smiling or feeling the temptations of men. More than that, they put Him way out in space in a makeshift Heaven where nobody could reach Him except the chosen ones. They created God in their own image. Weak, petty, and self-righteous. It made no sense.

Mavis excused herself early. "I got to go home. I'm driving Daddy to the doctor in the morning. He's falling apart. He needs his hearing checked and he's been passing kidney stones again. Doc wants to take a look at him."

"Kiss Rupert for me," I said.

"I'll do it. Hey, why don't you dance with the groom before you go?"

"I don't think so. I'm not very mobile. I'll just sit and watch everybody else cut a rug." The truth was, having been brought up in Calvin's church, I'd never learned to dance.

Mavis laughed. "Cut a rug? Where'd you learn that?" Walking to the door she looked back and smiled. "Call me in the morning, Andie. Don't go having that baby without me."

§

Finally, the bride and groom ambled toward my table. Libby chatted with nearby guests while Ray sat next to me. "Did you like the food?"

"The food, the music, everything was wonderful."

"I'm hurt Joe refused to be here for me," he said, narrowing his eyes.

I placed my hand on Ray's arm. "I'm so sorry. I tried to get him to come."

"Joe and I will always be brothers. Artury can't change that."

"Your family only sees what Calvin wants them to see."

"He's a monster. I've talked to Mama about it."

"You did? What'd she say?"

Libby hugged me from behind and spoke softly into my ear. "Maudy refuses to listen. She doesn't want to believe she's made a huge mistake about her Reverend."

Ray smiled at his bride. "Libby and I are renting the extra house on her uncle's farm in Burlington, and we'll stay there until she's done with her veterinary fellowship and I've passed the bar. Then we're moving to Virginia. You and the baby can always follow us. With or without Joe."

Libby tugged at her new husband's arm, anxious to mix with other guests. She floated to the next table while Ray kissed my cheek. "We'll talk later," he said. For one awful second, it struck me that Ray knew something he wasn't telling, a vague foreboding, a warning. The idea grew so strong, I became afraid to ask.

After Ray walked away, I sat alone and listened to thunder play backup to the band for a while, then made my way through the remaining guests and stood at the door. Watching rain fall in sheets, I felt a damp chill. The sun had gone down and patches of fog settled over the parking lot. I turned around to find Maudy, ice cold and rigid, eyeing her son as he danced. After refusing champagne for the umpteenth time, Maudy and Al drank their last iced tea toast to the bride and groom. I shook my head and walked back to my table. Minutes later, they had gone home.

The band played on while Libby and Ray danced and swayed to the music, staring into each other's eyes. I'd seen enough of what I didn't have for one evening. Waddling onto the dance floor with my purse, I squeezed between them. "Hey, you two, I'm leaving. Have a wonderful honeymoon."

Ray wrapped his long arms around me in a loving, brotherly embrace. "Are you driving home in this weather?"

"No, I thought I'd surprise my parents. Stay with them tonight." I said my good-byes and final congratulations, and then stood at the door again, waiting for the rain to stop.

The storm wound down to a drizzle. That was a good thing because I couldn't remember the row in which I'd left my car. Hurrying across the large, dim lot, it felt like I had parked in the next state. The blanket of fog only compounded the difficult trek over the asphalt. Approaching the car, I felt a gush of water hit my feet and I looked down. A wet stain spread across my dress. In an instant, I grabbed hold of the door and buckled over from a searing pain like nothing I'd felt before.

Somebody Help Me

Andie

It never crossed my mind to go back to the reception hall for help. I'd driven to Lexington from Winston-Salem so many times I could've done it blindfolded. It would take a full hour to get there, but this being my first baby and my first real labor, I assumed it wouldn't get much harder until I arrived at the hospital, just like Mavis had said. Besides, I'd become a single mother at the moment of conception, traveling my pregnancy with so little help it felt normal to take myself, just as I had to every doctor appointment. I'd call Mavis from my room at the hospital.

I've got plenty of time.

Maneuvering my large belly behind the steering wheel, I thought of my soft, cotton gowns that snapped up the front, my nursing bras, and the precious yellow sleeper I'd chosen to bring the baby home in. They were all neatly packed in the suitcase at home in the closet. I was two weeks early.

A hangnail moon hiding behind storm clouds offered no light on the dark roads, and the old car offered no heat. My wet feet went numb and I shivered, remembering I'd left my sweater on the chair in the fellowship hall. The night turned into sinister fingers of white lightning on the landscape, thick and raking the horizon, while electricity danced along the ground. It started to rain again. All I could do was try to concentrate on where I was going, suck my bottom lip, and bite down hard with every pain.

A taste of blood slid in my mouth. *This can't be happening. I'm dreaming.*

My bald tires hydroplaned and I downshifted between labor pains. "Damn it. Double damn it!" My contractions were approximately eight to ten minutes apart, near as I could tell. I couldn't see my watch in the dark and the car's dome light wasn't working.

Placing my hand over my mouth at the next contraction, I gasped into my palm. At 60 mph, the back tires slid and the car rotated a complete 360, taking out two mailboxes as I came to a dead stop. I didn't bother to survey the damage. I shifted into first, gunned the engine, and spun out on the asphalt. The old Javelin was no thoroughbred, but had turned into a thundering renegade on the open road, which was suddenly unknown territory. In the darkness and the pouring rain, the highway twisted this way and that, morphing into a narrow country two-lane. *Where am I?* It was hard to breathe.

Intense pain forced me to speed, searching for a familiar road sign. When I rounded a curve by an open field, a deer jumped into my headlights. I screamed and slammed on my brakes, but didn't push in the clutch. The car jerked and stalled. I started the engine again and pushed the gas pedal even harder as the pain became unbearable. Navigating my way through murky farmland it wasn't long before I hit a good-sized pothole, which raised the right side of the car up and brought it down with a hard thump, blowing out the back right tire. As I whipped the car onto the side of the road, the back end came around and the Javelin rammed into a deep ditch with fast-running water, back bumper first, headlights glaring up into a rain-filled sky.

I froze in my seat, gripping the wheel for all I was worth; my eyes clamped shut in fear. My head had hit hard on the steering wheel and warm blood dripped down my cheek, chin, and neck. The ditch was deep and the car sat almost upright. Slowly, I moved my feet and arms and pressed my belly in different places, hoping to feel a tiny fist or foot poke at my ribs. Nothing. I lifted my face to the sky. *God, help us. Please.*

The instant I pushed on my door, another contraction bore down and I screamed from the pain. Having already bit through my lip, screaming seemed the only thing to do at that point. Once the contraction ended, I figured I had about eight minutes to get out of the car, but my door was jammed shut. I rolled the window down and panicked at the sight of water rushing up to the bottom of the door. I twisted my head, seeking a way out. Grabbing my purse, I hung it around my neck and scooted to the passenger side, managing to get the door open but not far enough. A large thorn bush pressed against it, preventing me from opening the door wide enough to slip out. Getting on my hands and knees, facing the driver's window, I hiked up my dress over my waist and tucked it in my underwear so I could climb, thankful Mavis wasn't there to take my picture.

The car rocked slightly, creaking and grinding on its watery base. I sucked in a ragged breath and rolled the driver's window the rest of the way down. Clinging to the car, I climbed out into the swift water. The rain fell fast and furious. It stung my skin as I stood in the quickening stream and waded in water up to the tops of my thighs. My soles slipped on rocks and mud as I struggled for a foothold. Finding the edge of the bank, I crawled on all fours up the slippery slope. Clawing my way upright in the mud, I fell back into the water as the next contraction ripped through me. In an attempt to gain control of the situation, I took off my flip-flops and flung them. I was not drowning and I was not giving up. But I froze, sucking in another shocked breath as thick mud oozed between my toes and around my feet, suctioning me to the ground.

Through dead-of-night darkness and the torrential downpour, I saw the faint outline of tall switch grass growing two feet away. Painfully, I pulled myself toward it, and planted my feet in the grass for traction. A vehicle zoomed by and I screamed for help. The red moving tail of the car sped away as the Javelin's headlights pointed toward the Heavens, unnoticed.

A bolt of lightning cracked overhead, shaking the ground and splitting a nearby tree in two. It scared me so bad, I shrieked. Pee ran down my leg. Nearing the top of the ditch, I reached for the road, but the next contraction jolted me sideways. I grabbed my stomach, which sent me back down the muddy hill into the stream butt first, hitting bottom with a bone-jarring halt, and totally immersing me in three feet of water and mud. I stood quickly and sliced my foot on something sharp. Rocks, litter, a beer bottle, any number of things were thrown into ditches, and I would never know. Staggering, I sat in the mud on the steep embankment and looked at my foot. From what I could see in the dark, the wound appeared deep. A chunk of flesh and muscle on the ball of my foot flapped open. Blood oozed everywhere.

As I held the wound shut with one hand, I reached inside my purse around my neck and felt for the cotton hankies I'd taken to the wedding. I tied them together and wrapped my foot the best I could; it was difficult to reach my foot with a baby in the way. I hadn't worn sneakers the last couple months for that very reason. Suddenly I heard myself screaming during the next contraction, easing the pain if only in my mind.

A whole lot of determination, desperation, and a little courage pushed me back up that muddy bank. Slowly, step-by-step with my feet turned outward, I dug them into the mud to gain a foothold. It was a toss-up at that point as to which pain was worse, the contractions, my wounded foot, or my swollen lip I'd bit through moments before. The bleeding gash on my forehead was all but forgotten. Swallowing bile that came up bitter into my throat, I reached for a small tree with one hand. Time was running out; I expected my next contraction any second. Twisting my body, I sought to embrace the branch closest to me, but my effort cost me precious foothold and my weight became too great for the sapling to bear. Realizing I was in danger of plunging back down the slope, I braced my feet in the mud and made a frantic lunge toward the road. My belly collided with the muddy embankment and my fingers clutched convulsively at the elusive ledge. My arms felt as if they might separate from their sockets, as my fingertips were losing their grip on the bruising roughness of the asphalt. But my feet held fast in the mud and refused to budge. Inching my way up, I peeked over the top of the ditch. I was not about to let go. Pulling myself over the edge, my cheek scraped against the unforgiving blacktop and warm blood seeped down my neck. I rolled onto the road, tearing the skin off my forearm and knees, and shrieked through the next contraction. "Oh, God! God, please, help me!"

For a moment I sat on the road; at least I could *try* to walk for help. As I looked over the rim and into the ditch, the flash flood had turned my car fully sideways and moved it downstream, hanging it up on a tree trunk. The headlights were still on, the keys still in the ignition, and my new tires remained locked in the trunk. Water poured into the open window flooding the inside.

Rolling thunder followed another flash of light as if a pile of boulders had fallen on the road behind me. More thunder echoed off the land, repeated itself, and echoed again, the rain never letting up.

I had to get help.

At least it was a paved road. I trudged toward lights. *A gas station? How'd I end up here?* A new pain hit, sharp as a piece of steel slicing through me. More excruciating than the rest, it struck with a force so hard I couldn't stand until it passed.

Cold, barefoot and bleeding, my entire body racked with pain, I was determined to make it to the lights ahead of me. I pulled my dress out of my underwear. Fifteen minutes—I could do it. I squinted to see beyond the darkness, wandering farther down the road until my next contraction hit. Screaming louder than the whirling wind, I doubled over as the rain pricked my skin like the tips of needles. With the raging storm as my only companion, I kept walking. No car passed. No one would even miss me until morning. Moving my bare feet forward over small stones that covered the wet pavement, I winced with every step. My injured foot throbbed and I limped to keep pressure off it, but the sharp pain shooting up my leg disappeared as the larger pain of my next contraction drove up into my belly as if being impaled through my groin. When the pain weakened a little I staggered to a stop sign and braced myself by holding on. Weak and trembling, I had found my way to the lights at the end of the road.

It was a truck stop. By the time I reached the perimeter of the lot I saw long-haul truckers parked for the night in the shadows. Muddled watercolors of shapes floated inside the fluorescent-lit twenty-four-hour restaurant and convenience store.

Stumbling toward the windows, I got a good look at my reflection. With my dress ripped and covered in blood, I resembled Stephen King's *Carrie* at the end of the story. In the throes of hard labor, I doubled over again from the pain. Limping forward as the contraction eased, my hair and body camouflaged with mud, I clutched my stomach. My purse swung from my neck like a cowbell as I stepped close to a window. Three or four young women, hunkered down in a booth drinking coffee and smoking cigarettes, paid no attention to me. Dazed and in shock, I couldn't find the entrance. A waitress walked by and I put my bloody hand on the cold glass, speaking softly, my strength evaporating. "Somebody, help me."

Edging my way down the wall of the convenience store, I saw a vaguely familiar car parked under a light. Standing on the sidewalk, I gripped a trash can and a newspaper dispenser through my next contraction as the face that matched the car strolled out the door carrying a six-pack of Budweiser.

"Coot!" I stepped toward him.

"Good Godamighty!"

I stumbled and collapsed into his tree-trunk arms.

HANDS OF DELIVERANCE

Andie

Lexington Memorial Hospital was small and cozy, compared to the rambling Winston-Salem hospitals. I had chosen to have my baby close to home. When I visited the birthing units in my seventh month, they appeared homey and equipped with the necessary equipment for labor and delivery. I had imagined Mavis beside me, coaching and joyful, while my child was born into Dr. Eshelman's capable hands.

But it was not to be. I lay in shock, the gash on my head needing immediate attention and my foot badly wounded. I heard a technician say my blood pressure had dropped and that he couldn't find the baby's heartbeat. By the time they rolled me through the emergency room doors, I had fallen into delirium.

A voice echoed above me. "What's her name?"

Where am I? I felt the night pulling me and I yearned for silence.

An unknown figure leaned in close. "Can you tell us your name, dear?"

"Andie! Her name is Andie," I heard Coot say.

"Hold on, Andie!" another voice said.

Bright lights were suspended above me, and I felt the soothing heat against my skin. I shook my head. It was too soon and I had to wait for Mavis. The room and the sounds around me faded. I fell into a deep, deep darkness reaching for hands that motioned to me. They were strong hands with large, square palms. *Definitely a man. They have to be Joe's hands.* But they were strange looking. *Not Joe's.* They weren't Coot's hands; I'd felt his bulky hands holding me only moments before. *No, not Coot's hands.* The hands were not my daddy's; his were dark and hairy—and stubby. *Not Daddy's.* And they weren't Dr. Eshelman's hands. His hands looked like a woman's; long and thin, with hairless fingers. *They must be Joe's hands.* Reaching for hands that led me deeper into unconsciousness, I knew it wasn't Joe, although the image in front of me felt strangely familiar. A clouded face with a beard came into view. *Jesus?* It wasn't Jesus: there were no scars in the palms. Yet I felt as though a divine entity had sent this man, these hands, to me. As he reached for me one last time I saw he was missing the top of his left ring finger, down to the middle knuckle. *Have I seen these hands before?* Unafraid, I reached back. I felt the hands touch my own, comforting and gentle—I was dreaming. Or was I?

Fast and sterile, the Cesarean section was not the birth I had fantasized about one hundred times during the past eight and one-half months. The hours drifted by in a pain-free dream, quiet and restful, in the hands of a man I knew, but could not place.

But every dream must end, and every slumber has an awakening.

§

I turned my head ever so slightly to the left and saw Coot asleep in the corner and the clock above him. My mouth was dry and I swallowed painfully. My vision blurred; I felt the sheets beneath me—a hospital bed. My head pounded in time with my heart. Aching and swollen, I lifted myself slightly and found no mass of baby to obscure my view to the end of the bed. *This isn't real.* My foot throbbed beneath a massive bandage. A translucent tube snaked up into my nostrils and another was taped to the soft flesh of my uncut forearm and the back of my hand. A thick paper bracelet circled my wrist, and a ring of blue plastic machines beeped and blinked around me. I felt like I'd been ripped to shreds and sewn back together in record time.

"Coot," my voice just above a whisper. "Coot!"

Startled, he jerked awake and hopped to my side. "Hey there, little Mama. Don't look too bad fer what ya been through."

"Coot, where's my baby?" Barely audible, my voice sounded strange in my head.

"Hold on there, honey, I see yer mama running this way. I'll let her tell ya." He gestured for Dixie to hurry, his arm from his elbow down swinging in wide circles.

"What, Coot, tell me what? Where's my baby? Tell me. Where's the baby?"

Frantic, I struggled to sit as Dixie and Daddy scuttled in the door. "Where's my baby?"

"It's a little bitty boy, Andie. He's in the nursery. You'll see him soon," Dixie said, laying a cool hand on my face.

My voice ragged, my eyes wide and pleading, I said, "Daddy, my baby, why can't I see him?"

"He's sick, Rosebud. He's a little feller. Not as big as they thought he'd be. He's a bit premature. That's all. Your doctor is on his way to talk to you."

"Sick? What's wrong with him?" I thrashed at the sheets, attempting to move my legs out of the bed. "What . . . Where's my baby? I have to see him." I shoved my mother away, pulled the tube out of my nose and the IV out of my hand. "Daddy, please, help me. Help me up."

He took hold of my arms, and forced me to look at him. "Listen to me, Andie, you're sick, too. You think your daddy will allow anything to happen to his bitty grandson? Now quiet down. You've been through a terrible accident. Got a mess of stitches in your head and your foot has fifty. You've got to get better or you'll be no good for your little boy."

His words comforted me, but tears clogged my throat and I coughed, which hurt like hell. "It was awful, Daddy. I made a wrong turn, ended up somewhere, I don't know. Coot saved me."

"I know. He's a hero. Coot found your car early this morning, and pulled it out of that ditch. All but the very top was covered with water. He towed it to his garage. I want it hauled to the dump. You're driving a better car from now on, honey." He looked hard at Dixie as if the car issue was an old argument he'd just won. "You're damn lucky, Rosebud, you're damn lucky you're alive."

"Mr. Parks, I'm just going to make a few phone calls. I'll be down in the cafeteria if y'all need me fer anything."

Daddy laid his hand on Coot's shoulder. "Thanks, Coot. I do believe you got a pair of wings sprouting from your back and the hint of a halo behind your ear. Dixie and I are grateful."

Coot's toothless grin made Daddy smile. "Just lucky to be there when she needed me, that's all. I'm a-tryin' to get in touch with Joe."

I could sense my daddy didn't want to think about Joe at the moment, much less talk about him. I reached for Coot. "Call Mavis. Dixie, give Coot her number."

My mother stomped over to her purse to write down the phone number.

"I'll be back soon. Ya just lie there like yer daddy says," Coot said.

I blew him a kiss and let out a silent sigh. I'd be forever grateful myself.

Dr. Eshelman appeared in the doorway in his surgeon's green gown with a nurse who proceeded to reinsert my IV. I shot him an uncompromising look. "I want to see my baby."

He first asked my parents for a few minutes alone with his patient, then drew the curtain around us and dragged a chair to my bedside. When the nurse left the room he said, "Andie, I want you to know your pediatrician and I, we're doing everything we can for your little boy. He's a fighter, that one. He was small for his gestational age. The baby's problem has nothing to do with your accident, except your blood pressure put him into a bit of distress. He has what we call a hypoplastic left heart. The left ventricle failed to form normally. We need your signature for surgery. We'll take him by ambulance to Baptist Hospital in Winston-Salem immediately."

The shock of my baby's condition made my chest ache, and I pressed one hand against my own hurting heart. Scalding tears sliced down my face. "Is he going to live?"

Dr. Eshelman put a tissue in my hand. "Like I said, we're moving quickly and doing everything we can for him."

I glared at my doctor, my knuckles burning from gripping the edge of the bed. "I want to see my baby. I want to go with him."

"The nurse will wheel you down to the nursery before we take him. You can't go in the ambulance. I can't release you because of your injuries, and just having had a Cesarean section. In two or three days I'll allow you to travel to Baptist Hospital to see him. In the meantime, I'll keep you updated every few hours, I promise. I expect his surgery to be completed by tomorrow morning. We should know more then."

Crying hard in fits of sobs and hiccups, I pulled on the bed rails trying to sit, demanding to see my baby. I didn't care what my doctor said. When my hysterics escalated, Dr. Eshelman didn't wait for the nurse: he admonished me as he administered an injection into my hip. "Stop this. You've *got* to settle down. You're young and strong and your uterus is still intact. Plenty of chances for more babies."

"I don't want more babies! I want this baby!" Each part of me screamed in pain.

Dixie and Daddy had remained in my room and when Dr. Eshelman opened my curtain they approached him at once, their eyes desperate for answers. "Dr. Eshelman?"

After handing my chart to a nurse, he turned. "Yes?"

My mother's tears were in her voice. "Can you tell us anything more?"

Drowsy, I watched my doctor pocket his pen into his lab coat. He spoke softly. "I'll be honest with you, this is a very delicate surgery. I am concerned about Andie, as well. Let me ask you a question. Is she really married?"

My parents looked at each other, astonished. Dixie nodded. "Yes, of course, she's married. Why do you ask?"

As they waited for Dr. Eshelman's answer, Al and Maudy walked into my room at the perfect moment. Daddy's smugness showed. "Doctor, this is Mr. and Mrs. Al Oliver, my son-in-law's parents." He wanted them to hear my doctor's opinion of their son.

I closed my eyes. I needed to hear it too, and I didn't want anybody walking out if they thought I was awake. Dr. Eshelman didn't spare his honesty for anyone. "The baby is tiny. Birth weight was five pounds six ounces. I planned on a much bigger baby, but Andie suffered from toxemia; she retained too much water. She'll be fine after some time, physically. But she did not receive the prenatal care she should've had. She skipped several third trimester appointments; claimed she didn't have the money for them. Visits where I may have detected the baby's heart problem, or treated Andie's toxemia by checking her protein levels. I gave her gas money once to get home. She's poorly nourished; eats all the wrong things. I asked you if she was married because I never met her husband. He did not accompany her to a single prenatal appointment. I may be out of line here, but marital counseling may be in order. I'm guessing Andie has been under severe stress, even prior to the accident, putting both mother and child in danger. I can recommend a counselor, if you would like. Right now, she needs love and support. Nothing less." Dr. Eshelman did not take further questions. "Excuse me. I need to check on the baby." I opened my eyes as he turned on his heel and walked away.

Maudy and Dixie ambled out of the room, I assumed to go to the nursery. Al fell into a chair across from my bed. Daddy mumbled something about needing a cigarette. I knew he would never forgive Joe for this.

The shot finally took hold and I felt myself drowse into a fitful slumber, wishing for the strange hands to come soothe me once again.

BRIAN

Andie

My eyes opened just enough to see Mavis's dark shape solidify. She stood like an Amazon warrior in a snakeskin jacket and silver earrings that dangled to her shoulders. "He's a beauty," she said. Sitting on the chair next to my bed, she lifted my hand to her cheek. "He's a good looking boy, mmm-mmm, we be fighting the girls away from your door soon enough."

"I wanted you here." Salty tears streamed from my eyes again, burning the cuts and scrapes on my face. But the pain in my head that blurred my vision hours before had lessened.

"Shhh, now. I knows the whole story, 'cept what you want to tell me later. Ol' Coot's been telling the whole hospital. Right now I got a mighty fine looking wheelchair here and a nice nurse, and we're taking you to see your boy. Now you getting up outta dat bed, or will I have to drag you out? Whew, Andie, you a sight. You need a shower and your hair done, girl."

I smiled for the first time since Ray's wedding.

"That's my girl," Mavis said. She sped around to the other side of the bed to assist the nurse and set me upright. They eased me into the cold wheelchair, my body raw and stitched from head to foot, and then wheeled me to the small nursery. The nurse rolled me inside and told Mavis she'd have to watch through the window.

"Where is he?" I asked.

"Over there." The nurse pointed him out as she pushed me up to his glass bed that looked like a fish tank.

A wrinkled grapefruit head with tiny eyes and long lashes that curled up, he was so precious. Wires and tubes protruded from his little body. My arms ached to hold him. Lying on a white blanket with nothing on except a teeny cotton diaper and a cap, he quivered. My baby's body appeared scrawny, his skin loose and fleshy, like raw chicken skin. His blue-veined umbilical cord moved against his diaper. He looked frightened and lonely. It grieved me so deeply.

"My . . . baby," I whispered. "God. Please be with him." I tapped my fingers on the glass as he moved his arms and hands. "He needs me," I said. Misery welled up in my throat, choking me, filling my head with crushing regret and spilling out by way of more tears running down my neck, breasts, and splashing onto my empty lap. "Please, can I hold him?"

"He needs to stay in the incubator," the nurse said.

"He needs a miracle," I said. I leaned in as far as I could. My voice cracked. Please, let me hold him."

"I have to take you back to your room," the nurse said sweetly.

"Please, I only want to hold him a moment," I begged. I knew my little one needed me as much as he needed a miracle. Exhausted, my whole body ached, yet an alarm went off in my head. A powerful force, like a river of righteousness. "Nurse, this is important. Listen to me. Don't allow anybody from the House of Praise near my baby. I don't want anyone but family near him. Make sure Baptist Hospital knows that. I mean it, I—"

"Don't get upset, Mrs. Oliver. I'll write it on his chart as soon as I take you back to your room. Okay, honey?" Her tone was reassuring, and I nodded as she opened the door.

Mavis had waited with her hands and nose pressed against the window. Bawling into a wad of tissue she asked, "Did you name him?"

I momentarily broke out of my despair. "Brian. His name is Brian."

"That's a fine name," Mavis said. "Reminds me of that movie, *Brian's Song* . . . about that football player. He's got the same color hair as James Caan, you know, the actor who played Brian Piccolo." Mavis's grin widened in approval. "Brian. That sho' is a pretty name, Andie. Brian. Sounds like a handsome man's name. And Brian Piccolo sho' was handsome." She looked back toward the nursery. "A mighty fine name—Brian."

One thing struck me when Mavis wheeled me back to my room. The baby looked just like Joe. He was a day old and his father had yet to see him. "Brian." Breathing in his name, I moaned as the nurse helped me into bed. Recalling the movie *Brian's Song*, I realized I had named my baby after a dead man.

§

Dr. Eshelman walked into my room that afternoon at four. He said the baby had been taken to Baptist Hospital and that his surgery was scheduled for the next morning. If all went well and I was clear of infection, I could leave Lexington hospital on Wednesday morning. He would make arrangements for me to visit Brian during his stay at Baptist. My doctor's kind eyes, sympathetic smile, and positive nature gave me a small sense of peace. He also suggested I forget about breastfeeding. Brian would need to be fed intravenously until he could go home, and then he would require special formula for quite some time. He prescribed pills to dry up my milk. The pills didn't work. My breasts continued to cry.

"Crying and lactating at the same time. It's one way to lose weight, huh?" Mavis's well-intentioned humor fell on deaf ears. She had spent the day feeding me ice chips and Jell-O and refused to leave my side.

Finally, Daddy and Dixie went home to get some sleep and explain every-thing to Caroline. Al appeared exhausted and withdrawn and needed to go home and rest. Obviously, Maudy wished to do a little damage control on Joe's behalf first, because she cleared her throat and then said to Mavis in defense of her son, "Joe has put God first in his life. For that reason, I believe God will heal my grandson."

I waited. Maudy would soon find out she was preaching to the wrong person. With my eyes closed, I simply smiled listening to Mavis's reply. "That doesn't wash with me, Maudy. I bet Jesus thinks Joe is an absolute idiot for not being here for his wife and that he needs a good ass kicking about now. Tell you what . . . I'll call Bud's cousins in Boone; they'll do it cheap."

Next thing I heard was Maudy's heels clicking on the tile floor as she huffed out of the room.

§

Waking throughout the evening in peaks and waves of pain, my foot ached and my whole face throbbed like a mouth full of toothaches. Mavis ran for a nurse every time I cried in pain. With a groan, I struggled to hold myself over the edge of the bed as Mavis held a kidney-shaped basin to my head in time to catch the vomit. After she wiped my mouth and brow, she dropped to the side of my bed and buried her face in the sheets. My fingers caressed her soft hair. "Mavis, don't. I can stand anybody's tears, even my own, but I can't stand your tears."

"I blame myself," she sobbed. "I should've taken you to your parents' house after the reception. I almost lost you. I almost lost the only person in the world who loved me."

"Your daddy and Aunt Lula love you. You know that. And, it's not your fault."

In the quiet of the dimly lit hospital room, Mavis reached for my hand and poured her heart out. "Not like you do. I could always count on your letters like clockwork. Every Friday, I'd open the mailbox and there'd be your letter, smiling up at me. Sometimes you didn't have much to say, but you sent your love every week. It kept me going. After all we been through together, I wasn't there when you needed me most."

Mavis wept like I'd never seen her. Minutes later, when she reached for the Kleenex box on the sliding table by my bed, the door opened. In walked Coot with Joe behind him.

Mavis bent and kissed my hand and then sauntered toward the door as if on cue. She patted Coot's shoulder and he winked at her. I knew she was as grateful to Coot as much as anyone. But when she stepped past Coot she stood shoulder-to-shoulder and eye-to-eye with Joe, making sure he knew what she wanted to say. She remained silent and walked out, giving us a moment together.

§

"I brought ya a present." Coot blew me a kiss, then left the room.

Joe sat in the chair by my bed and looked into my eyes. It stunned me that he could.

"Hey," he said.

I turned my head away. Then I turned back to face him. "He's at Baptist Hospital. Getting operated on in the morning. Go see him, Joe. Promise me you'll go see him."

"Okay." He stood and kissed my brow, then sat again. I caught a whiff of his cologne. "I'm sorry, Andie. For everything." No tears, just a lame attempt to make peace with me.

How repulsive I must look and smell to him. I shoved my matted hair out of my eyes and behind my ears. Holding back tears, I replied in a low, tormented voice. "If you intend to leave me, Joe, now is not the time. I don't . . . I don't know how . . . if the baby . . . please, not now. Not like this."

"I'm not leaving you or Brian."

I searched his face. "How do you know his name?"

"Mama called me. It's a fine name." He stood again and put his finger to my lips. "Hush now, you need to rest. I can see you're hurting. Last thing you need is to worry about me."

"I'm not worried about you." I wiped my eyes. "I'm worried about our son. He needs us. You have to go see him."

"I will. First thing in the morning."

§

By Tuesday morning, the rain had not let up. A soupy mixture of mist, fog, and drizzling showers covered the sun. It was hard to tell where night stopped and day began. Time had lost its rhythm. From my hospital room window, I could see cars with their headlights on. The morning TV weatherman called for more flash floods in all counties of the Piedmont.

Mavis, having lost all track of time it seemed, had gone home at four in the morning for a bite to eat and a bath. She returned before breakfast, bringing with her the scent and chill of rain. Below her full-length raincoat she wore black, patent leather boots, the tops hitting above her knees. Her acid-washed denim skirt barely covered her long thighs. Raindrops glittered on her fro, and although the bottom of her sweater hugged her hips, it dipped in front revealing a shiny brown cleavage as smooth as a baby's bottom. "How ya holdin' up, honey?" she said, giving me a quick squeeze. Her long earrings dangled in my eyes as she planted a rain-soaked kiss on my forehead.

I blinked. "You don't need to turn tricks down here, Mavis. They give it away for free. Just ask Joe."

She ignored me, and hung her coat on the door. "Ray phoned earlier. They're going to Baptist to wait with Dixie. He promised to call and report any news about the baby." Mavis held a straw to my lips. The nurses knew better than to take over for her. "Drink this," she said. "We're thinking good thoughts today."

I nodded as she worked a brush through my hair, pulling it up to give me a sponge bath. Mavis was right. I didn't want to think about Joe or the baby's delicate surgery or that Libby and Ray had postponed their honeymoon because of me. I wanted to think about going home and setting up the crib, nursing my child in private, and singing lullabies into his tiny ear.

"Well, looky who's here," Mavis said. She smiled and motioned for Daddy and Caroline to come in. "Y'all can't stay but a minute, I gots to give Andie her bath. Hey, why don't you two head on down to the cafeteria. I hear they got a killer breakfast. Not as good as Dixie's of course, but I'm sure Andie would love some chocolate milk. It's her favorite."

Caroline squeezed my hand, the one without the IV tubes. Mavis offered her a tissue to wipe away her tears, but I could see Mavis's mind was suddenly elsewhere.

§

I would think back to that day many times in the years to come. The rain dripping down the windows, the gloom of waiting for word on my baby, and of course, Mavis—her shiny boots, her cleavage and her energy—bearing shimmering words of hope like a beacon in the darkness. How precious the memories, and yet how unthinkable. I came to understand the loveless life I lived, but no one talked about divorce in 1975. Not in the Bible Belt. No one except Mavis remotely considered that I should leave Joe. And I certainly didn't need Calvin to call me at the hospital that morning and pray out loud for my baby and my marriage, reminding me of my sacred duty to honor my husband and to bring up my child in the fear of the Lord.

I'd keep my vows, but I didn't want to.

Joe had sent flowers to the hospital. A bouquet of pink roses, my favorite. The card read, *I'm sorry, Andie Rose. Please forgive me for everything. I love you.*

Heaven's Bloom

Mavis

We watched the clock as the morning wore on. Bud and Caroline took off for the cafeteria while I kept Andie occupied, talking about how I would help her take care of the baby when she brought him home, and how Dixie might arrange a temporary nursery in her spare room. The doctor made it clear that when Andie left the hospital, she was to go where she and her infant son could be taken care of properly. I was thankful Andie agreed to go to her parents' house. And surprised. She'd been so determined to do it all by herself. For the next hour, I somehow managed to find a million things to talk about to keep our minds off the time.

Earlier, Andie told me Joe had promised to go to the hospital to see the baby. I knew better. Glancing out the window to check the weather, I saw the weasel in his daddy's truck. "Church Boy just pulled into the parking lot. He's in Al's truck."

Andie's face went white as a lunch plate. "Oh Lord, Mavis. Daddy's here."

I stepped out of the room and found Bud on the phone at the nurses' station.

My throat went dry. "What's happening?"

"That was Libby. Ray took Dixie home, she's all done in. I'm driving Caroline home and then heading to Baptist. I think it's best I avoid Andie's room altogether right now."

"What's happening, Bud? Tell me!"

Bud turned to me and smiled. "He's out of surgery. The best thing you can do is stay with Andie. Be there for her, Mavis, and I'll call you when I know more."

It wasn't a good enough answer and I followed him and Caroline as they rushed out of the hospital. I needed to hear some shred of hope to relay to Andie. But then, there he was. Joe. Strolling toward the entrance as if going on a picnic without a care in the world. He approached us on the sidewalk with a smile and a wave. It rolled through my head that Joe would've loved it had Andie and the baby died, solving all his problems. I think Bud and I shared the same thoughts because the next thing I knew Bud's face went sour apple green. Joe's Southern charm and good ol' boy manners wouldn't save him. I'd heard Bud say once, "There are times in a man's life when reason takes a back seat to justice." He was about to prove his point.

Quick as a bobcat after a rat, Bud leaped over a small shrub and into a bed of pansies. He seized Joe by his coat collar, hoisted him up about a foot off the ground like a fifty-pound sack of Dekalb corn seed, and threw him against the brick wall of the hospital. Joe struggled for air; his feet dangling like a puppet's while the morning's mist collected on his face.

I held Caroline back. "Let your daddy handle this," I said.

Bud's speech was deliberate, and he tightened his grip. "Your son is dying! It's what you wanted, isn't it? You're worse than an animal, you know that? Even animals want their offspring. I know what you're all about. I know you better than you think I do, you stinking son of a bitch. You don't fool me, boy. If you can't be a man and love her, be true to her, then I want you out of my daughter's life! You better start taking care of your wife or by God, I'll pay my skinny backwoods cousins from Boone to cut off your nuts and shove them up your shiny smiling ass. It's no threat. I don't make threats. It's a promise. Now, I've paid Andie's doctor and hospital bill, and I expect *you* to pay me back. You hear me good, boy, 'cause you obviously don't listen to anyone 'cept that mealy-mouthed ass you call a Reverend. We will not mention this incident to Andie, will we? Will we!" Bud waited for Joe to respond with a strained *no*. "You best hope that little boy makes it because if he don't, you ever come around my house again, I'll shoot you myself."

With that said, he let go. Joe dropped to the ground gasping for air, his eyes bulging. Bud stepped out of the bed of pansies, collected his youngest daughter—mouth opened to her knees—and left in a hurry.

I strolled over to Joe. He sat in a pile of cigarette butts in the hospital flowerbed with his hands at his throat, struggling to breathe. "That goes double for me," I said.

§

I didn't tell Andie about her baby's critical condition. Just that he was out of surgery, and it was a wait and see, moment by moment, in God's hands kind of thing. It pained me to watch her beg Dr. Eshelman to release her. He refused. He told her if she were able to hobble to the bathroom on her own by the next morning, he would allow her to travel to Baptist Hospital.

While I continued my bedside watch, Joe sat in the waiting room. When I left Andie's side, Joe went in and sat with her. When I returned, Joe walked back out. Neither of us spoke to the other and we refused to be in the same room together, knowing it was best to keep our mouths shut. For Andie's sake.

After the nurse gave Andie a good dose of Percocet, a small amount of comfort showed on her face as sleep claimed her. But when the nurse said she'd probably be asleep until morning, I grabbed my coat and drove to Winston-Salem.

I found Bud alone in the waiting room. The skin on his face drooped like his hound dog and his hands trembled. "The surgery didn't go well," he said. "This was a more serious heart problem than everybody thought. The surgeon said they don't save too many of these babies, if any. They don't expect—don't expect him to make it. Is Joe coming to see him?"

"I doubt it. I don't think that bastard wants to come within a day's drive of you or me right now. He's with Andie. Thank God she's sedated," I said, wiping my tears. I slid my arm around Bud's slumped shoulders and felt him shudder.

His chin dropped to his chest. He looked older, worn and thinned out around the eyes and mouth. I wanted to tell him everything was going to be fine, yet something stopped me. God, as He all too often does, had other plans.

§

We began our vigil, pacing back and forth, from the waiting room to the thick glass windows of the Neonatal Intensive Care Unit. Bud mentioned Andie's baby looked identical to his own son who had died in infancy. I didn't say anything because Andie insisted he looked like Joe. Of course, I knew Dixie and Bud had a son, born two years after Andie and two years before Caroline, and that he had died in Bud's arms three days after a difficult birth.

In silence, we waited until the wee hours of the morning. For news, any news.

And then on Wednesday morning at seven o'clock, a plump nurse in purple scrubs with rosy cheeks and a name to match nudged Bud awake in his waiting room chair. Her name tag read *Holly*, and I was grateful for her professional and sympathetic tone. "Mr. Parks. I am so sorry, sir, but the doctors are requesting someone from the family come and hold the baby now."

Bud looked at me and sighed, then nodded at the nurse. I was thankful Dixie had stayed home; I knew she couldn't handle it. Bud staggered like an old man to the little boy who looked so hopeless and small. I followed, assuming I would have to stand outside the window again, but the nurse helped us both slip into gowns and masks. I put my arm through Bud's as we made our way toward two rocking chairs. Nurses pulled tubes and monitors off Brian's body and wrapped him tight. I glanced at the clock. It was 7:20 a.m. when they laid him in his grandfather's arms.

I knew Bud's tears were for Andie. He loved her so. She had wanted a life like her mother's and deserved a better one than the one she had. He cried for his family. And he cried for his grandson, who he would never see again after that day. I slid off my chair and fell to my knees beside Bud, quietly witnessing the most precious moment of my life; this gentle man I'd known since I was a baby myself, holding the dying son of my best friend in the world.

"Well, little buddy," he said, "I don't suppose we'll be hunting or fishing or building you a tree house anytime soon. I know you'll have lots of fun up there. You'll meet your Uncle. He went up to Heaven when he was long about your age." Bud let his tears flow, unashamed. "You tell him his daddy misses him. I 'magine you'll see all kinds of folks you're related to."

I had never seen a heart truly break. But that morning, Bud's heart shattered into pieces as he gazed upon his grandson. "I guess . . ." He stopped for a moment, stricken with grief from some place down deep, and whispered, "I guess you were born on earth to bloom in Heaven."

At 7:32 a.m. the baby boy took his last breath. Bud bowed his head for a moment, and then pulled down his mask to kiss Brian's soft cheek. A nurse lifted the tiny body out of Bud's arms and carried him out of the room, and I was there. I was there to witness it all.

PART THREE

Heaven And Earth

OVERTAKEN

Reverend Calvin Artury

When word of Andie's accident and dead baby spread, I directed my congregation to pray for the family. I'm a compassionate man concerned for my flock, shepherding them into truth and light and the Glory of God. Without a doubt, the smallest mishaps can turn men and women away from the illumination of God's love. But the death of a loved one can cause the annihilation of a family. I'd seen it happen too many times.

I told my secretary to find Pastor DeSanto. I needed to speak to him. He would have to preach the funeral of the Oliver infant. I yearned to clone myself, to preach in two places at once. Leaving my church in the hands of Tony DeSanto while I conducted miracle crusades across the country was a difficult decision, but the only one I could make. Tony's sketchy past had been hard to trace prior to his graduation from seminary. But his titillating testimony had appealed to me during his interview.

When Tony said that God had found him at a tent revival in New Jersey of all places, it did not surprise me. God searches the highways and the hedges, the dark alleys and the corrupt side of town to find the harlots, the drug users, the destitute, and the troublemakers. He's desperate to not only show them the way of salvation, but to mold them into soldiers for the army of Christ. Which is exactly what happened to my Assistant Pastor. Intending to harass the small-time evangelist, Tony ended up on his knees. Soon after his commitment to Christ, he escaped a life of crime to pursue his true heart's desire. Become a pastor and go straight.

The young pastor's salvation story attracted the youth, and I slowly loosened the rope by which I controlled him, giving him more position and power. Aware that my own charisma drew men like Tony, I needed to know more about him. After discovering his connections to a New York organized crime family, it angered me, and yet had I a tail, it would've been wagging. Tony assured me his appetite for guns and glory was finished. But I suspected he was still a product of his past and would undoubtedly follow the lead of someone with bigger connections and, in his case, connections to the Almighty topped those of any New York crime family. And since *God chooses the foolish things of the world to confound the wise*, I fathomed someday I might need to tap into the contacts I knew Tony still had.

Mavis Dumass had become a threat to my ministry. Her message, demanding a meeting, was like a fly buzzing around my head. And to make matters worse, Maudy Oliver's phone call to report the death of her grandson gave me great pause. Tony needed to know the delicate situation regarding Mavis before the funeral. I had always felt it my duty to keep Andie safe within the walls of the church. She should've listened to me and given that baby back to God because, after all, God took it anyway.

Fannie's voice interrupted my thoughts, startling me. "Pastor DeSanto here to see you."

"Send him in." I straightened my tie and aligned paperwork on my desk at right angles.

"You wanted to see me, Boss?"

He was regal, from Italian and Jewish descent. Mid thirties. The first thing I noticed about Tony was his height, six-foot-four—far from ordinary. Skin the color of buttered toast and scarred over his knuckles, he had reached up to run his hand over his chin. He hadn't bothered to shave that morning. It was the first time I noticed a thin scar that ran along his jaw line. His dark locks fell to his even darker eyes. Dark blue eyes, in fact. The kind that hides things. Someone had hit his nose once or twice and left it a bit crooked, but other than that, I enjoyed Tony's look, a mix of Arch Angel and Montgomery Clift. Perfection seldom seen in a man. I also liked that he called me 'Boss' and that we shared a love for expensive clothes, jewelry, and fine leather boots. I had noticed his Christian Dior Crocs the moment he stepped into my office. But as hard as my Assistant Pastor tried to fit into the South, he simply didn't. And yet, like the rest of my handsome ministry team, Tony loved the women.

"Have a seat." I shifted in my chair and felt my shoulders relax. I'd been tense. Much too tense. "First, regarding the death of the Oliver infant, I'm allowing Joe Oliver to stay home this weekend from the crusade; he needs to support his wife during this time. We have bigger problems, Pastor . . . problems with Mavis Dumass. You and I had a discussion a few days ago about her. Do you have any information for me?"

"Sure, Boss. You wanted the name of her talent agent. His name is Dino. No last name. Owns an agency on West 58th Street. You also wanted her tailed. It's a boring log, Boss. She follows that Andie woman all over. Joe's wife, right? Miss Dumass seems harmless enough."

"Don't underestimate her, Tony. Never underestimate the hand of the devil."

Our conversation lasted long into the afternoon, and as I learned more about the elusive past of my new assistant, God uncovered every secret. His divine plan of what to do about Mavis unfolded before me like a Dead Sea scroll.

My suspicions were correct. Tony's New York family paid his seminary tuition. They financed him to keep him indebted to them. How absolutely ruthless! The dashing pastor broke down and revealed that he needed to pay back the cash he owed them. It's what drove him to the House of Praise in the first place. When he heard I was interviewing for an assistant, it was the open door he needed. Oh, the wondrous workings of the Lord! They never cease to amaze me.

New York didn't care if Tony was no longer a member of the Catholic Church. He wasn't a *made man*, after all. Just a low-level soldier for Satan, he'd said. He then removed his shirt and belt and unzipped his pants, revealing his knife injuries, bullet wounds, teeth marks, and deep scars where he'd had tattoos removed. He told me things about his life that would make most men grow pale and women faint. To New York, he was just a wiseguy who found a new religion. They were all betting on his failure and eventual return to the family. This information thrilled me and I found myself salivating as I contemplated the possibilities.

Tony agreed to yield his soul—completely. His pledge of devotion prompted me to make a few guarantees of my own. I detected that while religious prestige and making a name for himself appealed to my young pastoral assistant with a Mafia past, his dream of religious fortune excited him more. So I promised to share the secrets of my ministry's success, as long as he promised to walk in the divine will of God. And I would direct him in that endeavor.

In the meantime, the handsome pastor would host his own television show. God had already given me a name for it: *The Overtaken Hour*. How glorious to be overtaken by God's power! And as long as Tony showed respect, knew his place in the hierarchy of the church, and brought no reproach upon the ministry, I promised him freedom to pursue his own dreams and ambitions. Of course, he was required to tithe the profits on those dreams and ambitions.

I took one final leap of faith and told Tony many things about myself. With an arch of his eyebrow and a curl of his lip, he took it all in stride. The debonair young pastor with the shady past didn't shock easily. Unwise in the ways of the evangelical world, Tony's disadvantage became God's advantage and mine. I requested an unusual favor of him, along with making him an offer he couldn't refuse. I promised to pay off his loans—with only one string attached. As I suspected, Pastor Tony DeSanto didn't flinch. "It'll take some time to arrange, Boss, but I'll have the job finished within the month."

"Thank you, Pastor. Jehovah-Jireh will richly bless you. I assure you."

SILENT GRIEF

Mavis

I attempted to pull it from somewhere deep inside myself, but composure eluded me. Dread crept up my spine as I drove south in a blur of tears. By the time I reached the parking lot at Lexington Hospital, I had searched for and collected as much self-control as possible with only one thing on my mind. Andie. Bud had gone home to rest and gently relay the news to Dixie. We agreed I should get to the hospital immediately. Someone who loved her had to tell her. I arrived at nine and found Joe slouched in a waiting-room chair. He stood slowly and followed me. Church Boy knew, I think, because for the moment, he had nothing to say.

I had nothing to say to him either. Not until he grabbed me by the shoulders and whirled me around. I had no mercy inside me for the likes of him. A lone tear popped out of my right eye, slid down my cheek, and splashed onto my coat. "He's dead. Your son is dead. Happy?"

"None of this is my fault," he said. "I'm telling my wife. You can stay out here."

I bounded down the hall after him, grabbing his arm. "Oh no, you don't. Nobody wants you to tell her. You've done enough to destroy her spirit." Joe yanked out of my grip. I stepped in front of him, blocking his way. "Listen to me, Joe! If you don't want her to hate you, you'd better let me tell her. Believe it or not, I'm trying to help you out."

He hesitated. With a withering look of contempt, he agreed. "If you really want to help her, Mavis, then stop ragging on me."

"Don't worry. She loves your pathetic ass. Why she does, I have no clue. Nothing I say will put a stop to that." I could feel his eyes follow me to Andie's room.

"Nice ass," he mumbled.

I wheeled around to walk back and beat the shit out of him right then and there. But a nurse had laid her hand on his shoulder, expressing her sympathy. The blank look on Joe's face told me all I needed to know. What little marbles he had rolling around in his head were long gone. Joe truly believed every word handed down from the golden pulpit at the House of Praise. Losing the baby was his sign from God, confirming Calvin's prophecy that the baby wasn't God's will for them, and the tragedy occurred because Andie ignored that divine will. I was certain Joe suffered no remorse. That he felt no more to blame for Andie's sorrow than the man in the moon. Shaking my head, I clucked my tongue and waved the thought of him away with my hand as tears welled in my eyes. *That sick bastard is not my concern at the moment.*

§

Standing outside Andie's room, I prayed hard and gulped hard while hot tears slipped down my cheeks. I stood there and I stood there and I stood there, my heart blasting blood to my eardrums. I felt the hospital walls shaking and knew if I didn't sit down, I might have a stroke. Andie lay awake as I walked through the door. She blinked and studied my expression. Turning her head to the window she said, "Dixie's painting the baby's room that new color of green. Don't you think that'd be nice?"

I fell to my knees beside the bed. "Hunter green. I 'member you liked it. It's real pretty."

I felt boneless, crushed with sorrow, but when I looked up, Andie's eyes were dry. It was as if her despair had deadened her senses. She sat quietly until I began to weep great sobs of grief, as if I'd lost the baby myself. Although Andie could not cry or speak, she consoled me by stroking my hair. I crawled onto the bed with her, but she only shook her head as I tried to tell her. My words did not penetrate. Finally, my spirit exhausted, I took her in my arms and forced her to look into my eyes. "He died in your daddy's arms," I said. "Somebody who loved him was holding him." It was a small amount of comfort in such a time of utter sadness, but it shattered her barrier. She took a deep breath and yielded to the sorrow that overtook her like a flash flood.

§

It wasn't until after lunch that Joe poked his head into the room. Andie straightened. "Oh, Joe, Brian—my baby—our baby has died."

He walked toward me and said, "Think you can give me and my wife a few minutes?"

I slid off the bed, took a box of Kleenex from Andie's table, and walked out. I didn't go far. I stood just outside the room, listening to every word. I wasn't going to let that bastard tear her up any more than she already was.

Peeking around the corner, I watched Joe kiss her forehead. My stomach turned. His cry was a dry one, and I hoped Andie could see through his faked distress. He reached for her hand with his head lowered, his voice uncovering the sheer weight of his attempt to cry. "I didn't get to see him. I'm sorry."

She pulled her hand away. "But . . . you promised. I thought you'd gone to see him. I assumed . . . I mean, why didn't you go see him, Joe? You promised."

His head jerked up. "Because I love *you*. I wanted to stay near you. I've been thinking a lot about what I've done and I'm so, so very sorry. I knew your folks were with him. I've got a nice surprise for you. Reverend is letting me stay home this weekend for the funeral."

Andie only closed her eyes and wept until her shoulders shook.

It was all I could do to stand outside that door. No words or emotions could express how much I hated him at that moment.

Fingernails Down A Chalkboard

Andie

Joe didn't fuss when Daddy checked me out of the hospital and drove me to Winston-Salem on Wednesday afternoon. He agreed to meet me Saturday morning at Tussman Funeral Home and I agreed that he should handle the funeral arrangements with Pastor DeSanto. Concerned my strength not give out, I wanted to save my energy for the funeral. When I arrived at my parents' home, I found Dixie had bought me a new black dress, size 18, and had hung it on the bedroom door. The perfect welcome home gift.

Mavis had all but moved into Daddy's house to take care of me since Dixie lacked not only the nursing skills for my current condition, but the patience. Mavis switched on the shower, waited for it to warm up, then stuck me inside to wash my hair. I moaned, but the pain lessened as the hospital smell was scrubbed off my broken body. In the process, we both ended up with a shower and laughed a little. It helped to ease the sting, mostly in our hearts.

On Saturday, Mavis managed to pull my hair back into my signature ponytail. I was determined to attend my son's funeral, despite Dixie's protests. Mavis ignored Dixie, too, and slipped a pair of flip-flops on my swollen feet. My right foot, still bandaged, couldn't bear shoes.

"You sure you can do this, honey?"

I nodded to Mavis, my eyes pleading. "Just get me in the car."

She situated me in the front seat, and then slid behind me into the back seat of Daddy's station wagon. Dozing and jerking awake all the way to the funeral home, I wore dark sunglasses to block the bright sunlight blinking through the trees, distracting me from the silence and sorrow. It was brief, however. Rain clouds gathered as Mavis pushed my wheelchair into the funeral home amidst a glare of public sympathy. I felt her grudgingly position me beside Joe. Only twenty feet from my baby's tiny closed casket, I couldn't take my eyes off it.

Joe slipped his arm around my shoulders, smiling and chatting with everyone as if it were just an ordinary day. A new professional aura emanated from him. Wearing a custom-made suit, new leather boots, and a silk tie, he looked like a model out of the pages of *Gentlemen's Quarterly*. While I—bloated, bruised, and bandaged—had become by my appearance, a poster child for battered women.

"I'm sitting right behind you." Mavis said into my ear.

People from all over the Triad lined up around the block to pay their condolences.

"It's for the best, sugah."

"God needed an angel, precious."

Then there were those House of Praise people who interpreted the baby's death as an act of divine vengeance. "Will you be returning to church soon?"

Men and women whose lives had no semblance to mine, said, "Get over it, honey, and the sooner the better. You'll have another one." Three hundred people came and went in the span of an afternoon, expressing sorrow and concern for my loss, insinuating into my ear that he "was in a better place."

Dead words. Plastic words. Words with little sound and no significance. They filled the air around me, but did not diffuse an ounce of my explosive grief. Where were my sympathizers when my breasts oozed with no baby to feed? I had lost my child, my hope for the future, my life's direction, all in the same day. How does a woman get over the death of her baby? Tell me how, somebody! Brian's death was burned into my identity. I might get used to it, but never over it. And where were my well-wishers at four in the morning when I woke to find my body in a fetal position, hugging an empty womb? How does a woman experience motherhood in one day? One day without any of the splendor of it. Weeping in my wheelchair, I wanted to be left alone.

Maudy and Al sat on the other side of Joe, delivering bits and pieces of scripture and consolation to their son. The Oliver camp was divided, as Ray and Libby offered their sympathy only to me.

Libby spoke softly behind me. "I'm here if you need me."

I said nothing.

But I turned around when Ray touched my shoulder. His eyes rimmed with tears, spoke volumes. His voice cracked out a whisper, "I'm so sorry, Andie. I knew Joe would do this."

And still, I said nothing. Not even to my parents sitting next to me. At least I knew what Ray had been keeping from me. He had hoped, as I did, that Joe was not a monster.

I didn't feel like playing hostess at my baby's funeral anymore. The thought of sending thank-you cards to those mourners nauseated me. I resented rather than appreciated their presence, their comments, and their sympathies. Each teary-eyed long face who greeted me with a theatrical condolence agitated me, prickled my skin, like fingernails down a chalkboard.

All except Candace Cooper, my neighbor at Shady Acres. I didn't recognize Candace at first. Her teased-high hair had gone from Midnight Black to Champagne Blonde. But I'd seen her red-leather tooled boots and her leopard-skin purse many times from my kitchen window.

Ignoring Joe, Candace bent over and embraced me in my wheelchair. Overcome by Estée Lauder and cleavage, I started to thank her for coming, but Candace had something to say. She crouched down further, looked straight into my eyes and spoke softly. "Only women bleed. Men don't know what we go through in life. They put us in these situations and then wonder why we go crazy. I'm across the street if you need me."

"Thank you. I'll remember that." Of all the people who spoke to me that day, Candace made the most sense.

The door finally stopped whooshing open. Extra metal folding chairs had to be brought in. Those who wanted to stay for the service found a seat. From the moment I arrived at the funeral home, I sat with my legs crossed at the ankles and my hands in my lap like I'd been brought up to do. But I had reached my limit. Tuning my ears to the roar of whispers behind me instead of Pastor DeSanto's insensitive sermon, I stood. Hugging the memory of my baby was not enough. My insides ignited with desperation and anguish, and I pushed Joe's hand off my shoulder and my mother back in her seat. Staggering to the tiny blue metal casket covered in a spray of white roses, I pulled off the flowers, raised the lid, and lifted the lifeless body of my son. Holding him close and sobbing into my swaddled baby, all I could hear was one big gasp of horror from the room. The funeral director tried to console and coax me to lay my child back in the casket, but I pulled away, backed against the wall, and slid to the floor with my baby.

Mavis stumbled over Libby and Ray and a row full of mourners, while Dixie clawed at Daddy, screaming, "Do something!" I looked for Joe. He had turned toward his parents, shielding their faces and his own from the spectacle I was making of myself. My baby was cold and stiff; his little body felt like a doll. I stared at him. He was wrapped tight in a white blanket with a hospital hat tied on his tiny head. And then, it was as if I had woken up from a bad dream.

I gazed into the mass of spectators. It was Coot who pressed through the crowd. He approached cautiously, knelt down, and put his arms around me. "Git up, Andie, sweetie. Ya gotta put yer baby back. He's done gone on to Heaven."

"I . . . I just wanted to hold him," I said. "I didn't get to hold him or say. . . goodbye."

"I know, but ya gotta put him back, honey."

I kissed my infant son before allowing the funeral director to take him out of my arms and lay him back in the casket, tuck the satin blanket around him, and close the lid. Coot helped me stand and walk back to my wheelchair, but I hobbled past it and collapsed into Mavis's arms.

§

I remained between Libby and Mavis at the burial site. Afterward, Joe whispered into my ear that he would take his parents home; they weren't up for eating supper at my folks' house. That was fine with me. There were already too many people gathering at the Parks's residence, bringing more food and condolences than I could possibly manage.

Before sunset, I excused myself from the throng of sympathetic eyes and questions about Joe. I walked through the living room, through the bathroom-spray stench of flowers brought from the funeral home; a sickly sweet fragrance embedding itself into my memory. Facing the stairway that led to my old room, I felt my baby moving inside me again, an unseen presence filling me to the brim with grief. The thought crossed my mind: maybe I'd lost my mind after all. Mavis followed me as we ascended, holding tight to the banister, and taking every step, slowly, one at a time.

Ultimatum

Mavis

It was more than I could endure. Andie was not suffering another minute. Though Joe had turned me into a raving lunatic, I was determined to break them both out of Calvin's prison. At least Joe would have a chance to redeem himself.

Using the excuse that I needed to take care of things at my daddy's farm for a day or so, I put Andie to bed and then left for the evening. I was aware that Calvin was out of town, but I drove to the nearest pay phone anyway and dialed an unlisted number at the House of Praise.

"This is Mavis Dumass again. I really need to speak to Reverend Artury."

"He'll have to return your call." Obviously, Fannie had been given her orders.

"Get him on the line now, Fannie. Tell him I need to talk to him now or I'm calling the newspaper in the morning."

I waited a small eternity. Fannie returned every few minutes, curtly requesting I continue to hold. But standing in a gas station phone booth across the street from a Methodist Church, my knees went weak reading the sign in the front yard. *John 15:13 Greater love has no one than this—that he lay down his life for his friends.* I lit a fresh cigarette. My hands shook and I broke out in a sweat when a Southern accent, smooth as a buttermilk biscuit, seeped through the line.

"Mavis Dumass, I was expecting your call. Fannie conferenced me in. Can you hear me?" His performance was clear, calculating, cold.

"I hear you fine. When can we meet?"

"As you know, I'm in Richmond this weekend for a Sunday miracle crusade. I'll be in my office Monday morning. Say at nine?"

"Nine a.m. on Monday, but not in your office."

"Where then? I can't meet you in a public place. People know me; they'll talk."

"Calvin, people will talk a lot more unless you meet me where I say."

"Don't threaten me, Mavis."

"Threats? I haven't even started, Cal. Meet me at the Kopper Kettle Diner. I know the owner. He'll give us a private room. Come alone."

"Okay then. Make sure it's private."

"Of course."

Silence.

"Calvin?"

"Yes?"

"You can buy me breakfast." *Click.*

§

Ken Kopper told me I could use one of the booths in the back room he usually held for the supper hour. I thanked him and stuck a twenty-dollar bill in his shirt pocket. He smiled and set a pot of coffee on my table. Pouring a cup, my hands trembled. I knew I wasn't responsible for Andie's happiness, but this was different. I had the power to fix the mess she was in, plus unload some of my own demons, something I should've done a long time ago. Dressed in my best white jeans and matching jacket, I pulled lipstick and a mirror from my purse. Working my lipstick back into the tube, I tried to remove the annoyance from my face. He was late. I laid a napkin in my lap and waited. Unless he showed up soon, all bets were off.

A few customers sat in the front. The waitress talked casually to a couple at the counter while someone else dropped their fork and hollered for a clean one. The smell of bacon and sausage frying floated through the diner; I heard it sizzle whenever Ken or his waitress opened the swinging door to the kitchen. The customers were oblivious to my presence, which was a good thing considering the circumstances. My legs started to quiver. A side effect of the coffee and the anticipation of his face. I pushed my knees against the wall to still them.

He startled me as he slid into the booth, the smell of his cologne overpowering and nauseating. "Thanks for being so discreet," he said, his mouth curling into a smile.

"It's what I do best," I replied, keeping my tone cool. He peeled off his sunglasses. His familiar blue eyes stirred a vicious parasite of regret that I longed to burn out of me like holding a match to a tick.

He had pulled back his hair into a ponytail and stuffed it up under a ball cap. It shocked me to see him in blue jeans and a plaid shirt open down to the third button, revealing chest hair. A pair of Reeboks and sunglasses completed his disguise. Except for his gold watch and pinky ring, he looked like every other redneck that came into the Kopper Kettle for breakfast.

Calvin gave the restaurant a once-over. Satisfied he didn't recognize any of the patrons, he shot me a twisted grin. "Let's just have coffee. I have a driver waiting in the alley."

I tightened my lips, but a giggle sneaked through. "Oh, I don't think so, Cal. I want breakfast. This is my gig, hear?"

"Fine. We'll do it your way." His eyes widened as Ken limped into the dining room dragging his bad foot. Ken didn't so much as blink an eyelash when Calvin nodded hello. I ordered breakfast for myself.

"Just coffee, thanks," said Calvin.

"It's a shame. Kenny here cooks a mean omelet."

"No, thanks."

Ken winked at me and then headed back to the kitchen.

"Will he keep his mouth shut?"

"Who, Ken? Ken's a good ol' boy. Believe me, you can trust him. He hears lots of stuff in this diner. He's as safe as Fort Knox."

"Mavis, you look good. All grown up."

"Thanks. Sorry I can't say the same for you."

Calvin's grin changed to a look of impatience and disgust as he folded his hands on the smooth wooden table. He shifted in his seat. "Just what do you want exactly?"

"Mmm-mmm, in a big ol' hurry, ain't ya preacher? Let's talk 'bout the good ol' days for a minute. I'm a little nostalgic today. Been watching that new TV show, *Happy Days*. You see that show, Calvin? All 'bout being in high school. I was pretty crazy myself back then. So young and desperate. Wanted to get out of the South so damn bad."

"Don't cuss around me, Mavis."

"Oh please, Cal," I laughed. "You said some damn nasty words to me once. Then I guess you forgot about that, huh? Course, you don't want a scandal. You'd deny it. Say I ain't got proof." I sipped my coffee. "Or do I?" Smiling, I raised my eyebrows. "Do I make you nervous, Cal?" I had the upper hand and studied his reaction, but he showed no emotion. Nothing but silence. "Ha! I knew it. Damn, I'm good," I slapped my hand on the table hard enough that his coffee splashed over his mug rim.

"Didn't I pay you enough?" he asked.

"Shuh, I'd say so. For me, bein' a poor young black girl scratching and clawing my way to New York City, it was plenty of money. Lasted me a good long time. Still got some of it. I rented me a nice place in Manhattan. Cramped, but nice."

"A small price to pay to keep your mouth shut."

"And I'll keep it shut. It's not money I'm after, Cal."

"Then what? What are you after, pray tell."

"You pray, I'll tell," I snickered. "Here's the deal, Pharaoh; Miss Moses here wants you to let the Hebrews out of Egypt. In other words, I want you to let Joe and Andie Oliver go. I want you to kick the entire Oliver family out of your church. Leave 'em alone. Let 'em go free."

"What have you told Andie?"

"Nothing about you. Just what I seen Joe do in Philadelphia."

"Yes. I heard about Joe's indiscretion. How do I know you're telling the truth?"

"You don't. Unless you use your all-powerful gift of discernment, or voodoo, or crystal ball, or whatever it is you use. I don't want anything from you, Calvin. I want as far away from your sorry ass as I can get. But my best friend in the wide world is in love with Joe Oliver. God only knows why. All she wants is a quiet existence, a home, children, the good things in life people like you and me don't deserve. She can't get it 'cause you got a hold of Joe's balls."

"And if I don't let go?"

I reached across the table and jabbed my fingernail into his bare skin scarcely above his chest hair and unbuttoned shirt. "You're letting go of all the Olivers. You're doing it now, or I will be your worst nightmare, Cal." I sat back down. "You thought I wasn't smart, didn't ya, preacher man? Thought I wasn't witty enough to protect myself. Course I didn't know how big you were bound to get. You're quite famous these days, ain't ya? Folks sho' would be disappointed to know you're just a fake and a phony, like all the rest of them big TV preachers you're competing against for folks's money."

"Mavis, I don't think you know what you're dealing with."

"What . . . the Almighty?" I laughed again, staring at the dent my fingernail left on his chest. Ken brought out my breakfast. The silence was stifling. Calvin's eyes blazed hot as I peppered my eggs and buttered my biscuit. "Cool it, Cal. God don't want you found out. It wouldn't sit well with all the people He's honestly trying to save. Lots of good folks out there, seeking a true God. Not the kind you're selling." I knew he wasn't about to discuss theology or debate his imagined integrity. "Besides, I'm just as much to blame, keeping my mouth shut all this time."

"So let me get this straight. You just want me to tell the Olivers to leave my church. Tell Joe to fall in love with his wife. Live happily every after. That's all you want."

"Damn, you're a smart man, Cal." I leaned into the table. "Now you go and fix the mess Joe and Andie's in. That boy is addicted to sex, but not with his wife. I want you to pay for professional counseling outside the church. Do whatever it takes to keep them together and Andie happy. Like I say, let 'em go free. You'll never hear from me again."

"I'll think about it, see what I can do."

"You think real hard, preacher man."

"How about calling me Reverend Artury from now on?"

I chuckled. "From now on? I hope to never speak your name again, you sorry excuse for a holy man." My chuckle turned to laughter. "Oh, Cal! You a goddamn joke. I ain't calling you nothing but what you are. A joke."

Calvin's massive palm reached across the table and locked onto my wrist just as I put a forkful of eggs up to my mouth, causing them to fling back on the table. The force of his stare pushed a lump into my throat. For a pale second I barely breathed; our eyes fused while the heat of his hand throbbed against my wrist. "Listen you little nigger whore, I'll do what you want. But let me tell you something. You ever threaten me again, or so much as breathe the air within 100 miles of me; it'll be the last breath you ever take. You get that?"

I shuddered, but I would not let him see my fear. I yanked my hand free of his painful grip, refusing to give in to the tears that stung my eyes. "And I'm giving you an ultimatum, you motherfucker. Leave me and the Olivers alone, or I will take my story and evidence to every major newspaper and TV station in this country and ruin you overnight."

Calvin stood and threw a twenty on the table. "Here's for breakfast. Go back to New York, Mavis. I'll take care of the Olivers. You keep your mouth shut and we'll all be free at last—free at last."

"Thank God Almighty," I responded. I didn't look at him again. I picked up the twenty, stuffed it in my cleavage, and took a bite of my biscuit, waving him away like a gnat flying around my head.

He pulled his ball cap low on his forehead and exited the way he came in.

§

As soon he was gone, I ran to the toilet and threw up all I had eaten the past twelve hours. Slinking back to the booth, I pushed my food away and laid my head on the table. My body shivered and I clutched at my sides. It wasn't until Ken turned the corner that I allowed even a single tear to fall.

"You okay, Mavis?" Ken cleared the table around me.

"Yeah. Give me a minute." I pulled the twenty out of my cleavage and handed it to him.

"Keep it," he said. "Breakfast is on me."

"No, actually, it's in your toilet. Sorry. Food's great. It's the company I keep."

"I didn't hear a word. You look whipped."

"Not quite. Not yet."

No Compromise

Reverend Calvin Artury

A low groan rumbled inside me. I crawled into the back seat of my Cadillac and told Percy to drive me home. I needed to change clothes. Calling Evan on my car phone, I felt my blood boil. Was it all a test? Had I failed my Lord and Savior in some small way?

It was a bitter moment.

Evan said he was in the middle of something, and I told him to get off his wife and contact Silas and Pastor DeSanto and meet me at the church office in an hour. "Don't be late!" I prayed and took deep breaths to soothe myself, but my hands clenched into fists. My teeth ground together as I replayed the past hour in my head, and my knuckles pounded the seat while a few of my flaxen hairs turned white on the ride home. I hated not being in charge, but I had to let her think I was at least considering her demands. Tension coiled around my stomach and bowels. I turned my face to the Lord and sensed the warm blanket of the Spirit covering me from head to toe. I would not succumb to her—I would not compromise.

"Hallelujah! I'm on the Lord's side!" I cried out. "I have nothing to fear! Nothing to worry about!"

God *was* on my side. Unfortunately, Lucifer had planted himself firmly on the other. I was quite aware the bigger my ministry, the bigger my problems. I also knew my miscalculation of the shy, soft-spoken, poverty-stricken black girl was my mistake and Adonai-Jehovah would require me to rectify it.

Time To Leave

Mavis

I left Kopper Kettle Diner and drove to Salisbury. I had promised Dixie I'd gather up the baby toys and gifts, and take them to the Goodwill box. No need for Andie to go home to a trailer ready for a baby she no longer had. I had just enough time to get in and out before Joe came home from work at five.

The little trailer felt empty without Andie's smile. I hurried, but worked into the afternoon, making sure I gathered every blanket, bootie, and bottle. Opening drawers, closets, and looking under the bed, I tried to remember where she had it all stashed. It broke my heart to do it, but it would've torn Andie's heart clean out of her chest. I worried that she might never recover.

The phone rang and I hesitated. I'd already had a rough day, and I didn't feel like answering Maudy's annoying questions as to why I was there. Then I thought it might be Dixie, or Daddy . . . "Hello?"

"Mavis, it's Dad."

I sighed with relief, my cheeks hot. "Daddy? You okay?" I checked my watch; it wasn't quite four thirty. I had less than an hour to get out before Joe came home.

"Fine, fine. Came in to eat an early supper and got a phone call from somebody named Dino. Said he was your agent. Didn't give his last name."

I chuckled. "Yeah? What'd he say?"

"He said he's leaving town, not to bother calling him back. He wants you to return to New York. Said he's got you a job singing four nights a week. The opening act for big names who come to the restaurant."

I knew Dino meant "bar," but wouldn't say that to my daddy. "Which restaurant?"

"He didn't say. Just to come back. You're to start next week. Thursday night, he said."

"Okay, Daddy. Thanks for calling. Dixie tell you where I was?"

"Yuh, Dixie tole me. It's mighty nice, Mavis, what you're doing. Make sure you get it all. Poor thing."

"I will. See you at home tonight."

"Okay, darlin'. See ya later."

Finally—a real excuse to return to New York. I'd go home, start packing, and check bus schedules. After picking up the last piece of the crib and my purse, I locked the door behind me and nearly fell off the porch balancing the slats on one arm. Sweat popped out on my forehead and neck as I jammed and tied the crib into the trunk of Aunt Lula's Nova. I decided to take everything to the battered women's shelter before going back to see Andie. But just as I picked up my car keys, Joe pulled into the driveway behind me. *Damn it. All I needed was one more minute.*

He bolted to my car. "What are you doing here?"

"Dixie asked me to get all the baby stuff out."

"Dixie has no business asking you to do that."

"Take it up with Bud and Dixie. I got to go. You want to let me out of the drive?"

Covered in black grease, he stood no more than five feet away. I smelled his stench, a mixture of sweat, motor oil, and gasoline. He lit a cigarette and moved toward me slowly, like a big cat stalking its prey.

"Careful, you'll go up in flames the way you smell."

"Funny, all I smell is a whore," he said as he blew smoke in my face, paying me back.

But his contempt bounced off without leaving a mark. "Just let me out, Joe. I ain't in the mood for you today."

Joe spit his words at me. "You know, you break into my house—"

"Excuse me," I interrupted, my head bobbing and weaving while the rest of me stood still, "but Dixie gave me the key, and it ain't a house, it's a tin can, and it ain't even yours, fool. You don't make enough money to own anything last time Andie told me." I turned to open my car door, but Joe grabbed my arms, flipped me around, and started to gyrate against my white Calvin Klein's. He bit at my neck as he rubbed dirt and grease into my new jeans. It really pissed me off. "You have a bad day, Joe?" I asked, attempting to shove him away.

"Every day I'm not working for Reverend is a bad day. Why don't you and me go into my tin can and I'll show you just how bad I can be. Course you should know, you seen me in action. Got pictures to prove it."

"No thanks, Church Boy. Not interested. Now you letting me out of here, or do I have to use the neighbor's phone and call the police?"

"C'mon Mavis, you and me never got a chance to know each other." He held my arms tight against Aunt Lula's car and dug his greasy face into my neck and breasts. I could feel him getting hard, and that was all I could take.

"You disgust me! You got a sick wife in the bed and a dead baby just been put in the ground." I pulled my knee up hard and rammed it between his legs. Joe let go, doubled over and fell into the gravel drive, holding his groin. I leaped into the Nova, started it, and then cracked the window just enough for him to hear me. "You need a few lessons in foreplay, Church Boy. It ain't nice to force yourself on a lady."

Joe struggled to upright himself. "You ain't no lady, bitch! Don't come 'round me anymore, or I swear I'll ram my fist down your throat next time." Pounding two dents into the hood as I backed around his daddy's truck, he then lunged for my door. "You goddamn negra!"

I sped back to Winston-Salem. It was time to get out of North Carolina.

True and Unconditional

Andie

It felt like the rain would never let up. I'd lost track of the days. Mud everywhere, the Piedmont had became swollen and brown. Flash floods continued to pop up in every county. Cold and wet, the grass had little chance to grow and the fields were gray as the sodden sky. I got used to rain beaded on the windows. It was fitting. Sunshine just didn't seem appropriate.

Dixie screamed up the staircase. "Andie! Mavis is back."

Relieved to have someone else to talk to besides my mother, I flushed the toilet and stepped on the bathroom scale. One hundred ninety-two pounds. "My God!" I hop-walked out of the bathroom hunched over, keeping my weight off my bandaged foot. My stitches pulled and itched.

"Traffic's a zoo. God, will it ever stop raining? How ya feeling?"

"Better. Except I just got on the scale. Don't ask."

Mavis helped me ease myself back into bed and propped my foot on a stack of Dixie's chenille accent pillows. "You know, Andie, you're a beautiful woman."

I blasted her with a dismal look.

"No, you're not model thin, never were, never will be, but you got the most gorgeous face and skin I've ever seen. Perfect teeth, blue eyes that can haunt a person, and your heart is your best feature. You're not perfect, you're impatient and bossy, but you sure know how to love. Even the most insignificant creatures. I've seen you carry spiders out of the house and set them into the grass. More than once I've watched you give Bud's dog the last bite of your cheeseburger. You don't ask for much out of life. Just one filled with love, laughter, a home, and a good husband."

"And children."

"Yeah, and children," Mavis said softly, then took my hand. "You'll lose weight. Eventually. Use the puking technique. It works."

"As soon as my 200 stitches heal."

Mavis scooted off my bed and fell into the overstuffed Waverly-print chair that sat next to yards of white dotted Swiss covering my bedroom windows.

"My agent called," she said.

I covered my ears with my hands. "I don't want to hear this. It's too soon. Please stay. I need you." I couldn't look at her. I looked out the window instead, staring at the mammoth oak swaying in the March wind. The tree Daddy planted when I was a baby. The thought of her leaving me plunged like a scalpel into my heart.

"Please don't," she said. "I got to go. The only thing keeping me here is you. Dino called and talked to Daddy at the house. He told me to get back, he's got me a job."

"What will I do without you? I can't stay here. Dixie's driving me crazy. I swear she's in full-blown mean-o-pause! Hollers all the time. You'd think she'd realize we have more in common now since we both lost our sons. I want to go home. I miss the quiet."

"Then go. You're strong enough." Mavis moved back to the bed to sit close to me. "I went to the trailer today. I took out the baby stuff."

"I know. Dixie told me. Where did you take it?"

"To the battered women's shelter. They'll put it to good use."

I sighed. "When are you leaving?"

"Friday morning. Daddy's driving me to the bus terminal."

"It seems like yesterday I picked you up there."

"A lot has happened since then," Mavis said.

"Take me back to Shady Acres on Thursday. That'll give my parents time to adjust."

Mavis smiled. "That'd be fine. I'll take you home. Hey, I know Joe's been driving his daddy's truck, but what do you plan to drive since Coot took your piece of shit car to the dump?"

"Daddy bought me a Cougar. Brand new, well . . . used. Only a year old. Silver. Did you see it in the driveway?"

"Woo-hoo! That was your car? Good ol' Bud. Oh, I almost forgot. I got something for you, too." Mavis pulled a tiny box out of her pocket and set it in my lap.

"What's this?"

"I bought it at the diner where Aunt Lula works. It's just a cheap key chain."

"It's a microphone!"

"Yep. You 'member how we'd pretend you could sing and were my backup?"

"Hey now, I can carry a tune, I just don't belt 'em out like you do. I remember, though. You were always Aretha, or Diana Ross, or—"

"Tammi Terrell," we chimed in unison and laughed.

I held up the tiny microphone to my mouth as if I were about to sing. "Daddy made us each a microphone out of a toilet paper roll and a golf ball glued on the top. This microphone is about us, isn't it? It was our gig, nobody else could play." I relaxed and closed my eyes. "Our song, we sang it a million times. Over and over."

Mavis touched my hand that held my new key chain. "What'd we sing, Andie? What were the words to that Marvin Gaye and Tammi Terrell song?"

My eyes fluttered open, and I sang, quietly. ". . . *ain't no mountain high enough . . .*"

Mavis harmonized the last part and coaxed me through the verses. I listened to the lyrics, about loyalty and faithfulness, and realized the song embodied our devotion to one another. When we finished, a tender smile played on her lips. "That's your answer, Andie. Unconditional love." She looked deep into my eyes. "Hold tight to it, and nobody, not even Calvin Artury, can destroy you. You remember that."

§

By Thursday Mavis had packed my things and driven me home. I shuffled around my trailer and felt the emptiness of it. There was no baby to take care of. Not even a trace of one. Just emptiness. Cold and empty. I sat on my worn-out couch and held Mavis's hand. "Call me as soon as you get to New York. I mean it, call me."

"Come with me," she said. "I'll take care of you. We'll find you a job. You can divorce him and start your life over."

"You know I can't. I can't do anything until I'm healed up. I've got to have a plan. Right now, I have nothing but a little time on my side."

Mavis sighed. "My wish is that Calvin never hire Joe. That Joe grow a nut sack and leave that church."

I wiggled, trying to get comfortable. "Yeah, well, wish in one hand and pee in the other, see which one fills up first."

I loved Mavis's smile. I would miss it.

She stood. "I want you to relax and get well. I'll call you Saturday evening. Don't go back to church."

"Not until I'm well."

"That's my girl," she said, pulling me to my feet.

My tears were suddenly non-stop. "You know I hate good-byes. Come back to me soon."

"I will." Mavis held me as hard as she dared. "I love you."

"Love you," I sobbed. The effort of smiling seemed futile. "Sisters forever."

Mavis touched my cheek lightly, then opened my hand with the scar and kissed it. "And ever."

My arms tightened around her neck, like iron. My tears soaked her shirt. Attempting to pull from my grip, Mavis finally peeled me away. Momentarily frozen, I stood at the screen door, watching her back out of the drive. Better than a friend and closer than a sister, she held the key to my heart. Our affection for each other was a tender thing, tangible, like anointed oil, seeping into the cracks and crevices of our lives. A healing balm, soothing the cuts and scrapes of our trespasses. So why couldn't we live in the same town? Raise children together, share recipes, take turns driving our kids to school and piano lessons, complain about our husbands, the weather, and grow old together? All questions I would ask myself the rest of my life.

To Tie God's Hands

Reverend Calvin Artury

Joe stepped apprehensively into my office. Brushing away a strand of loose hair, his look was a vague, pathetic one. Eyes lowered, he cowered at the sight of Pastor DeSanto, Evan, and Silas standing to leave. No one acknowledged him as they walked out and closed the door.

"Joe, have a seat," I said, running my hand over my chin. "It's been a long week. How are you and Andie?"

"Better, thanks. She's coming home today."

"Good. Continue to help her get well. I'm busy this morning so I'm coming right to the point." I pushed back in my chair and crossed my legs. "I'm taking you off the team, and I doubt I'll be hiring you in the future. You need to work on your marriage—"

"Wait a minute! I don't understand!" Joe shot out of his chair. "I thought you were sending me to Los Angeles for training. Why? Why are you doing this?"

"Sit, Joe. You did this to yourself when you had your fun in Philadelphia. There's a scandal brewing. You and your family need to leave the church and I'll be generous and pay for counseling . . . for you and Andie of course."

Joe hit the chair with his fist. "This is about Mavis, isn't it? Damn her! Reverend, I've followed you around the country. I believed in you, done everything you asked me to do. Everything! I've screwed up lately, but not because I didn't love you. It was because of my own stupidity and carelessness. I've learned my lesson. I need to be here, not trying to work on a marriage I no longer want! I'm not like my brother. You know that. I did what Ray wouldn't do, even when we were kids! I want to make Heaven, be God's warrior, remember? When I was just fifteen you said I would be a warrior for the Lord some day. That day is now! Please, Oh God, Reverend, don't do this to me."

I sat silent and expressionless. It pleased me to watch Joe beg for his position.

"You know, I didn't cry at my brother's funeral. I didn't shed one tear over Andie's pain and suffering, other than what I had to fake. I felt no sorrow, none in the least, over the loss of our baby. But losing my position with you, it takes the air from my lungs," he said as his eyes turned watery, "I can't . . . I can't breathe."

"I have to let you go, son. Give you back your life without the church. I really have no choice." My words breached Joe's stare, breaking his will not to cry.

"Yes, you do. You have a choice!" Tears fell down his baby-smooth cheeks.

"You've tied my hands, son. You've tied Jehovah Nissi's hands."

"No! All my life I wanted to work for you, for God. I have nothing else! I won't let this happen. Please, Reverend. Don't take this from me. I've worked so hard. It's who I am. It's all I want."

Joe fell to his knees. "How will I live without this church? Without you?" He stared at me with bloodshot eyes.

I allowed the silence to hang in the air while he groveled at my feet. Still unmoved by his sad display of emotion, I opened my Bible to First Samuel. "Sometimes, Joe—to stay alive—we must become like King David and slay a few giants."

Mavis

I arrived at the Port Authority Bus Terminal in New York City on Saturday morning. As soon as my feet hit the concrete, I hurried to the nearest pay phone to call Dino's office and leave a message with his secretary. I wanted to thank him, even though he'd said he was leaving town. I knew Dino liked to be thanked and if he called in for messages, my *thank you* would be one of them. It was worth a few brownie points. Besides, I had questions, like what bar was I to report to on Thursday, and how did I get the job without an audition? Questions I'd thought about on my long ride home. Questions that couldn't wait another day.

"This is Mavis Dumass. I know Dino's out of town, but—"

"Mavis? This is Carla." Dino's secretary slaved long hours for her boss. She worked every Saturday to keep him happy.

"Hi, Carla. I'd like to leave a message for Dino."

"He's not outta town. He's right here. Wanna talk to him?"

"Um, sure, I guess so."

"Hello, Mavis! How are things in North Cakalacky?" Dino had never traveled any further south than Baltimore, and enjoyed poking fun at my Confederate roots.

"Funny, Dino. Daddy said you called and that you were on your way out of town or I would've called sooner. I just got back to the city. He said you had a job for me."

"What? I never called you, babe. Sorry. Bar business is dry at the moment."

"But . . . I came home because . . . you sayin' there's no job and you didn't call?"

"That's right. And clearly, I never left town. Come to think of it, somebody was in here looking for you yesterday. Some guy. Asked how he could get in touch with you; asked for your phone number and where you lived."

"You didn't tell him anything, did you, Dino?"

"Of course not. I don't give out information on my clients."

"What'd he look like?"

"Hell, I can't remember. White guy. Nice. Dark hair. Tall. Young Clark Gable-type."

"Did he have a Southern accent?"

Dino laughed. "No. This guy was from New York, definitely."

"Maybe one of Harry's friends wants me to take a few photographs. Wedding or something. I guess I need a job now."

"Sorry, Mavis. I'll be sure to call if someone's looking for a talented broad to sing in their establishment. Glad you're back from KKK Land," he laughed—nervous-like.

"Thanks, Dino. Just get me a job. I want to sing, not take pictures with Harry all my life. Why are you there on a Saturday?"

"Helping Carla clean up a mess. My office was ransacked last night. Bastards tore the place apart."

"God, I'm sorry. Anything missing?"

"Nah, nothing important."

§

Dog-tired, confused, and hungry, I climbed into a taxi and settled my suitcase and bags at my feet. "Nicky's Deli on Broadway, Lower Manhattan." Nicky's was a good place to hang out and collect my thoughts. Besides, my friend Lucy worked there. I hoped she could get me a job.

New York City always stirred my need for a good smoke. Twirling an unlit Salem Light between my fingers, I couldn't wait to get out of the cab. A chest full of stale city air filled my lungs before I placed the cigarette in the side of my mouth and flicked my lighter. I smiled at the skyline. The friendly comfort of skyscrapers and nicotine welcomed me home. I was glad to be back, job or no job.

Since Nicky's was packed, I figured I could make some pretty nice tips. I ordered a salad with no meat and light on the vinaigrette before asking for a job application. Sitting at a table, I thought about my apartment. I had called the guy I sublet it to and told him I was coming home early. He wasn't happy about it, claiming he'd already paid April's rent and that he was going to complain to our mutual friend Harry, who had introduced us. But when I promised to reimburse him and throw in an extra hundred, he agreed to be out the next day.

I took the last bite of my salad when Raoul, the manager, told me I'd landed a position waiting tables, starting the next day. Raoul seemed pleasant enough. An upscale deli, Nicky's would pay my bills until Dino could come through or I could hook up with Harry and start photo shoots again. Calvin's hush money had dwindled and I tried not to dip into it.

I checked my watch, then stepped out onto the sidewalk to hail one last cab for the day. "Corner of West 81st and West End Avenue," I said. After handing the taxi driver an extra dollar, I let my oversized suitcase drag behind me up the three flights to my apartment. It freaking figured—an all-night bus ride, a disappointing conversation with Dino, and my building's elevator was suddenly out of order. I was ready for a hot shower, clean sheets, and sleep.

And then it happened. The moment I slid my key in the door, I felt it. Like a bucket of water poured on my head, a bizarre kind of uneasiness flowing down my body. My welcome mat was missing and the door wreath I'd bought at a craft fair in Jersey lay in the hallway corner. I picked it up, hung it back on its hook, and quickly searched the hall for my missing welcome mat. A familiar cheap men's cologne, like something I smelled in Woolworth's once, hit me in the face as I stepped inside and switched on the lights. I sat my suitcases on the rug next to the hall closet, then turned and bolted the door behind me. As I walked around the corner into my living room, my mouth flew open.

"Oh shit!" The room looked like it had thrown up on itself. Sofa cushions had been tossed to the floor along with magazines, pillows, and my bookcase was flipped over. Pieces of my stereo peeked at me from beneath the debris. My record albums, opened and scattered, appeared as molested as my desk. Its drawers were left gaping, my papers strewn everywhere, someone had rummaged through it, caring less if they left a mess.

I stepped over a fallen planter with dirt ground into the rug and started toward the kitchen, my leather shoes clicking against the parquet floor. At the doorway I just stood there for an instant, too shocked to move. Counter drawers had been yanked out and upended. Others stood ajar as if they'd been rifled through. Canisters lay open on the floor; flour, sugar, and coffee spilled onto the linoleum. Melted Popsicles had dripped down the refrigerator from an open freezer door. I gagged at the smell of thawed meat. A broken bottle of Merlot lay on the countertop soaking into the grout. Broken dishes and glassware crunched under my feet, and the trash bag had been ripped open and scattered. The kitchen reeked of garbage. A stillness enveloped me, nothing moved, there were no sounds beyond those of the city.

Quickly, fury built and burned behind my eyes, but I swallowed hard, dismissing it. I had no time to get pissed off when there was such a mess to clean up. "When I get my hands on that guy, I'll strangle him!" I figured he must have been super-pissed that I'd asked him to leave early. He sure didn't seem the violent type. When Harry introduced me to Chip Atkinson, a student at The Art Institute, I thought he was a first-class nerd, a real honest-to-goodness Potsie Weber-type. I stomped back to my bedroom, grumbling. "Damn it! You just never know. A guy you think's nice and nerdy turns out to be a juvenile delinquent!"

I changed into clothes to clean in. Then I felt that bucket of water pour over me again like an ocean wave. Why would someone call me back to New York? Dino's office, my apartment. Both a mess. Standing in the kitchen with a mop in my hand, the impulse grew into full-blown panic—was someone looking for something? I dropped my mop and ran to the bedroom. Standing on a chair, I reached up and removed a ceiling tile, then felt for the handle to the metal army footlocker my daddy gave me years ago. Still there and locked. If someone were looking for my pot of gold, they didn't think to check my ceiling. I remembered how I had strained and pulled a few muscles lifting and tugging the heavy locker up into the rafters.

Hoisting myself into the small, tight crawl space, I reached for the key that hung on a nail in a supporting two-by-four. The light from the room below was enough to see by. I swatted away a few cobwebs and opened the locker. Nothing was missing. All the evidence I'd saved for the past six years, it was still there.

This is silly. Coincidence. I'd better call Andie or I'll catch hell. Clean the apartment tomorrow. Call Andie, and then go to bed. I'd been back in town almost six hours, made a few phone calls, got a job at a deli, and hadn't called Andie.

She picked it up on the first ring. "Mavis, I was worried! When did you get back? I've been in this tin vat of depression, soaking it up by the hour, waiting for your call. I guess I'm not as ready to return to the regular routine of living as I thought."

"Got home this afternoon. You should see this place. That guy Chip, he's paying for this mess! My apartment looks like a tornado blew through it! Worse than that, Dino never called me. Somebody's cruel joke."

"How awful! You could be here with me."

"I miss you, but I'm glad to be back. I got a job waiting tables. Nicky's Deli in Lower Manhattan. Nice place. I start tomorrow, Easter Sunday. Yippee, a paycheck. But I can't reach Harry. No answer. I've got to go to Jersey next week and see him."

"But now I can rest. You're in your apartment, your life is its usual chaos, and I can go back to . . . figuring out Joe."

"Call me immediately if you do. We'll bottle it and sell it. Make a fortune."

"Promise me two things," Andie said.

I lit a cigarette. "What's that?"

"First, send me copies of the pictures you took while you were here. I want to put them in my new photo album. Second, call me every day, at least for a while: I'm having a rough time. I should've stayed at Dixie's. She's crazy, but she kept my mind occupied."

"Sure, sweetie. I'll call you every morning before I head off to my glamorous new job of asking, *ya want chips and a dill pickle with that*?" Hearing Andie's laugh calmed my nerves.

"Thanks, Mavis. I know long distance is expensive, but it's just for a few days. I'll be waiting for your calls. Miss you."

"That goes double for me," I said.

§

Sleep deprived, I dragged myself out of bed the next morning. My promised phone call to Andie consisted of I'm-late-for-my-first-day-of-work-have-a-nice-day-and-I'll-call-tomorrow. A rushed shower, wet hair, and no makeup did nothing to accentuate my drab waiter's uniform of black pants, black shoes, and a white button-down shirt. I had changed my mind and stayed up until two in the morning cleaning the mess Chip created in his departure. Andie's obsession with keeping a spotless house had finally rubbed off. But Sunday morning came too early.

I bolted down the steps and shoved the heavy glass doors open, hoping to catch a quick cab. Two men stepped into my path.

"Mavis Dumass?"

A taxi stopped at the curb and then sped away empty.

"Yes?"

"We'd like to ask you a few questions." They identified themselves as detectives Watson and Derrick, New York City P.D. "Do you know a Chip Atkinson?"

"Why?"

"He's missing. We have your apartment as his address."

"I didn't *know* him exactly. He's a friend of the photographer I work for. He answered my ad to sublet my apartment and he used Harry as a reference."

Detective Watson asked, "What's the name of the photographer you work for?"

"Harry, Harry Philips in Secaucus."

"Can you tell us anything you know about Mr. Atkinson?"

"I saw him once. Before I went to see my family in North Carolina. I wasn't there as long as I thought I'd be, so I called Chip last week and told him I needed my place back. It pissed him off, but he said he would leave. I told him I'd reimburse him for April's rent. I haven't heard from him since. He was gone when I got here. The place was a wreck."

"Mind if we take a look around your apartment?"

"No, except I'm late for my first day of work on a new job."

"We won't take long."

"Okay. I'll take you up if you'll hurry. I stayed awake 'til two cleaning the mess."

The detectives followed me up the steps. "Anything missing?" Detective Derrick asked.

"No, not a thing. That's why I know he did it. He was a weird kid."

I opened the door and led the detectives inside. They took a quick look in every room, lifted a pillow or two, pulled open a few drawers, and peeked in a few closets.

Detective Derrick jotted a few notes on a small pad. "Tell me again the name of your employer who knew Mr. Atkinson."

"Harry Philips. Philips Photography, over in Jersey." That's when I saw both detectives eyeball each other at the mention of Harry.

"If you happen to see Mr. Atkinson, please call us immediately. This is our card."

"Yes, I will. Can I press charges for vandalism? He sure made a mess."

"We got to find him first."

"Is he in some kind of trouble?"

"Right now, he's just a missing person, according to his sister in Brooklyn. Just call us if you hear from him."

"Will do, officer," I said.

§

Without giving it another thought, I hurried into a cab, asking the driver to hoof it downtown. As I stepped out of the taxi, I promised myself I'd start taking the bus or subway to save money. Glancing up the street, I noticed a black Lincoln Town Car parked at the corner. A limo. A stretch. It had a sizeable dent in the left front fender, its headlight smashed on that side. I thought I'd seen it somewhere before. Dismissing my wild imagination, I bounded into the deli.

I'd forgotten how difficult waiting tables could be. Dropping a bowl of soup, mixing up two orders—one with cream cheese, one without—and watching a whole carrot cake slide off my tray and plunge to the floor, I figured it wasn't too bad for my first day.

After my shift, I scurried up Broadway to the subway station. Stopped at the light waiting to cross, I checked my reflection in the window of a building. That's when I saw it—behind me—the same dented Town Car. I patted my hair, lit my cigarette, and then stopped to buy a newspaper. Strolling toward the subway, I tuned my ear to the Town Car's defective muffler and low rumble growl. It stopped when I stopped. Rolled slowly as I walked. As fast as I could go without seeming obvious, I fell in line with a group of tourists spilling into the subway. Running to the train, I glanced over my shoulder. My eyes scanned each passenger in the subway car. Exiting at 79th Street, two blocks from my apartment, I felt foolish and mildly amused by my paranoia. But there it was again, lurking in the street, one block from the subway. As if it knew where I lived. Same black car, same dented left fender, same loud muffler.

It just sat there. Idling. Parked with no driver. I ducked behind the rush of pedestrians and reached my apartment building in time to bolt up the stairs ahead of my elderly neighbor. After a fast inspection of my apartment, I double locked the door behind me. I felt silly again. I grabbed my Salem Lights, lit one up, and mumbled while I smoked. "I can't live like this. I'm flipping out. Dang paranoid is what I am. Got to be tons of Town Cars in New York. They can't all be following me, even ones with dented fenders." Settling down for the evening with no further incident I ate a quick salad, took a bath, and fell into bed.

Lying in the dark, I recalled where I'd seen the car prior to arriving at the deli that morning. Parked at the bus terminal that Saturday, and then it had pulled up to the curb in front of my apartment, but sped away behind the taxi when the detectives showed up. I tiptoed to the window. The street was clear. *Coincidence.* "Go to bed," I said out loud.

§

"Another sleepless night," I said to no one. I felt as hollow as my voice sounded. Sitting on the edge of my bed I stretched, yawned, and tugged off my nightgown. Achy and exhausted, I pulled on jeans, a T-shirt and flip-flops. Thoughts of the sinister car were all but gone. I hunted for my keys and some loose change, then ran a pick through my hair. My shoes smacked the bottom of my feet trudging down the steps, heading for the newspaper stand and the nearest coffee shop.

Pictures of Saigon and Vietnamese refugees covered the front page of the *Times.* Leftover information on the jail sentences for Mitchell, Haldeman, and Ehrlichman dribbled over the second page. Standing on the sidewalk, I skimmed the newspaper while holding my coffee and bag of danish in my other hand. Chilly breezes blew a gust up my shirt, and a weak sun shone from behind puffy white and gray clouds; it was barely spring in New York. After a quick peek at my watch, I shoved the paper under my arm, then walked back to my apartment to call Andie.

There it sat. Parked in the street. The shiny black cockroach. There was no mistaking it. Like a peculiar dream, the car's engine started almost at the precise moment I walked by. I could hear the muffler somewhere behind me in the creeping traffic. It was too awkward to turn and look, but my peripheral vision caught glimpses of the car at my back and my intuition told me that the occupant knew exactly where I lived.

I stopped at the light a block from my apartment. A ragged woman smelling of old urine stepped out of an alley, her bad leg beating the sidewalk in a rhythmic limp. Her palm, open and extended, looked as unwashed as her face. "Can you spare a dollar?" she asked. I seized the opportunity to sneak a peek at the car as I felt in my pocket for change. I didn't recognize the driver: dark-complexion, maybe Italian or Latino. No one sat beside him. The side windows were tinted. It was impossible to see any passengers. Other than the smashed headlight and a missing front license plate, it was a limo similar to those seen on Broadway used by the stars. The grungy woman hobbled away. When the light changed I moved fast to trail the car without breaking into a run, but the vehicles following it shielded the back license plate from view. The car turned a corner and disappeared. Relieved and puzzled, I determined it had to be someone new to the neighborhood or my overworked imagination. The phone call to come back, Chip missing, it all wore on my nerves.

§

"Andie, it's your wake-up call," I said, lighting a cigarette.

"I've been up. How's sin city?"

I cleared my throat. Sitting on my bed, I couldn't think of anything witty to say.

"Something wrong?"

"No. Well. I guess. I keep seeing this car everywhere I go. A black Lincoln. A limo. The windows are tinted, so I can't see who it is. And I still haven't heard from Harry. In fact, the operator says his phone is disconnected."

"Why would anyone be following you?"

"I don't know," I said. I hesitated and blew a line of smoke at my ceiling tile, thinking about what lay above it. It wasn't the time to unveil my recent visit with Calvin and the history behind it. Andie didn't need more to worry about in her weak condition. "It's just my silly imagination. I suppose I'm just tuckered out. That kid Chip who rented and wrecked my apartment? He's missing. A couple detectives questioned me about him yesterday."

"Are you telling me everything? Mavis, I'm frightened."

I could've kicked myself. "It's nothing. Really. You remember how I always saw a bogeyman 'round every corner as a kid. This is the same thing. Forget it."

"If you say so. You call me if you find out what happened to, what's his name, Chip."

"I will. I got to run, sweetie. It's Monday, and I've got the lunch crowd."

"Keep calling me every day for a while longer. I need to know that car is a figment of your wild and wacky imagination."

"I will. Stop worrying. You okay, now?"

"I'm fine. And don't you worry about me either, Mavis. I'm going to get my life straightened around. Sooner or later."

"That's my girl. I love you, Andie Rose."

"That goes double for me," she said.

PREDATOR

Mavis

The next morning a blast of April air rattled the window. I glanced outside. The sun had disappeared into the bleak, cold morning. Even the air inside my apartment was cold and damp. Blustery weather ruffled the steel-gray waters of the Hudson and chased bits of paper and trash down city streets. The wind whistled around buildings as more rain clouds moved across the sky. "Damn. Sitting in the street like a black cat ready to pounce."

Maybe it has something to do with Chip. Scrambling for my purse, I called the number the detectives gave me. After a five-minute hold, an irritated voice erupted on the phone.

"Detective Derrick."

"Yes, um, this is Mavis Dumass. You came to see me the other morning about Chip Atkinson?"

"You heard from him?"

"No, but there's a car that's been following me for a couple days since we talked. It's sitting in the street right now."

"Stay there. Don't answer your door or go anywhere. We'll be right over."

But by the time the detectives arrived, the car had vanished. They told me they'd take another look around the area for the car in question and left me with a piece of advice. "Call us when you hear from Mr. Atkinson, not when you see a suspicious limo in the neighborhood." One of them cursed under his breath, but I pretended not to hear it.

My head hurt. Since my shift had changed to the supper hour, I kept my eyes peeled all morning for the car. Every five minutes I found myself staring out the window. It was as if the car had disappeared. Feeling more ridiculous than ever, I reached for my afghan and sank into my sofa after lunch. Stress and lack of sleep finally took its toll. With my promised call to Andie forgotten, I popped three extra-strength Tylenol into my mouth, washed them down with a couple shots of whiskey, and fell into unintentional deep sleep.

Hours later, I woke to rolling thunder, lightning, and eerie darkness. I'd slept through my shift. Hell, I'd slept the whole day away. I was irritated that nobody had called me. When I picked up the phone, the line was dead. I hit the lamp switch, but nothing happened. Gripped with panic once again, I unwrapped myself from the afghan and rolled off the sofa. I crept to the window. The neighborhood looked like a giant Gothic cemetery right out of an old movie and at the next flash of lightning, I saw it. The limo.

"Damn it! Go away!"

There was nothing to do except wait, and since I had no phone to call the police, I sat at the window in obscurity and watched—and waited. An hour passed and I checked my phone again. Dial tone! I didn't ask for the *Dragnet* detectives that time.

A young policeman in blue showed up at my door. Had it been under different circumstances, I might've asked him back for a drink after his shift. He was black and beautiful with a nice fro and a big smile. "Ma'am, I understand you're concerned a limo has been following you?"

"Yes, it was . . . I mean it is. Come to the window, I'll show you." The car was gone. I strained my neck, peering down both sides of the street. "I tell you it's been following me!"

"I found no car in the area that matches the description you gave. You say the front left fender is damaged?"

"Yes, and it *has* followed me, every day since Saturday. I—I'm sorry. It freaks me out every time I see it."

Sympathetic, the officer said he could do little except circle the area and make a report. I heaved a long sigh and thanked him, then inquired about the power outage.

"Electric company is working on it. Lightning blew out a transformer about seven blocks down. Keep your doors locked, ma'am."

After the officer left, I bolted my door again and searched for Raoul's phone number to apologize for missing work. Raoul didn't answer and Harry's phone was still disconnected. There was no way I was calling Andie. I'd freaked her out enough. Besides, what could she do for me in North Carolina? There was no one left. The loneliness of my life bore down like the storm outside. Sitting in the dark with my head in my hands, I watched the shadows as the black car drove down my street, returning to its perch, its lone headlight hugging the curb.

It finally hit me it really wasn't about Chip. It was about *me*. But I wasn't stupid and they were about to find that out.

The car was still there as it had been the night before and the night before that. They were shoving me, and every part of my obstinate self wanted to shove back. I took a slow breath. I had not anticipated it. It dawned on me, whoever occupied the car couldn't tell if I were home because of the power outage. Staring out the window, I prayed for someone to exit the car. It only hovered on the pavement, as if waiting for a sign of my presence. Outside the rain fell, and the city was as windy as it ever got, like the stirring blasts of God's breath. But not a soul moved.

I'd been dozing when voices in the hall startled me. Looking at my watch, it was almost midnight. I'd not lit a candle, a cigarette, or turned on a flashlight. Padding down the hall in my bare feet, I leaned my ear to the door. Not hearing or seeing anyone through the peephole, I scampered back to the chair by the window to continue my vigil, but the car was mysteriously gone. I didn't stop to think about it. I knew it was time to gather up the only thing someone might be after and send it to Andie.

Climbing onto a chair, I hoisted myself up, squeezed into the crawl space, flipped on a flashlight and collected my evidence. Quickly, I replaced the ceiling tile, then hopped down and moved the chair back against the wall. I had no time to waste so I wrote fast, explaining the contents. After a brief rummage through my desk, I found two books of postage stamps. I licked every last one of them, hoping it'd be enough to get my darkest secrets to North Carolina.

Unwilling to wait until morning, I decided to take advantage of the darkness. Since the car had not reappeared, I pulled my sweatshirt hood over my head and exited the back of the building into the persistent rain. My skin was cold as metal and my clenched jaw ached into my skull as I ran like a deer to the mailbox on the corner. Dense tentacles of fog slithered down the buildings, banding the city in a ghostly grip. The storm and the mysterious car had thrown me into my own private horror movie.

Arriving at the corner, I said a final quick prayer and dropped the only hand I had left to play into the mail receptacle. Walking back to my apartment, I rounded the corner when suddenly the city's lights flickered and came on, illuminating me. The rain had soaked my clothes, and the car appeared in the distance. It looked at me with its one headlight. Immediately, I turned around and scurried away from it and my apartment building. My pulse quickened as I glanced over my shoulder to check behind me. The one-eyed limo followed. Shrouded in the gloom of night and swirling fog, I breathed deep to ward off more panic. I could hear it. I knew my predator was there. Somewhere. Lurking.

Blocks away from my apartment, the limo and the sickly golden glow of its headlight swung around the corner, pursuing me, bouncing over sewer grates and the brick street. I backed into the shadows, out of the light, and wedged myself into the dimness of an alley. The limo stopped. My head snapped sideways, and I froze. Within seconds the demon car crept forward again, nailing me in my tracks. I couldn't see inside because of the streetlight's glare on the windshield, but the hunt was over. With nowhere to run, I waited.

It had stalked me and won. It slid forward again then stopped a short distance from where I huddled in the dark, its engine at a low rumble. The back passenger door opened and someone stepped out. The dark figure of a man walked straight toward me, his long shadow sparkling on the pavement behind him. Trapped, I turned to face my stalker head-on. He walked close to where I stood between a brick wall and a dumpster, his eyes flickering like candle flames in two dark windows. Popping a match with his thumb, he stretched out his arm and held it to my face. "Hello, Mavis. I'm surprised to see you out in this nasty weather."

"Who . . . why? Why are doing this?"

"Now that's Southern hospitality for you."

My voice cracked. "This ain't the South. Besides, Southern hospitality can kill you."

"We'll not talk about that right now. Let's take a ride, then you can invite me to your apartment for a drink and show me what real Southern hospitality is all about, since you're such an expert."

"I'd rather not."

"Mavis," he shook his head. "You have no choice." The gun, clearly visible in his hand, was pointed at my head. "Get in the car."

To Dream The Impossible

Andie

I woke to the sound of my own scream in the stark silence of the trailer. Disoriented, I sat bolt upright, trembling like a child beneath a blanket, my heart beating as if desperate to break out of my chest. For several moments I sat listening to my labored breathing with the sheets bunched in my fists and as frightened as I'd been the night of my accident.

Slowly, I became aware of my surroundings. The dim light from the lone streetlight in the trailer park slanted in through my bedroom blinds. Rain pelted the window. The clock ticked by my bed. The furnace hummed from the hall utility closet.

I fumbled for the chain of my bedside lamp. Shoving back the bedspread, I slid out of bed and limped to the bathroom. I wiped my mouth with the back of my hand, and pushed the hair off my forehead that had stuck to my bandaged head wound. This wasn't a dream about the baby; that much I knew. It was a nightmare that had wrenched me from sleep and bathed me in a cold sweat. All I could recall was a black car. Like the one Mavis had described.

Struggling to get out from under the weight of it, I hobbled back to my room and pulled my hair into a ponytail despite the snarls, smoothing it back with my hand. I grabbed my robe off the bed and looked at the alarm clock. It was nearly three a.m. Not wanting to return to sleep, I crept into the kitchen, opened a bottle of Pepsi, and then carried it to the living room. I needed to hear Mavis say, "What the hell are you doing calling me at this hour?" I needed to hear her voice, even if it grumbled at me sleepy and perplexed, I needed to hear it.

I think someone is following me, Mavis had said. For a moment I stood there, holding the phone, trying hard to shake off the pure fright that had settled over me. Mavis had been almost fearless as a New Yorker. But deep inside I knew *almost* carried no weight when it came to living and working safely in that city.

We'd probably get a good laugh out of her black car paranoia someday; have something hilarious to tell at parties and reunions. In the early morning silence of my trailer, those thoughts played havoc with my own imagination. Separated by miles, I sensed her distress with the same intensity I had once when we were in high school and she lied about a new camera she bought.

Her phone rang and rang and rang. Finally she picked it up. Or someone did.

"Hello? Mavis? Mavis, it's Andie. Are you there?"

Click.

"Mavis!" I assumed she was probably half asleep and had just hung up on me. Either that or I had dialed the wrong number. There was nothing I could do, at least not until morning. I replaced the receiver. "Go back to bed," I muttered. "Mavis is fine." But as I shuffled through the kitchen and crawled into bed, the sound of her voice filled my head.

Andie. So real it startled me.

Mavis wasn't okay. I didn't believe it. Not for a second.

§

I dialed Mavis's number several times the next morning and it rang off the wall. By noon, I stood glaring at my phone nonstop. For two days in a row I'd not heard a peep from her. "Damn it!" Realizing that yelling at the phone was stupid, I tried pacing. Mavis wasn't the most responsible person; it wasn't the first time she'd forgot to pick up the phone and call. More than likely her agent phoned her and they decided to meet. *That'd be just like Mavis to forget I was waiting by the phone.*

But no matter how hard I tried, I couldn't shake the uneasiness churning inside me. At one o'clock, I called Libby.

"Still no word from Mavis?" Libby asked.

"I'm worried sick. Her phone just rings and rings. I called information and got the number for Nicky's Deli, only to have someone named Raoul tell me he's pissed off 'cause she didn't show up for work yesterday. She just started that job. Why would she miss work?"

"Maybe because she's with her agent?"

"She promised to call me every morning, especially since she knows I'm concerned about what she said in her last phone call."

"Have you tried calling the photographer she works for?"

"I tried, but the line's been disconnected."

"What about her neighbors?"

"I don't know any of them." I paused. "I'm calling the police."

Libby's tone softened. "Want me to come to Salisbury?"

For the first time, my concern transformed into nothing short of panic. "There was something in her voice, Libby. I swear, the last time I talked to her she sounded scared. Mavis never gets scared."

"Is there anything I can do?"

"Not at the moment. I'll call you though."

I thought maybe I had the wrong number for Harry, so I dug out the New York City phone book Mavis had sent me for Christmas one year as a joke, as she was always trying to get me to move in with her. I opened it and ran my finger down a column of telephone numbers, searching for Philips Photography. *Harry Philips, photographer to the fashion district.* I dialed— waited. "This number has been temporarily disconnected."

"Damn."

Without putting down the receiver, I flipped through the phone book, determined the police district I needed, then dialed the number. A female voice answered, "New York P.D."

Quickly, I explained the situation, ending with the black Lincoln that had been following Mavis, and asked if the police could help.

"We can do a routine welfare concern check, ma'am. If you'll give me the phone number, address, description of the woman in question, we'll send an officer by her residence to make sure she hasn't had an accident or met with any foul play."

"Thank you." I paused. "She's my . . . she's my best friend."

"You sit tight," the woman officer said, sympathetically. "We'll do our best."

I tried to convince myself I was overreacting. Mavis was a grown woman, after all. Maybe she was on a shopping spree, buying more fancy-schmancy clothes, or in a prissy hotel with some musician having mad, passionate sex and I was a complete idiot.

Or maybe the nightmare was a premonition.

My watch read five o'clock when the police called back. "This is Officer Bender from the New York City Police Department." I recognized the woman's voice. "An officer drove by the apartment building on West End Avenue where Miss Mavis Dumass rents a third floor residence. It seemed secure from the outside. She didn't answer the door, but there was no sign of any problems, breaking and entering. Without a warrant, we can't go inside. According to our records, she did call twice and request someone come out due to the car you mentioned, a Lincoln Town Car. We searched the perimeter of the apartment building. None of our officers found the car in question. Wait."

The officer hesitated. I could hear her flipping through paperwork. She lowered her voice to just above a whisper. "I really shouldn't be telling you this, but our records show she was questioned a few days ago regarding the disappearance of the man who sublet her apartment. The missing person was found dead this morning in a dumpster in the Meadowlands. That's in New Jersey. It definitely puts a whole new light on this."

Silence.

"Ma'am? You still there?"

"Yes."

"May we call you if we need to ask more questions?"

"Yes, of course."

"If you hear from Miss Dumass, please call the New York Police Department."

Panic gripped me by the throat a little harder. None of it made sense. Why was the guy who rented her apartment murdered? And why was Mavis missing? "Believe me, if I hear from her, *I* will call you. I appreciate your help, ma'am . . . officer."

"Sure thing."

I hung up and stumbled into a chair, the officer's words replaying in my head. I knew it was crazy, but I couldn't let it go. I'd never be able to live with myself if Mavis was in some kind of trouble and I did nothing to help. Consumed with worry and an unhealthy dose of irritation, I was at an impasse of what to do until moments later, when the phone rang again.

"If this is you, Mavis, I'm letting you have it for making me worry like this."

"Hello, is this Andie Oliver?"

"Yes, who's this?"

"My name is Harry Philips."

"Yes! Mr. Philips. How did you get my number? Is there a problem with Mavis?" My throat, raw and burning, nearly closed up on me as I stood there hoping he had heard from her.

He returned my question with a question. "Did Mavis return to New York? She gave me your phone number and her father's back in February when she left for North Carolina. I can't reach her father, there's no answer."

A sudden sense of loss exploded inside my head; a loss so miserable that it throbbed like my pulse. "Rupert, I mean Mavis's father, lives on a farm and is usually out in the fields this time of day. Is there a problem?" Annoyed, I wanted him to answer my damn question.

"Well, yes, there is. I need to get in touch with her. I thought she was in North Carolina."

"She went back to New York a week ago, Mr. Philips. She said she tried to call you and couldn't get through. Actually, I've been trying to call you, too. The message says your phone has been disconnected."

"It's disconnected alright. My studio was bombed a few days ago."

"What?"

"Yeah. Blown to Hell and back. Everything I owned, all my equipment, film, negatives, client files, albums, everything, blown up. The police are investigating. I need to get in touch with Mavis. Some of her work was destroyed. And, of course, I need to tell her I'm out of business. At least for a few months. Thank God for insurance. You say she's in New York?"

"Yes. Doesn't she have your home phone?"

"My home was in the loft above my studio. I was out for the evening. Thank God, again."

Fear rose in my voice. "Harry, excuse me . . . Mr. Philips."

"Harry is fine."

"Okay, Harry, I can't find Mavis. I'm very concerned. The last time I talked to her, she was scared. Said she was being followed. Her agent had called her back to New York, but when she contacted him after she arrived, he denied he'd called her. Then she tried to reach you. I've been calling her apartment for two days. It sounded like she answered her phone last night and just hung up."

"That's strange. From what you're telling me, I'm guessing my studio was bombed before she returned to New York. She couldn't reach me because I'm living with my mother until the police investigation is over."

I held back my tears. "Mavis said when she got home it looked like a tornado hit her apartment. The guy who rented it left it a wreck and now, according to the police, he's dead."

"Chip? Chip Atkinson? That guy's a neat freak! He wouldn't have wrecked her apartment. I photographed his sister's wedding in Brooklyn. Dead? They say how?"

"No. Just that he was found in a dumpster in a meadow somewhere in New Jersey."

"Man-o-man, this is the pits! I *introduced* Chip to Mavis."

"The police questioned Mavis about him earlier. Why hasn't she called me? She promised to call every day."

"Mrs. Oliver—"

"You can call me Andie if I can call you Harry."

"Fine. Andie. I have a key to her apartment. She gave me a key when we worked together. I would occasionally have to—oh, what the hell—we slept together a while. She's a beautiful woman, as you know. I've told her over and over she's more stunning than most of the models in my photo shoots."

"You're right, she is. Harry, please, go see if she's okay. For me. Please."

"Sure. If I had known she had come back to New York, I'd have been over there already. I'll take a detective friend of mine. He owes me a favor. I think we need to play it safe. Damn."

"If you see her, tell her I'm pissed off and she'd better not do this again. Tell her to get her butt to a phone."

"Try not to worry. I know her hangouts. I'll find her."

"Harry, thank you. Bless you. I didn't want to come to New York to look for her myself. That city scares the shit out of me."

"I know. Me too."

For one split-second, snarly, cold fingers reached for the key to my heart. But I refused to let go of it. Mavis was fine. She had to be.

ABDUCTED BUTTERFLY

Mavis

Facing the back of the car, I felt the city streak past me with no way to escape. Tears bubbled from my eyes and terror dropped into my gut as if he were dangling me from the Brooklyn Bridge over the East River. I had fought him, but he had covered my mouth with duct tape, bound my hands behind me, and wrapped a loop of cord around my feet and neck before pushing me out of the car and into the alley behind my apartment building. The Town Car sped away. I never saw it again.

"Don't need your key," he said. "I found one on a guy named Chip. You know him? Poor bastard. Innocent prick, too. Just happened to be in the wrong place at the wrong time." I knew he was going to do to me what he'd done to Chip. Whatever he wanted.

He pulled me toward the building. I knew any sound I might make would burn up energy I couldn't spare. But I couldn't help it. He meant to kill me. *I don't want to die.* Allowing myself to go limp, I hoped to make it difficult for him and create some noise to attract the attention of anyone who might be in the area. It pissed him off when I refused to hop forward and he threw my head to the ground in a swirl of stars. Loose debris on the asphalt ripped a hole in my jeans and bit into my flesh. Tiny fierce stabs struck my skull. In a fraction of darkness, blood pooled in my mouth and I whined like a wounded dog, hoping it would take the place of my scream, but the pathetic little sounds amused him and he laughed.

In the wee hours of the morning, there were no sounds of help from New York.

Opening the service door, he lifted me by the cord, and dragged me like a bag of trash. My struggle was useless; my heels dug into the carpeted steps all the way to the third floor. With tape across my mouth, my voice was no more than a desperate rasp to inhale. Quickly, he opened my apartment door. A reeling blow met my temple, sending me to the floor. Pain and blackness ricocheted within my head, while bands of duct tape rendered me immobile. Breathing in ragged hysteria through flared nostrils, I gagged, my mind screaming as the blood in my mouth slid into my throat. Foolishly, I thought perhaps if my brain screamed loud enough, someone might rescue me.

The door shut quietly behind us. Once again, he rammed his gloved fist into my face, stunning me to another moment of sparkles. My knees collided off the wall beside me, like a trapped butterfly in a glass jar. Grabbing me by my hair, he pulled me from the hallway, leaving me lying in the bedroom. Cool air bled beneath the door. A blessed moment of solace. But my world faded in and out as I heard my phone ringing and ringing. He walked to answer it, his boots echoing down the hall like rifle shots. He picked up the receiver, replaced it gently on the hook, then walked back. And kicked me. Repeatedly.

"You willing to talk yet? We can rip off that tape."

I nodded slowly. He bent over me and yanked the tape off my mouth. "Please," I whispered. My vision was all but gone. I spit out blood. It dripped down my face and onto the floor. "Listen—to—me," I begged.

"Tell me. Tell me what I want to know," he demanded. "Where are they!"

Pain ripped through me, each breath like a knife twisting inside my chest, but I spoke slowly and softly, deliberate words, pleadings, nothing he wanted to hear, but things I had to say. I was done. *Now. Get it over with.*

"That's a lie!" In a quick instant, he tore open my sweatshirt and bared my breasts. Next, he stripped my jeans down to my ankles. As he yanked them off, my shoes came with them. I lay naked and exposed. The phone rang again and again, but he ignored it.

"You know, I have no intention of using this gun. Too noisy." He sat beside me on the floor and waited, staring at my naked body. The next thing I knew, my head met with the end of his gun, over and over again, breaking every bone in my face and skull into pieces—slaughtering me like an animal.

Mucus mixed with blood collected in my mouth under a new slab of duct tape, my only airway being one open nostril. In the next instant he forced himself inside me, grunting like an old hog. We slid on the hardwood in his sweat and my blood. Finally, my god finally, he finished and I lay beneath him, feeling his shallow breaths against the hollowed part of my neck. The pain engulfed me then evaporated as my heartbeat slowed. But my hope for survival was already dead. My body, broken in so many places, could no longer move. Perhaps he would leave me to die alone, but I was conscious enough to know he would not take the chance of being identified by me later. My thoughts were of Andie, that I had once said I would die for her. My only hope was that she receive the envelope in time.

Through the tiny opening of one swollen eye I saw he had rolled away from me. Still, I felt the weight of him. He moved in close again, laying the cold blade of a knife on my chest, between my breasts. He lit a cigarette, his face flaring visible for a moment before he smiled and pulled the tape off my mouth one last time. I had no air left in my lungs to scream, no voice to utter a sound. "Go sing in Hell, Mavis," he said, slitting my throat, as my mama took me by the hand and pulled me up to a more brilliant sunrise than I had ever seen.

A Long Night

Andie

Joe's suitcase fell to the floor of the trailer with a thud.

"You're finally home." I felt a rush of sympathy for him, despite myself. His eyes were red and sunk into his head as if he hadn't slept in days.

"I hope I don't have to go on too many of these business trips until he hires me."

"Me too. You've already missed three days with Coot this week. We can't afford it, Joe."

"I know what we can and can't afford. When can *you* go back to work?"

I looked at my husband as if I'd never seen him before. Limping to a kitchen chair, I eased myself into it. "It's only been a few weeks. I'll go back to work when Dr. Eshelman says I can." Fresh tears stung my eyes.

He threw a House of Praise envelope on the table. I opened it to find large bills tucked inside. I stared in disbelief.

"Reverend Artury figured we could use it since I've missed some work."

I felt strange about accepting it. Yet, I couldn't help but think about the past due bills I was going to pay. "Why cash?"

"Why do you care? It's five hundred friggin' dollars."

"Tell him thank you, for me."

"You can tell him yourself. When you return to church."

I changed the subject. "I can't find Mavis."

"What do you mean, you can't find Mavis?"

"She hasn't called me like she promised. I'm worried."

He pulled off his boots, then ran his fingers through his hair. "She lives in New York. You've never seen that city. The place doesn't sleep. She could be anywhere. Don't worry about her, worry about yourself. And don't you be making a ton of long distance calls, you hear?"

I hobbled to the sink and ran water for dishes to hide the sound of my tears.

Joe stretched out on the couch and sighed. "Did she say anything to you? Did she sound concerned about anything last time you talked?"

I hesitated. I did not trust him in matters of Mavis. He didn't like her, and Mavis detested him. I wasn't about to give Joe a reason to enjoy her disappearance.

"No, she promised to call me because I asked her to. That's all. I'm having a rough time since our baby died. In case you haven't noticed."

"I'm sorry," he sighed. "I'm just so tired right now. If you hear from her, tell her I hope I never see her again."

"Why do you hate her so? She's my dearest friend in the world."

"Because she always hated *me*. And because she turned into a New York bitch who thinks she's so much better than the people down here. She rubs me the wrong way. I've always known she was jealous I married you. Hey, maybe *she* wanted to marry you, you think?"

"That's not funny. Mavis is as straight as I am. She loves me because we've been friends since birth."

"Can we talk about something else? I'm beat."

"If the phone rings, let me answer it. I'm expecting a call from the photographer she works with. He went to check on her."

"Fine, you answer all calls. I need to sleep before I head to Coot's."

"Did you meet with TV people for two days straight?"

"What?"

"You said you—"

"Why do you want to know all of a sudden?"

"Just making conversation, Joe. Trying to keep my mind off Mavis."

"We met with executives at Panasonic and Sony."

"I forgot where you said you were this weekend."

"Los Angeles. My ticket stubs are in my bag in case you want to check."

"You need to start leaving me emergency numbers."

"And you need go back to church and start paying attention to what the Lord's doing in the crusades."

"Maybe I should," I said. "Maybe I should be at every one of them, watching out for redheads."

Joe mumbled as he flipped on the TV. "What was it the guy said at the end of that movie you love? I think it was something like, frankly, my dear, I don't give a damn."

§

Joe's voice on the phone sounded tense and tired. I didn't care. I wanted off the phone, in case Harry called. I'd waited all day for his call. "Coot needs me to work on an engine. Needs it rebuilt by the end of the week. I'll be home late," he said.

Coot yelled in the background "It's legit, Andie!" He'd volunteered his services; to keep Joe on the straight and narrow by promising to wrap his massive hands around Joe's neck if the need arose.

"Fine." I hung up.

Cocooning myself in the darkness of the trailer, I had all but chewed my fingernails clean off when the phone rang. Harry delivered a nightmare through miles of telephone wire. His voice was strained and cracked; I could hear his tears. He and his friend, a detective from Queens, had opened Mavis's apartment door and followed a trail of blood. With the bedroom door ajar, they could see her. He said the sight knocked him to his knees. Mavis had been beaten, raped, and murdered. Harry pushed the next few words past his vocal cords. I barely heard him. "Andie? You still there?"

"Mavis's birthday is next month. She'll be twenty-three," I said.

"Andie?"

"Yes?"

"The police are investigating; they want her father to identify the body. Should I call him before the police do?"

I replied, "No. Please don't allow anyone to call him. I have to tell him. Only me." I spoke slowly, my voice just above a whisper. "I'll be coming to New York with her father to make arrangements and bring her home. Where can I reach you? I'll need your assistance."

Harry repeated his phone number twice. I thanked him, standing silent for a moment after he said goodbye. The phone receiver slipped from my fingers and dropped to the floor. It would have hurt less if someone had taken a baseball bat to my body.

With my foot and head still bandaged, I managed to crawl to the couch where I sat alone, in shock, and unbelievable grief. Carrying a burden not even an animal should bear. The desolation of my life without Mavis melted me to my knees. Throwing my arms up pitifully over my head, I fell flat to the carpet and wept until it took every ounce of strength I had left to stand and stumble to the bathroom where I vomited. Weak, I lay near the toilet until I was finally able to stagger back to the living room. I'd lost my son and my Mavis within a month's time. I wanted to die.

§

At midnight, Joe arrived home. "Why are you sitting in the dark?" He switched on a light.

I blinked. The brightness hurt my eyes. I stood in stages, but I couldn't make my lips move. Finally, I uttered in the tone of a woman gone mad, "She . . . she's dead. Mavis is dead. Someone raped her, and then murdered her. Why would someone do that, Joe? What . . . what kind of a monster could do that? What could Mavis have done to make someone hate her that much?"

Joe caught my elbows as I went down. My knees buckled. My body had abandoned me. Awkwardly, he lowered me to the floor. I bent my face to my knees and wrapped my arms over my head, wanting to dissolve — evaporate. Nothing was worth living for.

After some time he managed to lift me into a kitchen chair. I pushed him away with the palms of my hands, then coughed and gagged again. There was nothing in my stomach. My voice raspy and faint, I shivered.

"You're in shock," he said. Grabbing Maudy's old quilt off the back of the couch, he wrapped it around me. "Come on, Andie, lie down."

"Leave me alone."

Joe pulled a chair close and stroked my hair. I sat rigid and cold and said nothing until he put his hand on my leg.

"I said, leave . . . me . . . alone."

"Fine. Try to sleep. I'm going to bed."

I heard only the faintest sound of him. The longest night of my life had just begun.

LIKE JOHN BOY WALTON

Reverend Calvin Artury

"Death and life are in the power of the tongue: and they that love it shall eat the fruit thereof," I said, smiling at Evan like the brilliant light of dawn. "Find Joe, tell him to stick close to his wife. We need to know what she knows."

Evan sat behind his desk and fumbled through files. "What if she leaves him after all this?"

I glared into Evan's golden eyes. "Then he better turn into John Boy Walton. You tell him that. Give him the week off. Make sure he wines, dines, coos, and woos her. I want her followed. Okay, enough about the Olivers. Let's talk about our television station at the next meeting with Silas. I want to increase the budget. *60 Minutes* wants an interview, and you need to follow up on that."

Reading every item, I marked them off the list with my new ornate fountain pen, a gift from a local judge and her husband. "Make sure we give a special love offering to the Gibson family. Bless their hearts, they lost their mama this week to cancer. Oh yes, I want to honor our mothers this year for Mother's Day. Special cakes or flowers, you decide. Remember to get the contribution in to Judge VanOrson's campaign on time. And Evan, don't forget, have your secretary schedule a meeting with the builder. I want the final touches on the Praise Buffet completed before the grand opening, during Camp Meeting services over the Fourth of July weekend."

I had decided it was no longer sacrilegious to partake of food on church property. It was profitable.

Taking my time, I replaced the cap over the nib of the pen and offered it to Evan who reacted as if it were a two-edged sword. I smiled, cocking my head slightly. "It's yours. I've got a drawer full."

I was pleased to notice the briefest of smiles flicker across Evan's face. I then handed him an envelope stuffed with cash. It was time to get back to business.

On A Day Like Today

Andie

By five a.m., I had called Libby. At seven, she stood at my front door. As I fell into her arms, a mournful wail like the sound of a wounded animal escaped from my throat. Denial and disbelieving chords of agony mixed into one long, sad cry. Streaks of mascara on the puffy, fair skin beneath Libby's red eyes told a story of her own sorrow she couldn't wipe away. We stood holding each other until Joe walked into the kitchen, moving around us as if my shock and grief were a common sight in his home. He opened the door to leave for work and smiled at Libby, but spoke to me. "I'll be home after work. Don't worry about supper. I'll grab a burger."

I ignored him.

He winked at Libby. "Tell Ray to call me. I might be able to swing a day off from Coot next week," he said, picking up the newspaper off the porch. "We can go shoot some turkey." After tossing the paper onto the kitchen floor, he let the door slam behind him on his way out.

My sister-in-law only shook her head in silence, her face blemished with emotion. I felt her shudder. Oblivious to death—certainly that of his son and now of Mavis, Joe started the engine to my Cougar and then peeled out of the driveway. The rage in my head was suffocating, but as I glanced at an article on the front page of the daily paper, I forgot about Joe for a minute. *Ken Kopper, Owner of Winston-Salem's Kopper Kettle Diner Found Dead.* He'd been shot in the head.

§

Libby helped me dress and eat a bite of food. I tried desperately to pull myself together, and swallowed a Valium to keep from falling apart. I had to see Rupert right away. I wanted to go to New York and see Mavis's body. I'd have to borrow money from Daddy, but I had to see what some animal had done to her. I would insist on it. Rupert could stand in the wings, but I could not live the rest of my life without seeing Mavis one more time. It was a decision I made in the darkness; in the early morning hours as I sat alone, listening to the sounds of the refrigerator and furnace. I had to see her one more time.

§

I crawled into Libby's truck and we were off to find Rupert, but the mail carrier had blocked the street. I leaned my head out the window to hear what he was hollering. "What'd you say?"

"I said I got a package here for you, Mrs. Oliver; it won't fit in the mailbox. Want me to leave it in the door?"

"Sure, that'd be fine."

Ralph walked a thick manila envelope up to the trailer and stuck it behind the screen door. I froze a moment, thinking I should get it. But my exhausted body rebelled against the thought of walking back to the trailer.

"Want me to get it for you?" asked Libby.

"No, no . . . whatever it is, it can wait."

"What do you think it is?"

"On a day like today, nothing important, I'm sure. Let's go."

§

I was silent. Memories of Mavis met me at every turn in the road. I rested my head against the truck window as Libby drove deeper into Forsyth County farmland. We passed a mud-splattered truck with a Confederate flag strapped across the grille, a rifle mounted in the back window, and cages filled with roosters in the truck bed.

"No wonder Mavis left the South, except the North wasn't any kinder to her," Libby said.

I gazed into the fields, remembering that Mavis had hoed and harvested tobacco to make money to buy school clothes; that she helped her mother take in laundry and iron shirts until every finger bore scars from the steam iron; that for twelve years Mavis walked two miles to the school bus stop, their farmhouse sitting just that far from the main road. With everything she encountered attending an all-white school, she had deserved the best in life and was offered a bitter cup. I prayed whomever did this to Mavis would fry in Hell—and soon.

The road to the Dumass farm twisted and dipped deeper into a valley. I smelled the Yadkin River as the land leveled out. Branches slapped the windshield of Libby's pickup as we bumped over a dirt road no better or bigger than a tractor path. I thought of Rupert and his quiet demeanor, his face rutted like a dried-up field, eyes that didn't blink much even when he smiled. Not much taller than Mavis, and dark like Daddy: they could've been brothers. This would finish him, and I had no idea how to tell him, how to begin.

Libby's eyes grew stern and righteous as she drove. Despair and anger tinged her voice. "I don't understand why someone would do that to her. You sure Rupert's out here?"

"I've known the man all my life. We'll find him in his fields before we find him anywhere else." I could not answer the rest. There was no reason fit for speaking.

"There, pull over next to that post. I see him." I held onto Libby's arm as we stumbled down a slight hill where a weathered fence girdled the property. In a nearby tree, a young robin screamed for breakfast. Libby held the barbed wire open and I crawled between the wires next to a spider holding fast to her swaying web—a miracle of strength to keep her home together that for some reason God didn't give to me. The sound of a woodpecker reminded me of Rupert, the way they both beat their heads against all odds to survive. Stepping onto the fertile field, I watched him cultivate his tight rows with the same worn-out hoe I'd seen him use year after year; the blade bowed in, the handle made smooth and dark from his sweat. Like a plow mule, Rupert kept his eyes on the ground straight ahead of him. His tobacco grew no more than two feet apart near the river, which was his blessing. Yet I could not help but think, his bountiful crops, his way of life, his blessings had come to an end.

Rupert was hard of hearing. I knew calling out his name was fruitless so I waited for him to finish, recalling how Mavis and I used to string tobacco leaves on sticks and hang them in the barn to cure. The gum made our hands brown and stuck to our skin like school glue. Libby and I moved further into the field, walking on weeds and dirt Rupert had hoed up. I think he heard us then because he stopped and turned around to find us only a few feet behind him.

He didn't say, "What's the matter?" or "What happened?" He said, "It's Mavis. She's dead." The back of my neck prickled. Men like Rupert who lived so close to the land seemed to know those things before anyone else. I nodded. Libby caught him as he fell to his knees with his arms folded around his head, hiding his face and crying like a lost child. I fell into the dirt next to him. Libby crouched by both of us, handing me a tissue. Rupert pounded his fist on the ground and cried out. "Why, God? Why Loretta, now Mavis . . . please answer me, God!"

"Matthew five and forty-five." I said. "*For He maketh the sun to rise on the evil and on the good, and sendeth rain on the just and the unjust.* It falls where it falls. Rupert, remember what Job said? *Though he slay me, yet will I trust in Him.* It's the way of things. We have to trust Him. I don't know why my baby had to die either. I've walked around like a crazy person for days. I think our challenge is not to make sense of their deaths, but to show the purpose of their lives." I began to sing. Though not the powerful pipes of Mavis, my voice floated over the tobacco field like smoke. *Farther along we'll know all about it, Farther along we'll understand why, Cheer up my brother, Live in the sunshine, We'll understand it, All by and by.*

Rupert stood, took hold of my shoulders and kissed my cheek. I managed a faint smile. He pulled his red bandana handkerchief from his back pocket and wiped the dust from his face, as though it would make the world the same as it had been the week before, the year before, or the hour before we walked into his field. "God speaks to me through the mouths of babes. Let's get on to the house. Lula will need telling before hearing it from someone else."

Rupert and Libby all but carried me to the truck. I had to get to bed and right soon. He would have to break the news to Lula without me. An emotional woman, Lula would take days to calm down. Rupert sat in the bed of Libby's pickup as she drove him home. I said goodbye from the truck window informing him I was accompanying him to New York on Sunday. When he started to protest, I stopped him. "Nothing can keep me from going. Nothing."

. . . ain't no mountain high enough . . .

§

I arrived home that afternoon and found Joe squatting on the front porch, polishing his boots. "You left work early?" I asked.

"Yeah. Thought I'd take you with me to Mama's for supper, and I bought your favorite ice cream. It's in the freezer."

His mouth moved, but I heard nothing. Staring at the screen door, I recalled the envelope the mailman delivered, and that I'd asked Mavis for copies of the pictures she took while visiting in North Carolina. "Anything for me in the mail? Ralph stuck a big envelope in the door as I was leaving with Libby, but I was too tired to get it."

"Nothing important," he said. "Coupons and a free sample of toothpaste. That brand I don't like. I threw it out."

"Oh," I said. "Just as well."

Amazing Mavis Grace

Andie

Harry Philips met Rupert and me in Newark and escorted us to a waiting taxi. Rupert, subdued in his seat, studied the New York skyline. "How could anyone like it here? Constant noise, and can't see a tree or a blade of grass nowhere. Mavis wasn't like Loretta. She sure had dreams far from the farm."

I nodded, but I knew that long before Rupert did. Oblivious to the sights before me, I paid little attention to the city during my first ever taxi ride, only reading the street names, *West 71st, West 72nd, West 73rd . . .*

Harry was tall and rawboned with a likable smooth face. It was obvious why Mavis had been attracted to him. His gray temples, square jaw, and almost Southern mannerisms gave off an air of genteelness. He explained that after the police finished their investigation of Mavis's apartment, he had hired a cleaning crew to scour and repaint before our arrival. I hadn't thought about the mess left in the wake of her death. Thankful for Harry and his support, I invited him to North Carolina for the funeral. He politely declined. He was leaving New York City. I completely understood. Mavis's death had changed the direction of his life. Of all our lives.

Rupert retrieved Mavis's keys at the police department. A kind policewoman requested that he collect not only her body, which had been held at the Center Street morgue, but also her personal effects. The property manager wanted to rent the apartment by the first of May.

Harry asked the cab driver to pull up to the curb and drop us off at the entrance of Mavis's building. Promising to pick us up in a couple hours, Harry left us standing on the sidewalk. He was on his way to Chip Atkinson's memorial service. Alone in New York, Rupert and I looked out of place—like a couple of turtles in the middle of Times Square. I slipped my arm through his, both of us leaning on each other for strength. "You ready?" I asked.

He nodded.

I squared my shoulders and we ascended the stairs since the elevator was out of order. Rupert had trouble with the key. The lock seemed stiff, as if new, but he finally got it to fit and the door creaked open. We stepped into the last home Mavis had known, and closed the door behind us.

The whole apartment was smaller than I had imagined, but cozy. I walked into the bedroom by myself. The air was dank; the electricity had been shut off. Sunlight streamed through the windows. The room smelled of antiseptic and cleaning fluids. I stared at the foot of her bed. The place Harry said he found her. I dropped to my knees touching the floor where Mavis had lain, dying. A soft breeze blew into the room from somewhere. *Give her of the fruit of her hands; and let her own works praise her in the gates.* I began to think that maybe we don't become that impossible Proverbs thirty-one woman until after we die. The fruit of Mavis's hands became evident as my attention was drawn to her framed photographs covering the walls in every room of her apartment. A virtual gallery of photography.

I got up before Rupert could see my tears. Wandering from room to room, by the time I walked into the kitchen, he had already emptied half of it into boxes. The place was spotless. The crew had done a good job. I refused to think about the blood and the mess and got busy helping Rupert. Mavis was to be cremated, and the following day we would carry her ashes back to Winston-Salem. Our home. A city where the streets had good Southern names, like Marshall, Reynolda, and Silas Creek Parkway. The city I wished Mavis had never left.

I poked my head into the bathroom. All white and chrome, I emptied it—tampons, deodorant, Tylenol—into the trash. Drawer after drawer, her closets and her desk, we boxed it all or threw it away. I pulled down every photograph, took them out of the frames, and would carry them home along with her photo albums. Professional pictures she took of people and friends in New York. People I didn't recognize. A little girl and a man I assumed was the girl's father, or maybe her uncle. And I found Mavis's backpack. Her camera was missing, as well as any rolls of film. Rupert discovered a couple items he wanted, and I took a few more things. Odd things, really. I picked up the blue afghan her mother had crocheted for her and a few pieces of costume jewelry. Furniture and remaining boxes were left for the Salvation Army. By five o'clock, we had collected what was left of Mavis's possessions and closed the door behind us.

That evening, Harry took us to Nicky's Deli for supper. The staff gathered and expressed their condolences, while Raoul picked up the tab. A new waitress served cake for dessert as Rupert stirred sugar into his coffee. "I believe the police are doing all they can," he said.

For the first time, Harry showed his frustration. "Then where the hell are the results? Those damn cops call every damn day and tell us what they've produced. You know what they've produced? Jack shit. They've done nothing." He lit a cigarette with a steel Zippo and took a long drag.

"It takes some time to make headway in an investigation of this magnitude, I would imagine," Rupert said.

Harry stuck out his lower lip and exhaled a cloud of smoke over his face. "Look," he said, trying to contain his anger, "if this were my daughter, I'd . . ."

I smiled as Rupert reached across the table and patted Harry's arm. Harry needed a lesson in self-control. "I may be a quiet man, and I may even seem a little distanced from all of this. But one thing you must understand, Mr. Philips. There's a vast difference between this fast-paced world you and Mavis lived in and the one to which I am accustomed. I have no doubt that someday the person who did this will stand before God for his crime. Whether now or in the hereafter, it does not matter to me, sir. God knows who murdered my daughter. His vengeance is worse than mine could ever be. That is enough for me. It has to be."

§

The next morning, I walked alone into the room where she lay. The morgue was blue, steel, and sterile and smelled like a high school science lab. And it was cold. Ice cold. The attendant watched me limp to the table. He brought the sheet down from Mavis's head to her shoulders, and then left the room to give me privacy.

I prayed for strength. Holding back tears that had formed under my eyelids, I reached into my purse, pulled out a pair of nail scissors and a tiny envelope, and snipped a lock of Mavis's hair where the blood had dried. Her face distorted and her body swollen beyond belief, she was nearly unrecognizable, and I stood there holding her stiff right hand watching her face, as if my love for her might bring her back. But the deep wound at her neck the coroner did his best to close, shook me to my senses. Feeling the scar across her palm, the pain in my heart became a sick and fiery gnawing. I gripped my microphone key chain in one hand and Mavis's hand in the other, and cried out loud. "I'm so sorry, Mavis! No matter what it costs, or how long it takes, please, God, please uncover the monster who did this."

§

The grave's timeless smile creases every skull, but her smile was gone forever. The cremated remains of Mavis Grace Dumass and her mother were laid to rest under a monument placed above fields of new tobacco. It was the most majestic, and yet the most lonesome grave on earth. Next to the site, weeds poked through piles of dirt and around a few excavated rocks. On soft hills in the near distance, a length of white oaks and hickory brushed the sky. The bottomland waited to be hoed. Only the coarse grass and thistle near the tiny cemetery had been bush hogged and rolled to an appearance of cleared land.

Daddy dug the grave with his backhoe under a large oak. He also built a three-foot high picket fence that surrounded the site, and ordered a pink granite stone with the dates of Mavis's short life chiseled deep beneath her name, and her mother's on the opposite side. Rupert was grateful and offered to pay for it, but Daddy wouldn't hear of it.

No burial was more impressive. The air was spiked with the smell of fresh-turned earth as the mourners broke the silence of the desolate farm, singing low, sorrowful songs and weeping in the muted, slanting light. I stood next to the stone, my flip-flops caked with red dirt, my bare legs spotted with mud. Dr. Goodwin in his black suit, stood at the headstone and bellowed long and loud about the mansions in Heaven that God had made for his children. "From dust thou art made and unto dust thou shall return," he said. I only half-listened until Lula sang *Amazing Grace* with sorrow borne from unfathomable grief, causing chills to ripple down every spine. Those around Lula joined her, singing and swaying as if drunk on spiritual wine. I closed my eyes, imagining an angel standing in our midst—a real Arch Angel of flesh and blood, full of the Spirit and fraught with anguish, wielding a vengeful sword at his side. I felt a closeness to God at that moment, knowing Mavis was home, and that no one would ever hurt her again.

Lula continued to sing with her face to the sky. The sun set over the trees, blue sky against brown earth. The possibilities of a God became evidence of a real one that incredible evening. After placing the ashes of Mavis and her mama in the ground, I slipped off my flip-flops and laid them on the grave. She had bought them for me when she came back to Winston-Salem, just a scant few weeks before. For over an hour I remained there, holding hands with Libby and Ray. Joe had refused to attend, and I was glad. I didn't want his sympathy.

Almost as silently as they had assembled, the hushed crowd slowly broke apart. Looking for Rupert, I turned to walk the long path back to the house in my bare feet. I hadn't seen him during the funeral. And then there he stood, alone on a grassy knoll. He spoke first to his folded hands and then to a silent horizon before approaching me. Pulling me into a hug, he whispered into my ear. "Be careful, Andie, be very careful." He didn't make any sense and I didn't ask, but the strength of his arms was firm and persuasive, and I kissed his soft, tear-stained cheek. I knew Rupert was broken and tired. He needed rest. His sweet concern for me was not important at the moment. I was on my way home to pack and leave Joe for good.

PART FOUR
And The Earth Was Without

July 1975

EVERYTHING I WANT

Andie

I packed my things, made three trips, and moved back to Winston-Salem and into my old bedroom. For weeks afterward, I endured Joe's endless telephone calls at all hours. Begging. Pleading for me to come home. Beseeching calls from Maudy woke me every morning. An endless supply of roses arrived every payday. Cards and letters, all from Joe. He was wooing me. I had to admit, it felt good. He nearly swayed me, but I held firm. Mostly because of Daddy and Dixie, truth be told. I decided to file for a divorce—until the day Pastor DeSanto called to explain he had been counseling Joe daily for months. He said that he understood me, and agreed I had every right to be angry at Joe's infidelity. His trespasses. Then he said, "What about forgiveness, Andie? How many times did Christ tell us to forgive?"

"Seventy times seven," I answered sheepishly.

"Withholding forgiveness and love is not Christ-like, Andie. God would forgive you. He's forgiven Joe. How can you do less?"

When the doorbell rang the next morning, it was Joe—on his knees, in full-blown tears and a new and improved declaration of love. Gripping a handful of freshly picked roses from somebody's garden, he held up the bouquet and said, "A peace offering." This time, his promise included working toward my goal of a better place to live. I wanted to believe Joe's new confessions of devotion. I wanted it more than anything. Standing in the doorway with my arms around Joe, I looked back at Daddy. He only shook his head, gave me a look, and walked away.

"She's a glutton for punishment," Dixie said.

That same day I moved back to Shady Acres in unbearable summer heat. Two dozen pink roses and a Hallmark card sat on my nightstand. When I lifted the roses from the box a large thorn pricked my ring finger. Blood dribbled down the back of my hand and I stood there watching it forge a path through the hair on my arm, mesmerized by its tiny trail. I couldn't move until Joe hollered for me to get the lead out and help him unload the car. He needed to hurry and pack. It was Friday and he was already late.

Left alone, my mind swirled with images of Mavis. I spent my time disappearing down endless corridors of my past, drowning in recurring memories, and rediscovering the blessed comfort of food. I was not one to indulge in the unacceptable behavior of alcohol and drugs, but I did participate in the tolerated addiction of overeating. Pounds of carbohydrates, fats, sugar, and caffeine. And to appease my husband, I found a job serving the lunch crowds at Newberry's, a popular local restaurant. The cook sent me home with boxes of leftovers. Although my mind stayed occupied the four hours a day I worked, nights and weekends became a feeding frenzy. I refused to answer the phone, watched non-stop TV, inhaled massive amounts of food, and then fell into a coma until it was time for work the next day.

Watching Joe pack yet another suitcase, I twirled my ponytail around my fingers, sighed, and trailed him back and forth from room to room like a forlorn puppy. "Can't Calvin find you some help? Give you one night a week off, one weekend off? For crying out loud, he doesn't even pay you."

"You don't get it do you? I'm a disciple of Christ. My reward is in Heaven. Besides, nobody knows the audio equipment like I do. I *can't* take any time off. Monday is trio practice, Tuesday choir, Wednesday quartet, Thursday I edit tapes, every Friday we leave for a crusade. It's as hard on me as it is on you, Andie. Once I'm a full-time employee, it'll ease up. Promise."

"We need to talk about moving to Winston. You said we'd talk about it."

Joe slammed the lid on his new suitcase. "Then you get a better job. Or wait until I'm making twice what I make at Coot's garage. Then we'll talk about it." He kissed me. "Go spend the weekend with Mama. At least she has an air conditioner. See ya Monday."

Sitting on the edge of the bed in the quiet, I cursed my inability to get on with my life, then looked at myself in the mirror. Moments later I was out the door, it was bargain night at Hoggy's Barbecue.

§

Libby said she knocked several times before she panicked and drove to the nearest pay phone to call Maudy, who arrived at my trailer moments later with her spare key and a bad attitude. I could hear it the moment she pushed open the front door. "Andie? Where the heck are you?"

When Libby opened my bedroom door, Maudy pushed her out of the way and gasped, "Lord, sugah, wake up. It's noon. You sick?"

"She's not sick. She's hung over!"

"Hung over? Libby, Andie don't drink. Ain't a drop of liquor touched those lips as long as I've known her."

"Not booze. Food. Look at this place!"

Candy bar wrappers, Krispy Kreme boxes, and KFC carry-out tubs littered my bedroom. I had amassed piles of empty soda bottles, an assortment of Burger King bags, and pizza boxes in the kitchen. My refrigerator and freezer were empty, except for a half-eaten two-gallon container of butter pecan ice cream. I had stashed empty pie pans from the restaurant and Styrofoam containers from the past week's lunch specials in the sink since the trash was full. My otherwise spotless single-wide smelled like rotting fruit.

I rolled over in my sweat-soaked bed, opened my sleepy eyes, and wiped my cottonmouth. "How'd you two get in?" I could hear Libby doing something in the kitchen.

Maudy cupped my face with her hands. "Sugah, you need to get up, get a shower, come home with me and Al for a couple days, get away from this stinking depression you're in."

Libby stomped back into the bedroom. "This place smells as bad as you look! Andie, get out of that bed and into a shower, and I'm not taking no for an answer. You see yourself lately? You look like shit—sorry, Maudy—but she does."

"Stop it, Libby!" I said. "What do you know about what I've been through? You've got a good man, an education, a pretty house, and good job! And you wear a size two! What do you know about suffering?"

Libby walked around my bedroom picking up trash. "Quit feeling sorry for yourself. You're a food junkie, and *you* are still alive. But you won't be long if you don't stop. Your heart's going to give out before you're thirty. And you can still have more babies. Mavis would be ashamed of you! How dare you destroy her good name and memory like this? Have you even been to see Rupert since the funeral?"

I moaned and buried my face in my pillow. Libby knew her words were the shot in the arm needed to rouse me from my sugar stupor. My pillow muffled my words. "I've been eating like this since I married Joe."

"Don't blame Joe," Maudy said.

Libby snickered. "No, you're right. It wasn't Joe who put the fork in her mouth, but he caused her pain. Where is he now? Go on home, Maudy. I'm taking Andie to my uncle's farm with me for a while. She needs to sober up, do some real work, and lose weight."

"Libby, I—"

"Thanks for bringing the key, Maudy."

Maudy looked at me trying to pull myself out of bed. "Hmm, well, you know where I am if you need me, sugah." She leered at Libby, the daughter-in-law she didn't like. "So, Libby, now that you've taken over, I suppose you'll stick around and clean this vomit-smelling mess of a trailer, too?"

"Already working on it," she said, ushering our mother-in-law out the door. Libby then called Newberry's, and told the manager that I quit.

I sat wide-eyed at the kitchen table, I couldn't believe she did that. "I can't quit my job, Joe will be furious."

"What does he care? If he cared about your health he'd be here, trying to save you instead of letting you dig your grave with your fork. Besides, that restaurant's turning you into Porky Pig and I'm not about to watch it happen." She flung three Hefty bags full of garbage into the park dumpster before writing Joe a note and telling him if he wanted to talk to me, I'd be at the Stewart farm in Burlington for a couple weeks. Then she stuffed my suitcase and me into her truck.

§

For weeks, dark skies had skipped off to the northeast, leaving the arid Rowan County dirt begging for rain. I found it strange the rain came in torrents the day I rode out of Salisbury with Libby. She stopped at the Exxon station on the edge of town to gas up her truck and call Dixie. My mother told Libby to keep me until I was well. I knew what that meant. Dixie couldn't deal with me. Not like I was. I gazed through the rain. My stringy hair lay against the truck window and dark rings of sadness circled my eyes. My body was a bloated mass of fat and flesh with bands of grief twisting around my head that cut off my ability to reason. It was a good thing Libby drove like we were both eighty years old because my stomach and bowels churned from the massive amounts of food I'd ingested. She stopped the truck twice so I could vomit on the side of the road. "I don't believe in God anymore," I said, my face chalky and my lips swollen.

"Yes, you do." Libby handed me a tissue to wipe my mouth.

"If there's a God, then why don't He do it?"

"What? What do you want Him to do?"

I wiped my eyes with my shirtsleeve. "Why doesn't He make Joe love me?" I said softly.

It was the first time I'd seen Libby's tears. "Damn him," she said.

We rode in silence. Libby had become more than an in-law. She was suddenly my friend. My only friend.

"You want kids someday?" I asked her.

"Ray and I both want children. In a few years. After we move to Virginia."

"You *both* want children. What beautiful words. I envy you. I have to warn you though, the road to motherhood is paved with blood and tears. I feel like an old woman."

"I know," said Libby. "You've lived a lifetime already."

I rolled back to the door and leaned my head against the window again. "What's your family like? I don't know much about the Stewarts other than meeting them at your wedding. I figure since I'm staying with you a while, the least you can do is tell me about your family." I yawned, slid down in the seat, and propped my knees against the glove box.

Libby smiled. "Not much to tell, really. I was raised Catholic, as you know. Baptized as a baby. My family never ate meat on Fridays or missed a confession or Mass on Sunday. But they never criticized those who did. The Stewarts are saturated with religion quite like the Olivers. They love Ray. I know Maudy and Al would've preferred Ray marry a girl like you."

"I'm not sure how to take that," I said.

Libby sighed heavily. "Don't take it wrong. Ray and I are on your side. I don't have answers for you, Andie. I can only offer you a place to stay while you clear your head."

"And get sober," I said.

Libby winked. "Yeah. And get sober."

§

Ray and Libby had moved into the "extra" house, as they called it, lower down on Byron Stewart's property, near a stream—a painted white farmhouse in a stand of oak and poplar trees. While Ray studied for his law degree, he also worked hours to infuse new life into the 100-year-old extra house, repairing old woodwork, heart-pine floors, and drafty windows. The blessing for Libby was the large enclosed porch off the side that Ray had turned into her veterinary office.

Libby drove up her uncle's gravel driveway toward the house, passing fields layered with fresh manure. Near the tool shed, Byron worked to unclog a geriatric spreader, and in the pastures his horses nosed for grass. I spotted a couple paints moseying toward the barn. On the tilting porch of the extra house, Libby's orange cat with one chewed ear sat on the swing with a mouse in its mouth. A simple life. I wanted it. I'd been paralyzed with grief and too full of sorrow at times to even weep. It was a new day. I fell asleep early that night with no supper. I slept hard. My first dreamless sleep in months.

§

Early the next morning, a weak moon shared the sky with a rising sun casting skinny shadows behind Libby and me. Walking up the brick path to the horse barn, Libby chattered as if she'd been awake for hours. She opened the barn door and grinned. "Grab that shovel."

Twice the length and breadth of the house, the barn's small windows, when opened, allowed drafts of warm air to stir up scents of sweet hay, alfalfa, and of the animals. For days, I cleaned stalls, piling manure high, while Libby shoed, walked, brushed, and walked the quarter horses again. Insisting I follow her on rounds to nearby farms, we often trekked a mile or two around the barnyards. Watching my tiny sister-in-law lay hands on sick animals, performing her own healing capabilities, I became a captive audience, along with Libby's big yellow dog, Buttons.

"We got a cow about to give birth tonight. You interested?"

"Are you kidding? I'm there," I said.

§

Outside the glowing warmth of the birthing barn, the chilly night air pressed fingers of rain against the windows. As the temperature dropped, a smoky fog covered the ground and I pressed my own fingers against the cold glass, remembering the stormy night I gave birth. The sounds of the calf beckoned me back to where the newborn curled in the straw at its mother's feet. Watching the proud mama lick her baby clean, I felt a peace I'd not felt in a long, long time.

Exhausted, but triumphant, Dr. Libby Stewart-Oliver patted the cow's nut-brown rump. "You have a beautiful baby boy, Thelma Lou. Good job." Libby picked up the obstetrical handles she'd used earlier, and I leaned against the wall, staying out of the way. Watching the calf, after several unsuccessful tries, wobble to his feet and root for milk, I didn't want the evening to end. Babies of any kind moved me like nothing else, it seemed.

Libby maneuvered in and around the barn stall, and was even more stunning in her cotton shirt, Levi's, scuffed boots, and denim apron than her church clothes. She came from a long line of horse people. I think her family's money had something to do with her career choice. It was clear she loved her animals.

"You're incredible," I said.

"And you're crazy. Working in cow, pig, and horse shit all day is not incredible."

"Not just that. You live on this wonderful farm, you're a doctor, and you have Ray who adores you. It's incredible, because it's everything I want and can't have."

Libby scrubbed her hands and glimpsed over her shoulder. "Ray and I will always love you whether or not your last name is Oliver. So here it is all wrapped up in a pretty bow. You chose the wrong man, that's all. Sooner you accept that, sooner you can get on with life."

"Maybe. Sometimes I think its a demon that's dug its claws into me."

Libby shot me a smirky look. "Now you sound like the pious Reverend. You're the one who won't let go. What Ray and I have right now is all we need. Even if he never passes the bar exam, we'll still be content. We want that for you. Contentment."

"Thanks, I know you do. You put up with me."

"Right. I do. Now hand me my medicine bag. Let's leave this girl alone with her baby. I'll check her in the morning before we head out to rounds at five."

"In the morning? Are you serious?"

Libby laughed. "You want breakfast or do you want to sleep in?"

§

After another particularly long night, watching a brood mare deliver her shiny black colt into Libby's competent hands, I opened one eye when I heard a knock at my bedroom door. My showered and dressed sister-in-law poked her head inside and said, "Morning, beautiful! Miss Verbeena's got a sick cow. Want to come with me?"

I didn't hesitate. I'd come alive on the Stewart farm. It was a life I loved— country and clean air. I hated punching time clocks in drab, tacky offices— stuck under fluorescent lights, stapled to a desk chair, glued to a typewriter. And I hated waiting tables of foul-mouthed truckers or happy couples with children in high chairs. Throwing on my clothes and stuffing a biscuit in my mouth, I ran out the door after Libby.

We rode five miles down a dirt road and turned left at a sawmill. Verbeena Crawford's farm spread out over the next hill with a driveway full of ruts that snaked between fenced pastures. Several dozen Guernsey stood in the fields, swatting flies with their tails.

Libby downshifted her truck. "You received a phone call last night?"

"Yeah."

"Was it Joe?"

"No."

"You want to talk about it?"

"No." I rubbed my neck and craned my chin to the side.

"Your business. Don't mean to pry." Libby parked next to the barn. Buttons hopped out of the truck bed to chase a few of Verbeena's chickens. We followed the sound of the sick cow to a straw-filled stall; Verbeena had brought her in early from the pasture. Libby squatted, resting her butt on her heels. She pressed her ear against the cow's belly and groaned right along with the cow.

"What's wrong?" I asked.

"Shhh," she said, patting its taut tawny hide. "I'm hearing . . ." Libby placed her stethoscope on the cow's abdomen. "I can't tell for sure, but I think it might be twins."

"Twins." A shiver shot down my spine. "Lucky girl."

"Don't say that," Verbeena answered grimly. "Twins might do her in."

Libby rose and flipped through a notepad she carried in her apron. "She's due in six weeks. I'll be by in a couple days to check her for Toxaemia. In the meantime, keep an eye on her. If she refuses to eat or won't move when you herd her to the barn, call me right away." Libby handed Verbeena directions on what supplements to add to the cow's feed to increase her energy. "See you in a week, Miss Verbeena."

"Send me a bill," she hollered as we walked out of the barn.

"Will do." Libby yelled back. With a shrill whistle she called her dog, and like Buttons, I obediently followed her to the truck. Libby's gift was in her voice—able to calm the skittish horse, soothe the injured dog, or ease the wounds of her disheartened sister-in-law. Libby in action was pure magic, and I was dumbfounded by it all.

Return To Oz

Andie

In the process of waking early, eating balanced meals, and walking five miles a day, I had lost fifteen pounds in a month. My mental attitude brightened living in the rolling hills of Alamance County. Joe had called twice to check on me. But it made no difference to him I hadn't been home in a month, and he sounded less than enthused when I told him I was ready to go back to church.

I walked to the barn and found Libby feeding the horses. "I don't think Joe wants me to come home yet."

"Ooohhh, but wait until he sees your new body," she said, grabbing my baggy jeans at the waistline.

"I need to lose another fifty before *he* notices. I've done this to myself."

"Just be happy. That's why I brought you here, to get happy again."

"I am," I said with a troubled smile. "I appreciate what you and Ray have done for me." I paused. "I told Joe I'm going back to church."

Libby foraged for the right words. "I'm not sure that's a good idea." She worked her pitchfork faster. Sweat rolled down the sides of her face. "I guess I see things different than you, after all." She stopped and leaned against the barn door. "Damn, Andie, what happened?"

"I see things different, too. Especially since you brought me here. I left Joe after Mavis died because I thought my marriage was over. Then I realized I wanted my marriage to work more than anything. Listen to me Libby, the Joe I married is locked inside him somewhere, and I'm determined to find him. It's true I almost lost my sanity hoping to find some shred of evidence that he wasn't lying to me again, and that he really did love me. But it seems my marriage is far better when I'm *in* church than when I'm out. Calvin called me here."

"That's the call you didn't want to talk about?"

I nodded. "He assured me if Joe is to be successful for the Lord, we shouldn't have children. He said that's why we lost the baby. It was God's will that he died. Calvin wants me to come back, be involved in the ministry. Maybe even work for him part-time. He said our marriage could be healed. I want you to know, I'm not putting my marriage at risk any longer. I'm not having kids. Ever."

"Are you crazy?" Libby didn't buy it. "You're a natural-born mother. Even more than me. You've wanted kids all your life. Why—"

"It's more than just about Joe! I shouldn't expect you to understand. You didn't grow up in Calvin's ministry. You've never had him lay hands on you and shriek that you'll blaspheme the Holy Ghost if you leave the church. That's been inside my head, Libby, since I was a kid. Nobody's ever called you on the phone and told you that you're doomed for Hell if you leave your husband. I live with that and the threat of missing the rapture every damn day of my life! I wake up every night in a sweat with Calvin's voice inside my head. Do you know what it feels like to have personal prophecy screamed in your face? Calvin has made the House of Praise the air we breathe. As much as I hate saying it, I've never had a life outside the walls of that church!"

I glared at Libby. I knew she had never experienced the full measure of Calvin's power. "He prophesied to me on the phone. He said God showed him I will die a lonely old woman in a mental institution if I leave Joe again. Said Hell is my destiny if I lay out of anymore services or abandon my church; that he saw it in a vision. Calvin might very well be crazy, but how do I know for sure? How do I know that? You've seen miracles happen in his services same as me. You tell me! How do I know it's not me who's got it all wrong? He's controlled our souls, minds, and bodies all our lives. So you tell me, since you're so stinkin' smart, how to stop it now!"

"I guess I've never allowed anyone to manipulate me like that. Nobody controls *my* mind, and I refuse to live in fear! Thank God for my sane family."

"Damn it, Libby! I'm happy for you. But I'll never have what you have here. And if God can forgive Joe, then so can I. I can't give up on him! I just can't! This is the life I've chosen, and it looks like it doesn't include kids. Joe's put up with me laying out of church all this time. He has stayed married to me even though I left him with no intention to go back. I owe him this."

"YOU OWE HIM? I repeat, are you crazy? I think you're the one who's done the putting up with! Hasn't he slept with more women than you can shake your fist at?"

I screamed in my defense. "He's all I got, Libby! He's all I got left! I have to make my marriage work and if Calvin's offering to help me do that, then I'm going back to that church, crawl if I have to, and ask God to forgive me in front of that entire congregation, pledge my loyalty, and say or do anything he wants. I'll kiss his bare ass if I have to! Don't you get it?"

"No. No I don't. You *are* crazy. You talk out of both sides of your mouth. You're not who I thought you were." Libby threw her pitchfork into a hay mound and hoofed it to the house.

I called Dixie the next morning and asked her to pick me up and drive me back to Salisbury. Leaving the House of Praise for good meant leaving Joe *and* God. I wanted things back the way they were when we were first married. Repenting would either make Joe happy or piss him off, because then he'd have to make it work. Calvin and I, together, would give him no choice. And better to err on the side of righteousness, just in case. The years I'd fought against Calvin and the church worried me. It was time to get right with God.

§

I did exactly what I told Libby I'd do. I returned to the next Friday night service at the House of Praise. Weakened from my losses, I wept uncontrollably in my seat. When Calvin finished his fiery blast from the pulpit, he called for the sick and afflicted to come forward, and form a "healing line." Then he whipped around and pointed in my direction. I stood instinctively. He had pointed at me. I knew it. Instantly, two male ushers rushed to my pew to lead me to the altar.

Calvin's hands shook above his head as he wailed, "The angel of the Lord stands beside me, speaking into my left ear. He's bidding you to come. Come child, come back to Jesus. Walk that aisle. Your sins have found you out and now is the day of repentance. Though your heart be black as coal and your trespasses be as scarlet, the Lord will wash you white as the most perfect snow. Oh sinner, come to Jesus! Backslider, come to Jesus! Cry holy unto the Lord! You can be set free by His mighty power. There's power, power in the name of Jesus. Come home, come home, ye who are weary, come home."

In bone-deep tradition resembling the multitudes who had done it before me, I walked the aisle like the broken woman I was. Barely able to stand in front of Calvin, raging grief tore through my heart with one question. *Why? Why, after losing my baby and then Mavis, why do I have to go through this, too?* I swallowed the scream that rose in my throat. It was not sorrowful repentance, but hope that made me walk that aisle. Hope for love, for adoration, for all the good things in life that had evaded me from the moment I married Joe.

"Lift your hands high, my dear sister. Mean this prayer, and God will hear you, Andie." Throwing his head back, he directed his prayer heavenward.

I repeated the sinner's prayer after him. "Oh God, save my soul. Take away my heavy load. I'm sorry that I've sinned against you, but I'm coming back. I'll serve you, Lord, the rest of my life. Deliver me from all my sin. Set me free, Lord Jesus! I believe You died on Calvary for me, and I believe in Your shed blood. There is power in the blood to wash away my sins, all my sins!"

Calvin flailed his arms, shaking, hesitating to touch me, as if the moment he laid hands on me God would send 1,000 volts of electricity through him. "Now, Andie . . . say, come into my heart, Jesus. Come in, Jesus!" With an ear-splitting high-pitched hoot and a holler he slapped my forehead and I fell to my knees, screaming for Jesus to forgive me. Forgive me from what, I wasn't exactly sure, but I felt strangely compelled to cover all my bases.

"If you meant it, He has come back to you. Jesus is yours. Hallelujah! A backslider has come home!" A victory for Calvin, he reveled in his conquest, jumped up and down, and sang like a squeaky hinge, "*Victory in Jesus . . .*"

Then he instructed the ushers to raise me to my feet. "Do you want to say anything, my dear, dear sister?"

With tears streaming, I said what he wanted to hear. What they all wanted to hear. I promised loyalty to the cause of Christ. I swore to assist the ministry as Joe traveled for the Lord. I confessed into the microphone that Reverend Artury was the chosen one to save the world for Jesus and that he was God's vessel for mankind's last hour. I even went so far to say, without being coaxed, that I believed Reverend Artury to be the thirteenth Apostle. My statement sent up praises and shouts from the members like I'd never experienced in all the years I'd attended his church. When the crowd settled down, I promised to submit to my husband. Calvin reached out and folded me into his arms, hugged me, and called me his little lost lamb. I didn't recall him doing that before. To anybody. Ever.

He surprised me by calling Joe down from the audio control room. He told him to stand next to me at the altar. Calvin laid hands on both of us, blessed our union, and told us to embrace and show our love as man and wife. Joe hugged me, but I detected his sigh and dismissed it. It was, after all, the beginning of a great healing. Healing for soul, mind, and marriage. A huge weight lifted from my shoulders as the congregation cheered for the marriage miracle happening right in front of their eyes, though few had known it was in trouble in the first place.

Like a chemo treatment, Calvin slapped my forehead one last time burning out any remaining evil spirits. I fell backwards because I knew he would want that, and was lowered gently to the floor by two male ushers who stood close by. The congregation sent up more shouts to God for allowing the wayward and backslidden sinner, specifically me, another chance to come back into the fold.

I briefly opened my eyes to find Calvin standing at my feet as I lay on the carpet. He crossed his arms against his chest and pointed a finger at the congregation. "This is what happens when you fail God, people. If she had died in a car accident on the way here tonight, she would've opened her eyes in Hell."

Once again, the 1,000-member congregation shouted thanks to the Lord for saving me, but Calvin continued his warning. "She almost didn't make it back. She almost lost Heaven. God almost turned His back on her." He lifted his arms high in the air, threw his head back, and shouted at the ceiling, "Thank you, Jesus! Thank you that You saw fit to save our Andie from the gates of Hell and the fire of your damnation!" He started to sing again, "*There is power, power, wonderworking power, in the blood of the Lamb . . .*" making his way to the line of the sick and suffering people who had been standing patiently for over an hour to receive their miracle.

§

After my humiliating return to Christ, I followed Joe out the back of the church, my eyes avoiding the stares of those still condemning me for failing God to begin with. Certainly, Julia Preston, Evan's wife, was the last person I wanted to see. Joe walked away as zipper-thin Julia caught me in the lobby and smothered me in a honey-bun hug and a sweet-roll smile. I had no choice but to endure it. I guessed we were the same age, yet she appeared much older with her beige up-do that wouldn't budge in a blizzard. Mascara-caked eyes— everything about the woman was overdone: makeup, perfume, double-knit pantsuit, and square gold earrings the size of tithe envelopes. Nothing about her spoke the truth, and I suspected gaudy Julia was a carefully veiled loose woman from her tongue to her toes.

She giggled. "I swear, Andie, you are the most beautiful thing I ever laid eyes on." Overpowering described anything that had to do with her and that included flattery. From his pulpit, Calvin once said Julia was a fine example of a Proverbs 31 woman, a woman we should all aspire to.

Behind Julia loomed Sylvia Turlo in her black and white usherette uniform that matched her black and white hair, teased and sprayed reminiscent of her 1962 graduation picture, I was sure. I couldn't imagine two more depressing women to run into. Sylvia's glance sharpened and an icy scorn sparked in her eyes. "Welcome back, prodigal daughter, to the army of the Lord."

I summoned a smile.

Sylvia hugged me the way someone would hug a leper, but her deep voice dripped with honey. "Silas said you were back. I was thrilled to hear it." The wife of Silas Turlo was also a loyal spy for Calvin. She kept a close eye on the lives of House of Praise employees and volunteers, should anyone make a move to retreat, quit the church, or slack off in their duties. "Julia and I have prayed for you every day for a year. Haven't we, Julia?" Then she was gone, saying she had important church business to attend to.

I had always looked at Julia and Sylvia as martyrs. Both sneered at any activity not church-related. The church was their very existence and they expected the same from all the ministry team wives. I heard Julia give her testimony once. She openly admitted to being so busy recruiting volunteers that she had no time for picnics, parties, or social events of any kind. Any free time she managed to squeeze out of her schedule was spent in prayer, fasting, and submitting to Evan. Everyone laughed when she said it, but I knew she meant every word.

"You ready?" Joe had waited long enough for me to finish my conversation with Julia, and was wanting to go. She flashed a smile at Joe then cupped one hand around my chin. "Andie, call me next week. The Praise Buffet is serving free sweet tea in July. We can do lunch. Maybe you'd like to volunteer at the studio, or in the mailroom. Hey, I think you might like to work in our new state-of-the-art kitchen. I hear you're a wonderful cook."

"Sure," I said, elated to be back in my husband's arms and heart. But not necessarily happy to be back in Oz.

§

I never saw Libby and Ray much after I went back to the House of Praise. It wasn't long until Maudy told me Ray had passed the Virginia bar exam. They moved to Richmond shortly after that. I received a few phone calls from Ray from time-to-time. But my return to the House of Praise had created a rift between Libby and me. I had hurt her and I wondered if we would ever be friends again. The Oliver family had fractured a little more, and a little more of my heart broke off in the process.

March 1976
A WELL–CONCEIVED PLAN

Andie

For three years, Joe had traveled from Salisbury to Winston-Salem and back, eating up gas money, working weeknights, and leaving every weekend on a faith-healing crusade in hopes that Calvin hire him full-time for the ministry team. Even as a volunteer, he never took time off, attended every service, and made himself available at a moment's notice. I couldn't fathom why Calvin kept putting it off. It perturbed me only because it kept Joe in a foul mood. Calvin dangled Joe's potential church career in front of him like a carrot on a string in front of a jackass.

In the spring of 1976, Calvin flew to Nigeria, Africa, and during that week he gave the volunteer staff the week off as well. Two weeks prior, at a staff meeting, he declared all male employees must undergo a vasectomy as a condition of employment. He was adamant, instructing any man who had not had the *Procedure* to do so before hiring began when he returned. When Joe told me about it, he said he wanted to have his surgery during his *vacation* week. But what Joe didn't know was that Maudy had finagled an invitation for us to visit her brother, Dodrill, in Atlanta that week. I'd lost my pregnancy weight since spending the previous summer on the farm with Libby, and I'd managed to put a patch on our marriage by staying in church and keeping my mouth shut. Joe reluctantly agreed to take me to Atlanta.

It was our first-ever vacation since our two-day honeymoon. Time away from the pressures of church was like winning money and prizes on a game show, a trip to Disney World, or front-row tickets to a Bee Gees concert. Driving the six hours to Uncle Dodrill's house, I felt no burdensome chains of grief choking my thoughts and hopes. My tears were gone, evaporated by the onrushing wind in my hair riding along with the windows down. Courage and determination were like a rock inside me again, begging for that slim chance of happiness.

Dodrill Lee stood on his front porch, bald and covered with a collection of freckles. I waved to him from the car as Joe parked between rows of live oaks and crepe myrtle. Looking at Dodrill was like looking at Maudy. After all, they were twins. Dodrill and Maudy had come from old money, mostly gone. Squandered, was more like it, Maudy had said.

After catching up, Uncle Dodrill showed us around the house and grounds and said to make it ours for the week. Spacious and clean, the old two-story resembled the house I grew up in, only run down and desperate for a woman's touch. He employed a black maid and a Mexican gardener. "An illegal immigrant," he said with a smile. Our room had a connecting bathroom and the whole house was air-conditioned. It was better than a cheap motel in my estimation.

By suppertime, Joe was holding my hand and stroking my back. He took deep breaths and was able to sit in one place for more than five minutes. Since he had been confrontational for such a long, long time, I found it difficult to respond to his sudden show of affection. I had forgiven him, but it was hard to forget what he had done to me. Nevertheless, if I was going to stay married to Joe, I knew I would have to find a way, once again, to live with the past.

Exploring the 100-acre farm after supper, Joe pulled off and parked the car in a meadow of tall grass. We sat and listened to the wind and the shrill song of a Whip-poor-will.

"Makes me sleepy," I said.

He picked up my hand from the car's seat and kissed it. "Makes me want to forget about so many things," he said. I wanted to ask what he meant, but said nothing, not wanting to break his sudden spell of euphoria.

Strolling under an archway of live oak and pine, like a cathedral ceiling of glittering colors and light, we explored a different world than the one we knew. Softly fragrant and chocked full of sweetness, the air blew cool and refreshing. I had forgotten how good country air made me feel. Warm and in full bloom, spring had come to the Deep South. Joe and I climbed a steep ravine packed with kudzu and knotted as tightly as a latched mat. Laughing and tripping over tree roots, we heard the sound of water. To my left, a creek tumbled to the bottom, and a gentle waterfall spilled over neatly placed river rock.

Walking back to the meadow where we had parked, we stepped over and around thick underbrush that lay nearly impenetrable on all sides of us, as if God had spread an enormous swatch of deep green velvet over the ground. Wildflowers sprouted from every dip and mound, and I picked a bouquet of Queen Anne's lace for our room. Joe pointed to webs with huge spiders asleep in their silken hubs, and as always, the ever-present hum of cicadas rode high in the treetops. The idea of a life like the one Mavis led was no more a part of me than moving to Antarctica. Old daydreams flooded back into my head. The country life was the life I wanted for Joe and me. It'd been a long time since I thought about it, but I imagined our dream house again. I closed my eyes and saw it sitting inside its picket fence at the back of Dodrill's property, where the woods opened up and the creek swelled into a swimming hole.

At sunset I held Joe's hand while we strolled on the veranda, gazing across a pond that rested at the bottom of a long slope of dogwood and mimosa. Trout heads nipped the surface for food, creating ripples that floated to the water's edge. Vibrant sunrays bounced off the glassy water shooting hundreds of sparkles into the air. The fireworks continued until the sun sank behind the treeline. We heard Dodrill calling his dogs for supper. A night heron sang and I watched lightning bugs glow golden in the dark. I had all but stopped thinking about my life back in Salisbury.

That first night, we crawled naked into a soft, cool bed. It was glorious not to be forced to move from a sweat-soaked spot to a dry one. Air conditioning was a luxury we couldn't afford at home. Joe had said if his parents did without it for years, then so could we.

It wasn't long before Joe pulled a rubber out of the suitcase and laid it on the bed. I stared at it. Pill or no pill, when it came to birth control I knew Joe would never trust me again. When we started having sex again, Joe took no chances and always pushed me away unless he had on his rubber.

"Why do we have to use that?" I asked.

He shook his head. "We've argued about this for years. You know why."

"That's not what I mean."

Joe sat on the side of the bed. I could count his ribs, see the sharpness of his hipbones. Having just finished another twenty-one day Bible fast, he had wanted his constant praying and fasting to send a clear message to God—to speed up his hire date with Calvin. Joe's piercing green eyes swept over me as he reached out for his Trojan. "Almost ready," he said.

"What I mean is, I hate the way that thing feels in me. I always have. It hurts."

He stopped priming himself. "Damn it, Andie. You sure know how to throw ice on the moment. Can't you talk dirty or something?"

Glaring at his silhouette through the dim light that shone from the bathroom, I scarcely heard him. All I wanted was a child to love. Just one child. He had carved a niche for himself with Calvin and his band of marauders. He found his reason for living. And as much as I didn't want to believe it, I knew it wasn't me. Hiding my anguish, I pulled the rubber out of his hand. "Can this thin piece of latex really keep me from getting pregnant? One of the girls at the bank said she got pregnant even though her husband used these things."

Joe retrieved his rubber. "Unless they're defective, they work fine."

"But it's so thin. How do we know it works?"

He ignored me. It wasn't long before he hollered for his *raincoat* again. I wanted him to know it was painful, but I tolerated it instead. After a minute of watching my face wince while he thrust away at me, he stopped. "It really isn't good for you, is it? You've already been pregnant. How can this still hurt you?"

"It's uncomfortable. I hate rubbers. I told you, I've always hated them."

"You know, we haven't had sex in a week. You might pretend to enjoy it, at least."

He peeled off the Trojan. I suspected Joe liked the way my body felt, like when I was eighteen; the only difference being a few faded stretch marks and the thin purple scar that traveled from my navel to my pubic hair. Pulling me on top of him, his hands on my buttocks, he sucked at my breast like a giant, red-spotted puppy. I felt the tip of his bare penis slide between my legs, and my thoughts became tangled with desire and those of motherhood. Despite my feelings, insecurities, and all I had come to realize about my husband, I knew if Joe were gone, there would never be another man in my life. Refusing to consider I might be making the same mistake twice I allowed my desire to take over, also knowing that once Joe had his vasectomy my chance for another baby was gone. Holding my breath to keep up my courage, I forced his penis inside. It hurt for a second, but then something happened.

It was smooth and warm without the discomfort, like when we were first married. I moved into positions I never had before, giving him the kind of sex I was sure he fantasized about. He wrapped his arms around me making no attempt to pull out. I wanted to give him the best sex of his life; better than any woman he'd been with.

It seemed I succeeded. His hands explored me as if I were new to him, parting me, sliding into the depths of me. I trembled and gasped. He moaned as he entered me, again and again. I pulled him in tighter between my thighs and arched my back. The soft roundness of my breasts pressed against his chest and he shuddered in the dark.

Joe had once told me he never felt it necessary to kiss me during sex, and yet I gave myself freely to the passion of his mouth, the first such passion I'd felt from him since our first few weeks of marriage. I claimed every kiss and afterward he kept on kissing me softly.

"Andie?"

"Yes?"

"Did you come?"

"Yes."

But I didn't. Joe never waited long enough for me to have an orgasm. Only a few times in our marriage had I experienced that with him. What I really wanted from him was love and a few minutes of his time. At that moment, however, it didn't matter. I had something else on my mind. "Why can't we go rubberless every time?" I asked.

"No way, José'. We can't take another chance like that."

We can't because YOU don't want children. I rolled next to him and trickled my fingers down his back. "I'll douche it out. It won't stay in. It's so much more enjoyable for me when it doesn't hurt." Laying beside him skin-on-skin, I had offered him the believable repetition of perfect sex, and from a new and improved wife no less.

Joe nodded like a schoolboy. "You better get it all out. I don't want any accidents. I suppose you're right. It is nicer for me when you're not laying there like a corpse."

Returning from the bathroom, my cool skin covered him like a sheet fresh from the line, my bright eyes wide and pleading, I kissed him again. "No rubber just on vacation. A few days and that's it." I watched him nod, yawn, and close his eyes. Overwhelmingly victorious, I smiled in the dark, cool room as the drone of the air conditioner lulled us both to sleep.

§

Away from home, Joe woke every morning in a grinning, pensive mood. I delighted in it. We ate well and he put on weight. His skin tanned again and I felt certain every available woman at the next crusade would attempt to attach herself to him like lice on a first grader. I worked hard at enticing him to stay an extra day. But as the end of the week neared, his mood changed. He wouldn't tell me, of course, but I knew he had begun thinking about the church. The fear of losing his position plagued him. Eventually, Joe's anxiety took us home a day early. I suspected unless my husband walked Calvin's straight and narrow, he would one day find he'd been replaced as Chief Engineer. Joe's longing to get back proved to me he would never wander too far off that path. He had a relentless fixation on his work, and as long as his youthful stamina held up, Joe would remain faithful to his precious Reverend.

But I'd seen tough men turn tender around their children. I had to believe Joe would too if he had a child who loved him. The one-year anniversary of our infant son's death had just passed. What better way to pay back the demons that stole our first child than to conceive a second one? I was sure Mavis would agree. Those precious few weeks before Joe's surgery were my last hope for motherhood, and the one thing I knew how to do best was hope.

May 1976
AUNT WY

Andie

The word was out. The original volunteer ministry team, including singers and musicians, were to give notice to their current employers. They were to begin as full-time House of Praise employees on May 1, and were reminded that *The Procedure* within the inner circle was not an option. If you wanted to be part of the ministry team, it was a requirement. Knowing his congregation wouldn't entirely approve, it was all very hush-hush. Calvin never mandated it from his pulpit, but I knew of other young men within the congregation who were counseled and encouraged to have it done before marriage. Some did, and some I heard, flat out refused.

Joe insisted on scheduling his surgery when we returned from Atlanta, but I held off until Calvin agreed to pay for it. When Fannie finally called and told me to send the bill to the church, I called the clinic.

"The doctor is booked until the end of May," I said with hesitation.

Joe leaned back in his recliner and crossed his feet. "I'm holding you responsible if Reverend fires me before I even start! Why didn't you do this when I asked you to?"

"We don't have that kind of money, Joe. I needed a commitment from your employer."

"No, you waited until I had to scream at you to make the damn appointment!"

I ignored his hissy fit and washed the supper dishes. I had missed my period in April and wanted to have unprotected sex as many times as I could. A missed period in May would mean only one thing. My wish had come true.

"By the way, when are you getting a job? It's been long enough, Andie. Reverend isn't paying me enough for you to stay home."

"I found one."

"What?"

"I said I got a job. Candace Cooper hired me. Part-time."

"The Shady Acres whore? That trashy woman still doing hair?"

"She isn't trash. I used to think so, but people aren't always what they seem. Besides, you liked her plenty until you discovered her age. She's been sweet to me since our baby died. She bought the beauty shop by the Kmart. Asked me to work three days a week. Answer phones, make appointments, and sweep up hair. Easy stuff. And Julia Preston wants me to volunteer in the mail room at the church two days a week." I dried the last bowl and wiped off the dish rack. "If you need me I'll be across the street talking to Candace about my new job. Before I forget, your mama's having a surprise party for you next Thursday night to celebrate your new hire with Calvin. Act surprised." I slammed the door behind me. I'd been in a pissy mood for days. I had no desire to help Maudy with Joe's party. I didn't care about Joe's crossover into full-time employment with Calvin. In fact, I didn't plan to attend the celebration at all.

§

The women worked around the large table like quilters at a quilting bee. Outside the mailroom, doors to offices stood open and the sound of conversation spilled out to the hallway, creating subtle and pleasing background noise.

Judy peered across the table. "I just love attending the miracle crusades, don't you Andie, darlin'?"

You'd have to drug me and drag me. Opening mail, I ignored her and did as I was instructed. I placed prayer requests in one pile and letters that contained offerings in another. I could not answer her honestly. I had no desire to see Calvin act a fool in Atlanta, Philadelphia, Nashville, or any other city where he'd been scheduled to preach.

I sat across from Judy Childress and Carly Pruitt. Proud ministry team wives who wore their lonely lives as medals on their lapels and had created their own club. I also knew these women were a sympathetic group of Joe Oliver supporters.

Judy spoke again. "I'm sorry, Andie, have you been to a crusade?"

"No. Not yet."

The two team wives eyeballed each other.

"I've gone back to work and I'm too busy on the weekends," I said.

Carly's cheesy grin nauseated me. "Do you miss sex when Joe's out of town?"

I refused to answer. *It's none of your damn business.* I nodded politely. *Do you miss having a brain in your head*? I had kept my weight down, and although Joe was not as attentive as he'd been on our trip to Atlanta, we managed to make love at least once a week.

"Maybe, Andie, if you went to a few crusades, maybe you and your husband would be happier."

"What do you mean?" I asked sharply.

"Hush, Carly," Judy reprimanded.

Shoving my unopened stack of mail to the middle of the table, I then pressed my piles of prayer requests and offerings into the provided folders. For a church that preached so adamantly against gossip, it ran rampant—like an underground newspaper. I couldn't endure another minute in the stuffy mailroom with my insolent mail-opening partners. I carried my folders to Julia Preston's office. "I'm going home, Julia."

Julia's shoulder held a phone to her ear. A quick flick of her wrist signaled her goodbye, as if I were nothing but a fleeting shadow crossing the room.

I flicked my wrist back at her and rolled my eyes, hoping she saw me. Living in a constant state of irritability was not like me. Pure and simple, every damn person at the House of Praise got on my last damn nerve. Cussing like a truck driver was not like me either, but fuck that shit. I picked up my coat and purse and walked out without saying another word. Opening my car door, I glimpsed down at the volunteer clearance badge that had caught on my sweater. I forgot to turn it in. Turning on my heel, I ran back into the mailroom in time to hear my name spoken, which stopped me in my tracks behind a row of metal shelving units.

"Poor Andie," said Carly. "She has no idea her husband doesn't love her." Carly dumped a new mailbag of letters on the worktable. As unattractive as her personality, she had big hair, a big butt, and an even bigger mouth.

"How do you know that?" asked Judy.

Carly settled her wide rear-end on a mauve-colored secretary chair and looked around the mailroom at the other volunteers, smiling as if she were privy to secret information. "Joe told my husband and my husband tells me everything."

"My husband adores me," Judy believed out loud. She ripped open the next letter then asked, "Why doesn't Joe? Love Andie I mean?"

"Andie Oliver will never get right with God. Can't you tell? She's not into saving souls. Not like us. Not as dedicated to the ministry. She won't go to even one crusade. Reverend will find Joe a proper wife someday. Julia said Reverend wants the congregation to see Joe as the good husband that he is. When Andie backslides again, and you know she will, their divorce will be her fault. She will have failed God for the last time and Joe will be free to remarry. Reverend will see to it."

"I never want that to happen to me and Earl," said Judy.

"It won't, honey. We support Reverend Artury; we've sacrificed for the good of the ministry. A wife like Andie, who can't decide if she's in or out, that girl deserves the hell she's headed for."

I threw my badge on the floor and retreated to my car. My life went around in circles of regret.

§

I cringed opening Joe's first paycheck to find his starting salary was barely enough to cover our bills. Cheap rent and living at Shady Acres would save us. At least for a while.

Maudy's surprise party was mild compared to the keg party Coot threw for Joe the night before his surgery. Against the instructions of Joe's doctor, Coot and the old gang from the pool hall bought Joe enough beer to drown his sorrows for a month. The next morning, my hung-over husband paced back and forth, cracked his knuckles and bit his nails to the quick. Calvin gave him three days off work to recuperate. I had no sympathy. I hoped it hurt like hell, and told him it probably would.

Joe's procedure was scheduled for nine a.m. After a fast kiss goodbye, I left Joe alone on a table, his penis taped to his stomach, his legs draped and spread as if he were ready for a pap test. I giggled all the way to the women's clinic on the opposite side of the building.

"I'm Andie Oliver, here for a pregnancy test." The grin never left my face.

Dr. Eshelman had moved his practice to Charlotte, so I was in search of a new obstetrician. I figured the outpatient center would be as good a place as any to start my search. I peed in a cup and in a very short time, my suspicions were confirmed. The clinic doctor examined me internally, finding my uterus naturally swollen for an eight-week pregnancy. He handed me a slip of paper with a due date—on or around Christmas.

I was officially pregnant.

I paid my bill, picked up my lab results, and walked to the outpatient waiting area. Two hours later a nurse wheeled Joe, woozy and nauseous, to the recovery room.

"How ya feeling, honey?" I held his hand as he weaved in and out of consciousness.

"I think I should've stayed away from the beer last night. How long was I out?"

"You weren't really out, you just don't remember it. But long enough."

"Andie?"

"Yes?"

Now, Joe was a mean drunk, but he was even meaner drugged. "Fuck you," he said, slurring his words. "You'll never have a baby now. I'll never have to worry about it again. Despite what you did to me before, I won. You get pregnant after this . . . it ain't mine . . . and you can fuck off." He laughed a sick, feeble chortle, reeling from pain medication mixed with the previous night's alcohol.

My eyes narrowed and my anger seared hot. After bearing the church-women's ridicule, I wasn't about to take it from Joe. Not anymore. I leaned over and whispered into my husband's ear. "Do you remember what Dr. Eshelman said at my last doctor appointment? You were with me, remember? He said I wasn't to take birth control pills for a while. To give my body time to heal. And do you also recall you haven't worn a rubber for the past two months? I mean, I sure as shoot couldn't put one of those things on you. You remember all that?"

"Yeah, so?" Suspicion shone in his eyes.

"Calvin knows I'm not on the pill. You told him, remember? You tell him everything about us."

Joe breathed deep, long breaths and squinted, like he was about to be struck in the face.

"See this piece of paper?" I shoved the lab results in front of him. "I had a pregnancy test in this clinic. Today. While you were getting your nuts cut off. I'm eight weeks pregnant. Due at Christmas. Must've got pregnant down at Uncle Dodrill's. So guess what? This time, I guess it's *both* of our faults. Calvin will be happy, don't you think?"

Staring at me with a potent mix of horror and disbelief, Joe grabbed my wrist; his eyes rolled back in his head. He nearly passed out before I pulled out of his grasp. I stuffed the paper in his shirt pocket hanging on the recovery room door. "I called Maudy. She's coming to get you, to take you to her house. I don't want to wipe your nasty ass. You never offered me so much as a hug after my accident. Stay with your mama 'til you're on your feet. I'm going home. See ya."

When I turned to leave, a box of Kleenex flew past my head, missing me by a thumb's width. "You fucking cow!" he said.

I spun around.

Blood dripped down his chin. He'd obviously bit his tongue or his lip. His nostrils flared with fury and his eyes blazed. When Joe laid his head back on the pillow, a sinister smile spread across his face. His lips thinned. "*Vengeance is mine, saith the Lord*," he said.

I sauntered back to him, keeping my distance, and threw my next words like rocks. "I'm sorry to be so insensitive in your hour of need, *dear*, but I might as well tell you. The doctor . . . today . . . he heard two heartbeats in this cow's womb." Raising my hands, I mockingly tilted my head toward Heaven in praise. "The Lord's seen fit to bless us extra good this time. With twins."

§

The nurse at the clinic wrote several doctor referrals on a piece of paper. When I arrived home, I glanced down the list until I saw a familiar name. *Wylene Rose Oakley, M.D.* It was my aunt. I didn't know she was a doctor. I didn't even know she was alive. Dixie hadn't talked about her in years. How many people could be named Wylene Rose, I wondered.

So I called.

A pleasant female voice answered the phone. "Greensboro Medical Group."

"Uh, hello. My name's Andie Oliver. I found out today that I'm pregnant. I'm looking for a new doctor. I'd like to make an appointment with Dr. Oakley."

"I'm sorry, Dr. Oakley is not accepting new patients at this time."

"But—she's my aunt. I think. Please, may I speak to her? Tell her Andie Parks is on the phone. She'll know me by my maiden name."

The seconds passed like hours. As I waited, I thought about Joe. Maudy probably had him propped up on pillows. She hadn't asked me to join them for supper, but I had every intention of showing up while Joe convalesced in my mother-in-law's spare bedroom. I wanted to break the news to the Olivers while they babysat their son. I needed their help to soften Joe on fatherhood before I had to deal with him alone. It pissed me off that I had to *deal* with him at all. But I would not go through another hellish pregnancy. Not again.

I waited on the line.

Maybe I'd jumped the gun. Maybe Wylene didn't want contact with our family. It had been over twenty years since any of us had seen her. Suddenly, I regretted calling.

My thoughts were interrupted by Wylene's deep, scratchy voice. "My God, is this really Andie Rose Parks, firstborn of Dixie Anne?"

"Sure is. It's nice to meet you again, Aunt Wylene, even if it's on the phone."

Wylene rushed to the point. "So you need a doctor?"

"I'm eight weeks pregnant. Confirmed just this morning and yes, I need a new doctor."

"You had an old one?"

"Dr. Eshelman from Lexington. He moved to Charlotte."

"Know him. Great doc."

"Yes, yes he was."

"Well, bust my hump! I'm finally talking to family. I'm putting you back on the phone with Debbie, my secretary. Make an appointment."

"Thank you. Thank you, Aunt Wylene."

"You're welcome, darlin'. By the way, you married?"

"Yes, ma'am. Nearly four years now."

"Good. See you soon."

Debbie scheduled the appointment in a cancellation slot for the next day. My excitement at meeting the infamous Wylene Rose kept me awake all night. There'd be nothing Dixie could do to stop my relationship with my aunt should it develop. I was a grown woman, able to choose my own obstetrician, after all.

§

Wylene's office, located in the medical building annexed to the hospital, smelled like cough syrup and mimeograph paper. I signed in at the receptionist's window and had a seat on one of the green vinyl chairs in the sparse waiting room next to a metal rack of worn magazines and a plastic fern. Flipping through an old issue of *Redbook*, I glanced up at the peeling plaster. That's when the door opened. She had come to fetch me on her own. Filling the entire doorway, the full-figured, big-bottomed woman with reddish-blonde hair hinted at a sharp tongue and a flaming temper. An obvious undisputed doctor whom none would dream of disobeying. My mother once said her sister's husband died early in their marriage. I saw no ring on her man-sized fingers. It didn't take a brain surgeon to see what kind of a woman she was. Holding a cigarette in her hand, her face wreathed in smoke, Wylene appeared curious. The creases in her forehead gave her the look of an intelligent woman. One who spent too much time in deep concentration.

"Aunt Wy?"

Wylene's eyes shrunk to tiny brown dots and she nodded. "Come on. Let's take a look."

I walked to my aunt, kissed her cheek, and then followed her inside.

§

Wylene had Debbie clear the rest of the morning. My aunt sat behind her desk and sighed. "I'll be damned. You look like a smaller version of me when I was your age. Except you got them big blue eyes. Of course, I never took care of myself. You know what they say about physicians being the last to heal themselves." She held up her Virginia Slim. "Damn cigarettes. They'll kill us all in another twenty years."

I brought my aunt up to date about the family. I talked about my sister, whom Wylene had never seen. But she did recall Mavis as a little girl. She remembered I had shared a crib with Mavis at Dixie's house when Rupert and Loretta Dumass came to visit. Wylene took a deep breath when I relayed the chilling details of Mavis's death. And then of my child's.

"Hope you don't mind," she said. "I drove to Lexington last evening and picked up your chart. I know the office manager there. Doc Eshelman and I go way back."

"Of course not. I'm glad you cared enough to actually go get it."

"Are you serious? This is my dream come true, to see you again. You were two or three last time I laid eyes on you. I'm hoping our relationship as doctor/patient will be okay with your mama, though."

"Dixie doesn't know I'm here."

"That's up to you, darlin', whether you want to tell her."

I shifted in my chair. "What happened, Wy? Can you two ever forgive each other?"

"In my youth it was easy to see life in black and white. The shades of gray came after I'd been kicked around a few years. I'd be willing to bet Dixie still sees everything in black and white. You need to remember this, darlin'. Sisters never forgive one another. Usually, they just pick up where they left off. What happened was Dixie's temper. And mine. We said many things we didn't mean. Made from the same mold, us two. We're as different as we are the same. Dixie was ashamed of me, flamboyant sister that I was, and am. And jealous, I think. I had wealthy foster parents, the opportunity to go to college. Dixie didn't. She had numerous foster parents, none of them kind to her. But hey, she ended up with Bud: that's worth all the degrees hanging on my wall over there. Then your little brother . . . it was a bad time for all of us." She sighed. "When Dixie's baby died in '56, I decided to become a doctor, specifically an obstetrician. Now, here I am."

I nodded. "My mother never talks about her life as a girl. It's taboo."

Wylene cleared her throat and pulled her rimless glasses down from the top of her head, changing the subject. "I see you haven't any health insurance. Is that still the case?"

I proceeded to tell her the short version of Joe and his employer, Calvin Artury.

"We'll not worry about payment until after your baby is born. Or babies, as the case may be. Right now, let's head on down the hall to the exam room. Gotta take a look at you." Wylene shook her head, then spit it out. "Good God. How did you get hooked up in that God-awful church? I've heard stuff about that place. Seems like half my patients go there. No, don't tell me. I'm sure Dixie dragged you to Sunday school as a kid. We'll talk about it later."

§

I followed her down the tiled hallway. "I want to try to go natural."

"You sure about that?"

"Aunt Wy, I want to be awake and see my babies born. The natural way."

"That's a tall order, darlin'. I've studied your chart. It's apparent you suffered a great deal during the birth and death of your first child. I'm taking the safest route to deliver your twins, if that's what you've truly got in there. I'm not saying it can't be done; just that it's risky."

I suspected Wylene was not in the habit of arguing with her patients, but I wasn't any old patient. I was flesh and blood. And clearly bull-headed, like her. An advocate for natural childbirth, Wylene made me promise to follow a diet and exercise regimen to the letter of the law. Her law. She was explicit: if I missed one appointment, there'd be Hell to pay. My pregnancy was considered high-risk due to my history. She said she'd never lost a patient and wasn't about to start with me.

Under normal circumstances, Wylene would've referred me to a colleague. But I wasn't normal by a long shot. I had no money, no health insurance, and a set of twins on the way. Considering the trauma I experienced the previous year, the good doctor would not risk leaving me in anyone else's hands. I also suspected she'd inquire about my deadbeat husband later. She had no children of her own, but before she left me alone in the exam room to get undressed, her eyes filled with tears. Gratitude swelled in my chest. My aunt had come back into my life, whether Dixie liked it or not.

§

Wylene flew into the exam room. "Okay, let's take a look." She covered my knees with a warm blanket, keeping my top half draped and bottom exposed. "I'll agree with natural childbirth. At least for now."

"Thanks, Aunt Wy." I believed if I were fully awake, if I were *there*, nothing bad would happen to my babies. The cold table was a shock to my bare back. Spread eagle, feet in the stirrups, I shivered.

"You understand the risks?"

"Yes."

"Well then," she sighed heavily. Wylene palpitated the outside of my abdomen then laid a freezing stethoscope on my skin. "Yep, there're two in there! Heartbeats sound good. Blood pressure looks good. Drink lots of water and take those vitamins, is that clear?"

I nodded as Wylene pulled on her latex gloves. I sucked in a breath as she inserted two cold, jelled fingers into my vagina. She laughed and said, "Hold still darlin'. Let's see what we got. Ah, Doc Eshelman did a fine job on you. I must commend him. Cervix feels normal, looks good." Wylene finished examining me and patted my butt. "All done. Get dressed."

"Aunt Wy!"

"What? Your bare behind still looks the same to me from where I'm sitting," she said.

I dressed then opened the exam room door. Wylene stepped back inside and leaned against the door frame, her large hip forming an armrest for her man-like hand. She had powdered her face and applied fresh lipstick, a frost pink that only emphasized the lines around her mouth. Her brows were thick and dark and her eyes big and round, making her face appear doe like. Under her white lab coat she wore more white, from the large bow that held back her long, wiry hair, to the stacked heels that stuck to the bottom of her swollen feet. She was one giant snowball. A wall of white polyester. *How did she get through medical school*? I imagined her piss-and-vinegar attitude was a fortress of self-defense against the young and privileged men in her residency program.

Wylene removed her lab coat and suit jacket. Her slip strap fell to her elbow. The dark brows rose and she spit her gum into the nearby wastebasket. "I'm going on a smoke break. Want some lunch?"

SURRENDER

Andie

I slipped on a T-shirt and cut-offs, then drove to the Olivers. Opening the back door with a hesitant smile, I flopped into a kitchen chair and proceeded to rub my eyes with the flat side of my hands. It'd been some time since I'd seen my in-laws. Al looked dusty and tired, his overalls tinted with rust. Maudy's familiar housedress, wrinkled and worn, was missing a button.

Maudy nodded. "Andie."

"Joe in the back bedroom?"

"Uh-huh."

For the first time in my life, I wasn't received with warmth. Even the house felt cold, like a basement in winter. I tiptoed down the hall to the spare bedroom where Joe lay on a feather comforter, as I suspected, with his eyes closed. A bottle of Coke, *Hot Rod* magazines, and his Bible lay on the nightstand.

"Joe? You awake?"

He opened his eyes, but did not return my smile. Instead, he rose on his elbows like a dog sitting on its haunches and motioned with his head for me to come near, as if he might kiss me. Surprised, I side-stepped to the edge of the bed and leaned toward my husband.

Quick like a cobra, he spit in my face. "Get away from me."

I jumped back. Sprinting back down the hall, I fell into a chair next to Maudy, and grabbed a napkin from the ceramic daisy napkin holder.

Maudy softened her tone, knowing Joe had done something awful. "What'd he do?"

I held out the napkin. "What do you think he did?" Wiping Joe's spit from my face, I lashed out. "You coddle him anymore than you do and I'll find you breastfeeding him next time I come over."

"Andie!"

"You baby him, Maudy. He's a grown man! I'm eight weeks pregnant, in case Joe forgot to tell you." I stood to leave. "By the way, it's twins."

"Twins?" Surprise drained the blood from Maudy's face. The tension lessened. Maudy took in a quick sharp breath. "Aw now, he'll change. This is wonderful news, sugah. I'm sorry. I'm just preoccupied with Joe's mood. I don't understand why you wanted him to come here instead of taking him home to care for him yourself. Isn't this good news, Al?"

Al nodded and chewed his food.

I swallowed my despair. "He'll change? When, Maudy? When will Joe change? What is a Christian man supposed to act like? Do they all spit on their pregnant wives? He's cruel and insensitive, and the worst thing is . . . he knows it! You keep saying he'll change, but he's worse. Maybe you can talk some sense into your son. And some manners."

Al wiped his mouth with a napkin, and then stood to close the door to the hallway so our voices wouldn't carry to the room where Joe moaned with an ice pack on his groin. "I've had enough. I'm calling Reverend. I want this nonsense stopped. Andie, I assure you, next time you see your husband, not only can you take him home where he belongs, but you'll get the husband you deserve."

Standing at the open back door, I wiped well-deserved tears from my eyes. "After all this time I doubt it. I'm not sure I can live with him any longer. But it's my fault as much as it is his. I should've never gone back with him after Mavis died."

"Please, Andie, a baby needs his daddy. Don't give up on Joe." Maudy said.

I shook my head and crossed my arms.

"Stay for suppah, sugah. I got some smoked sausage in the skillet and some limas in the pot, one of your favorite meals." Maudy's feeble apology was like trying to heal a child's boo-boo with a kiss.

"Thanks, but I need rest. I start a new job tomorrow. Please drive Joe home by Wednesday. I'm sure Calvin wants him better for next weekend's crusade."

A hard line had been drawn. Maudy was no longer my confidante. I sensed a clear difference in my mother-in-law's affection toward me. Blood was, after all, thicker than water.

§

Al had indeed called the church as he said he would. Word got back to me by way of Maudy that Calvin was furious with Joe, and that her beloved son had spent the better part of an hour on the phone cowering under Calvin's rage, leaving him humiliated and quiet with defeat. On Wednesday, Maudy drove Joe home, but my attempt to talk to him was fruitless.

He scowled at my light-hearted talk and turned away. "Stop, Andie," he said. "Just . . . stop. Your fru-fru bullshit conversation does not make me feel better. I'll never be what you want. But Reverend made me see that it's both our faults. Let me get through this on my own, and stop talking to me about it. I've got a lot on my mind. Reverend told me to accept it. I said I would try. So you got what you wanted." His hands swatted me away like I was an annoying insect. "Now leave me be."

December 1976
A Date That Will Live In Infancy

Andie

Working at the Tease Me Hair Salon for Candace was a breeze. Macramé plant holders filled with dusty silk ferns hung like ratty ponytails around the perimeter of the shop. The windows dripped with humidity, and the walls were covered in posters—large headshots of models sporting the latest perm, cut, and color. Glass and chrome shelving separated my workspace from four stylists, two sinks, and a manicuring station everybody shared. Although the wage was minimum, Candace's playfulness and sense of humor got me through the first trimester, the sick part, filling my days with laughter and free regular haircuts.

"*Walkin', after midnight . . .*" I heard Candace bellowing out Patsy Cline's song even before she opened the door. The last words fell tunelessly from her lips as she hollered a howdy-do to somebody in the parking lot. Still the queen of poufy, her bleached hair curled down to her Barbie-doll breasts, which bulged above a lace brassiere that showed through her too-tight T-shirt. Tar Heel blue stretch pants clung to every curve in her tiny butt and long legs, and her signature western boots clicked on the tiles as she wiggled through the door with coffee and a box of Krispy Kremes.

My skin felt hot and tight. Embarrassed and annoyed, I'd already gained forty pounds. I smoothed back my hair, and ran the palms of my hands over my stonewashed denim tent. Second-hand, well-used, and covered in spots and wrinkles, my entire pregnancy wardrobe had come from a local thrift store in Fashion Maternity Hell. Ungracefully, I pushed my big-bellied body out of my chair and stood. "No more donuts, what'd I tell you?"

Candace set the box on the counter and picked up a rat-tail comb to scratch an itch on the top of her head. "Oh, stop. You look good."

"Yeah? Well, your belly's flat enough to iron my dress on. What do you know?"

Kicking inside the fertile cave of my uterus, the babies grew quickly, like a tiny rosebush with two buds. Pregnant all over, especially in my legs, I walked with a back-and-forth gait, like a penguin, unable to balance the mass of baby taking me over. Joe had yet to accompany me on a visit to see Aunt Wy. He met her only once—at Thanksgiving. It was a day of firsts. The first time Joe had been to his in-laws since before the death of our son, and the first time my aunt enjoyed a holiday meal with family in over twenty years. Dixie and Wy indeed picked up where they left off, as if no time had passed between them, and Joe promised Wy he'd accompany me on my next doctor visit.

§

Aunt Wy's receptionist read me Joe's rambling, panicked message as I signed in. *Please tell my wife and her aunt I had a church emergency and can't make Andie's appointment. I've got to catch a plane. I apologize.*

I felt myself blushing as I stepped into Wylene's office. I stood there, not knowing what to say moments before the phone rang. Wylene waved *come on in*, excusing herself to take the call. I was relieved. After she said goodbye to *Doc*, who was obviously a colleague, she mashed out her lipstick-smeared cigarette and unleashed a coughing fit. Getting herself under control, she sat back in her chair and wheezed in short little breaths. "I'm down to a pack a day," she said. Shuffling through a few files before drawing her eyebrows together into a frown, she looked up at me and said, "So, where is the little bastard?"

"There's a meeting somewhere. They have to catch a plane."

She leaned over her desk and ran the tip of her tongue across her lips, as if to collect her thoughts. Her face reddened into angry blotches that traveled fast down her neck. And then she said, calmly, "You know, when I first laid eyes on your husband I thought to myself, what an attractive young man. He's polite, cordial, even uses the right fork. Hell's bells, Andie. He's surface. Shallow. Selfish. I don't want him in labor and delivery. You hear me?"

I shrugged. "I can't imagine why I expected him to show up."

"Did you really think it would save your marriage? It didn't work the first time, why did you think it would this time?"

"I wanted a child. I guess I'm selfish, too. I tried not to want children, Wy. I really did. It was useless. Now I have no choice but to pay the price for these babies." I shivered at my words. "I had hoped if he were with me during the birth, he might, oh, I don't know . . . change? Find some love in his heart for his children. For me." My tears fell on my aunt's desk.

Wylene tossed me a Kleenex. "We'll talk about this later, after you're on your feet. Find a labor coach. Anyone except Joe."

I sniffed and blew my nose. "I've asked my friend, Candace. Somehow I *knew* this would happen."

I also knew my marriage frustrated the hell out of Wylene.

§

At twenty-two weeks the babies were so big, Wylene had to sew up my cervix. At thirty weeks, the stitches started to snap. With the exception of doctor appointments and trips to the toilet, I was on mandatory bed rest to ease the possibility of premature labor. According to Wylene, the twins would've had more room if I had stayed on the diet prescribed, a difficult request considering my sweet tooth. My contractions started around week thirty-one, as many as twelve an hour. With only medicine and my sheer will holding the babies inside, my uterus went about its business of contracting, releasing, and preparing for the blessed event.

§

At week thirty-seven my pains started again. Excitement and fear reached new heights as I lay in bed, listening to the morning's rooftop lullabies from the pelting rain. It shimmered in stripes of light under the streetlight. As the next pain hit, I screwed up my nose and mouth and bore down, watching my face turn crimson and purple in the mirror over my dresser. Twelve minutes later at the next contraction with the veins distended in my neck, it was time to call Aunt Wy, Candace, and then Joe at the church.

I met Joe at the door in mid-contraction with my suitcase in hand. Forcing a smile, he appeared concerned as his eyes met mine. Until he opened his mouth. "You picked the worst day for this. I take one afternoon off to help Coot pull an engine out of a tough-lookin' '68 Stingray and then *you* call me." Clearly irritated, he excused himself to take a shower. Which made *me* irritated.

Joe took his time in the bathroom. I couldn't wait any longer. I walked through the steam to use the toilet. "My pains are ten minutes apart, but my water hasn't broke yet."

He offered no compassion. "Don't flush. Wait 'til I'm out of the shower."

"If you didn't want to take me, why not just stay at Coot's?" I snapped.

Joe stuck his head out of the shower. His look of exasperation raked my skin. "Don't start that crap," he said. I heard him sigh deeply, as if trying to compose himself. "Have you picked out names for these kids?"

I imagined he was trying to be sympathetic. In the midst of a strong contraction I clicked my tongue. "Did you think I was waiting until the last minute to name them? Last time I waited for you, you weren't around. I named Brian by myself. Daddy and I picked out names for the twins last week. *Not* to worry."

Joe stuck his head out of the shower again to glare at me.

I met his eyes and flushed the toilet.

"Goddamn it!" he screamed, flinging an empty shampoo bottle at my head. It missed and crashed against the door. "I swear you were born to torment me!"

§

I didn't bother to give Joe the look of pure infuriation I'd planned after he threw my suitcase into the trunk and slammed the lid. I just wanted to get there. He drove me to the hospital like a taxi cab driver—without saying a word or giving any indication of his feelings. It was strange and sad that in some cosmic sense I could sit right next to my husband and not see him, feel him, or care. I tried to relax and concentrate on my breathing. In. Out. Each contraction hit hard, the pain unleashing memories of my previous labor.

Clouds the color of a deep bruise built on the horizon. Rain-covered cars approached from the other direction with their headlights on, and as we approached Greensboro the squall hit. Goose bumps covered my arms from the cool air of the defrost. The windshield wipers slapped back and forth, and the rain stirred up more terrifying recollections of that night. But Joe only stared straight ahead, wrapped in his own thoughts, while I timed the prickly silence between us and the minutes between my pains.

§

When Joe wheeled me into the emergency entrance, my contractions were still ten minutes apart. I fought against the seismic urge to tell him, *just go home*. Smiling with relief when Candace appeared in the waiting room, I let go of my urge and focused, instead, on the miracle occurring inside me. Candace got in step beside my wheelchair, her boots clicking out a familiar beat on the hospital tiles. "Let's do this!" she shouted.

A nurse took the wheelchair from Joe and pushed me down a long polished hallway to the elevator. Sweat dripped from my forehead and clung to the short hairs that had pulled out of my ponytail. I looked up at Joe and sighed. Standing there, he watched the nurse roll me into the elevator and nodded something meant as a quick goodbye, allowing the doors to shut between us.

§

My babies ended up taking their own good sweet-patutie time. Sweat plastered my stringy hair to my neck and cheeks as Candace first blotted her face then mine, jumping from one subject to the next, and hollering *breathe!* every time I winced in pain. "Baby number one's all wampy-jawed," she said.

I looked inquisitively at the nurse taking my blood pressure. "Face up instead of face down," she explained.

One hour rolled into the next as vicious contractions sliced through my groin. I shut my eyes while my hands crawled over my stomach and the inside of my thighs. When the umpteenth contraction ended and my eyes opened, Dr. Wylene stood overflowing in her shoes by my bed surrounded by a group of young nurses. Poised in a lime green suit under a white lab coat, her face oily, a pen over her ear, and her hair frizzed out of its ponytail, she said, "Are we enjoying our beautifully, wonderfully, totally natural experience yet?"

I stuck out my tongue and gave her the finger. She threw her head back and roared with laughter, rotating on her heel to walk out of the room. The nurses quickly smothered their smiles and followed behind her, but at the door she turned back for a quick second and said, "Strong women, Andie . . . may we know them, may we raise them, may we be them." Then she blew me a kiss.

The next two hours passed in a blur. I don't remember much, other than the nurses transferring me onto a rolling bed, clicking the rails into place, and wheeling me under the searing lights of a ball field. I reached for Candace. "Where are we?"

"In a bright room. Surgery. Everything's fine," she said, holding tight to my hand.

Wylene, in full surgical gear, examined me. "Andie, sweetheart, I'm giving you a spinal block now. Then we'll see what happens."

"Just get them out!" I moaned.

My aunt laughed and patted my belly. "Not only are we getting them out, you get to watch the entire performance in living color!"

Candace helped me sit on the side of the delivery table, my legs dangling. "You've got to be in the midst of a contraction when Wy inserts the needle, honey." She encouraged me to hang on. I dug my nails into the shoulders of the nurse standing in front of me, anchoring me through the procedure. Her sympathetic eyes sparkled above her green mask covering her nose and mouth. Bearing down, I screamed and felt as though I were sitting on my baby's head. In seconds my water broke, pouring to the floor and into the shoes of the nurse.

Candace hollered. "The dam burst over here!"

I lay back on the delivery table, my pain unbearable. Closing my eyes, I tried to conjure my vision of the hands. Those peaceful hands that beckoned me as I suffered from the pain of Brian's birth and death. I kept my eyes closed tight, yearning to see them again. The hands with the missing left ring finger. The hands that soothed me in my time of utter sorrow.

Listening to the footsteps of nurses marching in and out of the delivery room like a Marine battalion, I felt the numbness take over. From the waist down, I didn't exist. The nurses carried out their orders. They draped, swabbed, and quietly relayed my vitals and that of my babies to Aunt Wy. What seemed like days was only a matter of minutes when twin number one turned and everything around me shifted into high gear. I could see that Candace thoroughly enjoyed the moment, asking dozens of questions until I wanted to stuff her facemask in her mouth. The laughing and joking quickly subsided when Wylene sat at my feet. She was all business when slippery baby number one crowned and cracked through the shell of my womb. It was more than just a beautiful experience. For one split second in time the room exploded in blinding white light, letting me know I had once again laid at death's door to give life.

A boy. Moments after he was born my baby boy lay against my heart and I counted his fingers and toes, traced the precious curve of his puckered ear, and thought of Brian. Blowing a kiss to my new son and rubbing his back, I felt tears run down the sides of my face, pooling in my ears. Without warning, a nurse snatched him off my stomach and I reached for him, calling him back the moment before the next contraction hit.

"Next one's coming down the chute. No time to stop now!" Wylene shouted orders like an Admiral at the helm. Bearing down again, I groaned deep and long as another little head crowned. Within minutes, my baby girl took her place on my stomach.

"A girl! Candace, look, a girl!"

"A *big* girl. This lil' piglet's got more meat on her than her brother," she said.

My fingers gently stroked my baby girl's face and tiny hands.

Candace kissed my cheek. "How blessed you are. One of each. Your heart's desire. I'll go tell Joe." But all I heard Candace say was the word, *heart*. I panicked. "Check their hearts, Wy, please. Tell the nurse to listen to their hearts!"

"These babies are fine. We'll give you a full update in a minute. They look just fine. I didn't detect any heart arrhythmia prior to birth, nor do I suspect any now. Calm down." Wylene ordered the nurses to report the date, time, and birth weight as soon as they had it.

"December seventh, ten thirty p.m. for baby boy, and ten fifty-two for baby girl, Doctor!"

Wylene laughed. "December seventh . . . a date that will live in infancy!"

I listened for shouts from the nurses. "Baby boy is six pounds two ounces, six pounds six ounces for the girl." Almost thirteen pounds of baby in my body.

Wylene patted herself on the back. "Ain't bad for one day's work," she said, and proceeded to stitch me from the inside out.

A few minutes later, a nurse shouted from the next room where my babies were trying out their lungs. "Got an Apgar score of nine for each baby, Dr. Oakley!"

"See there? Near perfect, I'd say." Wylene peeled off her gloves and dropped them on the delivery tray littered with gauze pads, bits of suture, and a little piece of umbilical cord. She cut off the middle fingers of her bloodied gloves, stuck them inside her mask and handed it to me. "A souvenir," she laughed. She planted a kiss on my forehead and smoothed the hair off my brow, then whispered into my ear. "We were lucky. You can't be patched up again. Be happy with these two, darlin', because you're done."

"I know. Thanks, Wy. I owe you."

The nurse asked if I had the babies' names for the records.

"Dillon Jennings and Gracie Mae," I replied.

§

Horribly bloated from the pregnancy and pee-yellow from a bad reaction to the spinal block, I lay enormous against hospital-white sheets; not my most attractive state. My wedding set cut into my sausage-like fingers, my bangs hung in my eyes, and my long, scraggly hair fell in tangles on either side of my cream-puff face. But my ears were open way before my eyes, listening to the soft shuffle of nurses and the cries of babies from somewhere down the hall.

Candace's voice was dry and sharp as two sets of footsteps entered my room. "Hey, Joe." She paused. "And who are you?"

He filled the air with well-chosen words. "Pastor Tony DeSanto. Nice to meet you. I understand we have you to thank for helping her doctor deliver the babies the way God intended, when they said it couldn't be done."

"It was in God's hands from *conception*," she said.

"Where are they?" Joe asked. "Where are the babies?"

Someone stepped toward my bed. "Is Mrs. Oliver sleeping?"

Candace knew I was in no mood for the feigned concern of my pastor. "Off and on."

"She looks like she's had a rough time of it. Don't wake her," he said.

"I wasn't planning on it."

Joe's voice rang with agitation. "Candace. I repeat. Are the babies in the nursery?"

"No, Joe. They're down the street eatin' pizza. Hell yeah, they're in the nursery. Where do you think they'd be?" Obviously, Candace was in no mood to watch her language either. I kept my eyes shut, but imagined Pastor DeSanto and Joe exchanging glances of disgust.

"Excuse me, Pastor. I'm going to the nursery," Joe said, attempting to smother his Southern accent.

"When you're done staring at your young'uns, get back here and be kind to your wife," Candace said curtly as she left the room.

Joe cleared his throat. "She's Andie's friend. She's not saved."

The brazen pastor whispered loud enough for me to hear. "That woman is covered in spiritual darkness. My suggestion is to get your family back in church and keep them there. Watch Andie . . . what she does and where she goes. Keep her safe in the fold." His words, veiled as a request, were really more of a subtle demand.

And then the Tasmanian devil blew into my room. "Joe, get your butt to the nursery and see them babies of yours." I opened one eye. Aunt Wylene, her eyes ablaze, stood with her fists nestled so deep into her fleshy hips they all but disappeared.

Joe bolted out, like a third grader summoned to the principal's office.

"The little ones?" asked Pastor DeSanto. "They're doing well?"

"So far, so good. A nurse can show you to the nursery window if you'd like." Wylene examined my chart.

Pastor DeSanto grinned. "I can't believe I'm standing next to such a famous female doctor, who I understand might be the next president of the Hospital's Medical Board. You—"

"Don't patronize me, Pastor. I don't care for your contrived flattery, and I don't play ball with pretty-boy preachers. Furthermore, I'm not about to go to your church or give you one damn dime. I answer to a higher power than your buddy Calvin Artury. Now if you'll excuse me, I have patients to attend to."

Pastor DeSanto stood slack jawed—as if a junkyard dog had just bit him.

I finally opened both eyes. "I see you met my Aunt Wylene."

§

Dixie and Daddy arrived the next morning and wheeled me to the nursery. "There, Daddy," I said with a smile, pointing to my babies behind the glass. "Dillon Jennings. You did good naming him."

"You don't mind I named him after Matt Dillon from *Gunsmoke*?"

"Course not. You love that show."

"Rupert will love that you named Gracie after Mavis Grace," he said.

"They're good names," I said. "But aren't they the most beautiful babies you ever laid eyes on?" I watched my parents' reflection in the window.

Tears fell down Daddy's face and onto the nursery window ledge. He smiled. "Almost as pretty as you were."

"Prettier," said Dixie.

Double Your Pleasure

Andie

I had wedged a changing table next to the kitchen table, and shoved a tiny chest of drawers against the back door of the trailer across from the bathroom. Dixie slept on my couch five feet from the babies' crib, which had been squeezed into a corner of the living room. Exhausted by the end of the week, Dixie called Daddy to come take her home. Caroline, newly married and pregnant with her first child, helped out a few days after Dixie left. Our mother insisted she get some on-the-job training. And then Maudy came to help. During the day she was a blessing, but at night, I worked solo. Consumed with the constant care of my infants, I had finally filled my life with purpose and meaning as my days and nights became indistinguishable.

My weight climbed to 200 pounds; the pregnancy had taken its toll on my body. I felt stretched out, like an old leather shoe. Purple stripes lined my underarms, stomach, and back and the fat on my abdomen jiggled like a tub of sour cream. Swollen with milk, my breasts leaked while my joints ached from giving birth to two babies. I felt, in a word, ugly.

Joe, meanwhile, used every excuse imaginable to stay away from home, and managed to find ways to become more and more indispensable to the House of Praise. He held the babies for pictures Maudy insisted on taking to send to Uncle Dodrill, but quickly handed them back to me afterward. He worked around the clock, it seemed, following Calvin every weekend to whatever city that booked the next big crusade.

In my attempt to keep the peace, I forced myself to church on Sunday without any help while winter dragged on. The four-hour services were simpler to manage, however. I claimed one of ten cribs lining the back wall of the nursery, a large glass-enclosed balcony above the sanctuary. Audio was piped in, but the whole ordeal was easier to ignore sitting upstairs in that sound-proof room. As promised to my husband, his parents, and to Calvin—I showed up.

At home, glass bottles boiled three times a day in the sterilizer on top of the stove. The babies created buckets of dirty diapers. My only hope for clean ones was sending them to Maudy. Al became my deliveryman for everything from laundry to groceries, while I spent the first cold, dreary months of 1977 inside my trailer at Shady Acres.

§

By March, Maudy and Candace took turns baby-sitting, while I packed as many errands into my time alone as I could handle. My world of bathing, feeding, and diapering my twins included long nights with either Dillon or Gracie or both crying for hours. Joe learned how to sleep through their nights of endless bawling, but I walked the floor with a tiny one in my arms, a baby cheek to my lips, acquiring little sleep myself. When I could sleep, I didn't. Instead, I stood at the crib with its mobile of smiling, bald-headed moons and watched every move my babies made. For months after I brought them home, I imagined Mavis and Loretta bending over the balcony of Heaven, totally captivated by my twins. In time, the hole Brian left in my heart healed over. All that remained was a ragged scar, sensitive and tender, but no longer painful.

§

Spring came, and then summer rolled in with its blast of heat and bright blue skies. Dillon and Gracie grew into chubby, squealing babies who demanded their mama's attention and got it. Joe insisted that I go back to work. But Candace had sold her beauty shop to the highest bidder. The thought of office work nauseated me, but I had to make the effort. Promising Joe I'd look for work, I checked the classifieds every Sunday and mailed résumés I'd typed on a borrowed manual typewriter. *It won't be so bad*, I told myself. *I'll never move out of this trailer otherwise.* Cramped beyond belief, I yearned for more space.

The twins were healthy, full of energy and filling lots of poopy diapers. Their drooly smiles lifted my spirits, eliminating thoughts of Joe and my plans to leave him. My babies were my life, they were my loves, and Joe observed it all from a distance. Until one day when he thought no one was watching. Whispering sweet words of love and devotion to each one, like he'd once said to me, he picked them up, first Gracie then Dillon, touched their little head, and kissed them.

It was that moment, that tiny shred of hope that turned me on my heel. I would stay with him a while longer.

§

The call came. "Andie, we'd like you to start work Monday." Southern States Insurance Company had reviewed my résumé, interviewed me and then hired me for basic clerical work. A full-time position, it paid six dollars an hour. I accepted. Then something grabbed hold of my heart and twisted it. How could I leave my children with a stranger?

I walked into the living room where Gracie and Dillon shared a crib. Their milky-white hands were curled like pudgy little paws against a freshly laundered sheet stretched over several mattress pads. *The Long and Winding Road* played softly on the stereo. Chubby legs and perfectly shaped heads, the twins filled every void in my life. I couldn't get enough of them. I touched their soap-scented skin with the tips of my fingers. Their cherry cheeks, their vanilla eyelids, their entire bodies were a constant reminder of the miracle that had occurred within me despite the odds.

Weary, I sat on the floor, leaned against the crib, and nodded off while the summer's warm breath billowed the curtains around the open window.

§

While Joe had yet to change a diaper, I juggled childcare between two days with Maudy and three days at the Methodist Church in Lexington. My strength gave out by Friday. Saturdays were filled with washing clothes and diapers in a Hotpoint wringer washer on the Olivers' back porch because Maudy refused to buy a washing machine. The grueling work of hanging every piece on the mile of clothesline that zigzagged in the backyard by Al's shop drained my energy. Pampers were a luxury saved for church.

Daddy drove to Salisbury every Saturday evening, bringing bags of groceries and gallons of milk, while Dixie showed her love by sending along homemade pies or cakes. A diet was an impossible project for me, knee-deep in babies and working full-time.

I was a married, single mother. I said good-bye to Joe every Friday after church, while my overwhelming impulse to ask for a hug or a word of kindness hit me like a brick in the chest. Starved for his attention and any love I could drag out of him, I desperately hoped he didn't notice the effect he had on me. It'd been over a year since we had any physical contact, other than accidentally touching arms or shoulders as we squeezed through our small living space.

Watching his bus pull away, it didn't take long for reality to sink in. I had babies to care for, and they took priority over Joe, my self-pity, and his incessant need to follow Calvin around the country like a puppy dog on a short leash.

November 1978
JIM JONES MASSACRE

Andie

I turned up the volume on the TV. Gracie, almost two, fussed and squirmed, while Dillon tugged on his ear in the crib. Both babies had developed upper respiratory infections. After wiping my daughter's little nose, I placed a bottle in her mouth, gently rocking and patting to quiet her. The evening news brought the first shockwaves to the world that religious leaders and their megachurches could be deadly.

"Today, followers of American cult leader Jim Jones and the Peoples Temple, died in a remote South American jungle compound in British Guyana called Jonestown. Some members were shot, others were forced to drink poison, but most willingly participated in what Jones said was an act of revolutionary suicide."

The hair on my arms stood straight up.

"California Congressman, Leo J. Ryan, received many complaints from his constituents regarding family members who were followers of Jones. He responded with an investigation. Having received permission from Jones, Ryan traveled to visit the group's compound. The congressman toured the settlement and met with Jones. Yesterday, Temple members passed notes to Congressman Ryan's party, requesting to leave with them. Ryan agreed. At an isolated airstrip, apparently under orders from Jones, gunmen from Jonestown ambushed Congressman Ryan's party. Ryan and four others were killed immediately. Some of the Ryan party escaped into the jungle."

"Jones then ordered the 'state of emergency' he had so long anticipated. A carefully rehearsed mass suicide took place. Everyone, except the very few who escaped into the surrounding jungle, either committed suicide or was murdered. More than 280 children were killed. Jones was found at Jonestown, fatally wounded by a gunshot to the head."

I shuddered as fearful images built inside my own head.

"Jim Jones began his ministry in 1953 as an independent minister in Indianapolis, but by the end of 1971, he had moved his congregation to California. His main church remained in San Francisco, but a second was also opened in Los Angeles. The Peoples Temple peaked earlier in this decade to include as many as 8,000 members. Jones was once a popular community activist who contributed cash and coordinated volunteers to support causes and political leaders."

A cold wave of familiarity pulsed through me.

"Jones appeared with many prominent politicians recently, including State Assemblyman Willie Brown. In 1976, Mayor George Moscone gave Jones a seat on the San Francisco Housing Authority Commission. Governor Jerry Brown was also seen attending services at the Peoples Temple. Today, after the 914 tragic deaths at Jonestown, Willie Brown said, 'If we knew then he was mad, clearly we wouldn't have supported him . . .'"

If we knew then he was mad. If we knew then he was mad . . . the words played over and over in my head. Calvin's House of Praise had grown steadily as he and his ministry team traveled the world. The television mega-ministry flourished, and his popularity increased by mega-leaps and mega-bounds every week. It seemed he was as cautious as he was charismatic, and had no intention of starting a commune in a third world country. I was certain Calvin would never make the same mistakes as Jim Jones. Yet this news had struck me silent, leaving me with one question: *Could he be worse?*

August 1979
OPPORTUNITY KNOCKS

Andie

I was to celebrate my twenty-fifth birthday in two days, the twins were approaching three, and life in Salisbury remained the same—cramped, poor, lonely, and hot.

Working a full-time job, I learned very quickly that I could not support two children and myself on my pitiful salary. Not alone. Joe was being forced to stay with me—I knew that—and I was forcing myself to stay with him. Oh, what a predicament I found myself in! For three years, from age twenty-two until I turned twenty-five, there was no such thing as uninterrupted sleep. I had no time to challenge Joe, the church, or my long-forgotten dreams. I felt fortunate to find my purse and car keys in the morning, and charged into every new day believing God's rising sun would somehow light my path to a better tomorrow.

August temperatures hovered in the nineties, with humidity you could drink. Dillon and Gracie fussed at night, rolled on sweat-soaked sheets and woke several times for water. I took a long weekend off work, hauling the twins and 'twin paraphernalia' to my parents' house to escape the high temperature of the trailer park for a few days.

§

Daddy's old dog fidgeted on the porch and settled its gray jowls on crossed forepaws. His hoary eyebrows twitched, keeping tabs on the world around him. "Hiya, Pitch." At the sound of his name, the dog—which resembled a lean bloodhound with sleek black fur—looked up and wagged his tail, despite his infirmities. I rubbed his silky ears and wondered if Pitch ever had hopes or dreams. What did he hope for or dream about? Maybe all Pitch knew how to do was wait. Patiently. For food, shelter, love. I knew something about that.

"I can't take it anymore, Daddy. I've got to have a house, with trees and an air conditioner. Somewhere the twins can play outside on a swing-set, in their own yard, under a shade tree. I'm sick of doing laundry at Maudy's house. I can't afford the laundromat. I've got to move to Winston-Salem, get a better job, and find a house. If one twin sleeps in the crib, the other sleeps with me in the bed. Joe, since he's not home much, well, he gets the couch."

I was not about to say that it'd been over three years since we had any type of physical relationship. Obviously, Joe got his needs met elsewhere. Though I'd come to despise Calvin all over again, I knew he was the one person who held our marriage together. As long as I showed up for church every week, he would not allow Joe to leave me stranded, and I needed Joe's entire paycheck more than anything else from him.

"What would Joe say if you proposed moving to Winston-Salem?" Daddy asked.

"He wants to stay where he is. Says it's all we can afford. He doesn't live there half the time. He travels in air-conditioned buses, stays in spacious hotel rooms."

"Let me give this some thought. You know Caroline and the baby are moving in with us? And she's pregnant again."

"I heard. I'm sorry things have gone bad for her. Little Bonnie isn't much younger than the twins. It's awful what Caroline's going through." But as far as I was concerned, fighting alcoholism in a man was easier than fighting a man's god, especially when that god was Calvin.

Pitch blinked his soulful eyes and yawned. He shifted, but didn't stand, his hips so painful that he moved only when my mother made him. She declared he was an animal that should be carried down behind the shed and shot in the head. Indeed, Dixie only saw life in two colors—black and white. You worked hard and lived well, then you died. There was no gray area. But I knew Daddy loved Pitch. He'd never stand for Dixie shooting his dog. Suffering was a divine calling for him and his dog. And he was bound and determined to demonstrate his point. I saw myself following in his footsteps, not in the physical sense, but in the spiritual.

The next evening I relaxed, grateful for my parents' assistance with two fidgety, inquisitive, and perceptive three-year-olds. I treasured my children's innocence, their clean smell and the taste of their peachy-soft cheeks on my lips. They kept me in a sane boat tied to a solid dock when otherwise I would've drifted far from the rocky shores of rationality and sensibility. Gracie clung to me, but Dillon's curiosity and spirit of adventure kept me running. Eventually, the weight melted off my size 18 body. No one noticed as I shrunk. The excitement of looking attractive suddenly seemed as silly and frivolous as accent pillows and ankle bracelets.

I walked out to the porch where Daddy had been playing *Cripple Creek* on his banjo for the twins until Dillon crawled up onto his lap, begging to hear another ghost story. Gracie held tight to my legs and tucked her bashful face behind them. My three-year-old girl had become a thumb-sucking growth on my side.

"Gracie!" said Daddy. "C'mon over here and listen to Grandpa's story."

She walked in front of me with her hands behind her back, then leaned into me again. "Go on, honey," I said. "Go sit by Grandpa. I'll bring you some cheese, okay?"

When I came back from the kitchen, Gracie was perched on Daddy's knee and had about sucked the skin off her thumb. Daddy tilted forward, looked each grandchild in the eye, lowered his voice, then burst out with a *boo*! As always, Gracie shrieked while Dillon squealed for more.

I set a slippery plastic pile of yellow cheese near Gracie. She held her slice by the end, taking a tiny bite of cheese, and then dropping crumbs on the porch. I started to clean up after her the moment Dixie stepped out to join us.

"Let the child eat. I'll sweep it up later."

Guarded, I watched my mother belly-tickle Gracie who pulled up her little knees and folded in on herself, squealing and giggling. I sat in amazement as Dixie then kissed Dillon all over his chubby face again and again. I suspected she loved her grandbabies much more than Caroline or me, as I could not recall a time when she showed that kind of affection toward either of us.

"Your daddy and I have been talking." Dixie collapsed on the seat next to Daddy, the way she always did. As if she wanted you to know relaxing wasn't something she did or that any woman should do. "You know we love these babies. I agree with Bud . . . even though Caroline's moving in and costing us a small fortune, we need to give you a down payment on a house."

Moved to tears, I lifted Gracie back to my lap. "Oh, Dixie, I—"

"Hush. It's our gift to you, not to Joe. The house has to be in your name only. We're not so sure Joe will be around in the future and I don't want the two of you fighting over it. These children need a home, something other than the junk yard you've been living in the past seven years."

My emotions were mixed as we worked out the details. I was grateful for parents who cared enough to rescue me from poverty, and yet embarrassed that I needed rescuing in the first place. Unfortunately, I knew it would take both Joe and me working overtime to pay for a house.

§

Three days later I asked Maudy to baby sit. Choir practice had been cancelled and Joe was home. Opportunity came knocking and finding time to talk business with Joe was not a simple task. I needed to seize the time when it surfaced. The conversation quickly turned bitter. I fought hard against the tears I refused to let fall and bit my lip to stifle the outcry, but it was no use. "I need security!"

"You need your head examined if you think I'm moving closer to your parents!"

"Do you really think we can finish raising our kids in this trailer? We've got to give them a place to play other than a patch of dirt in a trailer park."

"You should've thought of that when you brainwashed me into not using a rubber!"

"You should've thought about brainwashing years ago when you went to work for Calvin!" I bolted to the bedroom.

"Good God, Andie!" Joe showed no signs of relenting.

I clenched my jaw to kill the sob in my throat. My skin prickled with resentment at the detachment that rang clear in his voice. Lying on the bed, my fight wasn't finished. I stood and my feet hit the floor like meat pounders. I stormed back into the kitchen where Joe sat reading Calvin's latest book, *The Deceived and The Damned*. He had taken to reading Calvin's books and tracts like a starved animal.

He looked up. "What now?"

I felt pain and loss twist inside me again. "I'm not stupid, Joe. I know you've been unfaithful to me since the twins were born and before that. Why does Calvin excuse it? Do you really believe God winks at your carefully hidden infidelity?"

With a visible force of will, Joe composed himself. His lips twisted into a cynical smile and he raised one brow. "Have you not heard a word of what I've told you these past few years? I used to worry about a lot of things I didn't understand. Not anymore. Reverend speaks the gospel truth. Reverend is my Shepherd. I am his sheep. He preaches private sermons to the ministry team when we're on the road. That's why you're so deceived. Your mind is saturated with darkness, you don't listen, and you don't care what God has to say."

"I care what God has to say, not Calvin!"

Joe quoted scripture. His voice was dry and emotionless. "*And David took him more concubines and wives out of Jerusalem.* The men of the Bible had many women. God allows men things women cannot have, according to the scriptures."

"You can't be serious!"

He spoke with quiet, iron control. "Your fat ass is staying in this trailer in Salisbury and I want you to leave me the hell alone about it."

Quoting scripture one moment and cussing the next, Joe's insults were no longer shocking and I forgot them almost as quickly as they flew out of his mouth. I simply swallowed my hurt. "But what about our children? Whether you like it or not, they can't grow up here!"

Once again he gave me that disturbing, totally unexpected smile. "Like I said, you should've thought of that a long time ago. You accuse Reverend Artury of manipulation, but everything you do is to manipulate me into something I don't want." Then he did what he always did to win an argument. He grabbed his jacket and keys and left.

There was a war going on in Joe's accent as he battled to unload his redneck persona. His smoking, drinking, and cursing had almost stopped. He'd become a religious zealot. Quiet and cold as always, he had submerged himself further into the teachings of the church and its leadership. His whereabouts were unknown to me for weeks at a time, only calling home on occasion from crusades all over the world. And yet, in front of the world, he played the role of husband and father. He told me I spoiled the twins. *Ridiculously over-protective* were the words he used. I didn't care what he thought. I knew every crease in their necks and every dent in their knuckles. My life with my children was profound and inseparable. The twins and I had our own secret language. A dialect Joe didn't care to learn.

October 1979
THE PANTS IN THE FAMILY

Andie

Saturday morning's air had chilled with the season's first frost. The real estate lady arrived at Daddy's house early. Mrs. Greer—the only name she gave—waited in the car. I left the twins with Dixie who made me promise to get back before noon so she could finish the second coat of wax on her floors.

We headed to Turner Street in Winston-Salem, driving past poor, stunted homes that hadn't seen a fresh coat of paint since Eisenhower was in office. Houses that didn't concern themselves with lush lawns, pretty porches, or roof repairs. Mrs. Greer's car coasted until it came to the 'for sale' sign on the corner where a small red brick house stood stiff and alone. The place looked forlorn and run-down: the painted white trim and eaves peeled like blistered skin, and the porch sagged in the middle. I pictured a tired, swayback nag. "It said *rambling ranch* in the classifieds," I said. "Looks like it's about to ramble on out of here."

Ignoring the goose bumps that prickled my arms, I stood on the porch and pushed the front door a little wider following Mrs. Greer inside and wrinkling my nose at the musty smell. I glanced back at the open door before moving deeper into the living room. Cold, dark, and dank, the air reeked—a thick, nauseating odor of something dead, decayed, and forgotten. Instinctively, I reached for the light switch. Nothing happened.

Faded wallpaper curled and peeled away in places, revealing cracked and crumbly plaster underneath. The floor creaked beneath us. I raised my eyebrows. *This house could be cleaned up and livable. Maybe.*

"The old man who lived here had cats. Lots of them." Mrs. Greer put her hankie to her face, covering her nose.

"No kidding," I said. Covered with yellow spots, the ceilings reminded me of my tear-stained pillow. "This house has a story."

"They repaired the roof last month." Mrs. Greer said. "But that's all they've done."

"You think?" Despite the cracked walls, stained ceilings, and ancient picture window with wavy glass, the room appealed to me. In the cobwebby corner to my left I could easily imagine a splendid tree with a thousand twinkling lights and many shiny ornaments.

"Try to see the possibilities." Mrs. Greer coughed.

"Can I see the kitchen?"

There were no appliances and from the looks of it, squirrels and mice had dined on a bag of grits left in the cupboard. Rodent turds rolled everywhere. "My mother would pitch a fit if she saw this. She's so meticulous about her kitchen." I wandered through the rest of the house. "Hmm, and a dead bird, too." A torn-up bird with its brown feathers was scattered over the God-awful brown carpet.

"At least we know where that putrid smell is coming from," said Mrs. Greer, as she poked her head into the bedroom.

I tried to remain optimistic. The place, admittedly, was a wreck. I had hoped to get a little more for my daddy's money.

Mrs. Greer appeared positive. "The owners are Lester and Effie Gerber. They'll carry the financing. They'll have to. No bank will loan on the place. It's got potential, doesn't it?"

That's what I wanted—potential. I stopped at the back door, frozen. "A fenced backyard. It's big. Look at that huge tree. The twins could have a tire swing and a puppy."

Mrs. Greer pointed to a large barn-like building against the fence. "Please notice the backyard shed is near as big as your one-car garage."

I couldn't imagine what I would need a shed for. There was plenty of storage in the house and garage. Certainly more than I had in the trailer. The walls, floors, and ceilings needed stripped and either repainted, repapered, or refinished. The thought of it made me more tired than I already was. It was once someone's home. The question was, could I make it mine? Mrs. Greer called my attention to the cabinetry and woodwork throughout, as well as the hardwood floors under the nasty carpets. Standing outside, I spied the elementary school at the top of the hill, within walking distance.

"I'll make an offer. I have to talk to my father first. He'll have to agree to do the work and donate the material. He told me to get a fixer-upper and this certainly is one. Maybe I can get it livable before my husband comes home from Africa in six weeks."

"Your husband's in Africa?"

"On business," I said. It often embarrassed me to say who Joe worked for.

Mrs. Greer opened the car door, but I had stopped at the curb, scraping the bottom of my shoe onto the grass. "Dog shit. I think somebody's trying to tell me something."

§

When I arrived at my parents' house, the smell of roast chicken and floor wax hung in the air. "Sorry, Dixie. I lost track of the time."

She pointed to the study. "Your daddy wants to talk to you. The twins are napping upstairs. Next time I have to wax the floors, you can do it for me. See how much fun you have with kids hanging on your legs." Dixie was addicted to housework like her friends were addicted to alcohol and men. The best thing for me to do was walk away, which is what I did. I walked into the study and plopped into Daddy's recliner, fingering the cigarette burns in the upholstery.

At his desk, Daddy leaned back in his chair and lit a cigarette. The chair springs squeaked gently. "Well, Rosebud? You find anything worth buying?"

Mustering my optimism, I relayed the details of the house, and then with vivid recollection I repeated my brother-in-law's prediction. "Ray told me once I'd have to become head of the home, wear the pants in the family." I took a sip of Daddy's strong black coffee. "I have to protect my children, provide for them."

He folded his hands across his chest. "Will he move with you?"

"I think Calvin will make him. Publicly, the ministry team walks a fine line. Unless I turn my back on the church first, Calvin won't allow Joe to leave me. So I'll continue to attend services to keep us together. I'm stuck. Unfortunately, I never consulted my budget when the pangs of motherhood fell on me. I need the money he brings in," I sighed. "It's become a marriage of convenience for both of us." I pressed both hands over my eyes. They burned with weariness. "But Daddy, Joe does care for the kids."

Daddy raised his eyebrows and took another hearty pull on his cigarette.

I stood. "It's hard to believe, I know. I'm assuming he'll want to stay with me for their sake. I've been saying for years, maybe someday I can get him out of Calvin's grip. I guess it's easier to hope, than to actually give up."

"Do *you* love him?"

I paused, not knowing what to say. "When Mavis died I wanted it to be over."

"That's not the answer I'm looking for."

"I know."

"Someday, the kids may need braces. The expenses get bigger when the kids get bigger."

"That's why I need his paycheck."

"I won't work over there if he's there."

I laughed. "He's never home. This house is for the kids and me. Not Joe. He won't appreciate it anyway." I walked to the door.

"And I won't miss *Gunsmoke*. I have to watch *Gunsmoke*."

"I know, Daddy."

§

Dixie and Daddy's check for five thousand dollars secured the house. At closing I had a twinge of guilt signing the papers alone; buying a house without Joe. It didn't last long.

I quit my secretarial job in Lexington, and said goodbye to Candace. Looking around the empty trailer, I knew I should've moved from Shady Acres a lifetime ago. I picked up Dillon and held Gracie's hand in the doorway. We'd spent many years there. Years that festered inside me like an infected wound. I closed the door for the last time. As I sat in the car and put the new house key on the old worn microphone key chain, I said, "Mavis, you hear me? It's been a long road out of here. Put in a good word for me, will you? I'm walking on eggshells again."

On the way to Winston-Salem, I stopped at the Village Tavern—an upscale restaurant—and turned in my new employee paperwork. My new job as Hostess would start on Monday. I had packed Joe's things, what little he kept in the trailer, and hauled them in boxes to the refurbished house on Turner Street. I girded myself for a new life with the twins, whether Joe decided to stay—or not.

§

When I met Joe at Piedmont Triad International Airport, he and the rest of the ministry team were preoccupied, moving Calvin and his luggage swiftly to a waiting limousine before tending to their own baggage. I forced a smile at Joe's surprised look on his face. I'd rarely met him at the airport, only when necessary. We walked in silence to the short-term parking lot and then I broke it to him quickly.

"You did WHAT?" He threw his bags into the trunk and slammed the lid.

"Daddy gave me the down payment. Why don't we just get in the car?"

"Do my parents know what you did?"

"Al helped me move. Yes, they know. They're happy for us. I also called the church and asked Fannie to contact Calvin in Africa, since I know he likes to be informed of everything that goes on in our lives. I had hoped he told you."

"No, Reverend didn't tell me! I doubt Fannie told him. He has more important things to think about. Your trivial pursuits are not on the top of his list. How could you do such a thing to me again? We have to live within our means! You can't do stuff like this without my consent!"

"Well, I did, and it's done. And it can't be undone. The house still needs work."

"Don't expect *me* to help."

"I won't. Aren't you the least bit excited to finally live in a house?"

"No. I'm not. Shady Acres was cramped, but it's all we could afford. How do you plan to make the payments?"

"I'll handle it. As usual, I'll take care of everything."

Joe walked through the new house, pointing out everything wrong with it. "I'm glad you own this rat hole, Andie. This is *your* problem. Not mine. Where are my clothes?"

"Why do you stay with me, Joe? You don't love me, why does Calvin force you to stay with me? Do you even love Dillon and Gracie?"

"Don't ask me stupid questions like that. I need to take a shower and rest. Do you have any idea how long it takes to get home from Africa?"

"I want to know . . . do you love your children?" I asked again.

Joe frowned, his face an effigy of contempt. "Of course I do. It's why I'm here."

"Then why don't you get a better-paying job, for their sake?"

Joe threw his suitcase down the hallway. Black scratches marred wood floors I had polished to a mirror shine. "You have no regard for the way I was brought up, do you? None. It's all about you, isn't it, what *you* want. You use the kids to get it. You've used them to keep me. Well, it's working. But I will NOT quit my job because you want me to. I won't get a *better* job, as you put it, so the twins can get a few extra toys, a new bike, or a trip to Disney World. I work for the church because I'm concerned about their souls. And if that means living in a lesser house, driving a lesser car, or a few missed meals, then so be it! You will not use one red cent of our tithe or pledge money on this house! Get that through your thick head!"

"Got it," I said. "I think I finally got it." Calvin had always preached that God wanted his children to have the best life had to offer. But the fancy suits, custom buses, expensive restaurants, and plush hotels that the ministry team was awarded did nothing for the families at home. It was all done to look as though God had heaped upon Calvin every blessing from above.

I listened to the sounds of Joe. Unpacking, cursing, tearing through our new house, looking for his *things*. Muttering beneath his breath. The newly varnished hardwood felt cold and smooth under my bare feet as I tiptoed to the backyard and sat in lonely silence on a lawn chair. Wild grief slashed through my chest wall, landing on the painful knot I called my heart. I placed my hand on my breast. My long ago vows choked me, as memories of a kinder Joe flickered behind my closed eyes holding back more tears.

Joe walked out to where I had curled myself into a wounded heap. He ignored me, and stood gazing at the storage shed. I managed to get into my car without allowing my tears to fall. The raw sores of my aching life needed something equivalent to the healing balm of Gilead. It was time to pick up the twins.

April 1982
MONEY COMETH

Andie

With the house finished as much as I could afford, I experienced for the first time a sense of pride in my home. But I could no longer depend on Daddy to help me. He had taken sick with asthma and his doctor forbade him to breathe fumes of any kind. My parents were suddenly at each other's throats, but that didn't stop Dixie from hiding Daddy's cigarettes.

I needed a better job. I'd fixed up my house with gently used furniture purchased at street sales and Goodwill, all while Joe traveled the world for Jesus on extended trips to Africa, Asia, Israel and Europe. My focus had turned from food to decorating my home. I had exchanged one sin for another and my paycheck wasn't enough to pay my maxed out credit card.

But the good news was that I was once again on speaking terms with Libby. One morning Ray and Libby knocked on my door holding a house-warming plant and a box of glazed donuts. I gave them a quick tour of the place. Impressed with my gumption while hanging onto the strings of a marriage, Ray praised me for my strength. "Mama said the house looks great. I had no idea you could do this."

Libby spent time in each room, asking me how I got the floors the color of elderberry honey, and where did I purchase such pretty woven rugs. Sunlight flooded through the new picture window as I showed her my gently-used couch and chair, reupholstered in a chocolate fake suede. "It's comfortable and wears well," I said.

"Andie, the house is lovely. You and your mama have such a knack for decorating. It's so clean and cozy, and I swear it looks like you paid a fortune for some of this."

"Not at all. Garage sales. Every Saturday morning. Even Gracie's piano. We bought it at an estate sale last week."

After discussing the work that had been done on the house, the conversation drifted to life with Joe, Ray and Libby's new farm in Richmond, and of course—the twins. Finally, over coffee, Ray asked me the question I was dreading. "What about you, Andie? What are your plans for keeping this place?"

I blinked, then cleared my throat. "I want to be my own boss. I think the entrepreneurial bug has bitten me. There's been no sign of a raise for Joe and I don't anticipate one. So I need to make up the difference. Running my own business is a better way to survive than what I'm doing. I need to build something for my family. I'm tired of working my butt off for pennies and making somebody else rich. I have no college, as you know, and have been stuck in minimum wage jobs for years. I also need to keep the kids near me while I work."

I blew my bangs off my forehead, then bit into my donut. "I can make these, you know. Common sense I got. It's the business experience and capital I lack. I guess I just need a break."

Ray smiled. He looked at his wife. Libby nodded. "I have what you need," Ray said. "I've got the capital. It's a risk and I'm not sure about you taking on a business; it's more work than you can imagine. I may never see a return on my money, but if you can do with a business what you've done to this old house, we'll at least break even."

I don't think I slept for a week after Ray and Libby left that day.

§

Joe, once again, didn't care to ask what I was up to. He never thought to question what my interests were, what I did when he was gone, or what my dreams or goals in life might be. His life was separate and apart from mine. My wants and needs took a back seat in a big bus. I forged ahead and secured a commitment from Mavis's Aunt Lula as my partner, and transformed myself into an entrepreneur, even if I didn't recognize it. Out of necessity, I became a business owner, and quit my job at the Village Tavern to put my business plan together.

Over the following weeks, Oak Hill Cafeteria was born. A mixture of soul food and good Southern cooking. Lula and I rented a postage-stamp sized storefront off Miller Road, not far from Baptist Hospital and Business Route 40. We worked non-stop converting the old store into a country restaurant. A breakfast counter with naugahyde-covered bar stools stood at the back, and I filled the front with mismatched wooden tables. Antique lace curtains hung in the large windows at the front. I knew the old-fashioned charm would draw customers almost as much as our good cooking.

The cafeteria was open for business from 6 a.m. to 8 p.m. daily, except Sundays. Meals after 4 p.m. were served family-style. Breakfast and lunch consisted of whatever Lula or I had a notion to fix for the day. Cream cheese stuffed french toast, shrimp and grits, waffles and fried chicken—whatever sounded good to us. Customers chose from three main entrées, and lunch included a dessert choice from one of Lula's cakes or pies that most women chucked their diets for. I wrote the menus on two large blackboards at either end of the dining room.

At suppertime, customers didn't need to order, and there was no need to keep track of who ate what or how much. I worked the counter while Janice, my only employee, served beverages and breads and kept the country buffet and salad bar full. Patrons served themselves until they had eaten all they could hold. One price fit all.

After a rocky start, the cafeteria earned a reputation both Lula and I were peacock proud of.

Eyes On The Prize

Reverend Calvin Artury

I was furious with Joe. The men on my team were instructed to control their wives, their spending habits, their loose lips, and keep them busy working for the good of the church. But Joe had never been able to rein in his wife from the day he married her. When I discovered Andie's frivolous business venture, I called Joe to my office. Oh, the heartache of the prophets! For thousands of years we have endured the trials of fire. Mine grew hotter every time I had to deal with the Olivers.

He sat across from my desk, averting his eyes and massaging the tension out of his palms. To be so coy and flamboyant with the women, Joe shrank around me like a penis suddenly gone flaccid.

"Do I have to fire you?" His empty stare didn't faze me. "Every time you go away she buys a house, or a car, and now a business? Money you should be putting into the work of God is getting sucked up by the materialism of your wife!"

"I hate to confess this, Reverend, but no matter how much I yell at her, I can't stop her. I didn't anticipate her success," he said, barely audible.

"Do you envy her? Her success?"

No response. Just another blank stare. I crossed my arms and waited, bristling at his cowardice.

He squirmed in his seat. "I hate having to stay married to her. My life is here, with you, in the church. Not out there playing *Father Knows Best.*"

The seriousness of his tone provoked a change in my strategy. "We're all feeling the stress of the ministry. Evan and I have set you apart, pulled you into the more private projects."

"I appreciate it, Reverend. It's just that—"

"Just what, Joe?"

Joe turned his head. "Nothing."

I stood and walked around to the front of my desk, then lifted Joe's hands and held them in my own. "You must remember you are a mighty warrior. You've been called into the service of the Lord. These hands of yours . . . they're anointed. I think you know, there's no middle ground in serving God. You're either in or you're out. No teetering on the fence. *Many are called, but few are chosen.* You were chosen by Almighty Jehovah to do battle for Him. Keep your eyes on the prize, Joe."

I kept my features deceptively composed. I wanted him to feel only my authority mixed with the tenderness of the Lord. "I have not heard from God as to ending your marriage. Andie is not to be put in harms way. The wrong kind of attention will bring the enemies of God to our doors to destroy the ministry. Don't be responsible for that."

When I wasn't preparing for the next sermon, leading staff meetings, or stuck in a barrage of business meetings, my mind drifted to the delicate situation surrounding Joe and Andie. Satan besieged me with thoughts of them day and night, robbing me of my much-needed time in prayer and supplication before the Lord. The powder keg had shifted from Mavis and now rested on the shoulders of the Olivers. Joe had no idea that I would've given my right arm to have Andie secured within the walls of the ministry rather than him. Oh yes, it was a delicate situation.

Into The Future

Andie

At six, the twins were all arms and legs. They loved wrapping themselves all the way around their daddy's waist and neck, and it thrilled me to watch them do it. My heart warmed whenever I found Dillon or Gracie in Joe's arms. More often than not, however, Joe arrived home frustrated and short-tempered, spanking them over trivial mistakes. One afternoon it was for leaving their bikes in the driveway. "Don't look at me that way. They're my children as well as yours. Sparing the rod means spoiled rotten children!"

"But you've got to show them love, too."

"I tell them I love them every day. They may be whining babies around you, but they'll not grow up to be heathens. Not around me."

Still, there were times when Joe was restless, when he hadn't slept in days, and any clamor, any creak, any stifled voice might rile the father they barely knew—a man who smiled one moment and screamed the next. He was a shouter; a weary man with constant headaches who insisted Calvin's worn-out ways of bringing up good Christian children was the only way; a tough talker who showed affection with cold hugs and half-smiles on Friday nights when the sun set behind the church and in the teary eyes of his children. Nights when ministry team families gathered around the big shiny busses, saying their good-byes. Dillon and Gracie watched the man they called Daddy load his suitcases into the bus. Children trying to be brave, careful not to make a spectacle or embarrass him when the air smelled like diesel fuel, when silence was their secret game and their gift to him, when all they wanted and hoped for was love from him. Nothing else. Just love.

It broke my heart and wore my nerves to shreds.

He said I needed to knock them down a peg or two, and I probably let Dillon and Gracie get away with a few more childish pranks than I should have, but all too often, I had to step in between them and their daddy. I had to. Shielding them from their father's dogmatic doctrine and his relentless refusal to allow them a normal childhood with secular music and Friday night sleepovers and birthday parties became a weekly event. I'll tell you what—as far as Joe was concerned, the twins were put on this earth to walk *his* walk and talk *his* talk. Become little Calvin clones he could be proud of. In time, the twins avoided him entirely. He picked on Dillon and scared Gracie to death. So I took them with me to the cafeteria, rather than leave them with Joe. He possessed no paternal instincts—just as Dixie had predicted so many years before.

§

Thankfully, my little restaurant thrived. It surprised everybody. In the time it took to transform the fledgling idea into a decent business, Lula and my relationship blossomed from our shared love and memory of Mavis into a strong friendship and partnership.

"Praise be, you jus' like Julia Chiles!" Lula said.

My life at Oak Hill Cafeteria bore about as much resemblance to Julia Child's as my legs did to Cybill Shepherd's. At least the rules for owning my own restaurant were clear, and I knew how to follow them; my routines set as a well-made banana pudding.

The seasons of my life came and went. My work was time-consuming and grueling, and I frequently despised my vendors and the long hours of paperwork. But the restaurant eventually turned a small profit, and I believed if I worked hard I could retire well before my fiftieth birthday. That if I could show Joe we were financially secure and independent without his job—maybe he would retire too and we could finally rebuild our lives. It was time to put my nose to the grindstone and work my ass off for the next few years. And that's exactly what I did.

PART FIVE
Form And Void

July 1987
THE DARWOODS

Andie

The Darwoods lived upstairs over the drug store, across the street from the cafeteria. The small apartment was home to Henry and his wife, Vernise, and their two children, Lloyd and Drema. Henry, a bus driver for the city of Winston-Salem, and his family were my regular customers. I fed them meals at half-price and sent leftovers to Vernise almost every week. For that, the Darwoods loved us back and considered us—family.

Dillon's friend, Lloyd, was the sweetest boy and talked with a lisp. His sister, Drema, played the piano and taught Gracie how to read music. For me, watching Gracie and Drema play together was like watching old reruns of Mavis and me. Typical ten-year-olds, the boys tormented the girls until Gracie came screaming into the cafeteria for Aunt Lula to make them stop.

But at the end of the day, Dillon and Gracie finished homework, read, or watched TV on the small black and white in the back while I scoured pots, mopped floors, and prepared menus for the next day.

"Dillon?"

"Ma'am?"

"Turn off the lights, pull the blinds." Ten o'clock. Work was over.

As alike as they were, however, my twins couldn't have been more different. Dillon's hair sparkled golden in the sun with waves that hung in his gleaming blue eyes. Gracie's pale and washed-out tresses were pencil straight. Dillon was G.I. Joe in a little boy's body. But there wasn't a tomboy bone in Gracie's frilly four-foot two inches. She was a girly-girl. Gracie's blue eyes with lashes tipped in pixie dust shined so bright, I could see them from across the room.

Fortunately or unfortunately, depending on how you wanted to look at it, the twins developed no real attachment to Joe. It bothered me that he never thought to talk to them about his travels, ask them if they had any questions about his job, or even inquire about their day at school. They had long ago learned when their daddy arrived home from a crusade to go straight to their rooms. Gracie had no problem with this. She loved school. Her grades reflected it. She'd learned to read by the age of four and had she not been so tiny, the school would've started her a year early.

Dillon, on the other hand, inherited my love of daydreaming and had no time to learn when there was so much to do outdoors. He loathed sitting still in church. He hated memorizing scripture and opted for the easy ones. I tried to help him, but I knew his sense of adventure meant that he belonged outside kicking a soccer ball or riding his bike. He barely squeaked by in school and I kept that fact hidden from his daddy.

Joe and I had settled into a relationship where I raised the children and he remained absorbed in church work. I still attended services once a week for appearance sake, and pretended Joe loved me; it got me through knowing his affections were displayed elsewhere. Most of the time, we hid in our respective corners. The awkward truth of the matter was, I used my children to ward off the loneliness of being abandoned by my husband for years on end and had come to value the life I had carved out for myself.

Like so many women, I lived a comfortable lie.

Libby had stopped bugging me to leave him. My life revolved around the twins and the propaganda I dished out to the public: that we were a typical American family.

After five years of backbreaking work and little time to think about myself, my weight hovered at an all-time low. One hundred twenty-five pounds. At thirty-three, I have to say, I looked better than I ever did. That is, when I found the time to fix my hair and makeup, slip into a dress instead of blue jeans, and shove my feet into heels instead of flip-flops.

When I was thin, Joe wanted sex from me. When I wasn't, he ignored me like a fat woman in a freak show. His inconsistent behavior had worn on me throughout the years. My life, as always, ran according to his moods. An occasional kiss, when I smelled fresh as a daisy, was abandoned when I came home haggard and worn out from a sixty-hour workweek at the cafeteria. By our fifteenth wedding anniversary, Joe's attention was more often focused on our new black lab, Prissy. And only the puppy paid attention to his tirades—Prissy-girl was the better listener.

§

"A trip to Hawaii? Are you serious? I can't leave the cafeteria."

"Lula can take care of it. You'll only be gone a week. It's Reverend Artury's first miracle crusade on the islands. He suggested I ask you to go," Joe said.

"Why?"

"If you don't want to go, fine. I just thought since it was our wedding anniversary, you might like a nice trip. God's promised a special anointing to those who attend this crusade."

"Oh, you mean God will tell the poor souls who can't afford to travel to Hawaii—too bad sucker, no anointing for you?"

"Your sarcasm is sending your soul straight to Hell. You know that, don't you?"

I had learned to ignore my religious zealot husband. Especially, his attempt to mimic Calvin's doomsday prophesies. "How can we afford it? All I make goes back into running the cafeteria, you know that."

"My way is paid, as usual. I cashed in a life insurance policy for you."

"You did what? Joe! It's all we had if something ever happened to you! With all the flying you do?"

His eyes flashed. "Who cares? Your daddy will take care of you. What difference does it make in the grand scheme of things how you get to go?"

"But, I—"

"There's no hope for you. Forget I asked," he said, as he walked away from me.

I blew out an exasperated breath and tugged at his arm. "Don't be an ass. I'm sorry. I apologize. Sure, it'd be nice to get away," I sighed. "Maybe we can spend some time alone?"

Joe moved closer and kissed my forehead. "Yeah. Maybe so. Besides, you look great; it'd be a damn shame not to show you off before you balloon back up to 200 again."

§

"The Darwoods are here!" somebody shouted toward the kitchen.

"They's a nice-looking bunch." Lula peeked out the pass-through window while dishing collards into a large serving dish. "'Cept Vernise. No self-respecting black Baptist woman I know wears pants in public."

"Be nice, Aunt Lula," I said. "I've got to ask them to take care of the twins for a week while I go traipsing off to Paradise with Joe. I feel so guilty."

"You deserve this! You go, leave this place to me. Iffen I need 'em, I gots a lady or two at the church to hep me."

I put my arms around Lula. "Thanks. Dixie's got her hands full with Daddy. He's been so sick. Maudy and Al are too old to keep up with the twins. Libby and Ray live so far away. At least with the Darwoods, the kids will be with their friends."

It was a first for me on many levels. The first time I'd been away from the twins for more than a day, the first time I saw the ocean, and the first time I attended one of Calvin's miracle crusades. Little did I know, it'd be the last time.

A GRIEVED SPIRIT

Reverend Calvin Artury

Rigid behind my palatial desk, I felt like the President granting an interview. I put down my notepad and smiled. My latest television studio office was much bigger than my church office. Plush and spacious, the grand suite was long past due. Persian rugs covered marble tiled floors. My designer had arranged priceless artwork, stately leather chairs, and elegant tables and lamps around the room. Secure as if the righteousness of Christ pulsed through my veins, I sat poised in my crisp, Dior shirt and tie, scowling at Evan like Almighty God at the Great White Throne Judgment.

"Joe got her to come," he said.

"She needs deliverance," I made my fingers into a steeple, something my mother always did. *Here's the church, there's the steeple, open the door . . . see all the people.* All the people. All the people except Andie. Resting my elbows on my armchair and peering across the desk, I reminded Evan that Mrs. Oliver had slacked off in her church attendance the past few months. It alarmed me.

"She'll be in Hawaii. Don't worry."

"What do you think she knows?"

"There's been no sign that Andie knows anything, Reverend. You've been following her for years. I could use the manpower elsewhere. Besides, wouldn't she have played that card by now?"

"Maybe. Maybe not. But I feel the tug of the Spirit. It is grieved within me. Either way, I want her in church all the way or . . . not at all. It's the only way I can be sure."

"If she knows . . . I trust you'll deal with it."

"If she knows, I will put my trust in the Psalms. *Be merciful unto me, Oh God, be merciful unto me: for my soul trusteth in thee: yea, in the shadow of thy wings will I make my refuge, until these calamities be overpast.*"

Aloha Crusade

Andie

Three weeks later, I was sprawled across a lanai beneath a sluggish paddle-bladed fan. The Hilton Hawaiian Village on Waikiki Beach was more like Paradise than I had ever laid eyes on. At the end of our ten-hour flight, the pilot had banked the plane over the island of Oahu. I kept my face glued to the window for my first glimpse of the ocean. I didn't want to miss a single view of the volcanic island with a molten, sunlit sea lapping around its beaches next to great green mountains and bluffs jutting toward afternoon clouds. Honolulu hugged the island's edge, like one giant sun-bronzed city. All I wanted to take home from this trip was a head full of treasured memories.

I sat up and grinned at Joe. "Let's go to the beach. I want a suntan. It's the only souvenir I can afford to take home."

"You go. But you need to show up this afternoon at the orientation. We only got thirty couples from church who volunteered to help on this trip. You'll be missed for that."

"I don't want to go to the service," I said.

"To the crusade? Are you nuts?"

I giggled. "I'll never be missed. I hear they're expecting a crowd of over ten thousand. Why do I need to sit in church when there's all of Oahu to discover?"

"Because you're a ministry team wife. You have no choice."

"I'd rather have my thumbs crushed in a vice and my butt crack sewed up."

"Don't give me any ideas." Joe said.

§

Before we left home I had glanced through the brochure entitled, *Rules of Conduct for the Ministry Team and their Wives*, and then threw it in the trash. Dressed in a modest bikini, flip-flops, sunglasses, and a straw hat, I tucked a beach towel under my arm and headed to the white sand of Waikiki while Joe slaved in the heat to set up for the group's orientation to be held later that afternoon in a hotel ballroom.

Flat-out on the beach, the sunrays soaking into my skin, I rolled over on my beach towel as the image of Mavis popped into my head so clearly, it almost spooked me. The New York police never found her killer. There were no fingerprints in her apartment. Whoever did it was truly a professional. With no motive, no evidence, the case was all but dropped. Harry Phillips moved to California. Rupert had become sullen and quiet, toiling in his fields, day after day. Daddy visited him sometimes in the evenings. Lula took him supper most days. The farm was run down. Old and worn out, Rupert's life had seemingly gone out of him.

"Oh Mavis," I said out loud. I wish you were here with me." The wind suddenly rushed up on the shore so fast and hard that all I heard was the sound of the ocean and two little words that filled my head.

I am.

§

"You look like a tomato!" Joe said.

Burnt from forehead to pinky toe, I pulled up my ponytail and twisted it into a knot to keep it from touching my back. "Just don't touch me. I'll be okay. Let me get into this sundress and I'll meet you in the hotel ballroom."

"I won't be sitting with you. Evan's in charge of the orientation, while the ministry team meets with Reverend in his suite."

"Figures," I said.

§

I sat in the last row, my back not touching the chair, thinking how ridiculous. It was too much like being in church. I was supposed to come to Hawaii for an anointing, but the truth was, I'd come for the sun, the beach, and the Mai Tais. Gazing around the room, it quickly became apparent what I was really there for. No other woman sported a sunburn, a sundress, a flower in their hair, or a lei around their neck like I did. Demure fashion for House of Praise women never fit me.

Evan stood at the microphone to make his do-it-or-else announcements. "Hope everyone is settled into their rooms. Shuttles will be available to take you to the Aloha Stadium tomorrow one hour before the miracle crusade begins. I need all ushers to report two hours prior. Just a reminder, if you did not read *Rules of Conduct for the Ministry Team and their Wives*, there are copies up here on the front table."

I rolled my eyes.

"Please remember," he continued. "If you plan to spend a little time enjoying the ocean, you are to wear cover-ups walking to and from the beach and under no circumstances are the ladies to wear revealing bathing suits. We are representing the Lord and our church. Remember, though we live *in* this world, we are not *of* this world. I would like to speak to Andie Oliver after our orientation this afternoon, please."

"I've been busted," I said to a little old lady beside me.

"Maybe it's nothing but a message from your husband, dear," she said, sweetly.

"No. It's assuredly not that," I said. I knew it was to threaten me with my husband's job for ignoring those rules of conduct. I winced as my burnt back touched the chair. Me getting Joe fired would give him the perfect divorce I'd ducked the past fifteen years. I'd lose my house *and* the cafeteria. Problem was, I was just squeaking by. I needed money from him more than ever.

Evan droned on. "Also, Reverend Artury wants to make sure everyone read the rule about sleeping in the same room with your spouse. It is not permitted on crusades, including this one. Remember, the team is working; this is not a pleasure trip. Professional sports team wives do not room with their baseball-playing husbands, and we are certainly better and more important to the Lord than a sports team."

"What?" I shouted. "It's MY pleasure trip!" Several people stared at me. I swept an angry glare around the room, silently confronting each church member in turn.

"If anyone has a problem with that, they should see me afterwards," Evan spouted off. "Men stay with men, ladies find a roommate with another lady. Please remember this ministry team and the volunteers must go before God in prayer prior to every service and consecrate their minds to the Lord. Mental preparation is needed for the miracle services. There are souls at stake."

"Mental brainwashing bullshit," I mumbled. Without thinking, I did something I'd never done. I stood and shouted. "But what does sleeping with your spouse have to do with that?"

"Mrs. Oliver, we can talk about it after the meeting."

"This is my fifteenth wedding anniversary, Evan. Are you serious? I'm not allowed to sleep with my husband?"

"The rules for this trip were plainly stated in your pre-registration packet. If you would've read them, you could've saved yourself some money and stayed home."

I yelled back. "They're stupid rules! *What God has joined together, let man not separate!*"

Volunteers and team wives gasped and murmured among themselves, breaking the dead silence in the large carpeted ballroom. Several couples nodded and agreed with me, but the rest were aghast I had the audacity to defy the illustrious Evan Preston.

Evan motioned to the back of the room and a large male usher grabbed me by my sun burnt arm and forcefully pulled me out of the room.

"Let go of me, or I'm pressing charges!" I yelled at the man who, had he wore green leotards, could've passed for the Jolly Green Giant, only he wasn't so jolly.

"You need to wait here for Evan," the usher said.

Struggling free, my blue eyes blazing, I faced him furiously. The bulging man backed away. I won the stare-down. Thankfully, the orientation ended quickly. The volunteers filed out, whispering and staring at me huddled near a wall divider of potted heart-shaped anthuriums. Waiting for his next set of instructions, the giant guarded my every move like a Roman soldier, and within minutes, I saw Evan bolting toward me with two ushers flanking him on each side.

"Andie, care to step over here, out of the way, so we can talk?" Evan led me to a more obscure corner in the luxurious lobby of the Hilton. "First, you misquoted scripture. You did not quote from the King James, the only true translation of the scriptures."

"Okay then . . . *what therefore God hath joined together, let not man put asunder!* Mark the tenth chapter and the ninth verse." I was never one to just read my Bible willy-nilly. I knew my Bible.

His yellow eyes narrowed with self-righteous annoyance. Evan grabbed me by the other sunburned arm. "Let me tell you something, Mrs. Oliver, we will not put up with your attitude and your defiance toward God. You will keep your mouth shut, or His wrath will definitely fall upon you and your family right here in Paradise. You don't want that to happen, do you?"

I couldn't believe it. He was threatening me. I yanked out of his grasp. "Let me tell you something, Evan Preston. You touch me again like that and I'll not call the cops, I'll call my daddy's relatives. For a six-pack and a twenty-dollar bill, they'll do far worse to you than what you'd like to do to me!" It'd been years since my first encounter with Evan when I'd thrown up on his fancy suit, and I'd never liked him since. His self-appointed deity was unconscionable. I felt liquid fire flow through every part of me as my hands twisted into fists.

But Evan only smiled, leaned in, and spoke slowly through gritted teeth. "Get this through your head, pretty lady. You and your family can and will be eliminated from the face of the earth in one swift breath from the nostrils of Jehovah-Elohim if you ever threaten me again or cause any further embarrassment to this ministry. Woe be to the inhabitants of your household! Your actions can and will cost Joe his job. He should've told you about the sleeping arrangements before you spent the money to attend your first crusade. So listen up. You either show up at the Aloha Stadium for the crusade, or Joe will need to seek employment elsewhere when he returns to Winston-Salem. You will not bring reproach upon this ministry. It's just that simple. And one last thing. Reverend Artury has requested a private meeting with you and Joe in his suite the night before we are to leave." Evan then smiled another cruel smile, turned, and walked away with his guard-dog ushers following close behind.

§

I staggered to the nearest water fountain and wet my face with cool water. I was ready to get on the next plane home. But I couldn't. Evan's threats were serious. "What do I do now?" I walked back to my hotel and took the elevator to the ninth floor. The sounds and smells of the island and ocean floated through the open sliding door in my room. I didn't care. I ran a cool bath, as cool as I could stand, filling the tub to the top and sinking into the water. Joe could sleep with 100 whores during the crusades, but not with his wife? It was no longer a ministry. It was pure bedlam. I decided to make it as easy as possible on myself until I could get home. I would lay low. Do as I was told. Go to the service, and then visit with Calvin in his suite on Friday night. Saturday morning I would get the hell off the island. That's what I would do.

After wrapping myself in a thick, terrycloth robe, I crawled between the sheets. My day was done. I was homesick and had never felt more foolish. I had a feeling I was just beginning to see the true depth of Calvin's power. He had manipulated Joe and me for years, even in our bedroom. And I allowed it.

§

I couldn't sleep. At three in the morning, I rolled over to my stomach and stuck my fingertips through the slats of the headboard touching the wall behind it. "I'm in Hawaii, HAWAII, and Joe's on the other side of this wall." I sighed, then got out of bed. I didn't have to share a room with anybody. Joe had at least allowed me that courtesy when he moved to another suite. I walked out of my dark room to the lanai. My arms folded, I sat on the plastic woven chair and propped my feet on the glass-top coffee table. The moon's shadows on the beach below were no longer mesmerizing. Was it courage or stupidity that kept me fighting for Joe, no matter what it cost me?

§

I woke with a migraine. I was supposed to meet Joe for breakfast in the hotel restaurant, so I eased myself into a tiny strapless sundress and slipped a pair of funky sunglasses over my puffy eyes. I walked barefoot past Calvin and Evan, sitting at a table in their shirts and ties, sharing business and coffee.

I watched Joe wrestle to say something that wouldn't upset me. "Couldn't you find anything else to wear?"

"Let 'em look."

"Please, do as you're told, okay? I can't lose my job because of you. And please don't embarrass me again in front of the members. Go to the service. Try to have some fun during the day. Stay away from church people."

I shouted, "Fun? Have some fun? I've come all this way—"

"Shhh, keep your voice down!"

I started over. "I've come all this way. We've spent all this money. I've been excited for weeks about this trip, hoping you and I could find some time to talk like married people, and it's ruined. All because you didn't have the guts to tell me about this separate bedroom crap."

"For God's sake, don't let anyone hear you. I didn't know he would enforce that rule until the day before we left. Besides, you had the rules, you could've read it. If I lose this job my soul is in danger. Yours already is. And if I lose my job, I will have blasphemed the Holy Ghost, I will have sold out. I'll no longer be under the protection of the church, of Reverend, of God. You don't know, Andie, you don't know what that means. It will destroy me. I could lose my life! Please, do what they want, just like you've always done. For me. For us."

My slit-eyed fury at Joe's drama was obvious. As always, he blew it out of proportion. Ignoring him, I spat my words. "If Calvin starts yelling at that meeting in his suite, be prepared. All you'll see of me is the back of my head. I won't sit there and take his crap."

"I don't have a choice," he said. "I have to take it."

His response shocked me. Joe was clearly shaken. I forced my lips together and blinked, speaking softly. "What's going on, Joe?"

He slumped back in his seat and drew out a long sigh. "Your explosions could bring permanent consequences, Andie. Please," he shrugged. "Please get through this without another outburst."

His plea tugged at my heartstrings, but misery throbbed in my gut. An old familiar bruise—misery—it restrained the words and reaction building inside me. I nodded instead, fully aware that my agreement rendered a temporary reconciliation. "We have to talk when we get home."

"Fine. In the meantime, act like a good team wife is supposed to act. How about it?" He kissed my cheek, then stood and walked away. Evan was expecting him at the stadium for sound checks.

I ambled toward a line of gift shops selling adventure tours, shark-tooth jewelry, and snorkel gear. Hawaiian print T-shirts, bikinis, and flip-flops hung on sidewalk racks. A woman behind dark sunglasses appeared from nowhere. "Can I help you with anything?"

I jumped. "No. No thanks." I suddenly didn't trust anyone.

Paradise Lost

Andie

The sun sank into the Pacific, dyeing the world crimson, but once again—I didn't care. We could've been in war-torn Cambodia; it all looked the same to me—a wasted trip to Paradise. I found no beauty in my surroundings. I just wanted to go home.

Instead of riding on the provided shuttle to the mammoth Aloha Stadium, I caught the city bus to avoid anyone I knew. Dressed in proper church attire and carrying my Bible, I found a seat as far up and away from the stage as I could climb.

A line of volunteer male ushers sat in metal chairs on flooring that had been laid in front of the altar. They held plastic buckets with gold crosses stenciled on the front, and wore dark slacks, ties, and frumpy white shirts. But Evan beamed with the presence of a politician, his navy suit crisp and tailored to fit his slender *GQ* frame. I prayed the lei of fresh lavender orchids circling his neck turn into a noose. He faced the assembly with his sleek, cordless microphone wrapped around his head, greeting us with a ringing shout, "Aloha, everyone! It is time to give your love to God!" Evan led the crowd in songs, praise, and an offering that lasted over an hour. Behind him, the service played on a gigantic TV screen for those of us in the cheap seats. It was like sitting in the front row. I'd never seen anything like it.

When the last song ended, applause spread, slowly at first, then soared to a deafening roar throughout the stadium when Evan bounced across the stage and hollered, "Please welcome, your Pastor and Evangelist to the world, Reverend Calvin Artury!" In the distance, his white suit sparkled in the light as he pressed his way toward the pulpit from the back of the nearly filled arena, shaking hands with those who came to hear him from the islands of Hawaii and the nations of the Pacific. He wore an open-ended ti leaf lei and mesmerized those who touched him. A woman with a white plumeria flower in her hair screamed, shook, and fought through the crowd—desperate to touch him. Finally, ushers dragged her limp body out of the stadium. I watched the giant TV screen as the flower fell from her hair to the ground and was trampled by staff.

The throng moved in. Forty minutes later, Calvin managed to push through the crowd in the midst of unrelenting applause and shouts of praise. As soon as his feet hit the sweeping fifty-foot stage, he twirled in a circle, his hands out from his side. I recognized the familiar spirit dance. 'Going into the vision,' or so he had always called it. His voice reverberated as though it were echoing through the Grand Canyon, adding to the mysticism of the moment.

"Satan!" He bellowed and spoke as a god. "You have no power in Hawaii!"

The crowd roared.

He screamed. "The pagan gods of these islands will bow to Jehovah-Nissi tonight!"

When the applause waned, he exhorted further. "Parasites that infiltrate the bodies and blood of their victims are like demons in the minds of God's people, sucking out every drop of holiness until you become like the walking dead. By using the nine gifts of the Spirit, I, Calvin Artury, God's chosen vessel, will uncover the atrocities of Satan this night! Pentecostal fire will fall! And I will bring to light, before this mighty service of God is over, the most inconceivable invasion that the minds of men and women can bear . . . complete and absolute devil possession!"

As the people jumped and shouted, Calvin held his Bible in the air, spoke in tongues, and pranced back and forth across the platform. Whirling around, he stopped at the edge of the stage and pointed to the crowd. "*God is a rewarder of them who diligently seek Him.* The same God who liberated the three Hebrews from the fiery furnace will deliver you if you tirelessly seek His face. I tell you tonight, deliverance is at hand. Demon-possessed people are sitting in this grand stadium, but will be set free by God through my hands. Miracles and healings will take place in this very service! The signs of Jehovah follow those who believe!"

His arms flailing, body twisting, he moved as if he himself were possessed by a demon. Calvin wailed for what seemed like hours. The people swayed, entranced with his every move. They shouted when he shouted. They screamed when he screamed. When he became still and haunting in his speech, not a sound could be heard throughout the enormous arena. The services at home didn't compare to the eeriness of what I was watching. The people in that Aloha crusade believed they were witnessing the supernatural. It was questionable whether the honest-hearted mass of humanity admired Calvin, esteemed him, or worshipped him. Everyone believed, ignoring the time on their watches and the crowd surrounding them. Everyone but one woman up in the cheap seats.

"He's pissed off about something," I said to myself and giggled. I had hoped he wouldn't notice me up in that nosebleed section, but within minutes, Larry, Curly and Moe showed up. Three bulky male ushers stood like Polynesian warriors behind me. Calvin glared up into the high balcony where I sat. "Bring her down!" he said.

Two of the ushers motioned for me to come forward.

"I can't believe this!" But as quick I said it, a burst of wind blew in from somewhere and the same voice I heard on the beach filled my head again. *Tell him what he wants to hear. Get off this island.* I turned, believing someone had spoken to me since the voice was louder than the applauding congregation of thousands. For a split second, it terrified me. A familiarity of Mavis caused my arms to gooseflesh. For one awful moment I sensed raw fear, but then I heard it again. *You can do this. God will protect you.*

Smooth like a satin blanket, a warm peace covered me from head to toe. I stood. Winding my way down the long stadium steps, I walked without fear between the two ushers escorting me forward. They led me through the crowd and up to King Calvin who immediately grabbed my head, his thumbs on my temples, his fingers wrapped tight around the back of my neck. Moving my head back and forth, he spoke to the congregation. "This woman has fought God for years. Her mind is bound by demons and she lives in darkness. I speak to the demons that bind her! LOOSE HER, Satan!" He screeched with the force of a madman. His body shook as his hands pressed me to the floor. I laid still, covered with a large cloth as I had on a dress. My hands over my eyes, I pretended to cry.

"Slain," Calvin shouted over the swell of the organ. "Slain in the Spirit!"

I had gladly fallen to the floor to get away from him, sensing if I lay there long enough, they might leave me alone. Humiliated in front of thousands that time, I shut my eyes tight and waited. There were too many people vying for Calvin's attention for him to linger too long over me. He moved on.

When I finally made my escape and reached my seat, the third usher who had been sent to retrieve me was still standing there.

"Let me guess. You've been sent to watch me."

The young man appeared to be a local. He threw his hands in the air and slid into the seat beside me. "Whoa, lady. This isn't my style, man. These people are crazy if you ask me."

He reminded me of a Hawaiian cop I'd seen on *Hawaii Five-O* reruns.

"My grandmother asked me to volunteer here. The woman goes to church a lot, watches this Artury guy on TV. I'd rather be at Waimea Bay. Big waves are coming in tonight. Man, if these people want to see God, all they have to do is surf the North Shore, and they'll see Him."

I smiled at the big Hawaiian. "Then do yourself a favor and get on up to the North Shore and see the real God. I won't tell anybody. Your granny won't miss you in this crowd."

"Thanks, lady. I think I will." He winked. "Mahalo." He stood and grinned, giving me the hang loose sign with his massive hand.

"You take care." I waved, envying him as he left.

The sweet Polynesian boy slipped out of the upper deck and was gone.

§

The last day was free time for most of the ministry team. Two hours before our meeting with Calvin, Joe and I walked the beach and found a straw mat left behind by a sunbather. Away from the eyes and ears of the church, we plopped down under a palm tree to gaze at the ocean.

A family built a sand castle several feet in front of us. The father, a tan young man, laughed, tickled, and coaxed his two young children down to the water. He hoisted them into his strong arms and walked into the ocean as they clung to his neck. It wasn't long before the mother, golden and beautiful like her husband, followed her family into the waves. All four splashed and frolicked in the surf as Joe and I watched in silence. I glanced at Joe. His face distorted, he looked as though he had just started the next world war. Regret oozed from his pores. I could almost smell it. Slipping my arm through his, I laid my head on his shoulder, something I seldom did. He felt rigid and unresponsive. In a voice strange and distant, he leveled his gaze at the ocean and repented. "Sometimes I wish I could do it all over. Learn how to love all over again."

"What would you do different?" I asked, aware of a Joe I'd never seen before.

"It doesn't matter now. I can't go back and undo it."

For the first time since the death of our child, Joe clenched his jaw and tears welled on the rims of his eyes. It bewildered me. Those sudden tears weren't forced. A large one spilled out of his right eye and dropped into the sand. "I have no choice."

"Yes, you do."

His gaze shot back to me. Embarrassed by his show of emotion, he grabbed my arms and squeezed tight, shaking me, hurting me. "No, Andie, I don't! You don't understand!"

I wanted to ask him what I didn't understand, but a young boy stepped in front of us. "Picture?" He snapped his Polaroid camera and handed the picture to me before I had a chance to say no. I gave him a dollar for it, and he took off down the beach to his next unsuspecting customer. By then, Joe had already sprinted halfway back to the hotel without me.

§

The hour of reckoning had arrived. Evan opened the door. "Come in. Sit. Over there."

He pointed to the couch and my mouth flew open. Spacious and filled with finery, the Presidential Suite at the Hawaiian Hilton Village was reserved for kings, presidents, and royalty. Reluctantly, I walked forward, my movements stiff and awkward. The room smelled of heavy doses of Drakkar. *This place must've cost a fortune.* I wondered what the congregation would say if they knew how elaborately he traveled?

Several rooms noticeably made up the suite. A door led into what I assumed was the bedroom, but it was firmly closed to my curious eyes. On the top floor of the Tapa Tower, the breathtaking view of Diamond Head loomed in the distance. Joe and I walked further into a room approximately forty feet long and twenty feet wide, the one wall made entirely of glass. Waikiki Beach stretched before us. Tourists strolled the beach.

I had made my own list of places to visit. Chinatown, the Polynesian Village, Pearl Harbor, all abandoned during my miserable week in Paradise. The week I was to celebrate my wedding anniversary. The week I had secretly planned to fall in love again. The week I'd hoped to discover I wasn't crazy for holding on so long for so little.

Calvin approached us wearing a pressed white shirt and linen pants and holding a folded shirt in his hand. He was obviously packing. Evan was packing, too. He stood like a war hero in the corner, with a Colt .25 automatic in a leather holster under his jacket. He made sure we saw it. I recognized the gun. My daddy was not only an avid hunter, but a gun collector as well. Calvin repeated Evan's request. "Please, have a seat."

Shoulders back, I tried not to think of the sermon that lay ahead. We sat in the center of the room on a gold satin couch, facing the beach and view of Diamond Head. It was my saving grace because just that quickly, I moved from Paradise to the fires of Hell.

Calvin tossed the folded shirt on a chair and said, "Don't speak unless you are spoken to. When you are called, I expect a respectful answer and to be addressed as Reverend Artury. You are not to ask to go to the restroom nor are you permitted to look at each other."

Around and around the couch, he stalked us as he spoke. " I have heard from the Almighty regarding your conduct and behavior. God will not be mocked. He has a message for you. Jehovah-Shalom is a jealous God and He wants your attention, and by everything that is in me, He's getting it, if only this one time in His presence."

His slow interrogating-like gait, meant to intimidate us, infuriated me. I glanced at Joe who stared straight ahead and shook like a wet puppy. The coward. It briefly crossed my mind to make a run for it, but I didn't. I endured it for one reason and one reason only. To return home to my children without further incident. Antsy to end the torturous crawl out of that room, I started to fidget, staring in the other direction, and tapping my toe on carpet as thick and velvety as marmalade.

"I said to sit still! *Be still and know that I am God*, saith the Lord of Hosts!"

I crossed my ankles and pulled my legs under me. It was the last time I would ever sit under the agony of Calvin Artury.

Like a madman, he licked his teeth. I fought the trickle of a chill on my neck when Calvin moved and stood directly in front of me. His left hand trembled, raising his arm to prophesy over me. Slobber leaked out over his lower lip and I heard something I'd never detected before—a low growl in his speech, like a wolf ready to devour me, or both of us.

"You've left your mind open to the devil. You're saturated in sin, carrying your own self-centered thoughts, Satan's thoughts. You must know, Andie, I did not learn my vast wealth of knowledge about God from any university or even the seminary I attended; Jehovah Himself came down and taught me. With the gifts he has given me, I have discerned your spirit. You think you are saved, but you lay out of church. Your haughty spirit rules over your husband instead of submitting to him. You have no respect for the Shepherds of God's sheep. Darkness has overtaken you and this is your last chance! God will not give you another! If you fail God after tonight, He will destroy you. I assure you, you will meet with a fate worse than death. You must make a decision. Either stand for the oracles of God or land in the bowels of Hell."

"Joe, you have disappointed God by failing to reel in your wife. You've let her go off and do whatever she wants. She deceives you and gets pregnant. Then God takes the baby and you allow her to become pregnant again. She is your cross to bear!"

I couldn't take it anymore. I prayed silently. *God, if Calvin truly possesses Your voice, then let me hear every word that comes out of his mouth. If he is not Your mouthpiece, then Lord, close up my hearing and allow me to enjoy the beauty before me.* I sat there, watching the sun, brilliant in its perch and glorious in its divine presence, warm the island and the hotels of Oahu as it sank into the ocean. His voice faded, like an echo at the end of a long hallway. My attention was drawn to a group of children playing with a Frisbee on the beach. A couple meandered down the sidewalk that wound around the tropical gardens and out to the ocean. An old man with a cane, wearing Bermuda shorts, socks, sandals, and a funny looking hat, combed the sand for treasures. Seagulls, the first glimpse of the moon, the lights of an airplane landing, or maybe taking off. Lucky them. The wind picked up and the palm trees swayed. Before I knew it, Calvin's tirade ended. Wringing wet, his shirt dotted with sweat, he had delivered his last blast of fire and brimstone, a private sermon for two.

But my eyes had been opened. Calvin Artury had built a congregation rooted in fear and false prophecy. He was nothing but a charlatan. I couldn't wait to get off that island, get on a plane, and go home. I think it was then that he saw me swallow a yawn.

His voice strained, he twirled around and grabbed his Bible from a table behind him. In one quick instant, sweat flying from his hair, he flung the thick leather Bible across the room, breaking a lamp. He raised his hands to Heaven and cried out, "Listen to me! You will miss the rapture if you continue this way. It is imminent! I am pleading for your souls!"

He could have beaten me over the head with his hefty King James and still not have made the impact he wanted to make. I sat with a blank stare on my face, waiting for his sideshow to end. I figured if Moses could throw the Ten Commandments down the mountain, Calvin's fast pitch with his Bible wasn't so bad. I'd get through it.

He stopped. Finally. Puked up his last few words. Nodding to Evan, he leaned back on his heels and then stomped off to another part of the suite. Evan rushed over and stood in front of us. Joe had to stay, but I was dismissed.

September 1987
Time To Choose

Andie

Pulling into my parking spot behind the cafeteria, I hit the sidewalk with a skip in my step. On the short drive to work, I had filled my hope bucket to the brim again. Since Hawaii, I hadn't been back to church—not once—and there'd been no backlash from Joe or Calvin. An intimate supper of roast pork and sweet potatoes baked in a slow oven at home. It was my night to pull hard in my tug-of-war. I hoped, after giving Joe an ultimatum, he would choose his children over his church. I had witnessed his remorse on the beach. A moment of regret, perhaps, but evident.

The air brisk, autumn had shoved summer aside with a blustery gust. Cool enough that flies were easier to swat, and mosquitoes no longer feasted on my exposed flesh. The leaves hadn't started turning yet, but the city had that change-of-season look to it.

I walked by two young boys on the sidewalk, gently tossing a football. An occasional boy or two could be seen hanging around when Gracie was at Oak Hill. The cafeteria's windows had been plastered with a few of the previous year's Halloween decorations. Gracie lived to decorate for any holiday. Lula usually had to pull the reins on her or she'd have every square inch of the windows covered, which meant Lula couldn't see what was going on outside. If anyone in town wanted to know the latest gossip, they ended up at Oak Hill Cafeteria talking to Lula Pudrow.

The bell jingled above the door as I rushed through. Several regulars at the counter swiveled on their stools and nodded or waved a slight hand. Oak Hill served as the breakfast destination for every construction worker and road crew within a five-mile radius. Men who needed a gallon of caffeine and one of Lula's pork chop biscuits to kick-start their day.

I sat at the counter to open the morning's mail.

Janice slipped an apron over her head. "Hey, boss." Janice Oliver had the same last name, but was no relation. "We been busy; that's good, huh?"

"Yeah, that's real good," I winked.

Janice was not blessed with a large number of natural graces. Her limp brown hair stuck to her forehead and her clothes hung off her wiry frame, but she was a bundle of restless energy. And Janice was dependable. She never called off work. I figured her sixth-grade education and fear of being unemployed motivated her to work as many shifts as possible.

Lula set a cup of her special brew in front of me. "You been missing all the 'citement."

I glanced out the plate-glass window and sipped at my coffee. "Someone moving in across the street?" I asked. A beehive of activity swarmed the building adjacent to the drug store. No one in the cafeteria took notice; the customers' eyes, all male, were fixed on me. I'd learned how to politely ignore them, since I knew most of their wives they went home to.

I smiled as Lula swiped at the counter with a worn rag, straining her neck to watch our new neighbors at work. Her eyes tapered to dark slits and the little pink fleshy parts of her lips fluttered as they always did when her mind schemed. "Looks that way. Couple fellas stopped by a few days ago, then again yesterday. Say they's preachers. Before they lef', they had the nerve to ask me if I needed saving. I huffed at 'em. Told 'em I belong to the biggest Baptist church in Winston." Shrugging, she patted at her iron-gray hair. "Seem like nice enough fellas though. All black mens, real nice looking, and friendly. Pastor name is Clete."

"First name basis already?" My smile turned into a soft chuckle. Lula, always looking for a new lover, watched as the men made several trips from a white van to the storefront they were changing into a house of worship. "Why don't you take the morning off, Lula? I'll finish the breakfast and lunch shifts today. I need to be out of here by two, though."

Lula didn't argue. She shed her apron and handed it to me. "I'll be back by two. Orders are in, jus' need to bus the tables. I think I'll mosey on over there and invite them new preachers to Oak Hill for supper. Maybe I can get Clete to carry me to the grocery then fetch me back here. Course that might be a little forward."

It took Lula only a few seconds to cross the street and approach our new neighbors with a wave and a warm smile. The men had loaded their arms with what looked to be black Bibles or hymnals. I shook my head and opened another bill. *That's all we need—another evangelist in the South.*

§

I stopped at the house to check my roast before heading to my counseling session with Joe. After the Hawaii crusade, Calvin insisted Joe and I counsel with Pastor DeSanto. I knew it was a ploy to get me back in church. Although I wasn't about to return for any reason, I *was* determined to wage one final fierce battle for the only marriage I would ever have. I'd endure a few more counseling sessions only because of Joe's rare display of grief on Waikiki beach. *'I wish I could learn to love all over again,'* he'd said. It rang in my head day and night. But I would never return to the House of Praise for a church service. Not ever.

Sessions with Pastor Tall, Dark, and Annoying only lasted a few minutes before he and Joe began discussing church business. Frustrated, I looked around the office while they talked. Getting rid of Calvin on Sundays had been a breath of fresh air. DeSanto, like a pack of Rolaids, spelled relief to many in the congregation. Live broadcasts of *The Calvin Artury Hour of Power* television show aired daily from the studio complex in Winston-Salem to the rest of the world, whether Calvin was in town or not, and Pastor DeSanto, the Ed McMahon of religious broadcasting, had become a celebrity in his own right. His TV spotlight grew brighter every week. Christian talk shows were all the rage—top-rated hits with evangelicals all over the globe.

Put off by their chatter about a newly purchased satellite, I interrupted their mind-numbing talk. "I hate this, Joe." My words exploded as if I'd spit out a red-hot pepper.

His defiant eyes set his entire countenance into a hard, firm expression. Feeling unimportant under his gaze, I studied his chilly appearance, searching for some warmth; some hint of the regret he had displayed so aptly in Hawaii. I was sick to death of my long list of sins, made public and thrown in my face on a regular basis—can't submit to authority, no dedication, a lying tongue. Even my previous weight problem was likened to an obsession with drugs or alcohol and explained that I needed deliverance from the demon of gluttony to ensure I never become fat again. Every fault and flaw was related to some hellish demon, attaching itself to my soul, causing my misbehavior. And, as always, the wrath of God was imminent. After years of religious domination, my tolerance for the evangelical lifestyle had not just worn thin, it had worn out. I had come to the end of my fraudulent counseling sessions.

No faults were laid at Joe's feet, except his inability to control me, and I sat thinking about that fact with my hands clenched in my lap while Joe continued communing with Pastor DeSanto. As if I weren't even there; as if nothing was more important than a new satellite.

Ignoring their conversation, I glanced around at the plethora of books and materials on Pastor DeSanto's desk, all written by Calvin. On end tables, bookshelves, stacked in corners . . . everywhere lay Calvin's edicts. Bible tracts, cassette tapes, the church magazine, and full-length books, delivering the power and majesty of God through the written word, the forces of demonology and devil possession—so-called anointed messages of prophecy spoken by the infamous Reverend. But nowhere did I see a shred of paper that could tell a husband and wife how to go back to their first love, to forgive each other, to sympathize and compromise and appreciate each other—to believe in the sanctity of their union, conquer their fears and rise above the hurtful words they'd thrown at each other for years. To love each other, as Christ loved them, as I had loved Joe at one time: unconditionally. My long suffering had also come to an end.

"I'm not afraid of him," I said, soft in my bitterness. Their silly babble about television equipment and taping schedules bored me to tears. I no longer believed in the power and magic of Calvin. In Hawaii I'd had my epiphany, my revelation, my own anointing. I smiled, which made DeSanto bristle, cease his conversation with Joe, and unwittingly turn his attention to me.

"What did you say?" The Pastor's face flushed with a grin. Joe smirked and I could hear him breathing. His embarrassment by me showed plainly on his face.

I drew myself up straighter, lifted my chin, and endured their feigned amusement. With flaming cheeks, I repeated myself without hesitation. "I said . . . I am not afraid of him."

"You shouldn't be. You should never be afraid of your husband. You're to honor him—"

"Not Joe. I'm not afraid of Calvin Artury!"

Everything had just become a great deal more complicated. Pastor DeSanto's face went bone white, his gaze everywhere but on me. He slammed his Bible down on his desk, knocking over his chair as he shot up and stormed out.

Joe followed, but first glared at me with the hostility of a rabid dog. I sat motionless, amazed at what I'd said.

A minute passed when Pastor DeSanto walked back in, alone. He cleared his throat to find his pastor voice. "I used to lead a violent life," he said. "I have a tendency to revert to it when confronted with disrespect and a blasphemous tongue. Most women I know would love to be in your position, the wife of a man who works so close to Reverend Artury. Go home, Andie. We'll keep working on your attitude."

My anger stirred, thinking about my wasted trip to Paradise. Suddenly, I came out of my corner with my fists raised. "My attitude? We're trying to save a marriage, and you and Joe spend our entire session talking about work."

He glanced upwards for a moment, as if seeking heavenly intervention. "Joe wants to include you when he talks about his work. He thinks you aren't interested, that you have no respect for what he does." His face was mocking. "Please remember this counseling is free of charge to you."

I stood, threw on my jacket and turned to the door. "Joe's had plenty of opportunity to talk to me about his job. The past fifteen years, in fact. So that's a bunch of crap. And it's never been free of charge, Pastor. I've paid for it over and over again. I've paid for it every day since I married him. Thank you for your time, but I won't be back."

Pastor DeSanto spoke like a well-oiled defense lawyer, halting me at the door. "Your accusations about Calvin are absurd, you know. We've heard what you've been saying. As a minister, I must advise you to be careful. The Bible says it angers the Lord when we speak evil of one another. Jesus Himself said we will be held accountable for every word we speak. If you have a problem with Reverend Artury, I suggest you examine Matthew eighteen and fifteen and handle it biblically."

I heaved with tears. The sound of my voice seemed to come from another mouth, and as hard as I tried, I could not stop even one word from spilling out of it. I had come to the end of *myself.* "Yes . . . yes, I know that one. *Moreover if thy brother shall trespass against thee, go and tell him his fault between thee and him alone.* Of course, just like he never did with me. Sure, I can abide by scripture. But there's one little detail you're missing. Every single word I've ever said about Calvin Artury . . . is true. So let's think for a moment, shall we? If God would smite me for telling the truth, then His word would not be true. Am I correct?"

"But you're a liar."

I hadn't intended it to go that far. Rage rose up in my throat and nearly choked me. It roared in my ears. "I'm not a liar! But I *am* an idiot for following Calvin as long as I did. Now you want to sling some *more* mud at me?"

"The Bible is clear! *Touch not mine anointed, and do my prophets no harm!*"

"Oh, but it's okay for him to harm us? He's not a prophet, Tony. No more than either of us. He's a fraud."

With a thunderous crack, Pastor DeSanto's fist landed on top of his Bible. I jumped, all but falling back into my chair.

"Get out, you whore!" The shock of his words sent me spinning before I could brace myself. It took everything I had not to let him see me stagger.

"Now there's a lie if I've ever heard one!" I spoke slowly and shook my finger at him like a mother would to a two-year-old. "You're giving yourself a stroke, Tony. Here's a scripture for you. *O give thanks unto the God of Heaven: for his mercy endureth forever.* Psalms 1:36. I thank Him for His mercy. I'm *sick* of living in fear! Do you hear me? I'm sick of it. I don't fear God because He might be throwing His next lightning bolt my way. I fear Him because I love Him. Like a child loves a good daddy."

"The scriptures command you to fear the Lord!"

Finally, my defiant posture melted like a forgotten burning candle. I turned back towards the door, grabbed the knob and twisted, but found I couldn't leave it there. With my last long-suffering sigh, I faced him to find he had darkened to blood red. "You keep pushing that fear, preacher. It'll keep folks in the pews and plenty of money in the offering buckets. But I'm not afraid of Calvin anymore. You tend to forget that God and Calvin Artury . . . they're not one and the same." I'd spoken the last word and closed the door on my way out.

§

We arrived home separately. Suppertime was long gone. My pork roast h. ⊥ burnt and the sweet potatoes withered to the consistency of shoe leather. I tossed the potatoes into the garbage and stood at the stove, picking at the dried pork.

Joe nearly yanked the breezeway door off its hinges as he stormed into the kitchen. He slammed his briefcase on the counter. "What . . . what the hell were you doing?"

I kept a fragile control over my composure and words. "It's time to choose, Joe."

"Reverend was always fond of you through the years, always concerned about your soul, and this is how you repay him?"

"Fond of me? About as fond of me as what? A boil on his butt?"

"He knows you want our marriage to work."

"What do *you* want? Do you want our marriage to work?"

He didn't answer.

I turned to the sink and ran soapy water into the roasting pan. "I'm never going back. Not for counseling, not for church. Never."

"Then I guess I do have to choose, don't I?"

"Please, Joe. Let's keep our family together," I begged. "You can be just as happy working for another company, another church if you want. You've got lots of experience now. Billy Graham is always looking for good technical people."

"I think you know what my answer is."

"You'll actually leave your children?"

"They can stay with you, but I'm not leaving them. I'm leaving you."

My stomach tensed, my heart skipped a beat, and I broke out in a sweat. I knew this day would come, longed for it and dreaded it, yet I had still hoped above everything for a miracle.

The door opened. Gracie and Dillon, dragging their coats and backpacks behind them, walked into their parents' showdown. Lula had dropped them off.

"Go to your room," Joe said. "Your mama and I are having a conversation."

"A fight?" asked Dillon.

"I said go to your rooms. Don't ask questions."

Fuming, I looked hard at Joe. The children's expressions broke my heart. They instinctively knew this was the end, and I watched them position themselves around the corner.

"It's time for YOU to choose," he said. "Life without me, or life with all of us in the church."

I weighed it on my mental scale. Life with Joe at the House of Praise destined me to more years of just getting by financially, a loveless relationship, and a doctrine I loathed. I'd lived that life for fifteen years. But an existence without Joe was certain inescapable poverty, yet it meant getting my children out of the grasp of the cult, offering them a choice. "For a fleeting moment when we were on the beach together in Hawaii, I saw regret in your eyes. I saw it, Joe. Whatever you're afraid of, it can't be bigger than both of us. Talk to me!"

"I'm fine, Andie. The only thing I regret is marrying you. And while I'm still in this house, those kids will go to church with me."

Dillon came running from the hallway. "No! I'm staying with Mama!"

I knew my son was heading for a whipping if he didn't stop. Quickly, I reached for Joe's unlocked briefcase and opened it, hoping to distract him. Something stuck out of the top of his Bible. A photograph. From the corner of my eye, I saw Joe lunge for Dillon.

"What's this, Joe?" I thrust the picture in his face. A young woman, posed against one of the ministry team's buses. Her name, *Gloria*, and phone number were scribbled on the back.

"Give me that!" Joe yelled. I had uncovered him in front of his children.

"Yeah, what's that, Daddy?" Gracie said, angry.

I held Joe's Bible in my other hand. He reached for it but the Bible fell to the floor along with more pictures of the same woman.

"You bitch!" he screamed, picking up his snapshots.

I stood in silence, staring at my husband's collection of *Gloria* spread out on my kitchen floor. I chose to leave the red lace panties inside his brief case. Finally, it hit me. *My God, our marriage never existed in the first place.* A soft gasp escaped me.

"I'm moving to the couch, then out of here," Joe yelled.

I ushered my twins back to their rooms and crawled into bed with Gracie. My little girl had seen too much already and had started having nightmares weeks before.

My tug-of-war was over. I lost.

February 1988
TIME TO LOSE

Andie

"Andie, turn that up!" Libby pointed to the tiny black-and-white TV in the cafeteria.

The local television station interrupted *Days of Our Lives* with breaking news. *"Jimmy Swaggart, one of America's leading televangelists, has resigned from his ministry after it was revealed he had been consorting with a prostitute. In front of a congregation of 7,000 in Baton Rouge, Louisiana, he confessed to 'moral failure' without actually going into detail. Swaggart's confession is even more scandalous, since he unleashed fire and brimstone against rival televangelist Reverend Jim Bakker a few months ago for committing adultery with secretary Jessica Hahn. Bakker was subsequently defrocked and fired from his multi-million-dollar Praise the Lord TV station."*

"This time it was Reverend Swaggart's turn to repent after officials from the Assemblies of God Church were given photographs showing Swaggart taking a prostitute to a Louisiana motel. Rival televangelist, Martin Gorman, who was also defrocked after Swaggart accused him of 'immoral dalliances' in 1986, turned him in. Gorman, who ran a successful TV show from New Orleans, launched an unsuccessful ninety-million-dollar lawsuit against Swaggart two years ago for spreading false rumors. He also said Swaggart was trying to undermine rival TV shows."

"The Jimmy Swaggart Hour is watched by as many as two million families and donations raised total about 150 million dollars a year. After the Bakker scandal, donations from the faithful dropped dramatically, and the same is likely to happen to Jimmy Swaggart's show."

"The resignation will also displease Republican presidential contender Reverend Pat Robertson. He is currently trying to drum up support in the Bible-Belt Southern states ahead of the Super Tuesday primaries on March eighth. Reverend Robertson has threatened to sue anyone who calls him a TV evangelist and prefers to be described as a businessman."

"Enough!" Libby cried, hitting the off button. "When will it ever end? Calvin is probably worse than of all them, yet there's not one scandal about him." I loved it when Libby came for a visit. I missed her. She spun around on her stool. "It has to hit Artury eventually."

"Yeah, but Calvin is way more careful than Swaggart and Bakker," I said. "Exposing a bad televangelist? It's not as easy as it sounds."

"With religion, it never is." Libby shook her finger in the air. "People are so damn gullible. The problem, I hear, is that TV evangelism raises billions of dollars. This is good news for Artury. He knows the evangelicals who followed these guys will look for a new preacher in TV land to send their money to. One who appears honest, with the backing of the Almighty. The church body as a whole will lose a few because of men like Swaggart and Bakker, but Artury's ministry is in a great position now. Their loss is his gain."

"In the meantime, my family falls apart," I said, serving Libby a grilled pimento-cheese and tomato sandwich and a glass of sweet tea. "You know, seventeen no longer seems old enough to drive a car, and yet that's how old I was when I married Joe . . . because *I* wanted him and because *Calvin* said our marriage was God's will. Then he held Hell over my head as I lied my way into parenthood, crash-landed into a business, and hung onto Joe way longer than I should have."

"You tried harder than anyone I know, Andie. Your marriage wouldn't have lasted as long as it did if Joe hadn't been out of town every week. Your lives went separate ways almost from the beginning. You tried everything short of slitting your wrists to change him. For what? A paycheck? Was it worth it? I don't mind telling you, there are better men out there than my brother-in-law."

I sighed. The truth made me into an idiot. "Please, Libby. Stop."

Libby sipped her tea. "Well, it's true. Not all men abuse their wives."

"But I'm not interested in men. Never again. And I'm not perfect. I realize that. I've made my share of mistakes."

"Joe being the biggest one. Don't say you'll never be interested in men again. You've got a big beautiful heart. Some wonderful man might get lucky enough to have you someday." Libby wiped her mouth with a napkin. "He still sleeping on the couch?"

"When he's home and that's not much. We never talk."

"You need to kick him out. It's your house, after all."

"Damn. I really do need his paycheck."

"Here, this will help." Libby handed me a check for one hundred dollars.

"Oh, Libby . . . I . . ."

"Forget it. Ray and I will help when we can."

She said goodbye, kissed my cheek, and left the cafeteria to drive back to her uncle's farm only moments before the phone rang.

It was Dixie. "Andie Rose, your daddy's sick. Can't breathe a lick. Wylene is with me. We're on our way to Baptist Hospital."

"What can I do?"

"Call your sister; she's a mess. Then pray, honey. Don't come to the hospital yet. I'll call you when I get home tonight. Wy thinks they'll keep him, run some tests."

"Please call me as soon as you find out anything."

On top of everything, those damn cigarettes were killing my daddy.

§

Over the winter, Lula Pudrow had fallen in love with Pastor Cletus Owens, the evangelist across the street. Pastor Clete had set up shop and worked to pull in as many new members as he could. Finding Lula was his fortune. She started attending Sunday services in the little storefront Pentecostal church, inviting several of her lady friends from the Baptist church. Before long, Clete, whom I hated to admit I liked, asked Lula to marry him.

Lula married Pastor Clete on a sun-drenched afternoon in March. Members of the Mount Zion Baptist Church, as well as Pastor Clete's small flock, filled Oak Hill Cafeteria to capacity. Janice and I cut and served a buttercream cake decorated with dogwood blossoms, while Gracie poured tea and coffee. Lula threw her wedding bouquet into Janice's hands before the happy couple left on a four-day honeymoon to visit Pastor Clete's relatives in Birmingham, but not before the good pastor promised me that Lula could work at the cafeteria until the Lord called him to preach in another town. My fervent hope was for God to keep the little storefront church across the street alive and well for a good long time.

Hours later, I covered my kids with their jackets as they lay on opposite ends of an old couch in the back room. I sent Janice home at midnight with a piece of wedding cake to put under her pillow. After cleaning up and preparing to open by myself in the morning, I was ready to pass out from exhaustion. Turning off the dining room light, I then locked the door. Standing in the darkness and peering out to the sidewalk lit with the muted yellow glow of the streetlights, I stepped closer to the window as the wind blew away a heavy cloud, revealing a full moon. As I stood there, watching, another cloud floated across the sky, blocking the moon from view. A brief glimpse of happiness. Just like my life.

Joe hadn't left as he'd threatened. *Libby's right. I should kick him out.* Except I knew I couldn't. Feeling myself dip into depression, I started chewing my lip. Money was tighter than ever. Recent vicious rumors about my cafeteria drifted inside along with the patrons—bugs in the soup and hair in the salad. Those were the worst. I had been battling to retain my customers, knowing the war to keep my little business afloat had just begun.

Andie

Daddy walked around with an oxygen tank dragging behind him. Aunt Wylene had moved her practice to Charleston, South Carolina, driving back every weekend she wasn't on call to help with Daddy's care. And Dixie got on everybody's nerves. No surprise there.

Nearly deafened by the ceaseless whir of dog-day cicadas, either Lula or I visited Rupert once a week. We stocked his cupboards and Frigidaire with a week's worth of groceries, a cold jug of sweet tea, and a pie. I figured the man was determined to work himself into an early grave, but I'd not let him go hungry doing it. The only time he left the farm was to visit Daddy and his oxygen tank. Rupert stayed out on the front porch since Daddy's big house made him edgy. The end of summer's blast of heat had dried out Rupert's tobacco fields before they even had a chance to thrive. The two men shared cigarettes and passed the evening playing the banjo and discussing the dry crop season.

Whenever Joe was in town, he never came home until well after midnight. But in the morning, after a shower and few words to the twins, he'd hop into his truck and drive off without uttering a single word to me. At least every weekend we were free of him. Dillon and Gracie adjusted to their daddy's brief appearances. At almost twelve, the adolescent pulls of school, friends, sports, and cheerleading occupied their time. The twins refused to attend church with Joe. I was happy about that, of course. I knew with visitation rights he'd take them, eventually. In the meantime, I made every effort to keep them busy and away from the pull of the church.

The popularity of Oak Hill took a nose-dive when a customer's bad case of food poisoning made it into the newspaper. A customer, we discovered, who happened to attend the House of Praise. Overnight, the cafeteria sunk into the red and struggled to survive. Monday through Friday few customers trickled inside. Fortunately for Lula and me, our loyal Saturday customers still kept us busy.

Patrons stood in the buffet line heaping their plates with butterbeans, baby peas, squash, collards, fried okra, ham, scalloped potatoes, slow-cooked roast beef, homemade applesauce, cornbread, buttermilk biscuits, sliced fresh tomatoes, chicken and dumplings, and more. Gracie, her tiny body wrapped in a flowered apron, bustled out from the back. She swept through the dining room, pausing at every table, "Y'all doing okay? You want lemon with your water?" She poured coffee, sweet tea, scanned the tables, and moved on, calling toward the kitchen, "We need them biscuits out here, Aint Lula!"

"Comin', chile!" Lula hollered back.

Another couple from the House of Praise had mysteriously begun eating at my cafeteria on Saturdays, despite the rumors. Lula said it was because they lived on the next block over. I doubted that was the reason, but paying customers were paying customers. They walked in and claimed a table by the front window. Tom Culver, a nettlesome sort of man, loaded his plate with meat and potatoes, while Millie his wife, silvery hair carefully coiffed, chose a slice of tomato from the platter in front of her.

Between bites of food, Tom found time to taunt me while I bussed tables. "You know, Millie, I think Andie needs to close this place and start cooking over at the Praise Buffet. Why, with her good cookin', loyal customers would follow her there and find true salvation in the process. Think they got anymore of them butterbeans back there?"

I walked to the kitchen, ignoring my arrogant customer. "Gracie, baby girl, take a bowl of butterbeans out to the Culvers. How that man can eat while he's talking non-stop is beyond me."

"I ain't a baby, Mama!"

"You used to be," I assured her. I patted Gracie's behind and watched her walk to the Culver's table with a large bowl in the crook of her arm.

"More butterbeans, Mr. Culver?" Gracie asked.

Tom nodded. "Thank ya, kindly." He smiled wide. "Hey, little gal. I heard your mama doesn't go to church anymore." His obnoxious chortle startled a few of my customers.

"Where'd you hear that?" Gracie cocked her head. Her eyes narrowed.

"Everybody knows about it," Tom told her, giving her a wink and adjusting his smudged eyeglasses while he chewed.

Gracie set the bowl on the buffet table. "My mama's busy, that's all."

Tom stuck his fork in his wife's uneaten chicken wing. "Not the way I hear it. I heard she's got herself into a peck of financial trouble. What's that scripture, Millie, about rendering unto Caesar?" The whole room overheard him, including me.

I flew out to the dining room and steered Gracie back to the kitchen. Moments later, I ambled toward the Culvers' table, gathering up plates, and smiling before saying my peace. Quietly. "Bad news always involves a former House of Praise churchgoer, doesn't it, Tom? Folks who leave that church shouldn't be persecuted for it. It's still a free country. You want to discuss my business you talk to me, not to my children. And frankly, my business is none of *your* business. Please don't bring your church dirt back into my restaurant again. Furthermore, Calvin can't afford me. I don't work for peanuts like the rest of his staff." The voices in the dining room grew quiet amid the clinking of silverware as I walked back to the kitchen.

"What happened out there?" Lula asked.

"Nothing a good ass-kicking wouldn't help," said Gracie.

"Gracie!" I tried to hide my approving grin.

Lula winked at me. "Folks 'round here feed on trash talk like that. They's a mean bunch, that House a Praise. My Clete wouldn't put up with it. Pastor Cletus Owens loves his people. What few of us they is."

I scrubbed especially hard at a few pots and pans in my galvanized sink. "Sometimes I think the whole church is out to get me."

Lula nodded. "Yes, Lawd! I believe it, too." She ladled chicken gravy into a serving boat. "You thinking 'bout talking to that man, Artury? Giving him a piece of what for."

"No. What can they do besides start more rumors? I'm staying put." I had no choice, really. Pouring myself into aching, mindless work was my only option.

Lula flipped chicken over in the huge cast iron skillet. "Whole thing sounds fishy to me."

Gracie sliced more warm biscuits and laid them in a basket. "What's going on, Mama?"

"Don't you worry about me, baby. You just worry about getting good grades, and leave the church gossip to your mama and Aunt Lula."

"Lawd-hep-me-Jesus." Lula chuckled. "Amens to that."

"Time to serve their pie, though," I said.

"Cain't you do it? Janice will be in soon, she can do it."

"Be sweet, Gracie. Keep your mouth shut, and show the Culvers you're not afraid. Hopefully, they'll leave you a nice tip."

"House of Praise people don't tip, Mama. They only tip their preachers. I wish they'd all eat at the Praise Buffet and leave the rest of Winston-Salem alone."

"Fat chance," I replied. "Fat chance."

§

Monday started another long workweek, and I wondered if my customers would return to the cafeteria. A handful showed up for the lunch special—pork chops and potatoes au gratin. I couldn't bear to let the curtain fall. Filled with conviction to make it work for my children's future, I ignored the fear in my gut and prepared Tuesday's menu.

At midnight I fell into bed, exhausted. Again.

Sometime during the night I felt his hand on my hip. I stirred. My mattress creaked in protest as he slid between my sheets. The warmth from him, now strange, gently reached for me. *Why?* I rolled onto my stomach hoping to convey the oblivion of sleep.

His fingers drifted through my hair. His seductive whisper was almost affectionate. "Once more? For old times sake?" But he spoke to the dark, as if his mind lingered somewhere else. I clawed the sheet, knowing he couldn't see my face. My mute lips refused him. A memory faded. A time when I adored him beyond reason.

Why would a husband try to make love to a wife he intended to divorce? Libby would say he tried because he could. Because I had not changed the locks on the doors and barred him from entering. Libby would declare it was my fault. That I should've known he'd attempt to bed me one last time. To dominate me once more. To prove he was special and cunning and worthy of a better woman than me. It was time to tell the truth. Tell it out loud.

He had never loved me. I understood that. There was nothing, no tears, nothing left. In the silence, I felt the same cold, untouchable heart that had possessed him for years. I was done with deal making and hoping for that last drop of love to show up. Joe had thrown me up against the wall of despair and tormented me with the hope of love for years, ruthless enough to use it against me for sex one last time.

Repulsed by his presence, I cut myself loose, finally. I wasn't sure where my new life without him would take me. I wasn't sure how I would survive. Even without his paycheck. But what I knew, without a doubt, was that Joe had lost himself, lost his conscience, and lost the love of his children before I completely gave up on him. Love, I learned, didn't conquer all. It forced me to see the miserable parts of my past; and then it denied me a clear path to revenge. I stopped believing for a life that made sense and in a God who had my best interest at heart. Love was nothing but an exhaustive, brutal joke. It was not, nor had it ever been, greater than hope or faith. Not for me.

I sensed the full impact of Joe's rage had not yet descended on me. That ending my dreadful marriage would come at an awful cost, like a vulture ripping away at my flesh piece by piece, exposing me down to the muscle, the vessels, and the bone. It would attempt to steal anything left of my hope and leave me with crushing grief, and no peace. It would cause me to doubt my salvation, the faithfulness of God, and to question my belief in the Almighty Himself. It didn't matter. Something went out of me—the addiction of a lifetime. I'd been weak, gutless, pathetic, and Joe had been that wretched habit I finally found the courage to break.

I turned over onto my back and hiked myself up on one elbow, glaring down into his soulless eyes. Forever the hypocrite, Joe smelled of alcohol. His naked body, stretched over my bed and blankets, repulsed me. I found my voice. Quiet, solemn, uncompromising, through clenched teeth. "Get out. Get out of my bed. Get out of my house. Get out of my life."

His fingers still fondling my hair gave it a vicious jerk, yanking out a handful as he sat and swung his legs over the bed's edge. "With pleasure."

The room's darkness shifted, turning from silky grays to patchy, watery blues. Joe ran his hand across his face, stood, then walked back to his temporary bed on the couch. He left behind the faint smell of his cologne on my pillow. A smell I had come to despise. The moonlight sliced through the curtains when he closed the door behind him. That same moon appeared on my wedding day so many years before and had followed me, protected me. Outside my window, under a dense canopy of stars, its blemished face was worn and sad. I felt kin to the moon.

I rubbed my head, the sting of him still painful. But he had stung me for the last time.

Sitting on my nightstand was a framed photograph of me, pregnant with a son I never knew, and of Mavis. We had stood with our arms locked around each other in front of the Mount Zion Baptist Church. Two friends; broken, battered, and torn apart. It sickened me. Yellowed and aged with cracks that burrowed deeper into my heart and memory every time I looked at it, the picture told a tale in the moonlight. Mavis had taken over the moon's job to protect me.

I crept into Dillon's room. Nine years had passed since we left Salisbury and moved to Winston-Salem. My children did not remember much about Shady Acres trailer park. I was thankful for that.

Sleeping hard with his back to the wall, my son filled the length of his bed. I sighed, looking down at him. He was breathing heavily, mouth slightly ajar. I brushed his bangs from his face and kissed his cheek, savoring his presence. Nothing gave me more joy. I was grateful to God for my children. Dillon shifted onto his back. A warm-sheet smell rose in the room carrying the scent of his clean pajamas, his sweet skin, and of his shampooed hair. A cheerful aroma, reminding me of when he was a newborn. It was the smell of home and of all things good. It was the promise of a better tomorrow, a different life than what we had. His voice ascended as a whisper. "Mama? Everything okay?" the words a precious smile on his lips.

I hesitated, then said, "Everything is fine. Go back to sleep, baby."

I knew in the morning he would not remember I had slipped into his room. After covering his feet, I walked into Gracie's room. My twins were my life; they were my loves and always would be. As long as I had Dillon and Gracie, I could go on. I would make a life for them, for me. I would thrive in this new life; I had no choice.

Crawling into the warm nest of Gracie's little bed, I molded myself to my daughter's back and breathed in the scent of her. I brushed my fingers against her hair; it felt the way it always had. Infant soft. Her baby face was creased with sleep. She moved her tiny body only slightly. I sensed the warmth of her love and my heart eased. I fell asleep within seconds.

In the morning listened as he went about his regular routine. When I heard his truck back out of the driveway, I found the strength to get up. I opened the curtains and the sky greeted me with a lush throng of blue and a fresh sense of direction. Guided by some inner compulsion, I looked down the long highway of my destiny. *Today is definitely the day. Time to pack him up, move him out, and change the locks.* It was time to live again.

PART SIX

And Darkness Was Upon The Face Of The Deep

October 1988
Workhorses

Andie

"Andie?"

"Hmm?"

"You 'member my sister, Donna Beth?"

"Sure do. She attends the House of Praise, poor thing."

"Well . . ." Janice hesitated. "She had an abortion last month."

I dropped my paring knife and stood frozen for a moment. Janice, who loved to talk non-stop, had been quieter than usual.

"Why?"

"I wish I knew."

In her twenties, Janice looked fifty. Nothing but freckles and bone, she'd lived a hard life; a life a dog shouldn't live. Residing in a single-wide that had been condemned in the 'sixties, Janice wandered into the cafeteria shortly after Lula and I opened. At first, we expected her to walk out after the lunch crowd. To our surprise, Janice was a workhorse and one of the best business decisions we made. After I fixed her hair and explained basic beauty tips, she turned out pretty under her ragged exterior.

The clatter of pots, pans, and a knife on a chopping board filled the kitchen for the next few minutes. Then, slowly, Janice walked toward me and blinked. "Is abortion wrong?"

I stirred the soup and chose my words carefully. "Some folks think so. I think it's horrible wrong if you're pushed or forced. In the end, it's a decision every woman makes on her own. I think it's personal. Between her and God and, hopefully, the father of the child. But then, I'm not the one to ask," I sighed. "I have a question, Janice."

"Sure, shoot."

"Did Donna Beth's husband get hired at the church? I remember the last time we talked about your sister you said something about her husband applying for a janitor position."

"Yeah, they hired him months ago. Thing is, Roger and my sister don't make diddly squat between the two of 'em. Didn't have money for a proper doctor. Some man who called himself a doctor all but killed her. Donna Beth ended up at Baptist Hospital; nearly bled to death. She cain't have kids now."

"That's awful."

"Donna Beth ain't but twenty-two. I'm dern sick about it."

I slid my arm around Janice's shoulders and squeezed. "Please give her my best. Tell your sister if there is anything I can do, to call me. Take them this pot of soup tonight."

"Thanks, Andie."

"Sure. You know I don't go to House of Praise anymore."

"You 'n Joe left then?"

"I did. Not Joe. We're separated."

"Oh. Ain't he still living in your house?"

"Yes. But it's temporary. He's moving out soon. It's only a matter of time."

"I'm sorry. I've heard rumors, I admit."

"It's okay. I'm ready for it to be over." After pulling more vegetables out of bins, I slammed the refrigerator door with my foot.

Janice ran water in the sink and kept talking. "I hear things. Bad things about that church."

"Like what?" My ears were wide open.

"Donna Beth volunteers in the offices, making copies 'n stuff like that. She's a good cook though and wanted to work in their fancy buffet, but she's having second thoughts. Donna Beth said they asked Roger to get fixed. They don't realize she cain't have more kids anyway. Nobody from the church even came to see her in the hospital. What's going on there, Andie? You 'n me never talked about it much. Why don't they want women to have babies?"

I sat at the counter and wiped my hands on a towel, then pulled a pack of Camels out of my purse. A pack Dixie gave me to hide from Daddy. I lit up and took the first drag from a cigarette I could remember. I coughed and noticed Janice staring at me. "It's a long story. According to Calvin, if you have children you're forced to divide your time between your kids and the church. Spend money on your kids, instead of tithing and giving it to the work of the Lord. Calvin wants all your attention and money. That's the short version, anyway."

"Oh," said Janice, slicing potatoes.

I recalled the church members I'd known for years. Trapped. Afraid to leave for fear of failing God. I suspected some had marriages similar to my own that, for some unknown reason, they hung on to. Fear of the unknown. It was no way to live.

After I coaxed a simmer from the bean soup, I sat at the counter and finished my cigarette. "Janice?"

"Yes'um?"

"You go to church? You saved?"

Janice tapped a fingernail thoughtfully against her cheek. Her face blushed, and she nodded. "Came close. Nine times. Nine Sundays in nine different churches. I'd cry and my tongue stammered some. I walked down every aisle. Had my name written in The Lamb's Book of Life. But I stumbled out afterward, still unsaved I think. I like to read the Bible though, especially Revelations, all about the rivers of blood and the Lake of Fire. Shit like that." She winked.

Biting my lip to stifle a laugh, I looked away. "You keep going, Janice. It isn't that hard. *Believe and ye shall receive.* It's called faith. You don't have to feel anything. You just believe you're saved. Believe it. That's all."

"That's all?"

"Yes." I smiled as I handed Janice a tray of ketchup, mustard, and napkin dispensers. "Salvation is a gift. All you have to do is accept it. You don't have to work for it. He takes you as you are. And you don't have to belong to a certain church, or get all cleaned up first, you know? You can get saved at home if you want."

"Honest?"

"*Just As I Am*, like the old song says."

"Wish I'd known that a while back." Janice fidgeted with the tray. "You know Donna Beth heard you were in a backslidden condition."

"Tell her not to believe what she hears. In fact, get your sister and her husband out of the House of Praise if you can."

"It's a pisser."

I tried to keep a straight face but failed and laughed out loud. "Yeah, that's a good word for it."

§

Gracie and Dillon were due home from school soon and they'd be hungry. My eleven-year-old twins grew faster than I had money for. Rag-tag clothes were in style and I was thankful—consignment shops and thrift stores were all I could afford. I remembered Mavis's fantastic sense of style, but the memory died when the same old disturbing questions surrounding her death surfaced. Every time I tried to free myself from the grip of the past, I couldn't seem to break the fire-hardened chains of that horrible day, thirteen years before, when she was raped and murdered in her Manhattan apartment. The case had died, as well.

Life with Joe remained a constant uncommunicative nightmare. I had boxed his belongings and left them on the porch, then changed the locks on the house. It was my house, after all. My futile attempt to force the inevitable only made things worse. After Joe beat the front door into splinters with a sledgehammer, my call to the police only resulted in embarrassment. Legally, it was Joe's home, too, and until we were divorced, I was told I had no right to force him out. I couldn't fathom why he insisted on remaining in my home, when I knew he hated it there. Except he'd said it was for the sake of his children. I gave him back only one key. A key to the new front door.

A bitter silence ruled the scraps of our relationship. He had let the twins know their mother was on her road to Hell. Ironically, I thanked God he was only home a few days a month. Something I used to complain about had become my biggest blessing.

Daddy's breathing worsened every evening as the sun went down. Dixie continued to hide his cigarettes and prop him up with pillows to sleep. Somebody needed to prop Dixie up every morning. My mother was not made for taking care of the sick. We all thanked God for Aunt Wy. It pays to have a doctor in the family. But nobody, not even Rupert, Daddy's best friend in the world, could stop Daddy's disease from worsening. Dixie was driving Caroline, Aunt Wylene, and me to drink. But I had a cafeteria to run, children to care for, and a heart to mend. An empty heart, emptied of tears. Nothing, it seemed, kept the world from turning.

A Ridiculous Delay

Reverend Calvin Artury

Do you want to know the truth? Well, here it is. Living perfect before God isn't easy. Something was missing. My ministry was under constant scrutiny, and I fought to contain each and every scandal within its walls. It often seemed not one member of my staff cared but me!

I collapsed into the deep hotel tub; steam rose and swirled, ghost-like, then clung to the marble tiles, gilded mirrors, and the crystal chandelier. I needed to soak the tiredness out of my aching joints. I was a minister of the Gospel, a prophet, an evangelist, pastor, and faith healer. I'd seen blind eyes opened, witnessed the lame come up out of their wheelchairs and run across my altars, pulled my fingers out of deaf ears that could hear their mother's voice for the first time. Casting out devils, delivering the unsaved into the arms of the risen Savior, I'd seen it all. But I had started questioning God. My body was aging. Anointed men of God weren't supposed to age. *Rock of ages, cleft for me, let me hide myself in Thee!*

My ministry had grown to crowds far surpassing any televangelist in history. Tourism in Winston-Salem and the cities of the Triad had developed faster than any area in the country due to the crowds I drew to my Friday night miracle services. Renovations on the church were near completion. I possessed money and power. I was on top. I had rid my ministry of every threat. They were either dead or in exile. I churned the soapy water with my hands. Sweat poured down my forehead and neck. It pooled in a deep scar that ran across my chest under my nipples. Every plan was precisely on time as Jehovah-Elohim had intended. But something was missing.

I longed for peace and privacy. A warm body to hold me, tell me I was a good lover. I wanted to kiss, passionately. Hump like a wild dog, feverishly. I was, in spite of everything, still a man of the flesh. Maybe it was the cold ritual of living in hotels that was getting to me. A hotel had performed essentially the same role as a prostitute. In, out, and on to the next crusade. It wasn't enough.

My blue eyes sparkled in the mirrored wall across from me. A bottle of the hotel's best sat next to the tub. I poured a tiny cup full. The warm drink soothed me from the inside out. I wanted to hole up for a few days. Spending time at the feet of God in prayer, fasting, and reading the scriptures, I had not slept more than four hours a night for years. I found myself watching too many TV news shows. It seemed every evangelical Christian was interested in the news. My end-time prophecies needed to reflect the politics of the day, comparing world events to prophetic scriptures, yet remaining neutral on many topics plaguing my congregation. I danced around moral issues and insisted if one lived holy before God, these things just took care of themselves.

In the old days, nobody questioned me. Proving my sovereignty over and over, I grew tired. Like children, my staff had become problematic. I assembled the team every morning in a large circle before taping the day's program. Praying over them, giving a word of prophecy to anyone who had allowed their loose lips to create friction within the inner circle. I had built an empire on the threat of Hell. *The Calvin Artury Hour of Power* reigned as the number one Christian Talk Show, and I wasn't about to let that slip away. But my past . . . my past plagued me, day and night.

Sinking under the water in the cavernous tub, peace and privacy surrounded me at last. Silence. The silence of death. I shot up, like a man out of a cannon. Dripping wet and shaking as if afflicted with palsy, I bounded toward my towel then shoved my almost-white hair back until it fell in drenched locks down my neck. In seconds, I had wiped the mist from the mirror and stood gazing at my sagging body. A harsh light swirled in the steam behind me. My tormentor appeared, the face hideous and revolting. I held my privates and laughed at him. "Satan, you have no power over me. I rebuke you."

Satan couldn't hold me prisoner. I had no fear of the devil. But if Andie Oliver held any evidence, any proof Mavis may have gotten to her, the effect on my ministry would be catastrophic. My eyes wide, I refused to entertain the demon with my phobia any further.

Wrapping myself in a towel I walked to the bed and sat on the edge, shivering as my skin glistened from the hot bath. "I miss you, Mama. Please, if you will, tell Vivi I miss her." I groaned for my long-dead wife. "Vivian." I spoke her name like speaking to the highest ranking angel of God. "You and I could've ruled the world. You were my best friend. My only friend."

Within the hour, I entered a waiting limo outside the Ritz-Carlton—my body poured into a girdle, my boots polished to a black diamond shine, and my Armani suit, tailored to a flawless fit and a new shade of blue. The dye had been made specifically to match the color of my eyes.

"Shall I take you to the Metrodome, Reverend?" My driver's voice echoed from the front.

I hesitated. If the sun had not set, it had long since vanished behind cold, dense clouds. City lights filtered through the limo's tinted windows. It was time to put pressure on Andie and end the ridiculous delay, waiting on one piece of country trash to show her hand—ridiculous! I spoke to my driver. "Minneapolis is waiting to see the power and glory of God, Percy. Let's go."

Son of a Bitch

Andie

The bell jingled above the door. I surmised the man and woman weren't interested in my Today's Special. I recognized the woman. They wore business suits and unreadable faces.

"Andie Oliver?" The man extended his hairy hand. "Are you the current owner of Oak Hill Cafeteria?"

"Yes. That's me. Mrs. Lula Owens is my partner. She's not here right now. Can I help you with something?"

"We're from the Health Department, here to investigate a complaint against your establishment." The woman laid her business card on the counter. Her plum-gray suit matched the color of her skin and the streaks in her hair.

"Excuse me?"

"This will only take a few moments, and then we'll send you a report."

I looked at the woman and laughed, "Who complained? No, let me guess. A House of Praise member. Right?" I crossed my arms. "Don't I have a right to know what it is?"

"The complaint will be in the report."

I squared off and blocked their way to the kitchen.

"We can do this quietly, or we can come back with the Sheriff."

I stepped away, regretting that I had left the kitchen in a mess. I tapped my fingers on the counter while the health inspectors rummaged through my back rooms. After fighting the rumors for weeks, one after the other, losing customers, struggling to keep my doors open, it had come to a show-down.

A half-hour later, they huffed out the door, giving me no indication of their findings. I grabbed the phone. Joe's extension rang twice at the television studio. "Joe! So you've lowered yourself to sicking the Health Department dogs on me?"

"Why would I do that?"

"To ruin me!"

"Don't be stupid. I had nothing to do with it."

"Well, just in case you did, I will fight the whole damn church if I have to! I can make a few calls myself you know, I—"

Click.

"Son of a bitch!" I slammed the phone on the receiver.

§

The report read worse than I thought. They forced me to shut down until a list of ten items had been cleared up—all of which took money, lots of money, to complete. Items like my ovens were old and hazardous and my refrigerators needed replacing due to faulty wiring. The report also mentioned bugs.

When I called the Health Department to complain, they agreed it was an unusual repercussion for a first-time offense and that fines were typically issued, but the inspectors had suggested the department close me down until their findings were rectified. They advised me to get a lawyer. Yeah right. With whose money?

It all made sense, though. Lula's husband, Pastor Cletus, discovered that both inspectors attended the House of Praise. I did as I was instructed. *Closed for Repairs.* The sign on the door drove away my remaining loyal customers to new restaurants. Janice went on unemployment and my reputation landed in the garbage, while more rumors floated around town that the place was infested with roaches. Lies all spawned from the House of Hell itself. The war was on.

Lula and I had prided ourselves on cleanliness. Though some of our utensils and kitchen appliances were worn, they were clean. Most days you could eat off the floors. Once we scraped together the money to fix the items on the list, a non-existent advertising budget didn't help the situation. The majority of our customers came to the cafeteria by word of mouth. I kept wishing for my customers to return and spread the good news that our tiny establishment was open for business again.

Why are they doing this? What do they want? I turned my attention to my children, buried in homework at the counter. The thought of it made me weak in the knees.

In the following weeks, Lula and I gave it our best. We worked the hours, utilizing Dillon and Gracie's help. Six weeks of closed doors had nearly ruined us for good. Lula told me to stop paying her for a while. She even kicked in a little money of her own to keep things afloat. Nonetheless, we'd taken a huge hit and our vendors were calling for payment.

Overwhelming Odds

Andie

My feet were cold, but it took too much effort to untangle the blanket and cover myself. I turned my head to the right so I could see the alarm clock on the nightstand. *Noon already.* I'd taken the day off. The cafeteria would have to do without me. I needed to think. I needed good sound advice. I needed to get out of bed. I rolled on to my back and stared at the ceiling instead.

Dixie, consumed with a sick husband, all but ignored me. Aunt Wylene, knee-deep in a new medical practice in Charleston, seldom called. Maudy and Al, in-laws who had once been my rock, avoided me like a bad case of the flu. I'd only seen Coot once or twice since my move. I heard his garage was for sale. My sister had her own miserable life. Caroline popped out babies with husbands who spent most of their time in unemployment lines or AA meetings. Ray and Libby's professional careers in Richmond had no time for my problems. My brother-in-law had done enough by setting me up in a business, giving me start-up money. But that business was failing. How could I face him? I hit the bottom of my list of confidants and came up empty.

I felt as if I had dared to risk what few women do. My family raised their eyebrows when I first told them I'd bought a cafeteria; they expected me to fall on my face. Instead of realizing I was trying my best, they ridiculed my foolishness. *An uneducated woman owning a business . . . whoever heard of such a thing.* Of course, they would've taken some of the credit had there been any success in the venture. Trouble was, since the Health Department fiasco, most of my time was spent sitting at a makeshift desk next to the refrigerator in the back room where past-due vendor bills, bank statements, and piles of paperwork gnawed me to death. I didn't have a clue.

I shifted onto my side, closed my eyes, and imagined God shaking his fist at me again. My breathing echoed in the quiet room, planning my next move. Wanting to get out of bed. Hoping I could.

I'd spent a gazillion hours at the cafeteria. My life as an entrepreneur didn't make it easy to find friends or keep them. Up to my nose hairs in running Oak Hill, it was easy to get by day after day and not think of myself as lonely.

Time stretched out like an empty road before me, a heavy burden rather than a glorious gift. Mascara marks and tear stains covered my pillowcase. I hadn't changed the sheets in weeks. Despite my overpowering fatigue, I hadn't meant to lay in a dirty bed until lunchtime. I forced myself up and walked across the cold floor, wandering room to room. Dust, clutter, and piles of laundry consumed every square foot. At four o'clock, I could add cranky kids into the mix. The messy house pressed on me like a weight, sending me back to bed and the cold side of my pillow. I crawled between the covers, pulled the blanket to my chest, and curled on my side again. The list was endless. There was too much to do.

§

Lula's husband apologized, but said he'd heard the call—from a new church, a bigger one. Pastor Clete packed up his wife and his hymnals and set out for Birmingham. Lula cried, hanging her arms out the van window, reaching for me one last time. "I'm worried 'bout Rupert. He's been feeling poorly. You look in on him, Andie?"

"I will." The old white van pulled away. Lula didn't want to leave. But the duty of a pastor's wife was to follow her husband. So she did.

Somehow, I managed to drive to the cafeteria every day, only to have a few customers wander in and complain the buffet wasn't what it used to be. I had become hostess, waitress, cook, server, and cleaning crew. I hated it. I smoked instead of ate, and caught myself staring out the front window at nothing I hadn't seen a thousand times before. Not noticing, and still less giving a damn that the window was greasy and the floor needed to be washed. Life was mostly emptiness. I'd close up early and the entire nonsense would repeat itself the next day.

Daddy gave me a steady supply of Camels—the extra packs Dixie wouldn't let him smoke—since I really couldn't afford them. Nerves. I could feel them skittering along the top of my skin. Joe was only home long enough to wash his clothes, talk briefly to his children, and pack for his next trip. He had become nothing but a boarder who slept on my couch and deposited money into my account. Twice a month.

All of it affected me as a mother. I felt the twins' embarrassment. I wasn't like other mothers. I had serious problems. Believe me when I say the House of Praise made sure the lies spread beyond the stained glass windows of the church. I wasn't included in school activities with other mothers. However relieved I pretended to be, it hurt knowing they all pointed and stared. My life was too large, too full of pain, too ominous to care.

AN APPEAL

Andie

Sadly, I closed Oak Hill Cafeteria with bankruptcy as my only option. Before delivering my bad news to my principal investor, namely Ray, I would make one last appeal. Desperate, I needed money. Breaking my own law never to return to the House of Praise, I decided to ask Calvin for help. Help for Joe's children at least. His threats to leave and divorce me were now thirteen-months old. Perhaps I could buy a little more time before I lost his financial help altogether. I'd agree to work at the Praise Buffet as a cook, maybe two days a week, and pay back any financial loan with interest. It was a genuinely good plan. I reasoned that many mothers down through the centuries worked in the face of evil, made great personal sacrifices, and appealed to their persecutors just to feed their children. I was no different.

My phone call to Fannie landed me an appointment the next day. I requested no one be in the room except Calvin.

§

Nailing a sign on the door, I closed the cafeteria for the week. Nobody would miss it, except the Darwoods across the street. They had been there for me, to baby sit and eat at my humble establishment, their children playing with Dillon and Gracie on the sidewalks in front of the place. It made me smile. Treasured memories existed, in spite of it all.

The day of my appointment with Calvin, I borrowed Caroline's spare Honda. My Monte Carlo was in the shop again. It had cost me more money for repairs over the years than the monthly payments.

At a quarter to five, the parking lots at the Praise Buffet and the House of Praise television studios were full. Parking was not permitted in the church lot except during service hours. I circled the lots several times and opted to park across the street at McDonald's.

Fannie greeted me in the reception area. I took a seat, recalling the first time I waited to talk to Calvin in his office at the church, pregnant with my first child; I was scared to death.

I didn't have to wait long. Calvin opened his studio office door. "Andie." The barest of smiles cracked his lips. "Come in," he said with irritation and an imposing jerk of his head.

I stood and ambled toward him. "Thanks for agreeing to see me, Reverend Artury." Stepping aside to let me pass, he quickly closed the door behind me. I heard him sigh as he leaned against the side of his desk and crossed his arms. He wore the same pricey gray suit I'd seen him in on TV that morning, his tie knot still lodged tight into his shirt collar, his blue eyes shining like buffed turquoise stones. His hair streamed to his shoulders and glowed almost white in the light from the window behind him. A pair of diamond cuff links sparkled like the ones in his ring. I didn't need to imagine what his second sigh implied. He pushed back his shirt cuff to check the time on his shiny gold watch. Obviously, his precious schedule was a tight one.

I smiled coolly at him over his massive desk and decided that shaking his hand was out of the question. As an alternative, I sat on one of his plush leather chairs and dug my heels into the thick rug.

Calvin moved to his desk chair, sitting slowly. "Was there something specific you wanted?" he asked, sounding indifferent. "If you weren't a ministry team wife, I would not have squeezed you in today. I understand Joe is still in your home?"

Nothing could stop the tremor of desperation that crept into my voice. "You know he is."

"Just what, exactly, do you want, Andie?"

I took a deep breath, as if I was about to jump into white-water rapids. "I would like some help. Financially. For Joe's children, if nothing else. We've not had a raise in twelve years, as you know. We have no benefits. Of course, you know that, too. My children have to see a dentist, and Gracie needs braces."

He made an annoyed gesture. "And your business, how is it doing?"

"You know how it's doing. It's failing. We're sure to lose everything." This wasn't the time to throw the blame in his lap. I blinked away my tears. "Joe has always been able to escape from our financial problems. Traveling enables him to remove himself from reality, forget about his struggling family at home. So I figure we have two choices. Either Joe gets a raise, or I get a loan, in which case I would agree to work for you as a cook in the Buffet until it's paid off." My humble pie did not go down easily. In fact, I felt as if I might choke.

"That's an interesting proposition. The way I heard it though, let's see, how did Tom Culver put it? Ahh yes, you said, 'The Reverend can't afford me, I don't work for peanuts.'"

"My circumstances have changed." My driving need to survive terrified me. I felt myself groveling. "I'd really appreciate your help." I reached across his immaculate desk, daring to put my hands on it, staring into eyes that sparked with impatience. "I have fought this ministry long and hard, and I'm about to lose. I know that." My body slumped toward him. I froze my blind, unbelievable wish to cry, beseeching him. Then with fury, righteous anger, and a ruined heart, I allowed my tears to fall on the shiny surface beneath me. "Please try to understand. I'm not evil. I'm not an awful person. I just don't want to attend your church. Can't you see that? Why didn't you just leave us alone a long time ago, let us remain a family?"

"My, my." I heard clapping behind me. "That was quite a performance, Mrs. Oliver. Brought tears to my eyes. What about you, Reverend?"

Evan!

"I'm sorry, Andie. Evan, I promised Mrs. Oliver we would meet alone."

"Sorry to interrupt, Reverend, but I need to speak to you a moment."

Calvin stood. "Excuse me." He exited quickly, while Evan insulted me with his sneer.

It was no performance. I had exposed my throat, laid my cards on the table, and begged a man I loathed for help.

Appearing distracted when he returned, Calvin sat in his chair, crossed his legs and leaned back. "There are technical difficulties in the studio. I need to go. Although my heart goes out to you, Andie, I must bend to the will of God, which is for Joe to do His bidding. There are millions of souls at stake. You have stood in the way of God's will for Joe all of your married life. You have hindered him and now you ask for mercy. If you had not gone into debt with a mortgage and a business, this would not be happening to you. I pay Joe what I can afford. I warned you both not to conceive a child. It was your choice to have these children. Now you complain you can't take care of them properly. It's time you pay the consequences. My answer to you is simple. *No.* I will not help you. You have failed Jehovah-Shammah one too many times. Your call to salvation in Hawaii was your last chance. I thought I made that clear. Whether or not Joe divorces you is up to him. But I cannot see him spending the rest of his life serving God and married to you. Joe knows the scripture. *Ye cannot serve God and mammon.* I'm sorry; I need to get to the studio. Fannie will see you out." He stood and walked to the door. The meeting was over.

My temples pounded and my throat felt tight. For a moment, defeat held me immobile. I swallowed my despair, while mentally quenching the fire in my brain and my fierce craving to see him nailed to his own cross. And then, rage, more powerful than anything I'd felt since Mavis died, swept through me with a force that pulled me to my feet. I walked toward him and stood as close as I dared. "I truly should write a book about all this someday," I said, allowing him to see my fury.

For the first time, anger sparked across his face. Swiftly masked, it was followed by something else. His nostrils flared slightly. Something darker. He replied, almost too quickly, too calmly. "You really think that's a good idea?"

Seconds passed. My silence intimidated him and it felt good. I stood straight and lifted my chin. At that moment, I would've sold my soul for revenge. "No," I said. "It was just a thought."

Calvin smiled an artificial smile, walked back to his desk and pulled out a small envelope from his top drawer. "Andie, why don't you go over to the Buffet and have a cup of coffee on me. In fact, have supper. I'll buy. Here's a meal ticket. Enjoy. It's what we give our employees for perfect attendance. Then go home, accept your future, and try to plan your life without Joe in it." He opened the door, a sure sign he wanted me to leave, then hesitated. "I expect you'll allow your children to stay in church?"

Read my mind, Calvin. Not just no, but hell no! "I'll think about it," I said.

"Goodbye then," he said as he ushered me out of his office.

Numb, my mouth refused to work. The only thing I could think of to say was—*shove the free meal up your pretentious ass.* Instead, I said nothing and walked away.

§

I stood in a daze. In one more minute I'd be in my sister's car, and then go home. And do what? Pay bills? Worry and panic over which ones to avoid so I can pay those most pressing?

My stomach growled watching Fannie get into her car; it was after six o'clock. I was hungry. *Oh, why the hell not?* I'd have to walk outside to get to the Praise Buffet, but that was better than finding my way through the complex. The rain spotted the sidewalk. It was only October. I hoped maybe Joe would stay until after the holidays. That would take care of Christmas money. Maybe. Hopefully. Gusts of wind picked up brown leaves and swirled them around my bare legs. I'd worn my only good dress, but hadn't bought pantyhose in several months. My hair blew into my mouth and stuck to my lip gloss. A crowd had formed a line waiting for open tables. It had become a popular eating destination. I debated, but got in line—a free meal was a free meal. Besides, I hadn't found the courage to go home.

"Table for one?"

"Yes, thank you."

The inner circle, which Joe had been a part of since the beginning, remained the same thirty men and their wives. They were the original hires, the first to join the ranks of the ministry team. But the new staff, the outer circle, had grown to well over three hundred. Too many to remember by name. Not that I wanted to. The attractive, young hostess dressed in a short skirt and tight sweater, gave me a polite, hostessy smile and handed me a House of Praise Bible tract to read while I waited. Calvin's smiling face covered the front of the flimsy piece of paper. A piece of marketing magic. I balled it up and threw it in a nearby trash can. The girl's eyes narrowed. "Our members have sacrificed to make Bible tracts for people to read."

I laughed. "You'd be luckier betting at the racetrack than handing that to me. Can I have a menu?"

The simple-minded hostess stared at me as if I had committed the unpardonable sin. I figured the poor girl believed Calvin walked on water.

"Menu?" I asked again.

She handed it to me slowly, as if my attitude was contagious.

"Oh wait, I've changed my mind. Can you just bring me coffee? I'll do the buffet today."

"Sure."

"In case I don't see you before I leave, here's your tip." Feeling sorry for the little hostess, I shoved a couple dollars in her hand.

"Thanks!"

"You're welcome. Here's one more tip for you. Get out of this church as soon as you can. Before it ruins your life, before you want any children, and before your husband, if you have one, gets sucked into working here. Run away and never look back."

The young hostess nodded, turned, and staggered back to her post as if I had hit her in the head with a two by four.

Set Free By A Mighty Hand

Reverend Calvin Artury

There was no technical problem. A Praise Buffet chef had become difficult and needed dealt with. I gave Evan liberty to handle it in the manner of his choosing, and then excused myself quickly. Rushing back to my meeting with Andie, I groaned with an awakening that sent me reeling. She possessed no evidence. She knew nothing. Nothing of what Mavis knew. Otherwise, she would've played that card right then and there during our meeting. But she didn't, because Andie Oliver walked in darkness.

I'd been waiting for years for that moment. The confirmation I sought God for. God had delivered me from my oppressor, set me free of her, and it was time to set Joe free of her.

Walking with purpose to the recording studio, I simply ignored employees who attempted to distract me in the hallways with their trivial compliments, comments, or problems. Hard at work in his usual spot, Joe sat among the flotsam and jetsam of the audio equipment, behind the soundboard, mixing music. I inspected the hallway to ensure our privacy and then closed the door behind me. "Joe, got a minute?"

"Of course, Reverend."

"I just met with your wife."

He clinched his fists. "What was *she* doing here?"

"She needs money."

"I'm sorry, Reverend. She's a depressing woman."

"You're miserable with her, aren't you, Joe?"

"Horribly." He turned in his swivel chair and stared into my eyes. "I can't stand her."

"It was not my will, but God's that kept you with her all these years. Hoping against all hope to save her soul from the flames of Hell. She was your responsibility as head of your home. However, I realized today she took that honor from you." I pulled up a chair and sat beside him, placing my hand on his shoulder. "I must tell you. God showed me in a new vision last night, an affirmation of all that I've been telling you these years. If you leave this church and go with your wife, leave my protection . . ." It was hard to see through my tears. I just couldn't stop them as I spoke to that beautiful young man. "I saw you Joe; I saw you drop into Hell with her." I lowered my voice. "It was a vision I will not shake for quite some time. You know you're dear to me. Not like some around here. You've been with me since you were a boy. I need you. God needs you. And you've . . . you've done wonderful things for Almighty Jehovah no other man could've done."

Joe wept. "I will never leave you, Reverend Artury. Never."

"Well, then. It's almost time to take flight, son. This is the day of your dreams. Your Red Sea is about to part. It'll be my personal blessing to watch you run all the way to the Promised Land! Your prison term is almost over.

Get your house in order. See an attorney and make your arrangements. The Spirit is telling me you can leave her for good in December. I'll let you know the exact day and where to move as soon as God reveals it to me. You have my blessing. I'm sure God will bring the right help-mate into your life." I patted Joe's arm, then stood to leave. "It's a good thing you confiscated the envelope Mavis mailed. Since nothing else has emerged, it looks like the ministry is in the clear. Messes like that often take many years to tidy up, to make sure nothing surfaces. You've paid for your mistakes. Time to end it and brighten your future."

I cemented my relationship with Joe. He had proven his loyalty over and over again. In less than five minutes I had pardoned all of his sins, set him free, releasing him from a loveless marriage. And just in case he had any notion of staying with her for his kids' sake, I sweetened the deal. Oh yes, I surely did!

"One more thing. I'm giving you a raise. Double your present salary. But no sense in making your child support any more than it has to be, so we'll wait until your divorce is final. And Silas will add you and the children to the medical and dental plan."

Joe fell off his chair. "We have a medical plan? Thank you. My life is yours, Reverend."

"No, Joe. It belongs to God."

JOHNNY REBEL

Andie

The Praise Buffet's spread of meats, potato dishes, vegetables, salads, breads, and desserts served in chafing dishes over Sterno cans, stretched the length of five ten-foot tables. Presented like a feast for the starving middle-class, this unexpected treat delighted my senses. Owning my own restaurant meant I seldom visited others. I approached the buffet timidly, taking my time, eyeing every selection. I deserved it, though a free meal was not much of a consolation prize.

Sipping coffee, I watched House of Praise employees and regular customers come and go. Gratefully, I'd been seated at a table in the back of the dining room next to the kitchen, hidden in an obscure corner of fake palmetto plants. At least if I fell apart, I wouldn't be a spectacle. When I called the Darwoods from a pay phone next to the restroom, the twins begged to sleep over. I said, *fine*. A night off from kids and an evening alone appealed to me. Returning to my table, I decided to go back for seconds and thirds. *Why not*?

Occupying my mind, I put my feet up on the chair across from me and read the newspaper as employees cleaned up before the nine-thirty closing hour. I peered into the kitchen again. I had hoped to have a modern kitchen someday. A fantastic kitchen, even better than Dixie's kitchen, like the kitchens in the magazines—like the kitchen at the Praise Buffet.

"You've been here a long time. Need more coffee?"

I looked up into the smiling eyes of a boldly beautiful young man. There was no other way to describe him. Somewhere in his twenties, he was like one of those chestnut-haired angels in paintings, only fully clothed. Perhaps it was the ringlets over his dark brows and about his neck. His long-lashed eyes were clear blue like the most perfect sky, and his lips sensuous and a little bit sad. Statuesque and athletically proportioned, he had broad shoulders descending down to an almost female waist. He could have been a rock star; so why was he serving me coffee?

"I'd love some."

"Well, hey, it's lukewarm and weak as dishwater, but what the hell, it's free, right?"

"Did I hear you say the H-E-L-L word in here?" I smiled wide. *He's delicious.*

"Damn!" he gasped. "Pisser . . . oh!" He stomped his foot and covered his mouth with his free hand. "Please don't tell on me." He giggled and wiggled like a young girl, like my Gracie. "I always screw up when I'm tired!"

I laughed. I needed to laugh. It felt good.

"I don't usually bring coffee. I'm the chef today. I noticed you've been back to the buffet three or four times. You must've been hungry. You work here?" he asked as he poured.

"I'm just wasting time. And no, thank God, I don't work here. My husband, soon to be ex-husband, does."

"Oh really? Who's that, may I ask?"

"Joe Oliver; know him?" I sipped the fresh brew in my cup.

"Know him? He's one fine-looking man, honey."

He's gay. How long has he been here?

"I've worked here four years and counting," he said.

"How'd you know I was about to ask that?"

"Eventually, it's something you just know. They've hid me in the kitchen, but that's okay. Oh, hell, it's a long story. Damn! There I go with the H-E-L-L again!"

Drawn to him, I smiled; I needed a new friend. "I've got time if you do."

"Sure. Why not? I'm at the end of my shift. Mind if I pull up a seat?"

"Of course not. My name is Andie, by the way." I held out my hand.

"Andie? Andie Oliver? The infamous backslider? I didn't put it together when you said who your husband was." He took my hand and kissed it.

"Yep. In the flesh." Captivated by his expression and character, I blushed.

"Well, Mrs. Oliver, it's a privilege and a pleasure to meet you."

"I didn't know they talked about me so much."

"Are you kidding? You're the butt of the jokes at the lunch hour. Ah, but who cares? They're all a bunch of prissy folks with Calvin's Bible tracts stuck up their fat hineys."

I laughed again. "I've told you my name, what's yours?"

"John. John Rossi. They call me Johnny Rebel, because I am one. Only I'm a rebel *with* a cause."

I smiled. "Let me ask you something."

"Only if you let me ask you something next."

I nodded in polite agreement. "Fair enough. Where're you from? You sound Southern."

"I am. I'm from the mountains, a small town west of here. I spent my early years in a two-stoplight town. Left home shortly after high school for Harvard. My family has money—shhh, don't tell anybody. Although, after getting to Harvard I wanted to become the next Galloping Gourmet, the next world-famous chef. So I dropped out, I know—shocker. What idiot drops out of Harvard, right? But I enrolled in culinary school, and now, here I am."

Harvard had failed to water down John's accent. Diluted but still country, he radiated a rare kind of male loveliness.

"And I'm gay," he said.

"So?"

"That doesn't bother you?"

"Should it?"

"I'm not allowed to attend services here unless I confess my sin of homosexuality in front of the congregation. Sometimes I slip in the back for the sheer orneriness of it. So, yes, me being gay bothers most here who know about me. Except Pete." He winked.

"Peter Collins? Head-Chef-of-the-Praise-Buffet-Peter-Collins?"

He waved his hand at me, as if shooing away a fly. "I've been in love with him for years, honey. My turn to ask you something."

I hesitated. "Okay."

"How involved are you here? Have you really backslidden? From God or from Calvin? And don't worry, the dining room isn't bugged. It's too big. The cameras are off. Believe me, I know."

"I hate this place," I answered quickly. "I hate Calvin. I shouldn't hate, I guess. It's a pretty strong word. Right now, at this moment, it's exactly how I feel. He's held onto Joe and ruled my family for . . . I guess sixteen years now. Sixteen damn years." I shook my head at the sound of it. "Anyway, I've always bucked him, kicked against the pricks, Calvin being the biggest prick, if you know what I mean."

John's head flew back and he laughed hard and long. "That's one I haven't heard!"

I laughed, too. It was as if I'd known him all my life. But the laughter stopped and we stared at each other in soundless sorrow. In that moment of silence, we understood our meeting was destined.

I tilted my head and grinned. "Well, I guess I'm a rebel, too. Since my youth I lived in fear of Calvin and of God's wrath. I made the mistake of never asking him for permission to scratch my butt like everybody else does around here." I leaned forward, resting my arms on the table. "Today I begged him to help me. My financial life is coming apart at the seams. Adding insult to injury, my marriage is over, too. Actually, you know what? It never began. Calvin never gave us a chance for a normal life. What's normal? I'm not sure what that is."

John sat quietly as I thumbed tears from my eyes. He warmed my coffee again, pouring from the carafe he'd placed on the table.

"I suppose the answer to your question is that I've never backslid. I love God and I've made many mistakes; even come short of the glory a couple times. I don't believe He intends for us to live like this, placing conditions on our salvation. Legalism runs rampant around here." I let out a small whimper. "Oh well, what's it matter? I can't change it. Frankly, I don't want to be labeled as an evangelical anymore. Or even a Christian. Religious titles and denominations are like poison to me."

"I hurt for you. But I hear you." John leaned in. "Your plight mirrors my own. You're safe for me to talk to."

"Safe?"

"Yes. Safe. There are spies here. Some of us want out, like you."

"Really?"

"We've all got a story and reasons why we're stuck or trapped. Once you're in, they erect an invisible wall. True, we're not planting vegetables and having orgies in a remote commune in Montana, Arizona, or Guyana. Oh, no. They manipulate you here by controlling someone you love. And as you know, Calvin doesn't require his converts to forfeit all their wealth up front. He bleeds it out of them one paycheck at a time."

Intrigued by our common ground I asked, "So what's your story?"

"Okay, since you've opened up to me, I'll tell you. Security knows I close late, so we're protected in here. I like you, Andie Oliver."

"I like you, too, Johnny Rebel." I looked at my watch; ten minutes after ten. I'd been sitting there for almost four hours. The Buffet had closed, but no one could see us in the dim corner where we huddled, hidden in the low lights of the dining room.

"You ever wonder why Calvin is so attached to all the males around here?" John asked.

I choked on my coffee. Reaching his long arm across the table, John gently patted my back while I coughed hard, spit, and then wiped my mouth. My eyes filled with tears again. Something had come unbraided inside me. A secret code broken, the mysteries of the universe revealed. I didn't so much as smile. Neither did John. A chill settled between us, silent and misty, like the weather outside. I glanced at my watch again. Ten-fifteen. In five little minutes everything I thought I knew about Calvin worsened. The fact that he preached against a lifestyle he practiced himself made him even more of a fake, a phony, a liar. "Of course," I said softly. "It makes sense. How did you find out? But . . . but he was married."

"Lots of gay men have been married. I think he might be bisexual, with strong homosexual tendencies. Or just a man obsessed with sex and anything he can stick it in. His marriage was a front. In case you haven't noticed, his personality draws both men and women. Get him alone and he burns with a smoldering sensuality. Some women turn into puppies just talking to him. Obviously, not you," John chuckled. "But I was fascinated with Calvin the minute Pete introduced me to this man of means and finery."

He turned his head and searched the near-darkness for any remote eavesdropper. "When Calvin crossed my path, I allowed myself to be seduced by his palate for the finer things in life. Within weeks the red flags came at me like flies on a dead deer. My mama taught me everything I needed to know about rich men, having been married to one. Calvin's Sinatra-blue eyes, his long blonde hair, broad chest . . . he just blew me away," said John. "I was lured and held hostage. Plain and simple."

Something broke loose in him. He poured out his heart as I sat, mesmerized by every word. Every rise and fall of his voice. Chestnut-haired angels weren't meant to be devastated, to live in pain. I could feel his longing to be free of the place.

His face reflected the low lights of the room. "Aside from his physical attributes, Calvin spoke like a politician, a man used to being admired and followed, and he was addictive, even when he wasn't trying to be. I could've listened to him for hours—preach or just plain talk—it didn't matter. His Southern aristocratic drawl, the way his pinky ring flashed on his hand. Of course there was the way he'd looked at me. He met my eyes directly, as if God had truly anointed him. Duped by his false sincerity, it was an honor, I thought, to be noticed by the famous Reverend."

"When Calvin offered me the job of assistant chef, I jumped at it so I could stay near Pete. He made the proposal even though he knew Pete and I had been partners for years. I had no idea Calvin would prevail in our breakup. Who knew he was gay? But money, in the beginning, was his trump card. Considering the bank rolls he carried in his pockets, I wagered no price was too high when it came to negotiating my salary."

I choked on nothing but spit and air when John told me that Calvin didn't flinch at his six-figure salary demand. "Joe volunteered countless hours for two decades from the time he was just a boy. His salary barely fed us," I said.

John shook his head. "I've heard the rumors. The original ministry team employees are horrendously underpaid and overworked. There was nothing you could've done about your plight, Andie. As you know, there's no board of deacons to complain to. No Human Relations Department. You certainly couldn't organize a strike. It was hopeless from the beginning."

I blinked. John was right. For all my hope, my path had been set in stone from the moment I said *I do.*

John had accepted Calvin's job offer, though it was small potatoes compared to his experience. John was used to his own limelight, and had tackled some tough jobs for his young age, which included a catered affair at the lavish home of Jim and Tammy Bakker, a one-thousand-dollar-a-plate fundraiser for Pat Robertson's presidential campaign, and pastry chef for a state dinner at the White House. Working at the Praise Buffet or joining the church wasn't a big deal. John also alluded to the fact he was raised by a Godly mother and had embraced salvation at an early age.

"It was the nagging warning in my head, the tiny hint that Calvin was in love with my Pete that evolved into an all-out war. He'd met him in Charlotte years ago, having frequented Pete's posh restaurant. Then one day, he offered Pete a ton of money to work at the Buffet. And like a foolish puppy I tagged along. After negotiating and accepting his offer, of course."

"Soon though, I caught on as to why he hired me. He knew Pete wouldn't go to Winston-Salem without me. Now, I can't get Pete to leave. For the past two years I've wanted to quit, but Pete's been brainwashed."

"I thought I knew how the televangelists of the world operated, having had to deal with many of their catered events in the past. These high-rolling zealots think of themselves first. The desperation of paying for television time can drive those with the best intentions to the gates of Hell to make the kind of money they need to save face and prove they're called of God. What disturbed me after coming to work here was how Calvin treated his employees, and even some volunteers, as if they're disposable. He's cruelty in motion. He finds fault with even their most successful efforts. Yet, I'll be damned. They still worship him like he's a god."

John rested his head on his fist. He pushed his cold coffee to the middle of the table. "Once I thought maybe I was wrong. Maybe Calvin is a perfectly nice man, a preacher who just happened to build a business empire. Maybe he's just too outspoken for his own good, or a beacon of human virtue dressed up in a designer suit. Maybe he's trying to get closer to Pete for honest business reasons. Ha! Truth is, Calvin's a tough guy. Not someone anyone should work for. Getting mixed up with Calvin Artury was the worst mistake I ever made. It had *whoa, mule, whoa* written all over it, but I refused to pull on the reins."

"And now, Pete and I are still broke up. Calvin makes sure of that. I stay on, hoping Pete will see my love for him. Except Calvin's goons stalk me everywhere I go. They're trying to drive me crazy. I know too much. I know Calvin's a homosexual." He ran his fingers through his curls. "Man, I sure could use a cigarette. Beware of Evan Preston, too. He rakes in a fortune making porno films and shipping them across country."

I choked again. "What?"

"Evan hired me once to cater a small business meeting in his dining room. I arrived early. But no one was home. I knocked and discovered an unlocked back door. I was new and naive at the time, so I went on inside to get started. To this day I could kick myself. I didn't see it coming."

"After two hours of prep work, I waited around for a meeting that never happened. I got curious and started to wander through the place. Homemade vidcotapes, three high-end video cams, and a dozen photographer's floodlights filled a large bordello-looking bedroom upstairs. A huge round bed sat smack in the center with electrical outlets every three feet around the walls. I thought to myself, hey, this guy is kinky; he's set up to make porno flicks. There were boxes of videotapes, all unopened. Perfect set up, really. They must use the church's equipment to make the tapes and its bank accounts to filter the profits, or launder it by some other means. Either way, it's made Evan and a few others very rich. I finally put it all together. The raw tapes would have to be edited first, but the equipment for that wasn't in the house. Then they'd have to send the tapes somewhere to be made into movies, before selling them to adult stores across the country."

John crossed his legs, leaned back in his chair and breathed deep. The silence in the room was deafening. I'd found a poor soul just like myself, alone and desperate for someone to listen. Somehow in helping John, I would help myself. Thankful when he started talking again, I found my courage. My eyes met his with sympathy. I listened to the intent of his heart that mixed with the pain of his discoveries.

John cleared his throat. "I went through Evan's desk and found a few bags of cocaine. They set me up. A few minutes later, all Hell broke loose. Long story short, I got propositioned. They wanted me to work in the 'porno department.' I laughed. That's when they threatened my life, Pete's life, and then beat me up a little to keep my mouth shut. By then, I was trapped, and they had my fingerprints on bags of cocaine. So here I am, years later, still working at the Praise Buffet, trying to figure a way out of this mess."

"Have you tried to talk to the police?"

"I can't prove a thing. They moved the porno production out of Evan's house. There's no one here I can trust. I'm a gay man who has hidden it from a homophobic congregation. No gays allowed. Not outwardly. Calvin told me if I admitted my past relationship with Pete, I'd be out on my ear or confessing my sins before the church. Without Pete, I have no one here."

"I'm your friend, John. Here. Take my phone number." I rummaged through my purse, wrote my number on a slip of paper, then handed it to him. "You're not alone any longer. I think you're very much like me. Like you said, trapped and trying to find a way out."

John smiled and studied the number. "I've memorized it. No need to save the paper." He rolled it into a tiny ball, popped it in his mouth, and washed it down with the last of his coffee. "I'll call you. Don't call me; my line's tapped. Yours may be, too; if not now, it will be."

He put his hand on mine. "Thanks for listening. Thanks for offering to be my friend, but it may be dangerous for you. Just today it got serious when I mouthed off that I'd had enough. Someone sliced my tires last night. I had to walk to work this morning. Again, I can't prove a thing. Who will believe this church that donates thousands of dollars to the politicians, the poor, and the community, is involved in anything illegal? Yeah, I need to leave, I just need to get over Pete and find a job out of state."

"Why hasn't Calvin fired you?"

"I've threatened to expose him. His homosexuality, his fling with Pete. They threaten me, I threaten them. On and on. Like I said, it's a mess. Without Pete to back me up, I haven't got a chance. Still, they're afraid it'll leak out, and just the possibility of my accusations being true might cause bad press and an unwanted investigation. By keeping me here, Calvin can watch me. Control what I say, who I talk to. Eventually, he'll use scripture and personal prophecy to justify whatever means he chooses to destroy his enemies. So watch your back."

"Destroy? What do you mean?"

He stumbled for words. "Well, hasn't he destroyed your family? I want you to remember this: Calvin has more than one judge in his pocket, members of the press, a slew of doctors, lawyers, a banker, and a host of men, professional and otherwise, who will do his bidding all in the name of the Lord, no questions asked."

"Good God. He *is* omnipotent. Can you go and live with your mother? She seems to be a very nice woman from what you said."

"Yes, yes she is. Salt of the earth, that woman. But I have family who have not accepted my gay pride, if you will. Except for one brother, the others hate my guts. It's been a source of contention for years. I stay away to keep the peace."

"Please, John, I want to be your friend. Can we meet for coffee and just talk some place other than here? We can at least lean on each other until you get out. I have no one who understands what I'm going through."

"Sure, Andie. Someplace other than House of Praise property."

Suddenly the dining room's eerie darkness frightened me. I shivered as I glanced at the Exit sign above the back door. That was exactly what I wanted to do. Exit. "I need to get going. Can I take you home, drop you off anywhere?"

"No, believe me, it's not safe. I'm telling you, these people are dangerous. There's more to it than I can tell you in one night. Look, they've switched off the lights in the lobby." John stood. "We need to leave. Security will be around soon. Let's go out the back so no one sees us together. That would mean trouble for you. If they knew I was talking to you . . ." He paused, grabbed his coat from a nearby closet, then turned to me with a strange glare. "He's a Godfather in a Mafia of holy men, Andie. Don't forget that."

"You're scaring me, John Rossi."

"I hope so. Keep your kids out of here. Like I said, we've no proof. They'll make our lives Hell if we spill our guts with hearsay. Without evidence, we have nothing. We start a scandal, we're dead."

"Dead? John, has he—"

John put his finger up to his mouth. "Quiet. We'll talk more about that later. Let's go."

I slipped on my coat and shuddered. John knew more than he was willing to talk about in one night. "I'm following you home," I said. "Don't try to stop me."

"Fine, I'm just a short walk from here. I live at the Southern Pine Apartments down the block. Look at the time; we really need to go. Stay at a good distance. I'm serious. Don't even appear as though you're following me. I don't want anyone to link us together." He kissed my cheek, then whispered in my ear, "Welcome to the enemy's camp."

I nodded but didn't answer. I wanted to hold him; my protective urges swelling and spilling into my heart. I wanted to help him escape, take him someplace safe. I wanted to make plans with him to expose the ministry. Instead, I slid out the kitchen delivery door behind him. John pulled his leather jacket collar up around his ears and bolted across the lawns. In the shadows under a line of tall trees, I ran to my sister's car parked across the street. The full lots at five that afternoon were suddenly a blessing; it appeared as if I'd gone home hours earlier.

After starting the car, I drove at a snail's pace. John had already walked the short distance to his apartment complex. Dashing between parked cars, he appeared skittish. I noticed the tenants parked nearly 100 feet from their building, so I backed into a long row of cars under a large weeping willow tree and switched off the headlights to hide my face in the darkness. I had promised to keep my distance. A dimly lit garden separated the dark parking lot from the apartments; a wide driveway looped up to the front entrance and then wound back to the lot and out to the street. The smell of recent rain on the pavement filled the car as I cracked open the window.

John walked into the light of the garden. I could see him reach into his pocket for his keys. Several more steps would take him to the verandah of the old remodeled building. What was once a charming hotel had been transformed into luxury apartments.

Seconds later, headlights from a black Mercedes plowed into the lot behind me. I quickly switched off my ignition and sunk low in the seat. The car sped past, bearing down on John. I watched him turn and stare into the car's headlights, then fall backwards. As if in slow motion, he struggled to pick himself up, desperate to escape the car's path. John lunged toward the steps of the building but the car managed to swerve around him and block his entrance. I covered my mouth to keep from screaming. The car's driver window came down and in the light from the garden, Evan Preston appeared with a gun in his hand and fired. In one brief moment, there was a flash from the silent gun just before John's head exploded and his body crumbled to the asphalt. The window rolled back up and the car flew out of the lot, speeding down the street, but not before I caught a glimpse of Evan at the wheel and Silas Turlo in the front seat. I would've recognized their faces in a line-up anywhere. Peeking over the dashboard, I choked on my tears. A quiet scream climbed in my throat, and I shook. Violently. I slid down on the seat of my sister's car and hid my face in my hands; terrified they would return.

At one o'clock in the morning, I lifted my head, slid the key into the ignition, and drove out of the lot with the car's headlights off. John Rossi lay on the driveway by the beautiful garden behind me. A puddle of blood pooled around his body, shimmering in the darkness. It sickened me and I vomited into my lap.

My left hand trembled driving to the gas station on the next block as my right hand dug into my purse for a cigarette and change. I lit my cigarette before attempting to call the police, and dropping my quarter. Twice. Holding back fiery tears, I managed to report the murder, anonymously. And then mustering every ounce of caution and courage within me, I drove home a different way. Visibly shaken and blinded by grief, I blinked against the glare of the few headlights exposing me at that early morning hour. My fingers had gone past numb to aching from gripping the steering wheel.

After driving into the safety of my garage, I broke down, pounded the dashboard, and wailed, "Why, God? Why did You choose me to endure this? Why not let me die? Why did John have to die?" After a good cry and tongue lashing at God, I unfolded myself out of the car and found my way to the bathroom and then to bed.

My conversation with John rolled over and over in my mind, until I put some of it to memory. *How much more can I bear? I have to come forward. But who can I trust? With all the officials in Artury's hip pocket, they might even accuse me of the murder. After all, I was there.* I reasoned that Calvin believed in his own divinity but his upper crust, his top brass, used him and his church as a cover for their own crime ring. Morning's first light dawned, but the image of John Rossi's body lying in his own blood burned inside my head.

An undisputed truth emerged. I had to protect my children and remain silent. I knew if I went to the police, they would find a way to discredit or kill me before I could testify against them. Evan and Silas would walk free and my children would get sucked up into the ministry almost immediately. I couldn't let that happen. Stumbling to the kitchen, I sat at the table and wrote it down just as I had witnessed it. Placing my own deposition into an envelope, I carried my evidence to the attic and hid it in the rafters.

I had no idea how or when, but if God was truly just, He would help me unmask the evil within the House of Praise when the time was right. I would not tell Joe what I saw. He could not be trusted. With any luck, he was not a part of Calvin's crime ring. I had no way of knowing. My fear for my life and the lives of my children locked the secret of John Rossi's murder into that impassable wasteland inside me. And only God had the key.

November 1988
Only God Knows

Andie

The first sign of an unraveling seam is that loose thread. As I stuck my hand into my pocket and discovered one, I thought about the seams of life that fall apart when you least expect it. The real unraveling of my life began the moment I met John Rossi.

John's murder made front-page news and headlined regional telecasting. The police pleaded for the anonymous caller to come forward. John's family, who lived near Boone, offered a rather large reward for any information leading to the arrest and conviction of his murderer. No amount was enough to move me to call the police. My children's safety and future were my number one concern; I remained quiet. The news reporter said that although John was a chef at the popular Praise Buffet, his family refused the House of Praise's involvement in his funeral services, which were private and being held at the family's church in Watauga County.

"Good for them," I mumbled.

According to the reporter, the House of Praise did not comment, other than to say John's presence would be missed and that he was a good employee. They added that they had only recently discovered his homosexuality and his murder must have had something to do with the gay community. I imagined Reverend Artury proclaiming John's lifestyle had caught up with him and that God had allowed his destruction.

§

Three weeks later, I closed Oak Hill Cafeteria for good. The landlord rented the space to a new owner. I worked relentlessly, packing up what was left in the kitchen and giving Vernise and Henry a few large jars of peaches, pickles, and mayonnaise. I hauled the rest of my canned foods home, knowing I would need them in the days to come. Selling what dry goods I could, I put the rest into boxes for the Salvation Army. I pulled the lace curtains off the front windows and had the sign over the entrance removed. A couple more carloads, a few swipes with a rag on the counter, and one last sweep. I was done. Standing with my hand on the doorknob for one final look, I closed the door on that chapter of my life.

The next day, I borrowed yet more money from Aunt Wylene and filed for bankruptcy, flushing away my dreams of early retirement, independence, and success. The sheer weight of my failure backed me into a corner of confusion. How could I fight the devastating sense of defeat? How long before I would have to leave my home? Why were Joe's clothes still in the closet and his tools in the garage? And I had no idea what was in the padlocked shed. He'd told me it was full of car parts, broken audio equipment, and back issues of *Popular Electronics*. I didn't care. I just wanted him out.

Walking alone into the enormous dark of my future, I retreated to the comfort of my couch. Except for getting the twins off to school, fixing a few meals, and tucking them in bed, I remained stoic and still, and mostly— asleep.

The Second Son

Reverend Calvin Artury

I took time to counsel my ministry team in the Sheraton Grand Hotel in Munich. On an extended tour through Europe, I laid the groundwork for the new millennium. God had come to me in a vision. The angel of the Lord told me lovingly, that I, like the Christ, was the Son of God. His second son. It was the most cherished moment of my life. But there were a few knots to untangle before enlightening my staff and congregation as to my most recent revelation.

I had been slow to give Joe the exact date to leave Andie, explaining I was concerned about his children and their salvation. I assured Joe it was just a matter of time and God would move on his behalf. If he would trust and obey, then his son and daughter would not perish in the flames of Hell with their mother. "Our Heavenly Father will give us a plan and they will be safe inside the House of Praise," I told Joe. "Andie will be left to her own self-destruction."

I didn't want to see Andie destroyed. I didn't want to see her soul enter Hell as I had seen so many others drop into the abyss of flames. She was a beautiful woman, just like my mother and my Vivi. But she had blasphemed. She was like a dog returning to its vomit. An apostate. It was out of my hands.

MORE IMPORTANT THINGS

Andie

I found a job, but it was short-lived. Emerging into the brisk November wind, I pulled up my collar, feeling the rough scratch of it on my neck. My old wool coat had been my protection against chilly North Carolina winters for years—just one more thing I needed to replace and couldn't afford to.

Plumes of my warm breath swirled in the cold air. I stood in the street, glancing back at the restaurant I'd worked in for two weeks, clutching my one and only paycheck. The owner at Goddard's Steak & Ale had offered to show me his culinary techniques two nights a week if I'd wait tables the rest of the time. But I'd been let go. He didn't want to let me go, except business had slowed because of the bad economy; and people weren't eating out as much. He explained he shouldn't have hired me in the first place. His mistake. He was sorry.

Sorry wouldn't pay my bills or put gas in my car. I sure could've used more notice. Walking forward, I joined the uninviting swarm of pedestrians. Goddard's Steak & Ale seemed like a good place to work. It would've kept a roof over our heads and food on the table, including some leftovers the chef handed out every couple of nights. Located only a mile from my house, I could've walked and saved money on gas. I grimaced, and then pushed my self-pity aside. I had real financial problems. Joe's check was all but spent. Even with my one paycheck, I had about four hundred dollars to my name. *What can I sell?* There wasn't much. My wedding set had been pawned long ago to pay medical bills. Second-hand furniture wouldn't bring more than a few dollars. My TV served as my only distraction and Dillon and Gracie's only entertainment.

Except for a gold mother/child ring Dixie had given me, the rest wasn't worth thinking about. I weighed my options. The thing I knew for sure was there was no way to find strength or courage stretched out on my couch. The kids wouldn't be home until four. I needed to walk and clear my head.

My parents were tapped out. Caroline's second divorce was final. She and her three little girls had moved in with our parents once again. They were driving Dixie to the nuthouse. *Where do I fit in? How can I burden Daddy with my needs, when my sister is in such a mess?* On top of that, Daddy battled emphysema daily. He was not my answer. A down payment on a house and three used cars had been his contribution to my life. Dixie had babysat plenty through the years. That and a free meal from time to time, they'd done enough. Like everything else, I kept my poverty a well-guarded secret.

I marched through the chilly air. *What would my life have been like if I had gone to college?* Cooking, however good I was at it, didn't create a career to support me. In some fields, women could get work almost anywhere and be pretty well paid. Except it had been almost eight years since I'd taken a test. How would I pay for school? No, I'd missed my college boat years ago. All I'd ever done was change diapers and peel potatoes. That fact came as a shock.

I'd reached the end of my rope focusing all of my time and energy the past several years on simple cooking skills. Owning my own cafeteria was one thing, but landing a job as a chef wasn't in my immediate future. The better restaurants in town were filled with degreed chefs. All men.

I walked for several blocks and then stopped in front of one of the more prominent bistros, hoping they might need help. Maybe a hostess. Or someone to empty the trash. I went inside and asked halfheartedly if they were hiring. The manager shook his head and said they'd laid off their hostess yesterday. *Just keep looking.*

Stepping out on the sidewalk, the cold wind kept me moving. I strolled past a convenience store and its rack of newspapers. Glancing down at the headlines, I stopped in my tracks. Picking up the Winston-Salem Journal, I stared at a picture of Calvin Artury and an unknown woman. A stunning blonde stood at a podium, addressing a crowd of Munich's most influential people. According to the article, the woman told of an assassin who attacked Calvin during his Berlin miracle crusade in a service where she had just given her life to Christ. *Satan had come into our midst,* the beautiful woman testified. She also stated the killer shot his gun repeatedly at Calvin from a distance of only ten feet, and not a single bullet hit him. *I believe an angel of the Lord protected Reverend Artury,* she said. The police arrested the assassin.

The newspaper also reported the police had questioned Calvin and his team regarding the incident. They searched their equipment as a matter of routine, but Calvin proclaimed God was with them. *We have nothing to hide, said Reverend Artury. We are here on a mission from God to save German souls for the kingdom of the Lord.* The article mentioned that if you sent in a twenty-dollar offering within the month, you would be the first to receive the tell-all book as soon as it became available. A full account of Calvin's harrowing experience in Germany, and the blonde finding Jesus through his ministry.

Focusing on the picture, I wondered how many more theatrics and lies I could stand. No doubt the entire fiasco was staged. Gullible Christians would soak it up by the truckload, fully convinced that Calvin was a modern-day prophet as they stuffed a few extra bucks into their monthly love offerings. After all, nobody could put tears in your eyes better than Calvin. I'd sat through his services most of my life and I was the first to admit, I'd been duped. After all, why wouldn't people believe him? He could still sell God better than Tony the Tiger sold Frosted Flakes.

The Germans called him the "Miracle Man." *God help us all. If they only knew.* I read on. The article stated that at the next crusade in Brussels, Joe Oliver, a long-time employee and resident of Winston-Salem, would give his testimony of how God prepared his life for ministry and had selected him as a young boy to win souls. *Reverend Artury said Joe Oliver is a type and shadow of King David in the Old Testament, chosen in his youth to slay Goliaths.*

Joe? At the sight of his name, I laughed bitterly. What might the people of Brussels think if they knew his children did not receive their report cards because their parents could not afford to pay their school fees? And that Gracie Oliver had cried herself to sleep because someone had made fun of her worn-out backpack and the holes in her sneakers? And that Dillon Oliver couldn't go on the school field trip to Asheville with his classmates because there wasn't an extra twenty dollars in the budget? Would our children's sorrows make the headlines in Brussels, along with Joe's testimony of being a high-powered follower of Calvin Artury? I stopped laughing and clinched my fist around the newspaper.

A hard-looking woman wearing a hideous hat, cracked open the store's door and pointed with her thumb to a portable black and white behind her. "Hey gal, you want to buy that paper or would you rather watch the news on my TV in here?"

I stuffed the newspaper back into the rack and kept going, grinding my teeth, and fighting a massive headache.

Joe had separated himself from us even though he'd not moved out, and I couldn't figure out what he was waiting for. Handsome as ever at thirty-five, he'd been a notorious bad boy for years, making a fool out of me and my way of life. Endless women had no doubt shared his bed since Mavis confirmed the first incident. I saw the snapshots he'd taken of his travels with Calvin that inevitably included models, actors, and debutantes. Joe had grown out of his country-boy skin a long time ago, learned how to conduct himself, toned down his twang, and had become nothing less than a suave and debonair evangelical pawn.

It was a surprise to see him in the paper with Calvin. No doubt the German blonde and Joe were *friends*. She looked like the kind of woman he would say was *just a friend*. Everything that had to do with Joe was a lie. From his fine tailored suits and gleaming leather shoes to the Gucci briefcase he carried walking out the door on Friday nights, as if he were from a world of privilege—all lies.

Abruptly, I turned around and started for home, reminding myself that, once again, I had more important things to worry about. I had to think about shelter. The utility bills were past due. Food. We needed groceries. I shoved my hand into my pocket and felt for my gloves—they'd fallen through the hole. And a better coat.

December 1988
Exodus

Andie

In 1972 my plan had been a simple one. To stay together for the rest of our lives. An impossible strategy anyone within the House of Praise inner circle would say, because darkness cannot mix with light, and sheep must be separated from goats. As hard as I had tried, I couldn't become one of them. My faith did not include the gospel according to Calvin.

I took the twins to my parents for a few days to enjoy some holiday distraction. But destiny brought the inevitable, just days before Christmas.

§

It was December 22 to be exact. I guess he couldn't wait until Christmas was over. I had driven home alone to wrap a few presents for the twins. There was no end to my nightmare. My eyes burned in my head. The house felt oppressive and stale, drifting from room to room. I assumed he was kidding when he'd said that since he wouldn't get any money out of the house, he'd take its contents. I would never assume again. The empty rooms stared back at me, gaping and bruised. Molested.

Except for the couch, the Christmas tree and a few presents for Dillon and Gracie, the living room had disappeared. My knickknacks, end-tables, lamps, TV, kitchen table, and the books I loved were gone, no doubt to be sold. Dust balls covered the floor where my bed and dresser had been. Except for the mother/child ring on my hand and the gold hoops in my ears, my jewelry was missing. No doubt, carted off to some pawn shop. He, at least, had left my clothes in the closet. The kids' bedrooms were untouched except for Dillon's desk; he took it. I opened the linen closet: three towels and a bottle of Children's Tylenol. He had boxed up every bit of toilet paper, cleaning supplies and soap, and wiped out the kitchen with the exception of paper plates, plastic utensils, and four antique plates on the wall he'd once said were ugly. He took every can, box, and food container except a gallon of milk and a lf loaf of stale bread.

Ie had also emptied the garage apart from a few old tools and a push mower that belonged to Daddy. The storage shed remained padlocked; he'd lef: a note, stating he'd return for the rest of *his* things later. A check for one hu. idred dollars lay on the kitchen counter with what looked like a letter he'd written to Dillon and Gracie. I opened it.

D & G,

I'll see you as much as possible in the future, but it's time for me and your mama to end our marriage.

Dad

The Grinch had come and stolen more than just Christmas.

Then I panicked and bolted up the stairs to the attic. After checking for the envelope hidden in the rafters, I lifted the lid on my hope chest and rooted through it for my photograph albums I had tucked under Mavis's blue crocheted afghan. *All of it*, I sighed, *safe.* I closed the lid on the chest that was once full of hope, and knew for sure it wasn't the relationship I mourned. Instead I grieved for the hopes and dreams I had once concealed deep within my foolish, daydreaming heart.

Joe's exodus came as no surprise—I'd been saying, *we're separated* for years. It certainly didn't devastate me. On the contrary. He had finally done something right and I was relieved. What surprised me was that I cried. I had no idea what lay in my future. The raw and icy silence between us had at last drawn its remaining breath. He had left quickly, tearing the house apart in a reckless and rebellious escape, like a mutt digging his way out of the dog pound.

A new silence broke me. I stared at the mess in the wake of his departure, longing for someone to hold out their arms to me but the raped house only stood in shock. Breathing deep, I tried to shake some sense into myself.

I brought the twins home and together we sacked out on the living room carpet, falling into a fitful sleep in the early hours of the morning. Though he was the only daddy they'd known, Dillon and Gracie's relationship with Joe was tenuous. I was quite aware my children were relieved to be rid of the tension that had permeated every square foot of our home like the odor of rancid meat.

§

The next day, Dixie gave me the bed and mattress from her spare room and a small TV. She had plenty to say. "I'd press charges. I'd get me a lawyer right now! I'd—"

"It's finally over, Dixie. Let it go."

Oblivious to the holidays, the kids and I clung to each other. Despite my parents' efforts to put smiles on our faces, the holiday season melted away with only memories of rejection, neglect, and a final blow of abandonment for keepsakes.

§

"Hello." I'd been mouth-breathing. My lips were cracked and my tongue was dry. My voice hoarse from sleep, I'd long since stopped caring about maintaining a brave face. Why did I sense the worst was yet to come? How could I be relieved and heartbroken at the same time? I had lost my biggest battles. Why couldn't my family understand no amount of fresh air or shopping or exercise would dispel my fear?

Dixie's daily phone call prodded me with always the same question. "You awake?"

"No, I was just dozing. It's okay though." Always the same answer.

Followed by a sigh of relief to hear that I was still coherent enough to put two sentences together, my mother decided to rescue me. "Your sister and I are out shopping and I thought of you, darlin'."

Why does her voice always make me weepy?

Hell-bent on trips to the mall, Dixie's sudden spending sprees were a diversion from Daddy's sickness, Wylene had said. I viewed my mother as a spoiled, anal, and neurotic woman. There was a time I would've given my right arm for Dixie's undivided attention; to go shopping together, paint her nails, or share a Coca-Cola at a lunch counter. But clean floors and neatly pressed clothes came first. More than once I woke to the smell of Murphy's Oil Soap and the sound of Dixie, mopping and rearranging furniture in the middle of the night. I had once wanted to crawl back inside her womb to feel surrounded by her love, but no longer.

"It's a lovely day. It'd do you good to go out for a walk. Get some fresh air."

"Um, I reckon so." There it was again, that damn fresh air and exercise—the answer to all my problems.

"Maybe I'll call later. You can come over for supper and talk."

"No thanks. I'm all talked out, and I've got to pick up Gracie in an hour." Silence.

"Well, alright then, call me if you change your mind." Dixie always fussed unnecessarily.

"Okay." Another silence. "Thanks, though."

Other than the low hum of the refrigerator and an occasional moaning pipe, my refurbished house maintained its silent treatment. All that was left was a bundle of heartbreaking memories, a plan for the future that became more and more vague every day, and abject poverty staring me in the face. A long time ago, I had loved him so hard and it didn't matter one bit. A difficult road loomed ahead, but he was finally gone and despite it all—I was glad.

March 1989
ONE FOOT IN FRONT OF THE OTHER

Andie

Who's pounding? Confused and half-asleep, I opened the front door.

"I've been banging on this door for over ten minutes!"

I looked around outside, still not fully alert. Bright and slightly chilly, I felt the cool air rush at my head. *Must be morning.*

"Well, you gonna move? Let me in, for God's sake, Andie."

"Sorry. I was in bed."

She studied my face before giving me a hug. "You look terrible."

"Thanks." I managed not to roll my eyes, but it was a struggle.

"It stinks in here. When's the last time you cleaned this place?" Dixie scrunched up her nose and marched around my house, opening windows, picking up empty cups and plates, and mumbling something about fat grams and calories.

"I'll do that," I protested.

"When? Next year? Go shower and pack a bag. You're coming home with me."

A shower.

"Where are my grandbabies?"

"At the Darwoods."

"How are you living? Lord knows, you ain't making any money."

"I'm on welfare."

"Oh, Andie, welfare? I never thought one of my own would . . . never mind. Go shower; we'll pick up the kids on the way to my house."

"Is Daddy better?"

"Yes, that's why I'm so tickled. Wylene referred him to a new pulmonary specialist who changed his medication. He's breathing easier, and wanting to eat!"

"That's good, Dixie. That's real good."

§

I felt almost human stepping out of the bathroom. The windows were wide open and the cool March breeze woke up my senses. I was hungry. Following noises to the kitchen, I shook my head watching Dixie's arms work furiously, taking out her frustrations with Comet cleanser and a rag. "I thought I raised you better than this. Your kitchen is a disaster." She looked me up and down. "How much do you weigh?"

My black stirrup pants were tight at the waist and butt. "I don't know, I don't look." I plopped my enlarged body down on a chair and sighed. "I've been such a pile of shit lately. I don't know what I'd do without you."

Dixie sat next to me. Her tone sweetened. "I need to tell you something."

"Good something or bad something?" I blew my nose into a wad of toilet paper. Kleenex, paper towels, and napkins were for people who worked for a living, not for welfare lowlifes.

"Good, I suppose. I've had a long talk with Wylene and your daddy. You know, darlin', we're all hoping he lives a good long time; I can't stand the thoughts of it being otherwise. But Wylene made me a proposition."

"Go on."

"If Bud goes before me, and barring any accident it looks like he will, your Aunt Wylene has offered for me to move in with her. In Charleston. I'd have to sell the house but Bud says that's good; I can save the money for my retirement."

"Sell the house? I can't imagine it!"

"I don't want to live alone, Andie. Hopefully, Caroline will get on her feet and won't need me so much. I love Charleston . . . it's my birthplace, you know. Wy's got a nice house, and plenty of money. We'll just take care of each other the rest of our days."

Plenty of money. That's what it was all about. Dixie had always been afraid of poverty, of going to the poorhouse. She'd been such a skinflint. Aunt Wylene meant security, especially when Daddy was gone. "It'll break my heart, but I understand. I'm happy for you, Dixie."

"You know, she's a prominent doctor now. Wy has an office in Savannah, too. Those old biddies didn't want her around when she was young but now that she's gone back as a famous woman obstetrician, well, you can imagine. She's the talk of Charleston!"

"You want that, too?"

"Lord, no. I want to see her enjoy it. I'll keep house while she works. We'll do fine. I'll be back from time to time. We're getting ahead of ourselves; this won't happen for a while. I expect to be spoon-feeding your daddy a few more years."

I smiled warmly at my mother. She had plans, and at her age that was important. To know where she was going and what her future held. It was more than I had.

"Let's pick up the twins," Dixie said, squeezing my hand and giving me an encouraging smile. "You know it's good to be around family. On second thought, maybe not the Olivers."

"No worries there. I can't get Maudy to answer the phone."

Dixie's give-a-shit meter fell to zero. She never liked Maudy. "She's just an old goat protecting what's hers and she's pissed off, is all. Promise me you'll get out? At least for some fresh air. You need to go back to work."

"Pinky swear." I was already pouring over the classifieds for a job, any job. No matter how I looked at it, welfare and Joe's random checks paid better than Burger King.

But Dixie was right. I needed to stop moping around with the ghosts of my past. My mother promised to keep Gracie and Dillon for the week, drive them to school and pick them up so I could look for work. Tomorrow was another day and I intended to start by confronting my estranged in-laws with the truth about their son.

§

Although I had gone to bed with a new sense of optimism, a harsh reality struck me; how difficult every moment would be, making a new life for the twins and myself. But the eggshells were gone, too. I turned my head. The left side of the bed was smooth, untouched. I smiled and hopped out of bed.

Staring into the mirror, I replayed old conversations in my head, feeling the effects of Joe's cruelty and every truth I knew and kept to myself about the House of Praise. I seethed. The poison inside me showed on my face. I winced at my reflection. My nose and chin had broken out overnight. Upon further inspection, I discovered lines around my eyes and mouth. I pulled back my hair and was surprised to find the first signs of gray mixed in with my darker roots. *Time to get on with life before I'm too old to care how I look.*

Thank God, Dixie had given me money to visit a salon. A few hours later, I had taken advantage of the two-for-one-special—a cut and a highlight. My makeover included a trip back to Salisbury to find out why Maudy wasn't answering my calls.

§

I drove onto my in-laws property and swallowed hard. Al meandered out of his shop and waved. Maudy flew out the back door and straight up to my car door, wringing her hands. "You shouldn't be here, Andie."

I stepped out of my car and stood under the shade of the large oak, wondering what happened to the mother-in-law I once knew and loved so dearly. "Why?"

"It's just not a good idea. We must support Joe. I hope you understand."

"Joe and I were married seventeen years, Maudy. Doesn't that count for something?"

I shouldn't have been surprised when Maudy pursed her lips. "And after seventeen years, you've left him little of his dignity. You've ruined him emotionally and financially, never giving him your full support in the ministry. His only peace was and *is* at work!"

"Did he tell you this? Did he tell you how many women he's slept with? How little money he made?"

She didn't hear a word. "You should've stayed in Salisbury." It was like hearing it come right out of Joe's mouth. "Lived within your means," she added in a practical voice. She ignored the *other women* part.

I clenched my jaw to keep from snapping at her and turned instead, to look at the sadness on Al's face. Whatever regrets were battling inside him had launched tears to his weather-worn cheeks. It grieved me.

Maudy clicked her tongue and sighed. "We're getting nowhere standing here, defending Joe to you. You're deceived, Andie. Go back to church and confess your sins at the foot of the cross. I'm not sure even that will get Joe back."

I jerked my head toward my mother-in-law, searching for any speck of warmth in her face. It shocked me to find nothing there but a sharp-edged tongue.

I threw it back in her face. "I don't want him back!"

She raised her brows. Maudy's eyes, no longer friendly, blinked hard. "That's good because as soon as you've been separated a year, Joe is filing for divorce."

I shook my head. "Well, that's great. At least somebody has the decency to tell me."

"He's got a good lawyer. I suggest you get one, too." Her tone softened. "I ask only one thing: please let us see our grandchildren from time to time."

I walked back to my car and stood with my hand on the door. "Sure, but not in church."

"That's awful, Andie. They need Sunday School."

"They can go someplace else."

Maudy's mouth was tight and grim. Her accusing voice stabbed the air. "They'll miss Heaven because of you."

Biting back rage, I squared my shoulders. She had put my children in the bowels of Hell because they didn't worship at the House of Praise. "My children are not going to Hell and you know it! Good God, Maudy, I've been a part of this family nearly all my life. And now you turn me out?"

"Andie, I really think you should go. Like I said, it's not a good idea, you coming here. You've done this to yourself, don't you see that? We can't side with you on this. It wouldn't be good for Joe. We've been told you're demon-possessed. They've admonished us to not allow you in our home again, lest a worse darkness come on us than what's on you. I can't have you here until you've made your heart right with God."

My God, they've threatened you. I crossed my arms and felt as if I were suffocating.

Al had been silent, but wiped at his eyes with his hankie. He stared into my face, as though sensing my conflict, and then broke into a tender smile before quoting scripture. "*For I hate divorce, says the Lord, the God of Israel. And I hate the man who does wrong to his wife, says the Lord of All.*"

Maudy looked hard at him, then gave us both a shaky laugh. "That's enough, Al." Her unexpected interruption was jarring, and I resented it.

But he continued. "*The LORD has been witness between you and the wife of your youth, with whom you have dealt treacherously; yet she is your companion—*"

"I said that's enough! We stand with Joe!"

"*—and your wife by covenant . . . therefore take heed to your spirit, and let none deal treacherously with the wife of his youth. Malachi two fourteen and—*"

"Al! Stop it!"

"I'm on God's side, Maudy. I don't stand with Joe or Reverend or you on this. Whether you like it or not." He moved and stood between Maudy and me, placing his rough-hewn hands on my shoulders and looking into my eyes. "Come see me anytime you want, daughter. You are always welcome in my shop. It seems the only place I have any authority. Kiss Gracie and Dilly Bean for me, will ya?" He kissed my cheek in goodbye.

"Thank you." I wondered if Al's back would break from the burdens he carried. He nodded, then glared at Maudy, as if daring her to speak. I watched him amble back inside his shop, his shoulders slumped in defeat.

Maudy waved her hand, dismissing him. "Al forgets the covenant we made years ago to stand by Reverend Artury, to save the lost at any cost."

"Well, fine. But it's costing you your family. Maybe someday you'll open your eyes and see the cult you're in. Ray tried to tell you—"

"Andie! We've been warned. Reverend is calling you the Dark Angel. Do I have to say it again? We stand with Joe."

I opened my car door. Tears ran into the corner of my mouth, although I didn't remember starting to cry. "How dare he call me that?!" I trembled until my legs almost buckled, but I gave it one last try. "Maudy, why don't you at least investigate Calvin for yourself? Start asking questions; see where it gets you." The look on her face was as if I'd suggested they shave their heads, pierce their noses, tongues, and nipples, and convert to Hinduism.

There was nothing more to say. Maudy turned, walked inside her house, and closed the door behind her. She never looked back.

January 1990
DIVORCE COURT

Andie

My wavering faith constantly reminded me of what God should do, or should have done on my behalf. I can't tell you how many times over the years I asked Him, why are you letting this happen to me? But then I'd remember, He had given me what I asked for. Children to love and nurture. Maybe that was the best He could do for me. And it was a hell of a lot more than some women had. Every week, I pushed self-pity aside and head-butted my future with all the enthusiasm I could gather, only to find the spark of God had gone out of me, and I was standing alone in the midst of yet one more fire.

§

"Caroline? Can I borrow your Honda again?"

"Sure, why?"

"It's Joe. He's stolen my car."

"Good God, Andie. Did you call the police?"

"Can't. It's registered to Maudy. We were making payments to her, but I guess that wasn't enough. They came and took it right out of my garage. They knew damn well I'd have no transportation. I got kids, for Christ's sake! Damn them all to Hell!"

"Did you miss any payments?"

"I don't know. Ask Joe. He was supposed to make them for me so I could keep the car. That was our arrangement. The only bill he had to pay. Obviously, he defaulted. Son of a bitch!"

"I'll have Mama follow me over to your place. This old Honda is just sitting in Daddy's driveway. I got both cars in my divorce settlement. Keep this one until you can get something."

"Thanks. I appreciate it. I know I don't tell you that enough. Bring the girls over this week; they can help me bake again. I wish I could help *you* more."

"Way I hear it, you got bigger problems than me. At least my worthless husbands didn't rob me blind."

"Yeah. We sure know how to pick 'em. Huh?"

Caroline laughed. "I should've listened to you, Andie. Gone to school. Learned a trade. Instead, I married the first man with money that came my way. Both times. And I'm still broke, divorced, and got three kids in the bargain. Hey, do you know where they're keeping your car? You got a key, right?"

"Joe called and warned me not to take it. Said he'd call the police, say I'd stole his mama's car. Besides, it's sitting in Maudy's front yard with a *for sale* sign on it."

"God, Andie. See you in an hour. *Damn* them Olivers!"

§

Joe wasted no time after the legally required length of separation; he filed for divorce exactly one year to the day he vacated my house. I was served with papers during the holiday week between Christmas and New Year's. Happy holidays to me.

Driving the borrowed Honda to my divorce attorney appointment with foreboding, I pulled in and parked in front of a row of two-story red brick buildings; everything about the place was designed to create an image of stability and prosperity. A bank stood across the street. A fancy coffee shop and dress boutique had opened a few doors down. Bookstores, restaurants, and real estate offices had proliferated the area as new development spread.

The sign on the door read *Blunden and Crocker, Esq. – Law Offices.* Daniel Blunden, Esquire's suite consumed the second floor. When I stepped off the elevator the office smelled like the inside of a new car. Rich leather chairs lined paneled walls the color of cinnamon and nutmeg. My shoes sunk an inch as I stepped onto thick creamy carpet.

I wore my best black trousers and my turquoise cotton sweater that had faded to the color of a robin's egg. Having sewed a mismatched button on the bottom, I stood helpless to stop my embarrassment. I stared at the receptionist's black pumps. Shiny as a new nickel, they reflected the underside of the girl's chair. A nameplate on her gleaming desk read Sandra H. She had milky skin, glossy black hair, and red nails you could only get in a salon. I waited. Staring at her perfect teeth, it hit me just how lacking I was in everything from hair to clothes to all-around first impressions. The girl finally spoke. "Name, please?"

Covering my button with my purse, I lifted my chin and pretended to have more money than I actually did. "Andie Oliver. I have an appointment with Mr. Blunden. At four o'clock."

At twenty past four, Dan Blunden opened his door and apologized for being late. I followed him into a stark office, all chrome and leather, immaculately clean. He had hair the darkest shade of red and stood at least as tall as Daddy, with a right-angle jaw and eyes the color of frozen peas—so much so that I couldn't stop staring at them.

He shrugged his slim shoulders out of his suit jacket and hung it neatly on a hanger on the back of his door, then pulled a file out of a cabinet before moving to his desk. He seldom made eye contact with me, but started talking all the same. "First, we need to discuss my fee. Seven hundred up front."

I took out my checkbook and wrote out the check. I had borrowed more money from Aunt Wylene, promising to pay her back sometime before I died. Wylene was only too happy to help me put an end to my marriage and told me to consider it a gift for my future.

"Tell me about your marriage, Mrs. Oliver. I'm sure you're aware modern-day divorce proceedings focus on money, not morality. But tell me everything."

I kept my features deceptively composed and told him my side.

A few weeks later, a court date was set for the first week in April.

§

Dressed in a conservative blue suit and a starched white shirt, Dan Blunden scribbled a final note on his legal pad. Although my water cup was untouched, he took a quick sip of his and waited for Judge Landis to nod in our direction.

The judge looked impressive and leaned toward his microphone. "Mr. Blunden, you may conduct your cross-examination."

Despite my best effort to control my breathing, I struggled to slow my rapid heartbeat. I glanced at Joe. Seated in the witness chair, he had leaned back and crossed his legs. His eyes were lethal and filled with contempt glaring back at me. He turned his attention to the judge with a satisfied look. My attorney's three months of telephone calls, and his law clerk knocking on the House of Praise offices, got him nowhere. A fortress of closed lips and bolted doors, the church refused to budge despite numerous lawsuit threats. Blunden told me he'd never seen anything like it, and for the first time in his life, he was thankful for his Catholicism. They were obviously out to shield Joe and crucify me.

Sitting beside my attorney, my shoe tapped nervously on the polished courtroom floor. Blunden rose and walked slowly to a spot in front of the witness stand.

"Thank you, your Honor," he said. He then focused his attention on his adversary.

"Mr. Oliver, how old were you when you met your wife?"

"Fifteen or sixteen."

"Where did you meet?"

"At church. The House of Praise, where I'm now employed and attend service."

"Had your wife graduated from high school when you proposed to her?"

"No, we started dating seriously *my* senior year. I proposed during her senior year."

"And you testified on direct examination that you were married on July 1, 1972, a month after your wife's high school graduation. Is that correct?"

"Yes."

"Where did you spend the first seven years of your married life?"

"In Salisbury, North Carolina. Where I'm from originally."

"Did you or your wife go to college?"

"No. I worked. She worked."

"What type of work did your wife do?"

"Um, she had several different jobs. Mostly clerical or in restaurants. I worked as a mechanic and volunteered for Reverend Calvin Artury until he hired me full-time in '76."

Mr. Blunden retrieved a stack of papers from the corner of the table where I sat watching.

"Did she work more than one job at a time?"

"Occasionally. She liked to stay busy."

"Stay busy, or make enough to cover the bills you couldn't?"

"Objection, your honor."

"Sustained."

My attorney continued his cross. "Were you also working two jobs?"

"Yes and no. I told you, I *volunteered* my time to the church while I worked as a mechanic for Coot McGraw."

"For the record, you stated you lived in a trailer park for seven years. Shady Acres in Salisbury, correct?"

"Yes, that's correct."

"How many bedrooms?"

"One."

"Where did your children sleep?"

"Objection! I see no relevance here."

"Sustained."

Attorney Blunden looked down at the top sheet of paper. "After your wife's employment with First National Bank of Salisbury, was one of her employers Southern States Insurance Company?"

"I think so. I don't remember the exact name."

"Did she also work three nights a week as a convenience store clerk?"

"Uh, yes, for a while."

Dan Blunden's eyes flashed with a hint of fire. "Would it surprise you to know that I have employment records showing your wife worked a combined average of fifty-five hours a week at the insurance company and convenience store *and* for the remainder of your marriage while she was self-employed? Did you realize she worked fifty-five hours a week for more than ten years as she raised your children, while you traveled extensively?"

Joe shifted in the chair. "I remember we bought a couple cars, she bought a business, and she bought a house I never agreed to while I traveled to Africa on a crusade for souls. She sure surprised me. I came home and she said, 'Guess what I bought?' We needed to make the payments. She *had* to work hard to help pay for *her* ventures."

Attorney Blunden took a step forward, ignoring Joe's snide comments about my purchases. "Would you like to review the employment records for yourself?"

"No," Joe responded quickly. "If the records are accurate, the math should be simple."

"Do you think she made those purchases because she wanted to make you miserable or because possibly she wanted to take a risk, find the American dream, make a better life for your family?"

"Objection!"

Joe ignored the objection of his attorney and proceeded to answer. "Andie didn't care what I wanted. Only what *she* wanted. She knew we had to live within our means. She knew what I made. She never biblically submitted to me. She did what she wanted to do!"

Attorney Blunden smiled at Joe and continued.

"Do you also recall that Bud Parks, your father-in-law, gave my client a five-thousand-dollar down payment and also paid for renovations to your new home?"

"Sure, and I paid for a new roof and a new furnace. So? Like I said, she always gets what she wants."

I couldn't stand to look at him. I tucked my balled fists in my jacket pockets and turned my attention to the initials someone had carved deep into the bench beside me.

"My point is, Mr. Oliver, that you are laying claim to all of the proceeds in the sale of the house. A house that is in her name only and part of her bankruptcy."

I was certain Joe had not heard about my bankruptcy until that second.

"I don't want to be dragged into her financial problems."

"Her financial problems are yours as well," Blunden answered. Joe flinched and glared at me while Blunden continued. "When was your first child born?"

"In 1975. He passed away shortly afterward."

"And was she pregnant again when you started full-time employment with your church?"

"Yes, with our twins."

"Did she continue working while pregnant?"

"Only at a beauty shop."

"Looks like twenty hours a week, according to my records?"

Joe looked toward his lawyer, an older attorney named Howard Carson. Carson didn't offer any help and Joe ran his finger along the inside of his collar. "Whatever the records show. I don't remember exactly."

"Did you continue to insist she work outside the home?"

"Yes. I told you. She had to. It was her decision to buy a business. That left us with virtually no extra income. She thought it would force me into a better-paying job. That's why she did it. And even though I don't make much, she hasn't worked for anyone else in years. Just wasted all her time in that cafeteria of hers. I wanted her to work a normal job. And I wanted her in church. She hasn't attended our church for years. She knows how important that is to me."

"How long did she own the cafeteria?"

He looked up and mentally calculated the passage of time. "About eight years."

"Have you had any other children during that time?"

"No, thank God."

My attorney put the employment records on the table and slid a thick folder to a place where it would be handy.

"Mr. Oliver, you testified that for the past fourteen years, you've received all of your income from the House of Praise. Is that correct?"

"Yes."

"What do you do there?"

"I'm the Chief Audio and Video Engineer for the television ministry."

"How many trips do you take every year with your employer?"

"Six long trips a year. Three to four short trips a month, usually. My income is sixteen thousand annually. I gave Andie copies of my tax returns and asked her to give them to you."

Mr. Blunden gave Joe a slight smile. "Thank you for your cooperation, Mr. Oliver. I have carefully reviewed every one." Then he opened the thick folder and took out a single sheet of paper.

"Are you familiar with a company called Peyton Broadcasting?"

"Sure, it's our production company."

"Are you an employee of Peyton Broadcasting?"

"No."

My attorney handed the sheet of paper to the court reporter who marked it as an exhibit. He then showed it to Joe's lawyer who put on his glasses, made a few notes, and passed it back to him. Blunden moved a few steps closer to Joe but did not show him the sheet of paper. "Are you J. N. Oliver, who is listed as employee number 7005 with Peyton Broadcasting?"

"Uh, I guess I am. I never considered myself an actual employee there."

"Yes or no will do."

"Yes."

"What do you make from Peyton Broadcasting, Mr. Oliver?"

Joe squirmed in his seat and stared at the sheet of paper in Blunden's hand before he said, "I'm not sure."

Without showing him the document, Attorney Blunden returned to the folder and took out another document, which was marked as an exhibit. After showing it to Joe's lawyer, he handed it directly to Joe.

"What does this page from the minutes of a corporate meeting of Peyton Broadcasting directors indicate as your contribution to Reverend Artury's television production company?"

Joe looked down at the paper and didn't answer.

"Take your time, Mr. Oliver," he interjected. "I want you to be sure about your answer. Remember, you are under oath."

Joe recrossed his legs. "An additional twenty-five hours a week to my work at the House of Praise."

Blunden picked up a different sheet of paper and handed it to Joe. "And what was your income from Peyton Broadcasting last year, in addition to your income from the House of Praise?"

"Twenty-five thousand." Joe's face grew red. "Who told you?" he sputtered. "What about the whore I'm married to? What about her? Doesn't sleeping with every guy in the neighborhood say she's an unfit mother?"

Howard Carson stood to his feet. "Objection, Your Honor."

"On what grounds?" the judge asked.

"May we approach the bench?" Attorney Carson requested.

"Yes."

Dan Blunden joined Howard Carson in front of the judge.

I heard Joe's lawyer say, "I didn't know about this . . ."

My attorney responded in a whisper.

The judge frowned, then raised his head. "Very well. Court will be in recess for thirty minutes while I consult with the attorneys in my chambers. Mr. Oliver, you may leave the witness stand but may not confer with anyone."

My attorney gathered his files. I leaned forward. "What's the problem?"

"This is good. They're circling their wagons. They need the judge to help them out of a tight spot. It looks like your soon-to-be-ex didn't provide his attorney with all of his income records. And I suspect his attorney forgot to tell him it all boils down to assets. Sit tight."

I grabbed his arm and whispered. "What about custody?"

Blunden nodded to the judge then turned back to me. "I have to go. Listen, from what you've told me Joe doesn't want those kids. And if he wants to fight for custody, we'll subpoena records on the length of time he's been out of town the past seventeen years. The courts want custodial single fathers to live at home with their children."

The two lawyers followed Judge Landis to his chambers.

One hour later, the judge spelled out the agreement for the record. "Mr. Oliver will pay child support of three hundred dollars a month per child through age eighteen with comprehensive health insurance and payment of four years' tuition at the North Carolina average for private institutions at the time each child begins matriculation. Alimony of another three hundred a month for two years or until Mrs. Oliver remarries, whichever comes first, and total indemnification for any unpaid taxes on returns through the current tax year."

My face flushed and burned. Joe's admitted loss included no further dissection of his income or assets. He had given up the ghost. As the court reporter prepared a transcript of the settlement, it was also agreed my bankruptcy not include Joe. I followed Dan Blunden from the courtroom.

"I'll prepare the paperwork and send it to your husband's lawyer by the first of next week," he said. "I wish I could've got you more, but we were lucky to get what we got."

"He won't pay it anyway."

"He has to. He's risking a jail sentence if he doesn't."

Joe and his attorney exited the courtroom and retreated in defeat. They rushed past us without speaking. I recognized Joe's temper brewing. Familiar with his body language, my stomach boiled and churned; a wave of nausea rolled over me. I gripped my purse strap until my nails dug into the heel of my hand. "He frightens me," I said.

"Your husband created his bitter pill. Now he has to choke on it."

"I know, and I appreciate what you've done. But you don't understand these people. They do what they want. Joe will never pay it. Never. And Artury will never open his books to the public or anyone. They'll retaliate."

My attorney softened. "Only way they can retaliate is to file for custody, which I doubt your ex wants to do. You're right about one thing; no one even cracked the door for me at the House of Praise. We're lucky Peyton

Broadcasting isn't under the protection of the church; they had to cough up his records. And we only guessed at his unreported bonuses. Hopefully, you'll get your support every month and won't have to go back to work at a convenience store. Go after him again if he refuses to pay. Call me; we'll put him in jail."

I sighed. "I don't have the money for more legal fees. I can't afford to fight him. Joe knows that. He'll pay what and when he wants, I assure you." Fear came up in my voice like vomit. "I haven't heard the end of it. He knows I'm wounded. I'm afraid I've just pissed them off more. Knowing he intended to hide all that money even when he was under oath makes me wonder what else he's hiding."

§

I stuffed the traumas of my life deep into the fractures of my past and tried to live again. Outward circumstances improved at a snail's pace. Inside, I remained dark and twisted. Constant nightmares suffocated any hope of peaceful sleep. Dixie labeled me permanently moody.

Relationships with potential husbands became an impossible undertaking in my mind. Nothing lasted. My deep well of mistrust was bottomless. At the first sign of interest from a man, my cocky reaction scared off the aspirant suitor. I talked to Aunt Wy about it; however, the well-meaning doctor only knew how to check for beating hearts, She had no idea what to do with broken ones.

Not wanting to see Joe when he came by to pick up the kids, I had them ready with their bags packed on the porch. My past tormented me daily—things I knew, had witnessed, and could do nothing about. It stalked me along paths of terror. Only my children and an iron will kept me from insanity. The best I could hope for was the bankruptcy judge to allow me to keep my house.

October 1990
Postmortem Divorce

Andie

Dixie cut up vegetables for soup while Caroline carried a bowl of broth into the next room to spoon-feed Daddy. Sitting at the counter reading the Sunday paper, I threw the wedding announcements on the counter. "Get a load of this."

Dixie slid her tortoise-shell spectacles from the top of her head down to the tip of her impudent nose and gasped. "Selma Rodriguez and Joe Oliver married at the House of Praise in a private ceremony on September first." Dixie's chin came up a notch and her delicate eyebrow arched above her glasses, her eyes still that soft gray, like rain clouds. She laughed to cover her annoyance. "Only took him five months. You think they knew each other before your divorce?"

"Maudy let it slip that Joe was seeing a girl named Selma who lived at Ilene Robey's boarding house. Before our divorce I drove past once . . . at two in the morning to see if his truck was there. It was. What happened to the scandals Calvin was so all-fired up about? I guess people don't question anything Calvin puts his blessing on these days, no matter what it is."

"There's no picture. What's she look like?" asked Dixie. "This Selma person."

"I've only seen her from a distance when she comes with Joe to pick up the kids. She's very young. I'm guessing eighteen, nineteen maybe."

"For pity sake, she's not much older than the twins!"

"But she's very pretty, and as you know, Joe likes 'em pretty. She's attractive— in a dark kind of way. Brunette. Tall. String-bikini body. The total opposite of me. Latino, I believe. She's from Mexico, I think."

My mother rolled her eyes. "How's she dress?"

I shrugged. "God, Mama, I don't know. I don't care. She wears, you know, the kind of clothes Joe always loved on women. Trashy. Gracie says she's quiet. No sass, I'm sure. I've never seen her smile. Gracie also said Selma loves her job at the Praise Buffet and that she never wants to have children. Good thing."

Dixie gently brushed my hair away from my shoulder. "I don't like her. She's got home-wrecker written all over her."

"My home was already wrecked. Selma had nothing to do with it."

"There is no home without children. I see no reason for pretty women like Selma to enter the workplace and forego motherhood."

"I've come to realize, Dixie, not every woman wants to be a mother, and not every woman expresses love with casseroles and a spotless house like you do."

But my mother couldn't stop. "Selma is going to need a thick skin, more than she bargained for. Joe doesn't come with a monogamous guarantee or an instruction booklet on how to keep him at home. She can't return him for a full refund!"

"My best to the happy couple," I said, raising a glass of iced tea. "Now it's someone else's turn to put up with him."

Dixie shook her head; her tone was coolly disapproving. "It's not natural to never want a baby. It's just not natural."

I stepped to the sink, ran hot water for dishes, and recalled those first months of marriage. When our suppers were full of leisurely small talk and nights spent, if not curled in each other's arms, at least touching—hands held in sleep, his leg flung over mine, keeping me warm. My few happy moments with Joe. The few fleeting moments I clung to for too many years. Our marriage had spun out of control like a barn caught in the path of a tornado.

"Joe loves to rub my failures in my face. He says he feels fragile right now, doesn't want to talk to me when I call him about the twins."

"If Bud were well enough to kick his ass, he'd feel a hell of a lot more fragile than he does now."

At that moment it wasn't my mother's loving husband and beautiful home I envied. It was her newfound confidence. Dixie had recently, through the power of Wylene's ceaseless persuasion, begun to see a psychiatrist and to think of herself as our family matriarch.

Tired, I rubbed my eyes. "I have to pick up the twins from school, and the furnace man is coming. It's broken again." I kissed my mother's cheek on the way out.

"When you gonna lose more weight? You'd look prettier as a size eight," said Dixie.

§

I grew despondent after subtracting the sum to fix the furnace from my checkbook. The repairman stuffed my check into his pocket. "Your warranty ran out last month. I'll let you put it on a charge card if you want," he said. "I won't charge you for labor."

I laughed, hoping the check I wrote wouldn't bounce and the furnace was truly fixed.

Later, the house warmed slowly while I peeled an apple at a kitchen table I'd bought for a song at a fire sale to replace the table Joe took when he left. My children crept in and stood behind me. I turned to see their somewhat smiling faces. My heart wrenched. They were so vulnerable.

Gracie leaned across the table, resting her pudgy hand on my arm. She'd stopped taking piano lessons since we could no longer afford them and painted her thumbnails apricot and the others a bright lime green. Her baby-blonde hair, parted in the middle and pulled back with butterfly barrettes, hung straggly below her shoulders. Her faded Madonna T-shirt had tomato sauce stains from the previous night's Chef Boyardee. "You okay, Mama?"

I believed it to be my job to paste a smile on my face, straighten myself with dignity, and free Gracie from worry. "Better every day," I said. That was not a total lie. I was better than the day I had the flu so bad I vomited blood. I was better than the day my water broke while Wy shoved a twenty-inch needle into my spine. And I was better than the day I felt the pain of losing Mavis would own me forever.

Dillon scratched at a scab on his arm. "Then why are you crying?"

I sighed. "Having to take care of a broken furnace, Aunt Caroline's car won't start again, and I guess I'm a little tired. Just things like that," I told my children.

Gracie bit into a piece of my shared apple. "Did you love Daddy?"

I raised an eyebrow. Neither twin had ever asked that. "I did, once upon a time."

"I don't know how I feel about him," Gracie said.

"He's your daddy. You're supposed to love him, I've been told. But respect is something folks earn."

Dillon's eyes stared away from me and his sister. I sensed his anger.

"Well, there's no sense in hiding that things have been tough. You're both smart enough to know we're struggling. All I have left in this world is you two. There's always a way. There are always good things just waiting for you to find them."

"Are we looking for good things?" Gracie asked.

Their faces lit with hope, and I, as always, plunged toward it despite my wanting to do otherwise. "Every day," I answered. I reached out for my daughter's face, cupping her chin in my hand, wanting to look into Gracie's eyes, and then wishing I hadn't. For a moment, just before my precious girl turned away, I peered past her little-girl eyelashes into blue eyes like my own, full of jumbled emotion. As though all the hurt and uncertainty inside were finally welling up and spilling over. Gracie couldn't suck back her tears, but she wouldn't let them drop either. So they just hung there like heavy dew on delicate grass.

"We tried to be what he wanted us to be." Dillon pushed back his hair and leaned forward, as if the weight of my pain rested like a cross on his back. His small face was knit into a frown of concern. It undid me. "But Dad talks about God too much," he said. "And this one time, I showed him a picture I drew of Grandpa Bud's hunting gun. He said I shouldn't be spending so much time with Grandpa."

"He didn't mean nothing by it, Dillon. He just didn't like my daddy much," I said.

"Why?" he asked.

"It's a long story. Too long for tonight. Remember, your daddy loves you. In his own strange way, he does. He doesn't know how to show it, is all. He was raised with love. Al and Maudy loved him. Really they did. Your daddy just loves Reverend Artury more than anyone. It's something we all have to live with."

"That's not fair, Mama." Gracie yawned, her tears had fallen despite her willing them not to. She wiped them across her cheeks into her hair.

I reached over and moved her bangs out of her sleepy, teary eyes. "I know, sweetheart. It's just the way it is. We'll survive. One thing you can always count on is me. I'll never leave you and no one will ever take you from me. C'mon now, let's get some sleep."

I stood and walked behind them to their beds. Dillon laid his arm on my leg, too tired to sit up for his nightly hug. I kissed my son and tucked Mavis's big blue afghan around him. Then I stepped into Gracie's room.

"Are we alright, Mama?" Gracie yawned again, and stroked her inner arms with her fingertips.

I paused, groping for a reason to fill my daughter with more hope. "Sure, you bet we are. Now, off to sleep."

But in the next moment, I turned my face away. Fear knotted in my stomach. I had known terror before, but that time it sat on the bed with me. I felt as though I could reach out and touch it. Being alone with despair was one thing. Being responsible for the two little bodies that laid on their beds, with no resources but what I had to beg for, was living a nightmare I could not wake up from. *My hope is that there is a just God. That someday, Joe Oliver, when you look up from the bowels of Hell you share with your buddy Calvin, you will fully realize what you did to me and to our children. That will be your real Hell.*

April 1991
THE WEREWOLF IS ALWAYS AT YOUR DOOR

Andie

I moved through winter like a rudderless boat adrift on the Cape Fear. Electric and phone shut-off notices arrived and were paid, by yet another gift from Aunt Wylene. Food stamps, along with extra groceries from my parents kept meals on the table. I found a new bag of hope in the spring when I hadn't heard from my bankruptcy attorney.

Wandering from the kitchen to the patio off the garage, my stomach burned. I gulped the last of my Diet Dr. Pepper and realized I hadn't eaten all day. In fact, I'd not eaten much over the winter and it showed. I'd shrunk four sizes. Instead of feeding my depression, I smoked cigarettes and drank diet sodas. Had I been able to afford stronger drink, I might have become an alcoholic. Food had lost its appeal. One thing about living in Winston-Salem—cigarettes were cheap. Especially when Dixie gave me carton after carton to get them out of the house.

I fished one out of my pocket and fired up Daddy's old Zippo, imagining myself as Ali McGraw in *Love Story*. I watched it every time it was listed in the *TV Guide*. I wanted to be Ali McGraw, the most courageous girl I'd ever seen, my body wrapped around Ryan O'Neal. I got choked up thinking about that movie; it had nearly killed me to see the longing in his eyes after her death, the yearning he carried around so plain for everyone to see, his love that meant never having to say you're sorry. I wanted that from a man. My hopeless romantic self. Pathetic.

At almost seven o'clock, sitting in a rocking chair with splinters, I watched the sun, low and pink, hover over the horizon like an iridescent bubble. The phone rang and I jumped to answer it. I'd been sitting a long time. The rocker had left its imprints on my arms and legs.

Caroline's voice squealed on the other end. "Sooo . . . how was your date?"

"You really want to know?" Trying to ignore the throb of old wounds, I agreed to go out on a blind date. I turned away from the window and dropped my cigarette in the sink where I'd been washing dishes before enjoying the sunset.

Caroline giggled. "Hickey is a nice-looking guy. He's ambitious and attractive and—"

"Then *you* go out with him!"

"Oh, no. I was married to his brother. That's enough."

"See what I mean? No girl in their right mind would date a guy named Hickey, which I might add, is exactly what he wanted to give me. Who would name their child Hickey? Tell me, who?" I filled the percolator with water and slammed it on the counter. "He spent fifty bucks at the Salad and Steak Pit, and then expected me to have sex with him in his truck bed at an X-rated drive-in. When I saw we were about to watch a porno, I pitched a hissy fit. I made him take me home."

"The truck bed? Really?" Caroline burst out laughing. "Did you?"

"No!" I didn't want to have that conversation with my sister.

"I can't believe he did that."

"Well, believe it." My heart skipped a beat. "I don't believe in true love anymore. Just the made up kind in the movies. I don't need a man to be happy, but I sure could use the income."

"A girl doesn't need ice cream to be happy, either. Or cheeseburgers. Or peanut butter fudge. They're comfort foods. Girls need comforting, Andie."

"I'll keep that in mind next time you try to hook me up. I'll go to Dairy Queen instead."

§

Loneliness. It wrapped around me at the oddest times. I had to admit I'd tasted companionship and I missed it. Having some kind of relationship. Caroline had meant well, even if her ex-brother-in-law was a skank. I wasn't sure I was ready to date, or that I ever wanted to again. I'd been so wrong about Joe; how could I trust myself to find the right man, for me and my children?

He'd treated me to lobster salad and a Porterhouse the size of his truck. I was uncomfortable—a welfare recipient eating steak and lobster. Hickey also promised me a drive-in movie where we would just sit and relax, sip some wine, and talk. As I slid out backwards from his woolly mammoth pickup that smelled like a greasy burger and fries, I disconnected the radio by bumping into loops of wire that sagged beneath the glove compartment. He helped me climb inside the truck bed amid litter and a blanket I assumed was clean. I had felt obligated to bring the beverage, so I brought out two bottles of cheap five-dollar wine from a Harris Teeter sack. "Red or white?" I asked.

His hair all liquored up with some kind of goop, he pulled a swig from a bottle of whiskey and raised a quizzical eyebrow. "You mind if I drink my Jim Beam?"

When the cartoons were over and *Tits for Tad* flickered across the gigantic screen, I quickly ended the evening, insisting I'd become ill and needed to go home immediately. Porno reminded me of Joe and I couldn't stand the thought of it. Besides, Hickey would've broadcast his score to every bubba in Forsyth County. Mister Caveman curled his lip and looked at me with a gleam in his eye and a disturbing growl. I'd somehow managed to let him kiss me only once, keeping him at arm's length afterward until I could make it home without a scratch.

§

I watched him order a Big Mac, fries, and two Cokes. Jasper Wenger, my old flame. At least that's how I remembered him. The crush I carried for Jasper in junior high before I met Joe unpacked itself from an attic corner in my memory. I often wondered where he was, how he was, and if he was married. I wished I had put on my lipstick, but at least my hair looked good. I tapped him on the shoulder.

"Hey, Jasper. It's been a long time."

"Andie? How the hell are ya?"

He still had the same pretty smile, though some teeth had yellowed. I noticed he wasn't wearing a wedding band. Still, there was no certainty on how reliable a ringless hand could be. In five short minutes I found out he lived in Kernersville, worked for UPS, and was engaged to Sherry Hoover. He had a little boy from a previous relationship that never ended in marriage.

His eyes were crystalline light blue, like a spring Carolina sky, and they looked right into mine as he shook my hand with a strong grip. The sizzle of the attraction sparked through me. Then he gave me the same big, broad, charming smile he had in high school and said Sherry was waiting in the car. He'd best take her a Coke.

§

While food from Dixie kept meals on the table, money from Aunt Wy barred the wolves from my door. Almost. I was slicing bacon the next day, when the phone rang.

"It's me, Jasper."

"Lordy, Jasper, how'd you get my number?" I smiled to myself.

"Called your old phone number from school and your mama gave it to me. She filled me in on your recent divorce."

"She did, did she?"

He coughed to clear his throat. "Andie, I was wondering, would you like to go out, have a drink, talk about some of the deadbeats we went to school with?"

"Why, are you suddenly free as a bird? Your fiancée toss you out on your ear?"

"No, not really. I just couldn't get you out of my head yesterday. I mean, I have to tell ya, I had a major crush on you through high school, but you had your head in the clouds for that guy from Salisbury who, according to your mama, has pissed on your parade every year since you married him."

I laughed. As usual, Dixie gave away more than my phone number. And then I sighed. *Jasper.* What did I see in his eyes at McDonald's? He had a sunny warmth and an adoring expression—and he was an old friend. It was a nice feeling I'd forgotten. To have some honest attention from the opposite sex. I suddenly forgot about Sherry Hoover. "Sure, where can I meet you?"

We agreed, seven o'clock at the Elbow Bar near Mocksville. A double-wide with a good dose of character that had been turned into a good ol' boys' saloon. And a good distance from Sherry's house in Kernersville.

He dressed in ostrich skin boots, a white shirt with rolled-up sleeves, and creased Levi's with a big ring in his back pocket from sitting on his can of Copenhagen. He asked politely for a Miller draft and ordered a glass of white wine for me as we made ourselves comfortable at the bar. "Leather skirt?" He touched my leg and smiled another lovely smile with sweetness in it.

"Yeah. My sister let me borrow it. I'm short on nice clothes these days."

"You look great."

"Thanks." My shoulders went limp.

Jasper had smooth hands, long fingers, and crinkly lines around his eyes and mouth. He couldn't stop smiling. He said he had attended a prayer meeting the past summer where he got saved. I said that was nice and could we talk about something other than religion. That's when I felt his blue eyes lock on me. We drank and laughed until midnight, creating a healthy curiosity between us. A little shiver of relief and a shimmy of guilt rolled down my spine. Old friends who had not seen each other in years. It didn't bother me he'd had a fight with Sherry, which is why he ended up calling me. He displayed a sincere air of sympathy about my divorce, expressed concern for my children, and nearly cried when I told him about Mavis whom he remembered from school. He talked about his little boy in a way that touched my heart. By the time he downed his sixth beer and I tipped back my third glass of wine, he put his hand on my leg again and suggested he follow me home. I agreed. The kids were at my parents' house, and I'd put fresh sheets on my bed.

I fumbled with my house key, turning it the wrong way in the lock as Jasper wrapped his arms around my waist and pressed his lips on my neck. My heart quickened and I felt a tingling, both pleasurable and horrifying, like the tickle of a spider on bare skin. Finally I opened the door. Leaning against the door frame, I allowed him to explore me with his hands and mouth. Forcing my problems aside, I pulled him inside and then to my bed, complete with my favorite rosebud sheets.

He whispered in the dark. "You sure you want to do this?"

"Yes." I didn't want to think about it. I had married Joe almost as soon as I was out of a training bra. I didn't want to think about all I had missed. Nor did I wish to give in to the guilt of being the slut I knew *they* would call me if *they* found out. It struck me funny that Joe could have countless affairs and still keep face with his family and church. But should I indulge in alcohol and a strange man on one heart-pulsing momentous night, *they* would plaster it across every I-40 billboard from Winston-Salem to Raleigh before morning, if *they* found out.

My blouse and bra slid to the floor. I felt the heat in my cheeks as plainly as I felt the coolness from the night air against my bare back and shoulders.

Sex, evidently, was not limited to monogamous relationships any longer. It was an awakening. Jasper would be my secret, my chance for sex for the first time in years. He would also be a prelude to a better life. Joe popped into my mind but I pushed him out, overwhelmed by a determination to get on with living, a force stronger than the memory of him and my own principles. Jasper moved over me. My eyes closed, then opened, then closed again. Within minutes it was over. I'd had sex with a man who wasn't Joe. My virgin voyage into the world of other men. My first look at a naked body I was unfamiliar with. My first sexual encounter of pure lust and not one drop of love. My first feelings of contempt for myself, and the first time I hated Joe for pushing me into a world I did not want.

In the dark, Jasper finally rolled off me. He could not see my eyes tightly closed, my teeth biting into my fist to muffle a cry, and tears like fallen angels dropping from my eyes.

§

After I had fallen asleep, Jasper slipped out without a goodbye or a kiss or even a note. In the morning I found nothing but a used condom on the floor. My head felt like it was coming off my shoulders. I stood, naked, and walked unsteadily to the bathroom. Gripping the sink, I looked in the mirror. My face looked rumpled, as though I'd tossed and turned in one bad dream after another for weeks on end. My skin was blotchy and red and my eyes were ringed with mascara and liner. They burned. Standing in the shower I felt off balance. My world tightened around me, threatening to suffocate me again. But it felt good to wash the smoke from my skin and hair, loosening the pesky bands of my past.

Later, I walked to the mailbox in my robe and house shoes. Nothing to do but pay bills. No Mavis to call and share my secrets, my big night, and my great realization that not all penises looked alike.

By three o'clock, my queasiness hadn't let up. I could still feel his razor-burn on my cheeks as I chugged a glass of Alka-Seltzer. After resting Daddy's old cordless phone on my nightstand, expecting to hear from Dillon and Gracie, I contemplated frying potatoes and onions, which Coot had sworn by when he was hung over.

Crazy enough, I didn't feel guilty, not one iota, about my sleepover with Jasper. He wasn't married to Sherry. The only real guilt I could muster was over *not* feeling guilty. I wasn't willing to sacrifice my future happiness to make a deal with God and remain celibate. If Joe could do it and have no repercussions, then so could I. But word traveled fast in the Triad, and I knew that, too. Raised in a fundamental church, my deeply ingrained morality and beliefs haunted me. Sensing vibrations of shame, my tidy world inside my head unraveled a little more.

Lying on the bed, nursing a headache, I stared at the plaster ceiling. A crack zigzagged like a road map from one side of the room to the other. I tried to rest, but sleep evaded me. The phone rang and my heart pounded.

"Andie? How was your date?"

"Fine. Are the kids okay?"

"Just fine? Your date was just fine?"

"Yes, Dixie. We met at a restaurant, had a nice talk, I went home. It was fine. Are the kids outside?"

"Gracie's knee-deep in homework, Dillon's in your old tree house. Glad you had a good time with your old school friend. Come get the twins, I need to take your daddy to the doctor."

"Is he sick?"

"We wouldn't be heading there if he weren't. Wy's coming from Charleston this weekend to take a look at him, too."

The question popped out with no thought of what I was asking. "Dixie? You ever have sex with anyone other than Daddy?"

"I hope you're not thinking of that until you remarry."

"I'm not marrying anybody ever."

"Fine. Come get your children."

She didn't answer my question. Just a minute before she'd wanted details. Dixie was either distracted or didn't want to talk about sex or her past, as usual. I purposed in my heart to always answer my children's questions about sex. The sacredness and the beauty of the act, the love it should involve with one person you've chosen to be with the rest of your life. Totally unlike my date with Jasper.

May 1991
A Patrick Swayze Face

Andie

Good thing I wasn't head-over-heels about Jasper. I never heard from him again. But he had whet my sexual appetite. For all my begging God to help me adjust to a new single life, I was left with a heightened libido and a new sense of loneliness. Though I had boldly proclaimed my mistrust in men, I wanted adventure, an escape. Above all, I needed to be held. Church, however, was no longer the obvious choice to meet men. I had also prided myself on my virtues of faithful wife and good mother and had never visited a bar alone. Everyone makes mistakes. Sometimes more than once, whether they want to or not.

§

Heads turned as I walked through the thick smoke inside the Purple Passion Bar. The yellow page advertisement made it appear upscale. Wearing my sister's black sweater dress that fit snugly in all the wrong places, I sat near a man at the bar and heard someone drop a quarter into the jukebox. *Friends in Low Places* began to play as the man stretched out a lean arm and a strong hand to introduce himself. In a low-pitched, silky voice he said his name was Gifford. A voice as smooth and pretty as Garth Brooks'.

Gifford was ruggedly handsome: a granite-like face and movie-star jaw tanned by sun and wind, earthy brown eyes, sun-bleached hair, and a tall, lithe body that had been conditioned by over fifteen years working construction; he'd mentioned his occupation. The sound of his voice coiled around my ears with the same lazy caress of the cigarette smoke that swirled around his Patrick Swayze face. My brain sucked up the look of him and allowed my heart to register a few flickers of pleasure. Sipping my beer like a lady, I felt a flush beginning in my cheeks.

I slid to the stool next to him and looked boldly into his eyes. In the dim light they appeared russet, mysterious, and aloof. The smell of his leather and musk aftershave generated a sense of eroticism that after two beers and a little teasing, made me braver than I really was. I plucked the cigarette from his mouth, drew a deep drag, and then replaced it between his lips.

"Thanks for the conversation," he said preparing to leave.

"Going so soon?" I teased, my lips parting in a pretty pout. My naiveness showed. I had no experience with men, let alone men in bars.

He hesitated a moment before answering, contemplating his empty beer glass, as if he were trying to word his reply with care. It didn't come out that way. "Men are just flies in a shithouse to you, aren't they, lady? You think all you have to do is throw up some flypaper and we'll all stick."

I sat there watching his cigarette flip up and down as he talked, thinking he wasn't quite as handsome as moments before. Embarrassed, I came to myself and blinked a few times, and then shot my pissed-off response in his face. "That's been my experience. First cockroach I ever caught, I married; the rest haven't been much better." I took a long swig from my beer bottle.

He stood. "Nice-looking gal like you shouldn't be in a place like this," he said, tossing a few dollars toward the bartender. "Anyway, I'm not interested." He removed the cigarette from his mouth and slipped it between my lips, just as I'd done to him. "Last drag is all yours," he said. Seconds later, his boot heels clicking the floorboards with a long, easy gait, he strode out of the bar.

My mouth curved into a humiliated smile. Another Garth Brooks song played on the jukebox. I sat listening to *The Dance*, and talking to myself in a throaty whisper to keep the tears away. "Oh, Mister-whatever-the-hell-you-said-your-name-was, you'll never see me in a place like this again. Ever." I took a final draw from the cigarette, flicked the ashes into the ashtray on the bar, then marched to my car. I'd never felt so disgusted with myself. But he'd done me a huge favor. I gave myself a hard swift mental kick in the butt, tucked my tail between my legs, and drove home.

Keeping Promises

Reverend Calvin Artury

I arrived at the Memphis airport ahead of schedule. My limousine driver drove through a few rural villages and suburbs on our way to the new coliseum in the center of the city. Memphis had braced itself for my miracle crusade.

Evan smiled. "The local news channels have broadcast your route from the airport to the coliseum. I purposely weaved our course through a few small towns, staying off the interstate."

"We can barely get through this traffic. Is there an accident or something?" I asked.

The limo driver looked into his rear-view mirror. "No, Suh. They're waiting fuh you to drive through. Hoping to get a glimpse of you. Suh, may I say how privileged I am to drive you in mah limo to da Peabody Hotel."

Silent, I nodded.

Evan's expertise in publicity and promotion had paid off. He was superb at stirring things up. As a result of Evan's efforts, the money rushed in like the mighty Mississippi and my popularity flowed at an all-time high. Even among those outside evangelical circles.

The intelligence of my Chief Executive Officer rivaled my own unwavering astuteness. Evan was still the same genius I'd met in 1964, in a bar in Nashville.

§

A newly ordained preacher, I had traveled to Nashville in search of used church pews for the new church I was building in Winston-Salem. I walked by a watering hole across from the Grand Ole Opry and felt the Spirit leading me inside where Evan Preston sat alone at the bar, celebrating his twenty-first birthday and graduation from Old Miss. He had pounded a few too many bourbon shots when I helped myself to the stool next to him. After failing to save Evan's soul for Jesus, I made a pass at him. Evan hit me square in the jaw and then apologized. Apology accepted, I explained I was a minister of the Gospel, and though I had a few flaws to overcome, I was building a religious empire. An empire for God that burned like an eternal flame in my soul. Evan laughed at me, but I saw something in the young graduate that mirrored myself. Evan's laughter finally changed to serious contemplation after I revealed my plans and promised to never again approach him sexually. Evan accepted my job offer.

I had kept my promise.

Although I preached Christians must live free from sin, the one thing I knew for sure was that God could not save the world without me and that He winked at my occasional indiscretions. As long as my priority was preaching the good news to the godless and converting the world to Christianity, of course.

I did the same. I allowed my CEO side ventures, all under the auspices of the church. And when it came to me, Evan looked the other way. Together we accomplished our goals—control and power over the Christian world for me—wealth, prestige, and lovely ladies for Evan. My ruthless business partner had enjoyed his abundant life in the church, and had held on to my coattails for years.

And what a magnificent ride it was.

Having pulled myself out of a North Carolina hick town and obscure poverty, I had indeed built an empire. I was the chosen vessel of The Most High. My charisma reached heights unknown to the Christian world. But in creating my megachurch, my mind had become weary. Tired of wavering faith, gossiping, and the constant backsliding of my followers, I gave Evan carte blanche to eliminate threats to the ministry. *The sword of the Lord, and of Gideon*, I called it. Evan was addicted to treachery and would be content as long as he was on the winning end. And I had created the ultimate winner's circle. There were no losers in the Kingdom of the Lord.

Closing my eyes to Evan's methods, I was vindicated by the swift justice of God in the Old Testament scriptures, and my own paranoia. I had no doubt Evan took advantage of my weakness. Riding toward Memphis that day, wasn't the time to think of such a slight flaw.

Jamming the two-lane roads, a throng of people and vehicles parked on sidewalks and grassy shoulders to ease traffic congestion. Sitting on their cars' hoods, in truck beds, on lawn chairs and blankets, the silent crowds gathered, clutching their dime-store Bibles, and positioning their loved ones in wheelchairs by the side of the road. Children on crutches, old folks on cots, the sick and afflicted waited patiently as the prophet of God passed by in the back seat of a limo. I wept, Oh, yes I certainly did. The Lord brought the scripture in Acts to my mind. *Insomuch that they brought forth the sick into the streets, and laid them on beds and couches, that at the least the shadow of Peter passing by might overshadow some of them.* I was the apostle, the chosen one they sought that day.

As the limousine inched toward its final destination, I recognized the familiar hallmarks of small Southern towns. A barbershop with a patched screened door, a hardware store, and a local grocery where folks were probably allowed to buy on credit. A white clapboard community center near a marble obelisk war memorial carved with the names of the glorious Confederate dead. I had traveled the world, but I had grown up in the rural South. It was for these backwoods towns that I bowed my head and prayed, vowing to take them all for Jesus.

A half-hour from the outskirts of the city I asked Evan, "By the way, have you heard from Percy Turlo? Did he get the pictures we need?"

"He got them. Don't worry. In time, Joe will have his kids back and they'll be full-time members of the church again."

I smiled, slipped on my sunglasses, and waved to the people on the street. "Dillon Oliver. He must be near fifteen."

Evan nodded discreetly as he looked over his paperwork. "Yeah. Good looking kid, too."

"Yes," I said. "Very. Reminds me of his daddy at that age."

LORD, REMEMBER ME

Andie

Listening to Daddy struggling to breathe, Dixie became a loose cannon. I stayed nights with her, hoping she wouldn't explode anytime soon. Caroline and her girls had managed time away with her ex-in-laws, who were taking them all to Disney World.

"Mama, you think we could go to Disney World some day?" Gracie's sheepish look about did me in. For a fourteen-year-old, Gracie grew solid as a fireplug. She had a turned-up nose that made her look even younger than her years and high cheekbones that gave everyone the impression she was stronger than she really was. A pretty face, a future beauty queen like her grandmother, Gracie also inherited her father's athletic arms and legs. Her intelligence was often more than I could handle. Both she and Dillon had been gifted, if that was the proper term, with my strangely compelling blue eyes.

"Some day, baby. Some day when things are better, when I've got a good job, and your grandpa is better." *When Pentecostals really do fly away.* Grateful for my parents' home, I had tagged it my place of refuge. A place I could go and hide, and even live if I had to. But Disney World was not in our future.

§

"Wy's coming," said Dixie, flipping through her *Southern Living.* "I'm hoping she'll stay until we see what happens with Bud." She had no idea the seriousness of her statement.

"Dixie, you have to believe Daddy's getting better."

"It's been difficult, believing. He can't climb the steps anymore. He sleeps upright . . . in the chair . . . in the living room. All night. Can't breathe." Dixie threw her magazine across the room. "Them damn cigarettes!" It landed safely a few feet from a large Waterford crystal vase, a Christmas gift from Wylene.

The horror of losing my daddy struck me like a padded fist. My breath caught audibly in my throat. "Dixie, the phone's ringing." My voice was hoarse. "Want me to get it?"

"No, could be the doctor. Or Wy. She's supposed to be here by suppah. I'll get it." My mother picked up her magazine on the way to the phone. A minute later she hollered from the kitchen. "Andie, it's Lula."

Lula? I had visions of her or Cletus sick, alone in a Birmingham hospital. Then it hit me like a boot to the head. *Rupert.* His kidneys. They'd been bad for years. Since Mavis was alive. I ran to the phone. Lula, through frantic crying and nose blowing, managed to report that Cletus had bought her a plane ticket and she'd be in Winston-Salem tomorrow. I surmised correctly: it was cancer, in his kidneys. Rupert lay dying at Baptist Hospital, and had been asking for me.

I prepared to leave. "Do we tell Daddy?"

My mother couldn't answer. This was a bad omen to Dixie. Rupert and Bud had been connected at the hip. Daddy always said he wouldn't die until Rupert had gone on ahead of him.

"How much more can this family take?" She shuffled back to the living room, not answering my question. She looked old as she fell into the chair by the fireplace. Everyone I loved was disappearing. *How much more can I take, Lord? Me—Andie Oliver—remember me?*

I stood out on the porch and gazed into the blackest night I'd ever seen. Staring at the sky, I found no trace of silver, not one star, a slice of moon, or even the lights of an airplane. I had never seen a sky so void and still, like a bottomless ocean. Hurrying Dillon and Gracie into the car, I knew my mother was in no shape to keep an eye on the twins, and they didn't need to be bothering her with loud TV or music for the next couple hours. After dropping them off at the Darwoods, I sped toward Baptist Hospital.

Lula wouldn't get there in time. When I arrived at the hospital I spoke to a floor nurse; death was imminent. Rupert Dumass had coasted into the winter of his life, running on fumes. No one had known he was bad off until a deacon who looked in on him every day or so, found him collapsed on the porch. A few members of Mount Zion Baptist Church had sat by his bedside the two days he'd been hospitalized. Two men and one woman—all deacons—told me they'd called the Holy Ghost into the room. That God would either raise Rupert up or see fit to take him on to his heavenly home.

I thanked them for their kindness, and they left me alone with him. As always, his hair was precisely parted with exact comb marks. The room's soft light illuminated his closed eyes. I couldn't sit or stand still. Rupert's thin pale body distressed me. Tubes and IVs protruded from every part of him. It distressed me because I knew my daddy wasn't far behind.

He opened his eyes. "Andie. So good to see you, darlin'." His voice was just a whisper. "Got blood in my urine. It's my time."

"I wouldn't miss your homegoing for the world, Rupert." Blinking back tears, I clutched his hand.

"Going to see Loretta tonight. And Mavis. I've missed them."

"I know you have," I said softly. " Please Rupert, when you see Mavis, tell her I love her, and I miss her so."

"Will do. I . . . I need to talk to you."

"Shhh. You sleep. I'll be here."

He closed his eyes. It was where I was supposed to be. Daddy would want me by Rupert's bedside. I wouldn't leave him until he'd passed. I sat in the quiet darkness, dozing. The light from the hallway poured into the room. The nurses paid no attention to me, even though visiting hours were long over. I stood, stretched, and walked to the doorway. The heart monitor near his bed gave off faint and steady beeps, breaking the silence like a lighthouse beacon. Every blip of light signified his soul—out on the ocean—searching for Heaven. My own beating heart in the cavity of my chest seemed too inadequate, too broken for anyone to find.

I peered down the long hospital corridor. A janitor shuffled by, rolling a bucket that smelled of disinfectant. I held my breath as the off-putting odors of urine and a dirty mop trailed behind him. I detested hospitals and every emotion they stirred within me. Sorrow, fear, and the pain of death.

I looked back at Rupert. The hospital curtains around his bed swayed as if blown by a slight breeze. There was no open window, no air vent near him. The pungent antiseptic I had smelled turned sweet, like a field of strawberries or a hive full of honey. I knew about these things. I'd heard Daddy talk about his mother and the angels she could see. Really see, unlike the fabricated hype about angels Calvin dished out in his services. I figured Rupert's angel had entered the room to prepare for his departure. I had no fear, only a sad anticipation of his death. I ambled back to his bed and the quiet click of the pump providing morphine to dull Rupert's pain.

We hadn't had time to prepare. My mother and daddy, Lula, me. In the deepest, most anguished corners of our hearts, we were all praying for his recovery. It was always hard to let go of those you loved. It never got easier for me.

I heard him moan. "Andie? Where are you, honey?"

I moved quickly to his bedside again. With a gesture unlike him, he touched my hand. In a voice worn smooth he said, "Evil . . . abides . . . near us. It is worse . . . than imagined." Rupert's effort to talk wasn't a final breath, deathbed statement. It was a message leaving me totally shaken, and I wasn't sure I'd heard him correctly. After all, they were the words of a dying man, probably not in his right mind. His eyes suddenly popped wide. Sunken in deep lilac hollows, they darted around as he spoke. "Open it, Andie. Promise me . . . you'll open it."

"Open what, Rupert? Open what?" Frustrated at not knowing what he was talking about, I yearned to climb inside his thoughts.

Closing his eyes and falling asleep under the power of painkillers, Rupert opened his mouth and, one more time, simply said, "Open it."

Confused and tired, I needed coffee. Maybe later I'd ask him again. What did he mean, *open it*? I felt around in my pocket for change. A used Kleenex, a quarter, a nickel, two pennies. Enough for coffee from the machine.

I returned to Rupert's room seconds before dawn, seconds behind the medical team that rushed in and swarmed over him like a cloud of bees. Captivated by the flat unbroken line, I crushed the paper cup in my hand, spilling the scalding, hot coffee over my fingers and onto my coat and shoes.

§

I arrived at my parents' home, dragged my weary body inside, and then collapsed. Too weary and sick at heart to even take off my jacket, I fell head-first into the couch. In the dark, listening to my own short breaths, a bleak hopelessness wrapped around my body like an old familiar blanket. The hours ticked by. When I woke, Wylene and Dixie towered over me in their housecoats. Someone had covered me with a quilt. "He's gone," was all I could say.

§

When I told Daddy, he worsened, turning gray as if on cue. He'd made a promise to his friend that he would not die first. He had kept his promise. As I relayed Rupert's last words to Daddy, he offered no explanation. He only shrugged. As if he knew what it meant. I didn't push it. I figured it was something private between him and his best friend, now gone.

Three days later, on a rainy spring morning, Rupert was buried beside his wife and daughter in the tiny graveyard on his farm. I served a lunch I'd spent two days preparing. Dixie could offer no help, as she couldn't leave Daddy home alone. A few churchwomen, along with Gracie and Dillon, had pitched in to serve and clean up.

After the last guest offered their condolences to Lula and Cletus, I walked back to the gravesite. As far as I could see, Rupert's overgrown tobacco fields rolled over the landscape. Like fireworks, memories of the Dumass family exploded inside my head, one after the other. I gazed up into the thundering clouds above and cried out, "Rupert! You're home now!" The clouds opened up, allowing a single stream of sunlight to flood the tiny cemetery. He'd heard me. I was sure of it. He made it to Loretta and Mavis. Heaven. I strolled to the house as if hugging some wonderful secret, my steps a little lighter, my heart—jubilant.

Lula greeted me on the porch, holding a box under her arm, her eyes filmed over with tears. I paused a moment. One tear fell fast before she could catch it with her hankie, splattering on her dress. "He want you to have all this, Andie. He love you like his own chile'. Your family was good to him. Rupert, he loved my sistah. Had a hard time of it, wanting to marry a black woman back then. The white folk wanted nothing to do with him anymo'. And some coloreds, too. Sho' 'nuff, your daddy loved Rupert and helped him buy the first sack of tobacka seed for this ol' farm." Lula wiped her eyes and handed me the box.

Inside laid Mavis's old camera that she'd bought with stolen lunch money, and the picture of her parents picking tobacco in 1970. I held the winning blue ribbon, a little frayed and faded, and choked back burning tears. Caressing it to my chest, I could not contain my grief. A whole family wiped out before their time. My memories of the Dumass family would never fray nor fade. The land, house and contents were willed to Lula, who promptly put it all up for sale to pay off Rupert's bills and back taxes.

August 1991
Live For Today

Andie

I woke on my birthday with two hungry fourteen-year-olds and seventy-five cents in my pocket. Joe's child support money, half of what he was supposed to give me, had dwindled. I couldn't even call him for a favor, like "Can I have some money to feed your kids?" After the divorce, the twins rarely talked about him. When they were little and heard his tires crunch on the driveway, they'd hide in their rooms. When he left them for good, there were no more spankings, but there was no extra food either. Not unless it came from Dixie. I tried to keep my mouth shut about their father, but undoubtedly they'd heard me bitch. We're not supposed to talk negative to our children about the missing parent, and I tried. I really did. But I wondered how much of a saint I'd have to become to successfully achieve that virtue.

I flipped through my wallet looking for a hidden or missed dollar bill. My driver's license, a school photo of Gracie, a folded coupon for Prell shampoo. Nothing. Only a nickel that had wedged itself in between the plastic window for my social security card and some crumbs. Credit cards long gone, a balance of five dollars and twenty-three cents sat in my checking account. I got busy fixing whatever I could find for breakfast. Within minutes, the twins sat to pancakes, the last of the Log Cabin syrup, and watered-down orange juice.

After homemade cards and hugs, they prepared to leave and I reasoned it was the way of things. Every year I became less while their friends became more. Dillon's voice had changed, sounding more like Joe than ever. Especially his laugh. "Mama, I'm off to Bobby's to play some basketball," he yelled as he stuffed his mouth full of pancakes. I noticed his wrist bones were still boyishly knobby. He had grown out of his clothes. Tall and handsome with thick wavy hair that grew as fast as his legs and arms, his eyes were fringed with the sort of lashes only boys seem to get but girls covet. His constant companion, Prissy, barked and followed close behind him everywhere he went. And of course, Gracie tagged along. Everyone knew of her crush on Bobby.

"Don't forget," I opened the door and hollered after them, "Supper at Grandma's!"

As the twins grew older, they became more aware of my problems and my pain. They showed their love for me by staying out of trouble, and I thanked God every day for it. In spite of the divorce and my poverty, their lives, at least, were almost normal.

§

I still drove my sister's Honda but had managed to take a little money from my utilities budget to buy two new tires for the front. I felt I owed that to Caroline. And the timing was good. I ran into an old friend at the Wal-Mart Auto Center.

"Well, I'll be damned if it ain't Andie Oliver!" He'd cleaned up, lost a few pounds, and got contacts. I hardly recognized him as I kissed his now clean-shaven face.

"Coot McGraw! What brings you this way?" I'd missed Coot and thought of him often. He'd saved my life and I felt a twinge of remorse for not calling him.

"Doing a little shopping, picking up a car part, and waiting on my new wife." He shot me a toothless grin. "Married Candice Cooper! Last month."

I squealed and threw my arms around his neck. "Congratulations!"

At that moment, Candace click-clacked her way into the waiting area of the tire center, her snakeskin boots drawing attention. "Whose that strange woman a-hugging my husband?"

"Candace!"

All three of us embraced, and I made them promise to come visit as soon as they'd settled into their new trailer. Candace had sold her rusted-out single-wide at Shady Acres and together, she and Coot purchased a shiny-new double-wide. I had lived next door to Candace for seven years and worked for her for almost two. Underneath Candace's floozy exterior, her first-class character had far surpassed most women I knew. Turned out, Coot was the best thing to happen to Candace and her daughter.

Coot's dentist was making him a new set of dentures minus the tobacco stains, he said. He also said he'd stopped drinking, sold his shop, and had semi-retired. Driving a truck a few days a week for a short-haul outfit and selling Shaklee products on the side, Coot and Candace were two of the happiest people I'd seen in a long time, laughing and talking as if they'd known each other all their lives.

At least someone's life has improved.

"I ain't heard from Joe fer near ten years now," Coot said. "I 'spect he's too good nowadays fer us folk in Salisbury. He's done fergot where he came from, who he really is. Yer better off, Andie. Time to find yerself a little happiness. Live fer today."

"Thanks, Coot. I'm working on it."

A timeless Barbie Doll, Candace wiggled toward me in skin-tight pants and a mohair sweater. "Still doing hair at home," she said. Happy. She used the word three times. "Kiss them babies for us," she said after another loving hug.

"They're not babies no more, but I'll do it." I watched Coot and Candace walk to their car, hand in hand. A miracle.

§

Live for today, Coot had said. Exhausting my search for a job, I finally succumbed to interviewing at convenience stores and truck stops again. The Pit Stop Truck Stop offered me a position, the only place I'd interviewed that paid a little more than minimum wage. Happy birthday I told myself. I filled out the new employee paperwork and vowed that as long as I had Dillon and Gracie, I'd fight the depression and find my way to a better life, a better job, a better place to live.

My little house had started to fall apart. I thought one day I might buy a condo with a bathroom toilet that didn't leak. Maybe rent a colonial without drafty windows and uneven floors. A cape cod with enough closets, a sunny kitchen, and a little screened-in porch where I could sit and read or talk to a friend. With any luck I'd get to keep my current house and completely redo it. I still managed to squeak out a few daydreams.

When I arrived home, the message light blinked on my answering machine. It was Ray. Libby had given birth to a baby boy. Micah. He invited me to Richmond, but it was his next statement that shocked me. "Daddy's ready to leave the cult, but Mama's holding on to the bitter end. Please call her. Try and talk some sense into her again. Libby and I are thrilled Micah was born on your birthday. Happy birthday, Andie."

I longed to see the new Oliver baby but had no desire to talk sense into my ex mother-in-law. Maudy had covered for Joe, enabling him his entire life. She'd shunned me for years. Any regret Maudy possessed wouldn't change a thing, lessen my pain, or make my life easier. No. I hoped the best for Al, but didn't anticipate Maudy would allow him to leave the cult. The few families who left the House of Praise, ended up in other cult-like churches someplace else, smaller but legalistic just the same.

I'd heard ex-addicts often rush back into the pain they long to escape. It seemed many who left the House of Praise returned because they were addicted to Calvin, believing they had a better chance of making it to Heaven sitting in his church. That kind of brainwashing wasn't easily shaken. As for me, church of any kind was not in my future. I would take my chances and stay home.

October 1991
As Comfortable As We Can Make Him

Andie

The Beatles' *Abbey Road* album ended and the cassette player clicked off. Music or an old movie acted as a sedative. I had been working double shifts, wanting to put Rupert's death and my daddy's illness out of my mind. I hadn't seen my family in a month. Until Aunt Wy called, waking me from a restless sleep, and insisting I come for supper.

§

A carved jack-o'-lantern frowned on the stoop when I pulled the car into the circle drive that evening. My mother and sister stepped out to the porch as I bounded up the steps. I offered my cheek for a kiss from Dixie and gave Caroline a quick hug. "How's Daddy?" An undertone of desperation had slipped into my voice.

"As comfortable as we can make him. He'll be glad to see you," said Dixie. Her voice sounded pitiful and strained.

"What does the doctor say?"

Caroline's eyes welled with tears. "His lungs are congested, and he's been coughing up blood. He's so weak; and Aunt Wy says we haven't seen the worst of it." Tucking her arm around mine she added, "It's chilly out here. Let's go in."

Once inside, I paused to glance around. For a sad moment, I studied the wood floor Daddy had laid himself; the banister he took so long to sand until it was the perfect color of walnut; the oak steps of the wide stairway he polished until you could see yourself in them.

"Give me your coat," Dixie said, looking in the mirror and patting her hair; making sure the wind hadn't ruffled it from its proper place. I shed my coat, handing it to my mother who acted as if everything were fine and dandy. "I swear, your coat's filthy."

I rolled my eyes at Caroline.

Dixie tried to smooth out the wrinkles and laughed strangely. "Where'd you get this old rag?"

"Um, you. You gave it to me for Christmas—years ago," I said.

"Get it dry cleaned; don't let me catch you in it again."

I studied my mother intently in the ornate foyer mirror. Then, sighing, I reached out and touched her shoulder. "I'll take it tomorrow. Promise. You okay?"

"You're worse than a man," she said, refusing to answer my question, reaching back and fluffing my bangs. "You'll just wear any old coat, as long as it's warm. Don't matter that it smells like smoke and has six buttons missing. And get your hair cut."

Wylene waddled to the foot of the stairs, carrying magazines and a medicine tray. "Excuse me, ladies."

"Oh, sorry, Wy," I said. We all stepped back, allowing her to pass.

"I assume you want your daddy awake so he can talk to you, hey Andie?" She climbed the stairs without waiting for my reply.

"That'd be fine," I said.

My mother talked as if we had all gathered for a picnic. "Did Wy tell you she delivered the Mayor of Charleston's grandson?"

"No, she didn't," I said. Aunt Wy had mentioned Dixie needed to see a shrink again. I swallowed and sighed. "I'm going upstairs."

"We'll be at the table," Caroline said as she put her arm around Dixie's shoulder and turned her in the direction of the kitchen.

I caught the blank stare on my mother's face. Wylene was right. This was more than she could stand. Dixie's mental health was deteriorating fast. Daddy's death would send her over the edge unless Wy could snap her out of it. Of course, if anyone could, it'd be my aunt.

I hurried up the stairway and quietly opened the door to Daddy's room, nodding to Wylene, who stood when I entered. "Is he asleep?" I whispered. I had nibbled off my lipstick on the drive over. Biting at my lips again, I eased the door closed as still as possible, holding my breath until the click of the knob echoed in the dark room.

"You can wake him. He's been asking for you. I'll be right outside if you need me."

I grabbed her hand and asked the million-dollar question. "Aunt Wy, is Dixie okay?"

"She's a looney tune. That's what she is. But then, it runs in our family. You're a little looney yourself, Andie."

"I know. Everyone likes to remind me. Dixie sounds like she isn't wrapped right."

"She's started her grieving process early. She'll be okay. It's the shock of knowing. I don't keep anything from her. She thinks I'm cruel. It's because I love her and now that I have her back in my life, I'm not losing her again. I want to get her through this."

I laid a grateful kiss on Wylene's cheek. "I thank God every day we found you, Wy. Please don't leave us."

"Not going anywhere, except to the hospital to deliver a baby or two. I've cut my office hours down to two days a week. I'll stay here the rest of the time. Until it's over."

My breath caught in my throat and I stared, speechless.

Wylene changed the subject. "Hey, I moved into the TV room in the basement. I love your old Janis Joplin poster. Her hair looks kinda like mine."

I whispered, "It's yours."

Wylene smiled. "Get on over there. I think he's awake, listening and laughing to himself, the old geezer. I keep telling him to get better 'cause he's been a real pain in my ass lately. He just smiles and tells me he's going to belt me later." Wy shook her head. "He's nothin' but a danged old redneck who's kept R. J. Reynolds in business. And what'd he get for it? Emphysema. Damn fool. But, hey, at least it's made me quit!"

"Wy, that's great! You've quit smoking?"

"Yeah. And little lady, don't let me catch you with one. I can still tan your hide!" She kissed my cheek and slipped out the door.

I tiptoed to Daddy's bedside and had yet another shock. Grateful his eyes were closed, I took time to adjust to the change in his appearance. One month had taken its toll. He had grown thin and bony, ravished by the disease, the flesh loose on his once-muscular body. His unshaven face lined and drawn, the accustomed tan replaced by a pallor, and his thick, wavy hair, once streaked handsomely with silver, was matted and as white as the sheets beneath him.

I smoothed out his bed sheet and straightened his blanket, then gently lifted one of his frail hands.

At my touch, he slowly batted his tissue-paper eyelids. "That you, Rosebud?" His voice sounded flat and lifeless and strangely hollow.

Tears glistened in my eyes, and I raised his hand to my cheek. "Yep, Daddy, it's me." I sniffed.

"My pretty girl." A warm glow replaced his dazed look. "I'd forgotten how much you resemble your mother. You're the spitting image of her. So glad you're here," he said. "How are the kids?" He began coughing and brought a tissue to his mouth. I released his hand and sat at his bedside. "I've missed you, honey," he said when the spasm ended.

"I've missed you, too, Daddy. No one can scold me like you," I teased.

"Life's been hard on you, hasn't it?" he asked with regret in his voice.

"It doesn't matter now. I just want you to get well."

"I was afraid of losing you, afraid Joe would change you into one of them House of Praise fanatics. You don't realize how much like your mother you are. Got that same stubborn streak. Just like my grandpap's old mule. I was foolish, Rosebud, allowing Dixie to take you to that church years ago. I drove myself crazy thinking I lost you to that place."

"You never lost me, Daddy. You're the King of all you survey, remember?"

His attempt to laugh saddened me. "Ah, yes. I'm the King of my castle."

"But I need you now more than ever. I have no role model for Dillon and Gracie if you leave me. There's nobody who loves me as much as you. If you go, I'll truly be alone."

He raised a hand and cupped my cheek. "You'll be fine. I believe there's a man to come, one who will cherish you. You've yet to find the love of your life."

"*You're* the love of my life, Daddy."

He turned up a corner of his mouth in another attempt to smile. That's when I saw something flicker in his eyes. His countenance closed quickly, as if guarding a well-kept secret. I turned away, wearied by it all. My voice quivered. "Oh, Daddy, I'm so ashamed for disappointing you."

His anguished eyes stared into the dimness of the room. "I've a lovely wife and two beautiful daughters, what man wouldn't be proud?"

He reached out to me and I clasped his hand again. "Remember when you insisted we were related to Rosa Parks?" I asked.

"I named you after her. Dixie insisted on *Andie*, though. I wanted you to admire strong women who stood for what was right."

"Strong women: may we know them, may we raise them, may we be them," I said.

"That's beautiful. You make that up?"

"No. It's something Aunt Wy said to me once. It's by an anonymous poet."

"My mother was a strong woman, too."

"Tell me about Grandma Parks. I was a little girl when she died. There's so much I don't remember about her. Dixie said Caroline looks like her."

"Oh my, she does. Mother had such a passion for life. I can still see her kissing my father goodbye at the rail station. His job on the railroad took him away a lot. He taught us boys the value of hard work." Daddy's voice drifted lower as he stared a blank stare. "There are times I can even hear her laughter, just as it sounded when we'd walk behind the mule during planting season. She was happy. Content in every circumstance. She died too young."

I smiled. "Yes, but she lived and died in peace. How wonderful. Think of all the women who grow old and never know such happiness. Such love. I'm sure I never will."

"Of course you will. When you least expect it, true love will seek you out." Daddy returned my smile with a sigh of assurance. "I'm going to see her soon."

"Don't talk like that. I need you. Please, don't talk that way."

"But I'm ready. Got to rest on my mountain." Gripped with another spasm of wracking coughs, he reached for me again. I held him a moment, propping up his frail body to ease the strain. The coughing subsided, like rumbling thunder fading into the distance. His head sank back into the pillow and he stared at his dresser as if looking for something hidden in a drawer. "I gotta rest. I'm glad you came, Andie; go be with your mother. She needs you. She loves you. I know she can't say it but I've been talking to her about that. We'll chat later, honey," he said feebly. Closing his eyes, he drifted to sleep.

In the quiet room I heard a train whistle in the distance. I stood and my eyes clouded with more tears. "Yes, Daddy. We'll talk again."

Leaning over, I kissed his cheek and he mumbled. "I don't want to lose you like Rupert did Mavis." I watched to see if he would open his eyes again. *He's dreaming.* I walked pensively down the stairway. Instead of chastising my mistakes, he had always encouraged me to believe a better life was just around the corner. It broke my heart.

§

Caroline sat in front of a blazing fire, her cheeks a pretty shade of pink. Wafts of her Sweet Honesty perfume filled the room like a cloud. She'd recently cut her hair short; it glowed a candied-red in the flickering light. Her expression, though, radiated frustration, and her personality mirrored that of Dixie's. She possessed a natural ability to demand our mother's attention. Sitting with her arm around Dixie, Caroline was like the monkey that never learned how to get off its mother's back. I noticed the grim set of my sister's jaw. She'd not fought a battle with weight as I had, but her three close pregnancies took their toll on her mental capacity. When she wasn't searching for her next husband, Caroline clung to Dixie.

Blinking away the remnants of tears, I wilted next to my aunt, and curled my body around one of Dixie's large couch pillows. The four of us sat in hushed solidarity. The room grew quiet, except for the crackle of burning embers. Finally, I tried to work some encouragement into my voice. "How could Daddy deteriorate so fast? Maybe the disease will slow down and he'll get to feeling better."

We drank our coffee and stared silently at the fire. I knew none of us believed in my hopeful prediction, and I couldn't help but wonder if we were all thinking the same thing. *How much longer?* Wylene stood and announced she'd take the first shift and sleep on the cot in Bud's room. Dixie staggered off to bed behind her with her lips clamped tight. I looked at my sister who glanced sharply about the room. "What's on your mind, Caroline?"

"How could you stay with him all those years?" she snipped, her voice sharp and accusing. "Especially when he was never home and doing God only knows what to whom? Why did you stay with him?"

I shrugged. "In the beginning, it was easy. I loved him. I submitted to him, believing what I was told—that submission was God's plan and the greatest gift a woman could give her husband. I was determined to bloom in the red dirt God planted me in. All to Jesus I surrendered. But I ran myself ragged trying to please Jesus and Joe while chasing silly daydreams of having what Dixie had."

The warmth from the flames served to unchain my jumbled thoughts. "You asked how could I stay with him knowing he cheated on me. Joe had turned me into a forgiving machine. Forgiveness was an automatic reaction to every suspicion. Always plugged in and ready."

A spark of absurdity faded from Caroline's face as she poured more coffee and snickered. "I thought you were either incredibly stupid or had secretly turned Catholic and become some kind of saint."

I smiled. "I became an expert at forgiveness. Forgiveness allowed me to believe the past was the past. That tomorrow would be different. By forgiving him, I was doing what Jesus said to do. So did that make me better than him? I tell you the truth, it just put off the inevitable. To survive, I told myself every day that Joe would one day wake up and realize I was the best thing to happen to him. It never happened."

Caroline raised her brows and unfolded a blanket to cover her legs. "I still think you were crazy."

After a broken sigh, I looked at my sister. "Maybe I was. Maybe I was crazy enough to think by forgiving Joe, I could separate the adultery from the man. As if I could remove it from his body like pulling a handkerchief out of his pocket. That way, I could justify my reasons for staying with him. And, here's the kicker. I always figured it could be worse." I rested my head on the back of the couch. "I married him hoping to build a home for us and for our children. I think we both failed."

We sat watching the flames, and I felt there was something else. Something Caroline needed to say to me. So I kept talking. Explaining the best I could.

"Was it a sin not to see my husband as he really was? Or was it a virtue?" I stood and walked toward the fire. "It was neither. I was a fool. That's a hard fact to live with. I often wonder if God really cares that much about women. It seems to me He's all about influencing men and *enslaving* women because Joe's life was full, and yet mine was empty. Forgiving my husband didn't change him. Loving him didn't change him. And unfortunately, having his children, even burying one of them, wasn't enough to change him. Not even a little bit. Joe's heart only beat for Calvin; never us. I thought someday Joe might come clean. Admit he failed us. How silly. For him to confess his failure as a husband and a father was a ridiculous thought. But it was my nature to fantasize until the bitter end where Joe was concerned. And I fought Calvin hard for Joe, rebelling against the church *and* God. Because of my rebellion, the threat of Hell nagged at me day and night. Always afraid of blaspheming or missing the rapture, I trembled at the thought. That, in and of itself, held me captive within the church and my marriage. It was a vicious circle."

Wanting a cigarette, I stoked the red blush of the embers and added another log. Extinguishing my yearning for an idyllic life, I smothered a groan. Tightening my jaw, I turned to my sister, spread my hands regretfully and shrugged. "I had nothing left to fight with. Nothing to overrule the stinking religion that presided over my life."

"Money was a great mistake motivator. Especially since you had none," said Caroline.

"True." I stared into the fire, as if standing at the edge of the Bottomless Pit waiting for Satan to push me in. "To this day, I have no power of persuasion. No way to fight that church." The image of John Rossi swirled in front of me like smoke; I could not explain the evil that twisted around religion as I knew it. "I used to bury my head in my pillow, trying to stop Calvin's prophesies from blaring in my brain. Joe proclaimed in front of God and everybody the failure was all mine. In a way, it was. I allowed the insanity to go on far too long. In the end, his measly paycheck kept me hanging on. Sick, isn't it?"

"I hate him," Caroline declared then looked away, pale and pink-eyed.

I blinked hard. "My God, did he proposition you? It wouldn't surprise me."

The fire's sparks reflected in Caroline's teary eyes. "I wanted to tell you for the longest time. I couldn't. I was seventeen and pregnant with Bonnie. He cornered me at your old trailer when I sat with the twins after they were born. He tried to kiss me. I just about belted him. Never told Daddy; he'd a killed him. I never want to see him again."

I heaved a sigh of disgust. "Neither do I."

February 1992
GOOD MEN NEVER DIE

Andie

I left Daddy with my mother and a hospice worker to go home and take a badly needed shower. I'd had little sleep, driving back to my house only twice. To pick up my mail, and to head over to the Darwoods to see my children. Vernise was gracious, insisting Dillon and Gracie stay with her family until I could return for more than a day. Except when I got home, I crawled into bed and sobbed. *He's only 60. I'm only 38. He can't die this young. How will I survive without him? How will any of us go on without Daddy? My God, enough.*

I couldn't sleep. Leaving my sorrow under the blankets and sheets clustered at the bottom of my bed, I crept down the chilly hallway, the dog following sleepily after me. Prissy, always the protector. The winter wind raged outside like two fighting cats, as I walked on a sigh in the quiet, empty part of night, feeling as if I were the only person in the world awake.

Tiptoeing to the kitchen window and gazing at the speckled shadows on the lawn, I watched the moon over Turner Street spill a waxy patina on snow piled around the edges of the driveway. Like most snow in the Triad it would disappear the next day, unlike my mood. Iced like a cake, the frost-covered Japanese Yews and boxwood laid dormant in their winter beds. Grand maples I loved, naked and cold, stood guard over my property. The neighbor's velvety lawns rose and fell away in the night. Their houses, small and varied—most of them still lacking attention—sat like silent witnesses to the goings-on in and around my house.

I felt the temporary peace of the neighborhood. All was well; I had forced my mind elsewhere, away from my troubles for one peaceful moment.

Early February, the winter lagged. A dreary, cold and wet season, it chilled me to my toes and I cranked up the thermostat to keep warm. But rage burned hot in my head and my heart. I wanted to open my mouth and let it fly, puke it up—everything I knew, all over Joe and Calvin. I kept my secret secured in an envelope in the attic rafters; a wretched, horrible secret John Rossi created the night he was murdered. I knew too much.

I longed to see the hands that comforted me as I gave birth to a dying child over a decade ago. I'd never forgotten them. Although the left hand was missing a finger, they were beautiful hands. Every once in a while the vision floated into my dreams. They still comforted me on my worst days. That vision seemed like another lifetime ago.

Daddy's health went to Hell in a hand basket after burying his grandson and then Mavis. It was no wonder. That's when he started chain-smoking three to four packs a day. His cigarette was like an extra finger—a permanent fixture on his body. Brian's death, a few weeks before Mavis was murdered, had knocked us flat for a while. Though my baby breathed his last breath in infancy, it was no less devastating. Nobody was surprised when the doctor said Daddy's lungs were like overcooked grits.

I had come to dread the days and silent nights. Early morning cast soft light about each room in my house. It was heartbreaking to know Daddy's house, the house he rebuilt, would have to be sold for Dixie to support herself through her old age. I yawned and fell into my recliner.

My garage sale wall clock chimed, mockingly.

Settling Daddy into the hospital bed that had been rolled into his study, Dixie insisted we remove his antique clock from the wall, claiming every chime wore on her nerves and stole time from us all.

I refused. "It's his Federal clock. It belonged to his mother. He loves that clock. Think of it this way: every chime should remind us there's still time for a miracle." But listening to his wheezes, I doubted it.

Dixie's mouth twitched at the corner. On the verge of tears, she gave me a small, scornful smile and walked out.

Pleading with God, I cried out, "We've been praying our hearts out! My family has been praying their hearts out." I lifted my head and glared at the ceiling. "Look at me, God!" I admonished Him, as if speaking to my children. "Why are You letting this happen?" The only sound was the clock's pendulum, ticking back and forth like the tail of time wagging on the wall. My eyes stung with new tears. Possessing no self-control or faith at that moment, I scolded the Almighty. "You know what? If You heal him, it'll prove we don't have to go to Calvin for a miracle." As I expected, no answer came. Daddy would die and leave nothing behind but a wisp of cigarette smoke and the silent legacy of a man who had once lived among us.

§

Morning's light filtered through the windows, and I found myself still in the recliner, wearing the same pair of sweat pants I'd put on days before, thinking I should call Wylene. Reaching for the phone, I pictured her delivering a baby, her face stern, speckles of sweat across her brow. I dialed her private number at the hospital. *What the hell, it's worth a shot.*

She answered on the third ring. "Andie?" she said, her voice filled with apprehension.

"He's fine, Wy. Worn out, but fine. I needed to talk to you. Sorry." I sneezed. And then I sneezed again.

I could hear her fax machine. "He may be fine, but you sound like shit," she said.

I blew my nose. "I caught a cold from Caroline or one of her girls. Listening to Daddy breathe, and taking care of Dixie—I'm exhausted. I went home for a couple hours."

"I'll be there early this afternoon by plane; I had an unexpected baby to deliver. I won't leave him again, I promise."

"I know. You've done so much already, traveling back and forth. It's been as hard on you as anyone."

"I'm a tough old bird; it's Dixie I'm concerned about." Silence. "Andie, you still there?"

"It's not the way I expected him to go, you know? He's drifting away from us, Wy. It's so sad."

"Stay strong for him, but more for your mother. Can you do that?"

"Of course. What choice do I have?"

"None, really."

I yawned. "The twins called last night; this has been hard on them, too. I have to go back later and check on Dixie."

"Don't you want one more night to yourself?"

"Maybe," I sighed. "I'm going crazy, Wy." I blew my nose again. "I'm losing my house in the bankruptcy, Dillon and Gracie will probably have to change schools, and now I'm dealing with Daddy. I can't sit on my butt and do nothing."

"What about your job?"

"They gave me a leave of absence. Until it's over." What was left to be said? My world was one giant catastrophe. Certainly not the way I had envisioned it so many years before. My body ached as I ended my call to Aunt Wy. I dragged myself back to bed, because only in sleeping did I find a small amount of peace. Peace that would allude me in the months to come.

§

The next day the sun refused to come up completely, casting dark afternoon shadows on the ground. I drove with my lights on, thinking my mood matched the sky. A savage, battleship gray. When I arrived at my parents' house, Wylene sat like a beached walrus in the living room reading the newspaper and wiggling her wide fingers in hello. Allowing my coat to fall on a chair, I headed to the smell of food in the kitchen. Wy had made a pot of Brunswick stew. I wanted to get my mind off Daddy. What better way than to eat a hot bowl of stew, and ask questions about Dixie that had nibbled at me for years. Wy followed me into the kitchen.

"Aunt Wy, since Dixie's asleep, can we talk a bit?"

"'Bout what? About how bad her hair looks these days?" She laughed.

"No, not about her hair. About her life. I know your parents died in that truck crash when you were both little, but did you know Dixie's foster family?"

Wy's large metal spoon slipped out of her hand and dropped to the floor. "No."

"That's all you can say is 'no'?"

"Didn't your mother ever talk to you about her life in Charleston?"

"I wouldn't be asking if she had."

"Then think, Andie. Might be she doesn't want you to know." Wy picked up the spoon and set it in the sink. "This isn't the time to be asking these questions."

"Can't you tell me anything?"

"Don't know much."

"Then—tell me what you do know."

Wy sighed. "You keep quiet about this. Don't tell a soul. Especially Caroline. She's not ready to hear it, and I'm not sure that you are either. Don't you think you're under enough stress right now?"

"It's that bad?" I shoved my soup bowl away.

"Bad enough." Aunt Wy wiped her hands on a towel and then poured herself a cup of coffee. "I need to sit for this; scoot over."

I moved down the bench to accommodate my large aunt.

She spoke quietly. "Believe me when I tell you, your mother's past has made her a little crazy in the head. I'm sure you and Caroline have taken the brunt of it over the years. You're smart, Andie. You already know Dixie was very young when she had you. You got to know her young life before Bud was not a happy one. Unfortunately, I learned all this years after it happened."

"Go on, Wy. I can take it. Tell me."

"Well," she sighed, "her foster parents were country singers and played the fiddle and the banjo. Traveled the Nashville circuit in the forties."

It answered my question as to why my mother loved to sing and knew every old song ever written. I smothered a smile, picturing the couple's rickety pickup rattling back and forth to the juke joints.

Wy sipped her coffee and swallowed twice. "They got mixed up in some gambling and drinking. Left poor Dixie when she was just a teenager with some elderly uncle across the street. One day the police knocked on the door. Dixie's foster father had been arrested for murder and her foster mother lay dead in Nashville. Seems he caught her in the sack with a guitar picker who played for Hank Williams. He shot them both and went to prison. They should've strung the old geezer up. I heard he died in a Tennessee work camp a few years back."

I stared into my coffee mug. "What happened to Dixie? She always made me think she was raised to be a socialite. A debutante."

Wy shook her head, then wiped a few crumbs from the table. "The woman was never a debutante. Your mother was thrown to the four winds, baby. From foster home to orphanage to the streets. She was sixteen when Bud found her behind a diner, digging for scraps."

My heart skipped a beat. I wanted to cover my ears.

"He carried her home like a lost puppy. Worst thing was . . . she was well into her first pregnancy. With you."

My mouth flew open. "What?!" My heart went numb with disbelief.

"Shhh! Not so loud. I don't want Dixie to hear us. And close your mouth, child. Don't go asking me who your daddy is, 'cause I don't have a clue. Nobody does. Dixie's never spoken a word about him. I'm not sure *she* knows who he is. Whoever it is may be dead for all we know. And don't you go asking her neither. This is not the time, obviously. Thing was, Bud loved her the moment he laid eyes on her. I saw a few pictures of Dixie from back then. She was a sight for sore eyes." Wy wiped her tears away with a napkin, and sat quiet for a moment.

"So your daddy, when he found her pregnant, dirty, and half-starved, he brought her home, cleaned her up, and married her. She loved him back. They went on to have your brother and Caroline. It's a wonder you were born as good and healthy as you were, Andie. But they've always loved you as much as Caroline. Maybe a sight more. You're special. You got a mind God gives to few people on this earth. I don't need to tell you how smart you are. Lord knows, they should've sent you to college. You could've sailed right through."

Aunt Wy's hands started to tremble, as if all of sudden it hit her that she'd hauled a monster of a skeleton out of Dixie's closet. She fixed me with a steely gaze. "My God, don't you dare confront either of them with this. Let Bud die in peace. He never wanted you to know. And don't go digging for answers. You might not like what you find. It might kill your mother if she knew I told you. The real reason Dixie and I fell out years ago was because I wanted you to someday know the truth. Dixie cut me out of her life because of it. Keep this to yourself, hear?"

I nodded and rested my elbows on the table, pressing my palms to my forehead. After what I'd already been through, knowing I had another father out there wasn't so upsetting. "I guess it explains why I'm the only one in the family with blue eyes."

Wy's hand rested on my shoulder and squeezed gently. "I've said enough. Leave the past alone, Andie honey." She stood and gulped the last of her coffee, turned to the sink, then stared out the window. "God is still on the throne."

A heavy sigh left my lips. I wasn't pulling anymore secrets out of Wy. Not that day. "Bud Parks is my father," I said. "He always has been. Don't fret, Aunt Wy. This isn't as upsetting as you think. Not after the life I've already lived. But you're right. It's no wonder my mother's a bit of a fruitcake." I walked to the sink, slipped my arms around my aunt's spare-tire of a waist and hugged her tight from behind.

Wy sighed. "Yeah, girl. Losing Bud might just put her away. He loved her so, and took good care of her. That's all that matters to me. Why don't you head on up to your old bed and take a nap."

"That's a good idea. I think I will."

§

An hour later, I stumbled out of bed feeling the strangeness of knowing I was not the biological daughter of Bud Parks. I shook it off. Nothing would ever change the fact that Bud was my daddy. Not even DNA. What felt curious was that I didn't care who my real father might have been. Wylene had given me a glimpse into my mother's past, a gift, and my heart finally softened towards Dixie.

The house was cold. Quiet. It felt like a funeral parlor. No doubt frugal Dixie had turned down the heat. Every room had that hospital odor. I moved silently downstairs and peeked into the study. The pungent mist from the humidifier hid the odor of a lifetime of cigarettes that had embedded their poison within the walls and Daddy's lungs. He was sitting up; Dixie had him propped against a fresh set of pillows. His breathing was gravelly; an endeavor that fluctuated with the periodic gust from the large tank near his bed sending oxygen through the tube secured under his nose. Every time I saw him, I cried. Non-stop tears. Not a way to live. For Daddy or for me. Rushing back into the living room, I sat on the recliner across from Wy. "He looks worse."

"More of the same, I'm afraid. Exhausting, wracking coughs that bring up blood. It soaked the bed."

I could hear the soothing thump of the dryer in the laundry room. "Where's Dixie?"

"She washed the sheets, then went to the grocery store. You still tired?"

"A little."

Wy nodded then rolled her eyes toward the kitchen. "I made coffee."

I poured a mug full and tiptoed back to the makeshift hospital room to watch him breathe. Watching Daddy breathe came second only to eating and sleeping.

"Rosebud." His croaky voice squeaked and he panted like a dog.

"What 'cha thinking, Daddy?"

"I'm thinking I feel damn puny, if you want the truth."

My coffee was cold. I set the mug on his bedside table and thought about the yellowish tar we attempted to scrub off the walls every spring. I pulled up the sheet at the bottom of the bed and started to massage his feet.

"Dixie used to tell me when you'd massage her feet like this."

"Really?"

"Uh-huh. You didn't know it, but I was always a bit jealous of you and your mother."

"Daddy, that's silly. Why?"

"You knew you had my attention, but you were always trying to get hers."

I couldn't speak.

He blinked. "Wish I could stand on them feet."

I covered his feet, then took his hands and held them to my lips, smelling the scent infused in this skin. All the Aqua Velva in the world couldn't cover it. It grieved me. I chose to think of him hunched over his workbench; spreading mulch in the yard; tuning his banjo strings; peering under the hood of his car; hunting with his dogs in full camouflage; picking, tying, and stacking tobacco with Rupert. Daddy worked his whole life, rarely stopping but for a smoke. A lifetime of hard work implanted into the cracks of his hands along with the nicotine. His hands made things last. Made things better. And if it consisted of wood, metal, or grew in the dirt, he made things beautiful.

But they were not the hands in my vision of years ago. Misty-eyed, I dismissed the memories. Had I known how cigarettes were killing him, I would've hid them, made him quit, begged him to stop. Calvin had said he would die an early death because he didn't go to church. His curse. Maybe he was right. Maybe he was right about a lot of things.

I grabbed his hands again, "Please, Daddy, don't die!"

"Good men don't die—" His breathing was too labored; he couldn't speak.

Avenge Us All

Andie

After several attempts to force-feed my mother, I gave up, leaving her to Wylene who slipped a spoonful of leftover stew into Dixie's mouth along with a Valium. There'd be no funny business with Aunt Wy around.

"Go on in and sit with your daddy, Andie. I'm putting Dixie to bed and then I'll take over for you."

I peeked around the corner and found Daddy frantic. As if he tried hard enough he could scream with his eyes. When he saw me, he struggled to breathe, his speech quick and toneless. "Remember the lockbox?"

"The metal box. Upstairs in your sock drawer. I remember." I had opened the box once, saw it was full of odds and ends, paperwork I cared nothing about.

His antique clock chimed. Struggling for breath, when the chiming stopped, he asked, "What time is it?"

"It's eight o'clock."

"In the morning?"

"It's nighttime. Don't talk, Daddy. It exhausts you."

"Not much—time left. Have to—tell you about Mavis."

My heart skipped a beat. I moved in closer. "What? Tell me what about her?"

He pointed. "Go up to my room. Get—my lockbox."

"Daddy, damn it, you're sweating. We can talk about it later."

"Pay attention—Rosebud. Get it. Get the—lockbox." He collapsed against the pillows. "Go!"

I jumped up and dashed out, but waited until I knew Dixie was sound asleep before I slipped in and rummaged through Daddy's dresser drawer. Minutes later, I held the box toward him as if he could hold it. I sat and placed it on the bed near his hand. The back of his fingers moved against the cold metal.

"Ah, you found it. Sometimes—your mother moves my stuff." He winked.

"Combination the same?"

He gave me a nod and a slight smile.

I pulled off the heavy metal lock and lifted the lid. A large manila envelope lay on top. "It's from Mavis? How? When?" My breaths short between my words, I sounded as winded as Daddy. I picked it up as if it was hot to the touch. It was addressed to Rupert and was definitely Mavis's messy handwriting.

"Rupert gave it to me—a few months ago, when he found out—he had cancer. He'd hid it—in his barn for years. Mavis mailed it—the day she died. Look—at the postmark. I've looked inside. She mailed—the same envelope—to you. Obviously—you never got it. Thank God. They might've—killed you, too."

Daddy fought for breath as I panicked. "Daddy, please, you shouldn't talk."

"Have to—darlin'. Have to—tell you. We kept it from you—believing you'd be in danger if they knew—if they knew you had it. It got—Mavis killed. I'm sure Calvin doesn't know Mavis sent the same letter—to her daddy. Course not—they didn't think—she was that smart. But—she was—she was." His wheezing worsened.

"Please, Daddy, stop. This isn't necessary now. I can look at it later." I sensed he teetered on the fringe of passing out from the effort of talking.

"No!" He coughed and settled back on his bed again, sweat pouring down his face. "Your kids—might be in danger now. You have to protect them."

"You're scaring me."

"I'm—I'm still not sure this is the right thing—to do—to give this to you. But you've got to know—what Calvin is—and what he's done. This may also explain why Joe is—the way he is. Mavis didn't know how to tell you—after losing Brian—didn't think you could handle it. Your children—need you to fight for them—like Mavis tried to fight—for you. Don't let Dixie—or Wy or anyone—see what's in that envelope. Hide it—until you can use it—against him. Use it Andie—but use it wisely."

My heart raced; I could feel the blood rushing to my head. "What's in it?"

Daddy pointed a bony finger at the envelope. "Open it."

Open it. Rupert's final words burned inside my head. My fingers moved as if I'd suddenly become old and frail myself. I pulled out the letter and negatives.

"Pull it—all out." His shaky hand moved against my arm.

I dumped out the rest and shuffled through black and white photographs: one young man after another, naked, on a bed, in various poses, with someone. *Another man?*

"There's writing—on the other side."

My eyes opened wide, staring at each one. Names and dates in Mavis's handwriting were written on the back of every one of them. "My God! It's a younger Calvin? And . . . I recognize this boy. It's goofy Gary, the kid Joe and I used to make fun of in high school . . . and Calvin . . . NAKED! My God, Daddy, he's naked! With these boys, on the bed! Some I . . . recognize . . . some, I don't. Mavis. She took these! That's what she had on him . . . why they killed her! Oh, Daddy, I'm . . . sick."

"Keep going," Daddy said.

"Why? What else is in here?" Before he could answer, I saw it. The picture that answered all of my questions. My lifetime of unanswered prayers. Why Joe and Ray were as different as peaches and black-eyed peas. Why Joe was obsessed with sex. I dropped the pictures and fell to my knees by the bed, burying my head in Daddy's drenched sheets. "He molested Joe. That bastard had sex with Joe!" I pounded my fist on the bed. Then I took the picture in my hand again and managed to study it.

"Joe appears to be about fifteen or sixteen," I sobbed. "My God, Mavis was Joe's age, which would've made me about fourteen. This must have been taken right before or soon after I met him. I think I was almost sixteen when

I introduced Mavis to Joe. No wonder she had the reaction she did! How did Calvin get her to do this?" I shuddered inwardly at the thought. "This sure explains why she didn't like Joe. She knew I didn't know about this." I moaned. "Oh, God, Calvin is a pedophile. And Joe doesn't care," I cried. "He doesn't care."

"A psychopathic—pedophile," whispered Daddy.

"Dillon! He can't get his hands on Dillon!"

Daddy's wheezing grew louder as he glared at me.

Stunned, I took his head and held it between my hands. I wanted him to look at me. "Why did you keep this from me?"

He closed his eyes, and I let go of him.

"Is there anything *else* I should know?"

He shook his head, soaking the pillow with more sweat. "Mavis's letter—it explains—everything."

Hanging on to the threads of life, Daddy could no longer speak. That indisputable truth caused me to swallow my anger before I opened my mouth. "Why did you hide this from me, Dad? Why? Why didn't Rupert tell me? I had a right to know! Rupert should've given me this, years ago! Tell me what to do! What now?"

Daddy's face was a blank canvas. There was nothing left to say.

I slid the pictures, letter, and negatives back into the envelope, and slipped out of the room and over to Aunt Wy who sat in front of the TV, acting as if she hadn't heard a word of it. Daddy's explosive coughing echoed out to the living room. It quickly turned to choking. Wylene shot to her feet, grabbed her bag, and rushed to his side to roll up his sleeve and shoot something into his vein. His face flushed a blood red as the cough came from deep inside his chest—a phlegmy, heart-wrenching sound that turned my face to the wall. I couldn't watch.

I fled to the kitchen, out the back door, and into the middle of the yard. Standing with my arms wrapped around the envelope, I gazed back at the house, my breath forming a white plume in the cold. Daddy's house and everything in it had become forbidding and unfamiliar territory. It all seemed blurred, unreal, like a picture in the newspaper. Angry and ashamed, I returned to the kitchen only to find my aunt scrubbing her hands in the sink.

"He wants to see you," she said.

"He's worse off, isn't he?"

"It's progressing." She sat at the counter to dry her hands. "It's time for the hard stuff. If there's any forgiving to be done, do it now." Clearly, Wy had heard some of it.

My insides lurched and I backed against the sink. Morphine—medicine to ease him over the threshold, from this life into the next.

"It'll be better for him. Better for all of you."

"Okay. Aunt Wy, but—"

"Andie. Go see your daddy, then go crawl into bed." She stood and pulled me into her big, soft breasts that smelled of Ivory soap and fabric softener.

"You'll feel better about things in the morning. I'll sit with him until midnight, then hospice will take over, or your mother, whoever gets there first. Dixie's getting some vital sleep for now. Caroline will be here in the morning."

Her body was warm and comforting. I didn't want to move from it. "Will you start it tonight? When do you know—"

"Hey now. You leave the doctorin' to me. Deal?"

I nodded. "Deal." I gave Aunt Wy another hug and ambled back into Daddy's room.

"Rosebud?"

I leaned in close. "What do you need, Daddy?"

"You have to do something for me."

"What is it, Daddy?"

Straining, he raised himself from his pillows. I felt his breath on my face. I didn't try to stop him from talking. I couldn't. I wanted to hear what he had to say.

"I'm sorry—I didn't tell you sooner. I only thought to shield you—from Mavis's fate. When I've passed—avenge Mavis's death," he said. "Promise me."

I thought a moment or two, and then whispered my life's darkest secret into my father's ear. "I knew Calvin was gay, Daddy. I did, I knew it. But I didn't know he was a pedophile. I witnessed John Rossi's murder. The chef from the Praise Buffet who was shot four years ago. I saw Artury's men kill him. I'm the anonymous caller. The caller the police have been looking for. I'm the only witness. Nobody knows. Except you."

I broke my secret knowing he would never be able to tell it. His eyes drifted shut and I worried he had used up what little energy he had left.

Then they shot open, and bore into mine. Rage and regret made him a king again. But only for a second. He lifted his head further and bellowed what I did not expect. "Promise me," he said. "Avenge us all."

I watched him fall back against the pillows, closing his eyes, gasping for breath.

"I promise," I said, in one quick breath. "I promise."

Evil Revealed

Andie

Steady white flakes fell quietly through the darkness. I needed to walk, despite the cold. I stuffed my gloves into the mended pockets of my coat, pushed through the door to the backyard, and bolted down the red-brick path. Moonlight illuminated the walkway. Dappled with fresh snow, the winter-dark lawn disappeared near the edge of Daddy's garden.

I stood by the tire swing watching the neighbor's chimney etch chalky white smoke onto a blackboard sky. Slapping my palms together, I blew streamers of warmth into my hands. It was colder than I realized so I crawled up into my old tree house; still solid as the day it was built. I didn't remember climbing to be so difficult. Huddled in the corner, I watched my breath in the frigid air and pulled out the envelope from inside my coat as if it were the normal thing to do.

Mavis had mailed it over sixteen years ago. Purposely forgotten by Rupert, and then at last given to Daddy to be stashed away in his lockbox. A box filled with tax forms, appliance warranties, copies of his will, and coloring book pages from Gracie. It was a miracle Dixie hadn't thrown it out. Truthfully, had Daddy not demanded I open the envelope, I never would have. My children would've eventually found it in my own box of letters, ledgers, pictures, and personal whatnots after I had passed on. My heart stuttered. My chest hurt. My gut clenched.

It was plain manila. Dirty. Some water stains. Rupert's name and address scribbled in black ink. I couldn't bear to open it again. Holding it tight in my hand, I looked up into the shadows of the tree house, struggling for breath.

Not now. I can't deal with anymore tonight.

But the ghosts from my past insisted. I noted the postmark in the moonlight. *April 3, 1975.* Mavis died on April 2. Harry found her the morning of the 4th. No one could have sent it but Mavis. *She dropped it into a mailbox the evening of her death. Why?* Climbing down slowly, I had to know more. It made sense that Rupert had given Daddy the envelope. Their plan to protect me, though hard to accept, was understandable.

Inside the house, Wy talked with the hospice nurse. I walked past them and sprinted up the stairs to my room with the envelope in my hands. It frightened me. I took out the letter, recalling that Mavis was not much of a writer. She had problems getting words and ideas from her head to the paper. I had written many of Mavis's school reports. Her penmanship was atrocious.

I brushed away tears, and then unfolded the letter. I recognized Mavis's loopy handwriting, smudged words on yellowed paper. Just like everything she ever wrote, the letter was barely legible. Even worse, it appeared as if she'd written it in a hurry.

Dear Daddy,

I send same letter to Andie. Except I not tell her I send all this to you, in case Joe gets my letter.

You know I wanted to be a singer and would've done anything to get to New York. I always say no when Andie asked me to go to her church. That cause I knew Calvin Artury already. When I was 16 and first learn to drive, I stopped at his church to walk around his wife's pretty grave and take pictures. Wanted to see big statue of Jesus up close. He seen me. We talked. He asked to lay hands on me. Get me saved. I say no. Told him my dream to be a singer and go to NY. He asked how I plan to get there? I say I take pictures, too. I read up on it.

He say I could make money. That he pay me. He taught me to use his camera. It's art, he say. I took pictures of him and a boy my age. I did not know that first boy. Ended up was many boys. He pay me lots of money. Nobody knew I took his pictures, not even the boys. Only Artury knew, until now I tell you and Andie. He took his camera back and thought I gave him all negatives. He counted rolls of film and thought he got it all back. But I buy extra film. Develop on my own. Two months before graduation, I needed more money. He say he pay me to take more pictures, but I say no. So he say then you sleep with me. So I did. Only once. He awful. But he pay me, so I'm worse. His money got me to NY City. I was 18 and stupid. He figure I just go away. Never come back. He was wrong.

Some pictures are Joe. He young and stupid, too. 12 boys in all. I don't think he forced them. Some did it cause of who he was. He say these boys were God's gift to him for his sacrifice. He bought them gifts, drugs, and booze. I saw. I did nothing to stop it. I'm sorry. It was wrong. I thought I could get more money from him some day. Then I thought I could use these pictures to make him let go of Joe for Andie sake.

I'm so sorry to send this, Daddy. I should have told on him. Somebody's following me now, I think it's Artury. He knows I got these. Whatever happens please forgive me. I'm stupid, I know. But I love you. Tell Andie, I love her. I try call soon as I can.

Mavis

P.S. I have something else to tell you, but has to wait.

Mavis never got a chance to call anybody.

The discovery of why Mavis was killed made my blood run cold. Calvin had her murdered, just like he had John Rossi murdered. I was sure of it.

I folded the letter with great care as if handling a priceless piece of history. Mavis had what he wanted. The photographs and negatives. Now I had them. If I threatened him or took her evidence to the police, I'd be dead before I made it to the witness stand. Who could I trust? No one. Somehow I had to use them to protect my children. And I would go through Joe to do it.

What was the P.S. about? What did Mavis never get to tell? I decided I would never know.

THEY JUST FADE AWAY

Andie

Stretched out on my old bed and dead-dog tired, I nestled myself inside a comforter with memories of Mavis's death like it happened yesterday. The dream began as a remembrance as real as watching home movies rolling inside my head. The year I turned ten and Mavis was eleven and a half.

I could see her long legs hanging out the window of the tree house Daddy built for me that summer. A castle tree house. Daddy was the king of all he surveyed and I was his princess. It was a perfect tree house, a wide floor of plywood nailed across two large limbs, painted white walls, and real shingles on the roof. I climbed toward her on a ladder from the garage leaned against the old oak.

The temperature climbed that afternoon, too. Muggy pretty much described it. Not a dog barked. No lawn mowers roared in our ears. Just the whir of cicadas up high in the trees. The only noise you hear when it's super hot, as if the rest of the world were taking a nap. Dressed in the nearly the same outfit as Mavis, shorts and a white T-shirt, I had pulled my hair into nearly white pigtails jutting out above my ears. I scooted in next to Mavis, who had swept out the bugs and leaves before I arrived. Her fuzzy black hair had been braided all over her head and wrapped in colorful rubber bands. I pulled at the back of my shorts. "Damn, it's hot. Got sweat in my butt crack!"

Mavis giggled and dug into a grocery sack. "I got apples and Clark Bars," she said. She pointed to the corner. "Got two bottles of Orange Crush, too."

"But looky what I got. I got something really cool," I said. I pulled up my old beach bag and unzipped the top. "You got three guesses." Mavis stood to get a look, but I folded myself over the bag. "No, you guess."

"It's a new pink bike, like the one we saw parked at the Dairy Queen."

"That's a goofy answer, Mavis. Guess again."

"The Everly Brothers. One for you and one for me."

"In your dreams, maybe."

"Archie and Jughead comic books?"

"That's close," I said. "Shut your eyes."

Mavis stretched her neck toward the beach bag again.

"Shut 'em!"

Mavis hemmed and hawed. "I'm hot. Jus' show me for crying out loud."

I set my bag in front of her and pulled out a wooden box with Parks Family Bible written on the lid. A wide blue ribbon was tied around the box to keep it closed. "Open your eyes!"

Mavis sighed. "It's jus' a Bible."

"I know," I said. "I scooted into the back of Daddy's closet, under his pressed shirts to get it. If Dixie knew she'd pitch a fit."

"It's Bud's? Hoo-wee, he gone kill you."

"Nuh-uh," I said, untying the ribbon. "Because you're not going to tell him. I've always wanted to see this. Looks like it's got a whole lot of years on it."

Someone wrote in pencil on the first blank page. I read the words to Mavis, "If God be for us, who can be against us?" I searched for my daddy's name among the pages of births, deaths, marriages, and baptisms. There it was— Bud Jennings Parks, born July 1932—like a page out of a history book. "Pretty Bible, though, don't you think?"

Mavis nodded. "Bud's still gone kill us if he finds out."

I handed the Bible to Mavis and continued rummaging through the papers in the bottom of the box, coming to a long slender envelope. The outside read *Come Help Us Celebrate,* embossed in gold. I opened it. Inside was an invitation to church services at the newly built House of Praise.

"Can I read it?" Mavis asked.

I handed over the invitation and watched her open it and read it.

"They probably don't want colored people."

"Why?"

"They think we're not the same as white people."

"That's silly. You're as white as me, Mavis." I held up my tan, bare arm to Mavis's and sure enough, we were the same shade of brown.

"Not good enough," said Mavis.

I shook my head. "Last time I used the toilet after you, your pee was the same color as mine. You're no different."

"You and I know that, but Mama said no white church in the South will have us."

"Then I don't want to go there," I said. "I'd rather stay at home."

"You should go to church, Andie. It gets you into Heaven."

"It does?"

"Mama says so. First Jesus washes away your sins, then Sunday school teaches you 'bout Heaven."

"Oh!" I exclaimed. "Wonder why we don't go then?"

"Probably 'cause your daddy wants to find the right church."

We took turns holding the Bible in our hands.

"Why can't I go with you to your church?" I replied.

"Not many white folk go there either, 'cept Daddy and ol' Miss Dinkens," Mavis said.

I slipped the invitation back into the pretty envelope, then laid the Bible inside the box.

"What's this?" Mavis asked. Her eyes sparkled as she held up a pressed flower.

"A rose petal!" I shouted. "Hand it over."

The heat had slowed Mavis's reaction time. She eventually got around to putting it in my hand. "The paper around it says, Bud Jr., died June 17, 1956. Who's that?" she asked, flashing me a curious look. Nutmeg freckles, like my own, marched across her light brown nose and sprigs of hair stuck out of her braids.

"My brother," I said. "He died when he was a baby."

Mavis lowered her head and mumbled, "I'm sorry."

"I'll ask Daddy to take us to this new church; maybe he just needs us to ask him. After all, my mother sure needs to go. I better get this back in his closet. I feel bad."

"You jus' wanting to read the Holy Bible. Nothing wrong with that."

"Still, help me, Mavis; before he gets home and whips my butt."

"Wait." Mavis pulled out a sharp kitchen knife she'd brought from home to peel the apples. "Let's do a blood pact."

"A what?"

"I want us to mix our blood, then we'll really be sisters. I hear Mama talk about it all the time, 'there's power in the blood.' She sings about it in church."

"Will it hurt?"

"A little, but here's some Bactine. We'll use it later."

I held out my hand and only winced as Mavis cut into my palm. Mavis gave the knife to me. In minutes, blood dripped from our hands and we clamped them tight.

"Repeat after me. I pledge to God, fiddle dee dee, you and me, on the shores of gitchee goomie—"

"Stop!" I giggled. "What are you saying?"

"Never mind. Jus' pledge you'll be my sister forever."

"I pledge to be your sister and best friend, 'til death do us part."

"Now we have the power, Andie."

§

Jerked from sleep, I opened my eyes. The familiar feeling of death pressed against my chest, while shadows from the oak tree outside crisscrossed about the room. The echo of her voice suspended in the air, pulled me to my feet. *"Go now. He needs you."* But no one was there. Only the wind outside and a sweet, sweet spirit filling the room like perfume. "Mavis?"

Suddenly, Dixie's scream echoed throughout the house. It broke the silence along with Wylene yelping like a frustrated dog at the bottom of the steps, "Andie! Come quick!"

I flew down the staircase to find the hospice nurse standing by Daddy's side, doing her best to inject him with drugs and assist Wylene. His whole face, blue as a leg vein, fought for a breath of air. Wylene's heavy arms attempted to hold him still enough to secure the oxygen mask over his mouth and nose as he struggled to sit up. Dixie, at her wit's end, tried desperately to calm him but she buckled to the floor taking me with her. Caroline stood in the doorway watching, helpless, sobbing, her heart grieved to hear Daddy's last breaths. Our nightmare was ending.

I couldn't stand it anymore. I let go of Dixie and pulled myself up. Crawling into Daddy's bed under the tangled mass of tubes attached to his body, I scooted close beside him, pulling what was left of his body against my own. "Daddy. It's okay. Time to go."

His hand trembled, tugging off the oxygen mask. "Forgive me," he said, gasping for air.

"Nothing to forgive, Daddy. I love you. Go on to Jesus. Go on."

He reached for my hand.

"It's time to go, Daddy, it's time."

Unyielding, he opened his eyes wide.

"No girl could ask for a better father. You're the best, Daddy."

With that said, he relaxed slightly. His lips parted and his head rolled back. My mother remained on the floor by his bed. Wylene tended to her, holding her.

It was then I felt him go limp, as if he were disappearing. The room swirled around me in a whoosh, like I had pulled a plug in a tub. His voice barely a whisper, only I could hear and understand him. "Good men . . . never die . . . they just fade away."

I cried my heart out. "Go rest on your mountain, Daddy. Let go. Let go."

Wylene helped my mother stand and grab his hand as he looked into her eyes one last time. I held him, watching Dixie stroke his face, wordless, but there.

And then everything stopped. One last breath, and it was over.

After some time, I slid off the bed, walked numbly past my grieving sister and stepped outside. I stood and stared at the sky. The forecast said rain, but the sun was shining. It was a beautiful day and my daddy was dead.

§

We held Daddy's funeral at Tussman Funeral Home. I had become all too familiar with the place. Lula sang between her crying jags. The room overflowed with flowers: bouquets in baskets of every size and shape, and vases filled with every fern and blossom imaginable. Cold air blew from the air ducts and I told the funeral director to turn up the heat. It was a funeral *home*, not a morgue. Coot and Candace stood with me near Daddy's open casket. Neither could look at his body for long. Thin as a rifle barrel, his face rutted with the wrinkles of a man twice his age, Daddy didn't leave much of himself behind. The funeral home did a good job considering what they had to work with. But nothing could fill in the ruts, wipe away the ruin of a million cigarettes.

A line formed and each mourner walked toward me, a little shy but wearing a warm smile. About thirty men Daddy had worked with at R. J. Reynolds showed up. I was surprised as the crowd grew. Some drove for long distances and I thanked each one for their support. A far piece from Boone, Daddy's cousins arrived in a station wagon and two pickup trucks. Timidly, they talked about their memories of him and what a good man Daddy was. In the midst of their awkward embraces, I wept openly, moved by their kindness. Luckily, only Coot asked about the Olivers. I told the truth. I didn't care if they showed up. I hoped they didn't.

Wylene, relentless in her attention, held Dixie in check. Wy was a rock. Caroline couldn't get a baby sitter for her girls and chased them around the lobby while her ex-husbands sat in the parking lot with the local men chewing and passing a flask. Gracie parked herself next to Dixie and Wylene. Dillon cowered alone in the back of the room, drawn, thin, and speechless.

Caroline finally stepped in and took over for me. I went and sat by my mother, feeling colder than before, like I'd been sitting on ice. Despite my bulky sweater and wool skirt, my face and hands were freezing.

"Here." Candace handed me her Styrofoam cup of coffee. "Wrap your hands around it."

I shivered. "I want to go home."

"Hang in there, honey," she said, stretching her long arm around my shoulders and rubbing my arm. It warmed me.

Gracie moved next to Dillon who sat on the couch like a lanky pup, his knobby knees pushing through his pants legs. I was worried about him, but he perked up when his sister sat beside him. I noticed Gracie took her grandpa's death amazingly well, telling everyone, "He's gone on to Heaven to be with our brother." But Dillon had idolized his Grandfather. When he was ten he tried to make his voice the same, even adopting Daddy's habits, good and bad. More than once I had caught my son with a cigarette; holding it the same way, then stomping it out with the toe of his shoe.

Gracie had put on her navy jumper and white blouse, a bargain find; Dillon wore a new gray suit Wylene bought him with a smart-looking blue tie. At barely fifteen, their faces showed the first signs of real maturity. They both sat straight in their chairs, seriously taking it all in. Watching them, I saw myself years before at Brian's funeral, sitting near that same spot.

Daddy's coffin, a beautiful engraved oak number Dixie chose the week before he passed, had been laid out on a carved table, like a pulpit, in the middle of the adjacent room. Moments later it was finally sealed. A blanket of red roses lay across it with words imprinted on a red satin ribbon in silver glitter. "Beloved Husband, Father, Grandfather, Friend." I looked away. A suffocating sensation tightened my throat and I stood quickly.

Dixie uncrossed her ankles. She'd hardly said two words all day. "Andie—"

"You need coffee?"

Through a mist of tears she nodded and attempted to smile, but her wide lips remained sullen and pale, her lipstick bitten off hours before.

"I'll be right back," I said. Dixie's color wasn't good overall. When I returned she had folded herself against Daddy's casket, her arms spread across the spray of flowers. I watched tears slip off her chin and the slow, pathetic shake of her head. Each sympathetic voice encouraging her to back away only made Dixie cling that much tighter to Daddy's remains. But Wylene and I knew it wasn't only her husband she mourned. The world Dixie Parks was accustomed to, the world Daddy provided for her, had come to an end.

§

The weathermen were off a few days in their forecast. It finally rained.

Too many people crowded inside the house. Restraining their chatter, they ate casseroles and Jell-O molds, salads with ranch dressing, and little finger-whatever-foods. Dixie reclined in her chair, stoic and alone; everyone was afraid to approach her. I sat on an ottoman a couple feet from her, watching each mourner who had come to eat free food. They stood back as if our grieving family suddenly needed quarantined. *That's right, just nod and smile; come too close and you might catch the flu, get a zit, lose your car keys. Catch our rotten luck.*

Feeling the dreaded obligation, I stood and attempted to circulate with folks I barely knew who had nothing left to say. They offered up pitiful, weak smiles and I kept thinking I'd lose all self-control at the next pasty face expressing their sympathy like that. But I decided not to embarrass my family. Not that it was any different from living with Joe, really. I had long ago perfected the trick of walking on eggshells. What I wanted was for everyone to sob like Lula. She, at least, knew the art of grieving and how to get it out of her system. Instead, every dry-eyed face in the room only mumbled and finished off the chicken pies and vegetable trays.

Dixie coughed softly, rose from her chair, and for a brief moment she stood with her arms at her sides, her gaze lost. "I need to wash more glasses," she said. Then she pushed up the sleeves on her sweater and collected herself before facing the fifty or so people milling about her house. What would be a long and terrible night for all of us was compounded by the grief etched on Dixie's face. I could see her hands shaking and I felt the utter terror of possibly losing both parents: my only lifeline.

After the last guest had licked his plate clean, the dishwasher packed, and the leftover widow casseroles were stuffed into the refrigerator, I walked down to the edge of the property behind the shed, and fell into a lawn chair where I wouldn't be found. Daddy's death had left another gaping, bleeding hole inside me. The pouring rain soaked my clothes and the chilled air numbed my body. I sat there hoping the cold would also dull my brain, as I bent my head over my broken heart. But when the rain had slacked to a drizzle, I stumbled back to the house, slipped into Daddy's study, and dried off with his worn-out flannel shirt. Sinking into his recliner that smelled of Aqua Velva and cigarette smoke, I pulled his banjo onto my lap, and gave in to the racking sobs that rocked me back and forth like an oak tree in the wind.

March 1992
A Raging Inferno

Andie

The misery of Dixie's loss lessened daily. No longer nursing a terminally ill husband, her mood improved, for which we were all thankful. Wylene had gone back to Charleston in an attempt to put her neglected medical practice back together on the same morning I received word that Joe had filed suit for custody of the twins.

I laughed, and then called my mother.

Dixie's voice blared through the line, loud and clear. "That's ridiculous. He's not getting custody. They're fifteen. What judge in their right mind would do that? I can't believe Joe is even trying this!"

"He doesn't really want them," I said. "I'm not worried at all."

"You call your lawyer?"

"I can't afford one. And I can't borrow any more money. I owe enough." If I had wanted to hire legal counsel, my mother would have to pay for it.

My mother knew it, too. "No, you're right. You don't need a lawyer. You've always been a terrific mother. Oh, Andie, I almost forgot. That envelope you left here, you know, the big one your daddy gave you and you taped shut. It's on the kitchen table. I boxed up everything for Lula's church bazaar and found where you stuck it in Bud's sock drawer. You might want to come get it. If it's not important, tell me, I'll throw it out."

"No, don't. It's important! I'll come get it."

Some women held onto their husband's things for years. But not Dixie. Daddy's clothes and personal effects were gone within the month.

"What's in it, Andie? It's addressed to Rupert."

"It's . . . not a big deal, just memories of Mavis. Don't open it, Dixie. It's mine."

"I won't open it, but come get it, okay?"

I had already hung up the phone. I figured the envelope was safer at Dixie's house than at mine, but I had to get over there in case my phone had been tapped. It was time to take the envelope straight to the bank and deposit it in a lockbox along with the notes I made the day John Rossi was murdered.

§

I pulled into the Wachovia Bank parking lot, a typical suburban branch bank with a drive-through window and an interior lobby. My escort into the steel lockbox area was a bank employee with *Jenny* on her name tag. She wore a wedding ring and maternity clothes, although the baby wasn't showing much. I commented on that and she said she had six more months to go. Her first child. She and her husband were so excited.

I thanked her for her time and gave her a quick smile before I walked out of the bank. With everything locked safely inside the bank's vault, I felt relieved.

§

My pre-paid attorney had stalled my bankruptcy as long as he could. The creditors' petitions to the court had to be heard. The call came. My attorney had completed the paperwork, filed it, set a court date, and then sent out notices. I called off work at the truck stop the Monday in March I had to appear in court. Although the hearing was scheduled for nine and would be over before I had to be at work by two, I'd be in no mood to wait on truckers buying smut magazines and traveling salesmen trying to pay for gas with maxed-out credit cards.

I staggered through the bankruptcy proceeding as one lost in a fog. Desperate to quit smoking, I chewed my fingernails to oblivion as the attorneys hashed out the details. In the small conference room downtown the only creditors to show up were Lester Gerber and his wife, Effie, who held the land contract on my house. Shooting glazed looks of pity my way, they spoke a few kind words I didn't comprehend after it was over. All I heard was due to the nature and size of my debts, my house went back to the Gerbers. I had thirty days to vacate the property.

§

I didn't remember driving home. I parked my car in the driveway and stared at the house, my house, a house I'd worked so hard for. It was a disaster when I bought it. Daddy had worked endless hours on it, and I had nearly scrubbed my fingers raw cleaning it. I would certainly leave it in much better condition than I found it. My loss was the Gerbers' gain.

Home—no, that was the wrong word for it. It wasn't a "home"—more like a dwelling place for ghosts. Perhaps the entities would leave me alone if I no longer lived there. Or maybe not. "Southerners own their haints," Dixie had said.

An hour later, I was still sitting in the car, in the garage, in the dark. Where would we go, what would we do? Anger. An emotion I always held at bay, kept bottled inside for one reason or another, shot through me with such force, the top of my head tingled. Getting out of the car, I switched on the light and looked around at the few tools Joe had left hanging on the garage walls: tools that belonged to my daddy. There it hung, by the window. A sledgehammer.

For years, I had ignored the padlocked storage shed in my backyard, caring less what Joe had hidden inside. He would often make a trip to the shed on the mornings he picked up or dropped off the twins. In fact, I considered it might be empty and he just wanted to torment me with a padlocked room. He'd put off cleaning it out and I hadn't cared. Until that moment. The more I thought about Joe knowing that Calvin was a pedophile, the angrier I became. The years I wasted on Joe infuriated me. I grabbed the sledgehammer, stormed to the backyard, and then took the past seventeen years out on the shed, pounding the lock off the door. The lock didn't break, but I busted up the wood so badly the planks fell apart and the door swung open.

I pulled the string that switched on the overhead light bulb and blinked with open-mouthed fascination. A poster of Farrah Fawcett with the protruding nipple hung on the back wall. The twenty by twelve-foot shed was filled with boxes of pornography; neatly organized, categorized, and alphabetized. Missing since the early 'seventies, a storage box I once used for my cookbook collection sat among dozens of boxes, all of them filled with smut. New VCR tapes by the boxfuls surprised me. Audio and video equipment had been stacked on metal shelving against the two longest walls. In my years of living with Joe, I'd seen that kind of equipment several times.

Furiously chewing at my lip, I recalled something John Rossi had said. "*I finally put it all together. The raw tapes would have to be edited first, but the equipment for that wasn't in the house. Then they'd have to send the tapes somewhere to be made into movies, before selling them to adult stores . . .*" In that instant my suspicions were confirmed and my heart sank. Joe was indeed part of Calvin's religious Mafia. He was perfect for the job.

I quickly regretted opening the shed. *What if Joe's also involved in drugs or something worse?* I couldn't hide drugs in a bank lockbox. And I certainly didn't want to be connected to anything illegal. I stepped over the boxes, then sat on one marked, "Los Angeles—Carmine's Adult Book Store." None of it made sense, a televangelist transporting illegal porn across the country. I searched the boxes for a name, or incriminating evidence connected to the House of Praise. They had covered their tracks. There was nothing. Nowhere. In the corner, a briefcase leaned against the inside wall. A large case. One like I'd seen Joe carry out the door on Friday nights. I opened it. It was filled with bundles of 100-dollar bills. For a split second I considered taking a bundle. I sure could've used it. I was also sure Joe knew exactly how much was in there.

I panicked. It was all on my property. Calvin's team of slick lawyers would pin it on me. And in the middle of a child custody battle, I had no desire to call the police. I hurried back into the house and pulled Mavis's old camera out of the box Lula had given me. It still worked. I drove to the drugstore on the corner for film and rushed back.

Not knowing if taking pictures would do any good, I snapped an entire roll of film inside the shed. It was the only thing I could think of to do— snap pictures of every box, piece of equipment, and the open briefcase full of money. Then I wiped everything down and put it back the way I found it before driving to the bank at a quarter to three, fifteen minutes before it closed.

Inside the vault Jenny asked, "Do you remember your box number, Mrs. Oliver?"

"Number thirteen, I think. One of the smaller ones." I pointed, and then eyed the room. Jenny pulled a card from the box. "If you'll just sign and date this."

Afterward, I handed my key to Jenny who inserted both keys into the lockbox. It opened.

"Do you want to take your box to our privacy area?" she asked.

"Yes, thanks." Looking over my shoulder again, I slipped the film and the old camera inside, followed by a quick goodbye to pregnant Jenny before dashing out of the bank.

Driving home my heart stopped, then started with a hard thump as I turned onto my street. Joe's truck was parked in my driveway. Tapping the brake pedal, I slowed the car to a near crawl. Aware of cold fear coiling in my stomach, threatening to liquefy my bowels, my grip on the steering wheel tightened. He sat in his truck, waiting. I smiled, trying to put on my best why-are-you-here-it's-nice-to-see-you face as I pulled into the drive. My foot had barely touched the driveway when his truck door flew open and he hopped out. Joe slammed the door, bolted toward me, then grabbed my arm with such force my teeth shook.

"What happened to my shed?"

"*Your* shed? What the hell are you talking about? And let go of me!"

"Did you bust it open, Andie? What did you see? What did you do? Huh? You bitch!"

"I've been in bankruptcy court all day. Last time I saw it, it was locked." I lied and walked into my empty garage, away from the eyes and ears of my neighbors.

"Yeah? Well, it's a damn good thing I can't find anything missing! But if someone wanted to break in, they'd take something, right? Wouldn't they?"

"Sure, just like you robbed me, right?"

Joe glared at me like a starved predator. He hit the button that closed the large door behind us and then lunged, spitting like a rabid dog, throwing me against the inside garage wall.

"Stop it, Joe! Get off my property! I'll call the police!" I turned around to run.

My head snapped back as if he'd jerked on my reins—which in a way, he had. Cutting off my air he had grabbed the back of my shirt, twisting and wrenching it tight around my neck. My arms flinging wildly, I managed to take hold of the door to the backyard patio and open it. Prissy bounded into the garage, growling and biting Joe on the leg. He kicked Dillon's dog and she yelped, running back out the door. In the process, my shirt ripped and Joe let go of me. I buckled, gasping for air, my lungs hurting. "You disgust me. You disgust me. I hate you," I said over and over from the garage floor.

Joe stood against the wall breathing heavy, his hands behind him as he collected himself. The clock on the garage wall read 3:30. The kids would be home in a half-hour.

Without thinking it through, I reached into my shirt pocket and pulled out the one picture from Mavis I'd kept out of the envelope. The one with which I wanted to confront him. I held it up. He walked over to where I cowered on the garage floor. Like pulling a weed, he yanked me to my feet and snatched the picture from my hand. An exposed Calvin lay on a beautiful bed of white down comforters beside a young Joe, whose bare back and butt was to the camera. It was Joe. That much I knew. And it was obvious Calvin was enjoying his crime with a confused boy of sixteen. I scooted back to the concrete floor searching for protection. In all the years I knew him, I had not feared Joe until then. He'd shoved me a time or two, hard enough to bruise me, and even choked me once. But the difference had become clear. I knew too much.

"I have all the negatives and the pictures. The ones Mavis meant for me to have. The ones you destroyed the day the mailman delivered her envelope to the trailer. I got them anyway; Rupert got the same envelope. I swear to God I'll use them to protect our children!" I managed to stand, sliding up the wall for support, pleading. "Stop this, Joe. Don't let this happen to Dillon, for God's sake! If you love your son the slightest bit, you won't let this happen!"

He didn't speak. He opened the garage door instead and ran to his truck. Bolting back inside and out to the backyard shed with a hammer, nails, and two six-foot boards, he nailed it shut. Nauseated, I remained standing but had wedged myself into a corner of the cool garage, not wanting him to follow me into the house or out to the street. When his pounding stopped, fear spiked in my gut. I willed myself invisible and prayed he would just leave, but he appeared in the doorway and slammed the patio door behind him. Once again, we were alone.

"Don't open the shed again if you know what's good for you. I'll be back for everything tonight," he said, before slowly setting his briefcase on the concrete floor.

Only a slight shiver contradicted my outward calm. I watched the scalding fury that had been simmering inside him escalate into blind rage but then, as if by magic, he turned into the monster I knew him to be. Knowing what he was about to do, Joe put his finger to his lips and grinned. In that split second our eyes locked and he hit me so hard I blacked out and wet myself.

§

When I came to, it was ten after four. Joe was gone and thankfully, the twins' school bus was late. I stumbled into the house and sat in the bathroom until I felt well enough to clean myself up. With a new bruise purpling beneath my eye, I held ice on my split lip and on my cheekbone that had cracked and swelled like an old baseball. Sitting on the couch in my tatty chenille bathrobe with coffee stains down the front, I waved to Dillon and Gracie as they walked through the door and tried to explain it away as a car accident. A lame excuse, but the only one I could think of. They were too young to remember the last time their daddy left bruises on my body, so I figured they might buy it. Gracie hugged me and promised to make supper. But the smarter twin wasn't always the one with the most common sense. After noticing Prissy's limp and the storage shed that had been broken into and boarded up, Dillon pulled the car into the garage and hung the sledgehammer back on the wall.

Before Daddy died I'd overheard his conversation with Dillon, making him promise to become the man of the house. He whispered to me after Gracie had gone to bed. "If he ever hits you again I'll kill him myself, Mom, I swear to God!"

It saddened me that it had come to this, and it hurt like hell to talk. "Don't worry about it, honey."

"Don't let him take us, Mama. Gracie and I won't stay with him."

The bruise on my face throbbed, but I halfway smiled and squeezed his arm. "Never."

April 1992
NOTHING BUT THE BLOOD

Reverend Calvin Artury

"She said she'll use them if she has to," Joe said.

"What exactly does she have?"

"She said she has every picture Mavis meant for her to have. Rupert Dumass got a duplicate of everything. We never thought Mavis was smart enough—"

"But she was, wasn't she? She sent a duplicate. How absolutely perfect!" I held the old snapshot Mavis had taken and stiffened, as though she had stuck her hand through the veil of death to assault me. "Call Percy. Have him come to my office. I need to find out if anyone knows about this besides Andie. I need him to send her a message from The Lord Most High."

Thou hast been my help, therefore in the shadow of Thy wings will I rejoice! For the first time in over a decade, I ended a service before ten o'clock. That Friday night in April, I cut my usual service in half, finding it difficult to even pray in tongues. Eliminating the healing line, I called for the unsaved, backsliders, and for those who wanted a closer walk with Jesus to come forward. But the sight of Joe with his hands raised at the altar sent me reeling. Our meeting before church produced alarming evidence. It quenched the Spirit in me.

§

After the service, I quickly retreated to my office and softly bolted the door shut behind me. I left word not to be disturbed. No one would dare. Stripping in the darkness, I turned to the mirrored wall. The moonlight filtered all impurities from my nakedness. I would spend the night there and allow the cleansing to be completed. It could not wait. I was due; it had been a long time since my last one. The last time I had felt the hot breath of God, searing my skin.

I pulled the ivory-handled knife out of my desk and sliced a line across my torso. Blood oozed down my chest, over my nipples and collected in my chest hair and around my erection. I dipped my fingers in the warm blood and covered each scar on my body. A cleansing. To be washed in the blood, God's blood—in me. The perfect bath.

I laid my body on top of my pristine desk, moonlight covering me in God's love. I shrank away from it, but it pulled me into a vision, clearer than all the rest. My face stared back at me. A boy's face. The first time I had been washed in the blood. My aunts had defiled my innocence with their big, sweaty bodies. The blood felt good.

"The sweet-sour smell of coition cannot be washed away with water. It must be washed in the blood," my turtle-headed aunt said. *Her lips twitched upward at the corners and her hair, what little she had, was wrapped in a cow pile on top of her head. She washed my limp nine-year-old body in a galvanized tub*

filled with blood from the slaughtered hogs. Her elbows stuck out like wings as she moved methodically over my tender skin. "This is God's child, he must be cleansed from all sin." She called to her sister. "Fetch a rag, Tilley. He's ready."

"Hey, hey Bea, 'member when Daddy took a shotgun to Mama and blew her to kingdom come? I 'member, sure 'nuff. Her guts 'n shit flew all over these 'yere walls. I'm the onliest one who slipped in it, and he laughed, 'member? And, hey, hey, you 'member it got all over our church clothes an ever'thang!" She snorted. "He made usuns clean it up. Hee-hee, I think I swallered some of it. Ain't funny. I oughtn't to laugh."

"No dear, you shouldn't laugh about such things. It's time to take our child to bed."

Tilley drooled. A string of spit slid down and off her chin and hung there, like suspended vomit. Her diseased eye rolled in its socket and her breath smelled like spoiled meat from even across the room. Narrow-witted, her head cocked to the side, she hobbled over to give the rag to Bea. Tilley leaned forward and looked into my young eyes. Her other eye had the dull blue look of a blueberry. Small, dark, dried up. Her finger moved from her cracked and crusted lips toward my face and hovered, waiting for Bea to allow her to plant a blessing.

"It's time, dear. Time to say good night to God's son."

"Can I take his picture first?"

"Not now, dear. Time to kiss him good night."

"Any whar I want?"

"Plant your blessing, Tilley. Any place you like."

§

The rain fell in torrents the last time I saw them. I was a grown man. A beautiful man, made in God's perfect image. It was a hot July day. I remember because it was my birthday. Approaching their peeling porch steps, I flung my suit jacket over my shoulder, undid my tie, and rolled up my sleeves. While one aunt shook with a palsy and the other chewed a cud of something between her gums, I sat on a step and read from the book of Leviticus. "*A woman that hath a familiar spirit, a wizard, shall surely be put to death, they shall stone her with stones; her blood shall be upon her.* I'm going to preach," I said.

They stared through me, like a couple of deaf mutes.

I'd come to pick a bone with two old women; to rid myself of an infected snake bite, a poison that had infiltrated even the most anointed parts of my life.

"Can you understand? I'm an overcomer! Quench not the Spirit, saith the Lord! Don't you see? The audible voice of God speaks to me and through me daily. I once was lost, but now I'm found. You chastised me, but He chose me. I crossed over into the Land of Milk and Honey and I found it. I found the sweet honey in the rock. Sucked out the sweetness and emptied the cone, tasted and seen that the Lord is good. He found no guile in *my* mouth, no He did not. I spend my days speaking in tongues, yes, true, the tongues of angels, and fall asleep easily every night with God's words inside me, His anointing upon me."

A violent storm erupted. Lightning cracked amid a fast and furious rain. I grabbed them up, two rail-thin old women, dragged them inside and kicked the door closed with my heel.

"Remember those Amen enemas you gave me? Cleansings, you called them," I said as I bound their hands and mouths. Pulling up a chair to their kitchen table, I spun my wet empty glass around and around on the oilcloth. Licking the inside of my mouth tasting the blood of vengeance, I traced the edge of the table with my thumb, watching them languish in the heat.

"You fell upon my innocent soul like worms on a corpse. In the middle of the night, when sleep evaded me, I turned to the scriptures for comfort, only to hear your voices and see your faces once again."

I stood and removed my belt from my pants.

"Did you know the Bible is the bloodiest book ever written? Of course you knew, you used it well. Your problem was that you had a form of godliness, and denied the power. Because that power and the undeniable truths of Jehovah God make you either want to kill yourself or the evil that was done to you. But God gave it to *me*. The power, the wonderworking power!"

Lightning hit the house knocking out the electric. I walked around and around them, swatting flies off their bare and bleeding hunched backs. Their stench was oppressive.

"When one has been beaten, the scars remain forever. When you become desperate enough to lose your past, your memory of who and why they beat you, your body screams out for the scars to be removed! Oh yes, I was an abomination before God. I looked into the mirror and saw a disfigured man, but now, I see nothing. Nothing but the blood."

As I slipped the ropes around their necks, the air felt like somebody's hot breath all over my body, sucking in and breathing out even under my clothes.

"I want to forget for all time and eternity where I came from."

Standing behind them, I stripped off my shirt and pants. Thunder pounded the ground outside as I sliced my torso, allowing my blood to drip over their heads. I began to sing, over and over. "*What can wash away my sin? Nothing but the blood of Jesus. What can make me whole again? Nothing but the blood of Jesus. Oh! precious is the flow that makes me white as snow; no other fount I know, nothing but the blood of Jesus . . .*"

The blood pooled in their hair and slid down their fly-dotted faces, crusting quickly in the heat. Their eyes followed me as I picked up my knife and ran the blade down along their cheeks and necks, and then jaggedly cut away at clothes and skin and muscle.

Walking away from my aunts' house, the parched red dirt road had become a gushing river of mud, flooding into my shoes, and pulsating like a severed bowel. I never looked back.

GOONS

Andie

Between boxing up the house, consoling my twins and promising to keep them in their school district, my job at the truck stop was a few hours of relief in my day. Keeping everybody else content left precious little time for my own happiness effort.

Wylene had returned to Winston-Salem to Dixie-sit. Diagnosed as manic-depressive, my mother had gone from elated relief to threats of suicide. After donating Daddy's last pair of pants to the Goodwill, she collapsed. Caroline and I took turns sleeping at the house, occupying her mind with the semi-normal parts of our own lives. And then Wylene announced the time had come for Dixie to sell her house. In order for my mother to heal, she needed a fresh start, away from the memories. I agreed, but my heart hurt to think about it. Once the house was sold, my safe haven would be gone.

The bruises on my face were healing. I had told my family the same whopper I'd dished out to my kids. But Wylene spoke her mind the moment she had me alone. "Next time, Andie Rose, make sure your damn gun's loaded. It'd solve all your problems."

§

During spring break the twins stayed with Dixie while I hunted for an apartment and crammed the last dozen years of my life into more boxes. The hourglass was running out. My thirty days to vacate was almost up. I doubted I could give Dillon and Gracie even a semi-normal life much longer.

Peaceful and silent as a cemetery, my yard and the dark house appeared bleak and ominous as I pulled into the drive. Trees cast shadows on the small weed-filled lawn. Blinds and curtains drawn, the familiar home I loved had become cold and foreboding. I parked in the garage and saw that Dillon had left the inside door to the breezeway partially open. I considered wringing his neck but he'd been under a strain since Joe left, feeling the need to be the man in the family and to protect me.

Prissy whimpered in the backyard, scratching at the garage door to the patio. *That boy! He left his dog out.* I opened the door and knelt down to pat Prissy, speaking in a soft, calming voice. She ignored me, whined, and tried to push past me.

"Come on, girl," I whispered, yanking on her collar. "You can't come in the house with muddy feet." Prissy was strong as an ox. She wasn't about to budge from the doorstep. She looked up at me with dark eyes like mirrors, as though something was wrong. Her paw prints landed on my jeans. "Damn it, Prissy, you're muddy! Stay, girl!" She jumped down, scratching and begging me to let her in. The frantic dog pushed her massive body forward, but I managed to close the door, leaning on it with a sigh while Prissy barked like her tail was on fire.

"I'll let you in later!" I walked up the two steps from the garage, tossed my purse in the corner of the breezeway, and then opened the door to the kitchen. Blinking in the dim house, frozen with shock, I saw the place was a wreck. Two men flipped on flashlights, moving toward me in the darkness. I backed up, my hands feeling along the door for the handle. From the obvious mess, they'd been searching for something. The glow from the streetlight illuminated a third man squatting on the floor behind them.

The door handle was cool and smooth beneath my palms. One bulging man stood so close I could feel his body heat. I pulled at the handle and pushed myself against the door to get away from him, but there was no room to slip through. And it was too late to run for my unloaded gun. I couldn't even remember where I'd stashed it.

"I'll be damned, the lady of the house!" I recognized the voice. A House of Praise ham-faced goon. Just as I turned the doorknob, the man closest to me thrust his hand over my mouth, smothering my screams. His other arm circled and squeezed my waist, cracking a rib, but the shock of what was happening overshadowed the sudden shooting pain.

"What should we do with her?" The man who held me, his breath hot in my ear, dragged me over to his companions. He smelled like he hadn't bathed in weeks and his hand on my mouth tasted of grease or gasoline. A shorter man shone his flashlight in my eyes and I attempted to turn my head, but he held the light on my face. "Joe Oliver always liked the feisty ones," he said.

Another flashlight to the front and right of me, blinded me. While the first goon's smelly hand held me tight, a stocky young man came close beside me. His voice tight, he stared with the unblinking eyes of a reptile. "Mrs. Oliver. We hear you been making threats to your ex-husband. We know you got something Reverend wants and you probably got it hid. After all these years, why not jus' leave things alone? You being an ex-team wife and all, Reverend don't want you hurt none. Not yet, anyway." His malicious grin displayed sharp white teeth. "Would raise too many questions. He jus' wants us to give you this message. If you show anybody whatever it is you got or put anything in the paper," he put his face closer to mine, "I promise you, you'll be dead before that paper comes out the next morning. That's a fact, ma'am. And Joe, too. Reverend's getting real tired of him being so much trouble."

He rummaged through my packed living room boxes again, but kept talking. "Reverend wants to know, have you shown anyone what you got?" I shook my head furiously under the hand of the reeking man that held me, my eyes wide with fear. "That's good. Reverend wants us to make sure you never do. He said there's no sense in asking you for it. But me and the boys, we thought we'd search anyway. Course, ain't sure exactly what I'm looking for. I don't suppose you'd just wanna hand it over?"

I gave no response.

"Didn't I tell ya, Hillard? She ain't obliging." He glared at me. "Well, now. Reverend suspects you're the only one who has it. So it's your job to make sure it stays hid. 'Cause if you ever threaten Joe or the church again, that cancerous tongue of yours will be cut out of your pretty mouth before we shove a knife up your ass and slice out your bowels. You'll jus' ooze all over your nice rugs here. And those kids of yours will never see their next birthday. You get what I'm saying to you?"

I nodded, recognizing him as Silas Turlo's oldest son. Insignificant-looking, dark coarse hair, Percy and his accomplices, Hillard Becker and his cousin Delmer. Thugs I'd seen hanging around the church parking lot. Their mothers were usherettes. I struggled when the tall one called Hillard moved his massive hands to my breasts. His laugh, abrasive; his breath stunk. "Oh, baby. Baby, you got some nice big tits."

"I wanna feel," Delmer said. I fell purposely to the floor as both men grappled at my chest. I heard my shirt rip, the buttons popping and hitting the floor. Delmer cursed at his cousin, "Goddamn it, Hillard, I want some! Hit her, knock her out!"

Hillard snorted. "Fuck you." His left hand still over my mouth, I could barely breathe. I felt myself getting sick. "You had the last one, I'm having this one; this one's mine!" With his right hand, he let go of my waist and pulled my right arm up behind me, maneuvering me through my pain. Prissy howled and barked at the back door. I prayed it was loud enough to alert the neighbors. "Go get that damn dog, Delmer, and shut it up."

"Shit fire! Ain't no time for foreplay, just let me at her." Delmer unzipped his pants.

Hillard grunted. "Maybe. After I get through. Now go shut that dog up!" But as one held my arms, the other tugged hard at my jeans, yanking them down past my hips. I kicked despite the pain, bucking like a wild horse, catching them off guard. They fought to keep me on the floor, cursing more at each other than at me. Suddenly, Dixie's antique dishes fell off the wall and shattered into what sounded like hundreds of pieces.

Percy slithered back into the kitchen. "You can both stop now. This ain't some slut downtown. Reverend will have your head on a chopping block. Whoa, Hillard. Stop. Cool it. Enough fun, fellas. Can't do nothing to her 'cept what he says to do. Besides, my daddy will have my ass in a sling." He bent over me as Hillard got a better hold and squeezed me tighter. "You scream again, or call the cops, or as much as mention we been here, you're a dead woman, you got it? If I were you, I'd keep my damn mouth shut. 'Cause Reverend, he don't make threats. He makes the promises of the Lord."

I nodded again and Hillard let go. I reached out a hand on the cold linoleum as nausea, sudden and violent, rolled through me. I couldn't stop it. The hot bacon dressing and salad I'd had for lunch scorched its way up my throat. Tears rolled down my face, and I spewed the contents of my stomach out at their feet.

Percy stepped back, his flashlight painting the floor with a harsh light. I crouched on the linoleum, soaked in vomit, staring at the faded knees of his blue jeans. The nausea subsided, but every breath I took was agony, and I wondered if they would kill me anyway. *Mavis. They did worse than this to*

Mavis. Feeling small, I felt tears dribble down my face, falling to the floor. They laughed and yanked me by my hair to my feet. I winced and moaned as pain shot through my head and chest from the grip they had on me once again.

"Aw, damn; she puked!" Hillard let go again, and put his hand between my shoulder blades pushing me forward in the dark. Afraid of walking into boxes, I stretched out my arm to protect myself. My belongings were strewn everywhere. But even walking hurt.

I tripped over a stack of newspapers and landed back on the kitchen floor. It was Percy who yanked my head back that time, his vile fist grabbing a handful of my hair.

"Just remember what I said! Next time, I won't hold these fellas back."

Hot tears dripped down the back of my throat. I saw the boot for only a second. It hit my head, opening a wound that was still trying to heal. In my delirium I heard them prepare to leave, kicking my things out of their way, using my toilet, and laughing. They flicked their cigarettes at me and called me a whore. The door slammed behind them and Prissy bounded into the room, licking my face in the blackness. They'd let the dog in to shut her up. Moonlight streamed through the window alongside the silence where I huddled on the floor, sobbing, smelling the grimy garage stench of their clothes, tasting the grit from their hands. I couldn't move. Each breath sent pain ricocheting through my chest, ribs, and shoulder. The room swirled around me as an echo of Mavis called out my name. As if she were on the other side of a vast canyon. *Andie Rose, you have the power . . . don't let him . . . destroy you.*

I've Got A Gun

Andie

In the morning, I cracked open my right eye. The left was nailed shut by the sharp spike driven through it or the linoleum my face was smashed against. My mother/child ring sparkled from the sun streaming through the windows. The glare hurt my eye and I rolled over to move away from it. There lay Prissy by my side, dried mud caked over most of her sleek black body. "Poor girl," I said, stroking my dog's paw.

I tried to push myself up on my elbows. Piercing pain knifed through my chest and shoulder. My arm didn't want to move, and my head threatened to explode. I fell to my side and then back to the floor. Panic rammed into my gut. Squeezing both eyes shut, I felt Prissy's head next to mine, whining like dogs do when scared. "Shhh, you're okay," I said to the both of us. Tears leaked from the corners of my eyes, as I pulled myself up and stumbled to the bathroom. Peering into the mirror, staring at my face, I heard the sound of thunder roll over my head.

Swollen and black-and-blue, my lip was split again; a tooth wiggled and bled. *Ice pack*. My ribs ached. Scratches, dark bruises and welts encircled my arms and torso. Lowering myself on the couch, I recalled the beating in detail and shook. This wasn't a guessing game anymore. The Artury Mafia had paid me a visit. A greater alarm rose in my throat. Had they known I witnessed John Rossi's murder, they would have killed me. Calvin didn't know Mavis's envelope was safe inside the bank vault, but it didn't matter. I always responded to fear and, once again, it worked. I had clearly pissed him off by giving Joe that picture, and the goons had succeeded in delivering his message. I'd keep Mavis's envelope hidden. I had to protect Dillon and Gracie. The pictures would never come out. But how long would they tolerate me being alive, knowing I had them?

I barricaded myself inside my house. The goons got in through the front door. I was sure Joe had given them the key, and I thanked God I'd never given Joe a key to the back door, but I wasn't taking any chances. I scooted Gracie's old upright piano against the door that led out to the garage and moaned in pain as I piled heavy boxes on top and around it. Then I jammed it tight with a coat rack, placing the pole on the floor between the piano and the opposite wall. After blocking the front entrance with more furniture and boxes, I locked windows, pulled the blinds, and loaded my gun. Then I hunkered down with Prissy on the couch; corpse-still with my gun in my lap, listening to the rain on the roof.

§

Scorching tears once again trickled down my face. I'd not been out of the house in three days, except to feed Prissy and let her out the front door on a leash to potty. I'd missed three days of work, calling off with the flu. Three days pay—gone. Three days wasted, not looking for an apartment. And for three days, I'd made excuses and left my kids with Dixie again. I didn't want the twins to see me. I sat immobilized with the phone off the hook. My head ached and my stomach growled. *Even Christ rose from the dead in three days. Guess I should come out of my tomb.*

I had two weeks to vacate my house. *Lord, how can I find an apartment in two weeks when I have no money for a deposit?* I stopped praying, unsure of how much I believed anymore. Shuffling into the kitchen in Gracie's pink disco slippers, I felt dirty. I'd gone too long without a bath and spent too much time with my mouth open. But the thought of Gracie gave me strength.

Opening the fridge, I stared at empty shelves and milk long past its sell-by date. At least Prissy had a bag of Purina. I scowled as I emptied a juice carton. Slowly, after forcing myself to eat a few Saltines and sip warm Diet Coke from a can, the terror subsided. Somehow, I had to put the divorce and bankruptcy behind me then get through the custody battle. I had to find a better job and an apartment for my twins and me. Move to Charleston, live near Aunt Wylene. Get away from Joe, the Olivers, and the whole church. My children gave me hope, pushed me forward, and kept my head clear. I had to start over. Make a new life. Without fear.

I felt the house dissolve around me, as my parents dissolved when I thought about them. There came a feeling of letting go, a feeling I welcomed. I had fret every month over how much money I needed to satisfy the mortgage. At least those worries were over. The other blessing—I'd kept my weight off. But it was effortless. Instead of stuffing my face, I'd forgotten to eat. "Someday this will all catch up with me," I said out loud like a slap from my hand. I never intended to commit suicide by neglecting my body, and yet I didn't give a damn.

The doorbell rang. I peeked out the window to the driveway. No car. A hard rain fell. I tiptoed to the front door, hoping it was just a friend of the twins. "Who is it?" I kept the door closed and bolted.

"It's Peter Collins, Andie. The chef from the Praise Buffet. You know who I am. Please, can I come in?" He coughed loudly, a wet, rasping hack like a shovel scraping sludge off cement.

I froze. "Are you here to threaten me? Beat me up? 'Cause this time I've got a gun."

"No. I'm not here to hurt you. I'm leaving town. I need to talk to you."

I opened the door a hair-width; the screen door remained locked.

He was in his mid to late forties, a large man yet hunched over like an old woman. Possibly ten years older than John, he appeared pale and in pain. Peter's massive shoulders filled the coat he wore. His broad chest and back hinted to his former size and beauty, and he had most of his hair, golden with gray and several shades lighter than John's. Calculating, edgy eyes took

392 ～ Pamela King Cable

everything in as if he were looking for an excuse to run. I could see he was nervous, and had probably lived the last few years looking over his shoulder.

The rain fell steady, not a drizzle, but sheets so dense visibility was nearly nil. A fog had rolled in. Thunder rolled across the sky and shook the trees in my yard. Peter pulled his coat collar up around his ears and gave me a look of desperation.

"What do you want from me?" I asked.

"I saw John sitting with you the night he died. I think you were the last to see him."

"No, you're wrong. His killer was the last to see him."

"Well, you're right about that. But I know you talked to him. And I know what they've done to you. Please, can I come in?"

Reluctantly, I opened the door and let him step inside.

"Still don't trust me, do you?" he asked.

I held the gun tight in my hand. "Hell, no. Why should I? Aren't you Calvin's lover?"

"No. Not for a long time. You can put your gun away. I told you, I just want to speak to you for a few minutes and then I'm leaving. Going to Florida. Sarasota. I'm moving in with my mother. In fact, you're my last stop. I'll be brief." He coughed again, and then wiped the rain off his face with a handkerchief he had pulled out of his coat pocket. "I stopped at the Buffet the night you were talking to John. I was there only a few minutes, but long enough to know he was pouring out his heart to you." He sighed. " I loved John Rossi."

"Yeah? Well, you had an awful way of showing it. You could've saved his life and left with him years ago."

"True enough. For that reason and many others, I'm finally leaving. Whatever John told you is true. Did you see who pulled the trigger? Are you the one who called the police?"

I only stared at him.

"No need to answer. I know who did it." His big-knuckled hand reached inside his coat again. He handed me a videotape. "My hobby has been making videos of Calvin's secrets. Put this with the rest of your evidence. I know you've got more. When you're ready, look at it and use it. But not until you're ready. In the meantime, if you ever need me, here is my mother's address and phone number. I'd prefer you memorize it, then get rid of that piece of paper. By the time they realize I'm gone for good, I should be on a bus halfway to the Sunshine State."

"Why? Why me?" I asked.

"I guess because I saw you with John that night. And I know they mean to destroy you. I can't be a Christian anymore. Not their kind of Christian. Don't worry, I've never told anyone I saw you with John. I never will."

"Why don't you go to the police with this tape yourself?"

"For the same reason you don't . . . threats against my family. I know too much. Nobody knows who to trust there. The church is crawling with spies.

Last year they broke my nose and busted a few of my ribs. John may have told you; they have connections in the police department and judicial systems. Any evidence you present could be destroyed before the trial. They'd come out smelling better than ever. People would flock to the church believing Calvin was being persecuted. People love to support the underdog. We'd both end up like John. Shot between the eyes and left in a parking lot somewhere. I don't want to die that way. My mother wants my casket open."

I didn't understand what he meant by his last comment, but wasn't about to inquire. "Why are you leaving Calvin; lovers' quarrel?"

"You could say that."

"What happened?"

"I had to find out for myself. He's a fake."

"I could've saved you the heartache. I knew that a long time ago. So did John."

"I didn't want to believe it," he said. "I had to know for sure. I don't know why no one's done this, but the idea came to me. I faked a message in tongues, just to see if he would interpret it. I prayed first, asked God to forgive me for what I was about to do, but I wanted to know if Calvin was for real. So I just jabbered something I made up, hoping he would tell me it was *not* the Holy Ghost speaking. Instead, he interpreted it. A long beautiful prophecy. How God's will for me was that I forget John who now dwelled in outer darkness, and that I must continue to work where God wanted me. On and on . . . a load of crap. At that moment I decided to leave and to edit a few choice meetings Calvin didn't know I'd videotaped."

I leaned against my empty bookcase, the gun still tight in my hand, the videotape in the other. "Hoo-boy, I thought I'd heard it all."

Peter wiped the sweat from his brow. "But I never stopped caring about John. This is my way to avenge his death. Hopefully, Andie, through you."

I could see him observing my bruised face. My lip was scabbed over, cracked and infected. A yellowish-green tint covered my right cheekbone. Black rings circled my eyes and my hair hung in a tangled greasy mess.

"You look like you could use some medical attention to that lip." He coughed forcefully into his handkerchief; sweat streamed from his pores.

"I guess. You sound like you could use a shot of whiskey yourself. You sound awful. My father passed away from emphysema. Are you sick?"

"I've got AIDS . . . advanced. Six months left, if I'm lucky." He coughed again. "This damn weather doesn't help. Calvin will never chase me. He knows I'm a dead man. He doesn't really want me around in this condition. It's okay. I just want away from it all. To die in peace." Peter reached into his inside coat pocket a third time and pulled out an envelope. "Here, I know you could use some money. It's a few bucks; not much, but it might help. I heard you're losing your home. I'm sorry, Andie. For all you've been through."

I set the videotape down and took the envelope from him. "I'm sorry, too, Peter. Thanks. Really, thanks a lot." Then I had to ask, "Is Calvin HIV positive?"

"No, he's clean, and so are the rest of his staff as far as I know. They're checked regular. He's a freak about that stuff. If you ever need to contact me, you know where I'll be. Unless it's more than six months from now, then you're on your own." He smiled sadly.

"Peter, how do you know they won't come after you anyway?"

"Calvin won't do that. Not to me. As long as I leave him alone, he'll leave me alone. He'll only go after someone if they can't keep their mouth shut, or they make threats against him, or one of the team . . . or the ministry. Like you did. So be careful. Use your ammunition wisely and only when the time is right."

I shook my head. "I'm not sure there will ever be a right time."

"You still believe in God?"

I sucked in my breath and looked away. "Not sure. I think so."

"Then there'll be a right time." He turned to open the door and leave.

I couldn't let him go without telling him. I spoke to his back. "Peter, John loved you. He did, you know. That's why he stuck around so long."

Silent, he nodded. He never looked back. "Take care of yourself, Andie," he said. With that goodbye, he disappeared down the street into a waiting cab.

I opened the envelope, and cried. A thousand dollars. Enough to lift my spirits and start apartment hunting again.

May 1992
Pack It Up

Andie

I deposited Peter's videotape into my bank lockbox. I couldn't watch it. It didn't matter at the moment. I even considered destroying everything inside the lockbox rather than pay the small monthly fee, but decided against it. And instead of hiding the key in the attic again, I strung it on a chain and slipped it around my neck.

I would not ask to move in with my mother. Going through divorce number three, Caroline had already packed up her three little girls and moved in with Dixie. With baby number four on the way, my sister's recent brief marriage wore on everybody's last nerve. Dixie wasn't stable; I guessed Caroline and I had caused her too much strain. As it was, we'd mooched off Dixie and Wylene enough. I had always tried to keep the worst from my family. My current homeless situation was no different.

I begged the Gerbers for an extension, another thirty days to vacate, but they refused. Their son had taken over their affairs and was not as kind as his parents had been. He told me the sheriff would be at the door on day thirty-one if I were not out. So I walked across the street to visit my neighbors, the elderly Grissom sisters. Two years previous, Ada and Edna Grissom had fallen ill with pneumonia. I had nursed and fed them both back to health. The spinsters took pity on me and the children and said we could live on their enclosed front porch until I found an apartment, which was good because the twins needed to remain in their school district with just a few weeks remaining in the school year. The fact was, no one wanted to rent to me. With a low-wage job and ruined credit, I was a risk nobody wanted to take. Really, I couldn't blame them.

Dillon, Gracie and I moved across the street into our neighbors' glassed-in front porch. The twins were allowed to take one suitcase and a few of their favorite things. The rest of our furniture and boxes were placed in a rented storage unit across town, the cheapest one I could find. Gracie's piano was donated to the Salvation Army and we gave Prissy to Byron Stewart, Libby's uncle, knowing one more dog on his farm wouldn't make any difference to him. We cried silently, driving away from the farm, leaving our beloved dog behind. Giving Prissy away was the worst part of the whole ordeal.

A fluorescent bulb blinked in the rust-pitted tin ceiling. The long, narrow room was crowded with old porch furniture that should've been burned years ago. Gracie and I gutted the room and scrubbed it. Dillon painted it a soft white and I added a lamp, a rug, and a single bed—politely refusing the recycled mattress the Grissom sisters offered. The porch was livable. Better than a cardboard box or a homeless shelter. I cleaned a small loveseat in the corner with upholstery cleaner and covered it with a quilt; Dillon slept on that and Gracie and I shared the tiny bed. We'd manage.

It was hardest on the twins. My heart broke, watching them get off the school bus. Every day they walked to the back door of their old house, waited until the bus turned the corner, then they'd run across the street to our current address, a room no bigger than their mama's old bedroom. They didn't want their friends to know they were homeless. At fifteen, any diversion from the norm was an embarrassment. Somehow, I had to believe it would make them stronger. Show them how delicate life is, and how one bad decision could throw everything off balance. They would learn from my mistakes.

I had resolved to make it through. Most days I drove from interview to interview before heading to the truck stop for work. I scoured the papers for a job that would pay enough to rent a decent apartment in their school district. Funny thing: cooking skills were not as marketable as computer skills. Competing with girls fresh out of college, my frustration escalated. And I drew the line on how much I told the Grissom sisters. Although the ladies had been kind and generous, I had no way of knowing if those two might be given to gossip.

Solitude had become a commodity, something to haul home along with whatever groceries I could afford. Bread, milk, peanut butter, and boxes of macaroni and cheese. Every morning I stifled the accusations in my head to listen for a still small voice I hoped still existed. During my lower moments, I prayed for Jesus to tell me what to do next, clear away the clutter of my life, and give me a reason to keep moving. There was no voice. Nothing other than the sounds of Dillon and Gracie fighting over the bathroom.

We took turns in quick showers at specified times of the day. I managed to hook up our little TV; it helped pass the time and warm the porch. Not wanting to impose in Edna and Ada's dining room, we took our meals to our room. The house had enough space for two families, but I insisted the children remain on the porch with me. Fortunately, it was free. I counted our blessings. We were alive. Living at times from hour-to-hour, I worked hard to make the best out of our miserable living conditions. But Gracie and Dillon felt my stress. I concluded if we were to survive, I had to find a place of our own, and quickly.

§

Standing in front of the dingy three-floor walk-up, my puckered brow dripped with sweat. The front door hung on one hinge and a pile of coupon magazines littered the stoop; the whole house tilted to the left. Frowning, I stepped back and looked at the building again. It was hard to believe the landlady lived in such a place. I pulled out the slip of paper where I'd written the address. *Yep, this is it.* A shot of hot wind blew down the street and I glanced in its direction. The humidity climbed. I'd tried calling Annabel Boggs numerous times throughout the day to confirm my appointment and though I recognized the name, I thought nothing else about her. Desperate, I figured my best opportunity at getting the apartment at the end of the street was to speak to the landlady in person. It appeared that unless I was prepared to sit and wait on the rickety stairway, I'd reached another dead end. Nobody was home.

I knocked on the front door again. My spirits sank. I didn't have anymore time to waste. I had to get to work. Crumpling the paper, I started down the steps that swayed under my feet. Just as I hit the sidewalk, I caught a flash of hair dyed a harsh, unnatural shade of red. It belonged to a woman moving between two parked cars. She crossed the street with her head down, and it wasn't until I stepped off the sidewalk that she lifted her eyes, saw me, and stopped in the middle of the road.

"Hello," I called out, raising a hand. "Miss Boggs?"

"Who wants to know?"

"We had an appointment today," I said, hoping she really was the landlady.

The woman scowled, then started walking again much more slowly. "I don't remember any appointment," she said.

I tried to coax a smile from her but failed. She looked a tidbit familiar, but I couldn't quite place her. My eyes narrowed. Upon closer inspection, her forehead was covered with red blotches, which shone through a thick coat of perspiration. A breeze tossed her hair around, which fell past her shoulders. The woman had not aged well, having painted a new face on top of the old one, which glared at me with suspicion.

"Well?" She lifted her dome-like eyebrow. "I said I don't remember any appointment."

"I called yesterday. I'm here to apply for the apartment down the street."

Shooting me a coolly annoyed glaze, the landlady walked up the stone steps and mumbled as she passed me. "I'm not interested in having you for a tenant."

"Why?" I asked sharply, suddenly behind her.

"I know who you are. You should've told me on the phone, saved us both some time."

"What do you mean?"

"I know who you are. I'm an usher at the House of Praise. I don't rent to demon-possessed people. Get off my property." She pinned me with a look that would've withered anyone else. Holding up her hand as if she had a magic wand that would make me disappear, she shouted, "I rebuke you in the name of Jesus!"

Crushed beneath her heel, I refused to move. "Miss Boggs, you don't even know me."

The landlady swept a strand of hair out of her eyes. "I know enough," she said.

"But I haven't done anything to offend you personally, have I?"

Her brick-red hair blew into her eyes again. Aggravated, she pushed it away and opened her lacquered lips. "I don't like you," she blurted. As soon as the words came out, her cheeks reddened. She stood as still as a post but I felt her fist in my gut.

For a fleeting moment I thought if Annabel could see I was not a horrible person, maybe sit down and have coffee together, get to know me a little, it would dispel the fear. I smiled grimly. "Maybe the problem is that you really don't know me, you're afraid of me. Why don't we at least go in and talk—"

"I'm not scared of dark angels like you!"

"Then why the hostility?" I shrugged. "And I'm not a dark angel."

The landlady shook her head. "I'll only say it one more time. Get off my property!"

Astonished by her animosity, I gave her a level stare. "Here's a little something to chew on, Miss Boggs. I think it's very sad you believe every word Calvin says, and that you allow him to control you with fear. You've not even thought to question the 'accused.' Again, ma'am, I'm no dark angel. I'm a mother with two children in need of a roof over our heads. And if you're an example of Christianity, I want nothing to do with it."

She turned, stomped up the steps, rammed her key in the door, and slammed it behind her.

I sulked to my car. As I pulled away I looked up at her apartment windows. Through tattered lace, hate-filled eyes peered down with a repeated warning to stay away. I drove off, defeated, but believing that there had to be a few innocent people who attended Calvin's church and knew nothing about his debauchery. I thought about Miss Boggs and how she had most likely spent her entire life dedicated to a madman and a ministry with no real regard for humanity. I prayed in earnest for those who still had a chance—to get out.

§

I did my best to quiet Dillon and Gracie's nightly sibling brawl so the two old ladies we lived with wouldn't think I'd raised a couple of heathens. After losing my temper and reprimanding my teenagers, I made tea and thought about calling Dixie, but dismissed it. Anxiety, my new loyal companion, followed me as I retired to our room to read the *Apartments for Rent* section in the newspaper. Nothing. Nothing I could afford. I beat my fist into a pillow, ashamed to see the small cloud of dust that rose in the lamplight. I was exhausted. My energy and constant hope, like my checkbook, were overdrawn.

July 1992
Temporary Housing

Andie

I suck at this. Saving for a rainy day was out of the question. All my days were rainy. The money Peter gave me paid bills, bought groceries, compensated a dentist to fix my loose tooth, and went to drivers' training fees for the twins. Probably another bad decision in light of my pressing financial status. The little porch got smaller and hotter in the summer's heat. The lack of air conditioning became maddening. The old ladies demanded more and more of my time, and the twins begged to stay with friends or Grandma Dixie. I had to get out by the end of the month. Even if it meant moving back to Salisbury.

I had two things going for me—free rent and no car payment. My sister had signed over the Honda as an early birthday present at the insistence of Dixie, who promised to give Caroline a "little extra money" from the sale of the house. Caroline then proceeded with plans to move into an apartment in Charleston with her girls. Dixie would never be free of needy, forever-pregnant Caroline. As much as they drove each other crazy, they fed off each other. There was no room in Dixie's life for my trials and tribulations, and I wondered if some of it had to do with the fact that Caroline was Bud's daughter, and I was not. What did it matter? My upcoming custody battle had ruined my plans to move to Charleston to live near my mother and Aunt Wylene. At least for the time being.

§

Dennis Dawson sold real estate and managed rental properties for low-income families. "It rents for three-seventy-five a month," he said to me on the phone. "We won't check your credit on this one. If you want to fix it up, feel free, but it's your dollar. No reimbursement."

All three houses he sent me to on the south side of High Point reeked of horrible smells: sour milk, cooking fat, and cat pee. Seas of dirty clothes, empty beer bottles, and leftover fast-food bags. A not-housebroken Chihuahua, tied to a bedpost, barked and bared its teeth. Rotting picnic tables, mangled bicycles, and rusted cars cluttered the backyards, along with a couple of pit bulls chained to a clothesline. Overall, the houses smelled like sewers. Disgusted with the way people lived, I got back in my car. I wasn't about to fix up another house whose tenant had left it a stinking mess beyond the capabilities of ordinary cleaning.

As poor as I was, I had limits when it came to housing my children. Driving out of High Point, the stately homes of Emerywood were a sharp contrast to the houses I'd just walked through. They were the homes of my dreams as a young girl. Landscaped yards and gardens, exquisitely decorated rooms, and the love of a faithful husband and fair-haired children to fill them. Stupid dreams, that's all they were, nothing more.

Finally, I found a winner in Kernersville. It wasn't pretty but it was clean and affordable, and Dennis was kind enough to waive the deposit. I'd been sweet to him. It wasn't until after I'd signed a three-month lease that he asked me out on a date. Politely I said, "No, thank you," as he handed me the keys and I smiled—sweetly.

I promised my twins I would work on getting them back into their school district, but at least Kernersville was better than the Grissoms' front porch. They agreed. So we said goodbye to Edna and Ada, packed up our few belongings, and moved into the tiny rental house on the edge of K'ville. I was hesitant to take the rest of everything I owned out of storage. Instead, I bartered a deal with Space Savers Storage and got my unit free for cleaning their offices once a week. That way I could take my time as my children and I adjusted to the little one-bedroom house that came "furnished."

The furniture was the kind used in motels, vinyl covered and uncomfortable. A rope strung off the back porch to a nearby tree served as my clothes dryer. The place had one small bedroom and a bathroom with no tub, just a shower stall and a toilet. We brushed our teeth in the kitchen sink. It would have to do. Gracie and I got the bedroom and Dillon won the pullout couch to himself. If the "roadhouse," as we named it, was cramped physically, it was cramped emotionally, too.

Our first night in the tiny house, I didn't sleep. I lay in my bed watching the shadows from the streetlight play across the ceiling, and the tree outside shiver in the wind. I listened to the rustling leaves and then to a dog moving on its chain. Far away, a truck geared down as it barreled up a hill. Loneliness had curled up beside me once again.

§

A September court date loomed over our heads, adding to our insecurities. Everyone was cranky. I had seen the last of my children's good moods for a while. Gracie's inclination to cloud up and cry whenever she got her feelings hurt played like a scratched Bluegrass record, and Dillon played his Pink Floyd tape over and over until all of us had become comfortably numb. Although the twins wrote and mailed letters to the Judge stating their desires to remain with me, the letters had apparently gone unread. I never heard a word from the Judge.

A new school created unwanted challenges for Dillon and Gracie. The only house they'd ever known had been taken from them, and their grandmother's house was now up for sale. Their world had been turned upside down, even though I fought desperately against insurmountable obstacles to keep their lives stable. I had kept more from the twins than they would ever know. We hoped the worst was over. But I knew it could always get worse.

At least there was a park across the street with basketball courts. A nice distraction for a fifteen-year-old boy with tons of energy and angry at the world. It seemed the teenagers of the '90s all owned video games. I didn't know the first thing about them, and my children didn't bother to ask for a luxury they knew their mama could not afford.

§

Dillon and Gracie kept their visits with Joe to a minimum. He had all the benefits of church pity, being the cast-off parent. He'd once boasted he was the lucky parent without the pain and suffering of raising children. Gracie didn't understand. "So why the custody battle?" she asked. Of course, I knew why and the slightest possibility of it scared me to death.

I'd always been the better parent, raising my children on my own. Surely a judge would see my dedication. That thought and the voices of my children was all that kept me sane in the coming weeks.

I heard that Joe and Selma had moved into a modern condominium in a new, picturesque suburb of Winston-Salem, not far from the church. I lay on my bed and rubbed my eyes, watching the wind push the curtains out from the window like a big belly. The afternoon heat should've made me sleepy, but I wasn't. I had to be at the truck stop in an hour. My unblinking eyes stared up at the blown-on, lumpy ceiling. We had settled in the best we could. It wasn't home, but it kept the rain off.

November 1992
TAKE MY LIFE

Andie

Winter came early. I dreaded the twins' birthday and Christmas. Happy families forced me to remember that I had none. *If I could stay away from everybody's kids, I'd be fine. If I could shed the memories. If I could just die in my sleep.*

I shut off the car. The air was soft and damp; the temperature hovered in the low fifties. Deliberately stopping a moment, I considered my mother's lawn. On a narrow residential street shadowed by tall trees, it contented me even in winter. The flowers wouldn't be back for months, the trees were skeletal, and the grass had become brown and dormant. But there was order. There was predictability. There was beauty and structure and energy. Considering everything I had lost, not a horrible thing to come home to.

Home. Something I no longer had. And there was a bid in on this one, this last home. An offer Dixie had accepted.

I slid the key in the front door and hauled my weary body inside. Chock full of antiques, the home my parents built together overflowed with security and elegance. Dixie would move some furnishings to Charleston and sell the rest. For her retirement, she said. Though Daddy declared himself King of his coop, Dixie had always ruled the roost. Aunt Wylene had filled the void and carried on the family traditions, left by Daddy. We had turned a corner; a new family chapter had begun.

So many years ago, I'd gone after the same brass ring my mother possessed, declaring to my family I would have it all someday. Someday.

My throat constricted. Well. I'd sure shown them.

At least my children weren't around to panic over, no trauma left to survive. Dillon and Gracie were gone. Only silence. What more could they do to me?

A shower of bills scattered across the entryway where they'd fallen from the mail slot. I picked them up. Most of them mine, I leafed through a few, then tossed the rest into the trash. What more could anybody do to me? The Federal clock on the wall ticked softly. It gave me chills, reminding me of Daddy's desperate attempts to breathe. The house was quiet. No one was home. I walked to the sunroom, sank into an overstuffed chair and closed my eyes. After the double shift I just worked, I couldn't say I even wanted to wake up in the morning. Dixie's note said she'd gone to supper with Wylene and Caroline and her girls to celebrate the sale of the house, and that they wouldn't have to vacate until the middle of January. We can enjoy the holidays together, the note said.

Sure, enjoy the holidays. Then where do I go?

I would lie, tell Dixie and Wylene I'd rented an apartment—had it all worked out—I'd stay in Winston-Salem, and work on getting my kids back.

That I was in line for a management position at The Pit Stop. I'd—be—just—fine. All lies. I wouldn't be fine. I'd never be fine again.

I could never move to Charleston, or anywhere else. I had to stay in town to take their calls, see my twins on supervised visitations.

I tried to absorb the judge's decision and piece together what had happened to me, thinking back to that black day only two months before. When the fist of God shook in my face once again.

§

At seven o'clock in the morning on September seventeenth, the sky changed from bright sun to smoke gray as a front moved in from the west. *Custody: one last hurdle to jump through, and then I'll find a way to go back to school and get a better job.*

As the kids slept, I drank my coffee and stood at the window gazing at the industrial neighborhood I had moved into. Our days usually began that way. I could hardly believe Dillon and Gracie were fast approaching sixteen. Gracie sprawled across the bed. A limp strand of hair covered her cheek. Smeared mascara under her eyes gave her a wild animal appearance. She'd been experimenting with Maybelline and Cover Girl the night before, attempting to master the art of eye makeup. There was a dance on Friday so she'd been preparing days ahead. Dillon's foot peeked out from under the covers. Their even breathing soothed me like one of Mavis's hymns.

Gracie had made the debate team in her new school, in spite of her new braces. Braces that Joe's dental insurance paid for. Braces he'd thrown a fit over when he found out he had to pay a large deductible. Braces that Dillon should've had, too, but didn't get.

Assured everything was going to be okay, I set a stack of buttered toast and a box of cornflakes, bowls, and spoons on the table. The tension of waiting for results of the debate team tryouts was over. Finishing my coffee at the table, I planned our celebration for that evening with pizza and our own family debate—should a certain set of twins get their driver's licenses for their birthday?

Already running late, I hurried to dress. Gracie and Dillon stirred from their beds. Ready for what would be my final battle with Joe, I told them to dress in the clothes I'd laid out for them. Their Sunday best.

Dillon complained his pants were too short. Gracie stumbled through the living room in her pajamas, flopped into our one and only chair, and batted her big blue raccoon eyes at me. Her hair a matted mess, she took deep breaths on the verge of tears. "What if that judge makes us live with Dad? I won't live with him! I'll run away, I swear."

"Gracie. Can't you see we're running late? That won't happen," I said.

My daughter's chin rested on her chest.

"Go wash your face! I want the judge to see how beautiful you are." I smiled at her. "Tonight we'll celebrate our victories and get pizza."

"B-u-t . . ." Her constant whining grated on my last nerve. "What if . . . if . . ."

"If a frog didn't hop he wouldn't bump his butt when he walked!" I felt a sudden twinge of uneasiness, and responded to her with humor instead of the panic that rose up in me like smoke from a smoldering fire. "Stop it, Gracie. Now get a leg up; we're late."

§

How foolish I'd been.

Judge Gina VanOrson severed my parental rights until such time as I successfully completed a rehabilitation program from unacceptable behavior with disreputable men, alcohol, substance abuse, and obtained employment that could support two growing children. Then she mentioned something about supervised visitation. It was ludicrous. I'd hardly been drunk more than two or three times in my life. And men? What men? What substance abuse? What?

The judge was clear. "While the decision is clearly in the best interests of the children, I'm certainly not a happy judge to have ruled in another mother being separated from her children. Even though Miss Oliver knows full well that according to the testimony of her pastor and various witnesses, she has brought her troubles upon herself. One cannot abuse drugs and alcohol and be a proper parent at the same time. Even with child support, Andie Oliver's small income cannot properly support herself and two teenagers. Children she has dragged from pillar to post. How did you plan to house these children on what you make?" The judge looked hard at me. "Why in the world would you put yourself and your children in such a situation?" she asked.

I blinked like a confused dog. I should've had an attorney. I should've borrowed the money from Aunt Wy. I should've gone after Joe for the spousal support he never paid. Shoulda, woulda, coulda. John Rossi's words came back to haunt me. *A judge in his pocket.* I had seen her in church, or at the Buffet—somewhere. I couldn't prove it, but something told me this was a judge Calvin Artury had in his hip pocket. Judges don't take fifteen-year-olds from their mothers, Dixie had said.

Dillon and Gracie stood outside the courtroom. An officer of the court was supposed to retain them at the door. But as soon he heard the verdict, Dillon slipped through at the first opportunity and ran toward the bench. "No! You can't give us to him and expect us to like it! He beats our mother. He nearly killed her last time, and I won't go! We won't go!"

Gracie followed. "Please!" she screamed. "Please, don't!"

The judge banged her gavel on her desk.

"Take my life!" I cried hoarsely, in a fit of hopelessness. "But don't, please don't take my kids!" My cry made no sense. Then again, none of it did.

But the sudden revelations of Joe's temper motivated the judge to require testing by court-appointed psychiatrists at our own expense. "You had a choice," Judge VanOrson admonished me as I sobbed while my children left the courtroom with their newly appointed Guardian ad Litem. "The pictures of you with these men do not lie. Miss Oliver, you need psychological counseling before you finish parenting these children. When I see you have been analyzed and fully treated by a board-certified doctor of psychiatry, I will consider reversing my decision. But not until then."

I sat in my car until the shock wore off. Until I could remember how to drive. Until I could remember the way home. Until I could put two words together and make them coherent. When I finally stepped through the door of my rented house, the question hit me like another boot to my head. *How the hell do I pay for a one hundred-dollar-an-hour psychiatrist?*

I picked up the phone and called Dan Blunden, left a message, and then collapsed on the linoleum. I'd walked into their trap with no defense. I'd foolishly believed I didn't need to waste what precious money I had on an attorney. Wanted to save it, instead, believing Joe didn't have a chance. Grief seized me by the scruff of the neck and wouldn't let go. I looked at my watch. Two thirty and still no word from my attorney who I couldn't afford to hire. "What the hell is he doing? Why doesn't he call me? These are my kids, for God's sake!"

Finally, the phone rang. "I'm so sorry, Andie," Attorney Blunden said. "You should've called me earlier." It was how he said my name that made the tear slip out. The first of many. It was too late. Too late to take my fight any further. He needed a retainer. A big one.

I had created a world of false optimism and blind ambition. I had, like Scarlett O'Hara, tried to find hope in an overworked field of weeds and radishes. I had failed. More times than I could count. I managed to dial Wylene's number. There was no answer, so I left a message. "Tell Dixie she was wrong." *Click.* I couldn't say another word. Sitting in the darkness, I replayed the court scene over and over. I had to stay sane for a few more hours. Dillon and Gracie were on their way home to pack. I would get to see them one last time.

Pictures. More damn pictures. Pictures of me and Hickey Gilbert drinking and kissing in his truck bed at an X-rated movie. Of Jasper Wenger kissing and fondling me in my driveway then walking into the garage with me in the middle of the night. Jasper, who had neglected to mention he'd joined the House of Praise—a short month before meeting me. A slick liar, Jasper, he testified against me, flat-out lied and said we'd used drugs the night he had sex with me. Drugs and alcohol.

They were the only moments of pleasure and passion I'd had in years. But my mistakes were made public. Documented and recorded and used to destroy me. What a *jasper* he truly was. The judge also passed to me a picture of some man whose name I couldn't remember. The two of us sitting together at a bar. The Purple Passion. They'd followed me more often than I'd realized, made me look like trash. In front of my children.

What frightened me the most was that Calvin suddenly had access to Dillon and Gracie. According to the judge and Joe's testimony, I was raising them to be agnostics. Unfortunately, I knew my twins were peacemakers. They'd never been rebellious teenagers. The cult would wear them down if they could get their hands on them for any length of time.

It was all my fault. I fumed and boiled over at the thought of Joe's infidelities over the years. Serious acts of adultery never brought up in court. I'd not been given a chance to talk about Joe or what was hidden away in my lockbox. Some of it—evidence that Joe and Calvin didn't even know I had. How dare they! But once again, it didn't matter. I'd been unprepared. Calvin's lawyers were ready for the kill. Paid in full by House of Praise money. And from the way it looked, conveniently displayed in front of a persuaded judge.

It was nearly dark before the Guardian ad Litem, her assistant, and a police officer drove Dillon and Gracie home to collect their things and say goodbye. My reasons for living were walking out the door with social workers. The damnable judge's final words to my children bore into my skull. 'Until your mother is well, it would be best to limit visitations. Give her the time she needs to seek professional help,' she'd said. I would be allowed two visitations a month in a room downtown under strict supervision but only when it was convenient for Joe as well. This galled me. My heart told me these weren't small children; they were smart teenagers who would find every opportunity to talk to me.

Heads down, the twins drug their feet out of the house. Gracie carried her bag and turned around for one more goodbye. I fell to my knees, as my legs could no longer hold the massive burden strapped to my back. Gracie dropped her bag, pulled out of the grip of the social worker and ran back for a final hug. Dillon followed her lead and the three of us embraced one last time. This final devastating blow was a knockout punch, taking my breath away.

I lay on that same spot on the floor all night until Wylene arrived early the next morning with Dixie. When Wylene pulled me toward her, I started to wail like I'd been doused with gasoline and set on fire. It began in the soles of my feet and worked its way through me. Wylene cradled me against her like a baby. "Andie." Her voice was soft. Rocking me slowly, she held me close while I cried my heart clean out of my chest.

I felt Dixie squat beside us, touching my face, my hands, and then she went to rubbing my hair. I moaned and wailed and cried until I had no oxygen left in my lungs, until my shoulders shook and my breath was shallow and panting.

They packed my things, which weren't much, into my car and moved me back into Dixie's house. Everything else remained in storage. I would stay with my mother until I could figure something out, save money, get an attorney. The fact that the judge mentioned she would consider reversing her decision upon my psychological evaluation, bought me a small measure of hope. But there was very little fight left in me.

§

Wylene blew through the front door followed by Dixie and the rest of the brat pack, laughing and excited about their move to Charleston. I excused myself and staggered up to my room. I opened a drawer in my nightstand and tossed back a mouthful of whisky, oblivious to the blast of heat traveling down my throat. I thought about dropping everything and hitting the road with my bottle of Jack Daniels and who-knows-where for a destination.

Surrounded by an empty bottle, an empty cigarette pack, an empty life, and what was left of my memories, I deteriorated in my room. Exactly what the monster prayed for. Calvin would spare no expense or influence to see that my children become indoctrinated into the House of Praise. He would consider it a major victory against the dark angel. Dillon and Gracie Oliver, his own personal trophies. I should have been a better mother; I should have put the needs of my children first instead of my own hopes and dreams that kept pushing me forward and then holding me back; making me hang on to what wasn't there in the first place. I had followed every hope and dream around like the poorly paid convenience store clerk I had become, begging for a break.

I crept down to Daddy's study while the inhabitants of the house slept. Curling into his recliner with another bottle of Jack, I slugged it down as if it were Diet Coke. My eyes burned. I rubbed the right one with my shoulder, then switched on the TV and went to work on emptying the bottle. A calm washed over me as the warm booze slid down and coated my insides. I blinked and tried not to think about my children but the thought of their faces would not go away.

A drop of liquid splashed onto my hand. I looked down at the fallen tear. Remarkably, I hadn't felt them roll down my cheeks and didn't bother to wipe them away. I screamed out with the pain and agony I'd tried hard to bury since the last day I saw them. "I'm sorry! Oh, Gracie . . . Dillon. I'm so sorry!"

A public service announcement blared in my ears. I nearly choked. *It is now eleven o'clock. Do you know where your children are?*

I stood and swayed slightly with a single thought; I knew I could stand there and gaze and do nothing—or lose it. For years, insanity hung around my neck like a talisman, dangling just above my heart until finally, it landed on it. I heaved the bottle at the TV. It shattered. Glass, booze, and my life flew in every direction.

February 1993
THE BARREL'S BOTTOM

Andie

A year to the day Daddy died, Dixie said her good-byes, good riddance, and farewells to Winston-Salem. She visited her husband's grave and then walked through her empty home one last time before she kissed me and made me promise to call her when I settled into my new place.

Caroline had moved earlier to her new Charleston townhouse. One that Wylene had set up for her. Wylene had made the statement that my survival skills were much better than Caroline's. Whether true or not, I was happy for my sister. Maybe she'd find a new husband to take care of her because somebody would have to do it, and I hoped it wouldn't have to be Wylene forever. I couldn't complain too much about Caroline when Wy had consistently been my financial back up as well. "I can refer you to a good psychiatrist, Andie. I'm sure I can get him to knock the price down a bit if you want to go that route, do what the Judge said to do. Of course, the court will have to approve of my choice."

"Not this time, Wy." Even at a reduced hourly rate, any psychiatrist was more than I could afford. I needed to find a place to live first, so to ease her mind I smiled and said, "I'll let you know. Just take care of Dixie." My mother had lost a few more of her marbles after the court system scooped up the twins and stole them away. She refused to talk about it, partially blaming me, I think.

"Not to worry, darlin'. I'll keep her busy with that ol' house of mine, cleaning and redecorating. She'll be in her element and I'll be the envy of the Women's Club of Charleston!" The good doctor wrapped her thick arms around me and gave me one of her bear hugs, squeezing hard enough to leave a few bruises. "You take care. You're stronger than you know. Don't worry about the twins. I grew up in a foster home, remember? You get on your feet first."

"Sure." My heart leaped into my throat, watching them prepare to leave. The big Mayflower truck, full of Dixie's antiques and furniture, was already en route to the Low Country house Wylene inherited over thirty years before. Charleston, birthplace of Wylene and Dixie, where they would live their remaining years. Together.

We embraced one final time and Aunt Wy shoved an envelope into my hand. I opened it. Five hundred dollars. It would help, for a while. I squeaked out a "thanks." Just one more amount to add to the list I owed her.

Dixie handed over her house keys to the realtor and closed the door for the last time. I couldn't bear to look back as I drove away. Tears trembled on my eyelids. I followed Wylene and Dixie to the interstate and watched them drive south.

Now what? Unbeknownst to my family, my Honda had become my home.

§

"Quit calling! I told you they're not here!"

"Joe, please. Let me talk to my son and daughter. Please."

"They can call you at work. You call me again, I'll get a restraining order."

"I'm not allowed personal calls at work, you know that! I've seen them one time since you took them from me. Once! You conveniently cancel every visit. When is it convenient for you? You make the appointment, I'll be there!"

"My schedule is as tight as it's ever been. Have you stopped to think the kids don't want to see you?"

"That's a lie and you know it!"

"Do I?"

"Why?" I cried. "Why are doing this? You never wanted them, why—"

"I have to go. I'm telling you one last time. Don't call here again. The twins can call you anytime they want. When I get back from my next trip, I'll try to squeeze in a visit. Until then, leave us the hell alone!"

§

I worked steady at the truck stop. It kept gas in my car and a little food in my stomach. I drove I-40 and I-85 with the sun rising or setting in my windows, skimming the outskirts of tobacco fields, suburbs, and small towns—me and my memories. Wherever I felt safe enough to park the car, I pulled over and slept, and then searched for cheap motels on the weekends.

By the end of March I still hadn't heard from the twins: how they were, or why they weren't calling. The Guardian ad Litem refused to tell me anything more than they had settled in with their father and were fine. *Bitch.* I had parked down the street from Joe's condo once to get a glimpse of them, but the gated community was well guarded and there was no way to drive into it without an invitation. After a few hours I left the area, feeling fully defeated.

All I could do was worry. *Were Joe and Selma kind to them? Did Selma give them a nice sixteenth birthday party? How was their Christmas?* It was our first Christmas apart. The first Christmas I'd not bought them a gift. *Did Selma help Gracie with her hair?* Gracie's poker-straight hair needed special attention as it sprouted in odd directions every morning.

All of it drove me mad. I had no way of contacting them. Of course, the kids couldn't call me either. I wasn't permitted phone calls at work unless my boss was gone. And I had no address. No regular access to a phone. But every day I drove past the Magnolia Monarch Apartments and read the sign. *Efficiencies. Rent by the week. No credit check.*

The Gerbers had sold my house on Turner Street. The new owners had taken down my pretty lace curtains and installed blinds in the living room, which were always closed. I drove past, straining to see inside, recalling something Aunt Wylene once said. *Every ten years in a woman's life, everything turns itself inside out until you can't recognize shit.* I didn't understand it at the time but her remark came alive as I drove past familiar landmarks, including where Oak Hill Cafeteria used to be. The restaurant and the buildings around it had been leveled into a blacktop parking lot for Baptist Hospital. The apartment over the drugstore where the Darwoods had lived was also torn down. I'd lost touch with Henry and Vernise Darwood. They were as any other I had loved, a fleeting acquaintance I would remember fondly. I drove past my parents' house, now owned by another comfortable couple. Children played in the castle tree house and a big collie dog chased a bird in the front yard. *Daddy would be happy if this family loved his house as much as he did.* Everything around me had gone through a metamorphosis. Except for the constant struggle to provide for my children, nothing was the same.

§

As much as I hated the House of Praise, I drove my Honda in the direction of the church and the vast grounds that included the television studios and huge office complex adjoined by the enormously popular Praise Buffet.

The hours passed as I sat in my parked car across the street from the TV studios that towered twelve stories into the sky. The sun reflected off the windows, blinding me. I lowered the visor and slipped on Gracie's too-small sunglasses. Every half-hour I got the urge to slip inside the studio and find Joe but then I'd think of his wedding ring. I was not only his ex-wife, I was an enemy of the church. They'd not allow me to step one foot inside. I pulled a cigarette from my pack of Carltons and lit it. Blowing a line of smoke out the window, I raked my ringless hand back and forth across the dash and wondered just what the hell I thought I was doing. Even if he was there, he had no intention of giving me a moment with Dillon and Gracie.

Two male employees walked from their cars toward the studio. Both stocky, like Daddy. I longed to see Daddy, have lunch at Ham's Restaurant in the smoking section, eat turkey Reubens, homemade chips with ranch dressing, and drink sweet tea.

At noon, small groups of House of Praise employees, some I recognized, walked outside. They stretched in the sun, then strolled to their discount lunch at the Praise Buffet. Calvin's inner circle was smartly dressed and every one of them, attractive. I let out a lungful of smoke in their direction. I'd never been a part of their church cliques. Three women in pretty dresses flirted with some of the men walking behind them. Most days I might've let myself feel homeless, childless, and worthless. That day, though, that day I felt almost superior to them, like Wonder Woman, like I could see through walls, jump long distances, and run like the wind, just from living hand to mouth.

Inhumanly alone, agitated and restless, I found myself chain-smoking until my throat was raw and sore. I inhaled the last of my Carlton and mashed it out in the overflowing ashtray. I put my key into the ignition and forced myself to think about a place to park for the night. My mouth was parched, and my breath, foul. I didn't care. Once I thought I'd never put a cigarette to my lips again. Those thoughts seemed suddenly foolish.

After another twenty minutes, my mind felt like a battering ram at my skull. My body ached from sitting up, awake, all night long. I eyed every vehicle that drove into or pulled out of the church lot. No Joe. I hated him, and maybe I would run him over if I saw him. But I longed for my twins, a home, and a family. I felt dizzy and pulled into the street without looking. A car swerved, missing me by a short foot. It didn't phase me in the least. Not even when the driver laid on his horn. I pretended not to hear as I sped away.

I was deathly sick of living in my Honda, sick of searching the highways and the hedges for a place to park so I could sleep. At night, icy fingers crept inside the car—menacing cold that crawled over my skin. I was sick of freezing, having to wake periodically through hours of darkness, turn on the car for a little heat, then turn it off to save gas. Sick of taking whore baths in gas station restrooms and washing my hair in dirty sinks. And it was tough to get out of a car to pee in the cold and dark, wherever I was parked. Once in a while, I was lucky enough to be at a rest area, but most nights a clump of bushes by the roadside served as my toilet. I tried to park in safe well-lit areas, but it became tougher to care. I woke every day to early-morning mist covering my skin and impaling my bones, knowing that at least the rest of me was stowed safely in a storage unit across from the Magnolia Monarch Apartments.

There was nothing to do but worry. Once I sat in the public library for a whole weekend pretending to read. I rested there, dozing on and off until a man in dirty plaid pants and bulbous-toed disco shoes pulled out his wormy penis and waved it at me. "What do you want me to do? Scream? Follow you home? What?" Nothing about the male population surprised me at that point. I stood and walked past him, shaking my head. "Find a better hobby," I said. I never went back to the library.

The day was passing me by. After an hour of driving around and using up what little gas I had left, I drove to Space Savers Storage, pulled in front of my shed, and sat staring at the number on the door. Q13. I considered renting another room at the Pinewood Inn with a color television and a remote. That way, I could lie on the bed, watch game shows and fantasize about winning a million dollars. Make a list of everything I would buy with it. Order pizza and drink beer until I was so drunk I couldn't remember my name. Write checks; blow through what little money I'd earned at the truck stop. Not think about tomorrow. Or next week. Lie on that bed and fade away, just like Daddy did. I didn't want to find another job. I wasn't an alcoholic or a drug addict, I wasn't addicted to men, and I sure wasn't crazy. I just wanted my kids back.

I drove out of the storage area and stopped my car at a red light. I knew I'd gotten my hopes up of seeing Joe and working something out to see Dillon and Gracie. For five minutes even, before he took them to church. At least once a week. I didn't want them around Calvin, but I was no longer in control. What would I say to Joe, anyway? "Congratulations on your new condo, I'm destitute and living in my car, but hey—you certainly look great."

I peeled out without waiting for the light to change.

I thought about calling Aunt Wylene. No, I couldn't change my mind on that. Wylene had her hands full with Dixie, and also with Caroline. My sister and her girls were five extra people on Aunt Wy's plate she had to worry about. Six after she delivered Caroline's next baby. A boy, I heard. At least Caroline was smart enough not to marry the new baby's daddy.

And my mother was spending money again. "It's going though her hands like water," Aunt Wy said on the phone. I was sure Caroline was helping her spend it. Wylene attributed it to their grieving process. Whatever. I was sure the boutique shops and malls in Charleston had two new favorite customers. Wylene promised to keep Dixie and Caroline's spending to a minimum. Good luck with that was all I had to say.

And then I told Aunt Wy another lie. A doozy. I said my apartment was nice, but I still couldn't afford a phone. She asked for my new address and I said, "Off Stratford somewhere. I can't remember the apartment number or name of the place." I told her I'd call her with it later, not to worry. I was *fine, just fine*. More big, fat lies in a sea of thousands. I didn't even open a post office box: I wanted no mail. No more bills, bank statements, and possible leads to my whereabouts. No forwarding address for creditors or predators.

Asking Ray and Libby for help was out of the question. I owed them enough. And no matter how I cut it, they were still Olivers. Shunned by the rest of the Olivers, that left only Lula. But Lula was nursing a sick husband in Birmingham. I hadn't heard from her since Daddy died.

I had no one. And for the first time ever, there was no one to turn to, talk to, or even ask for a free bed for the night. Not even Coot. He and Candace had moved to Nashville. Even the Grissom sisters had sold their home and moved into assisted living quarters.

Nobody could reach me. Not a soul knew where I was when I wasn't at work.

My car slowed itself and without thinking, I headed north to the Dumass farm. I had no idea what I would do once I got there. Driving past tobacco fields, small dried-up yards still struggling from the winter, and clapboard houses that needed a new coat of paint, my throat felt scratchy again and my eyes burned a little. I lit another cigarette and cracked my window, driving past the *For Sale* sign at the end of the long driveway that led to the dilapidated farmhouse once occupied by the Dumass family.

I turned the windshield wipers on high; the afternoon downpour started as it had every day for the past week. Turning off the radio and stopping the car, I felt the pain of loss tighten in my chest, and hesitated before walking to the gravesite. The gold plating on my microphone key chain had worn off years ago. The chain clicked with the sound of the hammering rain, swaying in time with the wind outside. The sound triggered a memory within me, like the rapidly fading echo of Daddy's clock over his deathbed and a few of his last words, "avenge us all." I'd always known some decisions alter the road in your life and others don't. It was then when one of those life-changing decisions pressed in on me. The pain inside my chest let me know my life had disintegrated to that moment. I glanced at the now-motionless keys. "*Unconditional love, Andie. Hold tight to it, and nobody, not even Calvin Artury, can destroy you.*"

Locked in my stifling, airless Honda, twenty years of unrelenting memories floated around me like flies on road-kill. I had lost it all. They'd stolen what meant the most to me in the world. My throat closed and my breath grew short. They meant to break me, and were doing a damn good job. But I had one last card to play. Switching off the engine, I stared at the key ring closely, as if trying to remember something that passed quickly through my mind several times throughout the years, yet knowing that pondering it further would be like pulling the thread again. Further unraveling my life.

The cooling engine ticked. I leaned back and closed my eyes, whispering the obvious truth, the truth I had turned my back on. "How many lives will he destroy until you do something about it? It's up to you, you idiot. When will you come out of your stinking coma?" My heart raced; I felt my pulse in my neck. It was difficult to breathe. To swallow. To think.

I pulled the keys from the ignition and gazed at the old farmhouse. The place had a disheveled appearance, pebbled and weedy. In the distance, the graves remained surrounded by a now weathered and peeling picket fence. *Picket fence.* I sighed. Tall grass and wild flowers grew around the headstones, their spindly necks reaching toward the hope of sunlight above the rain clouds. A strong gust of warm wind whipped my hair around as I forced myself out of the car and made the slow ascent to the gravesite.

Mammoth pines towered across the ridge. A scattering of faint images came to me out of nowhere. A little boy from a lifetime ago played near the site. Why? It was Mavis's resting place, after all. *Brian. His name was Brian.* I straddled the little fence, and then on bended knees I pulled a few weeds and brushed dirt from the grassy graves that had not been tended since Rupert died. I stood and the soaked earth pressed up through my shoes.

Stiff breezes whistled through the pines that surrounded a giant oak locked inside the fence to stand guard over the graves. The sky grew more threatening. Dark clouds changed shape every few seconds. I shook my head and dropped to my knees again; maybe I *was* crazy. A voice echoed over the tobacco field, as another gust of wind rushed up through the pines. *He killed Mavis.* It startled me.

The wind whispered more names. Names of the dead. Names that had battled the monster in life. Names the monster had devoured.

Ted Oliver, John Rossi, even Vivi Artury.

"Vivi?" I repeated.

Yes, the wind whispered. *Even Vivi. And Bud. Shall I go on?* The wind paused.

"No," I answered the wind. I stood with renewed strength, wiped my eyes and gave my head a swift shake. On the crest of the sacred hill, the wind preceding the worsening storm blew through my hair and clothes. A single sun ray sliced through the dark clouds, piercing the air with golden-yellow and white light. Suddenly another great stretch of sunlight broke free. Explosions of light, one after the other, split the Heavens open and rolled over the landscape. God had uncurled His fist and extended His fingers to shoot streams of pure radiance out of the clouds and touch the white picket fence where I stood. It took my breath away.

I don't remember how long I stood there before the clouds smeared the bruising colors of war overhead, erasing the light. Drops of rain hit my face when finally I came to myself and picked up my key chain. I had witnessed something achingly and overwhelmingly beautiful. God, in His own way, had spoken to me.

I brushed dirt off my rumpled coat and wiped away stray wisps of unwashed hair from my forehead. After straddling the fence, I walked briskly, purposefully to my Honda. Looking back at the graves one last time, I faced the turbulent skies. "Time to end it," I said.

It was my turn to prophesy. I made a simple vow.

To kill him.

Do As I Say

Andie

While I scribbled my resignation, something about leaving town, my boss asked for my forwarding address. A place to send my final paycheck. I gave him the address of my divorce attorney. A check for 350 dollars wasn't worth worrying about. If I was lucky, maybe the twins would get it eventually.

Night fell as I drove to the storage facility. The relentless rain made it difficult to see. *Q13 . . . there it is.* I winced getting out of my car as the rain bludgeoned my body; attacked me for being an unfit mother. I kicked the door open and started to dig through my stuff. Lamps, chairs, boxes and more boxes, bedroom furniture, the little black and white TV, Dillon's baseball glove, Gracie's books and board games, dishes and kitchen appliances, it all stared back at me, as if I'd lost my mind. I rooted through the memories. It made me sick to my stomach. The photo albums—I had to find them, and the gun—*where's Daddy's gun?* I knew how to shoot it. *Ah, bullets. They'll come in handy. And vodka, what box did I stash it in?*

On the way out I gave the supervisor the key to my storage unit and told him to sell everything in it. I couldn't clean his office or pay for the space any longer and had no way to dispose of its contents. I imagined my worldly possessions as income for some thrift store or garage sale. A source of comfort for the next needy woman's desire to design on a dime.

After stopping at a gas station, I bought a liter of Dr. Pepper and then drove up to the pay phone. Carefully cleaning the area on the dashboard where I had eaten my light supper of Twinkies and a bag of chips, I composed a script for my phone call to Joe.

Taking one last deep breath, I felt a great weight lift from my chest. Killing Calvin was a drastic step, but it was the only possible protection for Dillon and Gracie. I had lost everything and would end up in prison but it'd be worth it to save my children from a madman. Waiting two years, until they were of legal age when they could come back to me on their own would do no good. It'd be too late. I knew all too well the mental pull and brainwashing of Calvin. By then, I would have lost them to the church. I had no choice.

I flicked a few specks of dirt off my knees as the calm after the storm entered my soul. There was no hope left. A new husband would tire of my baggage and kick me to the curb, or begin his own cycle of abuse. I could survive without needing anyone's help and perhaps someday find a degree of happiness, but any way I looked at it, it was fleeting. I couldn't live like that and suicide was not an option. But if I had to live, then he had to die. He had swallowed my family whole and I was determined to have the last word. Even with a future behind bars.

For decades the monster had handpicked each unsuspecting soul to fulfill his fantasies. Money meant power, and power brought fame and control over any man or woman, boy or girl, of his choosing. He had allowed Evan Preston to create a Mafia, making it easy for him to enter into his own cruel and perverted indiscretions. He wanted Dillon, and possibly Gracie. The monster wasn't getting what he wanted.

They would find any means possible to discredit my story and destroy my evidence. They would use any method to prove I was a liar, but once Calvin was dead, what did it matter? Dillon and Gracie would be safe. That's all I really wanted.

I might as well be drunk when I call him. I took a long pull on the vodka bottle and wiped my mouth on my coat sleeve. Scooting to the passenger seat, I dialed Joe's number. I had to concentrate, the number was already fading from my memory.

It rang only once. "Joe?"

"What the hell are you doing calling me again? What do you want?"

"I need to talk you. Give me just five minutes, please. It's important."

"You got one. Hurry up, I'm on my way to the studio."

"Tell Calvin we need to meet. Just him and me."

Joe laughed. "Why would he meet with *you*? God, Andie. Calvin Artury is the most watched and beloved televangelist in the world. Haven't you listened to the news lately? We beat the numbers in Billy Graham's last crusade. President Bush attends our services in Washington, D.C., along with half the Christian Coalition. People love Calvin Artury, and nothing you do can hurt him. He won't meet with you."

Indifferent, I smirked. "I don't have a TV, Joe. I don't care how big everybody thinks he is. He's pond scum to me. Tell him this. Tell him I'm living in my car. I'm at the bottom of my barrel. The end of my rope. Tell him I don't give a damn anymore. I'm prepared to expose him unless I get what I want."

"Are you drunk?" The acid in Joe's voice came across loud and clear.

Driven to a whole new level of rage, I felt it course through my body, a violent scraping on the inside of my skin. "I got proof. I know who killed John Rossi. I saw it. I was there. I watched Evan pull the trigger and Silas Turlo was with him. I'm the caller the police looked for, begged to come forward. I can give them details. Peter Collins gave me videotape on his way out of town. I've no idea what's on it, but I'm sure it's good. Oh, and by the way, I still got all the pictures and negatives and the letter from Mavis. I'm sure he had her murdered. And when I broke open the shed that day you beat the hell out of me, I took pictures of all of it. The money, too. I got all the evidence I need, Joe. I know all about the church's illegal activities. I have evidence to put Calvin away. And a few others. Maybe even you."

Joe's voice slowed, his intention to cut me off—gone. "Okay. What do you want?"

"Certainly not you." It was my turn to laugh. "I want Calvin. Alone. I want him to meet me alone."

"Andie, I demand you tell me what you want from him!"

"You . . . cannot . . . demand anything from me! I'm not telling you ANYTHING ELSE, JUST TELL HIM TO DO AS I SAY!" I blasted into the phone. "I'm not explaining myself to an ex-husband living in a beautifully decorated condominium with a scrawny wife. I heard Calvin allows Selma to travel with you now. Sleep in the same hotel room. Probably to keep you faithful, right? How dare you make demands sitting there with plenty, even if it is bought with dirty money. You kept me in trailer-trash hell for seven years and doomed to poverty the rest of my life. It was ME, not Selma, who did all the sacrificing and risk-taking so you could party for weeks at a time with Calvin, you son of a bitch! Besides, they can't make threats to a woman who lives in her car."

My head hurt most every day. I was dehydrated, my bowels were a mess, I was sick with grief, and I hadn't had a shower, changed my clothes, washed my hair, or brushed my teeth in over a week. Delirium stalked me as I lost track of time.

"Calm down. I'm sure we can work this out."

"I'm not working out a thing with you, you fucked-up moron! I want to talk to Calvin, alone!"

"Let me pray on this, okay?"

"Well, after you *pray* on it, call your attorney. You're going to need one."

"Okay, when do you want to see Reverend?"

"As soon as possible."

"Listen, Andie, I swear to Almighty God, he's on his way out of town. He's probably in the air right now. He won't be back in Winston-Salem until next month. I'm leaving tomorrow myself. Trip to Zimbabwe. The church bought a jet. A 747 to travel the world and save the lost. It was the last prophecy God gave, through Reverend Artury, to be fulfilled before Jesus comes back. The rapture will take place soon. You know that. Why don't you give your heart back to the Lord?"

"Yeah, seems I read that somewhere in the Bible. Something about Calvin getting a big-ass jet in the end-times. Grow some balls, Joe. God never said that." I laughed.

"You never believed, did you?"

"I believe that you and Calvin stole my life. I believe Calvin and his mob are pedophiles, murderers, and God knows what else! And I believe Calvin wants to devour our children and you're willing to sacrifice them. That's what I believe, you sick, twisted, sack of shit!"

Silence.

"Dillon and Gracie, they're doing well, you know. Do you want to see them? I'll set it up," he said softly.

I hesitated and clamped my hand over my mouth so he wouldn't hear me cry. "Tell them I love them," I squeaked out. I couldn't take the chance.

"Sure, Andie, sure I will." He stalled for time. I heard him breathing hard.

"Tracing the call? I'm at a pay phone, you idiot."

"Andie! Listen to me! You can't make threats like this! You can't see him alone! They'll kill you! Reverend is worldwide. Untouchable. You saw John die; you *know* what they'll do to you. Do you want Dillon and Gracie to be without their mama?"

"What do you care? You took them away from me." I lit a cigarette and took a long drag. "Strange, seeing how you never wanted them to begin with. So tell me now. What day does the murdering, boy-fucking bastard get back? And you better fucking tell me the truth, or I swear to God I'll find you. You've seen me shoot, Joe. You know I don't miss," I said through a plume of smoke.

"He's due back on April 6, early in the morning. What are you planning?"

"Nothing unless he doesn't show up. I need to talk to him."

"What if he refuses? I can't guarantee he'll—"

"I'm only saying this one time! Tell Calvin to meet me alone. At noon on April 6. Meet me at Tanglewood Park, by the tennis courts. Rain or shine. They're busy all the time and wide open. I'll wait exactly five minutes. If he doesn't show up, every bit of evidence I've got has been duplicated several times. It's packed up and ready to go to TV stations, newspapers, and more than one police department and judge. I'm going to nail him, Joe, nail him to his own cross unless I get what I want."

"Andie, please, what is it you want? You want the kids back?" he asked, softening.

I want him dead. "I'll tell him when I see him," I said.

"Okay, Tuesday, April 6 at noon, Tanglewood Park, tennis courts. I'll tell him."

"Right. And, Joe?"

"Yes, Andie?"

"First man or woman I see from the House of Praise, between now and the time I talk to Calvin, the packages get mailed." I slammed down the phone.

Nothing had been duplicated. I couldn't afford to duplicate anything. I didn't even know how or where to start. But they didn't know that. Not for sure. I planned to let my attorney clean out the lockbox before my murder trial. Once Calvin was dead, who'd care anyway? Fuck them all. I pulled into the Magnolia Monarch apartments, parked in the back, and rented an efficiency apartment for the month. I had enough money to last until April 6. And then it'd be over.

Reverend Calvin Artury

I massaged the back of my neck feeling Evan's glare. My exhausted body wanted to be any place other than locked inside a plane with Evan and Silas. At 63 years old, I worked harder than any televangelist in history. Parting seas, moving mountains, and blazing trails into nations barely touched by the Gospel, I'd perfected the efforts of my competitors. Like Moses, I had to remind myself to *stand still and see the salvation of the Lord!*

It was my appearance that suffered. I had traded in my recent baldness for a beautifully coiffed toupee matching the blondeness of my youth, but there was nothing I could do about my sagging chin, save surgery. And who had time for surgery? Age was a downer, but I still found plenty of youthful energy when I hit the pulpit. The strength of Jehovah-Jireh! The Lord our Provider! My faith in God provided me with power from On High to withstand the long services. So on the trip to Zimbabwe, I had hoped to relax. Instead, I sat in an emergency meeting at 3,700 feet.

"She's bluffing!" I crossed my legs and laughed.

"I don't think she is, Reverend." Evan cleaned his Ray-Bans then placed them back on his head, gazing at the clouds below and then back at me.

"I'm not cowering to the wishes of that tramp! I did it when Mavis was alive: I'll not be blackmailed by white trash!" My voice thundered throughout the cabin as I intended.

By the time my private jet had stopped in Atlanta for business before heading to Africa ahead of the team, a frantic Joe had tripped all over his tongue in an effort to reach me. Evan intercepted the call and found the entire House of Praise office staff and ministry team riled up and speculating about a possible attack on the ministry.

Evan removed a notepad from his pocket and pulled off a pen cap with his teeth. "Get Joe on the phone again when we land, Silas. I want to make sure he's cooled down before the team boards the 747. I don't want him spilling his guts about this."

If my voice was the thunder, my eyes flashed with lightning. They bore into Evan. "So what do you suggest we do now?"

"We have to do something about Oliver. He's got to go."

I laughed again, an explosive sound that shook my seat. "There's nothing wrong with Loverboy." Leaning back, I gazed out the window. "I've known him a long time." Quickly infected by the thought of him a curious moan escaped my lips. "I can get him to do anything just by throwing a beautiful woman into his lap. He's been with me since he was a kid, Evan, and he's been loyal. Done everything you've asked him to do. She almost got him, almost made him blaspheme God. I went to the edge to yank him back! The edge of Hell. I've never had such an experience with Hell as I had taking Joe from Andie. To this day, it still burns in my soul. Never in my ministry have I suffered so, felt the flames licking the soles of my feet. He was almost there. It's a horrific experience to know someone you love is so close to Satan's pit, so close your own body burns as you grab him, rescue him from a wife who has sold her soul." I folded my hands behind my head and stretched my legs in the wide seat.

Evan shrugged. "It's not easy taking care of business when your boss has visions."

I pretended not to hear his disrespect and peered over my sunglasses. "Did you say something?"

"I said Oliver can't concentrate. And now he can't keep his mouth shut. Wants everyone to see how important he is. He's created too many problems. Demanding Fannie get you on the phone. What an ass!"

"He knows the consequences of his actions. He also knows what will happen to him if Andie goes through with this." My eyes narrowed into ice-blue slits. She could've circumvented what was coming to her. She could've had a better life had she stayed true to the church. The reality was, I loved Andie. I always had. But she had avoided me from the time she was very young. Even though I orchestrated her marriage to Joe, my plans to bring her into the upper echelon of the ministry ended shortly after. She never knew how I felt because she had allowed herself to be taken over by Satan at a young age. Ahh, yes, as Lucifer was once loved by God and fell from grace, so was Andie Oliver loved by me, only to become my dark angel.

I had lost her, but God gave me something in return. Her children.

I glared at Evan. "I think she's still in love with him, that's why I say she's bluffing. She wants Joe and the kids back, that's all."

Evan returned my glare. "I disagree. It's bigger than that. It's *obvious* she knows everything. We have to eliminate her and whatever she's got as evidence. Right away. We should've done it when we took her kids away from her."

"We would have, except YOU didn't want it to look *obvious*, remember?"

Evan smiled. "I'll call DeSanto, have him send out a few of his men to look for her. She has to be in town. She won't be far from those kids. I'll get the description of her car she's living in and where she works from Joe; maybe her employer can cough up an address." Evan turned his attention to Silas and grinned. "Think Percy would like to make some extra money?"

Silas had been quietly chewing his toothpick. He looked hard at Evan and wiped his sweaty forehead with his hand. "My wife and I would rather you leave him out of this."

"Come on, Turlo. The boy's got more guts than anybody I've seen lately. Besides, we got him a pretty wife, didn't we? Wouldn't you love to see Percy advance in position? Sylvia loves her new daughter-in-law, doesn't she?"

Silas and Sylvia's new daughter-in-law was a dark-haired beauty, barely eighteen. Her family had attended the Rochester, New York crusade. Like a love-starved hound dog, Percy fell in love at that crusade. Since Percy had proved himself valuable in service to the Lord, I prophesied over the girl's family; that it was God's will for them to move to Winston-Salem. There's not a better perk than a divine one. The girl's family sold everything they owned and quit their jobs, but became destitute in North Carolina. It was, of course, the perfect scenario. Their only hope of survival was employment within my ministry. In return, they allowed their daughter to marry Percy Turlo. He got his girl. Of course, I paid for the enormous televised church wedding and Praise Buffet reception. No, the Oliver disaster was not a job for a brute like Percy. I needed a professional.

"I'm not in the mood to clean up after Percy again," I snapped. "No, Evan, this is a job for DeSanto and his people. Percy's good, but he's not an expert at this sort of thing."

Silas slumped backward in his seat, stuck his toothpick in his pocket and sighed heavily.

I needed a drink. "I think you're right, though. I believe Andie knows everything. Evidence that could bring us all down, including the ministry. You want that?"

"Of course not. I'll let DeSanto handle it his way. What if he can't find her?"

I thumped my hands on my chest, tilted forward, and stared straight into the eyes of my top brass. "*Watch ye therefore, and pray always, that ye may be accounted worthy to escape all these things that shall come to pass.* You two better hope he finds her before I get back to the States or I guess I'll have to go play tennis at Tanglewood Park on April 6. With Andie Oliver."

If God Be For Me

Andie

He deserved to die. On the first night in my rented basement efficiency at the Magnolia Monarch, I sat and plotted his last breath. Dropping to my knees beside a mattress covered with greasy sheets discarded by a former tenant, I pushed the gun to the side of the bed. My fingers landed on a photograph. A white beach shaped like a crescent moon surrounded by an azure sky reflecting onto an ocean as smooth as sapphire glass. A string of tropical hotels banked the beach. A young woman with honey blonde hair and a man with sad eyes lounged on a straw mat, arms locked together. Printed neatly on the corner—*Andie and Joe, Hawaii 1987*—words now surreal. I stared at the snapshot.

Flies swarmed the overflowing dumpster outside my door. A multitude had made their way inside the airless room and tickled my skin as they fluttered over my pale legs. A rusted refrigerator with no handle vibrated next to a stove that had most likely seen its last scrubbing in the 'seventies. The stale scent of cigarette smoke rose from the floor where butts had been swept into corners, and the pungency of urine reeked from the tiny bathroom. Gold napless carpet bore the stench of feet from years of poor tenants. But the smell from the dumpster seeped in and filled the entire room.

A roach wiggled out of a fist hole punched into the fake paneling. The walls dripped with mold and mildew. There was no closet, just an old set of drawers with chipped paint and holes from a TV bolted to the top a lifetime ago.

The room was soaked in a sooty, vague darkness, and my eyes strained to adjust. I stood and opened the draperies once gold, now faded and water-stained. Dust flew into the air. There was no lamp. Just an overhead fluorescent I couldn't bear to switch on. But the dump was cheap, and I could rent it by the month.

I surveyed my remaining possessions. I'd brought all I had left to that foul-smelling hellhole: photograph albums, the blue crocheted afghan, a few clothes, toiletries, a pair of shoes, a liter of Dr. Pepper, and a loaded gun.

I lit my last cigarette then picked up my .380 automatic. *He needed killin'*—a valid defense in the South, my daddy always said. I figured Hell'd be worth it to see Calvin's face as I pressed the gun to his head. The world would be a better place with one less televangelist.

Moving to the edge of a metal folding chair, I sat wrapped in the afghan as the sun moved behind the drapes. Shadows crawled about the room. One of them belonged to me. The dark silhouette of my body dragged across the wall, inch by inch, stretching me into a brutal abyss.

I could hardly wait for April 6 because I had come to the end of it. There were no safe places. I unclenched my hands and looked down at a crumpled note I'd written to myself as if, in the dim light of dusk, I could read the words on the paper: "Only monsters kill." Would I be one if I killed one? I released the air I hadn't realized I was holding in my lungs. The room's stench overtook me once again. The urge to just stop breathing settled on my chest like an anvil. A peculiar quiet passed through me. It expanded from the center of my body. I wanted to speak and put the world in motion, but couldn't find my voice. I felt suspended in the silent room, as if drowning in a deep well. My voice had dwindled to nothing, and I pressed my palm flat against my heart, checking for a beat. Possibly I *had* died and gone to Hell.

A poem filtered through my head, surfacing and then vanishing. A poem, half remembered. Something about strong women. Blurred words at the far end of the long corridor in my memory. Words that seemed almost liquid, or smoke. There, but fleeting. The body of the poem beyond my reach.

Perhaps another hour passed, maybe three. Suddenly, it was as though I'd been given the gift of sight. I looked down at my crusty feet, at the pants I'd worn for a week; I could smell myself. Disgusted, I wiped tears from my dirty cheeks with both hands and shoved my matted hair behind my ears. I pulled Daddy's old family Bible from under the stack of photograph albums, traced the words, and choked out a desperate laugh. *If God be for us, who can be against us?*

The room sank into darkness. I sat for some time and then said to God with all the sincerity I could find within me, "I've been told my whole life— great is Your faithfulness. Where is Your faithfulness to me?" It struck me suddenly that contrary to what I'd been brought up to believe, the prayers of the spotted, the wrinkled, and the flawed never made it past the gates of Heaven. That quite possibly Calvin was right. God had finally turned His back to the cries of the damned.

PART SEVEN

And The Spirit Of God Moved

BEHOLD, I STAND AT THE DOOR AND KNOCK

Andie

Another night. The same old nightmares. The sorrowful sound of the wind. The roar of big city traffic. Dense, gray rain. A black car on shimmering pavement. The fright in Mavis's voice. A never-ending scream. The horror of silence. Children torn from their mother. Men who prey upon loneliness and stupidity. Endless phone calls from collection agencies.

Night terrors.

I woke tangled in sheets, sweaty and alone. I should've known my nightmares would follow me to that place.

I pulled myself up and drank warm Dr. Pepper, yearning for someone to love me, someone who could empathize with my aging body. Sick and exhausted after a fitful sleep, I thought how nice it would be to talk to another person—a steady, quiet, reassuring loved one. To share a recipe, discuss the weather, chat about the latest styles. Conversations I once took for granted. Instead, I sat in the muted morning sun and missed Dixie and Aunt Wy, longed for the swish of their clothes, the touch of their fingers on my forehead, in my hair. The faint scents of their perfume; the sheen of their clean skin in stark contrast to my own. I closed my eyes and pictured their child-like grins, felt their sense of fun and play, and the comfort of their presence. Their existence remained only in my memory as I rested my head against the wall.

I shoved back the blue afghan that once belonged to Mavis. The unfamiliar apartment had fallen silent. I didn't make a sound as I pulled on my wrinkled clothes. A bottle of shampoo, a bar of soap, toilet paper, a toothbrush, and a hairbrush sat in the bathroom, but makeup and clean clothes were a forgotten luxury.

I dispensed with a shower that morning, and with brushing my teeth or looking at my hair. *Good enough.* I crawled off the mattress and walked through puddles of fly-plagued sunlight streaming through filthy windows and an ocean of dust.

The quiet morning was a severe contrast to the nighttime sounds from the apartments around me. At night I left the window air conditioner running for some relief from the shouting, slamming doors, screaming kids, drunken adults, loud stereos and TVs. Only early in the morning did the place fall into a silent stupor.

Pausing by the window, I strained my eyes and searched for my car. I had parked it behind the apartments next to a few mangled grocery carts stolen from a nearby Food Lion. The car would soon succumb to an ancient carburetor; I had no spare funds for repairs. The mechanic just shook his head. "About a week, probably; hard to find anyone who still rebuilds 'em. But a rebuild . . . that'll cost you." I remembered my daddy working on his carburetor. "Runs like a champ," he'd say after he finished. I missed him. He'd fix my carburetor. He could fix anything, except maybe my life. *Not that he didn't try.*

The same day I moved into the apartment, I'd sold my Honda for next to nothing to a sixteen-year-old boy with a new driver's license. I knew Calvin's goons would scour the city for my car. They would kill me if they found me. I'd given a false name to the landlord at the Magnolia Monarch. When he asked for identification, I told him I'd lost my driver's license. He just winked at me and said, "Okay. Whatever." Time to hide. Just a month. No more calls to Dixie and Wy.

In the end, an old Pontiac provided my escape. A mangled trunk lid, a half-dozen crimps here and there, and patches of rust on the doors. The beater car had started; one hundred dollars cash for the 1980 Bonneville with two hundred thousand miles. No title, no license plate. I didn't want one. Wouldn't need one. I'd go out and start it from time to time. I'd take my chances and drive it one last time—to my rendezvous with Calvin at Tanglewood Park on April 6.

After brushing away dead flies and live spiders on the windowsill, I rested my chin on my arms and gazed at the forlorn car. My dreams had completely unraveled. *Truth, Andie. Tell the truth.* Pushing past the panic in my throat, the truth came out choking me. "The dream never began."

My new residence sat unceremoniously in a field of weeds, where the sharps of thorn thickets and scrawny pines snagged plastic bags and wet newspaper. Low-income housing. A row of wood-clad apartments. The ones underneath, like mine, being the cheaper basement efficiencies. The weathered length of the two-story building was a faded relic of unfulfilled dreams. Its exterior fading and falling away in mass, its windows broken, its doors gouged and stained from years of use. Laundry and plastic chairs bedecked the railings. The lawns were worn to a few stretches of unmowed weeds and dirt. In the front by the office, an in-ground pool had cracked and dried up and was strewn with dead leaves and somebody's old shoe.

I peered into the distance for the interstate truck stop. I'd surprised myself, how easily I could quit my job. Working afternoons and nights at The Pit Stop was no rewarding career although it had fed me, kept me going. I sure didn't miss its searing whitewash of fluorescent lights and weary travelers with bloodshot eyes, seeking gasoline, a restroom, and coffee to keep them awake. Like ghosts in the night—their origins and destinations were unknown. Some nights it was as though the truck stop and I existed on an unmapped highway to immortality. At least until the sun came up.

Three more weeks of waiting. Waiting for my life's mission to begin and thankfully, end. April 6—a day of liberation. Every ounce of hope had faded to black. Hope for what? For his plane to crash? For him to die of a heart attack? For another miserable soul to pull the trigger instead of me? I wouldn't last that long. My patience, along with everything else, had worn to a frazzle. I stared into the morning light. *Prison will be worth it to see him dead. The madness will stop.* "And my children will be safe," I said out loud.

I thought maybe I'd take a taxi to Tanglewood Park. The landlord could sell the old Pontiac with the busted carburetor to cover my electric bill. I'd leave Mavis's old blue afghan on the mattress for the next poor tenant, and mail my photo albums to my attorney. I wouldn't need memories anymore, or an attorney for that matter. I'd plead guilty. With pleasure.

I opened my purse to check my cash. A twenty, two tens, a five, three ones and some change—a total of forty-nine dollars to last until April 6. I shoved the cash back into the zippered pocket, and collapsed to the mattress to nibble at a dry, deli-case cheese sandwich for breakfast. My stomach was in no mood for it. I'd lost my appetite, when, last week? Last year, maybe? Tossing it into the cardboard box I used for garbage, I couldn't remember good food. Food sat like a rock.

I'd quit smoking. There was no extra money for even cheap cigarettes.

My photo albums lay open. A picture of Dillon in a football uniform stared at me and I rubbed my thumb over it. My heart ached so bad I had to stand and catch my breath, as if I'd been dropped into the deepest end of a lake and needed to paddle quickly to the top. Hard to believe God blessed me with two beautiful children, and then allowed them to be whisked away and put into Selma's care. Selma, of all people. Not much older than Dillon and Gracie. A woman who never bore children and didn't want mine.

I closed the drapes and took another deep breath. Glancing down at the albums again, I saw the old photo of Mavis and me—pregnant with Brian, in the Baptist church parking lot; our arms wrapped tight around each other. I'd been silly to think we'd grow old together. Another snapshot of the twins playing along a path at some playground I'd taken them to when they were little. *I had a family once.* Every picture was a loathsome reminder of my life and all that had happened. A reminder of how far Calvin could drive a perfectly normal person to commit a totally irrational act. I sighed. My tears had abandoned me.

§

The sun was already above the treetops behind the parking lot. I dreamed of stretching out in one of Maudy's redwood lounges, lifting my face to the sun, and making up for some of the sleep I'd lost the last fifteen years. As I reached for my purse to gather change for vending machine coffee at the gas station next door, someone knocked on the door.

I glanced down at my wrinkled knit shorts and tank top, then up at the clock on the wall. Later than I thought. Already noon.

Insistent, whoever it was, knocked again.

Confident I could defend myself, I pulled the loaded .380 automatic out of my purse and laid it on the bed. If I recognized anybody from the House of Praise, I'd not hesitate to use it. I'd also seen too many movies about drug dealers breaking into ghetto apartments in the middle of the day, or maybe it was a tenant who had watched me come and go, always alone. Fear had become as senseless as hope. *Might as well answer the door; let my attacker know I'm fully armed.* I purposely left the gun on the bed, in plain sight and at arms length. After all, I wasn't trigger happy. I didn't want to shoot an innocent door-knocker. "It's probably just a Jehovah Witness. Or the ghetto Avon lady," I mumbled.

Glancing out the front window over the kitchenette sink, I spotted a large rusting distant cousin to my own car. A relic from the era when mechanics knew how to fix carburetors. A nameless color, hubcaps lost into roadside history, and tires as slick as a baby's butt. The car was parked parallel to the apartments; I couldn't see the license plate.

I peeked through the peephole. It gave me a mottled glimpse of a man with a beard, hovering on the other side of the threshold. His image was blurred, and he was alone. Sucking in a deep breath, I refused to let my past infect my courage and clicked open the dead bolt. Cracking the door slightly, a face appeared above the heavy chain lock secure in its holder, and I found myself speechless.

Tall with wide shoulders, he wore khaki shorts, a black polo shirt open at the throat, and he held his sunglasses in his hand. His brown eyes stared directly into mine. His lashes were thick, his brow wrinkled, his jaw strong with a close-cropped beard and a well-trimmed matching mustache. His hair was as thick and wavy as my own but salt and pepper, and wind-mussed. On both sides of his face he had dimples you could fall into. Screwed in as firmly as bolts into a washer. His ruddy complexion shouted early forties. He was trim but not too skinny.

I'd never seen him before in my life, but he smiled as if he knew me. Mind-numbingly handsome, my mind went blank. I opened my mouth to ask what he wanted but all I managed was a squeaky, embarrassing, "Um, c-can I help you?"

"Yes," he said. Impossible as it seemed, his little off-kilter smile grew in intensity. "Marguerite Valdez?"

I tried to focus and not stare at his chest. I cleared my throat. "Who wants to know?"

"Sorry. I'm Matthew Callahan. Social worker for the county."

"So?"

"I'm looking for the Valdez family."

"Well, they're not here, and I'm not her." I practically spat.

He nodded, his eyes going past me, over my head and into the room behind me. I turned my head to follow his gaze. "I'm sorry, I was given this apartment number," he said. "Do you know her or anyone who might know her?" He'd seen the gun.

"No. Try Mr. Gibbs, the landlord."

"I did. He told me she lived here. Obviously he doesn't know who he's renting to."

"Well, I think he's drunk half the time." Silence. "Is that all?"

He hesitated.

More silence.

As I stared at the man who called himself Matthew Callahan, I figured he probably had a wife who cheated on him, which meant either his wife was a looney-tune or he was a rotten husband. Why would I think that? Not everyone cheats. At least I was still naïve enough to think so. *He's probably cheating on his wife. With this Valdez woman.* Strange, though, he was well groomed. Relaxed. Educated. I could tell. Through his well-spoken manners, he had a hint of a Southern accent. He just didn't fit the car he drove. Of course, who would drive a nice car into a neighborhood where folks drank beer for breakfast? And didn't social workers travel to the seedy side of town in packs? At least the wolves who took my babies did.

"Sorry. I have no idea who this Valdez person is. You'll have to ask somebody else. I hope you find her," I said in a pitch that could chip ice, waiting for him to leave. He didn't look discouraged. In fact, he didn't look put off in the least.

"Well, since I can't find the Valdez family, and since I'm a social worker, a traveling psychologist of sorts, do you want to talk about anything?" he asked.

Now I was positive he'd seen the gun. I stood there, not knowing what to say.

"Can I show you my identification and credentials? It won't take long." Charming and certainly friendly enough, he looked perfectly harmless. But then again, so had Jeffrey Dahmer. How did I know he wasn't one of Calvin's goons?

"Sorry. No."

He sighed. Frustration and disappointment were etched across his face, but he didn't budge. He obviously wasn't giving up easily. I admired that in a person.

"Look, ma'am," he said slowly, the steadiness in his voice some kind of anchor. "What's your name, at least? I'm trying desperately here. You look like you got a lot on your mind. I see you've got a gun. Your apartment appears empty. What's it all about? I really don't want to call the police." He shoved his hands into the pockets of his khakis.

My eyes turned to fire. "Mind your own damn business. No need to call the police. It's my gun. I have every right to it. Go away!" I slammed the door in his face.

"Just talk to me!"

My back against the door, I heard him yelling. Surely he didn't think I would open my door to a total stranger, let alone a serial killer who eats his victims.

I watched him through a slit in the dusty curtains over the kitchen sink. When I didn't answer, his gaze shifted slowly to meet my eyes behind the curtain. "If you're planning a suicide," he yelled, "you'll do it with me here banging on your door! Please, talk to me!"

Suicide? He thinks I'm suicidal? Lord knows, I've fought a good fight just to stay alive! I've no intention of—suicide? How dare he! Yet the bleak hopelessness I'd felt at three a.m. had become a mood I couldn't shake.

I ran to the bathroom. Wiping my forehead with a towel that was less than clean, I stopped to stare in the mirror. I was a stranger beneath wild-woman hair and sunken features. Gaunt eyes with dark circles stared back at me. I'd been dying a slow death, and it showed in my face like a lifetime of hard drinking. Smoothing my hair behind my ears again, I was appalled at the lines on my forehead and the dirt under my nails. I'd not washed myself since—I couldn't remember. I peered down at my torn and dirty clothes. I hadn't eaten a balanced meal in what? Over a year? My skin was pulled tight and I could count my ribs and see the hard curve of my hipbones. My belly caved in, and for the first time ever, my collarbone protruded. Spending a few minutes listening to him make a fool of himself would give me something to do other than roam through photo albums, wondering how to stay sane while being suffocated by the past. What would it hurt to talk?

I'd tried once to make an appointment with a professional Christian counselor. His fee was one thousand dollars up front. It didn't happen. Neither family wanted to deal with my mistakes and problems, or God forbid, help me expose Calvin. Once, a local Baptist congregation brought a nice offering to the house. I was grateful, but all it did was pay a month's mortgage. Band-Aids. Covering wounds. That's all the well-meaning churches were. Nobody, other than John Rossi, had wanted to sit down and listen to me. Help me uncover Calvin for the demon he was. Everyone was afraid of him. The world had enough problems to care about mine. *Why, out of the blue, does this man on my doorstep want to talk to me? Because he thinks I'm crazy.*

I opened the door again to shoo him away like an annoying cat. "Git! Go away and mind your own damn business!"

I watched him leave. *Good.*

A minute later, a tapping on the large window on the other side of the room startled me. He had walked to the east side of the building. *This guy just doesn't give up.* I opened the drapes. Just a little. "Go away! I swear I'll shoot you, drag you in here. Say you broke in!"

His eyes widened as I pointed my gun at his chest. I yelled louder. "Don't worry! I've never shot anyone who didn't deserve it." He shook his head and silently walked away.

But in another moment he was at my front door again with a heavy dose of frustration in his voice. "I'm not leaving, ma'am. At least give me your name so I can tell the police who you are when you're dead."

I opened the door just a crack, keeping it chained again. "You don't give up, do you?"

"You kidding? I'm an old mountain boy. Been around guns all my life. I'm just not used to a pretty lady wanting to use one on herself."

"What makes you think I'm going to kill myself? And don't call me pretty. You're wasting your fancy words. For the love of God, go away. Leave me alone!" I leaned against the door and attempted to close it one more time.

But Matthew Callahan thrust his hands through the opening, holding the door ajar the four inches allowed by the chain, his fingers on the inside of the apartment. "Ma'am, I *do* love God and I have a sixth sense when it comes to death," he said. "I see it all over your face."

I stepped back, my mouth wide open, staring at his hands. Where had I seen them? Where? *Please God, tell me where.* Thrown back in time, my mind moved at the speed of sound to a hospital room. Lights, doctors whirling around me, a baby quiet inside of me, my foot and head wounded, something placed on my face. Falling down a long dark tunnel of sleep, I reached out to the hands came beautiful and peaceful hands. Hands pulling me from the grip of death. Whose hands they were or what they meant hadn't crossed my mind but a few times since losing my infant son. The hands with the left ring finger missing down to the first knuckle—just like—the hands holding my door open at that moment. Those were the hands I saw, and the bearded face.

I reached up and unconsciously touched the small scar on my forehead then stepped forward, within inches of him. "My name is Andie Rose Oliver," I said softly. "May I see your identification?" Shock showed in his face at my sudden change of heart. He reached for his wallet and patted his body.

"Wait . . . wait right there. Don't close the door, please. It's in the car. I'll be right back."

He bolted to his car. In seconds he returned and shoved his driver's license and business card through the opening, showing me his social worker status after his name. I looked at them briefly and unlatched the chain as if I'd lost all fear, unlike moments before. All trepidation was gone. I had no thoughts of leaving the door open for my safety, and I promptly closed it behind us as he stepped into the apartment.

I couldn't help but notice his gaze sweep the length of my bare legs before it traveled slowly up to meet my eyes. I motioned for him to have a seat. "I'd offer you some coffee and danish, but the maid took the day off. So, Mr. Callahan, exactly why do you think you need to talk to me, since you can't find your Valdez person?"

He sat on the metal folding chair, the only chair in the apartment, leaned forward, and rested his elbows on his knees. "Please, call me Matthew. May I call you Andie?"

I nodded. Underneath Mavis's old afghan, my gun lay on the sheet. Loaded. Ready.

He smiled his beautifully crooked smile again. "You might as well sit, too. Let's talk."

A Plan In Motion

Matthew Callahan

I gave her my most charming smile. I had not expected this petite, ragged woman to open the door. I fully anticipated she would tell me to go to Hell and I would have to call for support on this unexpected new case. Undeniably sensual and beautiful under the pain of her life, I could plainly see she was in distress. A woman in a wafer-thin white tank top and plaid shorts long overdue for the trash bin, the top of her head barely came to my chin. Younger than me, by maybe a couple years: it was hard to tell. My training and experience told me she was close to exhaustion maybe even a mental breakdown.

I took in the room and the odor of poverty. I'd smelled it before. The apartment was as bare as I suspected. Swatting flies away from my face and arms, I was moved by her living conditions. And then I waited as she gave me another slow once-over, deciding I wasn't out to harm her. I found a metal chair and sat. A few seconds later, she slid down the wall, landing on a dirty mattress opposite me. Her stringy shoulder-length hair moved every time she did. A slight smattering of golden freckles dusted the bridge of her nose. But it was her piercing pale blue eyes that cut me to the quick. They sparkled with an unspoken challenge, as if daring me not to even think about moving toward her.

She had positioned her gun close enough to grab from under the blanket if she needed it. Swiftly, I realized I'd broken all the rules, ignored my training, and lost control of my own common sense. I'd never approached a person like her, in possession of a gun. So why her? Why now? I was unable to look away as she crossed her shapely legs and gingerly rested her hands in her lap. Her hands. I stared at her hands and her ring. From the moment she opened the door her expression remained guarded. There was an edge to her. But a glimpse of curiosity and a flash of warmth in her eyes broke her definite distance.

I had honed my people skills until I thought I could read most adults like a book, but Andie Oliver wasn't giving anything away. I wondered if she was naturally wary, or if the harrowing life experiences I suspected she had made her that way.

She remained silent, patiently waiting for me to begin. I shifted and waited through her silence, glancing toward the parking lot, deciding how to launch into something that made sense to her. I wasn't exactly sure where to start or how to convince her I was there to help. She blinked, her eyes watery. I had to say something. I supposed the beginning was best.

"Until a couple years ago, I lived day to day. I lost my daughter, Jessie, to a childhood disease in 1987. She was ten. I live in the mountains northwest of here and after Jessie died, I didn't come out of my house much. After counseling, and my mother kicking my ass out the door one day, I went back to work."

"I'm a grief counselor. I help people. People who hurt and need someone to talk to when there's no one left. It's what I do. You could say it's my calling. I've made a good living, and now I pass on what the good Lord gave me. My ability to make a difference. If even for a moment."

I felt the pain of Jessie's death again, and it surprised me. The cold reality in my mother's voice was still inside my head. My mother, Bobbie Sue. Assertive, a born leader, larger-than-life.

New tears filled Andie's flashing eyes. "Tell me more."

I smiled warmly at her and then cleared my throat. Shifting again in my seat I said, "The last time I took Jessie to Baptist Hospital her prognosis was six months. She lasted three weeks, which in many ways was a blessing." I looked away from her. Why was I telling her this? "My wife and I had divorced months before her death." I sighed and smiled again. "But Jessie . . . she was a fighter. 'Til the end."

I was taken aback when she jumped into the conversation.

"I know what it feels like to lose a child." Andie began the story of her life. As she talked, I realized she could not stop. A dam had burst and from it flowed a flood of words that must have been stored for years in the reservoirs of her mind and heart. From front to back, cover to cover, unfolding the lies, deception, and horrors. Her ex-husband, Joe, and his cheating heart. Reverend Calvin Artury, whom I knew of, his cult and his organized crime ring, all in the name of the Lord. Artury the Godfather, Artury the control freak, Artury the pedophile. The murder of her childhood friend, Mavis.

"Artury gave the order, I'm sure of it. I just don't know who actually raped her, slit her throat," she said. Artury's men were looking for her. She mentioned that, too.

Andie rubbed her arms. She appeared hopeless. Hopeless and helpless. And scared. But she wasn't crazy. I'd seen crazy and Andie wasn't it. I believed her. The truth was in her eyes.

"For a while I thought I arrived at the bottom of my barrel because I fell from grace," she said. Her gaze went to the ceiling, away from me. "But it wasn't that at all. It happened gradually. I've been numb with grief for years. Brian—that was my baby—Mavis, Rupert, then Daddy. My children. Important people were taken from me. It altered the course of my life. Before I knew it, an ocean of grief lapped at my feet. My entire existence became a blur of funerals, vegetable trays, condolence cards, and the odor of death. Normal people adapt to loss and death. I guess I'm not normal. When they took Dillon and Gracie, my belief in God and everything good toppled over in a gust of wind, like the fairy tale house made of straw."

My heart went out to her. I looked around at the dark apartment that smelled like decaying apples. I had to get her out. She didn't deserve this. The poor woman was emotionally drained. I rested my head against the wall behind me and slowly put my plan in motion.

Andie

A seed of an unspoken alliance was planted between us. In the few moments I knew him, I believed he was a man of feeling. One who had loved and had been loved. A man who had loved his child. I let my guard down, but kept a few things to myself, especially the murder of John Rossi. I was not ready to talk about that and every atrocity of my life with somebody I'd just met. I could sense he was being intentionally kind, deliberately calm.

Telling my story had been painful and further exhausted me. I pressed my back against the wall and followed the line of his shoulders, the way his polo shirt clung to his veiny upper arms like a second skin. I imagined him as the outdoors-type from his rugged appearance, deep tan, and the tiny creases at the corners of his eyes from squinting in sunlight. He filled the chair, made it seem small, like a child's chair. His gaze slid past me as he focused on the interior of the apartment, staring at my meager possessions with such utter compassion. I had a feeling about the way he looked at me, too. With unreserved sympathy. To the point I had to turn away from the raw emotion on his face. Matthew Callahan wasn't like anyone I'd met. Yet, I had no precognition a stranger—someone of his height, build, and good looks—would appear out of thin air and rescue me on a white horse. Joe had been handsome, too. Way too handsome. I would never go down that road again. Never.

Matthew

I stood, walked over and leaned against the countertop in the kitchenette area. It only took an instant to realize the tiny apartment was truly empty.

"Is this everything you own?"

"You're looking at it. Gave away the rest. No reason to keep anything but what meant the most to me. I doubt they'll let me keep my photo albums in prison."

I stared at her, astonished by her remark. She shot back. "What did you think I was going to do with this gun? Go on a damn turkey shoot?" I could see her biting her tongue; sure she hadn't meant to give away her future plans.

I walked back to the chair and sat. Planting my elbows on my knees again, I threaded my fingers together and stared into her eyes. Amazed at myself, I believed every word she said. I'd heard wild and crazy stories before. Many from women just like her. But she was different. Due to the certain danger she was in should anyone find out where she was, I immediately made Andie my own private concern. I would not report her to my department, which went against more rules, but I didn't trust everyone downtown. Andie needed protection, not exposure.

"I can help you."

"Help me how? Help me kill him?"

"No. Of course not. Help you put your life back together."

"Hmm. You feel that sorry for me? You a white knight or something?"

"No," I grinned at her quick wit. "It's like I said. God's been good to me. In return, I want to help people who are truly in need."

"And I'm the neediest thing you've got going today, right? I mean, since you can't find your Valdez lady person, whoever she is. Your damsel in distress."

"Marguerite Valdez is an illegal alien my department helped get a green card so she could keep her five children away from an abusive and alcoholic husband. She's thirty years old but they say she looks sixty. I never met her. I heard she learned to speak English in a few months. I'm filling in for a while in Forsyth County and the department head requested I look in on her on my way home. I am concerned she's not here. I'll have to call the county office and let them know. They'll start a search. With any luck they'll find her alive and well and working at one of the local restaurants where she interviewed."

"Sorry." Andie lowered her head. "I forget there are other women as miserable as me."

"Actually, few have lost it all. Marguerite still has her children. You're one of the few women I've met who have found your 'barrel's bottom,' as you say."

"Thanks for pointing that out."

"It doesn't mean there's no hope."

I watched her tap her bare foot on the carpet. "I was full of hope once. Passed it out like candy from my pocket, Mavis used to say." She stiffened. "You're not looking at an innocent child on a cereal commercial, you know. You're dealing with a middle-aged woman who's been through Hell, somebody with baggage—and plenty of it." She shook her head. "Wait a minute. You don't even know me. Few have offered me help unless there was sex involved."

"I'm here as a professional, Andie. I'm not here to solicit anything from you."

Andie

He blanched. I almost laughed. "I'm sorry for my bluntness, but you need to know you will usher in Armageddon if you go face-to-face with Calvin Artury."

"I've thought of it," he admitted.

"All of it?" I knew he had no idea who he was dealing with. "He's dangerous and powerful. Most people wouldn't believe it."

He nodded. "I believe you. I've heard things." Matthew gave me a hard look and a heavy sigh. "I knew someone who attended services there."

"Yeah? Who?"

He shrugged. "A friend." He changed the subject. "I've been fortunate. My children were loved and cared for. My son, Conner, grew up happy and healthy. I hate to think of Artury molesting any child, a child I can rescue."

Our eyes met. "You have a son? How many children do you have?"

"Just Conner. He's sixteen."

I sighed. *The same age as Dillon and Gracie.*

I could see his mind working. I doubted a man like Matthew Callahan had been celibate since his divorce. "How does your ex-wife feel about what you do? What about your son?"

"My marriage lasted ten years. She got sick of living in the middle of God's half-acre and of me devoting tons of time to social work and other people's marriages. Too bad I couldn't save my own," he chuckled. "My son is a wonderful young man. Attends school in Boston. Brenda, that was my wife, wanted to move back to her hometown, join a golf league and a country club. Home to her was the ocean, tennis courts, Boston. She's a good mother; we just wanted different things. When Jessie died, she'd had all the mountain air she could stand. She took Conner and moved away. After Jessie and Conner were gone, I lost myself. But that's been said already. My son visits me in the summer and on holidays. I've rebuilt my life to a degree of contentment. Now, like I said, I help others rebuild theirs. Someday I'll start a camp for underprivileged kids."

There was something strangely refreshing in the voice of a man who loved his children. I reveled in it until it stirred up the thick, raw emotion in my heart I didn't want him to see.

Matthew

I was concerned by how much I had revealed to a complete stranger, but I continued nonetheless. "I listen to my gut. Some say it's God talking. I don't know, maybe it's my inner spirit guiding me. I want to make you an offer." I felt myself blushing again when I realized the sexual overtones of my statement. I shook my head. "No. No. I mean a serious, honest, and non-sexual job offer." And yet, despite what I said, I felt a spark of sensuality. "I'm also a philanthropist, as my colleagues would say."

She scrunched her brows. "A what?"

I laughed. "Never mind. I anonymously seek out charities or deserving individuals. I've started a couple foundations. And, because I do everything from my home, I need office help. Do you have any clerical skills? Can you type?"

She appeared shocked, but nodded.

"Good. I have an overburdened secretary, Ivy; she's been with me now, well let's see . . . I guess since God was a boy. Poor thing. I work her hard and she's been pestering me for some help. She's also my housekeeper and manages things when I'm gone. She's a sweetie, though. She and her husband, Tobias, own a beautiful house on the property. Tobias manages our few employees, the vineyard, gardens, and the animals. I love dogs. You like dogs? Anyway, Ivy and Mother were roommates in college. I can't imagine life without her and Tobias."

"Andie, come stay in one of the guest rooms in my house. It's in the mountains near West Jefferson. The house and property have been in my father's family over 100 years. I'll protect you. Artury will never know you're there. And here's something else to consider. I've got connections, too. I can't promise, but possibly I can make arrangements for you to see your children secretly until we can straighten this whole thing out." I rubbed the back of my neck. Gazing into her eyes, I hoped I had assured her that I'd do my best.

She stared back and stroked her throat. Concern flickered across her face. Andie's round eyes blinked. Tears filled the corners until they slid down her cheeks. She shivered but remained quiet. I could see she was stressed to the point of collapse. Only from careful observation of her countenance did I sense a cheated youth. An accumulation of endured hardships intended for a woman far surpassing her age. Her body and mind needed rest and somebody to care about her. She needed a way out, and a way back in, if it would make her feel more secure. I wanted to reach out to her, but I stayed seated to avoid scaring her.

"Tell you what," I said. "If I can't help you, and you aren't healthy and on your way to wholeness after six months, I'll bring you back here and you can finish your plan. I won't stop you." I said it, knowing I could make a difference. Bring back some of the happiness she had been robbed of. Until that day, I'd made it my policy to stay away from anything to do with a beautiful woman. It wasn't because I didn't have the self-control for it, but it'd been ages since I'd been attracted to a woman and I didn't want my attention diverted from my work. Illegal aliens, parental abductions, abuse, domestic violence, custody battles, those were the cases I handled. Give me drunken parents to deal with and I was in my element. But a woman like Andie? She didn't need to witness my heartache on top of her own. It all hit too close to home.

But I couldn't stop myself.

Her face reminded me of a porcelain doll, albeit a sad doll with a dirty face and long-neglected hair. She wouldn't have much to bring with her, which was good because I was sure it smelled like the inside of the apartment, the sour odor of unwashed clothes and overripe fruit. A smell she had probably gotten used to.

"So, will you help me? You can call the county, not give your name. They'll tell you all about me. I come with references," I said and smiled.

Andie

He has a vineyard and a housekeeper? Say no thanks and get him the hell out of here.

We sat in silence for some time while I processed his proposal and white-knuckled the mattress beneath me. And then, with a deep breath, I took another run at him. "I've seen things go bad when it comes to opposing Calvin on any level," I warned, compelled to be totally honest. "Arrangements like these aren't the same as the ones in the movies. Not everyone ends up happy." I also hated the thought of getting caught up in anything I'd regret. I heard of women like me who were conned into an abusive lifestyle. Then I looked at his hands again. A sudden peace flooded my heart. Still, I reminded myself he didn't specifically need my typing skills. Countless qualified typists would be happy to take his money, stay in his guest room. He could probably nail Calvin himself if he knew where to look, who to talk to, and had the patience—and the balls. Nobody had ever had the balls to go up against the illustrious Reverend. "You can do this yourself," I suggested. "You can track down the people who know all about him. I'll even give you the evidence in my bank lockbox."

Matthew shook his head. "It's not going to be easy. These things take time. And I can't devote round-the-clock effort to this in the immediate future. However, quite possibly the two of us, working together, could put him behind bars. In the meantime, we can work on getting your children back."

I smiled when he mentioned my children again. "Where did you say you live?"

"On a farm in the Blue Ridge, near West Jefferson. I, uh, own property all over the state." He coughed. "My, uh, my work keeps Ivy and me very busy. Believe it or not, it can be a pain. There's lots of paperwork involved. So," he shrugged again, "I'm anxious to get started. You help me, I'll work for you. What do you say?"

"If you end up slitting my throat, I'll come back and haunt you. But I believe you. I . . . I've seen your hands before."

"Really?" He smiled with candor, but I didn't return the smile.

"It's the only reason I let you in here."

He smiled again anyway. A slow smile that stirred my emotions. Warmed me like I hadn't been warm in a long time. Matthew Callahan, my knight in shining armor. I felt it. I tried to ignore the sudden ringing thoughts in my head, but my heart let me know I was still a woman in spite of my rotten life. Still, if he was interested in something other than my typing skills, he needed to look elsewhere. I was well aware of his handsome face, yet it was his story and his desire to find my children that moved me the most. Taking him up on his offer, based on my emotions, would only lead to trouble. I rubbed the scar on my foot, reminded of the night I first saw his hands. "And another thing; it's been some time since I've typed."

His eye-crinkling smile deepened. The kind of smile that made men like Clint Eastwood and Sean Connery Hollywood legends. "No problem. I'll help you get started."

Maybe it was the sun, beating bright in the sky like a fiery-hot heart, or maybe it was because I heard birds sing for the first time since Daddy died. Then again, maybe it was simply the thought of the mountains. Or the echo of Mavis's words ringing in my ears: *That's your answer, Andie. Unconditional love.* I'm not sure what it was, exactly, that made me decide to go with him. I wasn't used to someone saying, *I really want to help you*, and I wished Matthew Callahan's eyes weren't shining with as much unrelenting hope as they were warmth.

"You ever type on a computer?" he asked.

I shook my head. "Nope. Don't worry; if you help me uncover that ministry for what it truly is, it won't even take six months to turn my life around.

Believe me, I've got plenty of evidence. I'll be out of your hair in no time and Calvin will be eating his last meal on death row. I hope." I stood and brushed off my clothes. "No one has ever cared enough to listen to me. I've never trusted anyone with everything I know. It *is* dangerous. I wasn't kidding when I said they're looking for me. You're absolutely positive you want to do this?" Silently, I asked myself the same question.

"I've never been more sure of anything in my life," he said.

I wished I could've said the same.

He began gathering my few possessions. "So when do we get started?"

"Started? Did I say I would go with you?"

"You haven't said you wouldn't."

I laughed. "I need a shower first. And a cup of coffee in the worst way."

"But will you take my offer, stay in my guest room? I'm not asking for a lifetime commitment."

I saw him wince. "Against my better judgment, I'll go with you. A commitment? I'll never give you one."

"Fair enough."

I looked at his left hand with the missing finger again, my hoped-for confirmation that he was truly sent by God. I didn't want to get wrapped up in his needs and wants. No doubt few women turned him down. I'd learned my lessons about men. When it came to protecting my heart, I could be as tough as a rump roast from an old cow.

"I call all the shots when it comes to Calvin. I know him best," I warned.

"Right. You're the boss."

"Before we go, I'd like to talk about wages. I wasn't able to give Mr. Gibbs a deposit for my electric with my first month's rent. And I've got to pay the bank for my lockbox next week."

"How's a thousand a week sound?" He grinned, as if it were nothing to him.

I nearly swallowed my tongue. "Now, I'm not complaining, but damn, that's a lot of money. Joe and I together didn't make that much money in the seventeen years we were married. I'm not afraid of hard work, but this isn't a sixty-hour a week job, is it? I can't do that again."

Matthew finished piling my photograph albums together. "You drive a hard bargain. Listen, you've had the weight of the world on your shoulders. How about you get rested first, take a few days off from all that worry. We'll talk about money later." He winked.

I nodded in slow agreement. After shuffling into the bathroom, I gathered my few toiletries before stepping into the shower. *Am I dreaming? Will he be gone when I come out?*

"I'm going after coffee," Matthew hollered. "How do you like it?"

"With cream," I yelled back. I looked into the other room and caught him smiling.

"I think I can handle that. I'll remember how you like your coffee from now on."

That's just what I'm afraid of.

True to his word, Matthew had two Styrofoam cups of coffee waiting by the time I showered and changed into a semi-clean blue denim skirt and a white T-shirt. He'd dug up a donut somewhere, too. Flicking a fly off my breakfast, I stuffed my few clothes into a plastic bag and stared at the donut like I'd never seen one before.

"Let me." Matthew reached across me and took the bag to finish gathering my things. The soft scratch of his beard brushed against my temple and his warm breath passed by my cheek.

I reached out with both hands and grabbed the donut as if grabbing a lifeline. I think he was somewhat shocked by my desperation. "Mmm. Tastes good. Thanks for this." I stared into my coffee cup. *Get a grip, Andie.*

"You're welcome. I stopped by the office here, paid your electric bill, and told the manager that the woman in apartment 12 was vacating today. I assumed you used another name to protect yourself. You're supposed to drop off your key. Ready to go?" He held my stack of photo albums and Daddy's old Bible under his right arm, and the folded blue afghan in the other.

His intelligence and generosity overwhelmed me. I looked around the stark room, collected my gun and purse, and left the sheets and mattress on the floor for the next poor tenant. This was either my last chance, or I was a lamb being led to the slaughter. But I was too tired to care. Any way I cut it, it was a way out, and one last risk I would take. I inhaled his clean, masculine scent. It had been way too long since I'd been near a nice man, let alone smelled one. If he noticed my discomfort, he didn't let on.

"Oh, wait. What about my car?" I walked to the window and pointed it out to him.

"Do you really care?"

I giggled. "No. I'll leave the key in it."

"Is it titled to you?"

"No, I bought it off an old geezer who couldn't find the title. He said if I fixed the flat, gave him a hundred dollars and got it out of his hair, I could have it. So I did."

Matthew laughed. "You're quite resourceful. Just leave it here. They won't be able to trace it back to you since there was no title transfer."

With my hair still wet from my shower, I picked up my plastic trash bag of clothes and took a deep breath. "I'm ready."

Matthew opened the door. "Just two hours ago, I thought I'd lose you to that gun in your purse. Don't worry, Andie. This is a no-brainer decision you're making. You just need time, patience, rest, and access to the right people. You've never had the right people to help you nail this guy."

Intending to walk out the door behind him, I gasped as he held the door wide to let me go first. He followed me into the light. I stood blinking for a moment, staring through bright sunlight, as if I'd been trapped in a cave for months. Placing my meager belongings in the back seat, Matthew then proceeded to open the car door for me but not until he reached for my hand, gave it a gentle squeeze, and in a soft reassuring voice said, "Today, Andie Oliver. Today your life has turned around. I promise."

SHILOH

Andie

Beneath his hand I felt his strength and heartbeat. I kept telling myself it had to be real. Traveling to Matthew's home was the emotional experience of an unexpected blessing of deep significance. A premonition of good things to come. A dream. God had been silent for so long. "Please be real," I whispered.

The wipers waged a losing war against a sudden spring rain as Matthew drove the Blue Ridge Parkway, and then turned onto Route 16. To my left, I could see the gray-blue water of a small lake reflecting storm clouds. I hadn't bothered to look at the sky much the past few months and I watched the rain as if it were the first time I'd seen it. Well-kept farms, soaring trees, and lush landscapes dotted the mountains. A few log homes appeared sprinkled high on the ledges to get the full effect of the panorama around them.

"My farm is special, and we're almost there," said Matthew.

"How many acres is it?" I asked, recalling the beauty of Byron Stewart's fifty acres.

Matthew cleared his throat. "I think the last surveyor said it was around five hundred."

I swallowed hard. "Oh."

We rode the rest of the way in silence.

Finally, Matthew grinned and patted the dashboard, as if thanking his car for the ride. "It's just over the next ridge. You can see this road was recently widened. Road crews cut out some of the mountain. It needs to heal before it looks good again."

I compared myself to the wounded road. I'd been scraped and cut, parts of my soul dug out and hauled away. I'd never be the same: just like the road. And it'd take some time to heal before I looked good again. Just like the road.

Matthew turned the car onto a narrow two-lane drive that wound up a steep mountain slope and ended at wrought-iron gates with a large *C* scrolled on the front. I looked at him.

"For Callahan," he said, and smiled. Above the *C* was the word *Shiloh*. We passed between two stone pillars that marked the entrance of the drive. The tires picked up gravel and pitted it against the underside of the old car, sounding like popcorn in a hot skillet.

Relief washed over me as I gazed out my window in awe. We entered an avenue of immense trees, tall pine and oak, great straight trunks thrusting up through a shadowy canopy of green into the sky. The trees gave way to a meadow far to the right where a stout white house stood in the midst of it. A good distance from the road, the house was surrounded by gardens and a picket fence like a sash on a dress. The two-story sparkled in a sudden burst of sunshine and I blinked, imagining great Southern ladies and gentlemen calling it home in the years before the War of Northern Aggression, as Joe had called that war. "Your house is huge and beautiful! It's familiar to me, somehow."

"Yeah?" Matthew laughed. "That's not my house. That's where Ivy and Tobias live. Their house was built in 1803."

"Oh, my. It's lovely. But it couldn't be familiar, could it? I've never been here before."

"Déjà vu," said Matthew with a chuckle. "That's what Ivy would say. It's certainly not the sort of house you would mistake for another."

I pointed ahead. "You've got a barn, a nice one."

"You know about barns?"

"My sister-in-law, Libby. She lived on her uncle's farm for a while. I loved the barn."

"I built that one. Well, I helped. It was Tobias's design; he built it. Tobias and Ivy have lived in that house we just passed since we moved to this place. Both houses share access to the property, including the barn and outbuildings." Matthew's voice, peaceful and calming, affected me like a drug.

My eyes grew heavy and I longed for sleep. "Is this a road or a driveway? It seems to go on forever."

"It's a private drive. I have a crew maintain it in the winter."

We rode to the far end of the meadow through more trees and into a clearing, ending at a parking area designated by several boulders placed between the gravel and a pale-green piney woods. The area was covered with fallen leaves and debris from the storm. I studied the parked cars through the rain-streaked windshield. In front of a long garage with several doors sat a dented Jeep, a large pickup truck in decent condition, and a tiny red sports car that looked new.

"I could've driven us straight to the front porch, but I want to leave this car here. We'll walk up. I drive this junker when I travel into bad neighborhoods. In case you're wondering, the Jeep is mine. It's great for running around the farm. The truck belongs to Tobias, and I bought Ivy the car last year for her sixty-fifth birthday."

"She drives a car like that?"

"When you see her, you'll understand why."

Matthew swung open the door and unfolded his muscular frame from the car. He ran around to my side, opening my door wide. I grabbed my purse and climbed out, stunned by his manners and gentleman ways. We strolled up the wide Pavestone walkway breathing the cool air blowing down from the mountains, so clean and exhilarating, layered with the spice of a freshly washed forest and its sweet decaying soil.

"Damn, it's quiet here," I said.

"Yes, isn't it peaceful?" Matthew smiled and said. "This farm is the craziest place you've ever seen. Folks here in Ashe County still call it the Christmas Tree Ranch; you'll see the trees in the back. It was once part of a larger estate. The house was not in the best condition when I took it over. My dad leased out the ranch until the renters passed on. I've spent the better part of the past fifteen years restoring it. I named this land Shiloh."

"I noticed the name on the gate. What's it mean?"

"Shiloh is Hebrew for *place of peace*. I had a great-great-grandfather killed at the Battle of Shiloh on April 6, 1862. He's buried here on the property. Fought for the Confederates against a brother in the same battle; he's also buried here. I'm a Civil War enthusiast. There's a good-sized cemetery on the property. It's where I want to rest someday, in the far-off future."

The word Shiloh and its meaning surged through me like an electric current, along with the date of April 6. The day I'd planned to murder Calvin. There were too many coincidences. The Pavestone turned into a short brick path as we passed through an arch of twisted wisteria and ivy cascading over a white trellis. I saw the clearing ahead. I held my breath as the house came into view, and then blew it all out in a gentle stream.

"Magnificent." The word bubbled from my lips. The enormity of the structure sent chills to my hairline. Though it sat half-hidden in its cloak of woods, I gasped. A turn-of-the-century rural manor house, a mansion, mixing a variety of styles that somehow managed to flatter one another: white clapboard siding, ionic columns, gingerbread gables, quaint dormer windows, a wide wraparound porch, and a front door with an enormous stained-glass window framed by carved oak wood. I could have stood and stared at it for the rest of the afternoon, admiring the tiny bits of glass that sparkled in the sunlight.

The woods leaned in around the house, which had been painted a soft almost buttery white. The shutters were a glossy black that contrasted nicely. Dark green ivy shrouded parts of the front giving it a rich antebellum look. A giant black oak curled up from the ground, arching over the front corner, while a growth of vine and clematis tangled around the porch. I thought of Gracie hiding beneath her messy Saturday-morning hair. Though not yet in bloom, rose bushes and azalea gracefully accented an old stone fountain in the front yard, and the lawns stretched out in front of us like a golf course.

"Tobias is particular about the grounds. I couldn't do this without him," Matthew said as we walked toward the house.

Mounting the steps to the front porch, I drank in the beauty of the rolling farm. Words finally escaped me. The covered entrance had been partially screened, breezy, and wide. Plush accent pillows in garnets and blues sat on a wicker porch swing in the corner near similar chairs, their white paint matching the floor. I walked to the far end of the house and leaned over the railing until I could see the cottage we had passed by only moments before. I had thought it large when I'd first seen it but compared to Matthew's house, it seemed like a child's playhouse.

Four barking dogs bounded up the steps to greet their master. "Come meet the Hounds of the Baskervilles." Matthew shouted and pointed to each dog. "Cookie, Max, Buddy, and Sissy. Their barking and wagging was relentless. "They'll settle down in a minute."

I laughed while Matthew whistled and shouted. "Last, but not least, is *my* dog. The only dog I allow in the house. She's been with me for years. This is Sadie, my Golden. She was my daughter's dog as a pup. She's the queen of dogs. Say hello, Sadie."

"They're all great. Where do they stay if not in the house?"

"There's a large kennel behind the barn. They're free to roam the farm most of the time. They're actually pretty well behaved, except when they meet someone for the first time. From now on they'll just nod and say hello."

We made our way past the dogs and into the house. I found myself standing in an immense foyer of polished floors, gleaming walls, and a perfect little marble-topped table with an ornate gilded mirror hanging above it. Warm and dimly lit, the foyer walls were covered in delicate rose wallpaper and antique paintings. Fresh flowers accented tiger oak sideboards. Deep crown moldings separated the walls from the creamy-white ceilings, and a gentle wind blew in through the screen doors behind us, along with the scent of warm rain and the sound of the dogs barking in the yard.

Scents of apple spice and coffee suddenly swirled around our heads as we walked further inside, the hardwood creaking beneath my feet like an old familiar song. The house oozed with history, like old houses do; a grandfather clock chimed the hour in a nearby room. Large double doors trimmed with more wide moldings led to rooms on either side of the entry hall, and far beyond the staircase on the ground floor, the hall extended to what I assumed to be the dining and kitchen areas. The foyer was not only spacious but also formal, and I stood gazing at the generous staircase curving gracefully up to the second floor. It was like something out of *Gone With the Wind*, with wide stairs, a carved banister and elegant spindles. If Matthew had listened closely, he would've heard the sound of my jaw dropping.

"I thought Daddy's house was big. This is really something," I said, trying not to call attention to the excitement that had risen inside me.

It was an impressive house but as I looked around, the feeling I had made a mistake fell on me like a cannonball. Until that morning, my life had spiraled slowly to Hell. It was too drastic a change. Skeptical, I tried to imagine the real reasons behind Matthew's kindness. The deep emotional sensuality of meeting him earlier that day gave way to real concerns calling me from a place more familiar. And then we walked into a kitchen like none I had ever seen. The recognizable aroma of cinnamon and butter greeted me like a couple of old friends. I would've been as proud as a blue-ribbon pie winner to have had a kitchen like that one. Pies and what looked like biscuits cooled on the counter; a fire burned under a large pot of something that smelled like chicken soup. As I stood in the midst of the fairy tale kitchen, Matthew's assistant, Ivy, floated in from a nearby pantry like Glinda, the good witch of the North, drifting into Munchkinland. I really wasn't in Kansas anymore. Or rather, my tattered black and white life.

Ivy and Tobias

Andie

Ivy was a strikingly beautiful black woman with toffee-colored skin and few lines. High, exotic cheekbones emphasized her pleasant smile and slightly crooked front teeth. The sunlight through the windows caught the sparkle of diamonds on her fingers and around her neck. Her dark sapphire eyes flickered like her jewelry: I had never seen eyes like Ivy's or a pierced nose. A tiny diamond in her right nostril twinkled and I caught myself staring at it. Her delicate, friendly face radiated warmth and strength. But her eyelids were enormous: great coffee-colored canopies fringed with dense, dark lashes. Nearly as long as Tammy Faye Bakker's, only more natural-looking.

"Andie Oliver," said Matthew, "I'd like you to meet my dear friend, Ivy Dumass."

I froze. My feet were glued to the floor. My mouth went numb as Ivy extended her hand.

"I'm so pleased to meet you. Matthew phoned ahead, a consideration he doesn't often bestow on me. Told me you were on your way." Ivy shook my hand and then lightly kissed my cheek. "Please excuse the mess, I'm baking pies and shortbread today."

I stammered my reply. "I . . . I'm sorry. I'm not sure I heard your last name correctly. D-u-m-a-s-s, Dumass?"

"Dumass is my married name. My maiden name was Boudreaux, from Louisiana. You know the Dumass name, Andie?"

"Yes." I looked at Matthew. "Mavis. Her last name was Dumass."

Matthew turned to Ivy. "Any possible relation to a Dumass family in Winston-Salem?"

"Could be. Ask Tobias. He's the one from North Carolina."

From her mannerism and speech, I presumed she was an educated woman. Ivy's intoxicating smile switched off my panic button. I became unusually calm, as if watching my conversation with her from a distance.

She wasn't the typically-dressed black woman in North Carolina. An orange swirl of beaded earrings dangled two inches from the bottom of each earlobe, gracing the length of her neck. She was adorned in an Egyptian hieroglyphic silk print dress that was more like a loose shift. A rainbow of colors, the dress reminded me of the Peter Max psychedelic posters I pinned up in my bedroom as a teenager. Mavis would've loved her. A matching turban covered her head. Little tufts of Brillo-pad-gray poked out at the back and at her forehead. She was a song in motion. "Oh! Love your earrings!" she said. Then she stretched out her arm like a child, and softly fingered my earlobes. "They're so pretty! Where did you get them?" Ivy's accent was a mixture of many, and the whiteness of her teeth dazzled under full lips that broke into a leisurely smile.

I reached up with my right hand to feel my small gold hoops and noticed Ivy's expression change, staring at the mother/child ring on my finger. "I'd forgotten I had these on. They were my mother's; she gave them to me years ago. I'm afraid they're the only earrings I own."

But there went Ivy's smile again, bigger than before. She motioned for Matthew and me to follow her. "Come, let's get comfortable." She led us through the arched doorway into a large room with tall windows, lavish moldings, exquisite light fixtures, and high-coved ceilings of smooth white plaster. Beautiful wool area rugs sprawled beneath my feet.

"You've got a parlor!" I declared, with a gesture of graciousness.

Matthew laughed. "Well, kind of. It's my office. I spend most of my time in here."

To rest in such a room, in front of a snapping fire with vibrant colors of reds and golds, suddenly it was all I wanted to do. On the wall, a series of small paintings drew my eye.

Ivy noticed. "Matthew's collection of the civil war artist John Adams Elder is showcased in here. Better light, you know. Much better light. Glorious battle scenes. Matthew says, and I agree, they're much too controversial for other rooms in the house."

Cherrywood bookcases ran the length of the room filled with old and new books, potted plants in blue and white vases, gardening catalogs, and a collection of antique glassware. The parlor simply reached out and hugged me. Two leather sofas faced each other. An old traveling chest sat between them as a coffee table. Staring at tobacco-brown sofas draped with soft plaid throws, I again imagined myself napping there warmed by a blazing fire. Or reading a novel on one of the high-back chairs with delicate embroidered fabric. I gazed upward at an elaborate carved plaque that hung over the stone fireplace: *The Pioneer's Creed: The Cowards Never Started. The Weak Died Along the Way. Only the Strong Survived.* I had to be dreaming.

Covered in white plantation shutters, the large windows appeared new. I walked to a window and moved the shutter aside. I wanted to see the room in the evening sunlight as it purpled and softened the room. Ivy helped me, and immediately the room grew warm and rich in hues of earth and fire as the sun set over the mountain.

"Don't look at the dust. Matthew doesn't like me to clean around him when he works," Ivy said, raising her eyebrows.

"I can always tell when Ivy's been in here," Matthew retorted. "All my work is arranged in neat little piles and I can't find zilch. I'm the kind of guy who keeps things forever. I have problems getting rid of my shit."

"Matthew!" Ivy said in mock disgust.

Without warning, I began to weep. Overcome with fear and missing my children, I whirled around to face Matthew. "I shouldn't have come; I don't belong here."

Softly, he touched my shoulder. "And you don't belong in jail or dead, which is exactly where you'd end up if you weren't here with me. Please,

Andie. You're safe here. Think about my offer." He stuck his hand in his back pocket and pulled out a cotton monogrammed hankie. Handing it to me, I touched his fingers. A calmness and needed peace once again flowed through me and I sighed deeply and with purpose, hoping to still the fear that had followed me there.

"Pie and coffee?" Ivy suggested, attempting to brighten the mood.

While we waited on Ivy's pie, Matthew sat at his desk to take care of a few matters that needed his attention. He told me to wander through the house, and to holler if I got lost.

Awed by the old mansion's magnificence, I meandered from room to room following its woodsy aroma. Everywhere grand and stately antiques stood in corners or sat on shelves. Antiques like Dixie never had. The upstairs hallway, decorated with more exquisite paintings and Persian runners, stretched the length of the house. In the first bedroom I came to, a white wicker birdcage housed two canaries that matched the lemon and white magnolia wallpaper, coordinating bedspread, and window treatments. Laura Ashley. I'd seen the print in a magazine. Finials carved in the shape of pinccones lengthened the curtain rods.

A graceful antique four-poster bed had been placed opposite a working fireplace. It was heaped with rolled quilts and embroidered blankets like a pile of logs in winter, and thick with a fresh laundered scent. A primitive table on four straight legs sat in the curved bay window. I looked out the window at shades of purple, yellow, and coral flowers like a tropical lei around the neck of Matthew's property. Through the branches of the black oak I could see a pond and Ivy's white house in the meadow.

"This is your room."

I jumped. It was Ivy, wearing a gracious smile. "Sorry, Andie, I must remember to let you know when I'm behind you. Matthew gets so upset when I sneak up on him."

"It's okay. I've been a little jumpy the past few months." I ran my hand across the bottom of the bed feeling the softness of the down comforter. "This room is lovely. I'm not sure I'll be able to sleep in here after what I've been sleeping in, though."

"Don't be silly. It's just a room. May I be so bold to say that Matthew is a knight in shining armor. You'll be fine now. Leave the rest to him. He'll work it out, whatever it is you've been through."

How did she know that's what I called him? "He's done this for other women? Bring them here, I mean."

"No. Never. I must say I was surprised when he phoned and said he was bringing you here. And a bit worried. But no longer." Ivy smiled and looked away. "He invites few people to Shiloh. Matthew keeps his distance from the public unless he's working on a case. I say the man is too busy taking care of everybody else. He forgets he has needs, too." Ivy prepared the room for my stay. "It's been all business for him," she said, her smile unceasing. "I've never quite seen him like this, though. You are a mystery, Andie. A mystery for sure." Ivy cupped the side of my face with her hand. "But my spirit is at peace. I'm glad he brought you to this place."

I returned her smile. "Are you a woman of faith, Ivy?"

Ivy turned down my bed and took two plush yellow towels out of an armoire, placing them in the adjoining bathroom. "Many faiths. My mother raised me in the bayou. Born in Tammany Parish, I was. My grandmother practiced voodoo, but my father, now there was a beautiful man. Father was of the Baptist faith. You can imagine the turmoil in our family. After my mother died, my father, a white man, mixed actually but looked white— college professor, a fine man, strong and of a character fit for presidents and kings—he took me with him. Schooled in Paris and London until his death, I lived in both cities. Then I came back to the States to finish my doctorate at Harvard, which is where I met Matthew's mother, Bobbie Sue. She was at Seminary. We became the closest of friends."

"And of course, at Harvard I met Tobias. We fell in love and worked hard for Doctor King during the Movement. Later, we moved south because I wanted to live near my friend, Bobbie Sue. My Tobias, he was fine with that. He said he would follow me to the Amazon if he had to. He's from here, anyway. I delivered Matthew and his siblings."

"How wonderful," I said. In two little minutes she had offered me her entire life story.

Ivy sighed, and then smiled again. "One day, over fifteen years ago now, Matthew asked us to help him on a benefit for cancer research. The three of us have been together ever since."

"You said something about Matthew's mother in Seminary?"

"Yes, she's a pastor. Hasn't he told you?"

I laughed. "I'm sure he was afraid to. I probably wouldn't have come with him."

"Not to worry, Andie. Pastor Bobbie Sue is a precious woman. She's a country lady who preaches in a little holiness church in Valle Crucis. White steeple and everything. You'll never see her on TV."

"Good," I answered quickly, then shook my head. *Why would she tell me that?*

Ivy moved gracefully about the room as if her feet were hovering above the floor. *Had Matthew told her about Calvin?* She seemed to know everything.

"My, I've been rattling on so. Coffee's been ready; want some?"

I looked at her and saw Mavis. She was Mavis at sixty-five. The physical resemblance was strong. Maybe because I wanted it to be. Their personalities were so much the same that I knew why I felt instantly at home with people I'd just met.

§

"This is way beyond what I had envisioned," I said to Matthew when I walked back into his office.

"It takes a staff to clean it, too," said Ivy. "I just don't have the time, with assisting Matthew and his charities."

"I can't imagine why," Matthew murmured.

"Can I help?" I asked.

"What do you think, Ivy? Andie can type and file for you. I'd like to give her a job while she's here."

"I've only been after you to get me some help for two years now. She can start tomorrow. We have the Governor's Ball coming up. I need help with the menu."

"I'm a great cook," I said. "I used to own a restaurant. Well, a little cafeteria really." I lowered my eyes, humble and somewhat embarrassed about my homespun culinary skills. I figured pinto beans and cornbread were far beneath what these people were used to.

"You don't have to cook for this ball, Andie, just help me plan it. But praise be to Jesus, if you can cook, we'd love you to do some of that around here. Wouldn't we, Matthew? I would love a big pot of pinto beans." Ivy cocked an eyebrow and grinned.

Matthew eyes lit up. "Ah, Tobias. There you are."

"Mattie, we have a guest, no?"

"Yes, come meet Andie Oliver, my friend who I met this morning. Andie, don't let him fool you. Tobias reverts to his North Carolina farm-boy mode of speech when talking with me. He was only educated in the North, where he *says* he lost his Southern twang."

Tobias shot him a smile and an expression of devotion. "Nice to meet you, Andie. Such a pleasure. Whatever we can do to make your stay with us pleasant, please speak up."

I nodded and smiled. I thought only high-class hotels said stuff like that. And he spoke to me as if he were speaking to a small child, soft with a touch of sweetness.

His pants didn't fit well; his steel-rimmed eyeglasses slipped down his nose, and he wore a khaki shirt and shiny brown boots. His disheveled style was endearing: a clear indication he didn't care for refinement. A glint of a diamond shone in his right earlobe. A compact man, not quite six feet tall, who by midsummer would probably look so black he was blue. His hair was the color of table salt; cut so short you could see his scalp at his crown. His nose lay flat against his face, and his lips all but faded into the blackness of his skin. Gray-green eyes peered out from beneath narrow upper lids coming close enough that I could see the length of his lashes, the deep lines in his forehead, and the pores in his skin. But what really pulled me in were his gleaming white teeth that flashed when he smiled.

I was drawn to the three of them. Like a baby to a breast full of milk. They opened their hearts, as well as their arms. If not for the deep slashes wounding my own heart, I would've thought I had died in that hellhole of a room at the Magnolia Monarch and landed in Heaven.

"Toby, you related to any Dumass family in the Winston-Salem area?" Ivy asked.

"Yes, tobacco farmers they were. Why? You know a Dumass, Andie?"

I started to giggle and then laugh. "Yes, yes, I do. Rupert Dumass was my daddy's closest friend. Rupert loved Loretta Pudrow, a black woman, all his life. Their daughter, Mavis, was my best friend."

"Rupert Dumass? Owned a large farm north of Winston, correct? All tobacco?"

"Yes," I laughed again. "That's him."

They smiled at my contagious laughter.

"My daddy's name was Bud Parks."

"Parks rings a bell, 'tis true. But Rupert I surely know. We lost touch many years ago. A regrettable thing. His father was Bertram Dumass. Bertram's brother, Denton, was my father—a white man who met my mother, Phoebe, a woman of deep color from the islands. She had very black skin. They were not permitted to marry in this state, as you know. My father never loved another; they were together until death parted them. I guess that would make Rupert and me first cousins. Mixed marriages run in the family, I suppose. Not the popular thing to do in the South during the last few decades. My parents kept to themselves, stayed out of towns, and away from people. Rupert and his father brought supplies often, remember, Mattie? I told you about the bad times. Let's remember good times tonight, shall we? By the way, my siblings are shades lighter than me."

"Ah," said Ivy. "That's true. Why didn't I think of it?"

"Because woman, your beautiful head is busy filling itself with love for me," Tobias cooed and leaned over to kiss his wife.

"True again," Ivy chuckled after his kiss. "But I remember now, the old pictures of you and your cousin Rupert. Pretty boys, both of you. One very white, one very black."

"Nah," said Matthew. "I've seen pictures of you as a kid, Tobias," he teased, turning to me. "Andie, he was so ugly his mama had to put a ham hock in his overall pocket to get the dogs to play with him."

"You bad, Mattie, oooh, such a bad boy," Tobias said and laughed.

The hilarity lit up the room. I talked into the evening about Rupert's family and of his death, about my love for Mavis, and a little about my own family. Ivy's deep-dish apple pie melted on my tongue and along the sides of my mouth. The coffee was rich and aromatic, scented with cinnamon and pale with cream. Kona coffee, Ivy had said. I recognized the Royal Doulton cup and saucer. My mother once owned the entire set.

The food, fire, and friendship were like being rocked to sleep as a child. My eyes met Matthew's several times during the evening, eyes that held a warm brown brilliance, making me shiver.

Ivy poured more coffee into my cup. "Would you like more pie, Andie?"

"If it's not too much trouble," I replied, holding my dish out with both hands like a homeless, hungry child in a soup line. "It's absolutely wonderful. I'd love the recipe."

I avoided talking about why I was there, and Matthew focused our conversation on the light side of things. I was grateful. As I finished my second piece of pie, my eyelids kept wanting to close. I saw Matthew looking at me. His voice invaded my thoughts. "Andie, you are welcome to go to bed anytime you want. Did Ivy show you the deep cast-iron tub in your bathroom? Why don't you go up and enjoy it, and then turn in for the night? We'll talk in the morning. By the way, Ivy agreed to take you to a few dress shops in town this week. You need clothes. It'll be an advance on your pay, okay?" He winked.

I smiled. "Fine, Matthew, that's fine. Thank you all so much for your kindness."

"Tis' our pleasure," said Tobias.

I said my goodnights to Matthew and Tobias, lingering a moment on Matthew's smile, and then following Ivy out of the room and up the stairs.

"This house is big enough to get lost in," I said. In tears, I turned to say goodnight. "I'm sorry, I'm just overwhelmed by everybody's generosity. I'm not used to anyone caring about me except my parents. But Daddy's gone now and Dixie, that's my mother, is living with my aunt in Charleston, and I—"

"I'm happy you're with us." Ivy said, pulling me into a warm hug. "Sleep well."

After a long tub soak, I climbed into bed. Fatigue rolled over me like a giant ocean wave. I slept at once, a deep, luxurious sleep. The first such sleep in over a decade.

Something Special

Matthew

I gave Andie a smile before she followed Ivy up to bed. A smile I hoped she'd interpret as a sincere apology from the world's idiot male population. I decided to send her roses while she worked for me; after all, wasn't Rose her middle name? I couldn't take my eyes off her. She was so needy. I suspected I had only been able to scratch the surface of what lay beneath her distress. I swallowed—twice—and reminded myself I had brought her to Shiloh for purely honorable intentions.

But she was easily the most beautiful female I'd ever met, and yet her loveliness wasn't the only thing about her that was so impressive. She was direct, which had captivated my attention from the get-go. She was also natural and free-spirited, non-judgmental, speaking her thoughts without an agenda, as if she had no notion of the exquisite grace she wielded or the subtlety hidden under her destitution.

I watched her follow Ivy up the stairs, noting the delicate curve of her waist. Although she wasn't tall, she carried herself as if she stood a clear distance above every woman in the Carolinas. I was also well aware I hadn't sent a woman flowers of any kind for quite some time.

She liked me. I'd seen it in her eyes even though she pretended to have a not-on-your-life attitude when I flirted with her in my office earlier. Actually, it was her cold-day-in-Hell stance that caught me off guard. Again I told myself that under normal circumstances, I would never get involved with someone from a case, someone who needed my help. My counsel. But these weren't normal circumstances. There was something very special about her. I wanted to know more. And more of what she knew about Reverend Artury.

A New Day

Andie

The next morning my eyes slowly drifted open with a dazed *where-am-I* expression to the sudden chirps of the canaries. Someone had taken the cover off the cage. Against the far wall stood an old-fashioned dry sink with a small mirror. My bare feet felt for the cool hardwood floor. The large T-shirt I'd borrowed from Matthew to sleep in hung almost to my knees. I crossed the room, my legs wobbly, feeling as though I'd been asleep for a week. With pulse-pounding certainty, I knew I would not recognize my reflection. I'd taken over another body, there was no other way to describe the feeling.

My eyes flashed back at me and seemed larger and bluer than usual. They held an expression of words in a fairy tale, an unnatural happiness, as if dusted with a bit of magic or like I'd drunk too much wine. My tangled hair set off an unfamiliar pale face like a frame around a cameo, glowing vague and ghostly in the old silvered glass. The wildness of my image was poles apart from how I usually pictured myself—plain, simple, okay for thirty-eight—it shocked me. For a moment I wondered if it was really me.

And then I let out a yelp. Matthew. His handsome face appeared next to mine in the mirror. Sadie, his dog, had followed him and softly wagged her tail against his leg. "I didn't hear you knock."

"I didn't. Sorry. I forgot my manners." He grinned. "How'd you sleep?"

"Like a rock." I smiled and allowed myself a small amount of pleasure in our shared moment.

"This house will do it to you," he said, pulling me away from my reflection and linking his arm through mine. "There's a lot more to see around here. Ivy has breakfast ready. She told me to tell you she hung a robe on the back of your bathroom door; will that do for you?"

"I'm such a mess. Give me five minutes."

"Just five; I'm hungry."

I watched him leave then padded into the bathroom. Ivy had also laid a pair of blue jeans and a soft flannel shirt on a dresser near the tub, and she had washed, mended, and folded all of my stinky clothes, including the afghan. *The woman is amazing.* A word I didn't say much. But every time I turned around, there stood amazing Ivy saying or doing something that sent me reeling. The jeans fit. I rolled up my shirtsleeves and slipped on a pair of house shoes she had set near the sink. Amazing.

After I dressed, my eyes were drawn to the wall near my unmade bed. Under a hand-painted landscape on canvas hung a very old embroidered sampler, matted and framed behind glass in an antique frame. *Stitched by Emma C. 1897 Great is Thy Faithfulness.* The miracle touched me; I touched it back with my fingertips.

§

Ivy lifted orange French toast and maple-smoked bacon onto plates. A simple breakfast served with strawberry jam, sliced pineapple and coffee, but it tasted like manna from Heaven. My hands trembled while I ate and Matthew read the newspaper. Neither of us spoke. I took in the quietness and enjoyed the view of the gardens. Sipping my coffee, I wrapped myself in the serenity. Not even my best daydreams compared to it. My body breathed— finally.

I offered to tidy up but Ivy told me I could help at supper. "Enjoy your first morning at Shiloh and explore the beauty around you," she said and smiled.

Matthew agreed and took me on another tour of the downstairs. At the far end of the house was a paneled library with an opulent marble fireplace, floor-to-ceiling bookcases of mellow aged walnut, an antique pool table, a gun cabinet, and more exquisite handcrafted cabinetry. A floor of black and white marble tile, set in a classic pattern of large diamonds, shone like glass. On the opposite end of the house, in the large living room where guests were entertained, whisper-soft colors, sentimental keepsakes, and a refined rustic charm adorned the room. Two carved busts of Civil War heroes I didn't recognize sat on the mantel over a mammoth fireplace made of river rock. More arched windows topped two sets of double French doors leading to a stone terrace.

"There's a swimming pool, weight room, and decks overlooking the gardens out that way." His voice sent waves of sweetness to my tongue and I savored the taste of his kindness. "When I decided to keep this property in 1979, people laughed and said sinking money into it was just the sort of foolish notion that would eat up my investments. But Mother loved it, and Ivy and Tobias bought into the idea of living here and helping me with my charity work. To me the house and grounds were full of potential. I believed I could do something with the place, as well as keep my mind and hands busy."

An older woman appeared at the door. "Mr. Callahan, phone for you, sir."

"Excuse me, Andie: my work never stops. By the way, Katy, this is Andie. Katy helps Ivy clean house three days a week." As Matthew walked away he smiled and said, "I'm always glad when Katy is here. She pays no attention to Ivy and leaves my shit alone."

Katy and I smiled at each other and exchanged pleasantries until she excused herself, listing the rooms she had to finish before noon. I thought of my little house on Turner Street. How I put as much love into that house as Matthew did into his. I'd been proud just to afford a gallon of paint. Then I stopped and counted. I'd moved into my house on Turner Street in 1979. *How could this be happening to me*? I almost skipped to the French doors. Opening them wide, I stepped out to the terrace and drank in the air, delicious, fragrant, and touched with a chill of early spring.

Descending a stone staircase down to a carpet-like lawn, I followed a pathway lined with berry bushes. The vast grounds rambled up to the thick forest in the distance, which rose into the horizon. I found the place intriguing. Wandering across the front lawn, I looked back at the house. A house of dreams. A castle. Beulah Land.

I passed by the fountain and found a path leading through a small wooden gate, and down another stone stairway. The house disappeared from view at the bottom of the steps. But there I discovered a secluded flagstone patio ringed with giant trees and a covered picnic area hosted by a massive stone fireplace. I stood in the center, truly awed. Southern white pine, black oak and hickory, an occasional yellow poplar and hemlock—the ring of trees surrounded me like the walls of a great shimmering canyon.

Nearby, a narrow creek ran down the slope. Beyond the creek, the land dipped then ascended among acres of Christmas trees that blended into the mountain. Nothing of civilization could be seen: no roads, no power lines, no buildings. I breathed in the beauty of it, and then stopped. I had to remember why I came and not allow the enchantment of the place to distract me.

I turned to go back, but the steep cliffs and peaks around me halted my steps. Daddy had told me the mountains were filled with generations of tradition and lore. *Who knew what real magic could be worked here?* I lifted my face to the sky, offering a spur-of-the-moment prayer of desire, soaking up the untold, undisturbed stillness of the history surrounding me. But my emotions roller-coastered, slamming into a wall of guilt again. *Oh, God. What if my children are living in horror? How can I endure even the possibility of it?* And yet I knew living at Shiloh was the best solution I had. The only help that had been offered to me. I had to rescue Dillon and Gracie from the church and bring healing and a sense of family into our lives.

The snap of a twig and a rustle of leaves drew my attention. Soft sounds of feet stepping on thick boughs of pine needles; flashes of motion and color flickering between the trees. He stood high on the hill and my breath caught in my throat. Ivy had called him my knight. His growing smile was as intimate as a mattress in an attic from a long time ago. Dressed like a lumberjack in a blue and white plaid flannel shirt rolled up to his forearms, faded jeans and work boots, Matthew took the stairs two at a time. Walking toward me, he smiled again. Gentleness emanated from him like a great glowing orb. A virtue I assumed he was born with. It radiated from his burning brown eyes down to his muscular legs. There was no other way to describe it. The delight over his face and the scent of pure pleasure he gave off was like a wild animal encountering a mate. I wanted to run from it, but couldn't. Matthew could've bounded off into the woods, slipped into the camouflage of the trees like a twelve-point buck, it wouldn't have surprised me

His deep, masculine voice cut through the quiet. "Whatchoo doing out here, Miss Andie Rose?" The sweetness in him was almost childlike. But the elegant ruggedness of him was like the Cedars of Lebanon. Coming to a stop, he stood tall and straight, his gaze searching for and finding mine. That split-second connection was of such enormous intimacy it had me walking backwards. In circles. Just to catch my balance. Hoping the extra space would soften the wild beat of my heart.

Never having feelings for anyone other than Joe, I felt my new self emerge. My heart suddenly changed its beat, and I walked out of the dark of my life into something else. Something so strong and intense, it resurrected my hope. I made a decision. *I'll stay. I'll stay with him until I get my children back, and Calvin is behind bars.*

"Ready to go to work?" he asked.

I smiled, tilted my head slightly and nodded, attempting to return his kindness.

With each step toward the house, my joy was made full. The dread dissipated. No longer alone, no longer watched, stalked, hunted. The familiar fretful strain evaporated. In its place, new emotions surfaced. In my wild and primitive state of mind, a mixture of the unknown and uncrushable enthusiasm was born. Maybe it was the first time I felt I had a chance at life. I was still exhausted, every muscle ached, and my spirit remained broken. But with every minute that passed, the peace that had started to fill my soul when I met Matthew seeped into even my darkest corners. A peace I didn't understand. My head said I should be afraid or at the very least, uneasy, but my heart wanted to sing.

For, lo, the winter is past, the rain is over and gone. . . .

The Gift of a Rose

Andie

Matthew led me to his desk, offering me his soft leather chair. He pulled up a straight chair next to mine, allowing himself access to his computer. He smiled and a nerve twittered in his cheek just above his dimple. When I sat, my knee lightly touched his. Even through our jeans, such closeness, however innocent, unsettled me. I forced myself to concentrate on the work ahead of us. He then handed me a yellow legal pad with letters he composed in the early hours of the morning: letters directed to department heads in various social service agencies and one to a family court judge—all acquaintances of the Callahan family. The letters didn't give anything away as to my whereabouts, or that Matthew was in search of information regarding my children. Just a few questions any social worker might ask about a set of teenage twins he'd heard had been taken away from their mother, and how it might set precedent in further custody cases. "A back door approach to obtaining any slip of information." he said.

Unrelated to our quest, he asked me to retype a contract, something about a land purchase he'd bugged Ivy to type for the past week. He said he would have Ivy show me the filing system and passwords to access his computer files. Matthew took a few minutes and explained basic word processing and I caught on quickly, finding I rather enjoyed it. But at the first opportune moment as he stood to root through his files, I reached into my front pocket, pulled out a folded piece of stationary and laid it in front of him. It contained a picture of my children and an address neatly printed in bold, precise lettering. "That's Joe's address. I drove through the security gate once and got a threatening call from him the next day. My visits were supervised. Visits that were always cancelled for some reason or another," I told him. "I phoned my attorney a few hours after they were taken from me to ask for help. He declined when I requested to make payments for any legal fees. I guess attorneys won't work on credit."

Matthew scowled. He poured us both coffee from a carafe on a nearby table. "I'll bet they threatened your attorney by the time you had called him." His expression hardened.

"Be careful, Matthew. Calvin's persuasive. He buys everybody off."

"I can't be bought. I know what he's worth; as much as I can find out on the surface. I never believed his slick TV message. Some gullible people, however, don't have the sense God gave a goat. How did you sit through that all those years? I mean, you don't seem the type." He sighed. "I don't mean to insult you. I'm sorry. It's hard for me to understand why thousands follow him, and seemingly, would die for him."

I sipped my coffee, hesitated, and then answered his question. "People are looking for God. When they see the miracles happen, they think they've found Him. They sit in Calvin's services with eyes like a deer's in headlights, sucking it up with puppet mentality. They want to believe it. He does their thinking for them, tells them what to say, read, sing, wear, watch on TV, how to act. His followers attach themselves to every word he preaches and follow it to the letter. It's their pass into Heaven. On the other hand, they don't know the evil going on behind the scenes, within his inner circle. Calvin is a strong-willed, domineering man who rules with a fist of steel. You can't question him or have any doubt or dissent, otherwise it's blasphemy. There *is* pressure through fear to believe him, and public humiliation if you don't. Those who leave the church are shunned and stripped of family, until they return and confess their sins publicly. I've seen it happen numerous times. I've experienced it."

Matthew shook his head in disgust. "That's what happened to you."

"Worse than that, really." I sat for a second, hesitant to tell him more. "Anyway, most who disagree with Calvin are made to feel as though they're stupid. Or backslid. Those who attend his services regularly are brainwashed. They're told they don't have the spiritual knowledge or experience to question him. In short, he gets people saved or re-saved, fills them with fear and trembling, then takes over their lives. It's a real shame, 'cause the youth are particularly vulnerable to his gift of persuasion and his feigned expertise. No matter how radical he is in his decisions or actions, the members will not criticize him outwardly. Even if there's mild disagreement, few have the guts to open their mouth. The congregation reasons that although he may be mistaken in some of his judgments, the overall good he accomplishes outweighs any minor flaws. After all, he preaches from the Bible. And the miracles, they happen. So who is going to argue with that?"

"I hear he gives thousands to charities all over the world. Food banks and such," Matthew said. "I'm sure there are good people who attend his church. Brainwashed or not."

"Certainly. If you're not employed there or part of his inner circle, you don't have a clue as to what's going on. And sure, his charitable notions look good, don't they? Fact is, Calvin's got a worldwide fan club that includes lots of rich and educated people. He's more than just a spiritual celebrity, now. Not realizing what they're actually doing, people worship him. He's the final authority. Nobody does anything but what he says to do. I swear, he can make the sweetest granny look like a demon from Hell if he wants to. Every week, he serves up God on a golden platter. He's gotten away with lies and corruption for years while the police and the government look the other way. Separation of church and state, you know. Whatever he wants, he takes. And good people or not, nobody challenges him. Last but not least, he can get your last nickel before you know you've dropped it in the bucket." I raised my coffee mug. "Someday, God has to stop this madness. As for me, I went through the motions just to survive. I thought I had no choice. Which was pretty stupid, looking back; I lost it all anyway."

Matthew inserted paper into the printer. "To be quite honest, your incredible insight and assessment of Calvin astounds me. It's obvious you speak from experience. You've lived through Hell because of this man. Perhaps God will use us to expose him for the world to see," he said, handing me a manila file folder.

"I hope so," I said.

Until I arrived at Shiloh, the constant abrasion of living had left me void of hope. When I accidentally touched the back of Matthew's hand, another dose of contentment ribboned through me. I contemplated telling him about John Rossi, but for some reason the trust wasn't quite there yet. There would come a time to talk about his murder, but God would have to write that moment on the wall. In the meantime, I kept it hidden.

§

Matthew left me alone the rest of the day. After reciting the long list of farm chores needing his attention, he said he planned to spend the day with Tobias and mentioned if I would like, we could have supper in town that evening. Though I busied myself typing and filing most of the afternoon, my nerves got the best of me at the thought of a date with Matthew. Several times I'd barely made it to the toilet. Besides I had nothing to wear. Until Ivy walked in with a box of Imodium AD and a smart little black dress she thought, "just might fit."

"Ivy, where did you get this dress?"

"I bought it at the mall in Asheville last week. It's way too small. My wide hips, you know. Been too busy to take it back. Matthew said you might be driving to town for supper. I thought you could use a new dress and there's no time for us to shop today. So, try on?"

"Oh yes, thank you. It's beautiful. But I'm afraid, I've—"

"No shoes? Size seven?" Black shiny pumps hung from Ivy's other hand.

"Are you psychic?"

Ivy laughed. Her accent turned as thick as Cajun gumbo. "No, Andie, I swan, just very observant. Tobias and I have made it our life work to take care of da Callahans. Salt of the earth. 'Specially Matthew. He's like my own. Dat man has smiled more the last twenty-four hours than I've seen in years. Now please, go try on." Ivy kissed my cheek, leaving a bright red tattoo of her lips. I took in her scent and smiled—perfume and pot roast.

The dress fit. Perfectly. Matthew phoned me to say we should be ready to leave by six. I picked the remains of *Really Red* toenail polish off my two middle toes, and then asked Ivy for remover and any extra polish she might have. I felt eighteen again. After a long bath, an attempt to fix my hair, and a fight to cover the dark circles that still invaded the space around my eyes, I was ready to call the whole thing off and hide in my room until morning.

"Andie?" It was Ivy again. "Some makeup and lipstick. I thought you might want to use it. And I thought you might like to wear these."

A pair of diamond earrings dangled from her fingers. She handed them to me and I let them roll around in the palm of my hand. "Ivy, I really shouldn't. I mean, are they real?"

"They're just earrings. Put them on. Enjoy."

"Thank you. Thank you so much. I'm so pale. I need the lipstick. But these, I'm not sure I should wear your earrings." I slipped them into my earlobes at Ivy's insistence.

"You're beautiful, see?" Ivy touched my face lightly, looking at me in the mirror.

I smiled. "The earrings are beautiful, not me."

"Silly girl. Learn to take a compliment. I bought them last year, on sale. Five thousand. Good price."

I choked. My eyes filled with tears as my hand covered my mouth.

"Just jewelry. I say again, enjoy. And this is from Matthew. He asked me to give to you."

My cheeks burning, I opened the shiny silver box. It was a bracelet. Pink pearls held together with a diamond clasp. "Oh," I whispered, running my finger over it. I bit my lip and blinked hard. *A gift? From a man I've just met?* The last gift I received from a man had been years ago, and at that moment I couldn't remember what Joe had brought me. Something made of olive wood from the Holy Land. It didn't matter because he took it with him when he left.

Ivy reached out and took the bracelet out of the box, then put it on my wrist. "Matthew hopes you like it. He thought you might accept it better if I gave it to you. He's so happy you're here. Come down when you're ready. He said he'll take his shower and then meet you in his study," she shouted, walking out the door and laughing all the way down the hallway. That's when it struck me like an arrow from a cupid named Ivy. Matthew wasn't the one pushing.

Guilt stirred within me. *This has to stop. I'm here to find my children, maybe learn a few computer skills, and start the process to uncover Calvin. Nothing more.* It was all very nice, and maybe I deserved a little of it, but it was not my way of life. I had to get a strong grip and wake up. Stop the ridiculous daydreams that had plagued me since I was a girl. I clenched my jaw. The reality was that our relationship wasn't going anywhere. I would tell Matthew that. Before the night was over.

Matthew

When I walked into the room where Andie waited, the soft spot I had in my head for her went down to my heart. From across the room, she was pretty. But from where I stood, she was beautiful. Pretty was a fact about Andie, but beauty was her force. She brushed her hair away from her face. Ivy's earrings looked stunning on her. Her lipstick was some shade of fifties red, probably borrowed from Ivy, too, but appealing. I noticed her arms were bare. The little pink pearls I gave her followed each other around her dainty wrist. She tilted her head to one side a few degrees, a look she'd given me before, one that was meant to be friendly, better than a smile, and she touched her earlobe. Her skin and face was full of light. Andie was as perfect, at least that night, in that light, as the diamonds in her ears.

"You're breathtaking," I said, without hesitation, as my heart pounded for mercy. Desire. An emotion I once thought I'd never feel again burned inside my chest, like an old Packard that hadn't been driven in years. My glance swept over her, appreciating her attractiveness and the femininity of her dress, black and elegant. When she was working in my office earlier, she had tied back her hair with a rubber band. Up close, her freshly washed hair fell from her head like molasses from a jar in glossy gold waves and bounced lightly around her shoulders. Her eyes, more sky-colored than bright blue, rose to me and held their warmth. The sight of her and the faster beat of my heart were welcome, like a ray of sunshine on a prison wall.

Andie

Surprised at his remark, my mind lingered on the way he said it, with sincerity, not false adulation. "Thanks. You clean up well, too." The very way he stood there told me he had made it in life. A man of great physical presence, he had dressed in the uniform of a man who knew how. Blue blazer, blue oxford shirt, khaki pants, all perfectly pressed and creased, he was all class. "Thank you for the bracelet; it's lovely. You're too kind. Since I'm your employee, does this constitute as sexual harassment?" I regretted my words after I said them.

But he opened his mouth and laughed, flashes of white teeth in his tanned face. "Sure. I do it for all the women I bring to Shiloh." He winked.

I punched him playfully in the arm.

"I'm glad you like it, but damn, doesn't that just beat all?" he teased.

"What?"

"I forgot to give you this." He held out a single rose. Deep velvety red and fragrant. "I figured since it was your middle name you'd like it."

I winced. "I really don't deserve these gifts."

"Not so. You *are* a gift."

Our eyes met, and in that unguarded moment I mulled over his flattery, sniffed the rose, and searched for a rebuttal to his compliment to no avail. The air hummed between us. "It's beautiful. Daddy called me Rosebud. They were his favorite flowers, roses. Mine too. I guess I should thank you for the compliment. Ivy said I should accept them more often."

"She's always right, in case you haven't noticed."

I raised my eyebrows and nodded vigorously.

Matthew offered me his arm. "Shall we go to supper?"

"I'm starved. Where to?"

"A little out-of-the-way place near Blowing Rock. I know the chef."

I took his arm and shivered. "Just for tonight, I'll stop being terrified. I'll sink into the few good memories I have and not the ones I've tried to forget."

"Then let's make more good memories for you tonight, shall we?"

"Alright."

He opened the door and we stepped out onto the porch. "Your chariot awaits," he said and grinned, offering his arm again. A fairy godmother had transformed my old rusted Pontiac into a BMW convertible. Royal blue and regal.

"Might be a little chilly." Matthew picked up a coat and a pair of gloves off a wicker rocker. "Ivy gave me these for you to wear, just in case. Ah, here's a scarf so your hair doesn't fly around."

Touched by their simple thoughtfulness, I fondled the coat, gloves, and scarf like an orphan child's first Christmas gift and tightened my grip on his arm as delicately as I could, walking to the car.

Every now and then Matthew looked over at me as we drove the Blue Ridge Parkway in comfortable silence, slowing down at the curves in the road, then accelerating. In the dim light, the hills once more took on the cloak of a well-told fairy tale. The sun played like a strobe light through the trees, until we ducked into the full shade of the mountains surrounding us. I pulled on the gloves, pushing down on the woolly spaces between each finger. The coat wrapped around me as if to say, 'don't worry, these people will take care of you now.'

The groaning sounds of the BMW, the drafts of nightfall's sweet air—they wove a subtle unfailing spell. The night air was alive on my face, like a young child's breath. It was a good thing he couldn't hear me singing over the noise, but I couldn't get the song out of my head that day. *He's like the wind. . . .* My heart sang all the way to Blowing Rock. Over and over I sang that Patrick Swayze song, substituting *he* for *she*, until the golden glow of evening faded into a blaze of stars that spanned a moonless sky.

If nothing else happened, the drive to supper that night would've been enough. The mood called for a new daydream. A fantasy. If only for one night. All the things I wanted to say—remind him of why I was there—were left at the house.

April 1993
A Forfeited Game

Reverend Calvin Artury

Disguised as an ordinary suburbanite in tennis shoes, sweat pants, a tennis racket slung over my shoulder, sunglasses, and a sweatband, I showed up at Tanglewood Park on time. Anxious to play a rousing game of tennis with Andie Oliver. DeSanto's crew surrounded the perimeter at strategic points while I remained close to the tennis courts. All eyes were fixed on me, ready to defend the Man of God—they had their instructions. Abduct the dark angel. Make certain that some innocent soul discover her body the next morning with her wrists slit in a pool of unforgiving red.

But she never showed. I waited fifteen minutes then stormed to a waiting car, furious. "She stood me up! That foul harlot!" Up until then no one dared touch me. Not a soul alive frightened me, had the audacity to question me, or possessed evidence to destroy my ministry and me. No one until Andie. And the worse thing was; I believed her. She wasn't bluffing and I knew it. I knew it because I had come to realize, she was just like me. She would stop at nothing to get what she wanted. She was my one wayward sheep. I had left the ninety and nine and went in search of her. But I would never get her back into the fold. Never.

All we like sheep have gone astray! We have turned everyone to his own way; and the Lord hath laid on him the iniquity of us all!

A Matter Of Trust

Andie

I felt as if we'd made little progress where Dillon and Gracie were concerned. My chance to kill Calvin had come and gone and I was concerned about the relationship developing between Matthew and me. For crying out loud, we weren't kids anymore. We were middle-aged and old enough to know better. I had learned that guilt and elation were like oil and water. The two didn't mix. But suppers with Matthew had been special. Ivy had certainly seen to that. I even cooked a meal or two in his unbelievably modern kitchen, remorseful that I enjoyed that, too. The rave reviews from my new friends surprised me, and I caught myself daydreaming that I belonged at Shiloh.

Matthew spent a few days in the fields with Tobias, having stated to Ivy that the farm had more immediate problems than the Governor's Ball. I resigned myself to printing invitations for the ball, filing stacks of paperwork, and typing letters every day: senseless and tedious work.

I'd finally had enough. I stood, stretched, and stepped outside. Accompanied by one or more of Matthew's dogs, I explored the grounds close to the house, found the old cemetery, the swimming pool, and the vegetable gardens. Matthew requested I not go to the winery or any public place without him. I understood he was concerned for my safety. It was quite a change from the life I had led and a welcome one, but it still filled me with a guilt-ridden conscience. I could not go one more day without hearing something about my children or I would go mad. Farm work and Governor's Ball be damned. My children were *my* priority.

The next morning after breakfast, I tiptoed into Matthew's office with the mail. Soft guitar music played through a hidden sound system.

"Hi, Matthew. Mail call." I raised the stack in my hand. "Ivy said it's your turn."

He smiled. "Come in."

I walked to his desk, my shoulders back in modest confidence. He took the mail from me and dropped it to his desk without even so much as a glance. "Thank you."

"You're welcome. Sorry to disturb you."

I turned to leave, but he stopped me with an abrupt but courteous, "Sit down. Please."

I took a seat directly across from him and crossed my legs at the ankles. My eyebrows rose with my posture and I asked, "What's up?" Not the question I really wanted to ask.

Matthew

A warm breeze ruffled the mound of papers on my desk, but Andie's eyes were fixed on the stacks of files that had slid to the floor; my paperwork buried me alive. She was freakish about neatness. I'd already learned that about her. *Could I get used to it? Do I care?*

Yet her eyes alone brought a breath of fresh air into my mundane life. The way she smiled, the way, despite her circumstances, she never seemed to tire. Her intelligence and wit, it brought energy to me. I shuffled through the report I needed to discuss with her. Information she needed to know.

"A few things," I said. "Give me a minute to review this report."

Andie

While he fumbled through his file, I looked around his office. A stocked bar with a tiny sink and refrigerator had been wedged into a corner. He kept a coffee pot or tea kettle running. His mahogany desk was nicked and dulled, what I could see of it. The top was covered with piles of paperwork, an array of pens, pencils, and a Civil War cannon paperweight made of iron the size of his fist. His business cards rested in a handmade decanter, probably painted by one of his children years ago. Diplomas from some college called Villanova, and certificates that read Family Psychology at the top hung on the wall behind him along with citations, thank you letters, and photographs of what looked like an island vacation. Maybe he liked to travel. He liked to read. I could see that. In addition to reference materials on various psychiatric disorders and books on grief, a small collection of old leather-bound books lined his bookshelves. *Probably first editions.* Framed photos of his son and daughter were displayed on his desk. He loved his children; I could see that, too. I felt warm around Matthew. Safe for the first time since the day I left the security of my daddy's cocoon to marry Joe. *If I could just get over feeling guilty about feeling guilty.*

"Sleep well?" he asked.

I nodded. "As always." I counted Mississippi's. Ten of them. I almost blurt out, *Cat got your tongue?*

But he opened his mouth, finally, and said, "Anything on *your* mind?"

"Dillon and Gracie." My answer was quick and sharp.

He picked up a pen and shoved himself away from his desk. "Andie, I need to tell you something." He rolled his pen between his palms. "I've done some investigating."

I shot to my feet and fisted my hands on my hips. "Without telling me? Why?" My question hung in the air, unanswered.

"Sit, Andie. Please?"

I sat, but not happily.

"Trust me. I know what I'm doing. My goal here is to not only return your children to you, but also keep you and them safe in the process. You're right about something. You're a wanted woman within the House of Praise. I have an informant who has spent the past two weeks attending church services there, and talking to people at the Praise Buffet. If you go to Dillon and Gracie now, they'll find you. Do you want that? They *are* looking for you, Andie, everywhere. No more shopping in town with Ivy, or suppers out. But I can't hold you here. You're not a prisoner. You can leave if you want, but let me stress that it's dangerous. You should consider yourself in hiding until we break this open and nail Artury to the wall along with everybody involved."

I narrowed my eyes, much as a mother might do to a rambunctious toddler. Then I softened. "Matthew, I've got to know about my children."

"And I'll tell you. I care about you, Andie. I don't want you going off half-cocked and end up with a bullet in your back. You're right about that place. I don't know why it's never been fully investigated, but I'm pushing now. I've been in touch with the Attorney General. I'm putting some pressure on, calling in some favors. Promise you'll let me handle things."

"I have so far, haven't I? I mean, I came here, trusted you, did as you asked, worked the past few weeks for you, waiting and hoping we'd make some headway on this, and you've done everything behind my back. You've got to trust me, too, Matthew. Now, how are they?"

"Okay, okay. When they were first taken from you they refused to go to church, for counseling, for anything. Within two days they ran away but didn't get very far. Someone from the church was then recruited to watch them every moment, from what my informant told me."

"Oh, Matt!" My heart dropped to the vicinity of my feet. I stood again and ran my hands through my hair, wanting to pull it out.

"Don't worry, relax, they're okay. They're smart, those two. Instead of trying to find you they ran to their Guardian ad Litem on their third attempt. They spilled their guts and were transferred to where they are now." Matthew referred to his file. "They're with a Mr. and Mrs. Henry Darwood in Winston-Salem. It's highly unusual, but they're living with an African-American family who evidently requested to take them in. The Darwoods went through the foster parent program several months ago and when they heard about your twins, they contacted the court. Seems they knew them? The Guardian ad Litem petitioned that Dillon and Gracie be moved to their home temporarily. The Darwoods live in your children's old school district but, thank God, the kids aren't attending the House of Praise for now. They refuse. It's been a blow for the church. Artury has everybody praying."

I had fallen back into the chair, wiping silent tears from my eyes. "Thank you," I said. "I can rest easy. Yes, the twins have known the Darwoods a long time. They're good people. Dillon and Gracie will be fine. For now."

"My informant reported your ex-husband's attorney is fighting this, but so far they're still in the Darwoods' home. I've got someone looking into the way the entire custody case was handled. As of now, Joe has four hours on Sunday he can take them to church, if he can get them to go. It seems your kids are resistant to it."

I grinned. "I'm sure the twins put up a stink about going with him. And if I know Joe, he's not pushing it. It's not Joe who wants them; it's Calvin. We can't stop, Matthew. We have to expose it all. But my kids are safe. Vernise and Henry love them. Can we get a message to the Darwoods, at least?"

"Can we trust them?"

"Absolutely!"

"Then I'll get word to them you are safe. That will ease their minds, I'm sure."

Steep Slopes

Matthew

I sensed a great load had lifted from her shoulders. She smiled and it warmed me. "How about a walk?" I asked, smiling back at her.

"Don't I need to get to work?"

I rubbed my eyes. "I've been up since four this morning. I need a break, and it's Friday. Ivy's gone grocery shopping. She won't need you today. Let's take a picnic lunch up to a nice lookout spot on the mountain. You like to hike?"

"Yes, as a matter of fact, I do. When I woke up this morning, the warm air came in the window and I thought about camping along the New River with Daddy, hiking up Stone Mountain or Hanging Rock, finding the waterfalls at South Mountain State Park, or walking across the swinging bridge at Grandfather Mountain—laughing in the blistering heat, sunburned, and covered with bug bites."

"Those are great memories of your father. You loved him."

"I adored Daddy. He was my world. He protected me as much as he could. I believe Joe would've done far more damage if not for Daddy putting the fear of God in him a couple times. He'd like it here."

More and more I loved the sound of her voice and her hint of an Appalachian accent. Suppers with her had been light and easy, avoiding the traps of family and heartbreak. For the first few days I treated her warily, as if she might be hot to the touch or shatter like glass. Day after day, as I got to know her, I looked forward to seeing her. Even mending fence with Tobias, I found myself yearning to be near her. Now listening to her talk so lovingly about her father, it made me feel closer to her somehow. "I'll get a basket of goodies packed. You might want to change into a different pair of shoes."

"Meet you on the back porch in ten minutes."

I laughed. "Back porch? Huh. And all this time I thought it was a charming veranda."

Andie

With the dogs trailing behind us, Matthew handed me a walking stick. "It's great for fending snakes off the trail," he said. I raised my eyebrows and he laughed.

We strolled past the barn and took a quick side trip to meet the horses. "Don't know if you like to ride, but we've got some wonderful trails. Here's my herd." Matthew pointed to every stall. "Smokey, Levi, Dan, and Judah. It was Tobias's idea to name them after the twelve tribes of Israel. Looks like we're on our way, except for old Smokey here. She's my mare."

"They're as magnificent as this farm," I said, rubbing Smokey between her huge eyes. I spied a large fenced area near the dog kennel. "What do you keep in there?"

"Look for yourself. Ivy's goats. Ivy loves goat cheese. You need to take a walk over to her house someday soon. She's a woman of many talents. That's why I latched onto her so many years ago. This farm belongs to Ivy and Tobias Dumass as much as it does to me."

Hearing the name *Dumass*, my abiding love for Mavis stirred within me. It struck me that the strange turn of events in my life might be Mavis's doing after all.

Matthew

I heard her breaths become shorter and faster. "This trail is steep," she said. "I couldn't have made this climb when I weighed 200 pounds."

"You weighed that much once?"

"Yep, more than once. You might as well know I wasn't always beautiful, as you so warmly call me."

"It's not healthy," he said.

"It's not pretty either," she said with a snip in her voice.

I stopped and looked back at her, knowing exactly what she alluded to. That men are pigs because men only love you if you look like a James Bond girl. "Right, it's not pretty. I know all about weight. I used to weigh fifty pounds more than I do now."

Increasing her pace to keep up with my long legs, Andie grew winded. "But it's not the same for a man."

"How so?"

"For a woman to disappear from her husband's sight, all she needs to do is become very fat."

"Sad, isn't it?" I said. "That some men are like that."

She didn't answer me. But I wasn't about to hike another foot until I said what was in my heart. We needed a pit stop. She needed to catch her breath. I put my foot on a fallen log beside the trail and leaned over, resting my arm on my leg. Staring at my feet, I kicked a patch of moss off the log and tried not to mumble. I raised my eyes. "Andie, do you know what unconditional love is?"

"You mean like I have for my children?"

"Yes, kind of. But I mean between a man and a woman."

"I think so. My parents had it, I believe. Mavis talked about it. I can't say I've experienced it."

"That's too bad. Because when two people love each other, whether fat or skinny, young or old, paralyzed or half their body burnt, love never wavers. It's always there, constant, growing every day. I don't mean to lecture; it's the teacher talking in me, I guess. Anyway," I winked, "skinny people are just hangers for their clothes." My attempt to say something witty bombed. She didn't respond other than to wipe the sweat from her brow and take a swig of water from my canteen. "Listen, I didn't mean—"

"Joe made fun of my weight all my young life," she interrupted. "He hated it. It made me worse, I think. I'm not sure if men can possess unconditional love. Maybe. A few. Very few."

I had no way to persuade her. Besides, was it necessary to try?

Yes.

My heart finally convinced me. It was more than a rescue. I had a sudden indisputable feeling of rightness. I stepped back. An urge to clutch her hair and pull her against my chest flooded my body. I breathed deeply and slowly until the craving passed. She was not just a needy woman I wanted to help out of a bad situation. It was more than that.

Oh, yes—so much more.

Andie

We continued up the steep slopes of Shiloh's mountain. His big boyish stride was hard to keep up with. When we arrived at the top, the view from the cluster of rock where we stood took away what little breath I had left. A bashful sun rose high in the sky, but the spring air did not lend one breeze in the heat of the day. The unusual warmth filled the trees with seemingly hundreds of birds. I sat on a warm rock as Matthew spread out a blanket. He pulled out a quickly thrown-together lunch of bread, cheese, two apples, and a bottle of Shiloh wine. "A fruity Riesling," he said. Filling two clear plastic cups with wine, he then set them in the sun. After positioning the food on a paper napkin beside our drinks, he sliced both apples. A light wind stirred the air. I ran my fingers through my hair and pushed wayward strands away from my eyes. In four months I'd have yet another birthday.

"Oh, and now the *piece de resistance*. Ivy's goat cheese." Matthew sliced the soft cheese into chunks while I watched, not saying a word.

We were alone in the clearing. It had been a five-mile trek from the trailhead. Soon the foliage would be fully green, and the number of hikers and tourists coming to the area would increase. But Shiloh's mountain was Matthew's private piece of wilderness, the mountain and the rolling sunlit countryside that lay beneath us and beyond. I allowed my mind to revisit the past as I gazed at a turkey vulture, gliding on a current above us.

"I'm sorry I didn't bring a white tablecloth or silver candlesticks," Matthew said and grinned. "Too much weight for a hike."

I didn't respond to his attempt to make me smile. Images from years gone by had returned. Scenes more familiar than the well-worn trail was to Matthew. Scars on my soul, rivaling the depth of the gorge below us.

"Okay, I've waited out the silence. Let's talk. What do you want to toast?" he asked.

I looked past him and up to the sky at the vulture circling us. "The death of monsters."

Matthew gave me a puzzled look. "A strange toast."

"It fits," I responded simply.

Holding up his cup, he proclaimed, "I suspect your meaning, and I agree. To the death of monsters. Religious and otherwise."

We touched cups and took a sip. The bread was soft and the cheese tart, but I could only manage a few bites. Matthew quickly drank a cup of wine and poured another. I nibbled my bread but wasn't interested in more food or drink. I stared at the sky. In my mind, events from the past demanded my attention like a circling flock of vultures.

"Neither of us has led normal lives, Andie." In his inept attempt to break the silence, it was the wrong thing to say.

"Normal? What's normal? Normal for me is waking up from a nightmare and realizing you're still in one. Depression was normal for me. Having my heart broke. Every day. That was my normal life. I've heard depression is repressed anger and frustration. I can certainly believe it. I ate everything I could get my hands on, and I couldn't stop eating. It was all I had. It's how I coped. I spent every extra dime, and money I didn't have, on food, and then on cigarettes."

Matthew shook his head, obviously upset. "I did the same thing when Jessie died. All I did was eat, watch old movies, and sleep the days away. Except I never ran out of money."

I turned away. "Lucky you."

He grabbed my arm. "Hey, let's talk about this. Money doesn't buy happiness—"

"Stop! I'm so sick of that overused and stupid cliché, I could puke. It buys a hell of a lot of happiness if you ask me! Do you know what it's like to have nothing? To live in poverty? To want a child so bad you almost die to get one? Do you know what it's like to have everything you hoped for and dreamed of yanked out from under you because some damn preacher said you were a dark angel?" I jerked my arm from his grasp.

Matthew's eyes filled with tears. A look I knew Joe's eyes were incapable of. He reached for my hand but before he could touch me, I said, "Let's go."

"What is it?"

"You don't know me or the world I lived in. How could you possibly?"

"Your folks weren't poor," he said.

"No, but I was. I couldn't afford to feed my kids, Matt! Not on my own. My parents helped me, sure, but they were nowhere close to having what you have here at Shiloh. And they had my needy sister and her five needy kids to deal with. How can you possibly understand me, what it was like for me, losing everyone I loved, being beaten and attacked in my own home first by my ex-husband and then by Calvin's thugs. Having evidence I can't use. They threatened to kill my kids, Matt. I lived in my car, for Christ's sake. Do you have any idea what that can do to a person? The hopelessness of driving around hour after hour, sleeping in a Honda; I cried until my head felt like it was about to split open. How could I possibly expect you to ever know what I've been through?" I had to stand. Move. Get away from the vultures.

Matthew

I helped her stand but I refused to move away, causing her to look up at me. Her light blue eyes pierced me as nothing had before. My heart broke for her. "I'm sorry. I can't imagine the horror you've experienced. And yes, I'm blessed I've never had to worry about money, but it can all be taken away from me tomorrow. I know that, too. We both know the pain of losing our children, of losing someone we love to a monster."

She paid no attention to me. Her hands were in fists. "Calvin put a curse on me! I've gone back and forth, over and over that muddy road, for years, trying to figure it out. What sin did I commit to make God wash His hands of me? I'm angry, Matthew. I'm really, really angry. I've asked God why? Why! Why does He only hear me when I'm screaming at Him!" Her fury was no surprise. She'd earned it. I longed to hold her. Reassure her. Treading the ground in circles, her eyes ablaze, Andie swung her fists in the air.

I grabbed her shoulders. "Stop, Andie. Look at me. You have a right to your anger. I'm not here to hurt you. I . . . I'm falling in love with you." Suddenly I was so in love my mouth refused to work, and I was positive she thought me a babbling idiot. She had caught me off-guard as I poured out my heart to fall at her feet. But I had to stop her anger and the only way I knew was with the love I felt for her.

She stared at me, breathing rapidly. She didn't utter a sound or even twitch. Her face had disbelief written across it. Finally, she shot me a smile with her eyes.

"Is that okay with you?" I asked.

"I don't want my bad luck to rub off on you, Matt."

"Let me worry about that. How about we turn your bad luck around?" I pulled her to me and hugged her. A friendly hug, not a romantic one. I was not about to force myself on her. Andie had experienced enough male dominance. Sexual and otherwise, I was quite sure of it. I didn't expect her to love me. But I would be honest with her every day for the rest of her life, hoping I would be in it. Even with all the fancy furniture, rugs, and crown molding, my home had become just a farmhouse to me. I'd been lonely a long time.

"I'm still angry, but you've made my life bearable," she said. "Thank you. And thank you for your kindness. I know your heart still hurts from losing your little girl. It was rude of me not to acknowledge that. That was a horrible time for you. I'm sorry."

"Talking about Jessie has helped me more than you know. Maybe I shouldn't have told you about the love part. I'm sorry, too. It just seemed the right time. You needed a diversion."

"It's okay. Really. It's all crazy, I know. This place and you within such a short time, but," she hesitated, "I'm falling in love with you, too. I'm certain of it."

My hand cupped the small of her back and drew her closer. Absorbing the depth of her grief and the horrors of her past, I dared to touch her face with my fingers. She drew back, surprised, so I bent and planted a kiss on her tear-stained cheek. Her skin smelled sweet, as sweet as the wine we drank only moments before. I kissed her again, on the forehead and was taken aback by the softness of her skin. The longer I stood close to her, the stronger my need to kiss her lips became. "Andie, you are all my thoughts and hopes."

Andie

Let him kiss me with the kisses of his mouth: for thy love is better than wine.
The Song of Solomon scripture rang in my head as his lips moved across
my skin, tasting my salty tears. My breath caught, tender on his cheek, and
I turned ever so slightly until my mouth was close to his. He accepted my
invitation, his hands warm and strong, yet gentle, at the back of my neck.
His third kiss was a real one; a kiss unlike any I ever had. A kiss that began
to chisel away at my anger.

Nigeria For Jesus

Reverend Calvin Artury

I startled at the sight of my own shadow. Never before in my ministry had I worried about my casual indiscretions. Until Andie didn't show at Tanglewood Park. Furious, I ordered Evan to get the truth from Joe by any means necessary. He put a gun to Joe's head. Joe pissed his pants, but stuck to his story. After Evan was convinced, I assembled my posse. It was quite possible that her threats were bogus, as there was no sign of a police investigation. Not one reporter showed up at my door. Maybe she *was* bluffing. Satan had surely taken her over. She didn't have a chance against me, and maybe she had realized that fact right before she took a gun and blew off the top of her pretty head.

Still, I ordered Tony DeSanto to dispatch five men daily to search for her. Additional men were posted to watch members of her family, as well as her children, hoping to see her surface. Tony discovered she had sold her car and quit her job, sending her final paycheck to an attorney who, after several visits from Percy Turlo, swore he hadn't seen her. Checking every flophouse, shelter, and low-rent apartment building in the city, someone found a beat-up Pontiac with four flat tires in the parking lot of the Magnolia Monarch Apartments. A few of Andie's belongings littered the back seat. An old sweatshirt, a magazine, water bottles, and a receipt with her name on it from Space Saver Storage Units. All of her possessions had been given to various charity organizations or sold by the owner of the facility. We got a small break when Percy shoved her picture in the super's face at the Magnolia Monarch. For one hundred dollars he blubbered that some man from Social Services had come in and paid her electric bill. That she vacated a short time after she'd moved in, leaving with the same man. But the super was too drunk to remember names or faces. Even after Percy beat him like a dirty rug, he still couldn't remember.

When I received word that Andie was still alive, I fell into a chair and massaged my chest. Within the hour I offered a sizeable bonus to any of Tony's men who brought her to justice. My connections within the county offices, the police department and legal system had produced nothing. Nobody knew who had taken her from the apartment. Or they weren't talking.

At my Monday morning staff meeting I pounded my fist on the conference table and declared, "As long as her children are in the area, she will be, too. I want her found!" Of course the congregation and my staff assumed I wanted to lead her to salvation again. Only Evan, Silas, and Tony's crew knew that Andie Oliver's days were numbered. I felt an enormous pull of the Spirit to protect the ministry. I would no longer tolerate derogatory remarks. Pure blasphemy; that's what it was. As apostle, prophet, evangelist, pastor and teacher, I was, after all, a five-fold ministry rolled into one man of God. *The Lord is my light and my salvation—whom shall I be afraid? . . . I will lie down and sleep in peace, for you alone, Oh Lord, make me dwell in safety.*

§

My newly remodeled 10,000-seat auditorium, packed to over-flowing, rumbled and vibrated from the beat of drums, guitars, and the full orchestra that accompanied the Men of Praise quartet. A powerful audio system, with Joe at the helm, cast their voices throughout the great sanctuary. Lifting their hands and bringing the congregation to their feet, the praise and worship leaders sang my new favorite song: *Our God is an awesome God!*

My boots barely hit the platform as I bounded out during my congregation's standing ovation. Without delay, I omitted all preaching and entered into full-blown prophecy. The Spirit inside my body blazed white-hot, shooting outward into my arms, burning my fingertips. My eyes rolled back, I flung my hands into the air and cried out. "The cross is appearing in a vision! Thus saith the Lord! I have sent my Holy Prophet, Calvin Artury, to you. For some this is your last warning. I will cut you off because you lie! You speak untruths about the Prophet of God, my son, Calvin Artury. There will be no Calvary and no forgiveness for you. I will not forgive you in this world nor in My Heaven. I give you the kiss of death this night, to never look your way again, saith Jehovah-Shalom. I called you unto holiness, but Satan is leading you straight to eternal damnation. I will destroy your soul as well as your body. You will open your eyes in the fires of Hell and scream the scream of the damned. But! I will serve you your last drop of mercy tonight!"

Dripping with sweat as the prophecy ended, I could not stop. "Oh people, cry out to Jehovah! Oh God, show mercy to your people! One more drop; please! How many sealed their doom tonight, God? Wait, Lord; don't tell me, I don't want to know. People, listen to me! If you fight God's church, it will bring death and destruction to your door. Remember, Jehovah-Rohi has killed before, and He will kill again. Oh yes, be assured dear people, He will kill again."

"We must wage war against dark angels who threaten Jehovah, threaten us! We must trample demons underfoot! These are the last days, and it will get worse, Saints of God, it will get worse! But, remember signs and wonders follow them who believe!"

I prayed loud and hard against the darkness I predicted was to come against me, bringing my congregation to a feverish pitch. My people cried out for God to uncover the dark angel who had made war against the House of Praise. I wailed from my new golden pulpit. "When you blaspheme against the Holy Ghost, you become as a demon from Hell. God has bestowed upon me the fruits and the gifts of the Spirit. I speak the oracles of God: I am Jehovah-Nissi's mouthpiece. He talks through me and I am here to tell you tonight that Andie Oliver is this ministry's darkest angel. If you see her, you need to report her whereabouts to a staff member, immediately!"

The power of the Spirit had passed through my lips into the congregation like a current. Their arms raised to the ceiling, eyes closed, the members reached as high as their faith would take them. I had dared to name her from the platform. I was not stupid enough to believe every person in my church agreed with me, and yet it was a risk I was willing to take. I wanted it planted into the minds of every soul sitting in that vast auditorium. She was God's number one enemy. When she turned up dead, the faithful would rejoice. They would celebrate the Lord's final battle and victory over the dark angel.

§

Within the week, preparations were underway for the largest televised miracle crusade in the history of my worldwide ministry. Africa. Port Harcourt and then Lagos, both cities on the southern coast of Nigeria at the mouth of the Gulf of Guinea. The first two weeks of August were slated for these giant campaigns for souls and for the Nigerian people to receive their miracles and the gift of tongues, to ensure their place in the rapture of the church.

Mammoth platforms were underway. Constructed by the free labor of Nigerian men and women, these vast altars elevated my entire ministry team several feet above the crowds. I prepared my script, making a new list of medical conditions, diseases, and infirmities to memorize, and practiced day and night in front of a full-length mirror. "There are 5,000 people here tonight with AIDS who will be healed!" I made a mental note to exclaim it with a little more exhilaration and authority. Mentioning AIDS lifted any African crowd to pinnacles of excitement. That, and witchcraft. "Witchcraft devils, oh sweet people, if you could only see what I see!" I looked in the mirror. I loved the way my body moved when I said the word 'witchcraft.' I felt on fire as I said it out loud, even in my private office.

"One thousand souls are afflicted with something the doctors cannot diagnose, but God knows every affliction, and He will heal what medical science can't cure! This is the miracle power, people. Take it! Be thou every whit whole!" I'd fine-tune it a little more, add the powerful new messages of prophecy I'd been rewriting, and be ready by the Fouth of July annual revival at the House of Praise. I had to practice all of it on my own people first. If I received the response I wanted, I'd take it to Africa.

I knew I could sell religion better than anybody. If given the opportunity, I'd go toe-to-toe with Madalyn Murray O'Hair and force prayer back into schools; overturn that damnable Supreme Court decision. I'd show her. I'd talk to Evan about it. If I could pull that off, I'd rule the Christian world.

CNN had agreed to send a team of reporters to cover the Nigerian crusade. Evan said to expect prime-time press coverage on that tour, along with an immeasurable outpouring of love offerings. I had instructed all three weekly House of Praise church services, the radio broadcasts, and the daily TV shows to devote time to taking up special offerings for the campaign. Record crowds of a million or more were expected to cram into the outdoor arenas. It would take millions of dollars to pull it off. Huge crates of audio and video equipment, blessed cloths, and translated tracts were prepared for shipment. It was the American invasion of *Onward, Christian Soldiers* on African soil.

Sleepless In Shiloh

Andie

The day had ended with the first words of love spoken, holding hands, and trekking down the mountain. But I didn't want to talk about the turn in our relationship. Not yet. I wasn't ready for long conversations and all the gooey stuff that went with it. My mind was too burdened to chase the dream of a life with Matthew. A life of having my every need met, and then some. As sweet as it sounded, it was too much to contemplate and I appreciated that he didn't push it.

Ivy returned to her house around six. Tobias poked his head inside the back door to say he'd finished mending the south pasture fence. He chatted with Matthew as I dished up Ivy's chicken and dumplings for supper. I handed Tobias containers to carry home, then Matthew and I picked up our plates and strolled to the sun porch. Dark wood beams, stucco walls, terra cotta floor tiles, a fire, and arrangements of fresh flowers—another talent of Ivy's—surrounded us. Sitting at a small table, both of us lost deep in thought, the quiet stifled any and all conversation.

Matthew yawned and stretched his arms over his head. "I'm heading to bed early. It's been a long day."

My voice cracked, and I cleared my throat, avoiding his eyes. "You deserve a good night's sleep. I plan to curl up in front of the TV for a while." I wasn't ready to see the inside of his bedroom. I wasn't sure I ever would be.

In further silence, we cleared our dishes and tidied up. Matthew's assistance amused me. I wasn't used to a man's help in the kitchen. He sensed my uneasiness, though, because he flipped the dish towel over his shoulder, put his hands on my shoulders, and said, "Please don't read anything into what I said to you today. Honesty is important to me, and letting you know how I feel is part of that. It'll only go as far as you want it to go. I'm committed to bringing Artury down, but I'm more committed to ensuring you find happiness again, whether it's here with me or someplace else. It's up to you."

"Thanks, Matt. Thanks for that." I gave him a weary shrug. "I guess I'm a scarred woman. Damaged goods. I usually accept what I'm offered, but no man has ever offered me much. It's a new experience. Please forgive me for not knowing where my head is right now."

"Understandable. Nothing to forgive. Good night," he said, and kissed my forehead.

I smiled in return. Listening to him trudging up the staircase, I felt as if I were dying from emotional malnutrition. I wanted him to come back down and dispel my loneliness. At supper I had the uncanny feeling I was looking through him toward some unspoken private sadness of his own. Quite possibly, we belonged together. When I thought about it, it was more than coincidence, our meeting.

"Mavis? You listening? Did you have a hand in this?"

§

I tossed and turned and reached across the king-sized bed. The sheets were cold. Pushing myself up on my elbows, I read the muted red glow of the digital clock—3:15 a.m. "I can't stand this." I slid out of bed and into the jeans and shirt I'd hiked in the day before, pulled up my hair, and twisted it unevenly back into a ponytail. Creeping out of my room and down the long staircase, I then slipped into a pair of boots and somebody's old Carhartt coat hanging in the utility room. Quietly, I turned off the alarm and unlocked the back door, and then headed to the barn. I had to find something mindless to do. Something to occupy my time until I could sleep. Lying wide-awake all night, I had examined not only the impossibility of it all, but also the improbability of living at Shiloh. And yet, knowing Dillon and Gracie were living with the Darwoods gave me a blessed sense of peace. Once Vernise Darwood knew I was in safe hands, my old friend would find a way to console the twins.

Overhead, the sleepy blue sky flickered dimly through night's haze. I switched on the barn lights. The horses stirred. Judah and Dan poked their heads out of their stalls. The dogs woke, but once they saw me, they stopped barking. I gave each of them a good scratch behind their ears as they found a place to lay in the hay to watch over me. I took off my coat and threw it into a corner, picked up a shovel and a pitchfork and got to work cleaning stalls.

Losing all track of time I didn't even notice the pink sky in the east. The morning air was cool and dry, but full of promises of good things to come. After singing the first line of Aretha's, *RESPECT*, I heard the sound of rustling feet causing me to almost jump out of my boots. I whirled around, hand to my throat. "Damn it! You scared me to death!" I swallowed back the tightening in my chest.

"G'morning to you, too," he said. His thick morning voice reminded me of peanut butter fudge. Smooth, rich, and sweet, with a touch of salt. "Tobias told me you were out here. I didn't mean to spook you. Keep singing. I like it." With one shoulder resting against the planked barn wall, Matthew's presence was like a hard punch to my gut, which rumbled at the sight of him. Six foot two inches of Southern gentleman, his handsomely bearded face was healthy-looking in the cold air, his silvery hair tousled by the wind. Dressed for working outdoors, he jammed one hand into the pocket of his denim jacket he wore over a gray wool sweater, and the other into a pair of soft, well-worn jeans molded to his long legs. Scuffed boots crossed at the ankles—*whew*. He appeared as though he'd just stepped off the runway for Ralph Lauren.

"No, sorry. My concert is over."

Matthew ran his hand over his mustache and grinned. He had an air of calm and confidence I liked. But it was his deep-dimpled smile that was most reassuring, and I felt a strange numbed comfort just standing next to him.

"Don't you think you should take a break? This is hard work."

His silky words added even more heat to my blush and I reined in a swoon. I'd never swooned; I'd seen it done once or twice, but no man had ever given me reason to swoon. Conscious of my gunked-up jeans, shit-covered boots, and sweat-soaked face, I forced my hands not to mess with my

God-only-knew-what-was-splattered-in-it hair. "Maybe you should wear a cowbell around your neck when you skulk. Whistle or holler or something." The problem was, I didn't know what to do with my inward reaction to him, so I pretended it didn't exist.

"Uh, was I skulking?"

"Well, you surprised me." He surprised me, sure enough. "Actually, you scared the shit out of me," I told him honestly.

"Speaking of shit. I see you don't mind putting your hands in it," he said.

I smiled and pointed to the clean stalls. "Well. I got the floors as clean as I could." Not able to stand motionless around him, I looked around for my coat.

"Stalls look good," he said. "I didn't know you like to work with horses. It's a wonder they let you guide them out. They appear relaxed enough." Matthew walked over to Levi and patted his large black rump. "They seem fine."

I lifted one shoulder and refrained from rolling my eyes, feigning indifference with the exact determination I used around the few men I scorned after the Jasper fiasco. It wasn't easy. I felt his tug on my closed heart, like a beetle opening a bud. He made me squirm. With thoughts, feelings, and vibrations I never had with Joe or experienced in my life, my magnolia heart blossomed. I shot him a grin and chuckled, "I don't know much about horses. But I sure can clean a stall. Yesiree, I've shoveled plenty of shit in my lifetime. Not afraid of hard work, I guess . . . or horse shit." *Oh my God, I'm rambling.*

He laughed. I smiled back and bent over to tie my boot. When I straightened and tucked my shirt into my jeans, I felt my head spin. I leaned against the wall, forcing myself to breathe slowly. Sweat ran hot down my neck, my chest, and over my galloping heart.

"I still think you're beautiful," he said, guiding Levi back into his stall.

Plain tuckered out and sore, I bit back a sigh and gave him the glare of a mother with teenagers. "Eau de Equine. It's my signature fragrance. You like?" I shook my head and snorted.

Matthew shot back. "I do. We should bottle and sell it. Put your picture on it."

"What a bunch of hooey!"

That time, we both laughed. Unlike my ex-husband, he had a sense of humor, and a clever mind behind his fine-looking face.

"Why are you out here? Tobias will have to find something else for his helper to do this morning."

His elegance intimidated me. "Sorry. I couldn't sleep. I think I could now."

"Then why don't you? I'll let Ivy know she'll have to wait another day for you to help in the garden."

Our eyes met. "Wonderful. I'll soak in the tub, then get some sleep. I just had to think."

"Did you think about me?"

"Mostly."

"Good thoughts, I hope."

"Wicked good thoughts," I teased. "But we need to talk."

"About?"

"Each other. Our families. I know only what you've told me, and that's not much. For instance, Ivy told me your mother was a preacher. Why didn't you mention that to me? And how did you lose the top of your finger? All we ever talk about is your work. I'd love to know more about your children. You haven't told me a thing about your siblings, and—"

"Whoa." Matthew placed his hand on my shoulder and grinned. "We'll talk. Later. You need rest."

"Okay." I blew out a breath. Stopping along the flagstone path, I bent forward to poke my nose into a dogwood flower hanging from a tree. Taking in the splendor of the place, I walked slowly to the house with Matthew following me. Spring perennials lined the walks while green buds sat ready to burst on every tree limb. Early morning sunlight percolated through the dense tangle of red maple and pine; the grounds of Shiloh were a peaceful idyllic scene from a Currier and Ives postcard.

"Better leave your boots and coat outside. Ivy'll pitch a fit if you take them in."

I laughed a tired laugh. "Her fits are milk toast compared to my mother's."

"When you get up this afternoon, I'll be in my office working. We need to make plans to retrieve the items in your lockbox. We'll go after hours so you won't be seen."

"You can do that?"

He rolled his sensual eyes and gave me a smile of amusement.

"Never mind."

I could barely hold my eyes open as I slid my tired body up the stairs, my socks making muted padding noises on every step. My wintery heart had truly warmed again, and I felt myself plunging into something far more entangling than a casual liaison. I was grateful to live in the same universe with such a man. A man so sure of himself and his rightful place in the world. A man like Matthew Callahan.

ICE-COLD INDIGNATION

Reverend Calvin Artury

In my office pouring through the scriptures, I spent time in the presence of The Most High. Remembering. I had laid myself on the altar as a young seminary student. Jehovah-Jireh had rewarded me with many gifts and blessings and lambs to sacrifice. I had given all. All to Jesus I surrendered. My cleansings occurred monthly back then.

Every time I touched a man.

My greatest peace occurred in my earliest childhood when I was seven, during tent meeting week. It was a special time for Mama and me. I was a good son, never leaving my mother alone—even when my father did. After a long, hot service under a canvas filled with wooden benches, straw, and the smell of sweat-soaked bodies, Mama and I enjoyed the swimming hole.

"Baptize me, Calvin!" Her playful laughter, her soprano voice encouraging me to swim into the deep, rang as loud and pure as if it were yesterday. The frigid creek water frightened me as a child. *"Go on, Calvin, no time like the present. Jump in!"* Her words surfaced to the top of my ice-cold memory. *"Gotta bale hay when the sun shines, baby."*

I jumped in. I sure did. More than anything I wanted to make her proud. But in the middle of my precious memories, a cesspool gurgled and seeped.

At thirteen, I discovered church camp, then kissing men. And no, I wouldn't think about my father's sisters. Vile women who had attached leeches to my soul. I'd not think about them.

Not ever. Not if I could help it.

Except for the cherished memory of my mother, women were the barbed wire of my life. Keeping me from the Kingdom of God, women were an inscrutable force to be reckoned with. They never left me alone when I walked out of covenant with God. Prissy females with painted faces and pointy breasts. Loose women who threw themselves at me and not just in a bar. They followed me around the church and I hated it. Mama had told me the sure way to Heaven was to preach God's word. I'd also started preaching to keep women at arm's length.

A new suit and shoes, my hair cut high and tight and neatly combed back with dashes of greasy kid stuff, I took pleasure in my look as a dapper young preacher. That's when I spied Vivi. She was seventeen and unreservedly happy. The prettiest girl I'd met that summer. Her coffee-brown eyes made me jittery just watching her sing. She was already saved and not among the girls who swayed their hips like belly dancers down the aisle between rows of wooden benches packed hip-to-hip with the saints of God. Girls in thin cotton dusters who had fixed their eyes on any evangelist in town for the week. Girls who pranced straight to the altars in sweltering tent meetings and summer revivals. I directed the flock of mostly women in the sinner's prayer, but was never sure if it was Jesus they sought, or me. Flinging their unsaved arms into the air for deliverance from all sin, they shook their breasts and jiggled their behinds in front of every red-necked boy in town.

Vivi was different. She played the piano for her church, was saved and lived holy, like my mother. To my surprise, she not only said yes to receiving the baptism in the Spirit, but to my marriage proposal as well. I went through with it, figuring I was only in it for appearance sake anyway. Godly congregations wanted their young pastors married off to a church member. I assumed Vivi would split once she had opened my Pandora's box. Besides, what did she know about being a preacher's wife? But what *I* didn't know was the clout Vivi's daddy wielded. In the end, I praised God for Vivi: my blessing, my opportunity to enter into the circles of the politically rich and famous. From where I stood, it was my big break and I took it. The results were sanctuaries filled with wealthy members, sinners to save, and a chance to travel the world.

Of course, I struggled with the scripture. After all, my followers expected a family man. Believe me, I tried. I'd married Vivi and tried hard. Sometimes it was good. But most times, having sex with Vivi was like trying to put penny loafers on a pig. To her credit, she never gave up. She loved me until the end. I just couldn't love her back. Not the way she deserved.

Fannie's voice interrupted my thoughts and prayers. "Reverend Artury, Pat Robertson's secretary is on the line, she's needing your reservation."

"Yes," I sighed. "Tell him I'll be there."

For months The Christian Coalition had been pushing for my participation. Political nonsense in my mind. My kingdom was not of this world, although I had publicly agreed with Billy Graham, that evangelical Christians should organize corporately with the goal of gaining control of congress, the judiciary, and the executive branch of government. Pat Robertson's Coalition sought to gain control of the Republican Party. I wasn't interested.

My plan to amass millions of dollars and take the nation by storm wasn't for political gain as was my colleagues. My desire to take the world for the cause of Christ was the eternal flame that burned in my soul.

Like my marriage to Vivi, I would attend the Road to Victory Conference for appearances sake. In truth, I despised them all—Fallwell, Robertson, Oliver North, all of them. Bloodsuckers on the mind of Christ. Their stealth tactics, however, were maneuvers I wanted to learn more about.

Currently too many meetings besieged me, and I was late for the next one. Lately, I'd found myself wanting to be just a country preacher again. Leave the business side of things to Evan and everybody else. But God had entrusted His kingdom into my hands alone. I had built it brick by brick and been rewarded plenty. My legal team had called this latest meeting. More accusations of illegal dealings. The church would never cease to be persecuted. From early Christianity until the present, endless harassment and scandal followed the children of God. And in the past few weeks, I had forgotten too many appointments. My dentist. My supper with PTL network executives. How embarrassing. Arriving in time for coffee and dessert. I'd even forgotten to schedule my trip to New York and the yearly meeting with my tailor. All I wanted was to prepare for my next sermon, spend time in prayer, and a soft chest to lay on. The battles of the mind escalated with every legal inquest.

"Your car is here, Reverend Artury."

Time for war.

I walked to my waiting car in a torrent of rain. The liquid needles bruised my flesh and soaked my hair. I had forgotten to put up my umbrella.

Strong Coffee And Intuition

Andie

Ivy's presence filled a room and overtook it. Most people liked her, despite or perhaps because of her habit of telling everyone exactly what she thought. Her boisterous laugh was contagious. It was plain to see why Matthew loved her. Her protective glance followed me to the coffee pot. "How you feeling? You slept a long time."

I checked my new watch, another gift from Ivy. "My goodness, it's one o'clock. I guess I have. Not hard to do here. I've missed a whole day, haven't I?" I poured myself a mug of Ivy's coffee, rich and strong, with a kick like a Clydesdale. I recalled Matthew saying he valued Ivy for her unfailing courtesy, forty-five years of friendship, and for her coffee.

"I know this is none of my business, Andie, and you've only been here a month. But time has no meaning when the stars, planets and moon line up . . . and all indications point the way."

"What are you talking about?"

"Matthew ask you to marry him yet?" Ivy beat three eggs into a bowl of coffee cake batter. "Have you thought of moving here?"

"It's only been a month!" I wasn't surprised Ivy knew. I couldn't help but smile at her inquisitiveness. "If you must know, he's not asked. I've got nothing to move, anyway." I sat at the kitchen table, drinking my coffee and folding towels I'd pulled from the dryer. The window rattled and I glanced outside to see rain clouds moving across the sky.

"Huh. Tobias asked me to marry him the week after we met. At your age, a month is plenty of time. You best be thinking about your answer because I know Matthew, and he'll be asking. The man is in love. He wants you here. You need to think about it. About commitment. Marriage. You know it was God who brought you to Shiloh."

"Other than my children, I've been thinking of little else. I don't know that I want to marry again. I've paid a steep price for my freedom." Fingering the baked warmth of the towels, I didn't want to have this conversation with Ivy. What I wanted was to crawl back into bed as my mind had become as weary as my body.

"You sure your enthusiasm to remain single isn't just to mask your fear of another bad marriage?"

I shot her a look of surprise. "Do you realize I was married for almost seventeen years with never a moment's peace? Always fearful of what would piss him off, what I was doing wrong. Now I don't have to answer to anybody. Besides, Matthew doesn't need my baggage."

"I'm not trying to sell you on Matthew's virtues; I think you know a little of what they are. He's good, forthright, nothing shakes him. I've known him since the day I delivered him into this world." Ivy greased her cake pan. "He'll not give you a moment's sorrow. Not if he can help it. Haven't you been at peace here?"

"Yes, of course." I pushed aside the towels, folded, stacked, and ready for the linen closet. "But doesn't everybody expect the wife to tow the line after the honeymoon's over? I tell you, Ivy, other than my daddy, all the men I've known wanted a maid or a sex kitten, not a wife."

"I don't know as I'd go that far," she said, as she poured out the batter. "Of course, I go by my own marriage, not other folks'. I met Tobias, married him, and we've been in the same bed ever since. We take turns, towing the line, as you say." She leaned over the counter and touched my face with her finger, leaving flour on my cheek. "I've prayed every day for fifteen years, God bless Matthew for bringing me and Tobias here to this place. And now He has, with you. Matthew needs you. And you need him."

"Oh, Ivy," I said, done in by the events of the past few months. "My mind is tired." I rested my head on my hand. "It's more than I want to deal with right now." My thoughts bit into my logic and reasoning. "This *is* a beautiful place to live." I chewed at my lip, remembering Shady Acres.

"It's a slice of Heaven, for sure. I can hardly wait to get back to the mountain when I'm gone," Ivy said. She opened the oven door, sprinkled cinnamon and walnuts on the cake, and then moved the pan on the rack. Her toffee arms shimmered with the flush of the oven's heat.

"All you have to do is decide what *you* want. But Matthew will help you, no matter what that is."

That was just it. I didn't know what I wanted—whether to give my heart away again and run the risk of another bad marriage, or to stay single and run my life the way I wanted. I had finally learned to look for lessons in life, not miracles. I thought I might enjoy a single life.

But the thought of becoming Matthew's wife, with all it entailed, made my heart leap inside my chest. His ability to make me laugh, his soft touch, his cool head, and his voice—calm as a morning sunrise. I'd fallen in love with him. That much was true. I reasoned Matthew was not like Joe, not by a long shot. Joe never made me laugh our entire marriage. He made me frown a lot, cry on too many occasions, and nurse a sorrowful heart nearly every day. I sighed. "Once you've married and suffered from it, you're not anxious to get back into it." Ivy didn't answer. She raised her penciled-in eyebrows instead and loaded the dishwasher. "Please don't mention all this to Matt," I said.

"Not to worry. I'm bad to listen, but I don't pass much on. Sounds to me, though, all that baggage you say you got, most of it needs dropped off at the nearest Goodwill box. Then once your children are here with you, you throw the rest out."

NEWS FROM HOME

Matthew

Mug in hand, Andie closed the door to my office and took a seat in front of my desk. Although her eyes sparkled like the blue light of dawn, in the warm shimmer of the afternoon sun she looked tired. Extremely tired, if the shadows beneath them were any indication. I'd worried all night, wondering how to tell her that another person she loved had died.

"What's wrong, Matt?"

"I received word from my informant this morning. It's—"

"Yes, we need to talk about that. Just *who* is your informant?"

"Nobody you know. Not yet, anyway. It's my mother."

"Your preacher mama?" Andie giggled like a little girl.

"You bet. My mother is an adorable woman who has begged to play detective for me on a number of cases. The woman has read every Ellery Queen ever published. She was perfect for the job. Nobody suspected her. At first I balked, her safety being my main concern. But she has done some great legwork on your behalf. She's a pretty smart cookie, and she's coming to supper Saturday night. I can't hold her back any longer. Mother's determined to meet you. She wants to see this dark angel I have hidden in my house. A dark angel she suspects I'm attached to."

"Oh, no! She's probably been filled with lies about me."

I smiled. "Mother is a woman of extraordinary faith and reasoning. She doesn't believe a word of it. Or much of anything else Artury preaches. But—"

"What? Are my kids okay?"

"They're fine. In fact, Mother met them when she delivered the message to Vernise Darwood. They're worried about you, but they're good. Mother said if you look anything like your children, you must be beautiful." Andie blushed. She had no idea of her loveliness.

"There you go with that word again. Thank God, they're okay."

"Mrs. Darwood told Mother to tell you not to worry. She'll take good care of your twins. Mother liked the Darwoods. They're quite aware of the gravity of the situation. In fact, they talked outside at the picnic table. We suspect their house is wired. Anyway, Dillon and Gracie never knew why my mother was really there. Bobbie Sue plays a great Avon lady." Andie giggled again. I loved the sound of her voice. "Andie, I need to tell you about your father-in-law."

"Al." Her eyes immediately teared up.

"Mother said they announced in church that he passed away last week. Heart attack. He died peacefully in his sleep. They're burying him today in Lexington. In a cemetery near his boyhood church." My heart hurt watching her tears fall.

"God took him." Her hands wrapped tightly around her coffee mug. "Al couldn't stand the hypocrisy. I just know it. He was the only person on my side. Although he was powerless to do anything for me, he loved me. He really loved me." She pulled a tissue from the box on my desk. "What hurts most is I can't go to the funeral, or even send a card. Selma will be there instead of me. Selma. He didn't even like Selma. It's so not fair."

She wiped her eyes. "I'm sure Joe will take Dillon and Gracie to the funeral. Maudy must be a wreck. I feel so helpless. You stayed awake thinking about how to tell me this, didn't you?"

My own eyes grew blurry with tears. "Yes," I said.

Her mouth opened slightly and I saw the slightest hint of fear. A protective impulse surged inside me, a compulsion to shield and protect her. I walked around my desk and took her to the couch in front of the fire. Pulling her against my chest, I tucked her head under my chin and laced my fingers into her hair. It possessed only the slightest hint of silver. Most of its rich color of honey was so gold it was almost red. I sensed her thoughts were of Al, an old man she once knew and loved.

She sat back to wipe tears from her eyes, and I felt her shiver.

"Are you okay?"

She shrugged her shoulders and was already falling forward to bury herself in my chest again. Andie looked like a sad little girl, holding on to my shirt. "Why?" she asked.

"Why what?"

"Just why," she whispered to my heart.

The room was warm from the fire. The wind had picked up and the first drops of rain hit the windows. I had made it a habit to open the shutters every morning, knowing she liked them open. I held her as tightly as I could. It was not much of an answer, but it was all I had.

Graveyard Wisdom

Andie

Matthew had gone to Boone for a meeting at the university. I sat for supper next to Tobias while Ivy announced we would avoid anymore talk about my inevitable marriage to their Matthew. "I'm not a pushy woman," Ivy said. "Besides, I am sure you and Mattie still have lots to talk about. There are things you need to discuss. We shall leave this romance to blossom in God's own time, hey Toby?"

"Whatever you say, woman. You know best." He winked at me and I winked back, grinning. Ivy and Tobias had become my friends.

After supper, I took a glass of wine and sat by the fire in Matthew's office. I found myself missing him and smiled, realizing it.

"Mind if I join you?" Tobias held his usual cup of coffee and piece of pie in his hands. More and more I noticed his resemblance to Rupert in his soft mannerisms and simple needs.

I motioned for him to sit. "Please. Join me. Put your feet up. The fire feels good."

"Ah, the smell and sound of hot embers. I love the songs only a fire can sing, don't you?"

"Yes. My daddy did, too. He made a fire every day in the winter. We often huddled around it when the electricity was out."

Tobias chuckled and then grew quiet. Together we watched it burn down to bright orange coals, pulsing like the glow of hundreds of fireflies until he turned to me. His smile broad and flashing, he said, "How do you feel about living at Shiloh? Do you like it here?"

"Yes, very much. I feel safe. More than I ever have in my life. But I miss my children, and I worry we'll never be able to find the right time to expose Calvin to someone who will prosecute him and make it stick."

Tobias straightened and sipped his coffee. "I understand why you did not go to the police. Men like the Reverend pay powerful lawyers to find ways to explain away evidence. Or they pay evil men to destroy it. You were alone. It must've been frightening."

"To say the least. It's been quite a journey. I all but lost my mind because I kept it inside me. I have the evidence I need but as of today, I've done nothing with it. No doubt Calvin will make up some explanation for his fall from God's grace."

"Hmm," Tobias groaned. "The man is an enigma." He rose to stoke the fire. "Do you think you've lost your ability to love again?"

I sighed. "I don't mean to be elusive as a wet fish. I really don't want to be like this. Hating the idea of starting over again. Of never giving Matthew what he deserves."

Tobias slumped back in his chair, his legs sprawled out. "I know Matthew. He doesn't think about you giving to him. He lives to give to those he cares about. To those he loves. His capacity for love is truly an amazing thing not seen in most men. Especially his love for God. A childlike thing, really. Yet strong and unbending."

I suspected Tobias was wise beyond his sixty-five years, Godly, a man I could trust, as much as my daddy and Rupert. I felt something special about him deep in my heart. I stood and wandered to the window, loving the exquisite house Matthew restored. A cool, green sanctuary in the middle of a meadow in the mountains. I treasured the view of the old cemetery from his office window, fenced in with granite posts and iron chains, bordered by ancient oak trees. The gravestones, low, some worn nearly smooth, dating back to the Civil War and the Battle of Shiloh, just like he had said. I'd read every one of them. *Blessed are those who mourn, for they will receive comfort.* It had been carved into the large piece of granite resting at the entrance to the cemetery. I thought about that scripture, sharing the fire with Tobias. In the window, the reflection of the flames lit up the more lonely and hurtful moments of my life.

I felt Tobias watching me. "When Joe and I were first married, I loved God in a way I doubt I ever will again."

"Ah, the inexperienced adoration of a new bride. Unfettered and blind as a newborn kitten," he said.

"But I can't find my faith, Tobias. I'm trying, but . . ." Choked by my tears, I couldn't breathe. "I can't find God anywhere."

Tobias rose from his chair, walked over and stood beside me at the window. "When you can't find your faith, when you can't find God, there's only one thing you can do."

"And what's that?"

"Trust Him. Be patient. Let Him find *you.*"

C.S.K.

Andie

I'd been asleep, sitting up in a chair in Matthew's office when I felt his lips brush a gentle kiss across my forehead, like a whisper. I stirred, smiling at him.

"I missed you," he said. "I raced home. I feel sixteen. Couldn't concentrate on the meeting. Not a lick."

Heavy and half-open, my eyes glanced at the clock. "You're home early."

"Right, but I see you're ready for bed."

I yawned. "I guess I am."

"Then off with you. I'll see you in the morning."

"Leftovers are in the fridge. Ivy told me to tell you."

"Good. I'm hungry."

"See you in the morning then." I wanted to stay up and talk, but at that moment I wanted sleep more. He kissed me again and pulled me into a brief hug. Then he smiled, turned me around, and pointed me to the stairs. I dragged my sleepy self up to my room and to bed.

§

Two hours into a restless sleep, my eyes snapped open. Something new and inevitable rose in me, like a fin above water. It circled my heart. It drew a line between the past and the present. At two a.m. I was determined to see him. *Time to spend the rest of my life in the future instead of the past.* I jumped out of bed and punched my fists through the sleeves of the silk robe Ivy gave me. Unaware of exactly what tomorrow held, I had a fresh sense of direction, which suddenly changed my silly daydreams into a goal. A desire. To belong to Matthew. Attempting to remove the tired look from my face, I added a little blush and brushed my hair down until it licked my shoulders. Dabbing a bit of perfume behind my ears and knees, I needed all the help I could get. Never having been to Matthew's room, I recalled standing in the backyard and pointing to his balcony and the French doors leading out from it. He told me it was his bedroom, and that the balcony gave him a full view of his property, adding only the cleaning ladies and Ivy had ever been inside. I wondered at the time, if that final comment was for my benefit.

After opening my bedroom door, I peered down the long, dimly lit corridor connecting to the hall ending at Matthew's room. The next few hours would determine the direction of my life. My house shoes slapped the bottoms of my feet and my robe flew out behind me. I arrived at his door and knocked softly.

No answer.

I knocked again. A little harder.

When the door creaked opened, his groggy face appeared. The thick hair on his bare chest was salt-and-pepper like his beard. He must've thrown on the denim shorts, because I couldn't imagine him sleeping in them.

Matthew

I thought I was dreaming until the knocking woke me. Falling out of bed, I nearly tripped pulling on my shorts. My heart beat as though I'd just run a marathon. When I cracked open the door, I couldn't believe she was standing there.

"Andie? Is everything okay?"

"Yes. I'm sorry to wake you. I couldn't sleep."

"What time is it?"

"Two in the morning. I'm sorry. I'll let you get back to sleep." She turned to leave.

It was one of those moments I knew there was a God. A God who gently reminded me that life goes on. It'd been a long time. The question was: could this old peacock still spread his feathers? She smelled of jasmine. I was suddenly wide awake. "Don't you dare leave me like this. Come in. You want to talk?"

"Yes, I do."

Andie

I stepped into a room resembling an exotic place and time. A carved mahogany bed, its four posts holding up a grand canopy, sprawled across the middle of the floor. Dwarfed by the enormous room itself, the bed's splendor caused my breath to catch in my throat. Matthew lit a fire, then walked over and switched on a lamp. Hanging next to massive bookcases that brushed the ceiling, a Civil War musket glowed in the firelight, as if it burned to tell its own story. Animal print pillows and chenille throws were tossed over an overstuffed chintz loveseat in front of the fire. *Architecture Digest, Field and Stream*, and his Bible lay on another old trunk used as a coffee table. A man's room. Family photos were lined up across the mantle under a twelve-point whitetail buck's head mounted over the fireplace.

Matthew excused himself and walked to his en suite bathroom. I sat on a wingback chair to wait. When he returned, he had pulled on a fresh T-shirt and I smelled the minty fresh scent of Scope. He was definitely a gentleman.

He stood in front of me and held out his hand. "Please, Andie, come sit by me."

My eyes swept over him as I stood and moved with him to the love seat. He was shiver handsome. I ached to feel the brush of his soft beard against my skin.

Matthew reached out and ran his fingers through my hair. Silently he leaned forward and I drank in the sweetness of his kiss, a slow drugging kiss that sang through my veins. I pulled myself back. "I want to talk about everything I've been thinking of," I said, my cheeks feeling flushed as he explored my face with his lips.

"You bring a list?"

The world shrank to the room about us. My emotions whirled and skidded. "Matthew, I'm self-conscious about my body. I'm not nineteen anymore."

"Neither am I. And your body is fine," he said with an edge in his voice, which meant I was annoying when I talked that way.

He cradled my face in his hands. "Your cheeks are soft as a baby's." And then he loosened his embrace and brushed his fingers through my hair. I think he started to realize I really did come to talk to him.

Matthew

My heart beat faster, needing her, wanting her. "I had no right to move so fast." I opened my mouth to apologize again, but she surprised me by laying one finger gently against my lips.

"Yes, you did." Her whisper was so sincere it nearly moved me to tears. "You had every right. You saved me from prison. You saved me from insanity. You saved me from Hell."

It was hard to breathe and I shook my head slowly. "How can this be happening?"

Her eyes were as blue as the tiny slippers on her feet. "I don't know," she said. Confusion clouded her countenance briefly then cleared. "I don't know," she repeated. "But I learned a long time ago, some things you can't explain. They're simply true."

I kissed her again, a succession of slow shivery kisses. Forced to come up for air, I moved to sweep her back into another kiss, but she pulled away, gasping to catch her breath. "I . . . I can't. What time is it?" She sat up, dazed. "What am I doing?"

"Kissing me," I said. Whatever else she had put on her list could wait. I reached for her again, but she held me off.

Her face flushed and she pressed her hands to my chest, pushing away firmly, and then to her cheeks, as if trying to cool them. "Godamighty . . . I mean . . . I hardly know you—"

"I believe you do know me." On that point, I was sure. I smiled and tucked a strand of her hair behind her ear. "I feel as if we've known each other a long time."

She gave me a shaky little laugh. "You're right. I knew your hands a long time ago," she said lightly, as if speaking to herself. With an inward start, I remembered she'd said that before. She'd not told me about her dream or vision or whatever it was about my hands, but I'd not told her a few things either.

"Although," she continued, breaking into my jumbled thoughts, "I *would* like to know you more."

I took a deep breath. "Of course you would. What an idiot I am." I raked my defective hand through my hair. "My name is Callahan," I said. "Matthew Wayne Callahan. At your service, I need hardly add. Oh yeah, I told you all that, didn't I?"

We laughed as Andie pulled herself up and leaned against the arm of the loveseat and rested her head in her hand. "Tell me more about Matthew Callahan," she said.

"Well." I cleared my throat twice and tried to calm my neglected libido. "You know about my mother. I've three brothers, Mark, Luke, and John. And a sister-in-law, Mark's wife, Patsy."

"You're kidding, right? Matthew, Mark, Luke, and John?"

"I never kid about my brothers. Remember, my mother's a preacher. My father, Court Callahan, died when I was very young. Actually, he was murdered. I grew up fast." I felt a punch to my chest as I said it out loud. I didn't think of my father often.

"Murdered? How horrible for you. You didn't stay a child long."

"I haven't been a child since the day I was six and a liquored-up swamp-dweller in Morehead City blew him away over a land deal. Dad owned property in several Southern states. Mother refused to sell his holdings after his death. Her second husband, Jack, was one of the first men in the state of North Carolina to sign a pre-nuptial agreement. My mother is a smart gal. Jack didn't care what Mother owned. He was a chef, catering meals for the racetracks from New York to Florida, including the Kentucky Derby. A happy, short Italian man, a Catholic who converted to Pentecostal Holiness. Can you imagine? A preacher married to someone who spent his life at the tracks. It worked. He was a good guy, good to Mother, good to me."

"I was an only child until Jack and Mother had the rest of the rascally bunch of males I call brothers. John loved him most, followed him everywhere. My step-dad died in '86, a year before my daughter passed away. Their deaths were hard on Mother. But she had her four sons, and a small congregation who have loyally sat their butts in her pews for years. I want to take you there soon. Would that be okay?"

"Yes. I'd love to go. Your family sounds like good people."

"They are." I looked into the fire feeling the pain of loss. "Hey, now. Tell me about the dream or vision you had of my hands."

Andie spoke slowly, as though brushing away the cobwebs from her memories, relaying in detail the story of my hands, fighting for her life and for the life of her unborn child.

"That's why you let me in the apartment."

She took my defective hand and pressed a kiss into my palm. "The only reason."

I caressed her face, then stood and stoked a gentle fire. "Now, I've got something to tell you. You asked me how I lost this finger." Sitting beside her again, my heart swelled with affection as she leaned against my chest, waiting intently for more.

"I lost my finger field dressing that deer." I pointed to the buck hanging over the fireplace. "I'd hunted all morning and got careless with my bowie knife. Those knives are made to cut through bone. It sliced right through mine. My finger dangled by a flap of skin, I nearly passed out. Thank God Tobias was with me. He administered first aid, wrapped it, and then flew back to the house, five miles away. You should've seen that man run. He looked like Jesse Owens reincarnated. Ivy called the paramedics, but by the time they got to me, I'd lost a few pints of blood. You ready for this?"

She nodded and I continued. "This may sound familiar to you, and even as I tell it, it sounds strangely similar to your experience. After my surgery, I had a dream, or a vision, or whatever you want to call it. I saw a gold ring. It sparkled in the shallow part of our pond, down by the edge of the meadow near Ivy's house. The next day I talked to my daughter, Jessie, on the phone; she was only eight at the time. I told her to go to the pond, to the rock where she fished with her brother. I told her to look real hard, near the edge, and see if she could locate the gold ring. Of course, she found it. She meant to keep it, but then Jessie heard about the auction at Baptist Hospital. She'd spent many weeks at Baptist. Jessie donated the ring. It surprised me an eight-year-old would want to do that, but . . . my little girl was like that." My voice trailed off. "Anyway, that was the last we saw of the ring. Strange thing is, it reminds me of your ring."

Andie sat in sheer astonishment, breathing deeply. "I have to tell you. My daddy worked for R. J. Reynolds. He supervised a committee to raise money for the hospital's building fund. They put together several auctions. Daddy bid on this ring as a gift for Dixie. My fussy mother didn't like the plainness of it, so she gave it to me. I never wore it much until I realized Joe was stealing my jewelry. Then I put it on my right hand and never took it off. I know it's stamped, I just thought it had something to do with the gold content or the maker."

"Check inside; there may be initials. C.S.K," I said.

Andie pulled it off her finger. "You'll have to look. I think I need glasses."

I held it up to the light of the fire. "You need glasses?" We chuckled as I reached for my own glasses on the table. Holding the ring toward the light, I smiled. "C.S.K. This is the ring. I'll be damned."

Her lips parted in surprise. "This is all too much. Day after day, the fate of our meeting becomes more and more obvious. Now I *know* I'm in *The Twilight Zone*."

"Andie, C.S.K. doesn't stand for the maker. It's the initials of the owner."

"You know who owned it?"

"I do. Ivy told me. Coretta Scott King."

"THE Coretta Scott King, wife of Martin Luther?"

"That's the one. The Kings and their entourage traveled through North Carolina in 1967 and stopped for about an hour to see Ivy and Tobias. Of course Ivy and Tobias didn't live here in 1967; they lived on a small farm near Mother. I think Ivy told you how closely they worked with the movement. Doctor King wanted to thank them personally and give them a token of appreciation for their work. A letter signed by him. Tobias has it framed on his wall in his den. Ask to see it whenever you get up to the house. Anyway, Coretta had used Ivy's bathroom to wash up and left her ring on the sink. When Ivy contacted her, Coretta told Ivy to keep it. Years later, Ivy thought she lost it and worried herself sick over it."

"One day Ivy told me the story but it was too late. I would've given the ring back to her but Jessie and I had already donated it, along with other items, to the hospital auction. Ivy felt better, though, knowing it had been found and used for a good cause. She just accepted its loss. Now here it is, on your hand." I slipped the ring back on her finger and kissed it. "On Andie Oliver's right hand."

"Ivy's never mentioned it. Do you think she's noticed the ring?"

"She saw it the moment she met you. That's how she knew you were supposed to be here. She said she'd let me do the telling of the ring story."

The clock read four a.m. "We've been talking a long time. Think you've heard enough about me for one night?" I asked.

"Yes," she said.

I certainly hadn't imagined the quickening of my heart as I looked into her eyes. Or the unusual quiver, low in my belly; a sensation that made me shudder again and again. That night, there were no shadows across my heart as Andie stood and untied her silk robe, letting it fall to the floor, revealing perfumed and powdered naked flesh.

THE JOINING OF SOULS

Matthew

I stood and pulled off my shirt, letting it fall on the love seat behind me. My eyes roamed her body; she wasn't skinny, but she certainly wasn't fat. I took in the soft roundness of her hips and her small waist. I pulled her to me in a warm embrace. Feeling her bare breasts against my chest made my heart thump erratically. For a second I toyed with a blonde wisp of her hair trailing down to her shoulder, my mouth grazing her earlobe. I skimmed my palm down her back, and she arched against my caress like a sleek cat.

Looking into her expressive eyes, I smiled as she blushed. "I can't believe I'm saying this," she said. "But I'm in love with you, Matthew. Every day I try to list reasons why I shouldn't be, but instead it deepens and intensifies." She trailed her nail down my bare chest.

I took both of her hands again and held them, prayer-like, in my own. "I want you to know, I'm not just committed to your cause, Andie. But to you. I not only love you, I'm giving you my heart and my life. I want you with me." I held her body close and nuzzled her ear again. "I want you in my bed."

"Just for tonight?"

"Tonight and always."

Covered with gooseflesh, Andie slipped under my blanket. I smiled, pulled off my shorts and then climbed into bed beside her. Slowly my hand moved downward, skimming either side of her body to her thighs. I was too emotion-filled to speak. The blood pounded through my chest as I kissed her soft lips, her neck, her ample breasts, then ran my tongue over her round belly and down to the velvet parts of her, caressing her with my mouth, worshiping her with my tongue. Her breasts rose sharply as she drew in a breath. I moved back up her body and she shivered. I took her hand, laying it on me, wanting her to feel me. "This is what you do to me," I said.

"Then love me," she said. "Dive into me, discover every inch of me."

I smiled, watching the faint outline of her, saying it. "Nothing would please me more." We lay in my heavily quilted bed, kissing here and there, wherever our eyes lingered in the dim wavy light of the fire-lit room. Finally, I moved on top of her and she guided me in, wrapping her legs around mine. I felt the tips of her breasts crush into my skin, hardening.

Her arms closed gently about my neck. She whispered, "Matthew . . . I need all of you."

I shuddered. "You have me, Andie."

We moved slowly, unhurriedly, like two people whose pent-up passions now begged to be released, shattering the remains of every wall and any fortress that had been built.

Andie's hands ran smoothly and slowly along my neck and shoulders down to the small of my back, then up my spine. I cupped my hands under her buttocks and brought her up as I forced my groin down deeper into her. She came, bringing me to orgasm with her.

We lay still, listening to the absolute quiet of the room, our breathing, and our heartbeats pounding in our ears.

"It's the first of many," I said, nuzzling her.

"Can I believe you?" Her breaths were short and fast.

"Yes. Always."

We dozed lightly until Andie had to get up and find the bathroom. The fire had gone out; darkness filled the room. Lying in the warm bed with her scent on my skin, even the thought of her was pungent. The morning sun was minutes from dawning but I couldn't wait until she was back. I snuggled her into my arms. Her small breath warmed my shoulder and her hand pressed up against my chest. She slept, catching each loving, mighty, fragile beat of my heart in her hand. And then just like that, she had received my spirit with absolute sleeping innocence.

I was a giant again.

Aside from the lucky sheet twisted around her thigh, she was naked and uncovered. The sun had come up and poured in through the slats of the shutters, bathing her in a subtle ray and tracing the silhouette of her legs, back, shoulders and neck. A silver key on a chain snaked between her breasts. A key to her lockbox she'd told me about, or perhaps a key to her heart. I propped myself up; studying every inch of her fair and delicate skin, my fingers fluttering over the swell of her hip. A sliver of grace, a love song, a statuette carved by unseen hands. Andie was, undoubtedly, the centerpiece jewel in God's crown.

She stirred and rolled over in the warm sheets, and my hand found the smooth curve of her shoulder. I pressed my lips to her neck and my groin to her naked buttocks. Everything fell into place. We lay there like two exquisite pieces of porcelain, broken and glued back together. At that moment we only needed one heart. I started to whisper in her ear but up came her hand, a bouquet of fingers, and touched my lips in the muted morning sun. "Quiet." she said. "If I'm dreaming, I never want to wake up." Lying amid sex-tangled sheets, I stroked her silky skin, and pulled her closer. She smiled. "Maybe we should get up, what time is it?" Her clever fingers slipped down between us, encircling me. "Won't we be missed at breakfast?"

I yawned. "Does it matter?" I was ready for sleep.

"I think you should bring breakfast back to bed," she said.

"And I think you've got a great idea, but let's rest a little first."

She snuggled back into my chest, and then copied my yawn. "Good idea." I watched her fade. Within minutes she had fallen back to sleep. I followed close behind.

§

At nine a.m. I slipped out of bed, showered, and took off for the kitchen. I would surprise her. Our first morning of breakfast in bed, just as she requested. I would spoil her the rest of our days. She had lived a horrible existence with a man who did not love or appreciate her; for the life of me, I couldn't imagine such a monster. The epitome of everything I had longed for and never believed existed, Andie had proven to my shattered dreams I could be loved again. Hurrying down the staircase, I caught myself whistling. I hadn't whistled in years.

I could've had my pick of eligible, single girls. I'd been introduced to hundreds of beautiful women all over the world. But that little woman lying up in my bed had no idea of my wealth, other than what she could see around her. And she didn't care. All she ever wanted was someone to love her and her children. And I knew that her ability to love me back was bigger than the mountain I lived on. My mother had always told me God would show me the path to the right woman's door. He'd done that and more.

"Snoring away?" Ivy asked.

"A regular buzz saw in a barnyard." I laughed, kissing her cheek.

Ivy knew. Of course she knew. I never slept late. When neither Andie nor I showed up for breakfast, she'd gone and peeked in Andie's bedroom and found it empty.

"Did you tell her?" Ivy's inquisitive eyes burrowed into mine.

"No. I will. Today." I sighed. "I promise, Ivy. Okay?"

Tobias sat at the breakfast bar, drinking Ivy's buzz-worthy coffee. He winked at me, as if I were still the twelve-year-old boy who followed him everywhere.

Ivy made a face at her husband. "What you looking at, Toby? You not think a man Mattie's age can love again?"

"Ha, woman. The older the bull, the stiffer the horn. Every man knows that."

"You wish," said Ivy.

PART EIGHT
And God Spoke

Handwriting On The Wall

Andie

I opened one eye when I heard Matthew close the door behind him. I lay in bed and stretched, then reached for the remote on the nightstand. The TV, half-hidden in an armoire that matched his bed, offered no diversion from his magnificent bedroom. In daylight, the room seemed less mysterious. I could see the red, ivory and brown accents clearly, and how the colors reflected Matthew's masculinity and style. I wanted to know everything about him.

My heart light, I had found him. A love like none other. The name Matthew Callahan filled me and I rolled over to bury my face in his pillow. *Intoxicating.* I savored the feeling of satisfaction he left me in. He had freed in me a burst of sensation hurtling me past the point of no return. I never dreamed his hands could feel so warm, so gentle. Or that his words could hang in the air between us like vows.

I switched off the television. The thought grew like a seed, planted only hours before, exploding in the silence of the room. The great love of my life wasn't Joe after all.

I laid there, wishing Matthew would forget breakfast and come back to bed so I could cradle in his arms. For him to move inside me again. *Making love was,* I giggled, *incredible.* I'd had a few orgasms in my life, but nothing like that. The desires and urges I thought I lost had pumped into overdrive. To be held so closely, loved so deeply, and then finding I wanted more— it was exhilarating. Delicious thoughts of him ran thick inside my head, pulsing through my squirming body, throbbing between my legs. I looked around his bedroom again, noticing every little thing that was *him.* In an instant, my love for Matthew became boundless. I crawled out of bed, slid my arms through my robe, and strolled to the fireplace. I wanted to look at every photograph, hoping perhaps there was one of his mother. I smiled going from picture to picture. A family who clearly cared for each other.

But then my eyes widened. *Oh God. It can't be. It can't possibly be him!* I tore open the frame, took it from behind the glass, and turned it over. Little brother, John Rossi, 1987. *It's him!* Quickly, I surveyed the rest of the mantel. Pictures of Matthew's brothers were lined up, one after the other, including three of John. The finger of God had reached down and carved it on the wall of my heart—the time had come to tell Matthew about the murder. *Why didn't Matthew tell me about his stepbrother? What does he really want from me?* The best night of my life became abruptly twisted. Something Matthew said on the mountain suddenly struck me like a fist. I hadn't put it together, hadn't even thought about it until that moment. '*We both know the pain . . . of losing someone we love to a monster.*' He was talking about losing John!

I dug into my memory to recall my conversation with Johnny Rebel so many years ago. John had mentioned his family, ' . . . *my mama—salt of the earth.*' That's where I heard it, from John! His brothers hated him for his homosexuality, but his oldest brother—did not. Right. The words played like a tape recorder. I found myself gripping the picture for all it was worth. It was him. *Johnny Rebel!* I snatched the remaining pictures of him off the mantel, as well as a picture of Matthew and John standing in front of a Christmas tree. Someone indeed led me to Shiloh. Meeting Matthew was no coincidence, but was it divine intervention or a set-up?

Andie. I heard my name called from outside. Loud and clear through the French doors. I didn't stop to think about it. Anger propelled me forward quickly, fearlessly, and I flung the doors wide open. Thunder rolled in the distance and the wind whipped the trees back and forth, as if all of nature had suddenly become frantic. My feet froze on the edge of the bedroom carpet, refusing to move out to the balcony. The hair on the back of my neck rose. I yelled at the sky. "Who is it? What do you want to tell me? What? What!"

A strange static filled the air, as a deep and solemn weeping rolled down the mountain. *"Avenge . . . us . . . all,"* the wind cried. In a blustery gust, the doors slammed in my face.

Terrified, I screamed and bolted out of the bedroom and down the hallway, "Matthew!"

In a matter of seconds he caught me as I collapsed into his arms.

§

I roused to the sound of Tobias's voice. "Get her to your bed."

Matthew carried me into his room and laid me on top of the sheets. I sobbed, as if waking from a nightmare. I managed to pull myself up and grab the box of Kleenex off the nightstand. Pulling in a deep breath, I yanked the quilt over my legs and stared into the room at nothing. Matthew sat on the bed with me, waiting and watching my every move.

But Ivy walked around the room, finding the photos scattered on the floor where I had dropped them. "Mattie," she whispered, holding one up, "I told you, you should've told her. She knew him."

Matthew took them from Ivy's hands. "You're right, Ivy, as always. I'm not sure why I kept it from her. Talk to me, Andie, honey. What frightened you?"

Ivy and Tobias positioned themselves on the bed, listening to my every word. I blushed. Matthew smiled and smoothed the hair out of my eyes. "It's okay. They know you stayed with me last night."

Ivy handed me another tissue. "Don't be embarrassed, Andie. God brought you here. He only used Matthew to drive the car. Loving Matthew is within the natural order of things. Tell us what happened. You have a bad dream?"

I reached for a pillow and hugged it to my chest. "No." Pointing to the pictures of John in Matthew's lap, my voice cracked. "It's those."

"Pictures of my brother, John?"

"Yes. Why didn't you tell me? You never bothered to mention his last name. It's Rossi, isn't it? Your mother's last name is Rossi."

"Yes. But everybody calls Mother, Pastor Bobbie Sue. Rossi is seldom used because some of the old-timers at church still think she's a Callahan. I don't know why I couldn't talk about John with you. In my heart I hoped you knew him, and yet, I hoped you didn't. God, Andie, I don't know, maybe I was afraid to ask you. I kept putting it off. John's murder has been painful for me to talk about. More painful than Jessie's death, I guess, because of the cruelty of it. Then I tried to believe it didn't matter if you knew him. Did you know John?"

I stared straight ahead.

Matthew sighed, exasperated. "Andie?"

"What!"

"Did you know my brother?"

"You could say that. Yes, I knew him. He was the Assistant Chef at the Praise Buffet. They didn't allow him to attend services. It was cruel, you're right. Cruel and inhuman what they did to him."

"Then you knew he was—"

"Gay? Yes. And he was warm and wonderful. Funny and full of life and hope. He was desperate to get the man he loved out of there. Peter, the head chef," I said, looking hard into Matthew's eyes. The tears flowed down my checks like a steady stream of anguish, my memory carrying me back in time. "And he loved you all." I turned my gaze to Matthew. "I had no true knowledge of Calvin's utter debauchery until I met John. I—I talked to him a long time that night. The night he died."

The color drained from Matthew's face. "What else, Andie? What else do you know?"

"I didn't know he was your brother. I didn't know. I didn't want to talk about what I saw. To you or anybody. I was afraid because if they knew . . . I . . . I had to protect Gracie and Dillon, instead."

"What, Andie? What did you see?" Matthew asked.

I hesitated and clutched my pillow. "I saw him shot by Evan Preston and Silas Turlo. I am the eyewitness. I called the police. I'm the one they were looking for. The one you were all looking for. Oh Matthew, I'm so sorry, I'm so sorry you lost your brother. But you should've told me! Damn it, why didn't you tell me?" I bawled into the pillow.

Matthew rolled his head between his legs. "I think I'm going to be sick."

"Sweet Jesus!" Ivy raised her hands. Her chin quivered and she shook from her head to her feet in a full-blown Pentecostal moment. "It was God *and* Johnny that led you to her, Matthew! It was! She's here for you, and to help you put them bad men away."

Tobias rushed to give Matthew a drink of water while he reeled from my revelation of his brother's killer. Tobias then put it all into prospective. With his arms around his wife, he smiled and looked at each of us. "After all this time, all our prayers, God has delivered the only witness into your hands, Matthew. One with whom you have fallen in love."

Finally, Matthew pulled himself up next to me and held me like a father would hold his child after a nightmare." Tell me everything, Andie. Start at the beginning. Don't be afraid."

§

As the storm outside grew in intensity, we moved to the sitting area near the fire. I settled into the loveseat beside Matthew and scooted to the edge, gripping the cushion so tight I thought my bones would snap. I spoke about the few hours I spent with John. Looking back on that night, I felt as though I was trekking alone across a vast desert. Sand and dirt whirling up behind me. After I finished, I felt a serious tug of pity for the desolation on Matthew's face. If his eyes had looked tired before, they were haunted at that moment.

Matthew finally spoke. "I'm sorry." His voice sounded scratchy and full of agony. "I should've asked you if you knew him. You had no idea John was my brother. The only pictures of him in this house are here in my room. And until last night, you'd never been in here. I was desperate to find my brother's killer for such a long time, and almost gave up. I never knew for sure but I always suspected that church had something to do with it."

"Now you know," I said.

He sighed. "Yes, now I know."

The room grew quiet except for the popping embers in the fire. We all just sat there for a while, locked in our own remembrance of John.

"Why didn't you help him, Matthew? Like you're helping me."

"He was a private man, as you can imagine. He had to be. My brother never let on how bad it was there. I suspected he wasn't happy, but I had no clue of the pain and danger he was in. I would've swooped down there and carted him back here. But he knew that, and he wanted to stay near Pete. I should've listened to my gut. I have a sixth sense about death; I should've listened." He looked at me. "Where is Peter, now?" he asked.

"On the night he left town, he stopped at my house on his way to Florida. He had seen me talking to John that night. Peter figured I knew who did it. Peter Collins bought his way out. With AIDS. He was dying; they let him leave. He told me he had six months to live, and that's been a year ago. He gave me a videotape Calvin didn't know he had and money to help me. I think it was his attempt to make some sort of restitution for the way he treated John. I don't know what's on the tape, I never watched it, but it's in my lockbox at the bank. Joe knows I have it, and they know I saw Evan kill John."

Tobias wiped his eyes with his hankie. "I remember Pete. When he and John worked in Charlotte together, they came to visit us. Stayed with me and Ivy while Matthew was out of the country. Bobbie Sue came to our house to see them, remember, Ivy?"

"Yes, sure do. But Mark and Luke, they done Johnny wrong. They—"

"I know, Ivy. Believe me, they know, too." Matthew interjected. "Mark and Luke feel they are as much to blame for his death as the man who shot him. Artury!" Making a fist and holding it to his heart, he turned to face me head on. "He will never, ever touch you! I will follow him to Hell before he or any of his assassins lay a finger on you! Ivy is right; we came together for a reason. Destiny . . . fate . . . call it what you want. I love you, Andie. Harm will never darken your door again."

I watched, amazed and stunned, as Matthew wept. Great masculine tears that fell and caught in his beard stubble.

"I want to thank you, Andie." His voice choked. He sobbed, as few men know how to do. Tobias reached over and rested his hand on Matthew's knee to comfort him until he was able to speak. "I want to thank you for being John's only friend. For loving him in his last hours. That's why, sweetheart, that's why God led me to you . . . and you to us. This *was* a divine meeting. Your Mavis, my John, seems like they worked a deal with the Almighty." Finally, Matthew was able to smile.

I pulled in a cleansing breath, moved by his raw emotion. "Yes, I believe they did. I stood in your room with John's pictures in my hands and I heard my name called through those doors." I pointed to the balcony.

"Outside?" he asked.

I nodded. "John's senseless murder filled me with rage so hot I ran to the doors. I wanted to confront it, scream at whatever it was calling out my name. I flung the door wide not thinking fast enough to be afraid, not until I heard that same voice crying and saying, 'Avenge us all.'"

Matthew looked at Ivy, who nodded, obviously indicating I had told the truth. He pulled me to him. "What do you think, Ivy?"

"I think you best do what they've asked of you, Andie."

"We'll do it together," said Matthew.

§

Ivy brought a tray of danish and coffee into Matthew's bedroom. I had curled up in Matthew's arms by the fire again. "Tell me about John," I said. "I adored him; he was, I don't know, regal I guess." I took a cup of coffee from Ivy and smiled.

Matthew's features became animated. "Skinny as a piece of celery when he was a kid. Remember, Ivy?"

"Oh, do. Pants all the time falling off his tiny behind. The boy had no butt to speak of."

Matthew laughed, and then sighed. "He was handsome, with hair that always looked like he'd just stepped out of a shower. Not an ounce of fat on him. Six feet of pure muscle. Strong. Well-defined arms. Women chased him for years. He didn't have an eye for any of them. That's when I knew. John was a star. Until he and Peter went to work at that church restaurant."

"His homosexuality split the family for years. He was afraid to tell Mark and Luke, and when he did, all Hell broke loose. It's been hard for me to forgive them for the way they treated him. I'm still not sure Ivy has." He looked at Ivy, who said nothing. "John could've come here, but he never wanted to cause trouble. Never wanted any of us to suffer a moment's pain for the life he led. My brothers live with their regrets now. But it's over. We laid him to rest beside his father. Jack loved him. It'll be truly over with your testimony, Andie. I vow to you, we will get your children back. I will put this madman behind bars."

Tobias perked up. "Can't work outside today with all this rain. Let's celebrate."

"Good idea," said Ivy. "I'll make a grand supper. We will celebrate Andie and Matthew's love. Good love, yes?"

I blushed as Matthew kissed me. "Yes, the best," he said.

Matthew

At almost noon, Andie went back to her room to shower.

"Ivy, please move Andie's things in here with me." I pulled my old Villanova sweatshirt over my head, while she placed John's pictures back on the mantle.

"Do you think she'll approve?" Ivy asked.

"I approve!"

We laughed. She had heard the question. And answered it.

When Ivy left my room, I pulled my old friend aside. "Tobias, I need you to make some calls today. Get in touch with Royster Bently at the FBI. If you recall, he and his wife had supper with Mother and Jack every month for years."

Tobias nodded and stroked his chin, making a mental list of my instructions.

"Set up a private meeting with Royster in town. Call your connections within the IRS. I want another investigation started on the Praise Buffet, Peyton Broadcasting, and any other entity not labeled as a church, including the private accounts of Artury, Preston, and Turlo—and whoever that Assistant Pastor is. I also want a meeting with the detectives who investigated John's murder, and the murder of Mavis Dumass in New York. In the meantime, I'll schedule another appointment with the Attorney General."

"This will take a little time, Matthew. We worked so hard to find John's killer before."

"Right, but this time I have an eyewitness. And we'll have our ducks in a row."

"When it's over, you'll marry Andie?"

"If she'll have me. When it is truly over."

May 1993
An Invitation

Matthew

Ivy sat with the remote on her lap, staring into Artury's face on the small television in the kitchen. Andie had developed a migraine after breakfast and Ivy sent her back to bed. Ivy shook her head so hard her earrings swung back and forth against her neck. "Isn't it staggering? Everyone in America has been touched by televangelism, if only by changing the channels on the TV. Poor Andie. She struggled all her young life to get out of Artury's pit, and it just kept sucking her back."

"I'm sure not all televangelism is corrupt, but you can turn that bastard off," I said. "If I have to listen to him much longer, I'll be tempted to do some evil deed myself."

"Your mama is coming to supper tomorrow night, you remember?"

"Make it simple. Don't fuss." I stood at the window with my coffee cup, soaking up the first rays of sun breaking through the clouds. The previous night's dream upset me, perhaps more than I realized. I had trouble getting back to sleep, so in the early morning hours I crept downstairs to pour a glass of milk and catch up on my reading. I couldn't concentrate. The events of the past few days were bittersweet. I'd made love to Andie, and in the process found the one witness to my brother's murder. How would I introduce her to my family? How could I tell my mother who she really was? At three a.m. I crawled back into bed only to lie awake, think, and watch Andie toss and turn in her sleep.

I finished my coffee and rinsed out my cup. I wanted to talk to Andie again, discuss everything. First, I would meet with Royster Bently. There was no point in discussing it further with Ivy. She would only engage in unlikely speculation and wander off into long stories about John as a little boy. I fetched my jacket, calling out that I was leaving and would not be back for lunch. A vacuum cleaner whined from somewhere within the house. Not sure Ivy had heard me, I called out again.

This time the whirring sound was switched off and she responded. "You call me, Mattie?"

"Don't make lunch for me, Ivy," I said. "I'm not hungry."

Ivy poked her head around the corner. "You home for supper?"

"No. Tell Andie I'll see her tonight. I've got work in town. Keep her busy. We had a restless night. And it's not what you think."

"Uh-huh."

"It's not." I couldn't help but grin.

"She be fine. I keep her busy. Go on now. Be safe, and get home soon."

§

Tobias had set up the meeting. I hoped Royster would be able to start the investigation purely on my word, as I had yet to recover the evidence in Andie's lockbox. But my mother needed prepared before she came to supper on Saturday. And then I wanted to do something special for Andie, something that would cement our relationship, our mission, and our lives.

I shifted my car into low as I drove into the parking lot at Valle Crucis Holiness. Stepping inside her tiny office at the back of the church, which doubled as an overflow Sunday school room, I recalled having to bring in more chairs every Easter and Christmas. Her desk sat under the window overlooking the valley and a small thicket of rhododendron and dogwood trees, each jostling for position in a patch of earth. Mother's office had once been a storeroom, and had recently been painted by the men of the church. Lurking beneath the odor of new paint, a disinfectant smell floated up from cartons of cleaning supplies stored there for decades. I ran my hand across her old, wooden desk. The color of thick honey, it had been used hard, with many scratches as ample evidence. I'd seen her practice sermons at that desk, and change a few diapers on it, too. She was a mother first, a pastor second. I loved that about her.

The members had purchased a new office chair for mother. A fancy model that adjusted in more ways than Pastor Bobbie Sue knew how to sit, her feet never touching the floor. I had paid a local carpenter to refinish the hardwood floors. Certainly, the tiny church and parsonage in Valley Crucis existed because of Callahan money.

My mother had given all of her boys their inheritance early and, in return, we kept the little church alive for her, even when its members dwindled. The church didn't advertise other than the sign in the front yard. Over the years the small congregation had seen moderate growth, due to a recently built fellowship hall and by adding a youth group led by Mark and Patsy. I worried my mother probably couldn't handle it if it got much bigger.

There was no computer; she wouldn't have one. An old rotary phone sat on her desk. Two six-foot shelves packed with books and Sunday school papers leaned against the wall. The walls, save for a picture of Jesus preaching His Sermon on the Mount, were clear of all ornamentation. Family pictures were on display in the parsonage next door. Nowhere close to retirement, she'd been a country preacher from the time her first husband, my father, brought her to the area in 1952. I couldn't imagine the church or my life without her.

I followed the smell of furniture polish and found her dusting pews and hymnals in the sanctuary. "Pastor, why don't you hire yourself some cleaning help?"

She ignored me. She'd cleaned her church for forty years and she wasn't about to stop any time soon. "Who do I owe for the pleasure of your company in the middle of the day?"

I grabbed her, locked her in a bear hug and planted a kiss on her forehead. A blush of tiny blood vessels spread across her pudgy cheeks. She was a short blocky woman of Irish descent. At sixty-five her wide impassive face wore a permanent smile and she was usually found in a housedress with matching earrings. Her white hair resembled sifted powdered sugar styled in something she called a French twist. Her voice was too loud and her heart was too soft. Bobbie Sue loved Jesus like a child loved a good daddy. Everyone who knew her—loved her.

"Just want to make sure you're not backing out on supper tomorrow night."

"Not on your life. Ivy cooking? I hear Andie is a wonderful cook."

"Ivy's making your favorite. Fried chicken and cornbread dressing. Andie volunteered, but I wanted her to be free to spend time with you."

"So why are you here?"

"I need to talk to you about Andie."

She motioned for me to join her on the front pew.

I sat, crossed my legs, and turned toward her. "Really, Mother, this is about John." I saw her stiffen, her eyes teary. I took my time and told her about the night Andie had seen John's picture in my bedroom. A half-hour later, she was still quiet, holding her emotions in check, as always. I took her hand and held it on my knee. "Mother, I know it was hard on you to go to the House of Praise and find out what they were saying about Andie. You've been a blessing to us both. There's no need to go back."

She breathed in shallow, quick gasps. "Good. After what you just told me, I couldn't go back. And I think it's best we keep this from your brothers for now."

"Agreed."

She looked into my eyes. "You're in love, aren't you son?"

"Deeply."

"Well, you're certainly old enough to know what you want. I'm anxious to meet her. Give her time, Mattie. From everything I've seen and heard, she's had a rough go of it. I trust your decisions. Just remember, she has children. They seem fine, even after what they've been through, but you may have many challenges over the next few months. I will pray God give you strength. But if God has brought her here as you say, then it will all work out. As will your plan to bring John's murderers to justice. Please, be careful."

"Your optimism is what I need. And your prayers. Thanks, Mom. See you tomorrow night around six." I stood and kissed her cheek again.

It hurt me to see my mother's tears fall, despite how hard she tried to hold them inside. She took my hands and clasped them in her own. "Remember, son. *Many are the afflictions of the righteous: but the Lord delivereth him out of them all.*"

Andie

Saturday morning brought renewed anticipation. My belief that I would see my children again, grew daily. Walking Matthew to the door, I caught him grinning from ear to ear. "You're all smiles today," I said.

"Am I?" He pulled me into his arms. "It's not easy saying goodbye to you every day."

"Then don't go. Stay with me today. I hate when you leave." I gave him my prettiest pout.

"If there wasn't so much to do, I'd keep you in bed all day. I hear we're to have a taste of summer this afternoon. Enjoy it. Ivy's got everything under control for tonight."

I lowered my eyes. "I'm afraid I'll never have many guests here. Everyone I know and love is either dead or gone."

"Don't worry. I've got a plague of relatives to make up for it," he said.

"What time should I be ready for supper?"

"Five. And wear something sexy."

"Not to meet your mother! She's Pentecostal Holiness."

"Yeah," he winked. "But she's a Methodist during the week."

I mussed his hair and kissed him a final time before closing the door behind him.

§

Matthew and Tobias came home early from their meetings, but refused to divulge any information to Ivy or me until they "had their ducks in a row," Matthew said.

I had to admit, I wanted to get it over with. Meeting the famous lady pastor, another mother-in-law candidate, it wasn't something I looked forward to. I kept busy by helping Ivy set the dining room table until I felt Matthew's gaze. It traveled upwards from my black heels to my black skirt, which I tugged downwards, then finally to my pink blouse. I turned to see his face and smile. His inspection lasted only seconds, but felt like a lifetime. He walked up and stood behind me, looping his arms around my waist.

"You look like the main course."

"Leave me be. I'm helping Ivy," I said, dropping a fork on the floor. He always made me as nervous as a teenager on a first date.

Matthew hitched up his pant fabric at his knees and squatted beside me, picking up the fork. I couldn't help notice that he winced at the noise his knees made.

"Your knees sound like walnuts cracking."

"I've been younger, I admit," he said.

I touched his face. "I wish we could've met years ago."

"We met when God wanted us to." After a gentle hug, we walked into the kitchen, where Ivy was sprinkling paprika on deviled eggs. Before he could reach the stove to taste Ivy's soup, we heard the front door open.

I placed my hand on his arm. "Matthew."

"Are you nervous?" he asked.

I shrugged one shoulder. Why couldn't she be anything other than a pastor? "My entertaining skills have atrophied," I said to give him some kind of reply.

"She'll love you. Almost as much as I do."

A voice I didn't recognize boomed from the hallway. "Where is she?"

A stout, little woman turned the corner and reached up anxiously to smooth her snowy-white hairdo. "There she is! You must be Andie. You were right, Tobias, she doesn't look a day over twenty-five!" The Pastor had been ushered into the house on Tobias's arm.

"Thank you." I blushed.

Matthew stepped in to offer a proper introduction. "Obviously, this is my mother, Pastor Bobbie Sue Rossi."

"Oh, Andie, thank you for giving Matthew here a new lease on life."

"It's my pleasure to meet you, ma'am. It's Matthew who has saved my life, though. And I thank you for all you've done on my children's and my behalf."

"No need! I am so proud to have been of service, especially now that I've laid eyes on you." We walked to the living room and Matthew served wine. I was stunned that a holiness preacher would drink real wine. Tobias joined us with a tall glass of beer while Ivy busied herself in the kitchen putting the final touches on supper. I grew quiet as the room hummed with happy chatter. Light conversation that flew over my head while I looked back on the past few months in awe. I'd met the dearest people in the world. Matthew's mother had put me at ease for the moment. She reminded me a little of Maudy. Sweet and religious, the pastor had a continual apple blossom smile and bluish-gray eyes that sparkled when she talked.

I grabbed my third glass of wine from the bar, as Ivy's voice boomed through the doorway. "Supper's ready!"

Matthew offered his arm to his mother. I took hold of Tobias's arm as he held it out to me.

"Does the church keep you busy, Pastor?" I asked.

"I should say so. Since Jack died, I have more than my share of work to do. It's hard to find reliable help." She winked at me, and then turned toward the table.

I didn't ask who the church slackers might be, and didn't much care. I might visit but I wasn't joining her church. Or any church. Not for a long time. If ever.

"Will you come to service tomorrow morning with Matthew? I'd love to show you off."

I swallowed my thoughts. "If Matthew goes, I'll be with him. Thank you, that'd be nice."

Matthew took his mother to her chair, holding it for her then pushing her up to a table set with fine linens, crystal, silver, delicate china, and fresh flowers. He then proceeded to seat me while Tobias sat at his regular spot and Ivy served. I had never been around formality like that. I almost forgot they were people of a different class. My parents seldom ate at the table, preferring their breakfast bar or TV trays instead. And until that evening, meals with Ivy and Tobias had been relaxed and casual. Suddenly, I was unclear how to act or which fork to use. I felt out of place. Like the silk purse made from the sow's ear. My hesitation showed.

"It's all for show," Matthew's mother whispered to me sipping her wine. "We're all just country, darlin'. We put our pants on one leg at a time, like everybody else." She smiled and placed her napkin in her lap. "I must say, after four visits to the House of Praise and their Hollywood production they call a church service, I was sure glad to get back to my little old-timey house of worship."

Lifting my chin and squaring my shoulders, I returned her smile, adjusted the napkin on my own lap, then drained my wineglass.

"Your children are beautiful reproductions of yourself. So well behaved. Just lovely young people."

That did it. I finally teared up. But Pastor Bobbie Sue reached out and squeezed my hand. "Trust the Lord with all your heart, darlin'. Lean not to your own understanding. God will work His wonders. I know the man upstairs personally. He just loves to show off. Let's say the blessing, shall we?"

We bowed our heads while the pastor prayed. "Dear Lord, please bless this food and the hands that prepared it, and forgive me, please, for any embarrassing words that shoot out of my mouth. Especially anything stupid I say to Andie, and thank you for bestowing to Ivy her exquisite culinary talent. Amen."

Everyone replied with a hearty, "Amen" and raised their heads.

But Matthew's mother threw up her hands and said, "Oh, shoot! I forgot!" She looked at Ivy and smiled. I heard Matthew sigh and put down his fork. The pastor waited until we all bowed our heads again. "Lord," she asked, "you still on the clock? Well, of course You are. You know Andie is here with us today. Safe. Keep her in Your loving arms, Lord. We pray a hedge of protection around her and her children. You also know today is a rather special day because we're pretty darn happy to have her here. So I do hope when I pass through those pearly gates, you got me a welcome home party waiting with folks at least half as excited as we are on this day. In your precious and Holy Name we do pray. And Amen."

I smiled and nodded at Pastor Bobbie Sue, whispering a "thank you," as she patted my hand. I suddenly forgot my uneasiness. Hearing a prayer like I'd never heard before, it was as if these people truly knew God better than anybody.

Ivy ladled tomato bisque soup into small bowls. Cornbread dressing, wild rice, and sweet potatoes were passed on antique platters. Fried chicken, green beans, a plate of deviled eggs, and a basket of steaming biscuits rounded out the meal. I suspected it was a special occasion.

"Ivy! I thought I told you not to fuss. This is the best meal ever! Tobias, did you make the chicken?" Matthew teased.

Tobias chuckled and Ivy poked him. "Mattie, you know Toby only know how to eat chicken, not fix it." Poised gingerly on her chair, Ivy was ready to rise whenever someone needed a fresh glass of ice water or needed more of anything. I missed Lula and silently vowed to find her once my quest was over. But I was touched by Ivy's servant heart. A woman who was no more a servant than anyone at the table. A woman whose education rose far above us all. A woman whose choice it was to serve those she loved, no matter what color she was or we were. In return, Matthew had given her and her husband part of his farm, more money than they could ever spend, and had made them his family.

We ate and exchanged standard pleasantries, and I was happy that my foot had not gone into my mouth, not even once. Taking a serving of rice to my plate, I grew quiet hoping not to weep, already knowing I would anyway, at least before the night was over. Except for the clinking of silverware on dishes and soft music playing through overhead speakers, a hushed atmosphere fell over the table. Matthew broke the silence by clinking his spoon on his wine glass and clearing his throat. He sat back in his chair and everyone relaxed with him. Color flushed his cheeks and his eyes appeared feverish. His words, however unbelievable, were perfectly clear.

"Andie, I know it's been a short time. We've talked about that, and the fact that we've lived long enough to know what we want in life. Well. I know one thing for sure. I know I want you. Yes, this was quick and I was going to wait, but I can't. You've given me life again and love. Love I so desperately wanted and needed. I'm saying I want us to have a future together." He reached into his pocket and pulled out a square, velvet box.

"I was in a great store today. I found this. It's an antique. I know you love old things." He stood and stepped toward me, got down on his creaky knee, between his mother's chair and mine and opened the box. He spoke with his eyes first, then held up a ring. A huge diamond in platinum. I gasped at my first glimpse of it. He moved in closer. "It was made at the turn of the century and worn by one of the Vanderbilts at Biltmore. A jeweler friend of mine in Asheville kept it in his safe for years. I realize we want Dillon and Gracie here with us before proceeding with marriage. When they're finally at Shiloh, when we have accomplished all we have set out to do—please, would you be my wife?"

I lifted the ring from his hands and held it. A slow smile erased my distress, and I managed a nod. Matthew slipped the diamond on my finger. I stared at this thing that had taken over my hand. "Okay," I whimpered, feeling heat rush into my cheeks.

"*Okay?*" everyone said in unison. Laughter rippled around the table.

I was overcome with so many emotions my head felt like it was about to spin off my shoulders. "I love you too, and I would love to marry you, Matthew. Someday. After Dillon and Gracie are here. And when Reverend Artury is in prison." I had stated the stipulation of my engagement. Everybody knew it. My own pre-nup. Even though he had already said it, I had just enforced it. I would be his wife only after we had met our goals.

The table of on-lookers broke out in applause. He stayed on his knee and reached for my face, trailing his fingers lightly down the sides of my cheeks. "I hope it's alright that I wanted the people I love most in the world to witness my proposal."

My face was covered in a hot blush of my own. "It's fine. How can I thank you—"

"Just love me in return." As Matthew held me in front of his family, my mind rewound to a moment over twenty years before when I had promised God I'd never love another. I sat there realizing God knows our promises aren't worth a lick, and that it took me over twenty years to figure out that out.

A round of congratulations filled the room, but pure pleasure registered on Ivy's face. "Dessert will be served in the living room," she said. I asked for another glass of wine instead. The talk remained light for the next hour, and I appreciated that. My life being what it was, there wasn't much I could say that didn't include sorrow, or death, or pain of some kind. When the evening wound down, Matthew asked his mother the question I had also been thinking.

"Is it safe to bring Andie to church? I mean, I would love for her to meet Mark, Patsy, and Luke, but—"

"There's nobody in my congregation who knows a soul related to anyone at that damnable House of Praise. She is as safe at Valle Crucis Holiness as she is here in this house." On that point, Pastor Bobbie Sue was clear. "We'd love to see you tomorrow, Andie, darlin'." she said. "And, welcome to the family."

"Thank you. I'm anxious for you to know my children."

"So am I. I'm sure they will love it here. A new start for them." Bobbie Sue turned to Ivy. "Thank you, Ivy, for a lovely supper, as always. Can I help you clean up?"

"No, go home and get your sermon ready for tomorrow."

"Andie, before I leave, I want to say something. I know we haven't mentioned John tonight, but Matthew has told me about your unfortunate experience. That you witnessed the murder of my youngest son. I want to thank you for coming into both of my sons' lives at a time when they both needed you. God has brought you here to us. For that, I am grateful."

"Pastor, once again it's me who's grateful. Truthfully though, I'm not sure I'm quite ready to attend church again. I think I've been hiding from God for a long time."

"You can't hide from God, darlin'. He'll hunt you down, grab you by the seat of your pants, and nail your backside to the church wall. I've seen Him do it. I'll see you in the morning."

"Yes, ma'am."

Valle Crucis Holiness Church

Andie

I paused and looked up at Matthew's mother's church with grief on one side of me and guilt on the other. The sting of laughter and music drifted through the stained glass windows and bounced off the bright blue sky. I fought the urge to run away from the white steeple pointing to Heaven, reminding me of my past. Peeking inside the cool darkness of the sanctuary before the service began, I felt a wave of nausea. *Sanctuary. Safety and refuge.* Inside its secluded walls, the church was supposed to offer protection to those who sought it. *Is protection even possible for me?* Through the front doors, the engraved words above the altar registered a measure of comfort: *Come to me all ye who labor and are heavy-laden, and I will give you rest.* I identified with the heavy-laden outcasts Jesus sought, although, resting inside a church was not something I had experienced.

Pastor Bobbie Sue smiled at a couple who walked in the door. "We're serving donuts and coffee in the lobby. Please join us. Just watch for sticky little hands that may have touched your seat before you sit down."

Did I hear her correctly? Donuts and coffee? I smiled as Matthew stepped up to shake his mother's hand. The pastor, in a flowing royal blue satin robe, threw her arms around my neck. "Andie! I've saved a front pew for you both."

"Mother, I want Andie to meet the family. Do you know where they are?"

"Getting ready for Sunday school, I presume. Don't be late for my sermon."

Matthew grinned. "She can make me feel twelve sometimes, I swear."

I laughed my first real laugh of the day, which eased the gnawing sensation in my gut. We walked to the fellowship hall and up to a tall man in mirrored shades and a black cowboy hat over a self-inflicted haircut, sitting on the hood of his car. "Luke! I want you to meet Andie."

He tossed his cigarette into the gravel, slid off his souped up '59 Thunderbird, and hoofed it right up to me with his arms extended. "I heard! Congratulations! She's a purty thing, Matt."

I smiled at the brother called Luke who had obviously seen one too many Johnny Cash concerts. He wore a black shirt, black jeans, and a matching jacket that appeared slept in. Not as put together as Matthew, Luke was at least friendly. A country boy with light, curly hair about his neck, who, I could tell, didn't give a flip what anybody thought of him. Matthew had called him a man with plenty and no responsibility, who lived in a constant laid-back state of mind and loved fast cars, fast women, and his family. And definitely in that order. A heathen who loved gospel music, Nascar, and Jesus, but couldn't commit to any of them.

"Nice to meet you." I said.

And then there was Mark whose classic allure reminded me of John. He was no hick. Mark and Luke had the same washboard build, but with a different presentation altogether. Mark's dark complexion made Luke appear pale and sallow. His ebony hair was short and gelled and he spun his sunglasses in his right hand. His wife, Patsy, had riveting dark eyes with jet-black hair styled almost like her husband's. They were the new youth pastors. A swarm of teenagers gathered around, and I longed for Dillon and Gracie to be part of them. I was so close to a normal life, and yet the reality of one still evaded me. Mark gave me a quick hug, then excused himself and his wife to get to their morning class. "See you after church, Andie?"

"Yes, stay for lunch!" shouted Patsy, herding her group inside. "We're having potluck in the fellowship hall." Her attention was quickly harnessed by rowdy teens. "Hush!" she yelled.

"You have a great family, Matthew. I sure miss mine."

"I know you do. Someday, we'll gather both families here. On the day you marry me?"

"Okay," I said. But as I stepped into the church, haunting memories hit me in the face like a heat blast from a casting oven. Fire-breathing sermons at the House of Praise, years of torturous sorrow, and the insanity it created. I stopped in my tracks. I couldn't speak, my vision blurred, and my legs gave out from under me. "I can't do this," I said.

Matthew assisted me to a folding chair in the lobby.

"I'll get her some water," said an older lady who stood at the back handing out church bulletins. By the time she returned, the color had come back into my face.

"I'm sorry," Matthew said. He was clearly upset with himself. "I should've thought more about this. I was so overcome with you, wanting you to meet my family, I didn't think of the effect a church, any church, would have on you. Do you want to go home? Let's go home."

"No, let me sit a minute. Just let me breathe. Can we just sit in the back?"

"Yes, of course. Mother will understand."

Scooting into a back pew, a children's choir was ready to sing. *A children's choir. How beautiful, how simple, how Christ-like.* My eyes closed and I imagined Dillon and Gracie sitting next to me.

Matthew

I prayed for Andie, asking God to give her strength. I prayed for myself, for God to direct my path and guide my steps in the days ahead. *A righteous man's steps are ordered by the Lord.* I'd read it and heard my mother quote the scripture many times. Andie didn't see how similar our lives were when it came to being raised in church. Just two entirely different churches.

I had carefully selected my suit and tie that morning, my first occasion in years to stand before the congregation with a woman on my arm. Andie looked beautiful in the pale pink suit Ivy had bought for her. Her pearl bracelet hugged her wrist. Her diamond, round to match the shape of her face, flashed as it caught the light. Wrapped around her finger, the lucky ring was right where I wanted to be.

I would call my son, Conner, to come meet Andie. I would love her children back to wholeness. I would give Andie and myself a family again, as soon as we could put Calvin Artury and his cohorts behind bars. Special Agent Royster Bently had started his investigation, considering the evidence I assured him we had. Several other officials also promised to turn up the heat on the House of Praise. Cases were reopened or begun anew. Having friends in high places was about to pay off.

Andie

"*Thy word is a lamp unto my feet, and a light unto my path.*" The children's cherub faces quoted the scripture before they sang it with everything they could muster. As their song ended, the first and second graders were herded off and the next ensemble, a handful of teenagers took center stage. The youth group belted out their well-practiced Amy Grant song, *El Shaddai*. I wept bitter tears. Those young people, who reminded me of my own children, sang their hearts out, over and over echoing the love of their creator. Twenty or so throaty bells tuned each to the other, a few raised hands, and some faces lifted to the ceiling. They sang to God, not to the congregation. Patsy played the piano while Mark accompanied on the guitar and semi-conducted. The congregation cheered and applauded, but I sat in further amazement. I'd been robbed of more than I knew. It was worship in its purist form. I'd felt it once before, the day Mavis sang at the Baptist Church in Winston-Salem, but I was too young and stupid to recognize it. The battle to eliminate my anger over wasted years had begun.

Pastor Bobbie Sue preached for forty-five minutes. Matthew checked his watch and whispered to me, "It's almost over."

"How can you tell?"

"At precisely twelve-twenty our organist will walk to the Hammond. Bernice fixes roast chicken for her family every Sunday. It's been her sacred duty for thirty years to end the service. *What a Friend We Have in Jesus* is her signal to Mother to quit talking so she can get home before her supper burns."

I almost laughed out loud.

When the organ echoed to silence, a sawing of coughs, the rustling of bulletin paper, and folks zipping up their Bible covers filled the gap. The pastor raised her hands in front of her tiny pulpit one last time to end the morning service. "Go with God this morning!"

A reply warbled back from the congregation.

"We hope you enjoyed our youth choirs earlier. The adults will be back next week. One last item. My entire family is here with me this morning. I want you all to meet Andie, my Matthew's fiancée. Welcome, Andie, to the house of the Lord."

It felt like I'd never been to church before, and it'd been a long time since I was anybody's fiancée. I smiled benevolently while the happy pastor swept her arm in a circle, indicating the congregation should stand. "Let's all sing my favorite hymn, *Blessed Assurance*. 'Cause folks, when you have Jesus, you have assurance. He will turn your adversities into advantages, and your darkest hours into glorious sunshine. I thank Him this morning; I praise Him, because what the devil tried to take from me, God returned seven times over!"

I shot to my feet and my heart leaped within me. This was what God was trying to teach me all along. If I could learn to trust again, I would find more than just my faith. I would discover my way out of my darkest hour and an end to my lifetime of unhappiness. God had found me, just like Tobias had said. I had started over. For me, going back to church was nothing short of a miracle. It was a perfect beginning. As the congregation sang, I was caught up in a vision, the third one of my life. Mavis stood in a white robe alone in the choir loft, smiling, watching me. And happy.

July 1993
THE STINK OF THE FISH

Reverend Calvin Artury

In my dimly lit office, I bent over my desk. Sluggish, stodgy, and mottled with new liver spots. I held my head in my hands, speculating whether I'd go bankrupt or to prison first. All over the world brokers and bankers watched my holdings and investments plummet. I was building another church to replace the remodeled one—three times the size and three times as plush—but construction had come to a halt. Television equipment was in constant change and flux; new state-of-the-art video and audio accouterments were needed every year. Airtime remained at a premium, and we'd recently purchased another satellite. And, of course, there was the jet and the new team of employees to maintain and fly it. I supposed it all added up. It wasn't my job to watch it all; there was no way I could. I wasn't yet in my glorified body. Plus the cover-ups and the payoffs cost me a fortune. It had gotten way out of hand. And everyone lied to me. Literally. Lied. Everyone!

I had maxed out my personal credit cards to make the past few payrolls. A staff of over 500 depended on me for their livelihoods. Some of the banks had called in their loans. Loans I had recently learned were in default. My billion-dollar ministry had dropped into the toilet.

Where's Silas?

I trusted my Chief Financial Officer and his staff of accountants to handle the finances of the church, the restaurant, the television studio, and Peyton Broadcasting. When the news of possible corruption hit, I sent for the president of my bank. But he was missing. Evan said he'd disappeared overnight. *Goddamn Evan can't find anybody these days.*

I spent the night combing my files. The North Carolina Attorney General had ordered me to preserve and submit all files regarding the television studios. Evan said it probably wouldn't come to a head until after the Nigeria crusades. I wasn't chancing it. I'd heard about those infamous FBI raids Jim Bakker and a few others had suffered through. I'd not be televised while handcuffed and led to prison. The only bright spot was that the congregation had not got wind of it. It wouldn't leak to the press until I was safely in Africa. God only knew what I would come back to. *Come back? No.*

The bank was foreclosing on my house. Not the small modest three-bedroom ranch down the street where I'd lived with Vivi. The one my congregation thought I lived in. I'd paid that old house off decades ago. The bank sent notices on the other one—the one in Atlanta with the 12 bedrooms and 1,800 acres of lavish gardens and golf course lawns. They also wanted my New York City apartment, the country place near Gatlinburg, and my chalets in Vail for my ministry team's use. That wasn't the worst of it. A new Forsyth County prosecutor was breathing hard down my neck, along with the IRS.

Evan and Silas knew about it weeks before, but had kept it from me. *Damn them! Who could possibly be fueling this persecuting fire?*

Mavis was dead; I had destroyed all enemies who could defame me. Peter was dead, long gone to AIDS. No threats of lawsuits from any of the young men and women I'd taken to my bed had ever surfaced. I'd seen to that. *Where is this harassment stemming from?* Who wielded the power to force the government's hand? The few who knew my secrets had plenty of their own I was prepared to expose, should they betray me. *Wait a minute. Where's Andie Oliver?* It'd been weeks since I'd had a report on her. "Fannie, get me Joe Oliver on the phone."

It made more and more sense. She was the only demon we had never fully dealt with. She didn't show up that day on the tennis court. She didn't show up anywhere. It was as if she had disappeared into thin air. I'd been foolish to stop the relentless search, thinking she was bluffing. How utterly stupid we'd all been. *Someone is helping that harlot.*

"Joe Oliver on the phone, Reverend."

I picked it up with a loud and fast, "Have you found Andie?"

"Um—no, Reverend. She's not been a priority lately. Should she be?"

"She has always been your priority, Oliver! Where are your children?"

"They're still in a foster home. I get them on Sunday mornings for service when I'm in town. I haven't seen them this week, but I know their mother hasn't seen them since the court took them months ago. Far as I know, she's dead. At least I hope she is. I think she may have killed herself or we would've heard from her by now. No one has seen her for months. As you know, she sold her car and all her stuff. Since then, I've checked everywhere. Andie's nowhere to be found, Reverend."

"You sure she's not in Charleston with her mother?"

"I'm positive. Her entire family has been followed for months. Pastor DeSanto posted a man at every possible place she could turn up. She's not been near any of them."

"If you hear from her, call me. Immediately. In the meantime, tell Selma you need to get ready for the Nigeria Crusade. Then *you* go look for Andie yourself. Don't stop until you find her. Don't you dare come back until you can tell me she's rotting in her grave!"

"Is there a problem?"

"Problem? The problem is your head's going to roll unless you find her! Andie is behind *all* of our problems!"

"What if I don't find her? We're leaving for Nigeria in a week."

"I know when we're leaving! This is your fault, Oliver! You never could control her! Listen to me carefully. You will not board the plane for Africa until you find your ex-wife. As of now, you've been replaced until you can tell me, without a doubt, that she's dead. Now do as you're told!" I slammed down the phone.

I had searched the files all night for incriminating evidence, and still didn't know if the prosecutor was only fishing. The blame game was about to begin.

Everyone left standing in the inner circle would profess their innocence and trade evidence for leniency the second it was offered. The irony was that Joe, my Chief Engineer, who was supposed to know everything going down inside the church, who had made a name for himself within its walls and in the world of audio engineering, couldn't afford a lawyer. Not the kind he was going to need. My top brass faced prison time, regardless. I didn't care.

For me, either way—a prolonged investigation or a swift and merciless trial—as the church's sole head, I would take the most heat. *'The stink of the fish starts in the head,'* rang in my ears. *Where did I hear that?* My mother, probably. Complaining about my father.

Stuff your briefcase with cash, disappear, and don't look back.

But I did look back for a moment. As I reached under my desk for my briefcase, I felt something. When I saw what it was, I clutched it so hard it bit into my palm. Vivi's cross necklace. It must have dropped off the picture on my credenza. I had hung it there years ago.

My beloved Vivi. My angel of light. Her skeletal hands struggled to pull off her wedding set. The disease had ravaged her, turning her inside out. Her hair was gone, her eyes black and hollow in bile-green sockets. I was sorry she had to die in order for God's work to continue. I had warned her not to open my Pandora's box. But she did, and she had threatened me. She wouldn't keep my secrets any longer.

She threw her rings at me. "No . . . more . . . lies."

Her action stopped my next breath in mid exhale. I stroked her ringless hand and cried. "You don't mean that, Vivi."

She could only roll her head back and forth on the pillow. "I . . . want the world to know," she said and coughed. "What you are." Unable to speak another word, she gasped for her final breaths.

"I can't stand to see you in pain." I turned and nodded to my private physician in the corner.

Within minutes the doctor injected glue-colored liquid into her arm. The room's light faded into the hue of death. "She's gone," the doctor said and glanced at his watch. "Time of death, nine-twenty."

"Angel of Death, take my Vivi to the mansion our Lord has prepared for her. No more pain, Vivi. No more pain." I collapsed at the side of her bed and stroked her body. Grieving, I cried out loud into the shroud of sheets.

"The coroner will rule it a natural death due to the progression of her disease."

"I loved her," I said.

The doctor ignored me, collected his bag and left the room.

Her wedding band sparkled on the floor. I picked it up and placed it on my pinky finger and my tears came to an abrupt halt. "If only you had believed in me, Vivian. If only you could've seen the plan of God for my life, you would not have had to die. We could've ruled the Christian world."

I laid Vivi's necklace back on the credenza. Walking swiftly down the thick-carpeted hall wrapped behind the substantial baptistery, I arrived at a private office few knew about. I disengaged the alarm and retired to my closet sanctuary to sulk and covertly nurse my self-pity, one shot of bourbon after another. Tapping the shot glass against my teeth, I breathed in the smell. *"Have Thine own way, Lord! Have Thine own way! Thou art the Potter, I am the clay. Mold me and make me after Thy will, while I am waiting, yielded and still."* I sang loud and long and then, the voice of God revealed my escape route. I emptied the bottle as a plan formed in the recesses of my mind.

In that inner sanctum was a wall safe hidden behind an oil painting of the Jerusalem skyline, given to me by Prime Minister Yitzhak Rabin on my third trip to Israel. Crisp, green large bills, folded into several wads lay in that vault. Stacked behind ledgers and computer floppies were hundreds in bundles. Stacks of cash. A slush fund to tip waiters, limo drivers, and escorts. Memorable service given to donating religious celebrities or political figures who came to town. Cash for side trips to Paris, Rome, Morocco, and expensive hotels on the way back from a crusade. Cash for the unexpected. I'd disappear without leaving a paper trail.

I flipped open my briefcase and dumped files, come-to-Jesus tracts and department reports onto the floor. Filling it with money, I then jammed several stacks into my pockets. I would take the cash from the Nigerian crusade as soon as it was converted into dollars. If anyone believed I could be sent away to rot in some hellhole prison, they had another thing coming. A smile tugged at the corners of my mouth.

As soon as it's over, send the staff home, and head for an island.

TESTIMONY

Matthew

Andie and I hiked the narrow footpath that wound up the mountain around rocks and weeds. The temperature dropped the higher we climbed. July heat was easier to handle in cooler elevation. Gazing over the landscape, I stood holding Andie in my arms. It appeared as if the sun had cut itself on a sharp hill and bled into the valley. Its blistering heat was merciless on the farm and animals below.

I felt an urgent need to explain exactly what lay ahead. Moving to a nearby rock, I sat and observed her as she crept to the edge of the overlook, and peered out over the deep green waves of the mountains surrounding her. "I think this must be what it's like on the open sea. I think I can see all the way to Virginia." I knew she was falling in love with my land and the mountains that surrounded it. She turned to me with a funny grin on her face. "I have to pee."

"There's a nice tree right over there." I said, laughing and watching her walk to a clump of bushes. "By the way, last week, the neighbor at the next farm told me he saw a couple black bear. And watch out for copperheads."

"Oh, great." She rolled her eyes at me. "That's just great, Jungle Jim."

I simply loved her.

Later, we collapsed near the trail, on a grassy knoll where we surveyed yet another panorama of the Blue Ridge. The afternoon wore on. Andie fell asleep in my arms. I savored my time with her. The rock behind me felt smooth under my back and the sun hot on my face. She snored as she slept, relaxed from toes to fingertips. I enjoyed the heat of her body, the strength she gained every day. I had called her "chiseled" the previous night, exploring her with love, but also care, wanting to make sure she wasn't too thin. She was a belle. She was supposed to be round and soft. The constant hiking and farm work had made her body hard. Including her heartache. It was proving more difficult to conquer.

"Andie?" She lay unmoving in the space we shared, her face warm when I laid my finger on it. I moved a strand of hair from her forehead. At her temple, her pulse beat steady and strong. I wanted to touch it, to assure myself of its strength and endurance. She shifted in her sleep and I felt her despair that, God help us, Artury find her before she had a chance to testify. I had given her the first bit of hope she'd ever had to shut him down but from the time she was a girl, grief and misfortune had trailed her like a scent. Andie was not a natural optimist. She slowly opened her eyes. The lines around them were new. They were inevitable, weren't they? I was forty-two, she'd turn thirty-nine soon. She had earned those lines.

Andie arched her back as she stretched, her small hands fisted white. She turned her face upward to mine, her eyes wide, and then she put one hand on the back of my neck and brought my mouth down to hers, kissing me until my entire body responded and I groaned out loud.

"Goodness," she said, checking her watch. "It's almost five. We need to get going."

"Not yet," I said, pulling her to me.

A glint sparked in her eyes. "You do realize the whole world can see us up here?"

"What world? Only miles of sky and trees up here."

"And bears and copperheads."

"Let them look. Let them all look." I kissed her again. My lungs gasped for air. Despite how I found her—broken, despised, and rejected, I was certain she loved me. Not just because I had rescued her, but because it was the only way she knew how to love—with all her heart.

With great effort, I forced myself to stop kissing her before it went further. Not something easy for a man to do. I leaned against the boulder, her back against my chest. "Andie we've got to talk. There are things we need to do. Now. Before Artury takes the team to Africa."

She pulled away. "Like starting down this mountain before the sun sets and the night wind turns us into giant Popsicles for those bears."

I took her hands in mine, pressing them to my chest, and warming them between my hands and the flannel of my shirt. "Every day we delay, we're a day behind in getting that bastard. A day further away from what we want. Bringing Dillon and Gracie to Shiloh."

"I know."

I released her left hand letting my own slide inside her shirt and up her back. "We have to get the evidence out of your safety deposit box."

"It's not that simple. I'm sure they're watching the banks."

"Ah, but so are the Feds. Artury would be pretty stupid to do anything in a Winston-Salem bank right now. And he's not stupid. Besides, the banks are on notice. They're tightening security as we speak. If being rich gets you one thing, it gets you in the back door. I know old Hootie Snitch, the president at Wachovia. We worked a deal on a tract of land near Pilot Mountain some time back. He's taking us inside your bank branch tonight. At midnight. After that, we'll get your testimony recorded and documented, along with the evidence. You'll have to testify what you saw, and why you waited so long to tell it. Our attorneys will help you."

"And then?"

"You won't be needed again until Artury and the rest go to trial."

"Oh." She nodded, watching a turkey vulture glide on a breeze.

It was easier for me, I knew that. I made life work my way. She never could have done it by herself. The beginning of our investigation to uncover the House of Praise and its leadership was a tremendous success. I only wished Andie knew how important she was to the effort. "Won't you at least try to call Peter one more time?" I asked.

"I will. After supper. I can't think anymore about this." She shouldered her pack, then pulled her cap down low on her forehead.

I pulled her into me again. "Hey, it's okay," I whispered. "We'll talk later. But we have to deal with it soon."

"I'm sure Peter's dead," she said. "If he's not, he'll be too sick to travel back here."

"Then we'll go to him."

Andie

I headed for the trail. I wanted to get the long nightmare over with. It had taken all my courage to survive the deaths of my loved ones and losing custody of my children. I had no idea what would really happen next. *Will God turn a deaf ear again?*

But I was right about Peter Collins. Peter had told his mother that I might call someday. He had mercifully passed away three months prior to my phone call that evening.

At midnight, our quest kicked into high gear. The bank president unlocked the back door of my Wachovia Bank branch. It was quiet as a tomb. Escorted inside by two police officers, Hootie then turned off the alarm and kept the lights off. Matthew and I followed them to the lockbox area, and stood near the security door. I recognized Jenny's cubicle. A picture of her walking baby girl sat on her desk.

Hootie retrieved the master key from Jenny's desk. He spoke quietly, "Follow me."

Matthew carried an empty canvas bag and glanced around. My nerves about got the best of me as I bit at my nails. "I've guarded this key a long time," I whispered, pulling it from around my neck and handing it to Matthew. His eyes sparkled in the dead silence of the room.

Hootie gave us our privacy inside the vault. Within seconds we opened the box. The treasure chest. My written testimony of the night John died, the pictures and letter from Mavis, as well as the videotape from Peter. The roll of film I snapped of everything in my shed, which included pictures of Joe's briefcase filled with money—Matthew slipped every piece of evidence into the bag. I hoped all of it and my testimony was enough to put Calvin away. Enough to put him in an electric chair. Enough to send him to Hell.

§

Royster Bently reported to Matthew and me the next morning that the pressure was getting to Calvin. According to Royster's sources, Calvin announced he would not be preaching at the House of Praise until he returned from Africa. I leaped and twirled around the room. My confidence spiraled upward, as my contagious laughter lasted throughout the day. With my spirit encouraged, I was ready to nail his coffin shut. Matthew told me of the immense manpower that had come together to force Calvin out into the open, bring all the evidence into light, and hit him hard in his pocketbook. The tide of public opinion was slowly changing. Word of the audits leaked out to the newspapers that, in turn, started asking questions of their own.

I arrived at the police station the next afternoon with Matthew and his legal team. They drilled and questioned me and took my sworn statement. My rehearsed testimony was flawless. Matthew, the FBI, and the Winston-Salem detectives assigned to the case reviewed the evidence and watched the videotape, and then presented it to an unbiased judge who accepted it and issued arrest warrants for Calvin Artury, Evan Preston, Joe Oliver, Tony DeSanto, and Silas Turlo. In addition, every official suspected of taking bribes from the ministry was under investigation.

Matthew would not tell me about Peter's tape. "Let's just say Peter Collins has a new star in his crown. He recorded the sins of the century. Enough to lock Artury up for an eternity."

But the warrants for their arrests were issued two days too late. Under the cloak of night, the ministry team and its executive staff had left the country earlier than anticipated. The warrants would be kept quiet and wait until they arrived back in the States in the middle of August.

August 1993
No Way Back

Reverend Calvin Artury

Suspecting the worst and keeping my suspicions to myself, I insisted my entourage secretly depart two days early for Africa. The non-stop flight had been fraught with terrible turbulence. Everyone on the plane had thrown up at least once, including myself. I had spent millions setting up and organizing the Nigeria faith-healing crusade. God would not forsake us.

Plagued with problems, the massive meetings drew record crowds. Heat created havoc for staff, equipment, and especially for me since I refused to wear anything but my three-piece suit. But oh, the smells! Open-air toilets, overripe fruit, unburied corpses, parched meat hanging in markets, and hundreds of whores in the streets. The putrid smell of unwashed bodies saturating the sweltering air nearly buckled my knees into the Nigerian dust. The smells of sin, wickedness, and of Hell.

After the first night, I returned to my hotel room in Port Harcourt and found a call waiting for me. The caller had refused to speak to anyone but me. A caller with the authority to push the right buttons. My inside man in the Winston-Salem Police Department. Tyrone Neban.

"Reverend Artury, this is Tyrone. Bad news. Warrants have been issued for your arrest. They got warrants for Evan and Mr. Turlo, too. They say they got all the evidence they need and testimony from somebody. Don't know who. I wasn't invited to that party. It's all hush-hush. The FBI is involved. You need top security clearance to find out anything in here. Man, I was lucky to get what I did. You want me to call Evan? See what he wants me to do?"

A guttural hiss escaped my throat. "No. Don't call anyone. Just talk to me."

"What do you want me to do about this?" The phone connection broke up; it was difficult to hear.

"Nothing. I repeat. Do nothing."

"You're the boss ..." his voiced trailed and the line disconnected.

I dropped to my knees like Lot in Sodom, praying for one drop of mercy.

Quickly, I came to myself. I had nothing to fear. Nothing to worry about. That's right. I was the boss, and I wasn't about to let anyone forget it. I would not tell anyone about the warrants, not even Evan. Evan hated me. *Let him fry. Let them all fry.*

§

The morning of the final day dawned like a fire in a hearth, so gold everything seemed cast of metal. The air was unfit for human consumption. I rolled over on my wet sheet and spat out a swig of piss-warm water onto the floor. The skin on my face had turned a fiery red from the scalding sunlight. Preaching, prophesying, and praying for the sick in the enormous and all-day events pushed my staff and me to exhaustion.

Long-legged and nearly naked, the young Nigerian man at the foot of my bed stared at me with murky and inexpressive eyes, his shirt barely covering his voluptuous chest. His pants, unzipped, had slid down to his hips. I reached out, stroked his cheek and thanked him.

The knock at the door startled me.

"One minute." I slipped into my pants and buttoned my shirt. I knew it was Silas who stood on the other side of the door as I opened it. "You alone?"

Silas nodded and rolled his toothpick from one side of his mouth to the other. He stepped into the room and glared at the young man spread across my sheets, then turned his attention to me. "You ready, Reverend?"

"Better question. Are you?"

"We're ready. Percy knows what to do. We're moving forward."

"God will be with us. This is His plan of protection, Silas. Don't be afraid. I am here to bring you a great deliverance, a wonderful, blood-working anointing."

Silas looked back only once, then closed the door behind him on his way out.

§

A storm missed the hotel that morning, but with it came unbearable humidity. In the sticky hour after Silas left, I heard the huge throng of people pounding the ground only 500 yards away. The heavy air reeked with human waste and I hated the thought of fighting the dust and mud around the stage. The reclining young man at the foot of my bed smiled seductively. The beautiful creature had heard everything, and nothing.

"Time for you to go." I handed him a hundred-dollar bill and watched him slip out the hotel window and climb down the fire escape, the same way he got in, disappearing into the sea of faces already jamming the sidewalks.

I picked up the phone and dialed the car waiting below.

"Yeah?" The static-distorted voice was almost a bark.

"It's me," I said.

"About time."

"Sorry. You know how it is."

"Who was with you?"

"Some comfort in my time of need."

"Are you ready?"

"Give me ten minutes."

Evan appeared agitated as I stumbled into the seat beside him. Whisked away in the dust and heat, the car moved slowly from the narrow alleyway to the street, and then into an endless mass of people we divided like plowing a soft field. Women balanced bundles on their heads and backs with their children following close behind. Men carried the sick and afflicted, while others rode on bicycles with no tires. An eerie silence settled inside the car in the humid afternoon air. The car dropped us off at a white cement block building used as a gathering place for staff to count the offering and secure it in a large portable safe. A conspicuous group of bodyguards with guns surrounded the perimeter. Once alone inside the building, we wiped sweat from our faces with wet cloths provided for us by the local pastors from that God-forsaken country.

"I'm going to check security. You need anything?" Evan asked.

A slight chuckle escaped my lips as I shook my head. His concern for my safety amused me. Our eyes met briefly. *I wonder what you're plotting for me, Evan? What form of death would you choose?*

"Everything okay?" Evan's eyes, suddenly dark as tarnish, spoke silent obscenities.

I knew my assistant had sensed trouble escalating the instant we left the States for Africa. Evan tried to reassure me in years past it would happen someday; someone would leak something to the media and we would have to prove ourselves innocent. All televangelists lived with the threat of exposure and would face it, eventually, he'd said.

A smile like a cancer spread across my face. I didn't answer. I just waved him out the door, then placed a pill on my tongue and washed it down with warm Coke. It wouldn't take long. I clamped my jaw as waves of pain receded to a tolerable level.

I hid in the sparse room, asking not to be disturbed. A normal request: I often *hid myself away*, praying and talking with God, sometimes all night for services like that one. But I wasn't praying. Not that time. I walked to the spot where Silas had told me he'd stashed the nine-millimeter silencer-equipped Luger. "For *mine* is the kingdom and the power and the glory." I slid it into my pocket. "Forever." I stepped out into the heat and the droning sounds of the quartet singing their worn-out gospel songs. Songs made popular by Southern Christian artists over a decade before. Songs that didn't make a bit of sense in that country, on that landscape, to those people.

I pulled my Ray-Bans out of my shirt pocket and slipped them on to shield my red, swollen eyes from the blinding sun. A migraine engulfed my entire head. Evan stood several feet away, sweating like a migrant worker in his white dress shirt, discussing security measures with several men in uniform. I motioned to him that I was ready to press through the crowd and make my way to the platform.

The sun's strong steady heat never let up. The old and the sick, a desperate lot, squatted like mice as close to the stage as they could get, hoping I'd touch them as I walked by. The smell of their poorly washed bodies drifted in and out as a light breeze rose and fell. A few babies cried in their mother's arms. Suicidal dogs with their ribs protruding mingled among the crowd, while hordes of grimy children swarmed like flies over the grounds. I wanted to be any place but Nigeria.

Silas motioned to Percy who took his place behind me. He had been proud to be the on-stage bodyguard since the incident in Germany.

Evan took center stage along with a Nigerian translator. "Good and kind people of Nigeria," he paused for translation. "I would like to introduce to you God's man of the hour, the final hour before Jesus Christ's return to earth."

Another pause. "Your evangelist from the United States, the Reverend Calvin Artury!"

I gazed out over the immeasurable assembly. There were no seats. Thousands, maybe a million or more people stood like trees as far as my eyes could see and began jumping up and down, raising their hands, praising and applauding as I was announced. The music played and the crowd's shouting escalated in sound and intensity. In the distance, firecrackers exploded. A hopeful mob of press, CNN cameras, and paparazzi from several American and British tabloids jockeyed for position to document my every word and movement.

But a sudden string of drool dripped down my chin and I staggered and stumbled up the steps to the stage. I felt ill. Julia Preston lingered near the entrance. She grabbed my arm. "Oh my God, Reverend, are you sick?" I shoved her away and she fell backwards into the arms of a portly man from the House of Praise. I recognized him as one of the members who enjoyed traveling to the crusades on their own dime. A group of devoted followers, retirees, a mixture of bankers, lawyers, and influential business people who came to testify to the Nigerians and lead them to salvation.

Percy, close behind, shot Julia a hard look then helped me up the steps. I rushed to the middle of the stage before anyone could pull at me again. Standing on legs that barely held my weight, I didn't speak. Anticipatory sweat rolled down my forehead into my eyes and I wiped it away with the back of my trembling hand before I tore off my sunglasses. Looking out over the dark knot of people, I watched the multitude grow quiet but restless. A peculiar throng, their mood was always unpredictable. A river of changing faces who waited impatiently for their miracles. I turned from the crowd.

Squinting in the bright afternoon sunlight, I scanned the faces of my staff and crew. Singers, musicians, and stagehands looked lovingly at me; some bowed their heads. They had given all, traveled with me the past sixteen years, and sacrificed their lives for Almighty God. With their whole hearts, they believed the power of Jehovah moved through me. That my silence was the great miracle anointing. That prophecy was about to spill forth out of my mouth.

Instead, I shouted with the voice of an archangel and with the trump of God. "And the dead in Christ shall rise first! *YOU* who are alive *and* remain shall be caught up . . . to meet the Lord in the air . . . wherefore . . . comfort one another with these words! Prepare ye . . . the way of the Lord!"

I spun back around to face the vast congregation.

But before anyone fathomed the reality of the moment, I pulled the gun from my pocket, jammed it into my temple, and fired.

That Old Serpent

Andie

I slept for thirteen hours the night Matthew brought me home from the Winston-Salem Police Department. Eight hours of testimony and questioning had totally worn me out. But my part was over. For the time being. When I woke, I found Matthew in his office, loading a gun. Matthew and Royster had decided that until they accomplished the demise of the House of Praise and its executive staff, they could not bring the children back into my life. It was too dangerous for all of us.

I kissed him good morning, feeling his beard against my face. A feeling I had become addicted to. "What's that for?" I asked, staring at the gun.

"I'm not taking any chances. You know the alarm system in the house; you remember the buzzer under my desk?"

"Yeah, so?"

"It goes directly to the police. They'll be here quick. They're on alert. We can't be too cautious at this point. I'm sure there are leaks in the department. I have no idea who might spill their guts, let Artury know where you're hiding. This is my .38 revolver, and it's loaded. It's in my top drawer. If I'm away, you keep it close at all times. You listening to me?"

I nodded.

He winked. "I know you can shoot."

"What are you thinking, Matt? Am I in more danger since giving my statement to the police?"

"Probably. Ivy and Tobias have agreed to move into the house for a while. If I have to go off property, I don't want you alone. Until Artury comes back from Africa, until those guys are in jail, I don't even want you to walk outside unless someone is with you. I'm sorry, honey, but you've got to realize the danger you're in. It's only temporary."

I sunk into the chair in front of his desk and pulled my knees up to my chest. "I can't wait until this is over."

Matthew

Paranoia was a contagious thing. I caught myself staring out windows and checking doors several times a day, making sure they were locked. My fingers slid over the gun barrel and my skin grew cold at the thought of using it. They would kill her if they found her. Not only to eliminate her testimony, but who knew what crazy church member was searching for her because she was Artury's dark angel. I turned away so she could not see the concern that lingered in my eyes, the fear in me she had yet to find.

As quiet as a baby's sigh she said, "My birthday is next week."

"Your twenty-ninth?"

"Try thirty-ninth."

"We'll celebrate here with Mother and the Brothers Grimm. Okay?"

It was Andie's turn to look away from me. "I miss my children. So much."

I hurt for her. "I know you do. Hold on just a little longer, sweetheart." I leaned down and kissed her, tasted her breath and inhaled her morning scent of lavender shampoo and Ivy's coffee. "Have I told you how beautiful you are?"

"Like a broken record. When will you be home?"

"As soon as I can. Although I'd prefer a morning in bed with you, I've got meetings in Boone this afternoon and supper with Royster in Winston-Salem."

"Come home as soon as you can."

"Count on it. Every precaution has been taken. I'll tell Tobias to let the dogs loose. They'll let you know if anyone is around."

Driving away from Shiloh, I heard the sound of her words in my head, the rhythm of her accent, and for an instant I thought about turning the car around.

Andie

After Matthew left for Boone I fried bologna sandwiches for lunch. My old cooking habits died hard. Ivy had gone home to gather her things. I hated the quiet of the house, especially with the sound of thunder outside. Sadie wagged her tail and needed to go out. "Come on, girl. Let's walk to Ivy's. We'll help her carry a few things back here."

I walked the flagstone pathway between the houses feeling its warmth from the heat of the day, and tried not think of anything other than what to prepare for supper. I found Ivy in her bedroom, putting clothes in an overnight bag. A room in bloom, it popped with the color of her gardens—russet, gold, and soft forest green. Her patchwork quilt flowed over the end of her iron bed like a waterfall. The scent of lilacs and beeswax filled the air; the room felt cool and welcoming. Nestled among her houseplants on a table under a bay window, family pictures sat on several of her handmade doilies.

"What you doing here, Andie? You shouldn't be out by yourself."

"I thought you might need some help. Ivy, I can't live in fear anymore."

"Fear . . . no. Common sense . . . yes. Tobias will bring the suitcases later in the truck. How about some iced tea?"

Ivy's white and chrome kitchen was function over fashion. Stainless steel counters, a well-used apron sink, and the largest refrigerator I ever saw stood in tight formation along the opposite wall from the stove and pantry. I sat at her laminate table and looked through her floor to ceiling windows at late summer iris beds. Top-heavy, bigheaded ladies, the flowers stood in regal posture, as if posing for an unseen Victorian painter. Sadie stretched out on the other side of the screen door, her buttery ears unfurled across the porch floor. I watched her twitch while I tried to relax.

Ivy poured glasses of tea then planted herself in a chair. "You holding up under all this?"

"You know, for the first time in my life, I'm fearless. Calvin can't hurt me now. Matthew's scared they'll try to kill me, but I'm not afraid. The police know everything. I'll do whatever it takes to put that beast away. Get my babies back. I guess, though, in answer to your question, some days are better than others."

On better days, I didn't have to remind myself to breathe. On better days, I was completely dressed before I had the urge to crawl back into bed. On better days, I even clipped recipes in magazines to save for later. Yes, some days were better than others. In spite of Matthew's love and constant attention, I knew nothing would come of our relationship until Calvin was arrested and my children were safe.

I slumped in my chair. I didn't trust myself to continue. I smeared my fingerprints on the frosty glass instead. Ivy's quiet demeanor disturbed me, as if peering inside my head. I drank the rest of my tea and stood too quickly. My chair caught on the tile and crashed to the floor. "I guess I am a little nervous. Best head back. You'll wait for Tobias then?" I uprighted the chair then made a beeline for the screen door, but stopped there. The sky darkened, the wind blew dust across the meadow and lightning cracked in the distance. Sadie sniffed the air and got to her feet.

Ivy walked up behind me and leaned against the door frame. "I want you to know, you must go on, no matter what happens. Even if your heart hasn't. You must find a way to put this behind you. Matthew deserves that, but you deserve it more. I don't mean for you to bury your anger. Just let it go. Let it go. I feel danger for you otherwise."

I nodded and pushed through the door. "Thanks for—" *Please, Ivy. Stop.* "—the iced tea."

Ivy followed me outside. She rested her hand on my arm. "You listen to Ivy. I feel things before they happen. Not see, just feel."

"Hmm, that's something. Come on, Sadie. Let's go. Looks like we got a nasty storm heading this way."

Ivy lifted her hanging ferns off their hooks and set them on the porch. "The wind is picking up. I'll be up to the house soon. Matthew due home late?"

"Yes. I'm making supper, that okay?" I pulled Sadie off the porch.

A smile spread wide across her ruby-red lips. "It's more than fine. See you in an hour."

Sadie looked at me before taking off and running ahead. "Slow down, girl!" Her legs moved like she was running on hot asphalt. Walking the path back to the house, I recalled that I locked the doors but I'd forgotten to set the alarm. It was easy for me to forget about the alarm. I wasn't used to alarm systems. Daddy never had one. It had not become a habit like—well, like locking your door. Whirling around and gazing back toward Ivy's house now far behind me, an overwhelming presence swept over me. The courage that surrounded me a few minutes before evaporated. Lightning flashed again, splitting a gray southern sky. Terror prickled my skin. Moving forward, I found my backbone. The roof of Matthew's house above the tree-lined yard came into view. I picked up my pace and sprinted to the back door, unlocked it, and stepped inside. Everything seemed fine. The house was quiet. I opened the door again and yelled for Sadie.

A voice crept up behind me. "She's off after a groundhog or a squirrel."

"Tobias! You scared me to death." I had nearly jumped out of my flip-flops.

"So sorry. I seen you as I came up from the barn. I let the dogs loose. Where's Ivy?"

"At your house, waiting for you."

"I'll fetch her and be back in a flash. Stay inside. I expect a downpour soon. Ol' Sadie runs off sometimes. She'll be back."

§

I kept busy putting supper on the table and breathed easier the moment Ivy and Tobias walked in. Watching for the dog, I peeked out the windows from time to time while we ate. "I still haven't seen Sadie. Where could she have gone? I hope she doesn't come back muddy and think she's coming inside."

Ivy cleared the table. "Huh, who knows? That dog! She worry Mattie to death, I swan. She think she's the queen around here."

Tobias leaned back in his chair. "I've got to get the horses in, close up the barn. Looks like it might rain all night. I'll look for Sadie while I'm out." He wiped his mouth with his napkin. "I'll feed the dogs and leave them loose, like Mattie said."

Tobias had been gone about ten minutes when I held up my hand, shushing Ivy, my ear cocked to the doorway. "Did you hear that?"

"No. Probably the wind. This house makes lots of noises. Besides, I thought you were fearless," Ivy said with a chuckle.

"I'm just a little jumpy, that's all. Matthew left his gun in the bedroom. I'll go get it."

"Uh-huh, well, don't shoot yourself in the foot. Mine's in the drawer here. We'll have a shoot 'em up time anybody messes with us."

I smiled at Ivy. Both of us, truth be told, were a little edgy. I took the stairs two at a time, and hurried to the bedroom.

Rummaging through every drawer, I kept thinking Matthew said he had slipped the gun into his top drawer. *Maybe he meant his desk drawer.* I figured I only half-heard him, with all his security precautions and long list of instructions running through my head. Rushing down the staircase, I opened the door to Matthew's office and stopped with my hand on the doorknob. The desk lamp had been turned off and the shutters were closed, which was strange. Walking slowly into the coldness of the study, a sudden, inexplicable chill shot down my spine. I breathed in an old familiar smell. Drakkar!

A hand came out from behind the door, and across my face clamping my mouth shut. He yanked me hard into him. "Looking for this?"

JOE!

He shoved Matthew's gun to my head. His eyes moved slowly over me, his smile broadening with every jerk my body made to free myself of him.

I tried to scream, but he held me tight. "If you so much as crack a smile, I'll strangle you," he whispered. My head against his shoulder, I smelled all of him. His foul breath, stale sweat, and his hair—the odor of rancid vinegar. I nodded and his hand moved from my face to my shoulder. His sneer made my blood grow cold.

"Please, Joe. You don't have to do this."

The house was cool, but he was sweating like a prizefighter. He had lost his good looks. Middle age, years of keeping secrets, and long fasts had done a number on his skin. The stress on his gnomish face and receding hairline made him appear a decade older than he was. He wasn't the man I once knew.

Joe stared at me with a found-you-bitch grin. "Nice place you're living in. Wasn't easy to track you down, until I thought about your daddy's backwoods cousins in Boone. Figured you might've headed this way. When I showed your picture around town, it didn't take long until somebody recognized you as being the new girlfriend to the richest man in the state. Give me the tape and the pictures, Andie. All of it. Now. Now, damn it! Give me everything!" He unloaded Matthew's gun, allowing the bullets to fall to the floor. "I prefer a good knife," he said as he threw the gun into the corner. "It's nice and quiet."

I heard a muffled noise coming from the hall. Joe cast a quick look toward the door, his eyes showing the slightest glimpse of fear. He obviously didn't go to Africa with the rest, and he sure didn't know I'd been to the prosecutor's office the day before and handed in every piece of evidence he was looking for. He pulled a long, serrated knife from inside his coat and swayed where he stood, blinking his eyes, the sweat beading like tiny pearls on his forehead. The afternoon light cast his already narrow face into hard, angular lines, emphasizing his frown. I told myself to breathe in and out as my ears were tuned to his laughter, low and harsh, followed by words I will never forget. Not for as long as I live. "Give me what I want," he said, "or I swear I'll cut you up worse than I did Mavis."

Joe's words hit me with the force of his fist. I drew in a sharp and painful breath, doubled-over and placed both hands on my knees to keep myself erect. I broke out in a viscous sweat and my legs suddenly felt like concrete posts as he ambled closer. My vision blurred. But I knew if I passed out, I might as well be dead. "Joe," I said, my voice small and shaky. "You murdered Mavis?"

"Don't be so surprised. I hated that bitch. She almost cost me my whole career." A sneer stretched across his face and he laughed. "God, you shoulda seen her. She looked like she'd been through a meat tenderizer by the time I got through with her. I fucked her, then I about cut her head clean off."

His words knocked the wind out of me, and then stabbed me in the heart. Cold, merciless fury sliced through the middle of me and I fell to my knees, clenching my hands into numbness, my face contorting into twenty years of pure anguish. "You filthy son of a bitch! You killed my Mavis!"

He mocked me. "You killed my Mavis. You killed my Mavis. You bet I did, baby. And I'd do it again for a lot less money."

"You animal!" I screamed. "You knew Calvin molested children. My baby died because of what you put me through, and I lost my children because of your lies! And now . . . now you tell me you . . . raped . . . and murdered . . . Mavis. You *lived* with me, *lying* to me all those years! *You're* the monster! You really think I'll hand over evidence that'll nail Calvin's ass to the wall, along with your own?" I started to laugh. "And I thought I'd lost *MY* mind."

"Living with you was my sacrifice to God." Joe coiled back like a snake, the knife gripped in his fist. The tip came within an eyelash of my neck, as his other hand grabbed hold of my hair, and held it tight. Yanking my head backward, he pressed the cold, steel blade against my throat, allowing trickles of warm blood to drip down my neck and soak into my shirt. "Get the damn tape. Or I'll be more than happy to slice your throat, too." He released his grip.

There was no time to think. I bit the inside of my mouth to appear unruffled at the mental pictures he was so quick to relay. As precisely as a debutante, I rose to my feet and felt the pressure of his hand at the small of my back, pushing me to Matthew's desk. I had to stall him. I searched for the alarm button, my stomach rolling; I thought I might throw up. "I have the tape. They're in Matt's vault," I lied. "But I don't know the combination. None of you are getting away with this. The police already know what's on them."

"God will protect us," he snarled as he stumbled back to the door, slammed and locked it behind him. "Now we can get down to business."

That was when I saw the blood. Bright drops of blood. On the floor and on top of his boots. I got a better look at his grimy, full-length oversized raincoat. Underneath he was dressed in a black suit with a charcoal shirt and tie, like a minister turned evil—crumpled, malicious, and red-eyed. A flask stuck out of his coat pocket.

I heard the noise again, like a whining pup, from somewhere in the hall.

"Now, then," He spoke calmly. "The tape and pictures? Get them now."

"It's easier for you to hate than to feel guilt or pain, isn't it? I told you, I don't have the combination. Matthew is due back in a few minutes."

Joe shook his head furiously. The sweat rolled down his face. His eyes flickered and he grabbed his head, as though he was nursing a migraine. It was impossible to imagine I had loved him so much, because at that moment I hated him beyond belief. My adrenaline pumping, I couldn't think clearly enough to remember which side of the desk the alarm button was under. "Why?" I asked, stalling for time, feeling under the desk's ledge.

Joe stiffened. "Why, what?"

"Why did Calvin want *you* to kill Mavis?" Two tears fell down my face onto my arm.

"It was God's perfect divine will, not the permissible will, but the divine," he said, stiff and unmoving. "Reverend had a vision from God. We are the chosen. Jehovah-Nissi chose me. I was His hand. He used me to wipe His enemy from the face of the earth. We are special people. But I . . . I'm God's anointed warrior."

"Please, let me understand this. God wanted you to beat, rape, and murder Mavis?"

"No, just kill her. Like God killed Ananias and Sapphira in the Bible when they told their big, fat lies. Ripping her to pieces was my idea. Kinda cool though, don't you think? That bitch deserved it. I hated her. She started all this. Reverend just wanted her dead. Because of Mavis and you, though, I've lost my position, maybe my job. Everyone's in Africa but me."

I froze behind the desk. I wanted to kill him myself. Watch him suffer, the way he made Mavis suffer. And then I looked down at the blood on his shoe. I heard that curious muffled cry again, banging against a door. *The hall closet!* I finally put it together. *Shit!* He'd heard me coming down the steps and had shoved Ivy into the closet.

Staggering close to the desk, he scraped the knife's tip back and forth across his knee. It sliced through the fabric and his leg. Blood oozed down and soaked into his pants. Suddenly, he plunged the knife into Matthew's desk. "Why are you stalling? Get the shit! NOW!"

He would sacrifice me to his God because he was as delusional as his employer. Backing me into the corner between the wall and bookcase, he grabbed my arm and yanked the knife out of the desk. Pulling me away from the wall toward the middle of the room, his eyes bulged. His fingers released my arm then dug into my shoulders. Mouthing incoherent obscenities, he forced me to my knees and knelt behind me, filling me with a deep sense of terror. Despair washed over me in waves as Joe dug his fingers into my hair again, pulling my head back. His breath came hot on my neck as he jerked me into his chest.

"I can get you everything when Matt comes home!" I screamed.

"Never mind! I'll tear this place apart myself. First, though, I'm going to slit your throat, then I'll take pleasure in cutting out your tongue. It'll be my souvenir. I'll keep it in a jar of formaldehyde and display it on my audio board. Whenever I look at it, I'll smile. No more dark angel to wag her foul tongue and destroy the ministry." His whispered words added to the pain he inflicted as he yanked hard on my hair and forced my head back even further.

"You destroyed it, Joe. You and Calvin. It's over. Don't you hear me? The police know all of it! I was with the police yesterday. They have all the evidence! Our children. Please don't do this!" I choked back a sob, but he was oblivious to my words.

"You are, by far," he screamed into my ear. "The worst fuck I ever had! You know that? Goodbye, Andie." He brought the knife up to my neck—

—And the door blew open!

Matthew

I didn't hesitate from the moment I walked into my unlocked house and heard a man's voice through my office door. I kicked in the door and rammed into Joe from behind. We crashed into the wall. Andie screamed. I smashed Joe's knife hand against the wall. He kicked and bit me as the knife clattered to the floor, then pushed me back against the couch, but I threw a shoulder into his chest, spinning him backward. That's when Andie hit him in the head with the iron cannon paperweight from my desk, causing him to turn and gaze at me a few startled seconds, and then drop to floor as if all of his bones had suddenly turned liquid.

Andie ran to the desk and found the panic button, then into my arms. We both collapsed to the floor. I had worked part-time as a social worker for thirty years. I was not given to panic or violence. The last time I had to get physical was the day I laced up my steel-toed boots and walked into a roadhouse outside of Statesville some ten years before. I'd always known my heart and fist together were powerful, because there beside me was the one thing in my life worth fighting for, worth dying for. And she was alive.

Andie.

A pounding came from the hallway, like someone trying to push open a door. "Matt, it's Ivy!" I sprung to my feet and bolted to the guest closet. Not knowing how badly she was hurt, panic flared in my chest.

"Ivy! Stand back! I'm kicking in the door!"

When the door fell open we found Ivy with her hands bound and her mouth taped shut.

I pulled the duct tape off her mouth. "Be careful! He's got a knife!" Ivy yelled.

Andie worked to untie Ivy's wrists. "Her hand is bleeding."

I smiled at the woman I loved as much as my mother, helped her to her feet, and quickly pulled her into the kitchen to wrap her bloody hand in a towel. "At least we'll always have Ivy to watch our backs."

A swarm of local police and Agent Bently stormed into the house.

"I'm fine," Ivy said. "He just got my hand. I would've shot him dead with Tobias's gun but he cut me before I got the drawer open. Damn son of a bitch! Who does he think he is, coming in this house, all cocky, thinking he can order us around? Did he hurt you, Matthew? Andie, you're fine? Please tell Ivy you're fine."

Andie kissed Ivy's forehead. "I'm okay. But we need to get you to a doctor. You need stitches."

Sadie appeared at the back door and barked. I let her in and threw my arms around her neck. "I came home early. Thank God. I had a feeling I should skip supper with Royster. I called him and told him to meet me here. As soon as I arrived at the gate Sadie was waiting for me, barking her head off. That's when I knew. She ran ahead of me all the way back to the house."

"She saved us all," Andie said, hugging her, too. "Good girl, Sadie."

Andie

The police had picked Joe up off the floor. I heard someone read him his rights while the FBI scoured the grounds for additional intruders. He was conscious when they led him out the front door. Matthew sat with Ivy in the kitchen as an EMT treated her wounded hand. Tobias had nearly ran himself into a heart attack when he saw the commotion at the house from the kennel where he'd been feeding the dogs. Another medical technician treated him with oxygen.

I looked at Matthew and laid my hand on his arm. "Don't worry about me. I have to do this." I walked to the front porch where the police stood, cuffing Joe's hands behind him. I stared into the eyes of a madman, his mind seemingly gone. A purple goose egg swelled on his forehead and bled. More blood dripped from his nose, mouth, and chin. His eyes fluttered, and a low animal growl emanated from his lips as he slurred his words, "*And, behold, the angel of the Lord came upon him, and a light shined in the prison: and he smote Peter on the side, and raised him up, saying, arise up . . . And his CHAINS fell off from his hands. Acts twelve, verse seven.*" An officer grabbed Joe by the arm and pulled him away from me.

But I stepped close, inches from his face, astounded that no matter what, Calvin's followers believed they were right to the bitter end. Joe would never admit he was wrong. He would rather die. I could only think of one thing to say. "*And I saw an angel come down from Heaven, having the key of the bottomless pit and a great chain in his hand. And he laid hold of the dragon, that old serpent... and bound him a thousand years. And cast him into the bottomless pit, and SHUT—HIM—UP, and set a seal upon him, that he should deceive the nations no more . . . Revelation twenty, verses one, two, and three.*"

The policeman laughed. "She got ya on that one. Let's throw your nasty ass in the cruiser, get you out of these nice people's hair." Joe stumbled down the porch steps, and then wrenching himself free from the policeman's grasp, he bounded back up the steps, tripping, and coming within a hair of me before the officer grabbed him by the back of his neck. Once again, Joe glared at me and snarled like a wounded beast. "When Reverend Artury gets back from Africa, he'll deal with you."

I stared him down as I stood my ground.

"Then you haven't heard," the policeman said, matter-of-factly.

"Please, let me inform our prisoner." Agent Bently stepped to my side. He grabbed Joe by the coat and pulled him back down the steps. "Your leader is dead. Shot himself. Right in the head. Over there in Africa. In front of all those poor people. Crazy son of a bitch."

He had barely got the last word out when Joe spit in his face. "*Let God be true, but every man a liar!*"

Agent Bently threw Joe into the arms of several policemen surrounding them, then wiped his face with his sleeve. "You don't believe me? Look for yourself!" He shoved the front page of the *Winston-Salem Journal* in Joe's face. The headlines didn't lie. EVANGELIST CALVIN ARTURY, DEAD IN NIGERIA. "Get this slimy bastard out of here. And this time don't let go of him!"

Joe turned ashen white and his body wilted as he fell into the back of the cruiser.

The police finished their search of the house and grounds while the car, holding the man who murdered Mavis Dumass in its back seat, drove away.

§

Matthew confessed that the videotape Peter Collins had given me was horrendous and difficult for even him to watch. He said I had to know what was on it, in case it was shown during Joe's trial. It was clear video and audio of several staff meetings. And in one particular meeting, Calvin had given Evan approval to do whatever he wanted to John. At the end of the tape, ten minutes of old video recorded the most shocking evidence of all. The sound was distorted but good enough to understand most of it. Calvin laughed as he told Evan that he gave Joe permission to have *fun* with Mavis before he killed her. To consider it an employee benefit, a bonus. Peter had been a brave soul to slip in and push record during staff meetings. He'd been a very brave soul and no one knew it.

All of it sickened me. I couldn't turn off the light at night. I simply lay, watching the hours click by slowly. Eventually, my body demanded its due and I closed my eyes. But it was a sleep without peace. Matthew protested that I needed my rest, but my answer was always the same. "It means nothing at all to me that Joe will spend the rest of his life in a Federal penitentiary. Locking him up does nothing to get the pictures of what he did to Mavis out of my head. That will haunt me, the rest of my days."

§

We had been dodging interviews since the news hit about Calvin's suicide and Joe's attack. The press and cameramen camped outside the gates of Callahan property, clamoring for comments. Although Matthew and I had been able to steer clear of the media, soon our names were broadcast on every news program, channel, and in newspapers around the world.

The media was clear in their view of me. *Andie Oliver, scorned former member of the House of Praise, tireless champion of good Christians everywhere. Out to destroy scumbag televangelists the world over.*

At least the worst was over. Matthew insisted I still had to be careful of any remaining House of Praise crazies lurking about, but I didn't have to hide anymore. Finally, I was able to speak to my sister, to Lula, and to Aunt Wylene. But Dixie, it seemed, was always out of the house every time I called. I dismissed the excuses Aunt Wy made on her behalf. I had other things to think about. I missed my children. Matthew convinced me to wait patiently, a few more days, as he and his lawyers worked their magic with the court. Two weeks after Joe's attack, Royster Bently knocked at our front door. Ivy,

Tobias, and Matthew walked outside to talk with Royster and relax in the late summer evening air. A warm breeze blew soft on my face as I stepped out to the front porch with a tray of iced coffee and shortbread cookies.

"I thought you all deserved a report," Royster said. His silver-white hair stood up on end as though he had run his hands through it repeatedly. He had shed his coat and tie, but the warm expression in his eyes was comforting.

Matthew sat on the swing. "What do you have for us?"

I sat beside Matthew and took little sips of coffee, listening to the chains creak. A soothing sound compared to whatever Royster had to say.

"Thanks to Andie ... and to Matthew ... there were twenty-seven arrests."

"Thank you, Lord," said Tobias.

"Since Reverend Artury's death, the remaining church members have been scrambling to take up the slack and are pretty stressed out. They have no leader. A couple of the more innocent men on his staff tried to rally the few who showed up for service, singing songs, praying for their imprisoned leaders, hoping the truth come out. And the truth is getting louder every week. Besides all the murder and mayhem, you wouldn't believe the rest of it."

"More men and women have come forward with stories of Artury telling them God would heal them in his office, privately. But first they had to get naked for God to cleanse them. It was a mode of healing which had recently become popular. Many men from the church confessed to the police during questioning that Artury had asked to see their penises during marital counseling. Acted like it was normal." Royster shook his head. "The congregation has dwindled to about two hundred. Diehards who refuse to believe Artury's dead or that he committed the crimes reported by the media. Last week, those members waited inside the church, expecting the rapture to take place or for their Reverend to rise from the ashes. A few members were only too happy when the police finally took the initiative, forced everyone out, and padlocked the doors. Justice had come, but not in the way the House of Praise folk had hoped. I feel sorry for some of them. They're a sad lot. They halted construction on the new church. TV programs have been cancelled. Sponsors all jumped ship. There's a world full of hurt evangelicals out there."

Royster sipped his coffee. "I thought you'd also like to know about Joe."

I looked at Matthew, not sure what to say.

"Might as well tell us." Matthew said then turned to me. "This is all part of putting it behind us."

I nodded. "Okay."

Royster continued. "When Joe was interrogated, he said, 'You think I've committed a crime, but I haven't.' He still insists he is innocent, but does not deny he killed Mavis. When I asked him to explain how both these apparently contradictory statements can be true, he said, 'I was doing God's will; that isn't a crime.'"

I stood and walked to the edge of the porch, staring down the path toward the old cemetery. "You should let them know, Royster, that in dealing with

Joe, no one can argue logically with him because he uses the illogical to support his beliefs." I crossed my arms in front of me. "How could a sane man, or so he seemed . . . I mean . . . Godamighty, I lived with him for years and had no indication of his crimes. Of what he had done to Mavis. How could he kill a blameless woman so viciously, without the barest flicker of emotion? He was often cold, but I never had a hint he was the one who raped and murdered her. I should've known; I should've felt it somehow."

Ivy fanned herself with her good hand. "But you didn't know, Andie. Until Mavis could get you all the pieces of the puzzle, which is why she and Johnny led you here."

Royster set his glass on the table and locked his hands around his knee. "Well, Ivy, that sounds right to me. I suppose there is a dark side to religion that's too often ignored or denied. And there may be no more potent of a force than religious conviction. I've seen it before, and I doubt this is the end of it. Faith-based violence and craziness was present long before Joe Oliver, and it'll be with us long after Calvin Artury's death. The way I see it, Artury was a zealot, a religious fanatic, and outwardly motivated by the anticipation of a great reward at the other end—wealth, fame, eternal salvation—but the real reward was his obsessive control and the rush he received from it. I can hardly imagine God condoning such activities, much less that Artury could have had the audacity to seek His protection. Artury had a damn narcissistic sense of self-assurance about everything he did. I've seen it before in serial killers. A delicious rage quickens their pulse. Non-believers fueled Artury by their sins and shortcomings. People he considered lesser beings soiling the world. Issuing orders to kill in the name of God, he experienced something akin to the rapture every time he did it. Ecstasy. Killing himself was the ultimate ecstasy."

The air became still and hot. Royster's words stirred quiet emotion in all of us.

"Andie, Joe's been charged with the rape and murder of Mavis Dumass and the murder of Chip Atkinson. He's looking at a possible death sentence. Have you talked to your children?"

"No, but we've made contact with the judge. They're giving me back custody. We're picking them up in two days."

"Good. That's real good. I don't know how much they've heard, but I'm sure they're ready to come home. I'm assuming home is here, with Matthew?" He looked at the ring on my finger.

Matthew stood and slipped his arm around me. "Home will always be here for Andie and her children. Andie and I have a January wedding planned."

"Yes. Royster, will you and your wife please come?" I asked.

"We'd be honored."

"*For the Lord is good and His love endures forever. His faithfulness continues through all generations,*" Ivy said, rocking back and forth in her chair with her bandaged hand in her lap.

October 1993
Mama

Andie

Matthew and I walked past a café, smelling its hot apple cider all the way out on the sidewalk. A perfect match to the russet and lemon-yellow leaves on the trees, the V of geese overhead, and the signs in the drugstore window advertising Halloween candy on sale. Remembering Gracie and Dillon's costumes when they were little, how I labored over them, I smiled. My children and I had strolled through the streets of Salisbury, gathering candy and dumping the loot on the kitchen table. It was a good memory.

Hand in hand, I showed Matthew every place I had lived, replaying parts of my history for healing purposes. It all seemed different somehow. Coot's garage was gone. Shady Acres was surrounded by clumps of new businesses—liquor stores, pizza parlors, dark little bars and taverns dwarfed by giant dish antennas on their roofs. Beyond the city limits the houses thinned. We passed a used-car lot, a new barbecue joint, and a vacant strip mall broken by scratchy bits of trees and scattered cars parked on its concrete wasteland. Time had not been kind to the area.

Driving past the Olivers' house with its peeling paint and missing shutters, it had been a long time since I'd seen it. The sign near the road read, *For Sale*. I tugged on Matthew's arm. "Stop. Turn around. I need to see Maudy."

He pulled the car halfway up the drive. We spotted her on the porch. Before I opened the car door, Matthew squeezed my hand. "Be kind to her. She's the one hurting now."

I walked through unmowed parched grass and weeds toward the front porch. Unaware of her visitors, Maudy's eyes were closed behind wire-rimmed glasses pearled with fingerprints. A new metal glider had replaced her old wicker rocker. She was alone.

"Maudy?"

She opened her eyes. Maudy's entire body was drawn to the right and withered-looking. As white and thin as an eggshell, her skin sagged in on itself and her cloudy eyes appeared as if sleep had abandoned her long ago. Her hair was white and thin, a sheer scant of what it used to be. A pale pink sweater was wrapped around her now bony shoulders. She stared at her visitor, like she couldn't quite make out who I was.

"Maudy? It's me. It's Andie." I tiptoed up the porch steps. The house felt old and I could hear the hum of memories.

Her mouth twisted as she whispered. "Andie? Oh, my sweet girl. It's you. I didn't think I'd ever see you again. How are you, sugah?"

I kissed her lightly on the forehead. "I'm fine, Maudy. I'm fine. Are you doing okay?"

"Well, been better. Had a stroke a few months back. They tell me the cancer's back, too. You know Al passed away."

"I know. I wanted to come to the funeral, but . . . it wasn't possible."

"He loved you, Andie. He really did. I do, too. I always will. How are my grandchildren?"

"They're fine." It was all I could say. I was scheduled to pick them up the next day. I hadn't seen them in a year myself.

Maudy lowered her eyes to the porch floor. "You know Joe is in prison."

"Yes, I know. Maudy, I think you should prepare yourself for a life sentence."

"Prepare myself? Life is what I gave to my sons. Life *isn't* living behind bars. Some judge is gonna take Joe's life from him." Her teary eyes darted around, then focused on me. "Selma's living out at Shady Acres."

"Really? Why?"

"She couldn't afford the payments on the condo with Joe in jail, and she lost her job when the Praise Buffet shut down. Came here for a while. Then Ray moved her skinny butt out to your old trailer. It was available for rent. Can you believe it? I think she washes dogs for a living, or something strange like that."

I smiled wide. *What comes around goes around.*

Half of Maudy's face smiled back. "She deserves it," Maudy whispered as if the whole world was listening. Her hands trembled reaching for a tissue in her pocket. "But I'm to blame, Andie."

"Hush, now. It's all over."

"No, let me speak. I'm to blame. Al knew it. I think he forgave me, though. Before he died. I made Joe the way he is. I pushed him. To be better than his brothers. It destroyed him. I'll have to live with that. But it's you who has paid the steep price to get us all out. You." Maudy sighed then took my hand and held it in her lap. Her voice was shaky and feeble. She strained over every word. "I'm so glad you stopped by today, sugah. I think about you a lot. I apologize for the way my son treated you; the way we all treated you. Reverend Artury destroyed us all. Our family. All but you. Please go on for us, Andie. Go on for me, Al, Ted, and Joe, God help him. Make something of your life out of this mess. You're the one who can do it. The one God has chosen to heal the wounds. I'm sorry for everything, sugah. Go on. Find true love and have a good life."

I wept cleansing tears. I felt as if God were taking a scrub brush to my soul, wiping away the grime the Olivers had left behind. It helped put it all into perspective. Now I could truly—go on.

"Where are you going, Maudy? I see the house is for sale."

"To Atlanta with my brother, Dodrill. He's got plenty of room. I'll stay there until the Lord calls me home. To Heaven. At least that's where I hope I'm going."

"Of course you are. Of course you are."

A column of blooming chrysanthemums grew in a large terra-cotta pot near Maudy's feet. I picked an orange one. I opened my purse and pulled a straight pin out of the tiny sewing kit I always kept handy. A carry over from my days when things were mended—not thrown away to buy new. I pinned the flower to Maudy's sweater.

"Remember when you attached a flower to my high school graduation gown, Maudy? I believe you said 'Your gown needs a little color, sugah. It's from the family, because we love you.' I love you, Maudy." I kissed her again, then turned and walked to the car. And to Matthew. I didn't look back.

"Let's go home," I said.

§

Almost a year had passed since the day my twins walked out of our dingy rented house at the edge of Kernersville. Thinking about that day, I closed the clinic door behind me harder than necessary. Matthew and I walked through another set of glass doors and into a drab reception area, where a dozen or so people sat on black plastic chairs lined against white walls.

The receptionist seated behind the low gray counter wore a parrot green dress, bright orange lipstick, and feathered back hair. "May I help you?" she chirped.

"I'm Andie Oliver and this is my fiancée, Matthew Callahan. I have an appointment with Dr. Fitzgibbons."

The woman peered at her computer screen through round glasses sitting at the end of her pointed nose. "One moment," she said, clicking away at her keyboard. "You're here to pick up your son and daughter."

I smiled at the bird-like woman. "Yes, we are. The sooner the better."

She slid a sheet of paper toward me. "Sign here, please. And I'll need to see some ID."

I pulled out my new slim leather wallet and extracted my driver's license.

The woman cocked her head to one side and examined it. I figured I passed because she gave it back with a smile. "Dr. Fitzgibbons is picking up your children from the foster home. She should be here momentarily." Handing me a clipboard, the woman's nasal voice became irritating. "In the meantime, I need you to fill out this form, please."

Matthew had found two seats between a round-shouldered, middle-aged woman and a young Hispanic mother holding a sleeping toddler. I took the form and wrote my name, address, and other vital information, then hesitated at the line marked FATHER'S NAME. I sat there thinking that Joe had been a father in name only; certainly not like my daddy. I wanted to write *none*, but scribbled Joe's name and moved on.

It was easy to be angry over losing my children for almost a year, and I was. The judge had treated me like the criminal. "Seems she punished the wrong parent," I mumbled. My case was a set up; I knew that. But it didn't make it any easier to forgive the system.

I scrawled my signature on the bottom of the form, rose from my chair, and carried it back to the bird lady. I'd taken my seat again when the door at the front of the reception area opened. "Andie Oliver?" said a dark-haired woman in flower-patterned scrubs. "You can come on back."

I jumped to my feet, then looked apprehensively at Matthew.

"I'll be right here. You go. This is your time." He reached for my hand. "I love you."

"I keep forgetting how wonderful you are," I said, smiling.

"Go get our kids."

Our kids. He said 'our kids.' It was amazing to me that Matthew, who had never met Dillon and Gracie, wanted them—when all their lives their own father wanted little to do with them.

I turned and followed the woman down an antiseptic-scented corridor to a small office, my heart pounding. A plump, pleasant-faced woman in a navy-blue pantsuit greeted me. "I'm Bella Fitzgibbons," she said, holding out her hand.

I shook it. "Andie Oliver."

She gestured to two black vinyl chairs in front of her large steel desk. Three diplomas on the wall testified to the fact that she'd completed college and medical school and was a board-certified pediatrician. "Please, have a seat. I have a few things to go over with you, then I'll get the children."

I could only nod, my heart felt as though it were bursting.

The doctor gave me a gentle smile, then drew two forms out of a brown folder and attached them to yet another clipboard. "First of all, I need you to sign these forms and custody papers, verifying the children have been returned to you. I'll make sure you get copies." She handed me the clipboard. I scribbled my signature across the bottom once again.

"Can I see them now?"

Dr. Fitzgibbons smiled. "Don't worry, Mrs. Oliver. They're with a social worker who's wonderful with teenagers. They're as anxious as you are. But I need to ask you a few questions."

I pulled my brows together. "Like what? Is something the matter?"

"Routine questions and explanations," Dr. Fitzgibbons said soothingly.

But I refused to be soothed. Alarm bells went off. "What do you mean? What needs explained?"

Dr. Fitzgibbons hesitated. "Well, I need to discuss a matter with you." She tapped a stack of papers on her lap, straightening them into a neat pile. "The Guardian ad Litem reported Dillon has been rather, well, difficult."

My jaw tensed. *Screw the Guardian ad Litem. Screw her.* It was the same word Dillon's teachers had used about him during parent-teacher conferences. I took offense at anyone sticking a negative label on my son. "Difficult how? The Darwoods have no complaints."

"To those he doesn't know, isn't familiar with, he doesn't listen. Outright refuses to quiet down. He's been hard to handle and isn't doing well in school. Gracie also seems to have retreated inside her own little world. She won't come out of her room without being coaxed." I'm sure Dr. Fitzgibbons saw the fury on my face because she quickly said with a smile, "However, she makes excellent grades."

"This would've never happened to them had the courts not taken them from me!"

"We agree, Mrs. Oliver. Be that as it may, their resistance to human contact concerned us, so we took them to Brenner Children's Hospital for a thorough evaluation."

It sounded to me like everyone within the court system was trying to cover their ass on this case. The door opened abruptly and a tall, middle-aged man in a white coat walked in. Dr. Fitzgibbon's face registered relief. "Dr. Vincent Starling, our staff psychiatrist who specializes in adolescent behavior. He can explain it much better than I can. Dr. Starling, this is Mrs. Oliver. I was just about to review the problems we've encountered with her twins."

More problems? I shook the doctor's hand, impatient to get to the bottom of it. "What exactly are the problems?" I demanded. "Is something physically wrong with them?"

The doctor nodded hello with his practiced smile, his gray eyes somber as he seated himself in the chair next to me. "We ran a complete battery of tests. Gracie's not gaining weight the way she should, and she's developmentally behind for her age. She's sixteen years old, but she looks and acts like a child two years younger. Dillon, on the other hand, though he's thriving physically, is definitely a hyperactive child with an attention span problem. Stress and the situation with their father have not helped their mental state."

Anger ran a path from my head, down to my spine, and then dipped into to my toes. I wasn't in the mood to play the blame game. "Again, doctor. What, precisely, is the problem?"

"Both Dillon and Gracie have developed forms of Attachment Disorder."

"And what's that?"

He tapped his long fingers together. "All children need to form a strong attachment to one main caregiver. They did that with you, but you were torn away from them. Plus the events surrounding their father's imprisonment have made them both unstable. If that attachment with you isn't reestablished, and soon, the children could develop more severe behavioral problems. Both can be bright and cheerful teenagers on the outside, but they've also exhibited very deep lows. Of course, you know the Darwoods. They have been excellent foster parents. Children appear to thrive in their care. And even though Dillon and Gracie knew them previously, being taken from you the way they were; it's been rough on them. They do cling to each other."

The problems Dr. Starling described to me would be solved once I took them back to Matthew's farm and spent every day with them. I would call Vernise. Get the real story from her. One thing I knew for sure: Vernise and Henry's love had saved my children.

"Dillon needs weight management and someone to work with him on a daily basis to help him concentrate on one thing before moving to the next." The doctor flipped through the pages of a medical chart. "When their bond with you was broken, their progress as thriving children slowed to almost a standstill. We need to mend that bond. You must be patient, Mrs. Oliver. It will take time to ward off future problems. I understand you are engaged to Matthew Callahan?"

"Yes, that's correct."

"I know Matthew. He has worked with me in placing difficult children. I would say if it was anyone other than Matthew, this new man in your life would not be a good idea and I would strongly suggest you take some time to be alone with your children. However, I've been to Matthew's home. That is exactly the kind of place they need. And Matt's a good man. Take the rest of the school year and stay home with them as much as possible; help them to feel secure again. Home school them. Invite other kids into the house. Then introduce your children into a new educational system next September."

I leaned forward. "You said we could avoid future problems. What problems?"

"Again, mental deficiencies and challenges that would need psychiatric treatment. At this stage, however, let's be thankful you got them back when you did. Like I said, they need stability. In a year or two, they should be looking at colleges: they're both bright. Security, that's the ticket. And love." The doctor pushed his glasses up on his forehead and rubbed his nose.

"That's the ticket for all of us," I said.

"Yes, we understand it was a nasty divorce, filled with a great deal of anger. The twins felt all that. I've followed the stories in the paper. I've read the police reports. What they did to you was nothing short of brutality. I've counseled numerous patients who have suffered as a result of that cult. At least two a week, since its demise. I questioned whether or not you were capable to take your children again, making sure some healing had taken place in your own life. But in talking to Matthew, he assured me you were the most capable of anyone he knew. You must be a strong woman, Mrs. Oliver. I wish you only the best in your future. You and Mr. Callahan."

I smiled. "Thank you."

"As far as your children are concerned, be extremely patient and empathetic, and hang in there despite all of their fussing and fuming and pushing away. Even at their advanced age, this separation has held them back in many areas."

I wanted to ask Matthew about suing the court system, specifically Judge VanOrson. *Why rehash it? We needed to go on, like Ivy said, like Maudy said. Go on.* "They've got me. And Matthew. And Ivy and Tobias."

Dr. Starling smiled. "They're lucky children."

"Anything else?"

The doctor lowered his glasses and issued me a final warning, as if driving his point in a little further. "The worst thing would be for the twins to be alone again."

"They were taken from me; I didn't abandon them."

"I understand that. Just don't get so caught up in a new relationship—"

"Stop. I know what you're saying. My children are my priority."

"Fine. I want to see them in six months."

"Is that all?" I wanted to get my kids and go home. I didn't need to be told by this guy how to take care of my children.

He handed me a sheaf of papers from his folder. "That's all."

I shoved them into my purse, snapped it shut, and shot him a feeble smile. "Good."

Dr. Starling rose and circled his chair to open the door. "It was nice meeting you. Good luck." He shook my hand again and left the room.

Dr. Fitzgibbons raised her eyebrows and smiled, as if the need to bring the twins back from the brink of mental destruction was a cheery thing to contemplate. "Well, now. Why don't I go get them and you just stay here. I'm sure you're anxious."

"You have no idea." I sighed. A wave of nervousness washed over me as Dr. Fitzgibbons bustled out. I couldn't sit still, so I stepped outside the door and waited. Within minutes I heard the sound of their Reeboks plodding down the tiled hall. They turned the corner and my heart swelled as if I were watching my deceased children being raised from the dead. Dillon dragged his jacket behind him, his rugby shirt hung out of his jeans. Gracie's eyes were downcast, her arms folded in front of her. Her pants were too big and her shirt was too small.

"There's your mama," said Dr. Fitzgibbons.

I cocked my head and smiled through my tears. Reaching out to them, my hands and arms ached as I moved slowly forward, propelled by an undeniable force, a mix of excitement and apprehension. The twins ran into my arms knocking me backwards. For a quiet minute, the only sounds in the hallway were tiny noises of affection. Sweet kisses, hugging, and sobbing.

Dillon was an inch taller. "Mama, we missed you so much."

"Please don't let them take us away again," cried Gracie. "Please!"

"Don't worry, darlings. It's all over." Tears streamed down my cheeks. "Nobody will ever take you away from me ever, ever again." I kissed them repeatedly and ran my hands over their faces and necks. "Besides, look at you both; you've grown! You're sixteen! Dillon, you're taller than me! Let me look at you. You're shaving?" His smile was boyishly affectionate.

Tears glistened on Gracie's pale, heart-shaped face. Her complexion had become very sallow. "Mama, I've missed you terrible. I didn't think we'd ever see you again."

"Oh, Gracie, we'll be together, always." I wiped my daughter's tears with my hands.

She latched onto my waist and wouldn't let go. "Can we still see Vernise and Henry?"

"Of course you can see the Darwoods. Anytime. And they can come to our place, too. They're family now." Strange how they thought Gracie was so distant to human contact when she so clearly loved the Darwoods. But Gracie was tiny, and so thin! The only fat on her body huddled in her cheeks. Her hair was freshly permed and a bit frizzy, the short hairs falling about her face—she looked like a large raggedy doll. A new retainer sat in place of her braces.

Dillon rambled on. "Mama, I got my drivers license. Vernise made me eat broccoli; it's okay as long as you put Velveeta on it. I'm starved. Do we have a place to go?"

"We do, and it's a wonderful place. A farm in the mountains. And I've made some new friends." We cried, hugged, kissed, and jumped from one subject to the next. Nodding to a small group who had gathered to witness our reunion, I guided my children toward the door. With my arms around them, we walked to the lobby where a waiting Matthew stood beside their bags.

"Best of luck to you all," I heard Dr. Fitzgibbons say as the door closed behind us.

January 1994
Vows To Last A Lifetime

Andie

A cold day dawned. Mist rose from the forest floor, creeping up tree trunks and along bleak, leafless limbs. Like an old woman's hair, tendrils of gray fog spiraled down the back of the mountain. Later its peaks would compete for prominence in the colorless winter sky. I had become acquainted with Shiloh and its changing expressions.

Unable to fall back to sleep, I woke before daybreak. Gazing into the bathroom mirror, I found it hard to ignore the nervous blue eyes that stared back at me. My eyes questioned, "Are you sure?" I blinked the sleepiness away, fastened back my hair, brushed my teeth, and then rinsed my face in cool water. My face, like the rest of me, had become strong yet soft. Even the pleated corners of my eyes. After applying lip gloss and running a few determined brush stokes through my hair, I lifted my chin. "I'm very sure."

Turning from my reflection, I shivered. Winter in the mountains was majestic and still; its frigid night air extended into the early morning. I felt the chill in the house still hanging on with all its might. Humming under my breath so not to disturb my sleeping family, I slipped into jeans, a sweatshirt, and house shoes. I smelled coffee. Soon the sun shining through the windows would warm the second floor. Before long, activity on the lower level would warm the downstairs.

Ivy had made two pots of coffee. The norm since the kids had arrived. I stepped over to the French doors leading out to the back porch and decks and faced my dark and shadowy reflection. I gulped down my first mugful. Feeling jittery already, I supposed I hadn't really needed the caffeine. The wedding was the next morning. There was still lots to do. Gracie needed shoes to match her dress and I had to tell Dillon to pick up his tux at three. The events of the past year left minimal damage. I knew total healing could only happen over time. That day, though, there was no terror. No nausea. No ghosts of the past waiting to devour my children and me. No more funerals. No more thinking about death. Not that day, and certainly not on my wedding day. My memories were no longer bigger than myself. I'd forced such things into the back of my mind, and looked straight ahead. I had to check myself to keep a hysterical tickle from escaping my throat. If I laughed, I might never stop.

The gurgle of the pot drew my attention. *Ah, another cup.* I needed more coffee after all. I pulled out a chair and sat in the temporary quiet of the morning, wrapping my cold fingers around the deep mug. I thought of the past few months since the twins had come back into my life. It had been a little rough at first; they kept Matthew at arms length, while warming up to Ivy and Tobias right away. Shiloh was like Disney World to Dillon and

Gracie. My twins explored the farm and the mountain, warmed quickly to the animals, and found something new to do every day. It was intense therapy living at Shiloh, waking up to their mama's voice every morning. It had taken long talks to sort everything out. They called Vernise and Henry regularly, and Matthew had sent a limo to bring the entire Darwood family to Shiloh to spend a few long weekends. But what broke through to the twins was the love and attention Matthew showered on me. The interaction between Matthew and myself was a new experience for my children.

At Christmas, Conner came to stay a few weeks. It was a magical time. Every room simply glittered. The first floor was decorated with Christmas delights; candles in every window, and wreaths on every door. Ivy's blooming Christmas cactus sat on Matthew's desk. Boughs of holly and Charles Dickens figurines lined the fireplace mantels, while greeting cards framed the archways in the foyer. Huge trees lit up the windows in several of the rooms and Ivy's special hand-crocheted tablecloth covered the dining table. Red and green china added Christmas color to every meal. Mark and Patsy's youth group sang carols at our front door, and Matthew's friends and colleagues sent endless gifts, some of which included trays of candies, cookies, and lush pink and red poinsettias; it was like walking into the glossy pages of *Southern Living* magazine.

The boys hit it off. Both Conner and Dillon loved action movies and Matthew bought them enough videotape to keep them occupied for a week. Matthew and I were elated with a full house of noisy children and holiday hoopla. The perfect Christmas had arrived. We slept in Heavenly peace. Finally. Even Ivy and Tobias seemed a little younger with the kids around.

Gracie had gained a little weight. Home schooling was the right prescription. Dillon had met a girl in town, Diana. They would all be juniors together at their new high school. Other than a few tantrum outbreaks of not wanting to step foot in a church again, I felt things had gone smoothly. We didn't push them when it came to church, but at least they agreed to attend Mark and Patsy's youth group once a month. It was a start.

When I finally sat them down and told them the story of how Matthew and I really met, the twin's final resistance toward their future stepfather broke. They both cried, but it was Gracie who bolted into Matthew's arms. He picked her up and hugged her tight, her legs dangling. From that moment, I had my children back for good. And although no one could take Jessie's place in Matthew's life, I think it thrilled him that Gracie found the one soft spot in his heart left vacant when his daughter passed away.

My son stumbled in for coffee, wrapped in his blanket. "It's cold enough to freeze a fart!"

"Dillon!" Yep. I had them back.

§

The next day began with more frigid temperatures, but a flurry of activity warmed the house quickly. The plan called for a big breakfast, a private and simple morning ceremony, and a light lunch after the wedding with a few immediate relatives. The formal reception and buffet, with a much larger guest list, was scheduled to start at six at The Grove Park Inn in Asheville.

Matthew fried the potatoes, while Conner turned bacon in the pan and hollered at me as I walked into the kitchen. "You're not supposed to see Dad until the ceremony!"

"That's a little old-fashioned, Conner. I think we'd like to have breakfast together, especially since you're cooking!" I hugged him from behind. "But you need an apron."

"No way! Get that faggy thing away from me."

"Conner!" Matthew shook his head. "Many great chefs are men. And just because your Uncle John was gay does not mean he was less of a man. Got it?"

"Sorry, Dad. But do I have to wear an apron?"

The smell of bacon brought Dillon and Gracie to the table. "Mama! You shouldn't see Matthew until the wedding!" Gracie squealed.

"Geez, what a bunch of old fogies we've raised!" I said.

"Let's eat!" Tobias pulled up his chair to the table.

"I love this kind of heart-stopping breakfast," said Matthew.

Everyone talked at once. Ivy laughed at Gracie's jokes; Conner and Dillon discussed their girlfriends, the Super Bowl, and Nascar, and in that order; Matthew and Tobias debated about how much firewood to cut for the week. With great satisfaction, the loves of my life ate bacon, sausage, grits, fried potatoes, eggs scrambled in cheese, biscuits smothered in apple butter, and drank lots of rich, hot coffee. The kind of breakfast you fix when there's a house full of children and family and love.

I recalled what Bobbie Sue said that first Sunday I attended her church. *What the devil stole from me, God has given back to me, seven times over.* He did that for me, too. I prayed silently, thanking Him as I sat at the table and watched my miracle. *Her children arise up, and call her blessed; her husband also, and he praiseth her.* Maybe that Proverbs woman wasn't so crazy after all.

Matthew

There would be no honeymoon. We'd been "honeymooning" for a while anyway, I'd said to Andie. I planned to take her on a trip later, after the kids had gone back to school in September, when everyone was stable and secure in their lives at Shiloh. I'd cut back on my work with Social Services. I had a family. I was needed more at home, and it felt good to be needed at home again. I envisioned traveling more later, but not until Andie was ready.

I was concerned about her. She had her down days. I suggested therapy, but she resisted. Andie had major trust issues with anyone she didn't know, her own form of Attachment Disorder. She had told me she believed in God but wasn't sure God could be everywhere all the time, if that made any sense.

It was all she could do to endure some days. Even with the kids back. I'd seen her staring at a picture, obviously taken long ago, of herself and Mavis. And her mother wasn't speaking to her. Neither of us understood why. The past was too dark and too big. She had told me about Mavis, and I'd seen the scar in her hand. I had to remember that her pain had been greater than mine.

Sadly, Calvin Artury's threats weren't eliminated by his absence. They were locked within the dungeon of Andie's mind. Over the weeks I did my best to put salve on her wounds, but all I had were Band-Aids. I needed answers. I started a search of my own. A search for the faintest ring of truth. Who was Calvin Artury? I had my suspicions and I wondered if it was something Andie could handle. And yet, I knew she needed the whole truth to heal completely.

Andie

I sat in the room Ivy assigned to me, feeling the warmth of the morning sun through the windows. A time when new life began. A life as Mrs. Matthew Callahan. I had debated about changing my name, but I no longer wished to be known as an Oliver. *Andie Rose Callahan is a good, strong name.*

My suit lay on the bed, pressed and ready. Shoes, hose, jewelry, flower; my wedding ensemble waited for me to shed my housecoat and slippers. I relaxed in the chair, dismissing the memories of my first wedding day so many years ago.

Gracie pulled her long, burgundy-velvet dress over her head. "Mama, did you ever think you weren't as pretty as Grandma Dixie?"

"Why do you ask me that?" I stood to zip up my daughter's dress.

"Because I've always wanted to be as pretty as you."

"Oh, Gracie Mae, you are the most beautiful girl. Not only are you far prettier than me, you're way smarter. You've just turned seventeen. You'll be applying to colleges soon. When I was your age, all I could think about was marrying your daddy. I no more thought about college than I thought about the shape of Albania. Live your life for yourself, Gracie. Make your own way. Then fall in love."

"I'm happy for you, Mama. But you still haven't answered my question."

"You mean about Grandma?"

She nodded.

"It's true, your Grandma Dixie was beautiful. With my mother, I was always lacking something . . . something that would have made me nicer, prettier, thinner, and popular by her standards. I suppose I never thought she loved me as much as I loved her."

"I know you love me, Mom."

"Well, good, 'cause I'm late for my own wedding and I need you to go tell the boys they'll have to wait a few more minutes."

"Oooh, I can hear them now. Women!"

§

Conner and Dillon in black-tie, attempted to straighten Matthew's white one. When I walked down the grand staircase, Matthew's eyes glazed with tears. To the compliments of my family waiting at the bottom, I wore a white wool suit with velvet cuffs. Carrying a pink rose and a picture of Daddy, I wanted him with me on my wedding day, even if I had to imagine it. Matthew embraced me. We looked at the smiling faces around us, both of us holding back tears.

"Don't cry, Mama," Gracie said. "I'll be a mess before tonight."

"Okay then," said Matthew. "How about marrying me this morning, Andie?"

I could only dab at my eyes and nod.

Tobias drove the limo to the church in Valle Crucis where Bobbie Sue stood in her white robe to perform the ceremony on that cold January day. Friends and both families had gathered to witness the union of two souls. The church was simply decorated and held its warmth. White candles in glass sconces lined the painted ivory walls and cast a golden glow on the altar and on every face. The pews were trimmed with sprigs of pine branches tied together with gauzy ribbons. There were no flowers, just my rose I carried and a candle on the organ to represent the souls we missed: Matthew's daughter, Jessie, John, and both of our fathers. And of course, Mavis. No one sang, nothing was read. It didn't seem necessary.

Luke played his guitar as Matthew and I walked in together. Caroline and her new husband, Herman, along with my four nieces and two little nephews huddled at the back in case they needed a quick restroom exit. And there was Coot and Candace; it was so good to see them sitting next to Lula and Clete. I smiled at Lula and blew her a kiss. Of course, Royster Bently and his wife attended. I felt he deserved a seat of honor: he had believed me. The Darwoods sat in the second pew beside Aunt Wylene, whose favorite color had changed to bright orange. She looked like an early Easter egg. My mother wasn't there. She had come down with a cold, Aunt Wy said. Another excuse, I knew. But again, I put it out of my mind. Dixie wasn't speaking to me and I didn't know why. I refused to allow her to ruin the day.

Matthew's family and close friends sat in the adjacent section, while Dillon, Gracie, and Conner stood at the altar beside us to participate in the ceremony. Our vows were short, sweet vows—vows to last a lifetime. Nothing fancy, nothing to record in a book of poems. But they rang of truth and of a deep abiding love. There wasn't a dry eye in the sanctuary when I slipped a wedding band over the stub of Matthew's ring finger on his left hand. Soon, the steeple bell rang loud and long as Mr. and Mrs. Matthew Callahan ran to the waiting limousine, our children following close behind in the wintery morning air. It was a grand day, indeed, despite Dixie and her continual need to forever get under my skin.

March 1994
END OF THE LINE

Matthew

After the wedding a reporter managed to snap a picture of Andie and me, together with Dillon and Gracie—a picture that appeared on the front page of the *Winston-Salem Journal*—a newspaper that landed on the table of the Forsyth County Jail lunchroom—a table where Joe Oliver sat eating his hamburger. I was told that the newspaper slid into his lap like a bomb, exploding his insides into soup as he stared at the picture. He spent the next three days in the infirmary with the newspaper fisted in his hands.

Andie and I agreed that her life was a fascinating study in the mysteries of God. We talked long into the night that Calvin succumbed to the same end he had plotted and planned for her. It all stood out in our minds as a miracle. Many House of Praise members who had exalted themselves and called her a dark angel were scattered to the four winds, nursing wounds and trying to make sense of their beliefs. For Andie, a new life had begun, with me. And so, it was a shock on a particular March morning, nineteen years to the day she buried her baby boy, that I received a phone call from the prosecutor's office.

In addition to their charges of murder, Evan Preston and Tony DeSanto were accused of drug running, organized prostitution, and pornographic film pirating with cash filtered through the church. Pastor DeSanto, they'd found out, had worked for a New York crime family for the better part of thirty years. Joe, wanting to soak up some of the leftover money and prestige, worked for DeSanto and Preston in a starving-man-near-a-buffet kind of way. He knew the details of their operation the prosecutor needed for the upcoming trial.

But Joe refused to talk about DeSanto's Southern Mafia with Preston at the helm. Eventually, though, he agreed to a plea bargain. The trial was due to start in a week, but Joe had changed his mind again and was no longer cooperative. Unless he could speak to Andie. He would trade the death sentence for life in prison; tell everything, if he could spend ten minutes with his ex-wife.

Upset by this news, I consulted my attorneys, as well as my doctor about the repercussions of such a meeting for Andie. I was still working on closing her wounds. Busy with day-to-day living, running the house and farm, and taking care of business, I didn't want all we had accomplished to come crashing down because her maniac ex-husband demanded to see her. Andie had absorbed a great deal of office work to lighten Ivy's load as she and Tobias had taken on the task of tutoring the twins. We all agreed to keep this news from the children.

But after days of discussion, Andie decided if seeing Joe would put Preston and DeSanto away forever, she'd go. As long as I was with her, she would hear what Joe had to say, put it behind her as quickly as possible, and once again we would go on with our lives.

Andie

I had been told Joe was in his sixth month of psychiatric evaluation and counseling. They'd said he'd been deprogrammed, that he was remorseful. I was about to find out.

The windowless room, painted thundercloud-gray, fell quiet as Joe was led in like a dog on a chain and told to sit. I felt no fear or hate, yet neither of us knew how to start. I tried a noncommittal nod. Decked out in prison-issue orange, Joe simply stared. I folded my hands and put them on the metal table. He might have done likewise had his hands and feet not been cuffed.

I had no intention of ever seeing him again. But Joe, an accused murderer, had made a bargain. A private meeting with me, not Selma his wife, but me in exchange for information. A killer should not be allowed to make deals or bargains, I had said to Matthew.

I broke the silence. "You asked to see me?"

"Yes."

I nodded again, waited for him to say more. He didn't. "What do you want from me?"

Joe maintained his stare. "Do you know why I'm here?"

"You killed Mavis Dumass and Chip Atkinson, and I hear they got you for the rape of a minor."

I glanced around the room. The District Attorney, seated on a nearby chair, flipped through his files; a prison guard with stovepipe arms and a chest like a gun cabinet stood behind Joe, and a ferret-looking man reeking of garlic, Joe's lawyer, sat in a corner. Matthew leaned against the wall, purposely behind me in Joe's line of sight.

But Joe only stared into my eyes. "I had no idea she was seventeen, and it was consensual sex," he whispered as if nobody could hear him except me.

I shook my head and said to the attorneys, "Do I really have to listen to—"

"Please, Andie Rose. Stay. Please don't go."

"Don't! Don't you call me that! Tell me what you think you need to say so I can get out of here!"

Joe spoke quickly, "I followed him because I loved him. I loved him more than anyone in the world. I did as I was told. I believed he was who he said, a Son of God." He paused. "I was willing to give my life to God, so it seemed to me I should also be willing to take a life for God."

"I know that," I said. "And you disgust me." I could hear his Southern accent had returned.

"The warden here told me that out of suffering have emerged the strongest souls; the most massive characters are seared with scars. I disagree. Artury mentally beat us down to where there was no hope of recovery . . . we became as warped as him. So many of us, twisted and no longer recognizable as what we once were. I disgust myself." There was a faint tremor in his voice, as though some emotion had touched him.

I didn't believe him. I had no sympathy. *Why am I here?* My week had started off happy, working with Ivy, planning and preparing for Matthew's birthday party. But there I sat at a bolted-down table across from my ex-husband who had raped and murdered all I held dear. I didn't care about his scars. Or his suffering. "Why did you ask for me? What do you want?"

Joe looked like an aging playboy, shrunken, with graying hair that was combed, but unwashed. His teeth were cigarette-yellow, his skin leathery from years of playing by hotel swimming pools and too many long nights in windowless coliseums and dark hotel rooms. His reward for his Calvin-mandated Bible fasting was skin that hung off his body like an eighty-year-old man and internal organs that had begun to give out. I'd been told on my arrival at the jail that he'd been beaten up twice by inmates, and that he'd been passing blood through his urine and bowels ever since.

"I'm gonna die in here."

"I hope so." I said then sighed. "I'm sure Selma wants to see you."

"This has nothing to do with her."

"And it does with me? She's your wife, Joe. You need to talk to *her*, not me."

Joe leaned forward. "I have to tell you something."

"Why should I care what you have to say?" I was done with his tortuous maneuverings, his quest for an edge, his twenty-year search for a way out of marriage, his overblown sense of importance. I had moved on.

Matthew, perhaps sensing my thoughts, had moved where I could see him and shot Joe a warning glare.

"You think you detest me? You can't possibly hate me, Andie, as much as I hate myself."

"You're damn lucky they're letting you live," I responded, giving him my best I-don't-give-a-shit glare. "Unless you refuse to cooperate."

"I know what I have to do. There's a lot to be told. I want to see my kids. Don't I have a right to see my kids?"

At that, Matthew peeled himself off the wall. "You gave up that right years ago. You're not only a failure as a father, you're a disgrace to the cause of Christ."

Anger from the audacity of Joe's statement made me tremble to keep from laughing hysterically. He was the last person in the world I wanted around my children. To discuss visitation rights after what he had done, it made the bile in my stomach churn and rise into my throat. It was as if he hadn't heard a word Matthew said. Joe's eyes never left mine, and I fought off the desire to leap across the table and scratch his eyes out.

But he kept his stare constant. I didn't like what I saw. Though his eyes were, as one would expect, lifeless, I saw something else there. Something beyond the vacancy. A hint of shame. A pleading. There was regret there, maybe. Remorse even. It surfaced quickly, which surprised me.

I looked up at Matthew and nodded. He frowned, but he knew Joe wanted to be alone with me, and that I would give him that moment.

Matthew signaled to the guard and the attorneys. "I'll stay here for her protection. Everyone else can wait outside."

Rising from his seat, Joe's lawyer spoke for the first time. "Anything my client says is off the record."

The lawyers picked up their briefcases and files, and then followed the guard out the door. Matthew sat in the corner, graciously giving Joe space to finish what he so desperately wanted to say.

I knew the guard and attorneys were behind the one-way glass. They'd all be watching.

I shrugged. "Well?"

"Mavis told me something before she died."

I put my hands up to my mouth and blinked hard.

"She was barely able to speak, but she told me you were to take care of her child. 'Tell Andie,' she said, 'to take care of my little girl.'" He sighed. "It's been many years. I'm sure she's no child now, but Mavis said her name. I never forgot it. Believe me, I tried to forget it. At first I didn't believe her, but I figure folks don't lie on their deathbed. Mavis said, 'Her name is Suri. She lives on 14th Street. Greenwich Village.' Mavis . . ." Joe hesitated and took a deep breath. "She said to tell you, it's Calvin Artury's child. I guess so you'd understand why she never told anyone. I didn't want Reverend to know he had a bastard child. A negra child. It woulda ruined him. I had to protect him." He brought his handcuffed hands up to his down-turned face. The chains rattled as he wiped a tear from his eye. "It didn't matter in the end."

Joe wasn't lying. I was as sure of it as I knew my own name. He had reached out and gripped my heart with a cold hand. I shriveled in my chair, as though my mind was incapable of absorbing any further shock. Matthew stood and walked up behind me, resting his hands on my shoulders for support. I waited to see if there was more. There wasn't.

I remembered the first two years after my marriage to Joe. Mavis had stayed in New York, not wanting to travel back to North Carolina to see her parents or me. Even when her mother passed, she stayed in New York. Everyone thought Mavis was busy working on her career. All along, she'd had a baby. Her one time with Calvin as a seventeen-year-old girl had landed her pregnant and in the middle of New York City.

"Why?" I held my tears in check, not wanting him to see me cry.

"I told you, I did what I was told. I was just a hit man."

"I know that." I looked up. "Why are you telling me this now?"

Joe turned his head and studied his reflection in the mirror. Looking back into my eyes, his voice grew quiet, and desperate. "Hopefully, by telling you this, you'll help me see Dillon and Gracie. They're my only hope for sanity in here. I've no right, none at all, to say I'm sorry. I've said it countless times and never meant it. These months in here have cleared my head. You were right. I threw my life away to chase after a man I thought could give me a life better than the one I had with you. Now the best I can hope for is some kind of relationship with my kids." Joe pleaded. "Help me, Andie. Please. I want to see them. I need them," he said.

"Wow," I shook my head. "You're really something. You *need* them. Did you ever stop to think through the years that they needed you? That they needed, oh, I don't know, something like love, affection, attention, a kind word at the end of the day? Now you want *me* to help you have a relationship with our children. After you all but ignored them for years and then ripped them away from me. Sure, Joe, and we'll be one big, happy family, at last." I glared at him. "I wouldn't help you dig your way out of Hell, which is where you've ended up."

"Please." The anguish etched across his face changed to a guise of self-repulsion. He began to slam his forehead repeatedly on the metal table in front of him. In a flash, Matthew yanked Joe's chair away from the table while the guard flew into the room, grabbing Joe's hair and holding his head at attention.

I remained seated, undaunted by his sideshow. I looked at the guard. "I'm fine. Please, let him go." He backed away, and Joe's chin fell to his chest.

The D.A. gave Joe his two-minute warning. "Wrap this up, Oliver."

I rubbed the scar in my hand. How could I forgive him for what he did to Mavis? Joe's head bled from his table tantrum. Blood dripped over his eye and down his cheek. I had no feeling for him. Yet, to move on, have the life I wanted, I would have to forgive him. I would have to let the anger go. Really go.

"Joe," I said softly. He lifted his head and stared into my eyes again. "Dillon and Gracie are all grown up. When they were babies, they cried for you as you walked out the door every Friday. Asked me all the time where you were. They know what you've done, why you're in here. It's what you've done to their mama that's hurt them the most. You'll be damn lucky if you *ever* see them again. But they know where they can find you. If they want to see you, I promise I won't stop them. As for me, take a real long look; it's the last time you'll ever see my face." I stood to leave. "Thanks for telling me about Mavis. In some small remote corner of the universe, you've redeemed a tiny piece of yourself. Maybe after twenty years of rotting in some hellhole prison, you'll have made a bit of progress toward redemption. It's up to God in the end. Will I forgive you? I suppose I'll find that out then."

Matthew put his arm around me and we headed for the door.

"Andie!" Joe called out, breathing heavily, his voice a mixture of torment and tears. "I . . . I did love you once."

It galled me that he still wanted the last word.

My back to him, I forced myself to laugh and walked out of the room. But after crossing the threshold, I stopped and turned around to look into his eyes one last time. Holding the door open, I spoke each parting word slowly and for all to hear. "Frankly, my dear Joseph, I don't give a damn."

Joe shot up from his seat. His ankles and hands shackled, he fell to his knees, and that's when the last door finally slammed shut between us.

PART NINE
Let There Be Light

We are each of us responsible for the evil we may have prevented.
— James Martineau

April 1994
FARTHER ALONG

Andie

Spring had come to the mountains. Ivy's jonquils popped out of the ground along with hyacinths and tulips. The trees leaned to the east, their leaves and branches spread out in supplication toward the morning sun. Tobias set the sprinklers to pirouetting on the lawn. The soothing landscape of Shiloh had become home.

Ivy fried chicken for an after-church picnic on the grounds. Matthew had booked a gospel bluegrass band as lunchtime entertainment.

It was time for church. When Matthew and I walked into the back of the sanctuary, greeters shook our hands, spoke pleasantries, and chatted about the fine weather. Ivy and Tobias strolled down the middle aisle and laughed with the members. A few deacons and elders sat like proud peacocks with their flock of grandchildren in the pews behind them. There were no rules, no frilly church decorations, just lots of folks scooting across pews to make way for friends and family. Babies cried; expectant mothers popped up from time-to-time to use the restroom or to take their small children to do the same. Nobody looked twice. Nobody cared. I sat in my family's favorite pew and smiled all the way through my mother-in-law's sermon that lasted a whole forty-five minutes. Gracie, Dillon, and Conner huddled with friends in the corners of the sanctuary. A giggle escaped my lips periodically throughout the service. *I'm happy. Really happy.*

We sang a song that brought Dixie to mind. *Farther along, we'll know all about it, farther along we'll understand why, cheer up my brother, live in the sunshine, we'll understand it, all by and by.* I had sung it to Rupert in his tobacco field the day I told him his daughter had died. Dixie had sung it to me as a little girl. I thought of my mother a lot. And wondered.

"Don't forget about water baptism next Sunday," said Pastor Bobbie Sue. "Pray the river is a little warmer this year. In the meantime, let's all head outside. The ladies have prepared a delicious lunch, and we got ourselves a little bluegrass band on the lawn."

I had made it through. Just.

§

"It's a church picnic, not a hanging." Matthew made me laugh and I waited while he tugged his yellow tie loose before shaking a deacon's hand. The large double doors at the back stood open. God had turned on the sun to preheat the mountain. Steam rose from the cars in the parking lot, and the freshly mowed field next to the church smelled sweet and rich. A nearby thicket of dogwoods swung gently in the last puffs from the early morning's storm. Everyone appeared happy and content as they rounded the corner, making their way toward the fellowship hall. I got busy helping Ivy put out platters of chicken at two rows of picnic tables covered in long white tablecloths. At least until Matthew walked up and slipped his arms around me. "Anybody tell you how beautiful you are?"

"Matthew, people are staring!"

"Let them," he said as he nibbled my earlobe. "I love you, and I plan to tell you every day for the rest of our lives." His words deserved a kiss and he got one.

"Now leave me be, I'm helping out this morning." I smiled at my husband as he walked away, allowing me to get to the business of serving chicken and uprighting vases of wildflowers upset by the wind.

A blanket of quiet fell as Pastor Bobbie Sue requested the families gather around the Lord's Table. Pleased with the day and their place in the world, my new family joined hands and looked up toward the mountains. Their benediction was a simple one. That Sunday it was Matthew's to say. "*I will lift up mine eyes unto the hills, from whence cometh my help.*"

The congregation responded together, "*My help cometh from the Lord, which made Heaven and earth.*"

Matthew concluded the prayer. "*He will not suffer thy foot to be moved: He that keepeth thee will not slumber.*"

Everyone replied, "*Amen.*"

"Amen," I responded alone.

Later that afternoon as I poured tea at the table, I caught a glimpse of Dillon and Diana holding hands, sharing a plate of food on a blanket under a tree. Gracie flirted with a group of young men, all competing for her attention.

"Just like her mama: a beauty queen," Matthew said.

"That was Dixie, not me."

"She's you, Andie. She's you," he said as he walked off to join a group of men who were discussing the crop season and basketball scores.

I wandered among the tables. A group of children swarmed around me playing a game of tag. The boys' white shirttails hung out, already grass-stained, their jackets stashed somewhere. The girls' bows were undone, their hair falling out of tidy braids or ponytails. A three-year-old boy tugged on my skirt, wanting to be picked up. I hugged him close, and then released him to play with his siblings. Strolling over to a blanket on the ground, I plopped down and lifted my face to the warm sun. A softness hung in the air. It was the sort of magical spring afternoon meant for lingering. My eyes closed. I wanted to soak in the moment. I wanted contentment. I wanted much more of a sense of peace. But a dark presentiment began creeping into my daily thoughts, waking me even at night. A restlessness clung to me. Questions about Calvin's life and death ran deep. I opened my eyes and forced myself to smile. It was over, I had to believe it.

The late day air grew cool. I folded the blanket, threw jackets to my kids, and then helped my husband load the car.

"I've got a surprise for you," Matthew said as we drove home.

I yawned. "What is it?"

"I can't give it to you until Saturday. I just want you to know it's coming."

"Oh, that's nice. I'm ready for a surprise but now I have to wait a week?"

"The kids are off to the Darwoods' house on Saturday. Ivy and Tobias are taking Mother shopping and to supper in Asheville. We'll be home alone."

"You're not getting kinky on me, are you?"

Matthew laughed. "Not unless you want me to, sweetheart. It's a nice surprise. It'll be delivered on Saturday."

"And what do I do until then?"

"You wait. You wait and see."

May 1994
THE KNOWLEDGE OF GOOD AND EVIL

Andie

The first Saturday in May settled across a sunlit countryside. I stood at Matthew's office window, watching yellow finches at the feeder. Against a backdrop of brilliant orange sky stretching across the pasture from the west, a car barreled up the gravel road past Ivy's house and the meadow. Plumes of dust kicked up behind the tires, making it difficult to see through the sun's rays. Matthew walked up behind me, slipped his arms around my waist and whispered, "She wants to see you. Go out and talk to her."

My knees grew weak. I gave Matthew a quick glance. He winked and picked up his newspaper, tucked it under his arm, and headed to the front door with his mug of fresh decaf.

My surprise.

Wiping sweaty hands on my jeans, I slid into my flip-flops and walked out on the porch. The sun's glare blinded me until I made my way down the steps and past the fountain to the end of the brick walk where the driveway stopped and trees filtered the evening sun. The car parked, and a familiar bubble blonde hairdo peeked above the steering wheel. "Dixie." My heart leaped in my chest. "As I live and breathe."

My mother stepped out of her car and walked toward me holding something in her hands. "Andie Rose." She nodded. "I brought you a present."

Daddy's banjo. As she handed it to me I absorbed her immediately. A little older, a few more lines around her mouth and on her forehead, but she was as pretty as ever. Slim for her age, my mother had held together well. "Thank you. I . . . I haven't seen this in such a long time."

"It's yours, now. He'd want you to have it," she said, laying it in my hands. Peering down at Daddy's banjo, I knew he had loved it with his whole heart. It was an immortal piece of him.

When I looked up Dixie had already walked ahead of me, making a beeline toward the house. "This is some place. I almost got lost trying to find it." Her eyes widened as she stepped through the front door. I expected a comment from the green-eyed monster of her past, but she only smiled and said, "What a magnificent home, Andie. I'm very happy for you. Maybe you can take me on a tour later?"

"Sure."

"I met Matthew last week."

"So I gather." I carefully laid the banjo on a side table, caressing the warmth of it before ushering Dixie into the study.

Matthew gave my mother a quick hug. "How are you, Dixie? Want a cold cola? Or a glass of wine—"

"A glass of wine sounds good. Whatever you have. That'd be nice. Thanks."

Dixie seemed nervous, rubbing her arms, stepping to a window that over-looked Callahan farmland, and then eyeing every nook and corner and wall filled with Matthew's things and a few new things of my own. "I think about the twins every day," she said. "I want you to know I couldn't find them, and I had no idea where you had gone. Nobody told us they were with the Darwoods. How are they?" she asked, both of us wanting to embrace, neither knowing what kept us from it.

"They're fine. You remember they were taken from me for a while. Gracie and Dillon are living here with me now, all grown up, nearly."

Dixie sat at the table as Matthew served us both a glass of Cabernet. I spent the next few minutes giving my mother a quick report of the past year of my life. She grabbed my hand and her eyes watered. Her first tear fell on her hand. Another fell on her dress. The others left wet splotches the size of nickels on her sweater. I handed her a tissue then laid my hand on her trembling knee to comfort her.

"I'm sorry," she said wiping her eyes, "so very sorry." Dixie's face looked pale and pinched. "Matthew came to Charleston to talk to me."

I looked at my husband who only raised his eyebrows. My voice cracked. "Are you mad at me, Dixie?"

"Of course not. I've missed you, Andie." My mother sobbed.

I rushed to her side, pulling her into my arms.

"I've been avoiding you," she said. "Avoiding the truth about my life and things you need to know. Things your daddy never wanted you to know. But we can't hold back the truth, anymore than we can hold back God's love. Matthew, he wanted *me* to tell you."

"Tell me what?"

"It's a long story. You know I never wanted to tell you about my life as a young girl."

I nodded. "Well, let's get comfortable. Bring your wine."

"Oh, Matthew," Dixie said as he assisted her to the sofa, "you go first."

"What are you two talking about?" I asked.

Matthew sat next to Dixie and I soon understood my husband possessed the resources to find out about anything he wanted. "Sweetheart," he said, looking at me. "I had to know more about Calvin Artury than what any of us were allowed to see. I'd wake up at night and my mind would race. During the day my head was weighed down with questions. Who was he? After what happened to my brother and to you, I became obsessed to know what made him tick. Maybe it was the psychologist in me, too, I don't know. Not a soul has successfully investigated his past. He hid it quite well. A couple weeks ago, when I told you I was in South Carolina on business, I drove to Charleston and then to the Goose Creek area where Artury's really from. I discovered the truth about his childhood."

"Do I have to hear it?" I could see Matthew needed to give me his report. "Okay, tell me. I am a bit curious. He always said he had loving parents growing up. I never understood how he could become such a beast."

"He did have loving parents, it seems, but they died when he was nine, not nineteen like he told everybody. His parents burned to death in a house fire. Suddenly, everything that was right in little Calvin's world turned wrong."

My eyes opened wide and I stared at him, inquisitively.

"It's true," said Dixie.

I sat there wondering how my mother knew that, as Matthew continued. "Back then, technology didn't exist to determine how that fire started. Some old folks in town, I found out, knew the story. In particular, Artury's second cousin. I tracked him down and we met at the place where the house once stood. Young Calvin, an only child, was at school. There was a fight between Calvin's grandpa, who was running moonshine, and Calvin's holy-roller mama who wanted it to stop. His grandpa threw a mason jar full of the stuff at her while she stood next to a wood-burning cook stove. It caught both the stove and Calvin's mother on fire. Calvin's daddy stepped in and tried to save her, but caught fire himself. Neither parent made it out alive. The clapboard house went up in no time flat. Strange enough, the grandfather escaped and lived a while to become the town drunk, shooting off his mouth, telling folks how he'd killed his family, including his own wife, Calvin's grandmother. He said he shot his wife in front of his children. Guilt got the best of the old man. A year later they found him with a bullet in his head laid out by his smokehouse. It gets worse from here."

"Worse?" I rubbed my temples.

Matthew stood and retrieved a file from his desk. "Calvin went from being raised by loving parents to living with his father's sisters, two spinster aunts. This part I learned from a little widow lady who lived across the street from the old aunts. I believe her. She had no reason to fabricate it. She said she was ninety years old and that I was the first person she'd told. Nobody had ever bothered to ask her about what she knew, until I showed up at her door on a hunch. Anyway, she remembered Calvin as a little boy. When he was dispensed into his aunts' care, his life became threadbare and cramped overnight. He learned to survive by pretending, making things up, getting caught in one lie after another in school. He once told this old lady he firmly believed having children was a great waste of time."

"Well, it's no wonder," Dixie said.

Matthew looked at my mother. "I think you know, Dixie, that both aunts sexually abused him. Repeatedly."

I gave my husband a strange look. "How would my mother know that?"

Dixie took over the conversation at that point, her voice cracked and strained. "I'll tell you in a few minutes. It's true. They molested him until he was fifteen years old. Then Calvin got real sick. He almost died. But he watched Oral Roberts on TV and got healed, he told me."

"He told you? Dixie, I repeat, how do you know this? When did he tell you . . . why—"

"Let her finish, Andie." Matthew put his finger up to his lips, to sweetly hush me.

My mother's voice was shaky, which further surprised me. "A year later, when young Calvin was sixteen and well physically, but certainly not mentally, he ran away from his aunts, worked in honky-tonks, tended bar, and got blitzed about every night. Women loved him. He was truly a blonde bombshell. Every bit as good looking as Troy Donahue or Tab Hunter. He was a good dancer and could drink most customers under the table." Dixie coughed, as if her words had choked her. As if to hear them out loud made her ill.

Matthew interjected. "He had an IQ of 180. I discovered Calvin graduated with perfect grades. You know, it takes a genius to pull off what he did. He had the world fooled."

"Well, either that or a psychopathic madman," I added.

"True." My mother swallowed hard. "But after a year or two of sinful living, he headed for college. He hated women, mostly because of what his aunts had done to him. And then, remembering his mother's love of evangelism, he used his brain and some smooth talking to wheedle his way into Lee University, making few friends. He became charismatic and twisted."

Matthew took over the conversation again. "I sent an investigator to Cleveland, Tennessee. He found an old schoolmate of Calvin's. It seems Calvin believed kids were a necessary evil; that after you had them they should be raised by the state. On farms like animals. Then after they were disciplined and educated, only then should they be sent out into society to be productive and God fearing. It makes me shudder to think what would've happened if we hadn't stopped him when we did, Andie. He had a disturbed view of Christianity. His plan was to rule as much of the gullible Christian world as he could. The man honestly believed he picked up where Jesus left off. Sounds like an Anti-Christ, doesn't it?"

I sat and blinked, stunned at my husband's words.

Matthew poured more wine into my mother's glass. "Here's another shocker. There was a scandal."

"Can you believe it, a scandal about Calvin Artury?" Dixie snickered.

Matthew smiled at my mother. "The investigator discovered young Calvin was caught with his pants down around his knees. A freshman had professed his homosexuality to the wrong person. Namely, Calvin. Get a load of this. After they were caught, ol' Cal talked his way right out of it. Said he was experimenting with it so someday he could preach against it. That they really didn't sin, they just 'rubbed against each other's nakedness.' That it was just an 'indiscretion' on his part. What a crock of bull he must've laid on the administration at Lee. You know me, Andie, I don't care which side of the bed a man sleeps on, just be honest about it. But it was the 1950s and the student body ridiculed him; nearly drove him insane before he graduated. Why don't you tell her the rest, Dixie?"

A tinge of dread rippled down my spine, watching my mother set her wine glass on the table, scoot to the edge of the sofa, and start to talk. "So, by now he's in his mid-twenties and he goes to Parkers Ferry, which isn't far from Charleston. He's preaching in this tiny church, to about fifty members who know nothing about his past 'indiscretions.' One day he was eating at the local diner, and a young girl comes in, begging for food. Looked like a runaway. Calvin sets out to saving her soul. Before it was all said and done, he'd not only saved her soul, he'd bought her supper. The girl followed him around for weeks. He was kind to her for a while, but she was just a kid and got on his nerves real bad. He tried to get rid of her, but it didn't work. She doesn't leave, because now she's pregnant with his child. He puts her up in a boarding house and threatens to kill her if she tells who the father is. It's a wonder he didn't kill her. I guess his evil hadn't progressed that far yet. The girl, abandoned, and left to fend for herself, finally figures out he isn't about to fall in love with her, even if she is pregnant, so she hits the streets again. By now, she's eight months along. With you, Andie."

I stood and dropped my wine glass on the hardwood floor. Shattered glass and red cabernet flew everywhere. I bolted to the mirror on the wall. That's when I saw him, in my eyes. The same brilliant blue eyes. "Oh, God!" I'd been blind to the resemblance. The thought of him linked to me in any way—I wasn't sure I could live with it. I reached up to tuck a piece of my hair behind my ear and my hands shook. It started to make sense, why it was always so easy for me to get an appointment with him, why he kept trying to pull me back into the church instead of allowing Joe or his goons to murder me right along with Mavis. I twirled around to glare at my mother but only saw the torture she had endured in not wanting me to discover my lineage.

Dixie stood. Her words came out like a gusher. "Yes, you have his turquoise eyes. But that's *all* you got from him. At least you inherited my spirit and sense of goodness, a gene that was obviously left out of Calvin's DNA."

"My, God, Dixie! His blood runs through my veins! My children's! It's like I have a terminal disease and can do nothing about it! How could you! How could you keep this from me!"

Matthew quickly pulled me into his arms as I thrashed about the room. I buried my face into his chest and bawled as he spoke softly to my mother. "She's known for some time, Dixie, that Bud wasn't her father. Aunt Wy told her years ago."

I pulled away. "I never cared to even question who my father really was. It didn't matter to me. So why are you telling me now? Why? Why are you trying to ruin my life!"

Matthew fought to keep me still. "Listen to me, Andie! Look at me! Your mother's not ruining your life. She saved your life. Calvin wanted her to abort you, but she refused. Bud found her roaming the streets, digging for scraps. He took her home and married her, even though she was pregnant. God blessed you with a real father whose heart was big enough to cover it all. He loved you like his own. God saved your life to stop Calvin, don't you see that?" I could tell by Matthew's expression there was more. I fell back on the sofa with my husband still holding me close. "You need to know the rest," he said.

I nodded, fighting off waves of hiccups that shook my shoulders. Dixie sat with her hands around a wad of tissues and dabbing at tears; her feet crossed at her ankles as always. I suddenly realized this was harder on her than it was on me. "Okay. Tell me," I said.

Matthew took a deep breath, let go of my arms, and turned to face me. "Calvin was a murderer long before he built the House of Praise. No one knew it. You were all fooled. You remember those two elderly aunts who raised him? One day in the middle of the hottest summer in fifty years, the old widow lady who lived across the street, found them. Both hanging side by side from the upstairs banister. The coroner ruled it a double homicide. The killer was never caught. The old woman told me she knew better. She'd seen Calvin over there a couple days before she discovered their bodies. Said she hadn't seen any life around the place since the day Calvin left, so, being nosy, she knocked on their door. After two days of nobody answering, she broke in and saw those old women hanging like two sides of beef, swaying back and forth, covered with flies in the heat. He'd shaved their heads, beat them, and then sliced them open like slaughtered hogs. Disemboweled right over their parlor. She said it smelled so bad she about swallowed her tongue, and that she could still smell it from time to time."

"That old lady called the police. But before the police arrived, she did some more snooping. She found Polaroid snapshots they'd taken of Calvin as a little boy. Naked. And of each other naked. Doing stuff to him. Grotesque and horrible stuff. She still had the pictures, and seemed relieved to finally give them away. They tortured him, in unbelievable ways. He killed his two crazy aunts. Not that they didn't deserve it. I believe it was those two old biddies who had transformed him into a devil. That's what I want you to know, Andie. What your mother wants you to know. We want you to understand that not only were his problems self-inflicted, but his mental illness stemmed from what happened to him as a child. You have nothing to be concerned about in your own genetics. We are all products of our environment. Calvin certainly was."

Dixie's tears were nonstop. "Who knows why that old lady kept those pictures? She evidently never told the police what she found for fear of Calvin coming back and doing the same thing to her. He'd have done it, too. Matthew gave the pictures to me. I burned them."

My thoughts racing, I spit one of them out. The fierceness in my stare made my mother cry again. "Why did you go to his church in the first place, Dixie? Why take me there when you knew he was my father!"

"Your Daddy didn't know. Not at first. He had received an invitation to come to the church when it was newly built. An invitation he kept in his Bible for years. When he insisted we go to a few services, I couldn't bring myself to tell him who your father was."

I remembered the invitation. Mavis and I saw it when we were little girls. I still had it.

"After Bud and I attended a while, Calvin realized who *I* was, who *you* were. He approached me. Bud wanted to leave the church, leave town in fact. But Calvin wasn't about to let his daughter go. Not after he saw you. One night after a service, Bud and Calvin went head-to-head in the office. Calvin had the upper hand. There was nothing Bud could do. He was prepared to destroy our home, Bud's position at work, and anything he could do to keep you at the House of Praise. In the end, I was allowed to accompany you as your mother. He knew I would keep my mouth shut. Bud refused to attend much after that, and eventually quit. I went because of you, Andie. I attended that damnable church until you were grown. I attended to keep Calvin from harming my family. I only guessed what he was capable of, but I guessed right. What Calvin never anticipated, though, was your independent spirit. Your attitude toward him. Your wanting to pull Joe out. And now I hear Mavis had a little girl by him. That connects you to Mavis forever, Andie. Don't you see?"

My glare softened. I sat in stunned silence for a moment, and then responded with hope instead of anger. "I've always been bound to Mavis. But, I guess I have another sister, don't I?"

"Yes, I guess you do. Calvin's blood runs through more than your veins and Dillon and Gracie's. There's another girl out there somewhere."

The thought of Mavis's daughter thrilled and saddened me. "We need to find her."

Matthew smiled. "We do. And we will."

Dixie stood and walked to the window again. "Do your children see Joe in prison?"

"No, only Ray goes," I said. "And of course, Selma. It's best that way. I don't think Dillon and Gracie are ready. They've lived through it with me. The Olivers see the twins during the holidays. That's about it. It's a whole new family for me, for us. Matthew and his son, Conner. Ivy and Tobias. I don't know how I lived without them. Well . . . I wouldn't have."

Matthew took my hands in his. "I wanted you to know everything. And now you do."

"It wasn't the pleasant surprise I was expecting."

My mother faced me. "It takes more than DNA to be a father."

"I know that. This is all just a bit of a shock, Dixie."

"Andie. Don't you think it's time you start calling me Mama?"

I walked to the window and gazed out over the old cemetery with my mother. "I'll call you Mama, if you can somehow put it out of your mind who my father was."

More tears filled her red-rimmed eyes. "I did that for years, darlin'. Your father was Bud. He always will be." My mother peered into the distance. "What a beautiful cemetery with its simple white crosses and stones. I can nearly hear Maybelle Carter singing one of your daddy's favorite songs. He used to play it on that old banjo. Remember, Andie? *Will the circle be unbroken, by and by, Lord, by and by? In a better home awaiting, in the sky, Lord, in the sky?*" She sang softly and then stopped. "Andie Rose . . . will the circle be unbroken?"

I opened my arms wide and my mother walked into them. We clung to each other, woman-to-woman, bosom-to-bosom, and I smiled through my tears. "No broken circles, Mama. Not if we can help it. Not if we can help it."

Andie

Matthew stopped at Starbucks. I loved Starbucks. The drive to Fripp Island was long, but enjoyable. I made my husband stop our Range Rover at every antique store and winery from home to Beaufort, South Carolina.

"I told her we're on our way. Mama's turning seventy next year," I said as I turned off my cell phone.

Matthew smiled sweetly. "Yes, and *you* are turning fifty."

I pretended not to hear. Matthew's wrinkles had grown deeper. His hair, more salt than pepper, had receded from his forehead the past few years. He was heading toward the other side of fifty-five, but I shared in his contentment. The best years are still to come, he told me.

I flipped the visor down to check my face in the mirror. "Do you think we can get her to come to the anniversary party?"

"If I have to fly down and get her myself, she and Wy will come."

In January, we would celebrate ten years of marriage. Our children had planned an intimate party of family and close friends. I told Gracie that instead of sending an invitation to Dixie and Wylene, Matthew and I would take it to them. Mama and I had only seen each other for an occasional holiday throughout the years since the day she and Matthew filled me in on who I really was.

Matthew and I had traveled extensively. I finally got to stick my feet in a few oceans around the world. Wylene and Mama became too tired to take care of the house in Charleston any longer. They put the place up for sale and retired to a smaller home on the ocean. Fripp Island. A barrier island off the coast.

The driveway to their house was narrow and paved in crushed pink granite that crunched pleasantly under the tires. I spied Mama standing on the front stoop, waiting. Only God knew how long she'd been standing there. She waddled to the car, her frame a little shorter, a little wider. After years of living with Wylene, she had put pounds on her hips, arms, and behind. I thought I might say something to her about it, but I decided if she was happy let her eat all she wanted.

Mama didn't say 'hello,' or 'glad you're here.' She said, "Wy's gone to the store. I told her to go yesterday, but no, she had to clean the dern house yesterday, the old bat. So today she's got to buy a pie 'cause y'all are coming to visit. My pies ain't good enough for her; she's got to buy a pie! Hey, Matthew. How are ya, honey? You look a little tired. Why don't ya come on in. I got a bed waiting for ya both. How about a little nap before Wy gets back? She'll be there all day. Course, she didn't drive, you know. Can't see a thing, the old bat. Our neighbor man takes her to town once in a while, to the store and to the hospital to visit old friends. How's Dillon and Gracie? Andie, you look too thin. Lord, girl, what'd you do to your hair?"

Matthew turned to me and mouthed, "Can we leave now?"

I broke into an open smile and took it all in stride. After all, I wasn't about to change her. I went about settling Matthew and myself into our room. Later, I found Mama mixing up pie dough in the kitchen. "Matthew's taking you up on your suggestion to take a nap. How about you and me go for a walk on the beach?"

The Atlantic Ocean was as majestic to me as the mountains at Shiloh. Whenever I stood at the water's edge or the base of a mountain I was reminded of God's faithfulness.

"When did Matthew sell his property on Fripp?" Mama asked.

"Oh, you remember me telling you that, huh?"

She snorted. "I remember more than y'all think I remember."

Mama's dementia had started the year before. It was disheartening to think of her forgetting so much. At least one more time I would bring her to the mountains, back to Shiloh for the anniversary party, and to see her grandchildren before she forgot them.

Mama's clothes were Fripp Island casual—a sea-foam green, loose-fitting dress and low-heeled sandals she had pulled off to carry across the sand. Her hair was still a 1972 blonde bubble with curls in the front.

"I'm old, Andie," she said. She stopped walking. For the first time she reached for me first, hugged me first. I let myself be enveloped by my mama's arms. For some reason, the closeness left me feeling sad, perhaps even a little frightened.

"You're not old."

"I feel old. Wy retired, you know. Can't see anymore. The old bat is as blind as one. Oh, I think I already said that, didn't I?" She shrugged one shoulder. "Oh, well."

Mama took my arm and we walked on in silence, listening to the roar of the ocean. Seagulls glided on the wind like tiny white kites while the salty smell of fish washed up with the waves. The sand felt like wet cement between my toes as I stepped over a starfish caught in seaweed tangled at the water's edge. Leading Mama into the foamy waves that lapped at our bare feet, I loved hearing her laugh. She could still giggle like a schoolgirl. "Oh, my," she said. "Isn't this fun?"

Suddenly, her expression changed and her eyes went blank, like an erased page in a notebook. We walked on. "I can't drive anymore, so that means we don't get away much. Our groceries are delivered. Except when Wy can sweet talk the neighbor into taking her to Beaufort for a pie. We watch the ocean a lot."

I was surprised when she reached for my hand. "Did you hear Caroline moved again? She lives in Idaho. Of all places. It's her third . . . no . . . her fourth husband. But this one's a keeper. Who would move to Idaho? She's got six kids. They're good at giving her fits. Four girls, two boys, can you imagine? Comes around, goes around, eh Andie?"

"You gotta choose your battles, Daddy always said."

"He did?"

Dixie's life was what she had made it. Quiet. Living with her sister, walking the beach every day, hoping for visits from friends and children.

"What happened to you, Andie? Where'd you go for the year or so after we left North Carolina? Never could get a hold of you. We were worried."

I had explained it to her years ago. It had been disturbing enough to her then. After she told me Calvin was my father, I think she purposely put every bit of it out of her mind. We never talked about any of it again. "It's a long story," I said. "It's over. Not worth telling now." Not to Mama, anyway. It was time for peace in our lives.

"How are the Olivers? Have you heard from any of them?"

"Maudy died a few years back, remember? I told you. They buried her next to Al in Lexington. Ray and Libby have a son, Micah, and they adopted a little girl and called her Mavis. She looks like a little Mavis. They're coming to the anniversary party. You'll get to see them."

"Where's Joe? Did he ever remarry?"

My mother had deteriorated a little more since the last time I'd seen her. "Yes, Mama. He's still married to Selma. She lives in Salisbury . . . somewhere." That's all I cared to say about that. I smiled at my aging mother, turning her around like a child to walk back to the house. And then, like footprints in the sand, Mama's love washed over me and filled in the gaps, taking my memories out to sea.

§

Joe was in prison for life, with no possibility of parole. When it all boiled down, he was convicted of the murder and rape of Mavis Dumass and the murder of Chip Atkinson, but had turned state's evidence to avoid Death Row. Tony DeSanto was serving a life sentence, convicted of conspiracy in the murder of Mavis Dumass and Chip Atkinson, transporting drugs, and running illegal prostitution rings and gambling casinos. Evan Preston, due to my testimony and evidence, sat on death row and was near the end of his appeal process. He was convicted of the murder of John Rossi, and conspiracy in the murder of Mavis Dumass and Chip Atkinson. Further indictments included money laundering, extortion, bribing political figures, pirating videos, and the making and selling of illegal pornography. Had Calvin not put a gun to his own head he would've faced charges of tax evasion, and the rape and extortion of over twenty-two men and women who came forward after his death. He would've also faced charges of conspiracy in several murders. Silas and Percy Turlo were still at large, believed to be out of the country along with two million dollars of the church's money.

We were told after Calvin shot himself, they carried his body to a nearby building that within moments caught fire and burned to the ground. His cremated remains, what little the Nigerian government could find, were shipped back to the States to his closest relative, his second cousin in Goose Creek. The rumor was that the old man got drunk and walked to the town dump with a bottle of Johnnie Walker in one hand and the urn of Calvin's ashes in the other. Rumor also had it that he dumped the ashes over the garbage dump. In my mind, it was a fitting end.

§

"Ten years," I said, as I kissed Matthew.

"How about another forty?" he asked.

"Think we can make it that far?"

"Sure, why not?"

God's grace was sufficient. I had found God in the stillness of Shiloh's mountains, and love in the man who helped me save myself. At The Grove Park Inn our family gathered around as we cut our heart-shaped cake. I counted the number of hearts in the room that day. Sixty-three, sixty-four including my own contented heart. Plenty of hearts to love and to finish the journey together.

~ *The End* ~

Author's Note

Although there are many similarities, this book is not about me. My eyes are green, my dad never smoked cigarettes, and the father of my children was not like Joe. All the characters are fictional. They are not based on any person dead or alive. While many scenes were inspired in part by real life, all events and dialogue are entirely imaginary and/or wishful thinking. Any resemblance to real people or events is entirely coincidental. Although it was difficult to revisit so many dark places in writing this story, it does not change the purely fictitious nature of the work.

Sorry We're Open Diner does not exist, but there is a town in North Carolina called Welcome, and Mount Zion Baptist Church in Winston-Salem is not the same church as described in *Televenge*.

The following short stories in my previous book, *Southern Fried Women*, contain early versions of scenes in *Televenge*, or minor characters who tell their own story: *Pigment of My Imagination, Beach Babies,* and *Punkin Head*.

Though it is true this book is about the dark side of televangelism, it is also about the true light of unconditional love. Writers write about their passions, what moves them, what shoots out of them like a rocket. My key inspirational force is my spirituality. I am a seeker and the older I get, the more questions I have. I was married to a megachurch ministry team member for seventeen years. Under much distress, I left the church in 1988 losing everything in the wake of my rebellion, including my husband. I did not write this book specifically for a Christian audience. I wanted it to reflect the realities, the long-lasting devastation, and the horrific effects of legalism. For those who have left a manipulative situation or are thinking about it, I want you to know the great plan of redemption belongs to us all. No matter how desperate your circumstances, you can come out of a dark place, and into a life that is calling your name. God's mercies are truly renewed every morning, and He never, ever turns His back on us. No matter what anyone preaches from their pretentious pulpit. And that is why I wrote this book.

About the Author

Pamela King Cable is the author of the highly acclaimed collection of short stories, *Southern Fried Women*. Born a coal miner's granddaughter and raised by a tribe of wild Pentecostals and storytellers, Pamela is an award-winning author who loves to write about religion and spirituality with mystical twists she unearths from her family's history. As a young adult she was married to a megachurch ministry team member and attended years of megachurch services. She has taught at many writing conferences, and speaks to book clubs, women's groups, national and local civic organizations, and at churches throughout the country. *Televenge* is her debut novel. She lives in Ohio with her husband, Michael, and is working on her next novel. To learn more, visit www.pamelakingcable.com.